ANATHEMA

THE EATING WOODS, #1

KERI LAKE

ANATHEMA
Published by KERI LAKE
www.KeriLake.com

Copyright © 2024 Keri Lake

Cover art by Okay Creations
Editing: Julie Belfield
Map Art: Joshua James from Stardust Book Services
Section Break Art: Alicia @cheeky_lettering
Zevander Artwork: Alex @avoccatt_art
Castle Eidolon Artwork: Jonas from Stardust Book Services
Zevander & Maevyth Artwork: Zoe Holland
Chapter Heading Artwork: Franziska @coverdungeonrabbit

Warning: This book contains explicit sexual content, and violent scenes that some readers may find disturbing.

For those who feel lost in a dark and pathless wood.
Believe in the magic beyond the trees.

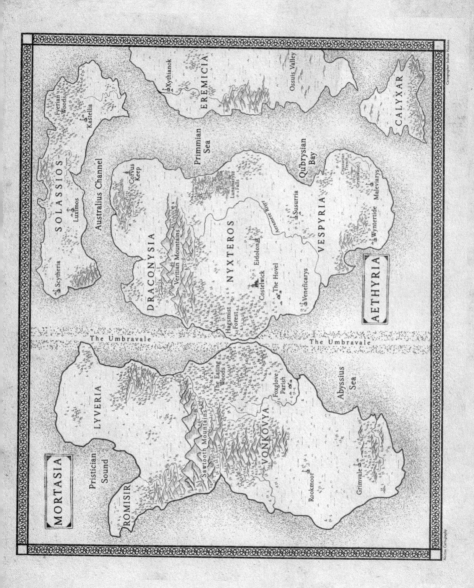

1

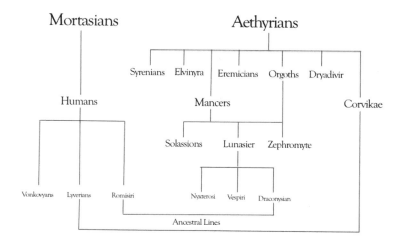

AETHYRIAN RACES

Corvikae [cor-vih-kai] – An ancient mortal tribe who went extinct due to genocide; worshipped the goddess of death; it is said that they have Corvugon blood; originated in the northern part of Nyxteros
Traits: Dark hair, light bronze skin, mortal

Dryadivir [dri-ad-i-veer] – A race of Aethyrians who dwell in the woods and can sometimes take the form of trees; highly intelligent and often sought for their knowledge; believed to be the ancestors of mancers; originated in eastern Vespyria
Traits: Rough bark-like or root skin, branch-like antlers, can manipulate elemental power

Elvynira [ell-vin-eer-ah] – Those who practice magic through

Nexumis; highly intelligent and often sought as advisors to the king; originate from the snowy island of Calyxar
Traits: Dark or bronze skin, white hair (some have red hair and pale skin), pointed ears

Eremician [ehr-ray-mee-shan] – Those who come from the desert lands of Eremicia; exceptionally skilled warriors whose power is the ability to manipulate sand and fire
Traits: Dark hair, scaly skin that can turn the color of sand, burgundy eyes

Lunasier [lune-ah-seer] – Mancers whose bloodline magic is powered by the moon; originate from Nyxteros, Draconysia and Vespyria
Traits: Dark or silver hair, pale/silvery skin, blue or golden eyes

Mancers/Manceborn – Immortal humans born with blood magic

Orgoths – Ogre-like beasts that are known for being extremely violent; do not possess magic but do possess exceptional strength; originate from Northern Solassia and Maleviarys in southern Vespyria
Traits: Muscular humanoid with green or blue skin, some have sharp tusks and pointed ears

Solassions [soh-lay-shuns] – Mancers whose bloodline magic is powered by the sun; originate from Solassia; believed to have been the first immortal mancers
Traits: Light bronze skin; blond hair; blue eyes

Syrenians [sir-en-ee-ans] - Sea dwellers with long black scaled tails and fins. They are described as mesmerizingly beautiful, but dangerous, as they are vicious and enjoy the taste of mancer

flesh. Found in the cold, dark depths of the Primmian Sea; some human seafarers have reported sightings in the Abyssius Sea as well.
Traits: Black or white hair, dark or pale skin, silver or gold eyes. Those that dwell below the Crussurian Trench are said to have black eyes and pale gray skin.

Zephromyte [zeh-phro-mite] – A cross between mancers and orgoths; highly aggressive and competitive; shunned by orgoths
Traits: Tend to look more like mancers but more muscular; some can look more like orgoths with less muscle

GLOSSARY

Abyssal binding [ah-biss-uhl] – the power to hold someone trapped in the caligorya

Ascendency [ah-send-ent-see] – a phase, similar to puberty, when mancers begin to come into their bloodline magic

Aura – Trace magic left behind that can be used to identify a mancer

Azurmadine [ah-zer-mah-deen] – An element found in the caves of Sawtooth, gives off a blue glow

Becoming Ceremony – a rite of passage for young women into womanhood and sexual maturity

Bellatryx [Bella-tricks] – Female warriors—half Solassion, half Zephromyte

Caligorya [cali-gore-ee-uh] – The dark space inside the mind

Caligosi [cali-go-see] – An animal whose hide is used to make leather

Cammyck [camm-ick]– A boyshort bodysuit worn as an undergarment

Cantafel [can-tah-fell]– A spell that allows passage through the Umbravale (only a few know of it)

Carnifican [car-niff-i-can]– A mancer who has consumed too much vivicantem and becomes violent

Catallys [cah-tal-lys] – Nocturnal creatures that dwell in the woods, a cross between a cat and a hawk

Celaestrioz [seh-less-tree-ohz] – Aggressive firefly-looking creatures with human faces

Chicklebane – a spicy herbal flower that serves as a muscle relaxer

Cleaving – the ability to transport from one place to another through walls and flat surfaces

Cor of Aethyria – The heart of Aethyria, thousands of miles below the surface, where the black flame burns hottest

Corvugon [core-vuh-gon] – A cousin of the drakon, a serpentine creature with four legs, feathers, a beak, and wings that breathes silver flames

Deimosi [day-moh-see] — Fears left behind from those who've died that take the form of shadows

Demutomancy [deh-mew-toh-man-see] – Altering blood; an outlawed form of magic

Dindleweed – A powerful aphrodisiac

Drake – a serpentine creature with four legs and no wings

Drakon [drah-cone] – a serpentine creature with no wings

Duoculos [dew-oc-you-los]– A condition that affects the color of the irises after injury

Emberforge – A ritual to ingest the power of sablefyre; extremely dangerous – can cause deformities in those who've reached the age of ascendency; has only been successful once

Fervenszi [fur-ven-zee] – A potent liquor

Firebleeding – Sprinkling flammapul on the tongue then making small cuts in the flesh and licking the wound to introduce the substance; causes extreme paralysis

Flammapul [flamma-pool] – A poison that causes extreme paralysis when introduced directly into the bloodstream/wound

Flamellian [flah-mel-ee-yon] — one who practices firebleeding

Forenzycaris [for-enzi-care-us] – A mancer who specializes in investigating murders and auras

Fragor [frah-gore] – A stone that can be detonated with the proper chant, causing large explosions

Glyph – Symbols that coincide with a specific blood magic; they appear as scars on the palm

Golvyn [gole-vin] – Half man/half rat creatures that dwell in the walls of castles

Highbloods – Highborn Aethyrians, wealthy

Initios [ini-she-ose] – A ceremony performed by royalty to kick off a celebration; a blessing

Keltzig [kelt-zig] – A unit of currency in the form of a silver coin

Koryn [core-in] – Large scaly serpents that inhabit moats and rivers

Lunamiska [luna-mee-skah] – My little moon witch

Letalisz [lay-tall-iss] – Assassins for the king whose identity is often kept secret

Liro [lee-roh] – A unit of currency (greater than a Keltzig) in the form of a black coin

Mageduell [mayj-do-ell] – A fighting technique that incorporates eldritch glyphs and bloodspells

Magestrolian [mayj-uh-stroll-ee-an] – An elite brotherhood of the most skilled mages; advisors to the king

Malevol [mal-uh-vole] – A demon spirit

Malustone [mal-uh-stone] – A golden stone that can inflict tragedy when given to someone

Mandrawyld Tonic [man-drah-wild tohn-ik] - a potent tonic with hallucinogenic properties derived from black mandrake and wyldwood roots

Mimicrow [mim-ih-kroh] – Birds bred by the Magestroli to serve as spies by mimicking everything they hear

Mortemian [more-tee-me-an] - Death collectors for the city.

Morumberry [more-um-berry] – A sweet berry that grows on vines used to make wine; the leaves are used to make oil said to ward off evil spirits; the flowers are part of the Nightshade family and highly toxic if ingested

Muripox [mur-ee-pox] – A highly contagious disease that causes unsightly boils all over the skin

Nectardeium [neck-tar-dee-um] – Nectar of the gods, a potent liquor

Nexumis [neck-zu-miss] – The ability to manipulate glyphs without blood magic; a practice used by the Elvynira

Nilivir [nil-i-veer] – Mancers who have lost their blood magic over time due to lack of vivicantem

Nilmirth [nill-mirth] – A potent truth serum that causes violent illness in those who lie

Pendulynx [pen-du-linx] – a long snouted mammal, smaller than an elephant

Prilunar Light – Light given off by the moon that helps nocturnal food grow and gives power to the Lunasier – A race of mancers whose blood magic is powered by the moon

Pahzatsz [pah-zahts] – A root, but similar to potatoes

Prodozja [pro-doh-ja] – The protective form of blood magic that appears in the form of an animal/insect

Primyria [prih-meer-ee-uh] – The ancient language of the gods, spoke by some Vespiri

Pyromage [py-roh-mayj] – A mancer who can manipulate fire

Quints [kwince] – A unit of currency (less than a Keltzig) in the form of a red coin

Rapax [ray-pax] – A child predator/pedophile

Rapiuza'mej et rapellah'mej - Loosely translated to *take me and ravish me.*

Raptacy [rap-tah-see] – An elixir, originally designed as a sleeping tonic, which heightens libido

Sablefyre [say-bul-fire] — An element of the gods, forged in the Cor of Aethyria

Septomir [sept-oh-mir] – A powerful septer that was used to create the Umbravale, powered by the blood of the seven

Serotonics [seroh-tonics] – Blood poisons often produced in illegal labs

Sexsells – Those who engage in sexual acts for money

Sickhash Root – A plant root sometimes given to children before bed to make them sleep

Spindling – A child born to Nilivir; they have no blood magic and cannot bear children (sterile)

Spirityne [spirit-teen] – Small fairy-like creatures that dwell in woods with human faces and stick-like bodies; highly aggressive; will attack in swarms

Umbravale – The ward created by the septomir that divides Mortasia from Aethyria

Vein – Deep lava trenches where the black flame rises up from the Cor

Venetox Steel [ven-eh-tox] – A strong metal said to have been forged in Nethyria

Veniszka [ven-iss-kah] – Aethyrian word for mortal witches who cast spells

Vivicantem [vih-vih-cant-um] – A nutrient mined from veins that is required for blood magic; without it, blood magic diminishes

Weavers – Herbal satchets used to ward off bad dreams and evil spirits

Wickens – Mortasian word for Spiritynes

Wrathavor - A forest-dwelling demon with a voracious appetite for human meat.

GLYPHS

Aeryz [Air-iss] – Wind's vengeance; a glyph that uses wind to knock an opponent back

Erigorisz [air-ee-gore-iss] – The power to levitate objects with the mind

Evanidusz [ee-van-i-duss] – To vanish into black smoke; to become invisible to the naked eye

Propulszir [pro-pull-zeer] – To repel powers; a protective glyph that prevents mind reading

Osflagulle [os-flah-jule] – Bone whip power – one strike can shatter bones

AETHYRIAN GODS

Deimos [day-mose] – A mortal who became the god of chaos and fire

Magekae [mayj-ah-kai] – God of alchemy and immortality

Morsana [more-san-ah] – Goddess of death

Pestilios [pest-ill-ee-ose] – God of pestilence and famine

Vivarya [vee-ver-ee-ah] – Goddess of fertility

Dear Reader,

If you're new to my writing, I want to thank you for taking a chance on my first foray into gothic fantasy. My goal is to create an enjoyable reading experience for you, so before diving in, I want to clarify what you can expect in this story.

My plots tend to be intricate and layered and while romance is one of the many elements I weave into the story, it is not the sole focus in this case. If you're anxious for the spice, it'll come eventually, but know that this is a slow burn. You will be tormented with pages of unbearable tension before we arrive at the climax, so to speak. Please take this into consideration as you venture into this world.

A word of caution …

This book contains a number of potentially triggering situations. You can find the full list of trigger warnings-with spoilers-on my website: https://www.kerilake.com/anathema-full-trigger-list

PROLOGUE

Two hundred eleven years ago ...

L ady Rydainn held her infant son close as she approached the glowing vein that, only days ago, had been a snarling fissure of black fire that cleaved the ground. With the two moons nearly as one, the chasm of violet lava had hardened to stone, leaving only the flickering remnants of that sinister flame. It was almost time to harvest the igneous rock, but they weren't there for the bounty it held.

They were there for the fire itself.

The men who typically guarded the vein from thieves lay in diminishing piles of ash, their bodies and armor charred to useless lumps of soot that scattered in the wind. Burned alive by a flame so hot, she could feel its radiance a half-furlong away. Sablefyre. An ancient element of the gods, forged eons ago in Aethyria's fiery heart. A single touch could turn a body to ash, and blood to stone.

And she had arrived to offer up Zevander, her second-born son, to it.

Not by choice, of course. Lady Rydainn would've sacrificed herself right there and then, if it would spare Zevander from such a horrific fate. Unfortunately, the mage who'd demanded the exchange wasn't interested in her pittance of an offer. He wanted her youngest son, and nothing more.

She forced herself to set her eyes upon the dark and corrupt soul, where he stood alongside her eldest son and husband, watching her every step from the edge of the vein. The man she'd come to know as the most dangerous mage in all of Aethyria. One of few who'd mastered the ability to control the otherwise chaotic sablefyre and discovered a means to harness its deadly and divine power. He'd once been the king's highest Magelord, a member of the exalted Magestroli, disgracefully dismissed on accusations of demutomancy—a dark form of magic decreed illegal by the king.

Cadavros. The mere thought of his name cast a shiver down her spine.

Yet, she and her husband had been forced to make a Faustian bargain with him, in exchange for protection against the Solassions who hunted their family. Ruthless warriors, known for their brutality and violence. Enforcers, who'd have made sport of their execution.

In their moment of desperation, the reclusive mage had approached the Rydainns with an offer they couldn't refuse. A powerful protection spell against those who sought their heads, in exchange for their firstborn's blood magic—a sampling Cadavros had claimed would be used in his studies.

If only Lady Rydainn possessed the power to reverse time. She would've chided her stupidity. Warned herself not to trust his lies. For, what he'd taken from her eldest boy was far more than a *sampling* of his magic.

Black, beady eyes, those deep soulless sockets, stared back at her, as if daring her to run from his ghastly form. There was a time he was said to have been handsome, but the dark and forbidden magic had taken a toll on him. Sank its claws into his flesh and twisted him into a wicked beast. From the top of his head breached long branching antlers, with horns that curled back. Deep grooves etched into his hardened skin reminded Lady Rydainn of tree bark, the black pulsing veins beneath said to house small serpents trapped inside his flesh.

Evil begging to be unleashed.

His appearance was the result of having performed the *Emberforge* ritual on himself, the same ritual he intended for her son. A rite that only young children were believed to tolerate without any permanent disfigurement, seeing as they hadn't yet gone through their Ascendency.

Beside the mage stood her husband and their eldest son, Branimir, whose similarly protruding black veins and coarse skin marked the horrific deformities of her first sacrifice only weeks before. A sacrifice that'd proven insufficient for the greedy mage, when Branimir had suffered the same grotesque mutations as Cadavros's. Though far from puberty and his Ascendency into blood magic, Branimir had already begun the physical transitions, before the flame had corrupted the seed of magic that'd taken root inside of him. And while his resulting deformities weren't as pronounced as those of Cadavros, they ensured her poor child would never know his true power—because once the black flame entered the body, it destroyed all natural blood magic.

Her demands to break the devil's bargain with Cadavros had proven hopeless, when he'd vowed to slaughter both boys should she fail to comply. Not an idle threat, given the many inquisitions she'd witnessed where he'd exerted his power with merciless cruelty.

Tears blurred her vision, her steps faltering as she drew closer to the vein. Her younger son lay sleeping in her arms, completely unaware of the night to come. A night that would forever change the innocent baby boy she so dearly loved.

For hours, she'd prayed to the old gods in hopes his fate might be changed, that he might somehow be spared. Alas, the gods had never answered, and darkness closed in on her as the moons slipped into the shadows.

Had she the choice, she'd have sooner taken young Zevander and fled to Mortasia, beyond the Umbravale that separated the mortal lands from Aethyria. A place believed to be nothing but a barren wasteland, brimming with famine and death.

There was nowhere to hide. Nowhere to flee.

The remorse in her husband's eyes failed to move her, the anger slinking its way through her blood with renewed fervor. After all, it'd been *his* nefarious dealings on foreign Solassian land that had sealed their family's fate. His unfaltering determination to elevate their social status, no matter the cost. She bit back the proud Lunasier magic pulsing in her veins that would've surely struck down her husband, had she the gumption right then. How easily he'd been convinced to offer their only sons.

Run, her head urged. *Save them.*

It was too late for Branimir, though. The eldest boy was the first to have suffered the ritual, and his darkened eyes had grown even more vacant in the fortnight since.

The sickly pallor of her eldest son's skin spoke of the hours since, during which he'd been locked away in the cells beneath the castle, as his father attempted to hide him from the world. *An abomination*, other villagers would have called him, and understandably so. What thrived inside of him wasn't a power of the gods, but a deeply rooted malice that'd grown stronger in the weeks since the ritual.

The notion of watching her jubilant baby, an echo of the sweet, loving boy Branimir had once been, suffer the same fate was an agony she couldn't bear.

Lady Rydainn's power trembled like a plucked thread, as rays of moonlight hit the sigil on the nape of her neck, penetrating the thick fabric of her cloak and eliciting a charge that hummed in her veins. It innervated every cell in her body, rousing a cold rush to her fingertips, where it begged to be turned loose. The moon affected all Lunasier that way, and Zevander shifted in her arms, as if sensing the vibration beneath his mother's skin.

It would've been years before his power would come to fruition, and she'd longed for those heartwarming moments of discovery that would soon be tainted by the poison of the flame.

Standing apart from her son and husband, she kept her distance from the flame, her breaths hastening as Cadavros approached her. She curled her fingers into Zevander, when the mage reached out a bony finger that appeared more like a branch than a limb and stroked its tip down her baby's soft, cherub cheek. A trail of blood followed, and Zevander stirred, letting out a quiet mewl that heightened as the small cut on his face deepened to a dark gash. One so frighteningly malicious-looking, she wondered if the tip of Cadavros's finger was tainted with death poison. The mage reached again, and on instinct, she jerked the baby away, shielding him with her hands. As she took in the unsightly wound, a seed of rage bloomed inside of her. Her kettled magic surged, winding around her bones and beating against her skin, demanding to punish the mage. Her baby screamed in her arms, his face red, limbs shaking. He'd hardly made a sound most nights, a contented baby from the day he'd been brought into the world, and it tore at her heart to hear his distressed cry then.

Fighting Cadavros was futile, though. With the power of sablefyre at his command, she'd be reduced to ash, like the guards who'd tried to fight him off when they'd first arrived at the vein.

A tear streaked down her cheek. *"Pilazyo. Orosj tye clemuhd,"* she whispered. *Please. I'm begging your mercy.*

Cadavros wordlessly slipped his fingers beneath the baby, and her tears turned hysterical when he gave a tug.

She yanked her child back to her, jerking the young boy to her chest. *"Nith! Nith hazjo'li! Je fili meuz!"* I will not do this! He is my son!

Zevander's outcry, as Cadavros pried the boy from his mother's arms, stirred her instincts. On a whim of madness, Lady Rydainn lurched for the beastly man who carried her son toward the smoldering vein, but a force struck her throat, knocking the breath out of her. Black smoke crawled from her mouth, choking out the words she'd longed to say. *Stop! I surrender myself!* Her unseen attacker held her there in its invisible grasp, while Cadavros didn't even spare her a glance.

Lord Rydainn strode toward his suffering wife, but as he neared, his leg snapped beneath him with the gut-twisting sound of splintering bone. His outcry echoed through the surrounding forest, and he fell to the ground, his limb bent wrong at the knee.

Branimir didn't move, his murky eyes vacant and lost.

In spite of the pressure at her throat and the lack of breath in her lungs, Lady Rydainn called out for her son, reached for him, but to no avail. Needles of terror prickled her spine, as Cadavros held the baby in the crook of one arm while stretching a roughly tessellated hand into the black flame that rose up from the glowing vein. The black ember he captured flickered in his palm, and Zevander's cries quieted, the child seemingly mesmerized by the sight as the mage held it over him.

Lady Rydainn whimpered and quailed, her knees weak with defeat, and before she could shutter her eyes from the horror, Cadavros shoved his palm against her baby's mouth, smothering him with the black flame.

Zevander kicked and writhed, his tiny feet dangling helplessly from his captor's grasp. A potent mix of rage and anguish shook her body, the endless stream of tears creating an irritating blur in her eyes.

Branimir shifted on his feet, all too aware of how ravenously that flame consumed, judging by the way he growled and slapped at his ears. As if he were feeling his younger brother's pain right then.

The trauma that both of her precious sons were made to suffer tore at her heart with jagged teeth. Tears spilled down her cheeks as she watched the black flames emerge through her son's skin, licking the night air like the dark tongues of serpents.

Zevander's struggle ceased, his body limp. The flames died, settling across the baby's flesh in wicked black swirls.

The darkness had accepted and branded him.

An eternal curse.

Cadavros lifted the baby and drew his noseless face over her son's naked chest. His mouth opened impossibly wide, and he shoved Zevander's head inside.

"No! Oh, gods! *No!*" A scream rattled in futile misery inside her chest, as Lady Rydainn watched in horror while the ghoulish mage attempted to consume her child.

The mage let out a boisterous roar and yanked the child from his mouth. He tipped his head, inspecting the black markings left on her baby's skin. A deep, guttural sound rolled in his chest, and he snarled, snapping his attention back to the flame. "*Quez sa'il!*" *What is this?*

Again, he looked back to the boy, running his finger over one of the markings on his chest. Growling, he struck the infant's face and tossed him into the flaming fissure.

"No!" The scream that echoed through the forest could've roused the old gods from their slumber, as Lady Rydainn shook and cursed their names, demanding they set her free.

Lord Rydainn howled in agony, crawling toward the vein with his horribly mangled leg dragging behind him. "You bastard! You fucking bastard!"

Cadavros roared again, smoke curling from his skin, his body trembling. He reached back into the flame, lifting the boy, who neither screamed nor cried. He didn't move, at all.

Agony clawed at her heart as she examined her baby from

afar. Eyes searching for a single sign of life. The blankets that'd swaddled him had burned away, leaving him completely exposed, his head cocked to the side, eyes still closed.

Was he alive? Oh, gods, let him be alive!

Snarling again, Cadavros held the boy in front of him, looking upon him with the kind of malice that curled her stomach.

"*Pilazyo.*" She shook with the plea. "*Jye suaparcz vitaez.*" *Spare his life.*

Lingering wisps of smoke drifted over the mage's face, and she caught the glisten of raw flesh across his bark-like skin.

It was then that Lady Rydainn realized: in his attempt to harm her son, he'd somehow suffered pain himself.

The pressure at her throat subsided, and sapped of all will, she crumpled to the ground. When those cloven feet stood before her again, she lifted her gaze to see Cadavros handing back her listless child, carelessly holding him by his arm as if he were nothing but a sack of meat and bones. Feeble arms outstretched, she reached back for him and cradled him against her. A searing heat burned her skin, but she refused to let him go.

"Is he alive?" Lord Rydainn's voice swelled with misery as he clawed at the ground toward them. "Does he live?"

She ignored him, her anger still too razor-sharp to care about his suffering, as she lifted her son to her face, noting the warm puffs of air coming from his mouth.

Thank the gods! He still breathed. On a tearful exhale, she held him tighter and kissed the top of his head. Her sweet child had survived being cast into sablefyre–a fate that would've left any other a pile of ashes like the poor soldiers.

Yet, he had survived. By the miracle of the gods, he'd been spared.

The babe awoke, and the once innocent blue of his eyes showed as a gradient of wine red with swirls of orange and gold that converged at the center in a black eclipse. The silvery wisps of hair that'd begun to grow in had burned away. Gone was the soul of a harmless, loving child. In his place lay the vestiges of an aberration that the gods would surely forsake.

Squirming in her arms, the child cooed and babbled, a peculiar sight, given what he'd suffered moments before. The gash at his face had blackened into a deep groove that mirrored the vein from which he'd been pulled. At the edges of the wound, smaller black veins branched out like rivulets on a map.

She ran a trembling finger over them, and on contact, she recoiled at the scorching pain that streaked across her skin. "How could you do this?" she whispered, lifting her gaze to her husband. "*How could you do this!*"

Lord Rydainn sobbed in the distance, and her hatred for him grew with every new discovery of her son's curse.

Branimir approached, his eyes wide with wonder. Tears in her eyes blurred his form at the memory of Zevander's birth, when the boy had looked upon his infant brother with the same curiosity. How precious and innocent it had been then, those memories nothing but a forgotten dream.

He reached for Zevander, running his finger over the marking on his chest, a curious black swirl that'd seemed to anger Cadavros. On closer examination, there seemed to be words written in ancient Primyrian embedded in the swirl in a way that reminded Lady Rydainn of a wax seal across his heart. Branimir's lips twisted to a snarl as he whispered the words that stabbed her conscience. "*Il captris nith reviris.*"

What is taken will never return.

CHAPTER ONE

MAEVYTH

The Village of Foxglove Parish
Present Day ...

The forest hadn't eaten in a while.

I peered past the macabre archway, into the depths of Witch Knell, the cursed stretch of woods where sinners went to die. It'd earned its name centuries before as a place where witches had once been sacrificed, its grim history upheld as a form of banishment for the heretics and morally corrupted. *The Eating Woods* the villagers called it, because sometimes the carcasses of those cast off were recovered along the edge, their bodies having been stripped of skin and flesh. Some so badly ravaged, only the metal cuff of their shackles confirmed them as banished.

Sharp bones and knotty sticks, covered in hoarfrost, twisted around each other to form the ominous entrance to the woods. Flanking either side of it, the gnarled and weathered oaks, smothered in icy webs of thorny briars, weaved an impenetrable wall that stretched for hundreds of acres to either end. A heavy gloom of overcast offered little light to see through the maze of crooked trunks that reminded me of corpses twisted in pain and reaching for the sky. Wild and hungry, the forest awaited its next meal, which was due to arrive at precisely noon.

I stared down at my weathered boots, the tips of which didn't quite meet the rocks directly below the archway, the boundary that, once crossed, awakened the monster on the other side. It was the closest I'd ever stood to the nefarious threshold, the doorway to whatever violent things happened within those trees. Curious as I'd always been to know what existed beyond it, I didn't dare set foot inside that misty labyrinth of trees. No one ever did, unless prodded by force, because The Eating Woods never returned what was given.

A wintry gust rippled the hem of my black dress, the tickle at my calves taunting my nerves. The cape around my shoulders did little to shield me from the punishing cold that gnawed at my bones. It wasn't the wind or cold that left me shivering, but the rumors of what lived amongst the trees.

Some villagers whispered stories of the wrathavor–a demon with a voracious appetite for human meat. They believed him to be a punishment from the indigenous, who'd been pushed from these lands to the north. Others told stories of wickens, small woodland fairies that housed the souls of scorned witches, who lured and scavenged the lost by mimicking familiar voices. Most in Foxglove Parish, including the governor, believed the angel of judgment dwelled in the woods and punished those who'd rejected their beloved Red God.

Whatever it was, it ate indiscriminately, because certainly not all who were banished were bad, seeing as the forest had been known to snatch a toddler once, or twice.

Even a small baby.

I was no more than a few days old when I'd been found abandoned before that cursed arch in a wicker basket, a single black rose upon my chest. No one knew who'd left me there, but every villager speculated that, whoever they were, they must have hoped the woods would eat me, as well.

Fortunately, someone had found me before then, and placed me on the doorstep of the Bronwick family. Otherwise, I'd have probably ended up like so many others who'd fallen victim to the forest's voracious appetite.

So many souls. Hundreds, maybe. The man I'd called grandfather, Godfrey Bronwick, was likely one of them. Said to have wandered beyond the archway after too much morumberry wine and gotten swallowed up in its misty depths.

Unfortunately, no one had braved searching for him there. Not even father.

Father.

A formal letter, held loosely in my fingertips, flailed for its freedom, while I mindlessly caught glimpses of the decorative calligraphy printed on the thick parchment. It'd arrived that morning in an envelope sealed in red wax with the royal stamp of the king. A fancy way of confirming that my adoptive father had been killed while serving the fanatical Sacred Men, the religious branch of the Vonkovyan armies that ruled with an iron fist over most of the continent. A small faction of defectors maintained a hold over Lyveria in the northern part of the continent, and my father had ventured there as a missionary, to convert the Lyverians for the glory of our good country.

Two months had passed since he'd gone missing, presumed to have been murdered by the defectors, which had left me and my sister Aleysia in the care of our step-grandmother, Agatha. An intolerant woman, who'd have probably tossed the two of us into the woods herself, if my grandfather hadn't insisted on otherwise in his last will.

"What now?" I murmured, as I stared through a mist of tears into the endless dark wood, trying to imagine what the future might look like.

Unwed girls without a father to protect their claim suffered one of two fates. They were either promptly forced into marriage. Or sent to serve the church as one of the Red Veils— clergy women ordered to worship obediently until death. Even if I'd wanted to be married, and I certainly didn't, the whole parish looked upon me as a pariah, so the odds of a respectable suitor were slim.

Which left only one option, and I'd have sooner raced straight into those woods than suffer the horrors I'd heard often befell the Red Veils. The least of which was having their tongues cut out for a vow of silence. As I understood, those deemed most impure suffered the worst indoctrination, often beaten into submission and made to endure long bouts of isolation.

Even then, pangs of anxiety clenched my chest at the thought of being sequestered from my sister, the only person who'd ever shown me love, unconditionally. She was the only person willing to see beyond the cursed baby left near The Eating Woods, in spite of what it meant for her reputation. As the blood heir of Grandfather Bronwick, she was more likely to be wed, though not to anyone of her choosing. Which meant, if I *were* forced into servitude, I'd only see her at the occasional Banishing, where all clergy were required to attend.

The many times Agatha had threatened to send me off to the convent to *glean some piety* had all but sealed my fate.

Neither option was appealing, but of the two evils I faced, at least marriage would've offered a life outside of the claustro-phobic temple where the clergy women were forced to reside. Worse still, as a Red Veil, I'd be at the mercy of Sacton Crain, the most senior member of the church, who'd undoubtedly go out of his way to make my life an absolute hardship. A man not only known for his unyielding expectations and veiled misogyny, but also, his unorthodox punishments, which included bare bottom spankings over his knee.

The paper crumpled within my tight fist, as I allowed myself to imagine such a thing.

I refused to be subjected to him.

Or any man, for that matter.

While I'd hardly known my adoptive father, nor held much love for him as a result of his constant absence, his mere existence had not only served as a buffer between Agatha and me, but had also protected me from ever having to consider life as a Red Veil.

His death was a tragedy in every sense of the word and for the first time in my life, I feared what lay on the horizon.

A damn fine mess you've left. And for what?

The ire I harbored toward my father was wrong, I knew that, but, damn it all, had he even considered the consequences? The mere *possibility* that he might've died and his family left to suffer the wrath of his beloved faith? That my sister and I would be placed in the care of the one woman in the world who loathed us more than the bone spurs she incessantly groaned about.

I wanted to scream into the void. To throttle fate with both hands for having dipped its poison-tipped fingers into our lives.

As I pondered the potential outcomes, the somber kindling of grief that simmered in my chest curled and lashed, fueled by my growing anger. A quiet flame that rose with a burgeoning need to be set free. Emotions I was forced to keep hidden for fear of looking possessed by evil, as girls were often perceived when they felt too much.

My fury refused to be smothered as a bleak picture rooted itself into my reality.

Damn you! my head screamed.

Though some may have been inclined to fault the defectors for father's murder, I didn't. I blamed the god who demanded blood. The *revered* god who ripped families apart and banished the innocent. An invisible entity, feared more than the creature that dwelled in the woods. The one to whom my father had pledged his undying devotion.

I glanced down at the letter, on the back of which, out of

resentment and spite, I'd written *The Red God isn't real*. They were words that scratched at my skull every time I knelt to pray. The same words that nearly spilled from my lips with every lashing I'd suffered for some obscure offense I'd committed against Him. To utter such a phrase would label me a heretic.

A witch.

Oh what fodder that would've given the whole damned parish, because had anyone found the letter, and what I'd written, I'd have been banished to these very woods. Of course, I could've burned it, and all traces of my blasphemy would've disappeared. But I longed to cast those words into the wind and see them carried to a place from where no one would be brave enough to retrieve them.

Into the depths of those starving trees that would eat them whole.

I opened my mouth for the scream begging to cut loose. The fury and frustration bound so tightly around my heart and lungs, it hurt to breathe. Mouth agape, I glared back at the letter through a veil of tears, summoning nothing more than a shuddering breath. The emotions remained strangled in my throat, like the many times I'd been forced to swallow them back in the face of ridicule and scorn and rejection. I'd learned at too early an age that the sound of a girl's scream drew nothing more than apathy.

Besides, what did it matter now, anyway? Father was gone. Our lives would never be the same from that day forward.

Mindless in my staring, the letter slipped loose and flitted just onto the other side of the archway, where it lay on the ground, oddly floundering like a fish in the dirt. The words I'd written trembled across the page, flickering in and out of view with each flutter of the breeze. Until the parchment settled, and a new phrase appeared where mine had been, in the same hasty strokes of my own handwriting. *God is Death*.

I frowned, my mind teasing the possibility that I'd inadvertently written that.

I hadn't.

God is Death? What did that even mean?

An unsettling wisp of confusion crawled over my neck as I reached out for the letter, daring my hand past that forbidden archway. I needed to see those words up close, to confirm that I wasn't imagining them.

I bent to retrieve it, and a hot streak of pain zipped across my forearm. "Dammit!"

Lifting my arm showed the sleeve of my dress torn up to my elbow, where blood trickled from a gouge down the underside of my forearm. A treacherous piece of bone, sticking out from the archway, held remnants of the torn fabric, confirming what had cut me, and a small piece of blood-stained lace slipped from its sharpened tip. As a sizzling sound rose over the rustling of the trees, I frowned harder, and as I watched, curls of white smoke drifted from the bone and once-red drops of blood seared to black.

Light shimmered across my eyes, the entire forest rippling with a translucent sheen. I gasped at the sight, my eyes fixated on the peculiarity, trying to discern whether what I was seeing was real. I'd heard stories of seafarers happening upon a glimmering wall, miles out from land, one that altered their navigation and sent them sailing right back from where they'd come. Those were the lucky ones, though. Others were said to have been swallowed by squalls that reached the sky, their ships never seen again.

As I cradled my wounded arm, a strong gust lifted the letter from the ground, carrying the stark white paper deeper and deeper into the dark trees. The errant breeze loosened my hair from its black rose clip, tousling the long and unruly tendrils across my skin like ghostly fingertips, tickling dreadful thoughts of what might happen if, on a capricious whim, the wind carried that paper into the hands of the governor, or Sacton Crain.

Or maybe it was the fear of not caring if it did.

Then, as quickly as it'd stirred, the wind died around me. As an eerie silence caressed my bones, I watched the letter fade from view.

Gone.

Glimpsing the blood still oozing from my cut, I turned for home to wash it.

A crackling sound caught my attention.

As before, I peered through the misty woods in search of its source.

Quiet. Calm.

Nothing.

The faint sound of a child's giggle rose up through the trees in a ghostly reverberation. "Maevyth," the voice whispered in whimsy, the sound of my name casting a chill across my skin.

I swept my gaze over the shadowy tree trunks, recalling a cardinal rule of the forest: *never answer to your own name.*

"God is death," it said, echoing the words on the paper.

A blast of blackness shot out from the arched entryway toward me, knocking me backward.

The frost-coated ground slammed into my spine, banishing the air from my lungs, and I turned onto my side, coughing. A treachery of ravens took to the sky overhead, the swoosh of their flapping wings punctuating their loud caws. They missiled over me as if they'd been spooked by something, and my own heart hammered inside my chest, my lungs rebounding with air.

At last, the commotion settled, and with panting breaths, I turned back to the archway. Only one bird remained, impaled through the breast by a sharp bone, a spike of malicious ivory, like the one that'd cut my arm. Fighting to catch my breath, I watched the helpless bird twitch and caw, its blood dripping over the pale white stones piled at the foot of the archway. A glint struck its eyes, drawing my attention to something unusual about them.

With an unwavering gaze, I slowly pushed to my feet and padded toward it, every muscle still trembling, but by the time I reached it, the raven had stilled. Even lifeless, the strange, silvery hue of its eyes was a striking distraction. One that had me questioning if it'd been ill prior to having been gored by the bone. The glassy, eldritch gleam, so cold and sharp, held my reflected form in a chilling glimpse of a world beyond. A place I feared to imagine.

Death.

And as I stared back at the poor creature, watching the blood trickle down the branches, a heavy ache swelled in my chest.

After a quick glance around to ensure no one was watching, I reached up, cupping my hands around the large bird's wings. Warm blood oozed down my wrist, mingling with my own as my tugging creaked the bones and wood of the structure. My arms trembled with the effort, but the bird wouldn't budge. Groaning, I tugged harder. "C'mon now. Come loose!"

Bracing my boot against the archway, I channeled all my muscle into the task.

A loud squawk sent me flying backward, and I let out a scream, tumbling for the second time. The bird lay on the ground beside me, its chest faintly rising. Blood trickled out of the corner of its beak, red against the ghost-white snow, as it writhed in distress. It somehow pushed to its feet and hopped two steps toward me before tottering to the side. Tears welled in my eyes, as the helpless creature opened and closed its beak, as if it tried to tell me what was wrong. I could almost hear it begging for mercy. Its wound was fatal, the bone that'd pierced its breast too big to have spared any vital organs, and its life was slipping away before my eyes.

Do something. Do not let it suffer.

My stomach twisted at the thought. I'd once watched Grandfather cut the throat of a days-old fawn that'd been gravely injured by a hawk. An act of mercy, he'd called it.

From the pocket of my skirt, I reluctantly removed a small paring knife that I kept for carving and fruit. One Agatha had tried to confiscate a few times with little success. Hands trembling, I slipped it from its makeshift cloth sheath and pushed to my knees to cradle the bird at my thigh. As it struggled against me, I exhaled a shaky breath and stretched its neck to slide my blade across the suffering creature's throat, flinching at the same time my stomach curled. *An act of mercy*, my head told me, but my heart wrenched a quiet sob from deep inside my chest. Until that moment, I'd never killed a living thing with my own hands.

What a terrible burden to watch something die.

CHAPTER TWO

MAEVYTH

F rigid breaths of remorse stuttered out of me in white
puffs, and I loosened my grip to find the bird no longer
stirred at my side. It'd gone cold and stiff already.

After a quick glance around, I wiped away my tears and gathered it up, cradling it in my arm, as I hustled toward the edge of
the wood. Beneath a winterberry bush, I found a flat rock and
scraped a modest hole in the dirt there. The bite of early winter
air thickened my hands, numbing them as I hurried to finish the
task. Once I'd dug deep enough, I laid the bird inside and buried
it. The toxic berries would keep the critters away, but for good
measure, I plucked a few, sprinkling them over the inelegant
grave.

The men of our parish believed the birds to be an omen of
death. They believed the same of me, too, so maybe I shared a
kinship with the foreboding creatures. It was said that, on the day
I'd been found near these woods, ravens had flocked around my
basket. I liked to think they were guarding me, but some thought
it a sign. A terrible sign.

The whole parish had branded me as cursed ever since.

The lorn.

The name that'd been drawn like a scar across my heart at my first baptism, when I'd devoted myself to their god. When I'd spoken the words that'd bound me to their merciless savior. But, just like the woods that ate voraciously, always hungry for more, my piety wasn't enough to earn their good graces. They still cast me off as something aberrant.

I could only imagine what they'd say about a silver-eyed raven.

Movement caught the corner of my eye, and I turned to where a small, thatch-roofed cottage stood at the edge of the forest, and a white-haired woman, half bent at the waist, gathered a cord of wood from a stacked supply. Enough for winter, which left me wondering how she'd cut it down herself. No one would've lent a hand, after all.

While I may have been shunned by the villagers, she was truly feared. *The Crone Witch.* Rumor had it, she'd murdered her husband and ate the hearts of children. I suspected she'd have been cast into The Eating Woods, like every other accused of witchcraft, if not for her healing skills that, years ago, had saved the governor's son from a bad case of somnufever. A deadly fate for most. Sometimes, The Crone Witch proved useful, garnering her more clemency than I'd ever been given.

As she hobbled back to her cottage, she paused en route and turned toward me. An inexplicable dread settled in my bones. Had she seen me? Would she tell someone what I'd done? If anyone found the buried bird, I'd be questioned. Probed. Possibly exorcised for bad humors.

I wiped my wrist against the black fabric of my dress as I puzzled all the possible consequences of my actions.

I could've unburied it. Tossed it back into the woods, but unearthing the dead was a sin and, in my book, even ravens counted as precious life.

The swooshing flap of wings interrupted my thoughts, and I

turned to see other ravens pecking around the ground for the berries I'd just scattered.

"Hey! Leave it! Go away!" I said, waving my hand to shoo them off. In all the fuss, I caught sight of a red banner with a cross in the distance.

The proclamation of the banished.

So focused on the approaching congregation, I didn't see Lolla, housekeeper and confidante to my step-grandmother, making her way across the yard toward me, until she spoke. "What in God's eyes are you doing, Maevyth?"

Startled, I turned to see her keeping a safe distance from the woods she seemed to fear would reach out and pull her in if she got too close.

She waved me over with her one good hand, the other arm had been crudely amputated by the Sawbones, a band of burly bottom feeders who collected debts on behalf of Governor Grimsby. Lolla, or Delores as everyone else referred to her, couldn't pay her taxes and had been forced from her family home. Grandfather had felt sorry for her, and had taken her in years ago to serve as a companion for Agatha, though my step-grandmother often treated the poor woman like a lowly house pet. "The governor is coming, and you're here frolicking by those wretched trees with those godforsaken birds. Please come. Quickly." Didn't matter that I was nineteen, a well-seasoned woman to those who kept track of such things, she still treated me as a child.

And for reasons I couldn't explain, I still obeyed.

Abandoning the grave, I hid my wounded arm behind my back as I made my way toward the older woman, and the moment I stepped within arm's length, she set forth with her one-handed fussing. The sleeve of her dress had been pinned to hide her mutilated elbow. Sawbones never hesitated to hack first and ask questions later, and their horrific handiwork spoke of their apathy in the task.

"By god, if anyone had seen you just now ..." she said, brushing what appeared to be nothing but the invisible wind from my skirts. Unlike the floral brocade that patterned the Egyptian blue corset over her brown kirtle, my dress was the simple black that I'd been forced to wear since I was a child. At my throat, dangled the signature black choker bearing the trinity cross that the governor had long decreed I should wear as a reminder of the mercy granted by our Red God. The same symbol my father would have been wearing when he was slaughtered in the name of the Sacred Men.

I ran my finger over one of the embossed flowers at her shoulder, longing for the day I might wear something so elegant.

Ignoring my caress, she kept on with her fussing and prattling. "My goodness, ravens, of all things. They'd have surely branded you a witch."

The villagers of Foxglove had branded me worse. After my arrival, we'd suffered the coldest winter in history, and food had become scarce. The following summer had yielded diseased crops that'd withered the harvest. According to them, I was the harbinger of famine, a mere infant responsible for blight. "You always said a witch held far more dignity than any parishioner."

Brows pulled to a pained expression, she shook her head. "Oh, for heaven's sake, I need to keep my damn mouth shut around you and your sister. Always fueling your feistiness. *Particularly* Aleysia." She tucked a stray hair behind my ear, the unruly curls refusing to stay put. "Those words will be your demise. Forget them. And any ridiculous comment I may have spouted off without thinking, while you're at it." As she reached for my arm, where my torn dress showed the blood still staining my skin, she frowned. "What in heavens ..."

"Cut myself on a branch, is all. Nothing serious." I didn't bother to mention the raven. Even as much as I loved and trusted Lolla, had known her since childhood, she feared the birds like everyone else and would've surely given me grief.

"Well, get it cleaned up. Can't have you looking this way for The Banishing." Lolla's frown softened as she stroked a gentle hand down my long black hair. "How are you holding up?" she asked, undoubtedly referring to the letter.

"In dire need of Grandfather's most potent batch of wine."

A smile curved her lips and she rolled her eyes. "Aren't we all. But there'll be none of that this early in the day." She rested her palm against my cheek and sighed. "It's nearly time."

The words I'd been dreading.

CHAPTER THREE

MAEVYTH

I gave one more backward glance toward the forest behind me.

"Come," Lolla said, locking her arm in mine and urging me across the stony road that divided the woods from the two-story cottage covered in moss and vine. Aside from The Crone Witch's hovel, the nearest dwelling was over two thousand paces away—steps I'd counted a number of times on the way to town—because no one else gambled to live so close to The Eating Woods. It just so happened to host the perfect soil for morumberries, which had made it impossible for grandfather to resist, in spite of the rumors of what lived amongst the trees. Our cottage sat on the outskirts of Foxglove, in the rural parts, far enough from town to feel completely isolated, but still close enough to feed gossip.

A weathered sign sticking up from the perpetually mist-covered lawn stood half-cocked in front, the paint for Black Sparrow Vineyards chipped and broken. My grandfather had built a legacy on morumberry wine, one that had quickly declined when Agatha had been granted ownership after his death. Debts had piled with her extravagant spending, and she was forced to sell off nearly all of grandfather's possessions, save for the cottage, which had since stood in disrepair. The care Grandfather Bronwick had put into the vineyard had withered with neglect and the berries eventually failed to produce. With what little money Agatha had left, she'd invested in a mortuary, deciding the dead would never leave her penniless. Grandfather's beloved wine cellar had become a morgue, and ten acres of the vineyard housed the dead in an unkempt cemetery. The remaining acreage of viable morumberry plants served as the primary ingredient for the oils and poisons Aleysia and I were tasked to make for Agatha. Yes, poisons. While many used them as an effective means to control rodents and pests, others found more ominous purposes for the little black vials. And what better way to ensure business than to forge a path toward death.

Once inside the home, Lolla hustled me past what had become the showing parlor, to the washroom. As I stood beside the water basin, dabbing my cut with a warm cloth, she scoured the cupboard for some healing cream. Nothing but snake oil, really. The stench of the toilet behind me, as if something had died in it, mingled with my rattled nerves over the impending banishment. The unsettling depth of my wound certainly didn't offer any calm, either, and I swallowed back the urge to lose my breakfast, as I watched the edges come apart with her cleaning.

"You don't think it needs stitching, do you?" I frowned at the fact that I could see enough pink flesh to knot my stomach. For as many dead bodies as I'd watched come and go, some of which I'd had to wheel into the morgue myself, I still couldn't handle the sight of blood.

"It's deep, but perhaps it can heal on its own. You're absolutely certain it was a cut and not a bite from one of those ghastly birds?" she asked and, to my relief, stopped prodding the damned thing with the cloth.

If it had been a bird's bite, the governor would've probably ordered my limb chopped off, as well.

"I'm absolutely certain." I lifted my arm to show her the nauseating groove there. "A bird would have to have quite a beak to accomplish that."

"Or teeth. Some harbor demons, you know."

"That's a new one." I snorted, fighting the urge to roll my eyes at yet another bit of superstition.

After a quick examination, she gave a nod. "Wrap it up as quickly as you can. It's nearly noon." She shuffled out of the washroom, and groaning, I swiped up the cloth she'd left and wound it around the cut. Using my teeth, I one-handedly secured it with a knot and yanked my black sleeve over top of it. With it properly hidden, I made my way up the staircase to the second floor.

While there were plenty of bedrooms on the upper level, Aleysia and I shared a room in the cold attic, up another enclosed staircase. The two of us would've been perfectly fine living on our own, but Vonkovyan law dictated that unmarried women were not permitted to own property.

When I entered the bedroom, Aleysia stood staring out the window, her deep burgundy dress a splash of color against the dull, gray walls. From the ceiling over her head hung small white sachets that were decorated in dried flowers and filled with herbs. Weavers. Aleysia and I made them to keep bad dreams away—an affliction from which both of us suffered. Wild, blonde curls fell about her shoulders–a contrast to my black *witch locks*, as Agatha called them. While my features may have been a bit darker to those of my older sister, her personality was far more reckless. A trait that rankled Agatha more than my cursed reputation. Having been father's natural-born daughter certainly didn't earn my sister favor in Agatha's eyes.

I ambled up beside her, taking notice of what had undoubtedly captured her attention. Beyond the window, two lines of clergy dressed in red and black robes—the Sacred Men—led what I presumed to be the prisoner, though he was hard to spot in all that lush and embellished fabric. Behind them followed two militant Vonkovyans, who resided in Foxglove to keep the peace. Garbed in peaked black hats, pauldrons and bracers, their black gambesons loomed like a shadow behind the red surcoats they wore.

A long succession of parishioners who had no choice but to attend followed after them. But it was the Red Veils I spotted in the crowd who held my attention, and the sight of them roused a fresh swell of anxiety. "Are we going to talk about father?"

"What's there to talk about?" Aleysia answered coldly. "I find it difficult to care for a man who was absent for most of my life."

"I understand, but you know what this means, Aleysia. I suspect you'll wed fairly quickly. But I'll become one of them." I nodded toward the women with their high red veils that served as a prophetic omen to what little freedom I'd enjoyed up until that letter had arrived. "Agatha would see to it."

"Have I not vowed to protect you, Sister?"

I recalled the days of hiding in Grandfather's cellar and the pinky promises whispered in the dark. "Since we were children. But how would you accomplish that now? My future only diverges one of two ways, and there isn't a soul in Foxglove Parish who would chance a marriage with *the lorn*. Even if there was, that fate is only fractionally better than the other, as far as I'm concerned."

"*I* will marry and I will claim you as my ward."

"Only if your husband *allows* such a claim," I argued.

"Oh, he will." She smiled, as if she were already aware of her unnamed suitor's intentions. "But let's not talk about that now. I'm exhausted by the worries of father's death."

A mutual sentiment. I'd traversed all the emotions the moment I'd read that letter—sadness, fear, resentment, and downright anger. But unlike my incautious older sister, I couldn't turn off my thoughts so easily. Not even with the distraction of the congregation slowly making their way toward the edge of the forest.

"Do you think the Sacred Men wear anything under those robes?" Aleysia asked, her unseemly question breaking the silence between us. "Or do you think their nether regions just sway back and forth as they walk? Like the snout of a pendulynx."

As much as I fought my amusement, I couldn't help but smile. "What had to die in your soul to imagine such a horrific visual? And what in seven hells makes you think it's as long as a pendulynx snout?"

She sighed, tucking her bottom lip between her teeth. "A girl can dream."

Biting back a laugh, I shook my head. "Disgusting. Truly."

"You're lying, if you say you've never once thought about it. The way Sacton Crain leans against you ..." She took hold of my dress, leg wrapped around mine, and circled her hips against me. "And how are you my dearest Penitent?"

Sacton Crain had always avoided me like the plague, which suited me just fine, but I'd heard he'd gotten a bit too playful with some of the young girls in bible study. The thought of what he might've done behind closed doors roused fresh anger, but before I could dwell on it, Aleysia needled my ribs with her fingers, snapping me out of thoughts with her tickling.

Wrestling her grip, I let out a laugh, and she clutched me harder, humping my leg like a damned dog.

"No, one moment. I'm almost ... just another ... I promise–"

"You are positively repulsive!" I let out a howling laugh, pressing my palm against her shoulders to dislodge her from my body.

"Oh, Red God ... oh, merciful lord of lust ... I'm gonna ... I'm gonna ..."

"Girls!" The boisterous voice stiffened my muscles, and with a lingering chuckle, Aleysia slowly released me. "The day of Banishing is not a laughing affair."

Clearing my throat, I rolled my shoulders back and turned to face the wretched woman who stood at the top of the attic staircase, wearing an ecru smock under a juniper green kirtle and leaning on a tired old cane. If my features were said to be intense, Agatha's were severe. She often wore her silvery hair pulled back into a harsh knot at the back of her head, drawing attention to her dark, sunken eyes that appeared black in some lights, and her thin gray skin stretched over sharp bones. Like one of the many skulls her eldest son, Uncle Felix, liked to collect.

"Sorry, Agatha," I said.

Aleysia curtsied, a show of mocking. "Yes, terribly sorry. Banishing is a day of misery, particularly for the accused."

"Watch your tongue, girl." Agatha held out a pointed finger with a long yellowing nail she often used to stir her tea. "If not for your grandfather's merciful heart, both of you would be living in squalor."

"We'd certainly be happier," Aleysia muttered under her breath, and I elbowed her side.

"Fix your chemise." Agatha's order was directed at Aleysia, who often wore her underdress off the shoulders.

Aleysia seemed to grind on her words, and her jaw shifted as she yanked the fabric back up onto her shoulders.

"What of the oil supply?" the old woman grumbled, plucking a piece of lint from her skirt. "I'm expecting great demand after today's ceremony." In her tireless efforts to regain her squandered wealth, Agatha had Aleysia and I convert the fruitless morumberry leaves into oil, which was said to ward off evil spirits. A claim Agatha herself had made when she'd lied and told everyone that I'd suffered a possession last winter.

I'd come down with a high fever and had fallen into tremors as a result, but leave it to Agatha to associate my illness with the occult. At the very least, morumberry leaf oil was wonderful for the skin when bathing, and it smelled as delicious as the berries.

"We have a full crate. I suspect it'll be plenty," I said, having been the one to bottle them myself the day before, after Aleysia had run off somewhere.

She tapped her finger against the top of her cane. "And what of the Snake's Tooth?"

The oil was a ruse, mostly. Agatha's more lucrative endeavor was poison. A deadly byproduct of the morumberry flower that, when crushed into a fine powder and consumed over time, created clots in the blood. Grandfather had long used it for rat poisoning, but it so happened to have the same effect on humans, as well. Sometimes, it caused heart attack. Other times, it caused stroke, or an embolism in the lung. Because the outcome was never the same, no one suspected anything sinister, and Agatha never went out of her way to make her poison known. Still, she managed to generate business, both in and outside of Foxglove.

"Plenty." Though my part was indirect, as I never sold the goods, the guilt weighed heavily on me. I tried to tell myself those who purchased the powder were ridding themselves of rats, in one form, or another. Still, I'd learned, over time, to add crushed nasturtiums in order to reduce the potency, which helped ease my conscience.

"You better hope it's plenty. Now hurry yourselves along. If you're late, consider yourself excluded from supper." Lifting her gaze, she waved toward the weavers dangling about the room. "And get rid of those damned things!" With that, she hobbled off out of view, and Aleysia let out a groan.

"I swear, if she were to get a good fucking, just once, she'd be a whole new person."

I snorted a laugh and crossed the room for my hooded cloak, which made me feel less naked in the crowd.

Once dressed, the two of us descended from the upper attic to the second floor.

At the sound of a whistle, both of us turned toward where Uncle Riftyn strode up from behind, adjusting the cuff of his jacket. "Aren't you two a sight for sore eyes."

His lips curved into a lopsided grin, springing forth the dimple in his cheek. Agatha's most beloved, if the woman were capable of such a thing. With his sandy brown hair and bright blue eyes that he must've inherited from his birth father, he was a startling contrast to his brother, Uncle Felix, the resident mortician who spent most of his time in the cellar with corpses. Tall and gaunt, Uncle Felix looked every bit the undertaker, and his slow, dark eyes and perpetually sullen face often sent a chill down my neck.

"Why, thank you, Uncle." The flirtatious edge of Aleysia's voice drew my attention to the bottom lip she practically chewed away.

"Step-uncle," Riftyn corrected.

"Yes, *step*. You look very handsome, as well."

Staring back at Aleysia with a wily grin, he gave a courteous nod and strode off.

I sailed a disapproving frown at my sister, goaded by the lingering smile on her face. "Strange. He makes the distinction as if step implies he isn't a relation, at all."

She shrugged, fluffing the curls that fell into lazy ringlets over her shoulder. "No blood relation."

"That matters?" While it was true that Uncle Riftyn and his brother, Felix, weren't related to her father by blood, having been born to different parents, they were still family. Bound by marriage. A relation the church recognized as no different than blood.

"Matters for what?" She slid on a pair of worn black gloves, feigning ignorance.

Instead of answering, I studied the grace in her movements, the blithe indifference to what anyone may have thought about her. Aleysia had always been beautiful, desired. Her golden hair was said to have been spun by angels when she was a baby. It made sense that any man, even Uncle Riftyn, would find her attractive. Had we not suffered the fate of becoming Agatha's wards, she might've been courted by the most desired men in Vonkovya. Perhaps even married to one of them, as was custom.

Broken families were considered undesirable, though. A punishment of The Red God. And those cursed with a godless daughter, as I was often referred as, ensured we'd never find good standing in Foxglove.

"I'll see you at the woods," she said, passing me for the staircase.

CHAPTER FOUR

ZEVANDER

Zevander had grown weary of the hunt.

He stalked toward his prey, who stood pressed against the cave wall where the fool had trapped himself in a poor attempt to hide. A black leather mask concealed the notable scars on Zevander's face, and the hood of his cloak shadowed his identity. Not that the man he chased would ever have the opportunity to disclose such details.

"Please! I'm begging you! Whatever you want is yours!" The man's overfed body trembled beneath a fine silk nightshirt stained by the vintage wine he'd been guzzling when Zevander had startled him earlier.

Had the pathetic creature known who Zevander was, or what he'd come to collect, he'd have probably bashed his own skull against the rock wall behind him to be spared the pain that awaited him.

Zevander strode closer, removing his glove, and held his palm upright. Summoning magic was as fragile as thin glass, and yet, he'd learned to traipse the finer edges with a sickening ease. His skin held intricate carvings, cicatrices of ancient glyphs that called forth the sablefyre slumbering inside of him.

He only needed to give it purpose.

The older man before him collapsed to the ground and held up his hand in defense, shielding his face in futility. As if he had the power, or strength, to block what was coming. As Zevander had learned of his prey, the elder man's magic was turning useless rocks into precious jewels and amulets. A skill that'd served him well in the bustling kingdom of Costelwick. The soft blue glow of the sigil on his forehead not only alluded to the terror pulsing through him right then, but confirmed his bloodline as Lunasier. Like Zevander's late mother, who'd also been Lunasier, his power was born of both moons.

A golden ring sat in the folds of his pudgy finger, and Zevander reached out, snatching up his hand before he could lower it.

He stared down at the chunky white stone, with its tiny flecks of silver moondust embedded into the gold band. *Vivicantem.* All mancers required the coveted nutrient, formed naturally in the Cor of Aethyria and mined once a moon cycle from deep lava trenches known as veins.

Forged by the very flame that had marred Zevander's flesh.

Consuming the element awakened the inherent powers that all manceborn acquired from their bloodline, but because of the difficulty of extraction and high demand for the element, only the wealthy could afford the vivicantem-infused foods and drinks, grown on farms and orchards owned by the king. Without it, power was useless, an atrophic muscle inside the body that could do nothing but wither over time.

The unauthorized mining of it was a crime punishable by execution, so those who couldn't afford it eventually lost their magic, while wealthy hoarded the precious mineral. Wearing it as jewelry to boast their status, a sickening reality that prodded Zevander's rage as he studied the purity of the stone. Nothing but ornaments to decorate their gorged bodies.

"Aethyrians starve while you flaunt your riches," he said, tossing the man's hand aside.

The man took hold of the index ring and tugged. "It's yours. You can have it. Enough to last you a month, at least."

As he struggled to remove it, Zevander raised his palm, and a black mist swirled and shifted to an obsidian flame in the center of his hand. He unclasped his arm bracer, showing where a scorpion, seared on the back of his palm and wrist, rippled as it came to life beneath his skin.

The man's eyes widened. "Are you a high mage?"

Zevander snorted at that. "Worse."

Realization seemed to dawn on the man's face, as his brows pinched together. "You're a Letalisz."

An assassin for the crown. Most of Zevander's prey were commissioned by the order of the king, and he'd learned to dispense of his quarry with a very skilled slice of a blade.

But he hadn't come on orders of the king, and he had no intention of drawing his blade. The brand of magic he intended to inflict on the man was forbidden in the kingdom, an ability Zevander had managed to disguise for most of his life.

"Why?" The man shook his head. "I've done nothing wrong. Why me?"

"Because you breathe." Zevander threw his hand forth, sending a blast of flame over the man, whose screams and cries of pain echoed throughout the cave.

Within seconds his flesh and bones had burned to ash.

Zevander plucked a dark, red sphere that sat atop the pile, and deposited it into a satchel at his hip. Bloodstone. Derived from a form of demutomancy, the practice of altering blood–an outlawed magic that had cursed Zevander's family for centuries. Had anyone known he possessed the forbidden power, he'd have been hunted down and brutally destroyed by the king's Imperial Guard.

Through the remains of the ash, he rifled a finger in search of the white stone hidden there. The gold band had melted away in the flames, leaving only the chunk of vivicantem.

Zevander studied it for a moment, then plopped it into his satchel alongside the rest of the man's remains.

CHAPTER FIVE

MAEVYTH

A cold wind blew through the hood of my cloak, as I stood beside my sister, rubbing my hands together to stave off the frigid bite. On the other side of me stood Lolla, and next to her, Agatha and Uncle Felix. All of the parish, perhaps two hundred people in total, had gathered around Governor Grimsby and Sacton Crain, whose long white hair danced about his face as he stood upon the Prudence Rock.

"Under the eye of our merciful Red God, Caedes, we offer the soul of this sinner." Hands raised to the air, he looked skyward, and I glanced around at other parishioners, whose heads were tipped back, eyes closed as if they felt some divine presence amongst us. If The Red God was watching, then he surely had a morbid side to him. "May his sacrifice please our Lord–his bones to reinforce our good faith, his blood to rejuvenate our hearts, and his soul to cleanse our transgressions. For we are an imperfect reflection of our sacred father, and it is our duty to repent and redeem ourselves, or forfeit The Red God's protection when The Decimation is upon us."

The Sacred Men believed the end of mankind would arrive in the form of total destruction and complete blackness, and that

The Red God would deliver them to the Eternal Light. They also believed the more sinners they thinned from our community, the purer their devotion.

I felt like a liar standing amongst them. A traitor for the skeptical thoughts in my head that I didn't dare speak aloud. Not even to Aleysia. At that point, I'd already suffered plenty of scars for transgressions against their god. All carved into my back and legs by Sacton Crain, or the Vonkovyan guards who sometimes doled out the punishments. So, I played along, pretending to worship as all others, because nonbelievers were also sent to The Eating Woods.

Peering over my shoulder showed the parishioners standing behind us, keeping a wide berth with their eyes turned away from mine. Years ago, I'd caught wind of a rumor, that looking me in the eye could bring bad luck. No doubt, they'd have gladly traded me for the prisoner who faced banishment, their suspicions being that I embodied the evil they feared most.

In spite of myself, I turned back around, sparing them the discomfort.

An arc of red hid the accused from my view, the high hoods of The Red Veils, effectively blocking out his naked form. All banished were stripped down, divested of all possessions, so I was grateful for the obstruction, even if their presence gave me hives. It was rare to see the clergy women, who wore long red vestments with red veils meant to signify their love and devotion to the faith. They rarely left the temple, as socializing was undoubtedly a bit more challenging without the means to speak.

I ran my tongue across my teeth, trying to imagine its absence.

At a stirring beside me, I caught a glimpse of Aleysia holding Uncle Riftyn's hand, her fingers curled in his, in a way that seemed more intimate than comforting. As disturbing as it was to see their hands entwined, I couldn't ignore the distraction of my heart stampeding in my chest, the tickle of nausea stirring in my belly. The ceremonies always made me anxious, but for some reason, the symptoms seemed far more exaggerated this time.

Or perhaps it was just the cold seeping its way into my bones.

Between the row of parishioners and the Red Veils which separated me from the prisoner, all I could make out was the top of his head, his hair dirty and disheveled. How unbearable the chill must've been on his exposed flesh obscured by all the heads in front of me.

As I understood, he'd defected against The Red God and country. A family man who'd gone on a raving tirade, claiming the Governor and Sacton Crain were frauds and murderers, and that the Sacred Men were nothing but a cult. He'd also threatened to burn Governor Grimsby alive.

Unfortunately for him, threats weren't tolerated in Foxglove Parish. Particularly those against the governor.

A glance to the left showed the prisoner's wife and young son, standing off at a distance. The woman sobbed into a kerchief, while her son, perhaps no more than seven years old, looked on, undoubtedly confused by the scene. She'd have been forced to attend The Banishing, because refusing would've placed her alongside her husband. Hard to say what would've happened to their son in that instance—most wives simply kept quiet and obeyed the laws.

Of course, they'd be homeless afterward, lucky to survive the winter, because the wives of the banished weren't permitted to own property. A cruel fate.

Unbeknownst to Agatha, I sometimes snuck bread and warm broth to Mrs. Chalmsley, whose husband had also been banished to Witch Knell. After having lost their home, she'd found refuge in the old granary that'd gotten damaged in a storm a few years back. I'd have to find a way to scrounge extra for the distraught looking mother and her child.

"Stripped of all possessions," Sacton Crain kept on, "this man shall be judged as all on the day of reckoning."

From a small brazier whose orange flickering I could see between bodies, he lifted a branding rod into the air, and the first twinge of panic gurgled in my throat. Breathing through my nose, I screwed my eyes shut to the sound of sizzling flesh, but could not block out the roar of agony, tempered only by the bit that'd been placed in the prisoner's mouth.

"Daddy!" The boy cried out, and I dared to glance his way. Tiny hands reached out as his mother held him close, burying her face in the small child's chest. Teeth clenched, she let out an angered cry, drowned by the dying sounds of suffering. There was nothing she could do, though. To interfere would've placed her in the same fate, leaving her child completely alone and defenseless.

"And now, we offer this sacrifice to the angel of judgment," Governor Grimsby said. "Should your blessings favor us with a mild winter and bountiful spr-"

The woman in front of me let out a wild scream, and at the hard clutch of my wounded arm, I looked up to see the prisoner standing before me, his naked and dirty body trembling, eyes wild. The branding of a B that'd been seared into his cheek glistened with raw and swollen flesh.

Muscles stiff, I couldn't move, my breathing hard and erratic as I stared back at him. On his hand, just below the metal shackle, I spied a five stars and moon, the symbol of the old gods, inked onto his skin.

His eyes rolled back to terrifying white orbs, which emphasized the dark circles where he must've been punched. "God is Death," the man rasped, and in the next breath, he was ripped away by the Vonkovyan guards.

The phantom mark of his icy grip lingered, as I stared down where he'd grabbed me.

Voices around me grew distant. I turned to see Aleysia speaking, her lips moving, but I couldn't hear what she was saying.

A path remained clear ahead of me, offering a view of the

robed men dragging the prisoner to the archway where I'd stood earlier, when I'd read those very words on my father's death announcement. Words I hadn't written.

One hard shove knocked the prisoner onto the ground at the other side. As he scrambled to his feet, the guards blocked the archway, preventing his escape, their sharp rods pointed at him. One of them sneered, jabbing at the man with his bayonet.

Everything moved slowly and fluidly, as if I were under water.

A nudge from my left drew my focus to Lolla, who asked if I was alright. Beside her, Agatha wore a repulsed expression.

With my muscles seized in shock, I couldn't form a single word.

The silence shattered beneath a gurgling outcry.

The Vonkovyan guards broke away, opening the view of the prisoner on his knees, blood oozing around the guard's rod impaling his chest.

An invisible force yanked the banished man backward, into the depths of the woods.

A guttural cry of terror echoed from the forest, and an object flew through the archway, landing at my feet.

As I stared down at the five stars and moon on the man's degloved hand, my breathing hastened, the view shifting around me.

Blackness filtered in.

CHAPTER SIX

MAEVYTH

"That had to be the most grotesque thing I've ever seen in my life." Aleysia dabbed a cold cloth against my temple, as I sat in the parlor of the mortuary and watched a small crowd mingle. Much of the parish had apparently departed after the ceremony, but about half a dozen women stayed behind. Agatha's few acquaintances from town, undoubtedly on the hunt for gossip about the bedeviled Bronwick girl who'd passed out. And looking to buy the morumberry oil that I should've been selling in the kitchen right then.

Seeming to catch onto my preoccupations, Aleysia sent a quick glance over her shoulder, toward the women who gawped at the two of us. "Don't mind them, the gossipmongers."

"They look at me as if I just crawled out of a grave."

"Well, you *do* look a little peaked." The smile on her face faded when I didn't reciprocate. "You're peculiar, is all, Maevyth. And nothing invokes fear quite like the peculiar." Gentle strokes of the cloth calmed the clammy pangs of shock still gurgling in my chest. "Though, I do wonder what language that was." Through the chaos still swirling in my head, Aleysia's comment snapped me back to the moment.

"What? Who?"

"The prisoner. When he grabbed you, he spoke strangely. Some are calling it the devil's tongue."

"He spoke … Vonkovyan. What do you mean? He said–" I paused, not daring to say the words aloud, for fear that she might've thought me crazy. I'd heard those words clear as day, though.

"Unless he was talking in reverse, that was *not* Vonkovyan. It was entirely unsettling."

A flare of cold danced across my arm where he'd touched it. How couldn't she have understood his words, when they were so undeniably clear? Worse, how could he have possibly known what was written on the back of that letter?

"Maevyth." Agatha's stern voice snapped my attention toward where she hobbled alongside a tall, husky man with graying hair. Perhaps in his fifties, or so. He wore a tailored burgundy brocade jacket, and a matching high-neck waistcoat with all the trimmings that told me he came from wealth. "I'd like to introduce you to Mr. Moros."

Introduce me? Agatha never introduced Aleysia, or I, to anyone who mattered. She considered the two of us a burden and an embarrassment. A roadblock to high society. "He's recently returned to Foxglove Parish," she kept on. "He owns mining companies stationed in the Sawtooth Mountains and Lyveria, but his family is here."

I didn't bother to ask what he mined. After the events of earlier, I had little energy to care. Reluctantly, I pushed to my feet to greet him properly, but he rested his palm against my shoulder.

"No need, dear. That was quite a horrific event earlier. I regret that you had to bear witness to such a thing. Rest, rest." One small squeeze of my shoulder, and he released me.

"It's a pleasure to meet you, Mr. Moros."

"The Moros name is a staple here in Foxglove. A *good* family name." Agatha gave an approving nod, as though she had any awareness of what made a good family.

I feigned a smile, less impressed by that bit of trivia. Names meant nothing to me, as I meant nothing to most. But also, I was suspicious. Because …. *Why should I care?*

"Aleysia, would you mind assisting Lolla in the kitchen?" Agatha offered an uncharacteristic adoring glance toward my sister, further stirring my suspicions.

"Lolla despises me being in the kitchen with her," Aleysia challenged.

"Perhaps you will simply do as I say without argument, dear." The dissonant warmth in Agatha's voice had both of us glancing at each other, the concern clear in Aleysia's eyes.

I offered a subtle nod to her, because who knew when Agatha's smooth cordiality might crack?

My sister snorted, eyes on Mr. Moros as she sauntered past. "Yes, Agatha."

Once out of the room, Agatha rested a hand against the man's shoulder. "My apologies. She hasn't been right since her father's passing. It's quite hard on a child."

A lie. Aleysia had always been that way. Father's death seemed to have pulled very little emotion out of her.

"No harm done. I'm certain your son's passing has affected all of you, in some way, or another."

"Stepson," Agatha corrected. "He was Godfrey's boy."

"Ah, yes. Of course." With a nod, Mr. Moros turned his attention back on me. "I'd like to invite you to brunch tomorrow, if you'd be so kind as to indulge me."

A quick glance at Agatha showed her lips tightened, and she gave a curt nod that sent a spiral of alarm across the back of my neck. I opened my mouth to speak, suddenly speechless as it occurred to me why she'd introduced us. Agatha had never cared to socialize Aleysia and me. Particularly me, with my reputation. And prominent businessmen didn't spare young women a glance without intention. "I'm afraid I can't. Bible study."

"Oh, I'm certain Sacton Crain would be happy to postpone." The clip of Agatha's tone told me she wasn't happy with my response. "Of course she will join you, Mr. Moros. You honor our family with such an invitation."

"No, I really–"

"Excellent. I'll have a carriage sent to retrieve you." He rubbed his hands together, and I noted rings of various colorful jewels along his fingers.

I'd once heard Agatha call a villager a whore for all the jewelry she'd worn. I should've brought it up just to nettle her, but my throat was still clogged with shock.

"Wonderful, how is noon?" Agatha actually smiled that time. In all the years I'd known the woman, I'd never seen her smile. A new wave of sickness crept over me, as I listened to the two of them settle plans on my behalf.

"Noon is magnificent." Mr. Moros lifted my hand to kiss the back of my palm. The moment his dry lips pressed to my skin, my stomach flipped on itself, and on instinct, I retracted. The older man regarded me as if I'd slapped him across the face, and his eye twitched. He straightened upright and adjusted his cuffs, clearly ruffled by my rejection. "Until tomorrow." On those parting words, he gave Agatha a chaste kiss on the cheek and walked away.

"What is this?"

"Your future." She fussed with her sleeves, as though the conversation meant little to her. "You didn't honestly think I'd carry the two of you the rest of your lives, did you?"

"You intend to marry me off to a man *three* times my age?"

"That older man offered three times the amount that a man your age could even dream of bidding."

"You ... *sold* me?" The word caught in my throat, while I fought to hold back the emotion gurgling in my chest. *Sold*. It sounded so cold. Like a worthless necklace of which she longed to be rid.

"How exactly do you think betrothals work, dear? You alone will help dig us out of this god-awful debt that your grandfather left behind."

Grandfather hadn't left behind debt. She'd acquired it on her own, a point I would've loved to have thrown in her face and laughed about, if I weren't so enraged.

"You have cursed this family long enough," she went on. "Fortunately for you, Mr. Moros isn't an entirely superstitious man. Between you and your sister, I should earn enough dignity to show my face again."

"You're selling Aleysia off, as well?"

"Yes. I have someone in mind, though I've not yet proposed the idea. But he's a disciplined young man who might keep her in line. Break that unbridled nature of hers."

"I won't." Had we been alone right then and not watched by the straggling few parishioners who'd stuck around, I wondered if I'd have had the courage to smack her, as badly as my palm itched. "I won't go. I refuse."

"You don't have a choice. He's already paid. The man desires an heir, and you will give him one. And besides that, the entire parish saw that prisoner grab your arm and speak some foreign tongue. They're convinced the two of you shared a devil bond. A few have already demanded a proper exorcism. Should you refuse Mr. Moros, well, I suspect you'll find yourself at the mercy of the faithful."

"He was delusional. Everyone knew he'd raved about … about the …"

"The what? You can't even say it, can you? You play along well, Maevyth, but the truth is, there is a sliver of denial that you can't help but pick and pick, and pick." She hobbled closer, setting my nerves aflame again, and lifted a small tendril of my hair. "I remember the day your grandfather found you on the doorstep in your bassinet. I begged him to get rid of you, and he refused, the fool. Do you think it's any coincidence that both he and your father met an early demise? Or that we've suffered only slightly less than the poor?"

An angry breath shot out of me, her accusation like a slap to the face. "Are you suggesting I'm at fault for these things?"

"I'm suggesting that you consider your choices. You have no future in Foxglove Parish, unless you long to live in the temple with your tongue severed. I've certainly no intentions of suffering the burden of your cursed existence, waiting for your knight in black armor to come and sweep you off. The best you can hope for is to marry a respectable man like Mr. Moros. And who knows, perhaps in time, he might help earn you favor in this community."

"I don't care about the favor of this community. Or Mr. Moros."

"Then, what do you want, Child? For the Governor to strip you bare and prod you with a branding iron? Be careful. What little respect your *adoptive* father bestowed upon you, as a hero of the faith, can easily be swept beneath accusations of witchcraft. Be prepared to leave at noon tomorrow." Sneering, she hobbled back toward the group of women standing off in a corner.

Ruffled by a flurry of new gossip they stared back at me, whispering amongst themselves.

I knew how quickly whispers could travel. How devastatingly serious they could turn. I lived it every day.

Agatha placed her hand on the arm of one of them and, with a glance back, whispered something that seemed to intrigue the woman, the way her brows lifted in surprise.

The betrothal, no doubt. It was sickening that it took a suitor to spare my reputation, my future. How tragic that a woman's worth equated to the depth of a man's pockets.

Having had enough social interaction for one day, I made my way up to the bedrooms. A figure at the top of the staircase brought me to a halt, and I gave a half smile in response to Uncle Riftyn grinning down at me.

"You're not much for social gatherings, are you?" He plodded two steps down, pulling a cigarette from his pocket, and paused beside me. A thread of tension wound through me, as he remained too close, and I descended one step, clearing my throat.

Placing the cigarette between his lips, he smirked. "I don't bite."

"Excuse me," I said, slipping past him, and made my way to the attic, where I skidded to a stop on finding Aleysia pulling on the sleeve of her dress. Frowning, I glanced back toward the staircase, where Uncle Riftyn had been moments ago.

She turned, smiling back at me. "Tired of haggard old women and men with wandering paws?"

"I just saw Uncle Riftyn a moment ago."

"You did? Hmm. I had to take this wretched corset off. Couldn't breathe. Do you remember the days when we'd roam around the house in nothing more than a shift? I can't tell you how much I miss–"

"Agatha sold me." I hated the tremble in my voice, the frailty in my words. That the wretched old woman could've so easily crawled beneath my skin that way.

"What?" The mirth on her face slipped into an icy stare. "What did you say?"

"She sold me to Mr. Moros." Biting the inside of my lip failed to keep it from trembling and the sting in my eyes threatened tears.

Her jaw shifted. "Tell me you're joking."

"I wish I were." The urge to tell her more, that Agatha had planned to sell her too, tugged at my chest, but doing so would only upset her more, and I needed Aleysia's level head to help me think of a way to get us out of this. I needed her to problem solve instead of clamping up into denial.

"She can't do that. I won't let her do this. That wretched snake of a woman! If only The Red God had spared grandfather for her."

"Aleysia. Stop. You're only making it worse."

"Worse? Did you glimpse the man by chance? It cannot get any worse, Maevyth. I could feel the awful things that must've slipped through his mind. The vile things he would do to a young and innocent girl."

"And so, what am I to do! Sever my own tongue and beg the Red Veils to take me in? That'd certainly be the easiest solution!" The harsh tone I cut loose revealed only a fraction of the chaos inside of me, but I instantly regretted raising my voice to her. "Please tell me."

"Run. We could run away." Even Aleysia had a flicker of uncertainty in her eyes. Running was foolish, after all.

"They'll hunt us. He's already paid."

"There must be somewhere."

It would've been principal for Governor Grimsby. He once had two men, lovers, hunted down and humiliated, tying them naked to a post in the town square, before he'd banished them to the woods. Two insolent women escaping marriage, what he considered to be a holy union of souls, would enrage the man. It would inspire a holy crusade after the two of us.

I shrugged and shook my head. "The woods? That is the only place they wouldn't dare."

Eyes stern, she crossed her arms. "Enough of that, Maevyth. You're speaking of suicide. There are other options."

"Like what?"

Her brow kicked up. "Like poison in his drink. A little Snake's Tooth over the course of a couple months ought to do it."

"What?" I stared back at her, searching for any trace of humor in her eyes, and found nothing. Nothing but apathy. "Are you mad?"

"I'd sooner watch him choke and bleed from his throat, than

imagine you in his bed." She stared off, a slight smirk playing on her lips, as if she were imagining such a thing right then.

"No. I'll not put either of us in danger." I paced, my mind spinning with thoughts. So many thoughts. We couldn't run. We couldn't change Agatha's mind–the woman valued coin more than sentiment. More than life, it seemed. Any resistance would only get us punished, or banished, if the governor saw fit, and if he opted to show mercy, the alternative of becoming a Red Veil was about as clement as a blade stabbed in my throat.

Or tongue, as it were.

I taunted my head with the possibility of marriage and what it would mean for me. I'd hold higher rank than Agatha, as a married woman. The community would be forced to respect me. Acknowledge me. "He owns mines in Lyveria and Sawtooth. He's exceptionally wealthy." I could hardly believe those words had fallen from my lips, but they rang true, nonetheless.

"What are you saying?" Her lips twisted with repulsion. "You're actually going to *consider* this? Foxglove Parish has plenty of fine *young* suitors—"

"Who wouldn't spare me a glance. Think for a moment, Aleysia. As a married woman, wife of a *wealthy* man, I'll have rights. I can secure guardianship for you. Make you *my* ward."

With a snort, she rolled her eyes. "Guardianship as my younger sister. How ridiculous. And why would I want to live in Mr. Moros's home?"

Swallowing a gulp, I leveled my gaze. "Because she plans to sell you, as well."

She pinned me with an incredulous stare and gave a slow shake of her head. "No. Uncle Riftyn would never allow it."

"Uncle Riftyn?" That she would've even considered him as a possible solution, a savior, made me want to slap some sense into her. "What does he have to do with anything?"

"He cares for both of us." Chin angled high, she busied herself, straightening the sheet on her bed that they'd undoubtedly crumpled with their tryst earlier. "Perhaps the only one in this house who does. He will speak to Agatha on our behalf. She adores him. She'll listen to him."

My frustration stewed, her ignorance grinding at my patience. "You're delusional, if you think Agatha will entertain such a request. Or anything else involving you and her son."

She whipped around, eyes narrowed on me. "What are you implying?"

"Stop toying with me. I see the way he flirts with you. Touches you. I'm certain it wasn't coincidence I stumbled upon the two of you alone up here."

While her right eye flickered, as it normally did in heated arguments, there was a spark of worry there. A kernel of doubt hidden beneath all that denial. "You're the one who sounds mad now."

Head tipped back, I groaned. "I'm your sister. I'm the only family you've got left. No lies, Aleysia. He may not be our uncle by blood, but he *is* a relation, and Agatha would sooner watch you suffer than risk her reputation."

Brows tipped, she sat on the bed and chewed on her fingernail, the worry finally chipping away at her. It hadn't been my intention to throw her into the same preoccupations that plagued my head, but I certainly wasn't willing to entertain her fantasies that Uncle Riftyn would have anything to do with this. "Then, what do we do? I can't survive the solitude and silence and celibacy of a Red Veil. The very *thought* of such a life … it would be absolute hell." Her hand shook as she gnawed away at her nail.

Sighing, I sat down beside her and gently tugged her finger from her mouth. "We do as I said. I'll secure my place, and I will have the authority to request that you live with us."

Eyes closed, she huffed and shook her head. "I can't …. I can't let you do this. I don't *want* to do this."

I gave her arm a squeeze, drawing her eyes to mine. "She told me she would find someone suitable to breaking you, Aleysia. I can't watch that happen. I won't. Mr. Moros is respected. Perhaps he's kind."

It seemed as if I were watching all stages of trauma and grief flash across her face, and the way she stared off almost looked like she'd lost hope. "When is all of this supposed to happen?"

"Marriage? I'm not sure. I'm to join him for lunch tomorrow, though."

Frowning, she stared down at the floor. "How are you so resigned to this? I would be crawling out of my skin right now."

"It seems I don't have a choice."

CHAPTER SEVEN

ZEVANDER

A frigid wind beat against the hard leather mask covering the lower half of Zevander's face, as he made his way down the dark and empty street toward Black Salt Tavern. Even that far from the Citadel, he made a point to disguise his identity.

Whispers reached his keen ears. Villagers who both loathed and feared him, breathing their words of faith into the air as he passed. Ridiculous prayers that faded like mist in his wake. The cursed Lord of Eidolon. *A demon*, they called him. Better that they knew him for the curse than the killings he carried out at the king's behest.

He was evil, after all. Only a soulless creature could take life so swiftly and easily as he did. No remorse. No emotion. Nothing but a trained animal, forged from pain and suffering.

Two radiant moons illuminated the dusky sky, blanketing the ancient city in a silvery glow. Tall gothic spires of shops and cathedrals sliced through low lying clouds, their shadows stretching over the worn cobblestone streets whose wet surface splashed against the soles of his sturdy leather boots.

Black caligosian leather, named after the fierce creature

whose hide was used to make it, clung tight to his body, the thick cuirass keeping him warm against the oncoming winter. The black hooded cloak he wore swept behind him, concealing the black Venetox steel sword that any savvy thief would've loved to swipe from his back.

Brisk strides brought him closer to the tavern, and he turned his head slightly, avoiding the stares of those who stumbled out the entrance. Drunks who dared to stare longer than they should've. Most respectable villagers tended to avoid him like a bad case of muripox, which suited Zevander just fine.

Just outside the building crouched a young boy, no more than a decade old. His gangly arms and pale skin revealed a map of pink veins that identified him as a spindling child. Born with no magic in his blood, at all. Two black horns stuck out from the top of his head, curving backward, their short length confirming his youth. Another unsavory trait of spindlings, ensuring they were often viewed as savages, as most Nyxterosi children had their horns cut at birth, the stubs usually hidden beneath their hair.

Aethyrians often possessed unique powers specific for their bloodline, gifted at birth, making them manceborn, or mancers. Much of the poor, living in the squalor of the The Hovel, couldn't afford the vital vivicantem required to sustain their powers and, over time, the blood magic languished, diminishing to nothing. Those born with blood magic, who suffered a severe vivicantem deficiency and consequently lost their inherited powers, were called Nilivir. While they still possessed the longevity that set them apart from the mere mortals who resided in the deadlands of Mortasia, they were looked down upon by highblood Aethyrians. The worst were the children born to them, spindlings, who were often treated like animals and used as slaves, in one manner or another.

Fiery red eyes, common for spindling children, stared back at him as he approached.

Once inside the tavern, Zevander swept his gaze over time-weathered wooden booths that sat mostly empty, save for the relentless few still up at that hour. He clocked every being, from one corner of the tavern to the other, and sighted an older man with dark tawny skin and long white hair toward the back. His tall, pointed ears identified him as Elvynira–a common sight in Nyxteros, but what wasn't common was the skill that he possessed, one that set him apart and had perhaps caused him to lose his mind.

For years, he'd served as one of the king's most prominent mages, a respected member of the elite Magestroli, whose specialty was interpreting ancient codices and scrolls. He also possessed the power of foresight, a curse, as he'd often expressed, which made him privy to fearsome visions. Revelations that had turned the brilliant mage into an ale-guzzling recluse.

En route toward him, Zevander unbuckled the baldric at his chest and removed the scabbard holding his sword, but didn't bother to remove the half-face leather mask, which left only his eyes exposed.

"You're late," Dolion rasped and glanced around the tavern.

Zevander slid into the booth across from him, resting his sword beside him. The single, black steel pauldron at his left shoulder, just beneath the cloak, felt bulky in the narrow booth, but he ignored his discomfort. He didn't bother to address the man's comment, either, as he reached into a pocket of his leather jerkin and removed that perfect, red spherical stone he'd collected. With shaky hands, Dolion accepted the stone and, from somewhere beside him, lifted a slim leather box that he opened to show five other stones–each a varying shade of red.

Every one of them a life Zevander had taken.

Dolion held the stone up to the lantern beside them on the table, out of view so as not to rouse the attention of anyone else. "The power of an entire bloodline cast in one stone," he said, as he slid the object into a small depression beside the others.

"A patriarch reduced to ash." Not that Zevander gave a good

godsdamn for the greedy mancer. He just liked to remind Dolion that it was he who had risked his ass to acquire those stones.

The mirthful expression on the older man's face faded. "I do not take pleasure in such thoughts. However, some deserved their fate. Parading around in jewels while their people starve."

"Yes. Some deserved it. And some did not. I suppose that it's not your conscience that must reconcile, but mine."

"I didn't know you had one."

"I don't."

Dolion chuckled. "Well, you do possess an incredible power, my friend."

What he possessed was nothing incredible. Sablefyre consumed. It drew cravings out of him that he didn't care to entertain. It was madness in the making. An unfortunate fate. One he'd hoped to spare himself from by collecting the stones that would fuel the most powerful scepter in existence. The septomir—an impressive weapon that Dolion had advised was powerful enough to banish the dangerous black flame from his body.

In his furtive glancing around, Zevander caught sight of a man he'd noticed when he'd first walked in, sat in the corner of the tavern, his hood pulled up over his face as he lifted his tankard for a sip of ale. Zevander's stare lingered a moment, and he studied the slow and easy movements of the stranger, who set his drink back down, not bothering to look up to allow Zevander a good look at his face. Making a mental note to watch him, Zevander resumed his scanning over the thin crowd, to a man sitting adjacent to him and Dolion.

On his forearm, he bore the mark of a predator. *Rapax*. Those who took advantage of children in one form, or another, either by sexual favors or abuse. The marks were issued by the Imperial Guard to identify them as molesters, and most served time in the mines of Solassia.

Having spent time there himself, Zevander was all too familiar with his kind.

A distant voice chimed inside Zevander's head. *"Knees, Boy."* Cold stirred in his chest as the image of him on his knees flashed inside his head. *"Open your mouth."* The flavor of ash and embers burned his tongue. *"Now swallow."* His fists tightened, and Zevander squeezed his eyes shut on the horrible scene in his mind. *"You belong to me, Boy, from this night on. And what hell you will suffer."*

"A new vision came to me."

Dolion's words interrupted Zevander's thoughts, and he opened his eyes to see the man across from him marveling his stones, seemingly oblivious to his surroundings.

Zevander unclenched his hands, noting the deep bloody crescents in his palm.

"A forest." Dolion prattled on, slipping the case of stones into his pocket. "One of thick mist and shimmer. A stone with silver markings." He lifted his tankard for a sip of ale, his shaking hands nearly spilling the drink over the rim. Hard to believe, a time ago, the old man's visions were respected and sought out by the king himself. He'd disgraced his once revered bloodline with his mad ravings.

Dolion signaled the barmaid, who sauntered over with two tankards of ale that she slammed onto the table, her gaze never wavering from the mask that covered Zevander's face. Most tended to fear him. The smart ones, anyway.

The moment she slipped away, Zevander leaned in toward the man across from him. "The forest you speak of is Hagsmist. Need I remind you, crossing the boundary is forbidden." At the end of Hagsmist Forest, just before the land fell into the sea, stood The Umbravale—the imperceptible ward that'd been weaved by the great mages centuries ago. The only portal into the mortal world, guarded by the king's calvary.

"In order to break your curse, I require the *full* complement of stones. All seven bloodlines."

Zevander had crossed continents to retrieve the stones of the many races that made up Aethyria–Orgoths, Elvynira, Solassions, Lunasier. Those whose bloodlines were purest, the descendants of the ancients, whose combined power, when harnessed by the septomir, was said to have formed the very boundary Dolion wished to cross into the mortal lands. Lands believed to have been nothing but a wasteland, as no Aethyrian could've possibly survived there. Not that anyone cared to cross, as Mortasia had always been known as a land flourishing with disease and famine. Diseases said to wreak havoc on blood magic—which made it illegal, by order of the king, to breach the boundary.

"What could possibly exist in the land of death, old man?"

"I do not know. I only know my visions are never wrong." He kicked back a long swill of his drink and wiped his mouth on the back of his hand.

"Whatever blood I find there will have no power. It would be useless."

"Not useless. Even without magic, blood is life. Life is what the scepter requires. The seventh bloodline might very well be mortal, *a mere mortal*, for all we know." Dolion threw back another sip, his dark brown skin reddening by the moment, and he signaled for another drink from the barmaid. "No one knows entirely what, or whom, the seventh bloodline originated from. It's a mystery that, to this day, baffles the magehood, but the moment it is reunited with the other stones, its true power will be known. And once in hand, I will possess the most impressive scepter in all of Aethyria. Far more powerful than Sablefyre."

"Seems like a lot of power for *one* man."

"Perhaps, but a necessary one. I've told you what I've seen."

"Yes. A plague. Courtesy of Cadavros," Zevander said in an unimpressed tone, hoping the mage wouldn't break into one of his long tirades again. "Except Cadavros is dead. Long dead." The evil that had bestowed the curse upon Zevander had long been extinguished. Destroyed by the king himself—or so the annals went on to say, anyway.

"You believe what they tell you, *Letalisz.*" Fortunately for him, he spoke the word low enough that Zevander didn't feel the need to rip his tongue out for having said it aloud. "And it isn't a simple plague. Creatures, the likes of which we've never seen, will ravage our villages. Insects will spill from the mouths of children. The Citadel will burn."

"Is it not these ravings that got you kicked out of the Magehood?"

"Cadavros will return. The Black Pestilence is coming! I promise you that. He will bring famine and death!" He slammed down his tankard, and a quick glance around showed the few still left in the tavern stared back at them. Dolion cleared his throat and sat back in the booth.

Another furtive glance, and all those curious eyes turned away.

Zevander fought to contain the mocking remark itching to break free. "Look, I don't give a good fuck what you do with those stones. So long as you pay me what's promised. And if you're lying about it, let's just say it'll be worth breaking some laws to watch you suffer."

"I resent your insults."

"Resent all you like, but don't fuck with me. Did you bring what I asked?"

Dolion reached into the pocket of his vest and tugged out a milky white substance that sparkled in the lamplight. Pure vivicantem. While the stone he'd taken from the highblood could've provided enough vivicantem to last a good month, or two, the liquid form was much easier to consume, and the measured dose ensured he wouldn't absorb too much of it. Too much was toxic. And turning the stones to liquid was a power only a select few were granted permission by the king to carry out. Those same few were required to live on castle grounds, guarded by the Imperial Army.

Given the protections and restrictions of the men guarding the vein, along with those who mined it, how Dolion came about acquiring the vial was a mystery that Zevander didn't bother to question.

"It isn't laced with anything, is it?"

"Straight from the vein."

"Good." Zevander tipped his head back and squeezed a half dropperful onto his tongue. Cold tingles rippled through his body, casting a shiver down his back, and he let out a grunt as the liquid sent a burst of pleasure to his muscles.

Too much resulted in poisoning and poisoning led to madness.

One half dropper of pure vivicantem would last a week.

Zevander tucked the remaining supply away into his leathers. The stones he'd scavenged from the ashes, not meant to be consumed in rock form, would prove useful in other ways.

"Mortasia." Dolion stared down at his drink. "It is said to be dangerous. A wasteland of mortal suffering and death."

"Trying to talk me out of it, are you?"

"Of course not. It is the only way. But should you fail ..."

Zevander hiked an elbow on the back of the wooden booth. "Have I failed you yet?"

"No. You've done well. And your reward will be freedom from the flame." The elder mage reached into his coat and fished out a small scroll that sat in his outstretched palm. "There are only three high mages in all of Aethyria who know this cantafel." The spell for the ward. Not entirely sought out by the Aethyrians, who'd sooner fling themselves into a vat of molten lava than cross into the mortal lands.

"And you're the lucky third." Frowning, Zevander opened the miniature scroll to view ancient words written in black ink. He recognized enough of the old language to know it was a passage spell.

"I trust you can speak it?" Dolion asked, tapping his finger impatiently against the tabletop.

"My mother was Vespyri. Born of the ancients. Yes, I can speak it." He rolled it back up and tucked it away in his pocket beside the vial.

"Good." Dolion leaned back in his chair, chin cocked indignantly. "In my vision, I can see a forest from a bedroom window. An archway made of bones."

Zevander groaned and shook his head. "You better not be sending me on a long trek through the mortal lands for this one."

"I can count on you to retrieve the stone, then?" *Retrieving it* meant boiling the blood of a victim into a hardened mass, which they expelled out of their mouths before the body combusted into a cloud of black dust. Something the overzealous mage couldn't seem to bring himself to say.

"You're asking me to venture beyond the boundary, a crime punishable by execution, and retrieve the stone from what has only ever been described as hell." Zevander rolled his shoulders back. "Of course. I want this fucking fire out of my veins."

"What does it feel like? The black flame? The power of Aethyria's most dangerous element at your fingertips." The intrigue in his eyes sickened Zevander. Much as they, the high and holy mages, denounced the power, they were always intrigued by it.

"Imagine your cock in the hands of a pyromage, only it's your whole fucking body." He didn't bother to smile as the older man winced at the visual. "I'll caution again, you attempt trickery, and I'll personally see to it that you know exactly what it feels like to burn from the inside out." Grabbing his sword from beside him, Zevander pushed to his feet and strapped it beneath his cloak, then exited the tavern, noting the hooded stranger no longer sat at the booth.

CHAPTER EIGHT

MAEVYTH

The sensation of sharp needles piercing my arm roused me from sleep, and I lifted it into the dappled rays of moonlight streaming through the window beside me. Noticing a strange blackness bleeding through the bandage where I'd cut myself, a sickening cold filled my chest.

I hissed a shaky breath and unwound the sticky bandage to find an oozing wound on my arm beneath.

Oh, no.

Angry red flesh surrounded the gash, and the veins branching out pulsed a distressing silver with each beat of my heart. Silver? A cold panic crawled over my chest, as I stared down at the abnormal color beneath my skin. Deep red drainage leaked from crusty edges, and when I lifted it to my nose, the stench of it tugged a gag from my throat. I pressed on the corner of the wound, and a thick, black substance, swirled through with what looked like whorls of molten silver, oozed out of it. Gurgling in my stomach had me breathing hard through my nose to stifle the urge to retch.

As a child, I'd had the silly notion that I'd one day become a physician. Ridiculous, seeing as women weren't permitted to study medicine, but I hadn't known any better. It turned out to be a futile ambition on my part when I'd discovered I had a weak stomach for blood and death.

And what grave misfortune that, of all places, I'd end up living in a mortuary.

"*Help!*" A frantic scream broke me from my thoughts, sounding like it echoed from the vent.

I turned to see my sister's bed stood empty.

"*Please, someone help me!*" The voice arrived again, the intensity heightening to panic.

Aleysia.

I shot out of bed, wrapping my wound as I crossed the room toward the door, which I cracked open to find a dark and empty corridor. The pictures of grandfather's relatives added an eerie feel, like eyes watching me, as I made my way down the hallway toward the staircase.

"*Please! Someone! Oh, god!*" The voice cried out again, though I didn't entirely recognize it as my sister's.

"Aleysia?" I whispered, as I stepped lightly down the staircase to the lower level.

"*I'm begging you! Please! Stop!*" The voice goaded me through the kitchen, washroom, and pantry, only to find nothing but stillness in each room.

From the front of the house, a thumping sound drew my feet closer to the viewing parlor. Tiptoeing toward the entryway, I followed the sound and rounded the wall. On the other side, stood Uncle Riftyn pressed against my sister, her head thrown back, bottom lip caught between her teeth. A twinge of alarm spiraled down my neck, and he turned toward me, his lips stretched to a grin, just before he captured my sister's bare breast between his lips, never bothering to turn his gaze away from me.

Violent ripples of mortification pulsed through me, and I shuffled back around the wall before my sister could notice, wanting to scrub my eyeballs with soap and salt.

"Oh, gods be damned," I muttered as I made my way back up to my room. It was then I noticed the cries I'd heard before had stopped. Certainly not my sister's cries, with the risk of Agatha finding the two of them.

If not Aleysia, then who had called out for help?

Once back in my room, I paused by the vent, listening again.

Nothing.

Had I imagined it? Had my mind somehow conjured that sound?

Once settled in bed again, I turned toward the window, willing myself to erase the visual of Uncle Riftyn cornering Aleysia's body against the wall, his pants pooled at his ankles, their naked limbs tangled around each other. The jarring shock of it still had my heart pounding in my chest.

I'd never been with a boy that way before, not fully penetrated, at least, though I did have a crush on one of the boys from my parish. Slightly older. The son of a miner, strong and handsome. The day before he left to fight for the Vonkovyan Army, he'd walked me home from the village square, where I'd gone to feed Mrs. Chalmsley some stale bread and dried fruits. Along a wooded stretch of road, he'd asked if I'd ever been touched by a boy before. When I'd told him I hadn't, he said he'd never touched a girl, either. He asked if I'd allow him one small touch before he left for war, and I'd said yes. Right there on a deserted road, I lifted my skirt and let him touch me in that forbidden place. Had anyone caught us, we'd have been beaten for it, or worse.

Still, I savored the feel of his strong hands on my most delicate flesh. No rumors between us. No scorn or crooked faces judging us. Just a curious boy and girl.

I distinctly remembered his eyes, heavy with lust as he slid his fingers inside of me.

Eyes that had dulled, vacant and lifeless, when he'd returned from Lyveria, laid out on the concrete slab in Uncle Felix's examination room, with his throat cut open. While a feeling of sorrow had filled my chest, I couldn't help the envy he'd stirred. What freedom he must've felt when he'd closed his eyes and drifted out of that mangled body.

I never once spoke of our encounter—not even to Aleysia, who would've taken that secret to the grave.

As much as I loathed the nature of her relationship with our uncle, I'd do the same for her.

At the click of the door, I dared not look to see what I was certain was Aleysia making her way back to her bed.

Ungraceful footsteps clunked across the room, and I frowned at her blatant disregard. *Cla-clunk. Cla-clunk. Cla-clunk.*

Frustrated with her, I turned over in bed. "Do you have to be so—"

A cold, wet hand pressed to my mouth, and a scream ripped from my throat as I stared up at the horrid creature standing over my bed, whose pale, gaunt face carried a shadow of terror. The man from The Banishing, earlier. He released my mouth, leaving behind a sticky wetness that clung to my lips, prodding me to wipe it away, but my muscles wouldn't move. Not even my lungs, which held my last drawn breath. He lifted a shiny, skinless finger to his lips, quieting me. Half of his face had been torn away to raw flesh and bits of bone. Hysterics gripped my chest, allowing only small panting breaths, as I lay staring up at him, studying his ghastly features.

The door clicked again.

Behind the man, I watched Aleysia pad toward her bed, not sparing him a single glance. On passing, she smiled at me. "Oh. I thought you were asleep." Trembling, I turned only slightly, to see the man still standing there, while my sister approached him from behind.

Not an ounce of hesitation in her step. As if she couldn't see him, at all, she practically waltzed right up alongside him. The sight of the two standing side by side left me paralyzed in disbelief. What was this madness?

Do you not see him? I wanted to say, but I couldn't summon a single word.

"Are you all right? You look … pale." Aleysia reached down to draw her thumb over my mouth and frowned down at her finger. Wiping whatever it was away on her skirt, she rounded the bed, walking right through the man, who wavered in a cloud of black smoke.

An illusion. It had to be an awful, terrifying illusion.

An intense burn at my arm flared again, and without thinking, I lifted it, unwittingly drawing Aleysia's attention there.

"Dear god, Maeve, what happened?" She held my arm in her hands, the same hands I'd seen pinned to the wall by Uncle Riftyn only moments before. As she did so, the figure of The Banishing Man faded out of view, offering a small bit of relief to the turmoil churning in my gut.

I finally spoke. "I cut it."

"On what?"

I didn't answer at first, my head still searching for reason, answers for what had just happened.

"Maeve? How did you cut your arm?"

I couldn't tell her how it had happened. While Aleysia certainly didn't buy into the religious nonsense and superstition, she still feared that forest as much as anyone else. "I don't …" I lifted the back of my free hand to my lips that were still sticky and wet.

"You don't what?"

"Please leave me alone about it!" I wrenched my arm from her grasp, immediately regretting my tone, but, for god's sake, if she requested a physician on my behalf, there was a good chance I'd lose my arm on precaution alone.

"You do look pale. Is it possible that it might be infected?"

"I don't know. I washed it. I just …" Lifting my head, I scanned the room, making sure the man from before was gone. Truly gone. "I'm just tired."

"Will you let me look at it?"

Absolutely not. One look would surely make her worry. It'd made me worry. "You're not a physician. What good would having you look at it do me?"

"I'm your sister. I want to make sure you're all right."

"I'm fine." I turned over in my bed, wanting nothing more than to wipe my head of the terrifying visual that still plagued me. "Please. I just need some sleep."

"You'll tell me if it gets worse, won't you, Maeve? It's like you said earlier, we need to stick together."

"If only that were true," I muttered under my breath.

"What does that mean?"

"You know exactly what it means. I saw you and Uncle Riftyn. And be grateful it was me and not Agatha, because you'd surely find yourself standing before that forest with the Vonkovyan soldiers prodding your back."

An unnerving quiet settled between us, one that lasted too long, and I wondered if I should've kept my observations to myself. When she finally spoke, she said. "I'm sorry you saw us."

Despite the emotion I could hear in her voice, I still couldn't bring myself to look at her. "What are you thinking Aleysia?"

"I'm thinking that …. Well, that I love him."

I turned over in hopes I'd see instant regret on her face for having admitted such a thing. "Are you mad? Are you so glutton for Agatha's wrath that you can't help yourself?"

"We're careful."

I didn't have to respond to that, the way she instantly lowered her gaze from mine.

"Most of the time."

"You can never marry him, nor have children, unless you run to the farthest reaches of this godforsaken continent, and what life would that be, beyond the reach of civilization?"

"Better than here. But we'd take you with us." She rested a hand on my shoulder, and I wanted to grab and squeeze it into a mess as mangled as my heart. Damn her for always making complications so unbearably complex. "I've already spoken to Uncle Riftyn about it. He'll take us both."

Both? Had she lost her senses? "No. I won't."

"You'd stay here? And marry a man three times your age? One who undoubtedly longs for an heir, like every other man in this parish?"

The thought of that twisted my guts, but no worse than the vision of us three roaming the barren lands beyond Vonkovya and Lyveria, to the arctic reaches beyond Grimvale, or the scorching deserts of Romisir–the only place the Vonkovyan soldiers wouldn't bother to hunt us down, because every other creature that dwelled there surely would.

"What do you want me to do? You think I asked to fall in love with him?"

"You're the eldest, Aleysia. You're the one who's supposed to have the level head."

She spat a mirthless chuckle. "So, I come live with you and Mr. Moros in your elaborate manor, staring the man in the eye every day as he rapes you for an heir? Or worse, stay and let Agatha find a man to break me?"

I agreed with her. Every option was unappealing. "I don't have a solution. I only know that I don't trust Uncle Riftyn to follow through."

"You don't know him like I do."

"I'm certain of that." I rolled back over, facing the window again. "Your love blinds you."

"I suppose you'd have to know the love of a man to understand."

As stinging as her words might've been, she was right. Behind my ribs stood a graveyard of empty caskets. A chest full of name-less tombstones. An emptiness which afforded me a small measure of clarity that she refused to acknowledge. "And I think you're the greatest fool I've ever known."

Another long bout of silence lingered between us, and I glanced over my shoulder in time to see her wipe a tear from her cheek. It was rare that Aleysia or I ever shed tears. Our lives, so entwined with pain and sadness, made crying seem pointless. She lifted the blanket and, despite my protesting stiffness and refusal to move, urged me over, just as when we were little, before sliding her hand over my hip and curling herself into my back.

"Sing for me, Maeve. Just like you used to."

"I'm not in a singing mood." The stench of forbidden sex clung to her skin, clogging my throat.

"Please? Your voice always settled my mind."

If only my voice had the power to make her realize how foolish she was for falling in love with our uncle. "I don't want to sing."

"*Vayr mu dahlję?*" It was a song written in the old language, roughly translated to 'Go, my Darling.'

The first time I'd ever heard the song was the night I'd stumbled upon my father tucked away in grandfather's cellar, sobbing. I'd come to realize, after everyone had gone to bed, he'd sometimes retired there, in the depths of the cottage, singing the song as he drank morumberry wine. Mourning his dead wife.

I'd learned the words to the song in the common tongue, in hopes that I'd work up the courage to sing with him some night, but I never had the opportunity between his deployments to Lyveria and his eventual disappearance.

With reluctance, I sang the song she loved. For her. Fingers gripping my shoulders, she nuzzled close, as I reached the chorus and stared out the window beside me, up toward the stars.

"Go, my Darling, unto that place
Where magic still exists
Beyond the confines of this cruel world
As you will not be missed

Instead, I'll find you in a dream
Or a wistful plea on stars
Hours of suffering no more redeemed
For eternity is ours."

At the end of the mournful dirge, Aleysia kissed my cheek, then padded back to her bed. I tucked my burning arm beneath the blankets, mentally willing myself to ignore the pain. In the silence of my thoughts, I drifted deeper and deeper into the abyss.

CHAPTER NINE

ZEVANDER

J ust outside the Black Salt Tavern, Zevander paused,
listening. Only the rustle of dried leaves drifting over the
cobblestones. Eyes and ears perked, he scanned over his
surroundings, not bothering to call on his horse quite yet.
He clicked his tongue, the sound bouncing off nearby objects. A
number of Lunasier possessed the ability to echo locate as a
hunting technique, but Zevander had honed the skill over the
years. The image in his mind showed only the spindling boy from
earlier, who'd watched him from the shadows. Zevander lifted a
finger to his masked lips to ensure the boy remained quiet, to
which the boy nodded and returned the gesture. The child then
pointed in the opposite direction.

The mark of the scorpion that'd been branded into Zevander's flesh stirred a quiet hum, as he strode down the empty
street in the direction the boy had sent him. He could sense the
stranger. Near.

Zevander slowed his steps a few buildings down from the
tavern and turned into an alley. He paused again to listen, and his
keen hearing picked up on the slightest tremble of breath. The
stink of ale beneath the rot that carried on the air.

Prickling vibrations of fear radiated from a shadow beside him.

In as subtle a movement as he could muster, he unlatched the scorpion dagger beneath his cloak and set his hand on the hilt.

The shadow shifted like black smoke and took form, winding into the shape of the hooded man from the tavern. A black tendril lashed out at Zevander, but before it could wrap around his throat as intended, Zevander struck fast with his blade, cleaving it away. At a pained outcry, the black vapor dropped to the ground and morphed into a severed hand and forearm. The hooded stranger held up a bloody and trembling stump. Color drained from his face as he stared at the wound in shock, and Zevander struck twice more—across his mouth, the other across his throat.

Gurgling, the stranger fell to his knees and hit the pavement face-first, where he stilled.

Zevander knelt beside him and pulled back the cloak to check the back of his neck. Bestowed at birth, the stranger's sigil, the primitive symbol of the Suvary bloodline, glowed a bright blue across his nape. The same symbol worn by the man Zevander had killed a fortnight ago by order of the King. He'd been a bloodmage who ran an unauthorized business of crafting sero-tonics—potent poisons that held the power to taint the blood and destroy an entire bloodline. No doubt, the stranger had sought revenge for his slain kin.

Zevander tore away his glove and raised his hand, sending a blast of sablefyre that caught on the stranger's cape, devouring him in a matter of seconds. It burned so intensely that the pile of remaining ash was small enough to kick to the wind. He plucked the resulting bloodstone from the soot and pocketed it. Not that the stone was useful, or valuable, he simply didn't want to leave any trace of the stranger behind. And just like that, the unwitting avenger was gone. Not a shred of evidence that he'd ever existed.

Though, Zevander had grown fucking weary of the attempts

on his life. The constant need to look over his shoulder. While his identity remained unknown, for the most part, an occasional few managed to find him. Unfortunately for them, they never lived to carry out their vengeance.

The sound of shouts and clanging metal reached his ear, and Zevander turned back out of the alley. Halfway between himself and the tavern, the man who bore the predator tattoo fought to shove the young spindling boy into a cage at the back of his horse-drawn wagon. The boy kicked and shouted, his skinny arms threaded through the bars of the cramped enclosure. Most would've looked the other way. Even the Imperial Guard wouldn't have spared a spindling boy a second glance. In their minds, it was one less spindling on the street. The boy would feed the man's cravings and keep him away from their own children.

Unfortunately for the heedless Rapax, a bigger predator prowled closer.

The tattoos hidden beneath Zevander's leathers seeped through the coverings like black smoke and gathered in his palm, taking the shape of a black scorpion the size of a plum.

The man slowly straightened his posture, as the Letalisz approached, clearly uncertain whether, or not, he'd dare to intervene. Most didn't.

"You got no business here," the boy's abductor said, raising his palm in threat. "I'm warning you. Go on now." Not a single glyph marred his palm. The wily bastard might've possessed blood magic, but he certainly hadn't mastered any of his power. The stranger spun away from Zevander, but before he could take so much as a step in the other direction, Zevander released the scorpion onto the ground, and it grew to the size of a melon as it shot across the wet cobblestones after him.

With little effort, the scorpion caught his ankle, its tail winding around his legs, and its razor-sharp stinger thrashed and slammed down into the man's groin. The outcry that followed would've surely drawn a crowd in any other part of the city.

Zevander strode toward the writhing abductor, passing the boy who trembled and clung to the bars of his cage. The scorpion kept its hold of the stranger's cock, while the man shook and batted it with an unsteady hand.

"Get it off of me! Get it the fuck off of me!"

Zevander reached for the scorpion, and it finally released the man on a spray of blood, before slithering its way up the sleeve of his tunic. "The sting carries a poison that will ensure you never know pleasure again. Each time your cock fills with blood, all you will know is a pain that will have you begging for death."

Without another word, he left the man cupping his mutilated groin, squirming and sobbing on the ground, and swiped up the keys the abductor had dropped in his attempt to escape. A blast of heat radiated across Zevander's back, and frowning, he turned in time to see a tendril of black flame slithering from his boot, across the gravelly ground, toward the suffering kidnapper. His muscles lurched to reel it back in, but before he could so much as raise his hand, the flame consumed the man, who screamed and gurgled in the mere seconds before his body turned to ash.

Fuck.

Teeth grinding, he lifted his palm, calling the fire back, but instead of following his command, it streaked across the ground toward the boy in his cage.

"No!" Zevander took hold of the power with both hands, as it thrashed and snapped at the air, fighting to break free, to swallow up another life. He hauled it, hand over hand, winding it back, fingers cramping with his tight grip. Until, at last, the flame retreated, scampering up his sleeve and back beneath his skin.

With palms pressed to his knees, he stood doubled over, each deep, burning inhalation crackling in his lungs, as the flame settled inside of him. He let out a groan. While episodes like these, during which he'd sometimes lost control of the flame,

94

were relatively rare, it was enough to trouble him. A testament to the unruly and unpredictable nature of his power.

After collecting the new bloodstone left behind and tucking it into his pocket alongside that from earlier, he unlocked the cage, freeing the boy, and kept on toward the tavern.

A pattering sound at his back had him turning around to find the boy running after him, fastening the pants that slipped over his too-thin hips. Zevander kept on and whistled for his horse, a cursed stallion who was as dark as pitch. A breed only found on the harsh and violent plains of Draconysia. The clack of its hooves reached Zevander through the darkness, and it came to a halt before him, its eyes as black as coal and fangs dripping with the blood of a recent kill.

"I see you've been busy," Zevander said as he climbed onto the saddle, and to his dismay, he found the spindling standing alongside the horse. "Your master is dead. You're free to return to your family."

The boy lowered his head, his shirtless body trembling with the cold. "No family, My Lord."

Seven fucking hells.

Zevander held out his hand, and a blast of radiant heat engulfed the boy, leaving his body no longer shivering, skin red with the warmth that would last him through the night. "Find some shelter. And stay out of trouble." With that, he gave a light kick to the beast's flank and sent it on a lazy walk.

Up the street and two over put him on the path toward The Hovel, situated on the seediest outskirts of Costelwick, farthest from the citadel. Highbloods wouldn't dare venture to that part of town, where disease ran rampant and death waited in the shadows.

A strange sensation tickled the back of his neck, and he turned to see the boy running after him, his spindly arms struggling to hold up his pants.

Zevander groaned and turned his attention back to the road

ahead. He set his horse to a mild trot in hopes the kid would give up the chase.

* * *

Through the gates of the city, a stretch of weathered shacks supplanted the once artisanal beauty of Costelwick's most flourishing district that was now a faded and chipped remnant of its former self. Flickering gas lamps cast shadows on the decayed brick buildings and across the damp and winding cobblestone streets, where the haunting whispers of desperation echoed from the alleyways.

Zevander removed his mask. Hiding his face wasn't necessary in this part of the city. Nearly everyone in The Hovel bore scars in one form, or another, and no one cared who he was, or what he'd been cursed with. It was only the hideous scar that stretched across his cheek and branched into tiny black veins down his jaw and neck that still garnered stares, even in the worst corners of Costelwick.

The air was thick with sanitation fog, an enchanted mist that the highbloods released over The Hovel, to keep their diseases contained. Fortunately for Zevander, the flame inside of him burned away disease and infection, making him immune to just about anything he might've encountered.

An approaching wagon kept a slow cadence toward him. Mortemian. Death collectors for the city. The coachman sat hunched over, undoubtedly weary from a long day of gathering the dead. A leather tarp stretched across the back of the wagon and covered the bodies held within, bound for the vein. While Nyxteros boasted a high rate of immortality, the poverty-stricken villages on the outskirts tended to skew the numbers, which was ultimately good for the king. More bodies equated to more vivicantem, after all. While the sablefyre contained within the vein had the power to transform flesh into bloodstones in a matter of seconds, it took approximately seven years for a corpse to phase into the much-needed nutrient that was then harvested from the rock. For centuries, the highblood immortals had relied on the sickly nilivir and spindlings to ensure a long and successful bloodline.

Zevander stopped his horse in front of a brothel and dismounted. As he slipped his mask into one of the satchels of his saddle, movement caught the corner of his eye, and he twisted to see that damned boy running barefoot toward him. En route to The Hovel, Zevander had slowed his pace, thinking he'd lost the kid, but it seemed he'd kept on him.

Dragging a hand down his face, he groaned again, and as he stepped in the direction of the brothel, the boy fell into step after him. Zevander swung around, pressing a gloved finger into the spindling's chest. "Stay. You can watch my horse."

The boy gave a spirited nod and scampered to the mount, where he gently petted its chest.

On a huff of frustration, Zevander strode up to the once-grand house that had since stood dilapidated and in decay, its roof bowing and wood rotting. A place of dark fantasies.

Beyond the door, a curtain of perfume clung to the air, masking the heady stench of pleasure. Sexsells, clad in ornate corsets, lounged across settees and couches, the curvy beauties primed and ready. After the shot of vivicantem, Zevander should've been all too willing to accommodate them–every one of them. Instead, he felt only indifference to their half-naked forms lying about. After all, he hadn't come to the brothel for sex.

A voluptuous woman, breasts spilling over a black corset, sauntered up to him, her red hair wild and cascading over slim shoulders. To most, she went by Madame Lazarine, but Zevander had known her intimately enough to call her Ze'Kyra. "Well, hello handsome. Haven't seen you in a while."

"Where is she?"

The woman's face soured. "You're not taking her again, are you? We just got her back. She's our best girl."

"I'm sure you'll find another to take her place."

"My Lord, please. I'm begging you. We are a clean and safe establishment. The best in The Hovel."

He strode past her for the staircase. "Be that as it may, she's coming home with me."

"She alone will bring in enough coin tonight to keep mouths fed."

Pausing his ascent, Zevander reached into a small satchel hooked to his belt and tossed her a silver coin.

Capturing it in her palm, she stared down at it and back to him. "A keltzig. She'll make at least three times as much."

He fished for two more and tossed them to the woman. "Where is she?" he asked, already making his way up the staircase.

"Last room on the left. Just finished up."

At the top of the staircase, he found an older man fucking a brunette against the wall, and he stepped past the two, catching her leering stare. Moans bled through the doors he passed, the thumping of beds against the walls keeping time with his strides. When he finally reached the end of the hallway, he knocked on the door.

"Giv'me a minu, will ya?" A familiar voice, laced with the telling slur of the mandrawyld tonic she'd taken, came from the other side.

Pressing his ear to the wooden panel, he listened, and at the sound of a heavy thud, he slammed through the door and found Rykaia passed out on the couch. On the coffee table lay the evidence of what he feared—the substances she'd consumed, set out in small black vials. The white gown she wore carried the remnants of blood, and he lifted her arm for the fresh scars undoubtedly put there by one of her johns.

Unbeknownst to some brothel keepers, clients sometimes

enjoyed the practice of firebleeding–making small cuts into the woman's flesh and sprinkling flammapul onto their tongues that they dragged over the bleeding wounds. Once in the blood-stream, the flammapul caused slight paralysis and tightening of the muscles, including the pelvic muscles. For the sexsell, it was a terrifying circumstance that made them exceptionally vulnerable. For the client, he could do whatever he wanted and manipulate their blood magic for as long as the high lasted. Most Johns paid for hours at a time, not only to take advantage of the tonic, but to allow it time to wear off.

Zevander lifted the vial from the coffee table. Raptacy–a sleeping tonic by trade, but abusers of the elixir enjoyed the effects that turned them happy and horny just before falling asleep. She'd been using it for quite some time, and it might've been the reason someone as strong willed as Rykaia could've fallen victim to the flammapul. Another dark ampoule beside it—Vermis Eye—ensured she wouldn't have felt a thing or had any awareness of her surroundings.

He pulled the small vial of vivicantem from his pocket and filled the dropper to the halfway mark.

Taking hold of her jaw, Zevander tipped her head back and squeezed the fluid into her mouth. Pure vivicantem in the blood acted as a powerful stimulant for the unconscious, essentially banishing the tonics from the body. At first, she didn't move, but then her throat bobbed and her eyes shot open on a gasp.

Rykaia turned over in time to expel a torrent of vomit that landed on the gritty floor. Fingers clutching the cushion of the couch, she heaved and retched as the mix of tonics exited her body. With the back of a shaky hand, she wiped the stringy bits from her lips, and the moment she glanced upward, she rolled her eyes. "What brings you here, Brother?"

"I'm taking you home."

"And if I refuse?"

Zevander tipped his head, brow cocked. She knew the answer

to that. He'd carry her out, kicking and screaming, the way he had the last time she'd left home. And the time before that.

"Please don't make me go back. You've no idea what it's like."

He lifted her arm, turning it over for the cuts. "And this is better? Who did this?"

Frowning, she ran her fingers over the wounds, undoubtedly unaware they'd been placed there in her drugged stupor. What had made her such a coveted choice at the brothel was, although her magic was weak in her drugged state, she possessed the ability to absorb pain and emotions. For the depressed, the stressed, the physically tormented, she served as something of a tonic herself. Allowing a moment when they might experience sheer ecstasy and bliss for the first time in their lives. Pain eaters, her kind were called, as they literally consumed the agony with a particular touch, or kiss.

It was hell for Rykaia, whose mind somehow had to process all that grief and suffering, the aches and injury, the weight of which had prompted her to abuse tonics at an early age.

"I don't remember, so what does it matter?"

"What matters is that, one day, your client is going to take his blade across your throat. And by the gods, I would burn him alive for it. I want a name. Who cut you?"

She huffed, reaching for a small glass that held an amber fluid—nectardeium, or nectar of the gods. "I couldn't tell you," she answered dismissively.

Her insouciance grated on him and he ground his teeth. "Tell me, or I'll see to it you're locked in the dungeons."

"You would do such a thing, wouldn't you?"

His patience snapped, and he swiped the glass out of her hand and chucked it against the wall, where it crashed into tiny shards.

On a huff of a laugh, she leaned back, resting her arm on the back of the couch. "Feel better? That tiny bit of liquor costs a fucking quarter keltzig."

"Tell me now!"

"I don't know! I fucking lost my wits and everything turned black! I don't know his name, nor his face. It's entirely wiped out of my head." The rapid blinking of her eyes failed to hold back the tears welling in them. "I never forget a face. Ever. But I cannot summon a single image for who may have done this. It's peculiar. And, to be quite honest, terrifying."

"Pack your things and let's go."

Tears spilled down her cheek. "There's nothing for me back at Eidolon, Zevander. I cannot live within those walls with the memories I carry. The pain that suffocates me every time I walk past that room."

Though he hadn't been present for the trauma that plagued his sister, the pangs of guilt cut him inside. Still, as empathetic as he longed to be toward her, it infuriated him to see her destroying herself on potions and tonics that so often rendered her completely unconscious. Vulnerable. Ones that chipped away at her body every time she consumed them. Ones that, if taken in just the right dosage, could easily stop her heart. "Am I carrying you, then?" he asked in a flat, unsympathetic tone.

She rubbed a hand down her face and expelled a forced breath. "Fine. I'll go. And we will find ourselves back in this very place once I've grown weary of being locked away in that dreaded castle. Mere hours from now, mind you."

"And I will be here to carry you back home."

"You are a tyrant."

"And you're a pain in the ass."

"Aren't you weary of this, Zevander? Haven't you grown tired of watching over me like a beastly nursemaid?"

At a knock on the door, Zevander turned to see an older man, dressed in a fine brocade jacket that told him he was from the highblood neighborhood, where the wealthy resided. In one hand, he clutched a pair of shackles. In the other, a bottle of liquor undoubtedly meant to ply Rykaia. The sight of him stirred Zevander's rage.

The stranger's eyes seemed riveted on Zevander's throat, where his sigil undoubtedly rippled with brewing anger.

"Zevander don't," Rykaia urged, but with fisted hands, her brother strode toward the door, his power lashing through him like a blazing whip.

The older man skittered off, stumbling as he made his way back down the staircase.

Zevander watched him, the fury still hammering at his muscles, and he turned to his sister. "Gather your things. Now."

As she reached out for the black vials, he took a step toward her. "Not those."

"I need them. I'll be sick."

"Leave. Them."

"No! You'd do well to remember you're not my father!"

Growling, Zevander strode toward her and gathered her flailing arms to lift his much smaller sister off the couch by her waist.

Stretching forward over his arm, she reached for the vials he'd denied her. "Let me go! Let me go, you tyrannical brute!" she screamed, wriggling and kicking, as he carried her down the staircase toward where Ze'Kyra waited, her long cigarette perched from the ring holder on her finger.

Zevander stopped alongside her, his patience snapping like a thread as he wrangled his sister's arm and held it out toward the redhead. "Is this your idea of *clean* and *safe?*"

The woman's eyes widened, then seemed to sadden as she ran a painted nail gently over the wounds.

"Release me!" Rykaia howled, squirming in his grip.

"I'm sorry, I had no idea ... please believe me, Zevander. I would never put her at risk that way."

"You will never put her at risk again. She won't be coming back."

"I will! I swear–" Rykaia's words were cut short by Zevander's palm pressed against her mouth.

"If whoever did this returns, you will let me know." Zevander said through clenched teeth.

"Yes, of course."

As he strode toward the door, the spindling boy appeared there, his miniscule form hardly blocking his path. "*Godspit*," Zevander muttered and shoved his hand into his pocket for more coin that he tossed to Ze'Kyra. "Give the boy shelter."

"I swear on all of the unholy, if you don't let me go, Brother, I will bite your damn ear off!"

As Rykaia wriggled and squirmed, he tightened his grip, ignoring her.

"I am not some charitable poorhouse." Ze'kyra argued, casually leaning against the wall. "This is a brothel, Zevander. No place for a boy."

It wasn't. But most didn't visit Madame Lazarine's Brothel for young spindlings, they came for the busty women with wet tongues and silky hands, who sweet talked them out of coin. "Better than what he'll be subjected to out on those streets."

"Come, boy." Rykaia reached toward the spindling in the doorway. "Come here. I'll give you all the coin I have to come kick this beast as hard as you can in the groin."

The spindling glanced up at Zevander, whose expression must've been grave enough to have him frantically shaking his head in response.

"You are positively demonic! May the gods rain down–"

"Quiet, Rykaia!" Zevander barked, his patience wearing thin.

"I will not quiet!" She kicked his flank. "You are." She kicked him again. "Not my father!" At her third attempt, Zevander shifted her in his arms, hoisting her over his shoulder. With the tonics and liquor she'd consumed, the pressure in her sinuses would keep her from screaming, at least. "Release me. Please. I'm begging, Brother. I'm begging."

Again, he ignored her pleas. "That's enough coin to rent a room for the month."

Ze'Kyra glanced down at it again, as if only just realizing that. "And what am I to do with a spindling child running around?"

"I'm sure you can dream up some tasks for him."

"I'll let him stay no more than a week. *No more.*"

"Good enough."

"Come, darling. Help me with my tea." Shoulders back, she reached a hand out toward the spindling. "What is your name?"

The boy looked to Zevander, as if unsure, but at the Letalisz's nod, he followed after the woman. "Gavroche," he answered, taking her hand.

With that, Zevander dragged his kicking and screaming sister out of the brothel and into the cold.

CHAPTER TEN

MAEVYTH

Cold. So cold.

Every muscle in my body trembled. I lifted the covers higher, up to my nose and buried my head in the thick quilt. The heat of my breath deflected back to my face, an infernal warmth, but not enough. My chest expanded with a hollow cold that stirred a nauseous twisting in my gut. I wanted to call out to Aleysia, but I didn't dare.

Instead, I breathed into the blanket, beads of sweat trailing down my temple and neck. My heartbeat throbbed in my arm, pulsing in agonizing pain. Lifting it proved difficult, like trying to lift a heavy log, my muscles useless. I couldn't bring myself to look at it, for fear of what festered beneath the wet bandages.

Would I die? Could I die from such a thing?

The question followed me into darkness.

* * *

"Is it a bite?" The sound of Agatha's voice roused me from oblivion.

"It doesn't appear to be," a man answered. Uncle Felix, I

guessed, though it was difficult to discern over the pounding of blood in my ears. "It seems she might've scratched it, somehow."

"It's a scratch. She told me so," Aleysia answered, and I wanted so badly to tell her to be quiet. Not to say a word to either of them, but my eyes refused to open, and my voice remained trapped in my throat.

"Hush, girl," Agatha snapped. "She cannot lose the arm. She'll be worthless."

"Best you can do is wait and see, then. If it gets worse, we may have to amputate." The most I'd heard Uncle Felix say in all the time I'd known him.

The most horrific words he could've possibly spoken.

* * *

S creams.

Horrible screams echoed inside my head.

A young girl wearing what looked like animal hide reached for an older woman, who lay motionless on the ground in a pool of thick blood. The girl cried and wriggled in the arms of a man dressed in armor, like the age of old. I watched him carry her to the edge of the world, where nothing but a thick white mist stood beyond the rock. The young girl's cries turned hysterical, and she clawed at the metal of his suit in futility.

With little care, he threw her small body over the edge of the rock.

A flash of black swooped down from the sky toward me.

I saw my reflection in the shiny, black eye of a raven.

* * *

B linding brightness pounded against my eyelids, and I turned over with a groan. Painfully luminous, it had my eyeballs aching and my head throbbing. A cold sting pulsed through my arm, and with a whimper, I took in the state of my bandage, profusely soaked in black blood.

Worse than the night before.

A strange metallic scent, not like rot, or infection, struck the back of my throat while I unwound the dirty gauze. When I finally reached the end of the wrapping, I paused, confusion clamoring through my already aching head. The wound had closed, the skin contractured and pulled together into a fully healed scar, the edges of which glowed a strange silver. I ran my fingertip over it, noting the slight hum beneath my skin where I touched. The marking seemed to have a deliberate shape, though it wasn't until I turned my head a slight bit that I noticed the way the skin had tightened around the wound like vanes to a rachis, giving it the appearance of a feather.

How peculiar.

It didn't hurt. I no longer felt the delirium, or heat of a fever. I sat up, noticing Aleysia's bed empty and made. Squinting against the light, I rested my palm against the ache in my left eyeball and stumbled out of bed toward the dresser. In the mirror's reflection, my skin seemed paler than before, if that were even possible. I lowered my hand from my face and jumped back on a gasp. The lower part of my iris, ordinarily a deep, winter gray, had paled to an icy silver. I leaned in, my fingertips skimming just below my eye, and studied the aberration that almost appeared like a metallic fleck stuck to my eye.

"Oh, thank god, you're awake!" Aleysia's voice shot a startling jolt through my muscles, and I nearly poked myself in the eye. "Thank the ever loving and merciful god!"

Merciful god? Since when had she begun crediting him for anything?

I turned just as she crashed into me, wrapping her arms around me.

"I thought we lost you! I thought ... I ..." The tears in her voice had me frowning. What had gotten into her? As she straightened herself, I covered my strange eye to keep her from seeing it. "You ... you slept so long."

"Yeah, I had a hard time falling asleep last night. Kept waking up in the night, after you went back to your own bed."

Face painted in confusion, she shook her head. "After I went back to my own bed? Maeve, that was four nights ago."

"What?" Suddenly, I was the one confused.

"You've been practically comatose for days."

Days? I let out a nervous chuckle. "That's …. That can't be. It was just last night I was singing to you."

Her brows flickered, and she blinked away the shine in her eyes. "Uncle Felix said you were actually dead for eight minutes and twenty-seven seconds. He tried to revive you."

Dead?

How could that be? I'd had moments of lucidity. How could I have not known that I'd *died*? That cold feeling of disbelief swept over me again, and I stumbled back into the dresser, catching myself. "I don't remember any of that, at all. Just … moments of waking and sleeping. But it felt like it happened over the span of an evening."

"You came down with an awful fever. Mr. Moros arrived, and you were still in bed. I had no choice but to tell Agatha about the cut on your arm, so she had Uncle Felix look at it. Then you … you stopped breathing, and he started talking about wheeling you down to the morgue …. Well, I … I was beside myself. And then you started breathing again." Clearing her throat, she flapped her hands at her eyes as if trying to stave off the tears and pointed to my hand still covering *my* eye. "The condition with your eye is called *duoculos*, according to Uncle Felix. He doesn't know what caused it, but he said it's relatively harmless."

At that, I lowered my hand, somewhat relieved. "What does he think of the cut?"

"He told Agatha to monitor it. If it didn't get better, they were considering chopping it off. I'm just relieved you're better. You must be starving."

It wasn't until she suggested the possibility of food that I noticed the ravenous ache in my stomach. "I am. A little."

"I'll grab you some warm broth. Probably better that you take it slow. No big meals."

"Probably."

"Well, now you're awake, I can finally celebrate the victory of seeing Agatha absolutely beside herself with anger." The worry and grief in her eyes from moments ago cut to a wicked expression of satisfaction. "Thought she was going to have to return that money to Mr. Moros. She broke three good vases, according to Lolla." She chuckled and plucked the brush from the dresser, drawing it carefully through my hair. "Just imagining such a thing brings me joy."

"Happy to have obliged." I winced as she tore through a knot. "And Mr. Moros?"

"It seems you've not rid yourself of him. He's come to check on you every day, leaving chocolates and flowers." She gathered up my hair and brushed the roots, chopping at them with haste. "I hope you don't mind, I ate quite a few of the chocolates. Had to make sure they weren't poisoned, you know."

"I'm sure."

"Honestly, Maeve. I could cry of happiness right now." Without warning, arms enveloped me from behind, the pressure at my throat damn near choking me. "You looked absolutely terrible for a minute there. I feared …. Well, with father having …" The wobble in her voice told me she was holding back more tears. "And being here … alone …"

"I'm here." I gripped her arm still banded at my throat. "I'm not going anywhere."

"I'll go get you that broth. Stay put."

I nodded, and the moment she released me and scurried out of the room, I turned back to the mirror, staring at my eye. "Duoculos," I whispered.

The sound of a shout snapped my attention toward the

window, and I ambled that way, catching sight of two boys, perhaps no more than twelve or thirteen, across the dirt road at the edge of the forest. Though difficult to see from that distance, it appeared as though they were stomping on something. I squinted, noting a black object beneath the boot of the boy wearing a brown hat, and my heart shot into my throat when it occurred to me they were near the winterberry bush where I'd buried the raven.

"Oh, no." I shoved the window open on a creak, and a rush of cold air nearly knocked me backward. "Hey! Hey, you! Get away from there!"

The boys ignored me, keeping on with their violent stomps. A dark and wicked anger stirred in my gut. I opened my mouth to scream, yet nothing but a high-pitched screech escaped me. I slapped my hand over my mouth and backed out of the window, ducking below the sill.

What in seven hells was that?

A peek over the sill showed the boys stomping away, clearly not having heard me, at all. Or perhaps they had and didn't care.

But then they stopped, and one of the boys turned toward the forest behind them, as if he'd heard something.

I pushed to my knees, curious.

A flash of black flew past the boys and up into the sky. Looming over them, what looked like a colossal-sized raven flapped wings that must've spanned the width of a small cottage. My jaw creaked open as I took in the size of it. The creature exploded into a flock of ravens that cawed as they scattered off.

A scream jarred me out of my staring toward the sky, and I glanced down to find one of the boys clutching the edge of the archway, as though something was pulling him by his feet into the woods. His friend grabbed his shirt, tugging him the other way.

He lost his grip and flew backward, the impact knocking his hat to the ground.

I blinked, and the other boy was gone.

A cold sensation moved through me as I stared down at that now empty archway, with its ominous bones. An itch at my arm had me mindlessly scratching around my wound.

The other boy pushed to his feet and peered into the forest.

The itch turned to a burning sensation.

"Don't do it," I whispered, watching him step closer. Closer. The scratching of my arm became frantic. "Don't do it."

"Don't do what?" At the sound of Aleysia's voice, I jumped back, and it was then I noticed the inflamed skin around my wound and the blood trickling into the grooves of the scar.

I glanced toward the forest again, to find the other boy was no longer there. Only a flock of ravens pecking around the grass. I'd have thought the forest had taken him, too, but there was no sign of his hat, nor the black object they'd been stomping. No upturned dirt from where I could see.

"I thought ... there were boys at the woods," I said, the confusion in my head carrying into my voice. "I saw one of them get taken." It must've been the lingering shock that kept me frozen, staring. That scene looping inside my mind. "They were screaming. Did you hear the screams, Aleysia?"

"No."

Surely, she would've. As thin as the cottage walls were, we'd heard strange noises coming from the forest a number of times.

"By chance, did you happen to see a ... exceptionally large bird that ... exploded into smaller birds?"

"No. Did *you* see a large bird that exploded into smaller birds?" Hearing her ask that aloud had me shrinking into myself. How completely insane I must've sounded.

"No. I was …. I just thought …. Some fresh air. I think I need air." I finally turned around to see her holding out a bowl of broth and a slice of bread for me.

"I think you need some rest. Maybe some food," she said, prodding the food toward me.

"I've had plenty of rest."

"Yes, well, eat something before you slip into delirium. Though, I fear it's too late," she muttered under her breath.

"I could actually stand a quick walk first."

"What? No. You need to eat, Maeve. You haven't eaten in—"

I snatched the bowl from her hands and tipped back the broth, slurping it until I'd polished off the whole thing. Though, I immediately regretted it at the roiling in my stomach.

Aleysia's jaw hung open as she stared back at me and half-heartedly accepted the empty bowl, when I handed it back to her.

"There. I ate." I snatched up the bread and ripped a piece with my teeth as I stepped past her for the door.

"Where are you going? You should probably have someone go with you."

"I just want some fresh air. I'll be fine."

"Okay. Fine. But if you're not back at the toll of the quarter bell, I'm coming to look for you."

"Deal." I slipped out of my nightclothes, keeping my arm out of sight, and into my black dress and boots, then padded quietly down the stairs in hopes of avoiding Agatha. The moment my feet hit the lower level, I froze. A tall, gaunt figure stood at the foot of the stairs—Uncle Felix, munching on a sandwich of, undoubtedly, smelt fish and fig jam, as he was known to eat. He regarded me with a cocked brow before biting into his loathsome lunch.

Likewise, I bit into my bread.

He turned into the parlor, and I kept on out the front door.

The frigid air stiffened my muscles as I ran across the dirt road toward the woods, glancing up at the sky on occasion to make sure there was no terrifying colossus bird overhead. By the time I reached the woods, the birds that'd been pecking there scattered off.

As I neared the winterberry bush, I slowed my steps on seeing the undisturbed grave, no black object in sight. I swept my gaze over the area to find no footprints, no sign of struggle, or grooves, where someone might have been dragged over the dirt.

It was real. All of it was so real.

I turned back around toward the house and spied Aleysia staring at me through our bedroom window. I didn't have to see her face up close to know lines of worry etched her brow.

I'm losing my mind. I must be.

Breathe. Just breathe.

I closed my eyes and inhaled deeply, and on an exhale, I opened my eyes to a flash of silver buried in the piled dirt.

Leave it alone.

I couldn't, though. Against my better judgment, I knelt to the ground and dug at the grave, until I loosened what appeared to be a black and silver, scaled and oval object, roughly the size of a melon. An egg of some sort, judging by the shape of it.

But no sign of the raven I'd buried there.

Frowning, I looked back to the empty grave and the object again. I examined its rough surface, trying to imagine what it could've been.

Over my shoulder, I stared at the entrance to Witch Knell. Nothing lurked there besides an errant breeze that winnowed through the crooked limbs, but it was that eerie placidity that cast a shiver down my spine and urged me to turn away.

The egg sat in my palm, and I held it up to examine the silver lined scales on its surface. I stretched my left arm out enough to slide my sleeve back for the scar there and the silvery scales that also accented the feather's rough shape.

My mind puzzled the connection. The bird I'd buried. The cut I'd sustained. And now the egg.

"What have you got there, girl?" The gravelly voice from behind me sent a quiver across my spine like a tuning fork. I slowly turned to find The Crone Witch leaning on a wooden cane, much like Agatha's.

Up close, I could see the pronounced wrinkles in her skin and a scar next to her milky white eye that looked like she'd gone blind.

"I, um ... I found this. On the ground."

Brow quirked, she glanced to the grave and back to me. "You dug it up?"

"No. I mean, I saw it in the ground. And ... well, yes."

A wicked smile curved her lips.

"I'm sorry. I'll put it back." I turned to place the egg back beneath the bush.

"It's yours now, girl. You must take it with you."

"Do you know what it is?" The clang of the quarter bell startled my muscles, despite being distant from where we stood, and on instinct, I looked toward the sky again.

"It's your penance. A life for death."

"Maevyth!" Aleysia called to me from across the field.

"Coming!" I shouted back, but at the grip of my arm, I turned back toward the witch whose eyes were wide and blazing with urgency.

"What do you see, girl?" Her gaze fell to my arm, and she ran her fingers over the scar there.

I wrenched free, nearly dropping the egg tucked into my elbow. "Do not put your hands on me."

"You see the dead. You hear them speak to you."

"I hear nothing of the sort. Only those possessed by evil hear such things."

"Is that so ..." Her response made me pause.

"Do you hear voices? Or see the dead?" I asked.

"My sight is far keener for this world. I see a daughter, shunned by her kin."

"You don't have to have keen sight to see that."

"I also know that the delicate black rose doesn't grow well in these parts. Our winters are far too cold for its fragile roots."

I puzzled her words and their meaning. Everyone knew I'd

been found with a black rose, but maybe she knew something more. Something they didn't. "Where do they grow?"

"Where the gods see fit to plant them."

The way she talked in circles had my already muddled head spinning. "You believe in the gods. Not a single god, but many." Admitting such a thing would've been confessing to a crime.

"The god to which you pray fears the power of many."

"Lyverians worship many gods. Are you Lyverian?"

"Lyverians weren't the only ones who worshipped many gods."

"Maevyth!" Aleysia called again, impatience thick in her tone, and I caught a glimpse of her making her way toward the dirt road.

"Coming!" I shouted over my shoulder again, not daring to take my eyes off the witch. "And what happens if this egg should hatch?"

"It begs the question … what happens when the dead return from the grave?" Her dark chuckle sent a shiver down my spine. "Go now, girl. Wouldn't want you to get swept away like two curious boys."

My blood turned cold. "You saw them?"

"I see everything." The way she tipped her chin down, looking at me beneath her bushy white brows, had me backing slowly away from her. When I turned around, I tucked the egg behind my back so as not to draw Aleysia's attention to it.

"What are you doing by those woods?" Aleysia chided, as I padded toward her. "Was it not enough to have a man's skin tossed at your boots?"

"I was talking to The Crone Witch."

Her face twisted to a look of pure repulsion. "The Crone Witch? The woman who *eats* children, Maevyth?"

I glanced over my shoulder to see the old woman yanking a cord of wood from a piled stack of them with little struggle. "Don't tell me you're swayed by rumor now?"

"Of course not, but don't you find her just a little unsettling?"

"Yes, I do. I also find her intriguing because of it."

"You're beginning to concern me, Sister. And what in God's eyes are you hiding behind your back?"

"It's nothing." I pulled it from my back, cradling it in my arms. "Just an unusual rock I found by the woods."

"That doesn't look like any rock I've ever seen. And you intend to decorate our bedroom with that thing?"

"I'll keep it under my bed. I just thought it was interesting." I ran my finger over the scales on the outside, the texture reminding me of an enormous acorn.

"It's probably cursed if you found it near those woods. Better to keep it outside of the house."

At the sound of an approaching carriage, both of us turned to see someone coming up the road.

"No," Aleysia said beside me.

"Who is it?"

"Mr. Moros. Hurry inside. I'll tell him you're still ill."

"What if he's seen us?"

"I'll still tell him you're ill and can't accept company. Now, go."

I rushed across the yard and plowed through the cottage entrance, egg still tucked in my arm. At the top of the staircase stood Agatha, and my heart sank into my stomach.

"Good god, you look ghastly with that deformed eye. Yet, I see you're doing well now. And how timely. Mr. Moros has arrived to check on you. Such a kind man to inquire about you these past few days. Fortunately, he wasn't troubled by your appearance." She hobbled her way down the staircase, and I clutched the egg tighter, offering a smile to distract her from the object.

"I heard he paid me many visits. So kind."

She stopped alongside me, and in as subtle a movement as I could muster, I slid the egg to my side along my hip. Leaning in, she sniffed and crinkled her nose. "Heavens, you smell like a pig's pen. Go wash yourself. Quickly. I suspect he'll want to visit with you for a spell."

"Yes, of course." Lowering my gaze, I slipped past her up the staircase, and when I reached the top, she called out to me.

"And, Maevyth, he may want to examine you. A fair request given what he's paid."

"What do you mean, *examine?*"

"No need for undergarments, my dear."

CHAPTER ELEVEN

ZEVANDER

Zevander strode up to the iron-embellished door of Eidolon's keep, the ancient castle that'd belonged to his bloodline for centuries. Gargoyles perched at either side of the staircase, their wretched faces illuminated by torch sconces that blazed below them. Situated on the summit of Insidian Ridge, the black stone castle overlooked the vast darklands of Nyxteros and served as a monument of his cursed name. Whatever life had once pulsed through the veins of the stony castle had withered inside its cold, gray tomb walls.

Rykaia lay passed out in his arms while the clank of chains rattled, and the door swung open into the grand darkness housed within. Halfway back to the manor, he'd had to place a sleeping spell on his sister to keep her from screaming and trying to escape.

A biting cold swept over him, the castle lacking in warmth and welcome. The flame of a candelabra drew his attention to the staircase, where Vendryck, loyal servant of the manor, descended toward them. Lanky as he was, he lifted Rykaia from his arms with ease, her long silvery hair caught in a tangle.

"Lock her in," Zevander ordered as he handed her off.

"Yes, My Lord."

Zevander slipped his hand into the pocket of his leathers and retrieved the vial of vivicantem Dolion had given him, which he handed off to the servant. "She will need a dose when she wakes."

"Of course, Master." Vendryck gave a nod and carried her up the staircase toward her room. Having denied her the stimulants meant she'd likely go through her fits, as he called them. The last bout she'd suffered had nearly destroyed half of the castle's east wing. She could be as violent as a tempest, and sometimes Zevander had to restrain her to the bed. Other times, keep her confined in the dungeon, if she'd really gotten on a kick. He hated having to do that to her, but he'd always made every effort to keep her comfortable.

Groaning, he rubbed a hand down his face and followed after them, toward his own chambers. It'd been days since he'd last been home, with his hunts taking him to the farthest reaches of Nyxteros. He longed for a good night's rest.

Down the great corridor, he passed numerous portraits of ancient ancestors–going all the way back to the primordial Lunasier, the first of his bloodline. Unlike most Aethyrians, whose powers required the sun, theirs derived from both moons. Those cold luminous rays that ordinarily bathed his bloodline's powers failed to rouse them from their slumbered state in Zevander. While he could still feel his bloodline sigil when the moons were high, he'd never be able to summon those powers, not after they'd been corrupted by his curse. His father had destroyed the proud Lunasier in both Zevander and Branimir, by offering up the blood of his only two sons like family heirlooms he'd been entitled to barter with, forever tainting their once honorable inherited magic.

He kept on toward the room at the end of the corridor and opened the heavy iron door that led to an elaborate bed with finely embellished silk dressings–a far cry from the stone bed he'd been forced to sleep upon in his youth, while enslaved to the

Solassions. For reasons he couldn't quite grasp, he sometimes longed for the hard and sturdy surface over the softness and comfort of his bed.

Right then, though, he didn't give a damn where he slept, so long as he rested.

He removed his cape and cuirass from over the black tunic beneath, which was also made of leather, peeling the garments away and tossing them onto a rack built of anacitine–a bulky metal that attracted the magic in blood. En route back to the castle, he'd tossed away the stone of his shadowed attacker into the bog, and the scant drops of blood that remained on his clothing slithered over the leather onto the metallic surface, which absorbed it away, cleansing the garments of any evidence. The anacitine would contain the magic held in those drops of blood, effectively voiding its powerful charge.

From the satchel at his hip, he emptied the milk-white stone he'd gathered from his prey into his palm. Ten times the potency of what Dolion had given him in liquid form.

He strode toward an alcove in the wall and knelt before a small iron door, about a quarter meter in height, decorated in rusted silver. The Golvyn door. He knocked three times, as was expected, and the door was swung open by a pocket-sized being–half man/half rodent, with a long snout and beady squinty eyes. Though hairless, his ears, half the size of his face, and two long incisors gave him the rat features. He'd lived inside the walls of the castle since before Zevander had been born, through channels burrowed in the concrete that led to every room. Most castles included a Golvyn, though they were rarely welcome and often subjected to extermination spells.

"You called, My Lord," he said in a nasally tone, gnashing his incisors. While mostly docile, Golvyns could easily snap if threatened.

Zevander handed him the vivicantem stone. The Golvyn had

no use for it, as they didn't require vivicantem like mancers, which made them perfect safekeepers.

With a nod, the Golvyn tucked it under his gangly arm and scampered back through the door, which slammed behind him.

Zevander pushed to his feet and made his way to his own private bathing room, a vast expanse of arched, stained-glass windows and dim moonlight. From where it'd been built, wedged between the west tower and the great hall, if the sky was clear and both moons sat high, he could see the caps of the Veritian Mountains in the distance.

He reached out a hand, and curls of black flames fell from his palm, dancing over the water's surface, agitating the clear liquid beneath. Moments later, steam rose up from the flickering crests, and Zevander removed his trousers before stepping into the warm bath.

He leaned back against the curved, marble basin, letting the heat loosen his tense muscles, and closed his eyes.

Mor samanet, a whispered voice said through the darkness of his mind. *Death awaits.*

He shot upright with a splash of water and glanced around for the source of it, ears perked for the slightest sound.

Nothing.

What had happened outside the tavern, earlier, wasn't the first time he'd been targeted for a revenge kill. While those who'd attempted it had so far been unsuccessful, Zevander wasn't foolish enough to assume the ward he'd placed around Eidolon was completely unbreakable.

The same ward designed to keep Rykaia safe, as well, as much as she hated the castle.

And him.

At no further sound, he settled back in the water once more, the engulfing heat loosening his tense and aching muscles. He'd traveled to the northernmost reaches of Draconysia to Veneficarys in the south, in search of King Sagaerin's prey, dispatching him swiftly before receiving word from Dolion that the sixth stone resided in Costelwick. His battered body needed recovery and rest.

As he lay breathing in the thick steam, his body hardened with a need he forced himself to ignore. One he hadn't longed to entertain since he was an adolescent. Eyes closed, he exhaled and reached through the water, but at the nauseating twist of his stomach, he hesitated to stroke his hand down over the ten rods that pierced the underside of his cock, each one holding its own sordid memory. A time when he was forced, at too young an age, to entertain the appetite of the Bellatryx–a band of female warriors, half Solassion, half Zephromyte, who answered to the same Solassion king that'd imprisoned him and his father. The same king who'd ordered his father murdered in front of him when he was only a boy. The Bellatryx were violent women who enjoyed sadistic pleasures, and Zevander had been one of a dozen boys used for their entertainment.

His fingers skimmed over each steel bar, the metal carrying an enchantment to ensure he could never remove them. A promise that he'd never know anything but agonizing pain without them. As he'd grown into his manhood with each new decade, a new bar had been added. Ten piercings. An entire century of enslavement.

He'd been assigned to General Loyce, a brutal woman who'd been responsible for the deaths of three previous slaves before she'd gotten her hands on Zevander. The day she'd forced the first piercing, she'd sat fucking her own fingers, watching him scream in pain. Though each Bellatryx had had their own personal slave, a gift from the king, Loyce had enjoyed sharing Zevander.

Their moans echoed in his head, the phantom memory of their claws at his back, their teeth on his flesh raking over his skull with a vicious enmity.

Even years later, when the commands of those vile women

were nothing but a distant memory in his ear, he still couldn't bring himself to stroke his cock. Not even when it begged for relief.

It was especially difficult during the merging of moons, when his body naturally craved sex. A time when all Lunasier men, in particular, hungered for a hearty fuck, and their women ended up pregnant as a result. Those were the times when he'd find mindless release with sexsells. Emotionless sex that had him grinding his teeth to finish. A quick release.

Harmless trysts, because there wasn't a chance in seven hells he'd ever settle down with anyone. Even if he wanted the headache of a mate, and he didn't, no Letalisz had ever been granted permission to marry. It didn't matter that he was King Sagaerin's most skilled assassin. His loyalty was merely the price of living without exile. Otherwise, he'd have suffered the same fate as his father.

Zevander released himself and exhaled, tipping his head back to the edge of the basin and closing his eyes. While he'd never bond with a woman, he did long to enjoy the pleasures of one without the memories of his past destroying it all.

Willing himself to banish the thoughts pounding at his skull, he let his mind drift into the empty black void. Sleep he so desperately needed, but which had eluded him as of late.

From the silence, a voice called out to him.

Zevander! Zevander! It belonged to his mother.

The surrounding blackness lifted to a bright light that Zevander squinted against, as he placed the scorpion he'd just fed onto the grass. He watched as its stinger pierced a pea-sized spider in the abdomen, then gathered it to its mouth with pincers. Unbeknownst to his mother, he often played with the deadly critters that were known to kill with a single sting. While vicious toward their prey, they never stung him. Not even when he held them trapped in his palms.

"Zevander!" His mother called again, her voice impatient, and he turned to the vines of roses that charmed the outer stones of the castle,

climbing the wall to the window from where she peered down at him. "Come. I need you in the kitchen."

"Yes, Mother." The boy pushed to his feet and entered the castle, winding through rooms, and as he passed his young sister playing with her dolls, he paused to kiss the top of her head and kept on.

In the kitchen, his mother stood at the wooden chopping table, adding bits of raw meat to a plate already piled high. Blood dripped over the edge of it, and Zevander frowned at the thought of its copper flavor on his tongue.

"I need you to take this to Branimir for me."

Dread stirred in his gut. While he enjoyed seeing his brother on occasion, the dungeon had always terrified him. And those spiders. Ghastly spiders that watched him from the shadows of Branimir's cell.

"Can Rykaia come with me?" the boy asked, despite not wanting his mother to think he was weak at ten years old.

"No, love. Branimir's condition worsens, and I would not want her to become ill, as well. Besides that, she was nearly bitten last time."

"Branimir would never allow her to be bitten, Mother. He loves Rykaia."

One of Branimir's spiders had bitten their cat, Gwinny. Two nights later, she'd lay moaning, convulsing. She'd thrown up all over Branimir's cell, and Zevander had to retrieve her skeletal carcass, a task that'd left him retching the whole time.

That had been the cat, though, not their beloved sister.

"I'm sorry, darling. You're the only one who can do this for me." She sighed and ran a hand through his already mussed hair. "Your father should return soon. Perhaps Branimir will be better when he does."

Zevander gave a solemn nod, and his mother kissed the top of his head. She handed him the dish of bloody meat, and the boy began his trek down to the dungeons.

The air turned cold as he descended the stone staircase, and puffs of white expelled with each breath. His arms trembled, and he wanted so badly to drop the dish and run back up the stairs, but Mother would only make him return with another. When he finally reached the bottom stair, he stole a moment to catch his breath, then kept on, past the statues of his ancestors, and the cells at the end of the corridor, beyond them, to the wooden door of the dungeon floor.

He stared at it a moment before setting the plate of food down while he lit the firelamp sitting beside the door. Once aglow, he carefully lifted the door on a creak of its rusted hinges and held the lamp over the gaping hole, below which he could see a dirt floor about two meters down. He reached down and hooked the lamp on a nail of the ladder and climbed down the first couple of rungs. Holding himself steady, he leaned over the edge of the hole and grabbed the plate, balancing it with one hand as he stepped down one rung at a time. Halfway to the ground, he unhooked the firelamp with his free hand, letting it slide to the crook of his elbow, and made the awkward descent the rest of the way down.

Chittering noises and the sound of something scampering over the dirt sent a chill down the back of his neck. He raised the firelamp up high, illuminating the expanse of the space and the shadows that hung on the fringes of light.

"Branimir," he whispered. "I've brought your supper."

The shadows shifted, and a pale white figure crawled toward him on hands and feet. While his form was grotesque and terrifying, the sight of him brought a smile to Zevander's face.

"Zevander," Branimir rasped and smiled in return. His black eyes had sunken deeper, and what should've been the muscled form of a eighteen year-old adolescent was instead a thin and skeletal body that hadn't been properly nourished.

Not because his family hadn't fed him, but because they couldn't afford the amount of vivicantem it would've taken to improve his health.

His brother grabbed a handful of meat, shoving it into his mouth like an animal, and as he ate, Zevander looked over the space, catching sight of an enormous spider's leg and eyes that watched him from the shadows. So many eyes. He lifted the lamp higher and gasped. An entire wall of webs showed thousands of spiders—some small, some medium. "Bran ... are there more of them?"

A quick glance over his shoulder, and Branimir shoved more meat into his mouth. "I think they came from Gwinny. I saw them crawl from her body before you discarded it."

"They were inside her?" The thought of such a thing had his own stomach twisting in disgust.

"Yeah. They didn't actually kill her, though." He lowered his gaze as if shamed. "She turned wild. I was afraid she'd hurt Rykaia."

"You killed her?"

"Broke her neck. I'm sorry. Is mother mad at me?"

"No. Just scared, I think."

"She should be scared. You should all be scared." He stared off, then crammed another handful of bloody meat into his mouth.

"Why do you prefer that it's not cooked?"

Branimir chewed slowly, as if contemplating the question. "It isn't me who craves it. It is them."

"You share it with them?"

"They taste what I eat. They feel what I feel." He ran his hand across his skull, where small patches of baldness showed he'd ripped out his own hair. "I have thoughts ... very bad thoughts." His eyes shifted as he spoke, brows pulled tight. "I pray they are not my own, but I can't be sure." Branimir let out a whimper, and the spiders behind him shifted on the web as if nervous. "I don't want you to come down here anymore, Zevander."

"But you'll starve."

"I don't care. Let me starve. The silence of death would be welcome."

"Bran ... you don't know what you're saying. I won't let you starve. I refuse."

Not a breath later, his brother lurched, knocking the boy onto his back. An intense pressure struck Zevander's throat, as Branimir gripped tight, his eyes feral with rage. Spiders crawled over his shoulders and head.

"I could feed on you for weeks ..."

"Bran ..." Zevander rasped, clawing at his brothers hand. "Bran!"

Zevander shot upright on a gasp, every muscle locked with tension. He looked around to find himself surrounded by water that bubbled like a cauldron, boiling hot, though the heat of it had no effect on him, at all. Black fire licked the air in sporadic bursts that mirrored the twitching of his muscles, and he pulled the rogue flames back into him, cursing his lapse in consciousness.

He ran a trembling hand down his face, his breaths heaving. The day Branimir had held him by the throat was the day his scorpion sigil had first appeared. While the air had waned in his lungs, and the spiders had sank their poisonous teeth into his flesh, he'd thought of something bigger. Faster. Impenetrable. From the darkness, a venomous beast had risen and struck with no fear.

And from that moment on, the spiders kept their distance from Zevander and his scorpions.

The memory faded, the image sharpening to the rippling water beneath him, where his reflection stared back. Deep black veins branched from a black crevice that ran along his cheek, the unsightly black scar he'd had since he was a child. The branches crawled over his jaw and down his neck, to his collarbone and left shoulder. The curse that'd corrupted his blood. It longed to eat his heart, to turn him into the same vile creature that'd claimed his older brother.

How much longer before that day? He couldn't say.

Branimir's physical changes had developed immediately after the ritual. It was his mind that snapped without warning. In a single moment, it seemed as if he'd lost himself, giving in to the dark madness.

The thoughts clawed at him, sending a cold sensation across his chest, as if his lungs were crystallizing.

From the holster lying beside his leathers, Zevander unsheathed his dagger and carved a long wound into his thigh.

The pain seared through his muscles as the poison on the blade's surface swam deep into his veins.

The fucking hypocrite in him. That he could chide his own sister for what she did to herself, then turn around and contaminate his blood with deadly toxin, but he'd had the visions before. Knew the power they had over his mind. How quickly they could trigger an episode.

Branimir had always served as a source of unrest for Zevander, torment, unless he had something to pull him out of it, to distract his mind from the black vortex that threatened to pull him under. The more his attacks had evolved over the years, the stronger the poison required to break him of it, and the more Zevander began to believe his brother's fate could very well be his own one day.

No. He'd sooner cleave out his own fucking heart than risk what'd happened to Branimir.

He needed to track down that final bloodstone, or gods be damned, he'd take matters into his own hands.

He let out a hiss while the vicious toxin worked its way into his gut and up to his ribcage where it spread across his chest, swallowing the icy sensation. He grunted and groaned and trembled, as white hot pain devoured his muscles. Hands balled into fists, he let the poison tear his insides open in splitting agony that had him arched out of the water, until, teeth grinding, he shook with violent convulsions, his consciousness thinning.

Slowly, by the gods, the ghostly presence in his mind faded under the wild flame of suffering, and *finally*, Zevander could think of nothing more than bleeding it out of him.

CHAPTER TWELVE

MAEVYTH

Shoulders pulled back, every muscle in my body urging me to run from the room, I stood before Mr. Moros, who sat on the couch across from Agatha.

"I can assure you," the old woman said in a voice that scratched at my ears like nails on glass, "aside from the small imperfection in her eye, she suffered no other physical deformities."

In the last hour, I'd begun to appreciate those new imperfections that had now labeled me anomalous in Agatha's eyes.

"You're welcome to examine her further." She turned toward me, eyes sparkling with feigned adoration. "Maevyth, dear, lift your skirts so the good sir can assess you."

Dryness tore through my throat, my eyeballs bouncing between Agatha and Mr. Moros' shifting form on the couch.

"Don't be rude. Do as you're told, girl," she chided, ushering me with her hand.

"That won't be necessary," Moros said, much to my mortified relief. "I trust she's perfect."

"Well, not entirely so. There is the eye, and the scar she now bears on her arm. Grotesque looking thing, though it seems to be easily hidden beneath her dresses."

"Miss Bronwick," Mr. Moros said, not bothering to acknowledge Agatha. "Might I entice you to lunch, then tea in the gardens, this afternoon? A public affair, I assure you. A number of respected members of the community and their wives will be in attendance. Some who knew your father quite well."

While I was inclined to refuse, the prospect of having to listen to Agatha lament about my new imperfections one moment longer urged me to accept. Besides, *no* wouldn't have been an acceptable response to her, either, so in essence, I had no choice. I also welcomed the opportunity to hear about the adopted father I hardly knew, one whom Agatha had made a point to exclude from any of the family albums, or conversation. "I'd like that, thank you, Sir."

"Very good. Perhaps you might want to ... consider more comfortable attire." It was clear he meant my lack of undergarments, and clearing my throat, I nodded. With Agatha's dismissal, I darted up the staircase for my bedroom, and once inside, I performed a quick sweep for the egg I'd hidden beneath my bed. Thankfully, it remained tucked against the wall, where I'd hoped Aleysia wouldn't find it.

Once I'd slipped into my undergarments and corset, replacing the high-necked dress and cross, I headed back down the stairs. In truth, I hadn't yet been to the northern side of the parish, where most of the military and politicians resided. I'd heard there were far more amenities there, including a telescope, which I longed to see someday.

When I returned to the parlor, a new but familiar face stood chatting with Agatha and Mr. Moros. One of the executioners from The Banishing days ago. The one who'd snickered and stabbed the prisoner with his bayonet.

Across from them sat my sister, the anger in her eyes telling me everything.

He was the man Agatha had chosen for her.

* * *

A long and opulent table stretched from one end of the dining room to the other, and around it sat twenty-two of Foxglove's more prominent residents. Mr. Moros had claimed the head of the table, while I sat wedged between him and an officer, identified as such by the embellished uniform he wore. Across from me were the parish physician and his wife, who'd already assessed me prior to the lunch. The Governor's clerks, some of the women Agatha often gossiped with, one of the Sacred Men garbed in the telling red robe, and a few others I didn't recognize took up the remaining chairs. A sea of vibrantly-colored attire.

Meanwhile, I wore my usual black dress and choker, which I found oddly comforting amongst uncomfortable company. A second skin that made me invisible for the way their eyes skated over me with the same disinterest as if I were a dried and withering rose in a garden of bright tulips.

For most of the lunch, I sat through mind-numbing, political commentary and loathsome gossip of villagers, until a man two seats down finally asked, "I understand you made quite a discovery while mining in Lyveria. Is that true, Mr. Moros?"

Beside me, Moros frowned, raising a bite of too-rare venison to his mouth. "And how did you come upon this news?"

"News is my business, Sir." It was then I recognized the man as a scribe for the Foxglove Gazette. He'd come to the mortuary not long ago, scrounging juicy bits on why the vineyard had failed so miserably.

Moros dabbed his face with a napkin and cleared his throat. "I did, in fact, make a new discovery." From his coat pocket, he pulled a small vial containing three milky white stones, their surfaces sparkling. "The stones were buried in what appeared to have been hardened lava rock at one time."

"Any idea what it is?"

"No. I'm having it examined. Virtually indestructible, so it may prove useful as weaponry, if we can find a way to melt it down." After another long stare, Moros tucked the rocks away inside his coat.

"It must be dangerous mining so close to the Lyverians." The observation came from one of the women, dressed in a flamboyant pink dress. "I understand they collect the bones of their kills."

"Yes. The Lyverians are quite hostile, but the Vonkovyan forces have been gracious enough to guard our operations there. The good captain here has ensured we remain insulated from attack." Moros nodded toward the man sitting beside me, and I didn't bother to turn and look, as I could feel the whole table staring our way. "They're quite primitive, I must say. Using bones for weapons." He chuckled, dabbing his mouth again, before setting the napkin atop his empty plate. "As I understand, they worship some ancient goddess named Morsana. The Goddess of Death, and the bones are part of their many rituals."

One of the women at the table gasped so dramatically, I turned to see if she'd choked.

"Positively malevolent! Call it *cultural* all you want, but it's pure witchcraft, if you ask me." The speaker was an older man, sitting beside her, with tufts of white hair, and his gaze fell on me, as if I somehow embodied the evil to which he'd taken offense. "I must say, Mr. Moros, I was a slight bit hesitant to accept your invitation when I heard that *she'd* be in attendance." He gave a nod toward me, and I shrank in my chair at the sudden attention. "Are you aware of the girl's history?"

"I am. And I find your superstitions to be somewhat …" Moros lifted his glass of wine, pausing to smile. "Ridiculous," he added, before tipping a sip.

"Ridiculous?" The older man scoffed, shifting in his chair like he'd forgotten how to get out of it. "Were you not in attendance for The Banishing? Did you not witness the evil that lives within those woods?"

"The Banished spoke to her in tongues, for goodness sake." The woman in pink feigned a shiver that ruffled the lace of her dress. "If that's not proof of her malevolence, I don't know what is."

"Don't forget the young girl she murdered years ago," a woman on other side of the accusing man added. "Lilleven Pontrey, I believe was her name."

It was her name. One that I had thought of every day since, particularly so on nights when she'd sneak her way into my nightmares.

"And what about her?" Moros couldn't have possibly looked more disinterested, as he held his wine up, seeming to examine it with more curiosity than he showed for the woman's comment.

"Well, she was trampled."

"By Ms. Bronwick?"

One of the guests chuckled, but the woman who'd spoken wore a frown. "Of course not. The girl *willed* Lilleven into the road."

"By her own hands?" Moros continued to mock the woman, perhaps already aware of the rumor.

"No," she answered sharply, eyes narrowed on him. "By her *evil* mind. She spoke the words of the devil, and Lilleven ran in front of the carriage."

In the thick of an argument, I had told her that I wished she'd get trampled by a horse. No sooner had the words come out of my mouth, and she'd turned and walked into the road, where she'd gotten run over by a carriage. For the two years that'd followed, I'd refused to speak a word, believing I'd caused her murder. I'd believed that I really was evil.

Moros chuckled in response, his reaction earning another gasp.

"It's true! Lilleven's brother saw the whole thing. This girl is the anathema, *a witch*, and deserves banishment to The Eating Woods!"

Before I could breathe so much as a word, Moros rested his hand over mine, offering what I took as a reassuring squeeze, though my first inclination was to push him away. "It is apparent to me you've not ventured outside of Vonkovya—perhaps not even Foxglove Parish. There are no witches here, I can assure you. If you long to witness witchcraft in its purest form, observe a priestess from one of the Lyverian tribes. They'll have you shuddering."

"With all due respect, Mr. Moros," the older man cut in, "she is birthed from the same evil that resides in those woods."

"It is my understanding that the girl was found abandoned. A child cast off by a frightened mother, I presume. You call her an anathema, but I say it's a miracle she lived!"

The man *hmph*ed, glancing at me again. "Our Governor says she was not harmed because the evil recognized her."

"Your Governor is a kind but foolish man." The comment earned Moros a collective round of whispers. "I've traveled far enough to know that evil does truly exist. And I can assure you, this poor young lady does not harbor such malevolence. As for the girl who was trampled? Well, it would seem to me, she'd have done well to watch for approaching carriages before stepping into the road."

A hum of chatter followed, his words undoubtedly new fodder for gossip. Fortunately for him, he was a respected man.

Every part of me wanted to push his hand away, but perhaps my speculations were correct about Mr. Moros. Perhaps he was my key to freedom, somehow. So long as I played along.

"She's quite lucky to have such a kind and benevolent suitor, Mr. Moros. I'm certain you will make a fine couple."

Moros raised his glass of wine. "Thank you. I look forward to our nuptials next week," he said, and tipped back his drink.

Having just swallowed the water I'd sipped, I immediately coughed into my glass. "I beg your pardon, Sir. Next week?"

"Yes. I'm a man who gets things done. Why postpone the inevitable?"

"It'll be a glorious wedding!" the woman in pink exclaimed with an air of celebration. As if she hadn't insulted me only moments before.

"Indeed," said the captain beside me, patting my thigh beneath the table.

Frowning, I swatted his hand off and turned my knees to the side.

"Tell me, Captain," Moros said, drawing the man's attention from me. "I understand Lyverian rebels have crossed Sawtooth and seized Murkmire Parish in the north. What are your intentions there?"

The man beside me groaned. "Murkmire is nothing but wetlands and the poor who refuse to leave its sinking abysmal property value–certainly not worth our resources."

"But aren't you afraid of the message it sends? If one parish can be seized so easily, perhaps our defenses are ... *weak?*"

"I fear nothing, Mr. Moros. Should they dare to test our defenses, they will find themselves at my mercy." He turned to me, offering a slight smile. "Only those deemed worthy long to be there, I can assure you."

"Why are we fighting them?" I dared to ask, directing my attention to Moros and ignoring the strange implication in the captain's comment.

"Their land is brimming with resources. Wasted on such primitive creatures." Whatever credit I'd given to the man shifted with that one snide remark.

"If they've no use for it, can't you strike an agreement with them? An exchange of resources? Surely, we have something they, too, desire?"

"Of course we have what they desire," the captain said beside me. "Our women, namely. What they would do with such an innocent thing like you." Again, he brushed his fingers over my thigh, and I dug my nails into his hand, earning a quiet growl from him.

Turning completely away from the man, I faced Mr. Moros, whose expression, brimming with suspicion, told me he must've caught on to my struggles beneath the table. "I don't question defense in an attack, but seizing land seems ... hostile."

"They're a primitive people," the captain said in a bored tone, easing back into his chair. "Certainly not capable of civilized negotiations."

"But haven't you lost men fighting them? Good men?" I bit back the urge to defend my father, even if I'd never agreed with his position on religion.

"We have. And for just cause. The righteous are born to suffer in this life so they may be exulted in the next."

My tongue practically bled with the effort to keep my ever-sarcastic tone in check. Arguing against his point might've been viewed as an insult to the church. "It just seems to me that there would be peace between the two countries, if we were to leave them be."

The captain snorted beside me, and the entire table broke into laughter at my expense.

"Why, it seems your decades of brilliant strategy and victory has been usurped by a young girl who's likely never been outside of her own parish, Captain." The older man from earlier smirked before sipping his brandy. "Yes, perhaps we should leave the uncivilized brutes alone and let them live in peace."

Moros patted my hand the same way an adult might pat the head of a small child. "Perhaps one day you can accompany me to

Lyveria and see how these wild creatures have chosen to live, with their many gods who praise depravity and indecency."

"I look forward to traveling outside of Vonkovya, Sir. I'm certain it'll be enriching."

One of the servers, a young woman who seemed only slightly older than me, appeared at my side, filling my glass with the sweet tea that I'd only sipped halfway. I sent her a smile, which she returned with a nod, and in not paying attention, she over-filled my glass.

"Onith!" Glass clinked as she pulled the carafe back, taking my glass with it. The tea spilled across the white linens and onto my dress, which didn't trouble me half as much as it seemed to worry the girl. "Onith! Oh, gods!" Her mouth pinched together, and she shook her head, scrambling to dab my dress with a napkin she swiped from the table. "God."

"You bumbling imbecile!" Moros barked, scooting his chair back from the table as though it had spilled over him. "Take Miss Bronwick to the kitchen and have Shireen help with her dress." With a huff, he took my hand. "Truly sorry, my dear. I'll be sure to replace the dress."

"It's only tea. It's fine."

"Come, Miss. Please," she said in a thick accent. It was as she took my hand that I noticed the stark difference in skin tone, hers a more ruddy color, and the mess of scars scattered across the back of her palm. Horrific scars that looked as if she'd sewn the wounds herself.

I followed after her, through a set of french doors to a sitting area, and down a corridor to an expansive kitchen with pots and pans hanging from the ceiling, dozens of cupboards, and more cutting surfaces than one could possibly need. A white porcelain basin and spigot, connected to copper pipes across the wall, indi-cated modern plumbing that I'd heard was very common in the more luxurious manors. Nothing like the clunky well pump attached to the trough sink back home. Although, I couldn't complain too much, seeing as a number of the rural cottages didn't even have an indoor toilet. A welcomed amenity in the thick of winter.

The girl's hand trembled in mine, and she released me and scrambled for a lower cupboard, from where she removed a stack of cloths and a basin. After twisting a dial on the spigot, water spurted into the basin, filling it. She skittered across the kitchen for the pantry, then back again, rounding the corner for whatever stood on the other side. Presumably searching for Shireen.

"It's completely fine," I said, chuckling as I nabbed one of the cloths and dipped it into the awaiting basin of water. "I'm horribly ungraceful when it comes to food. I'd have spilled something on it at some point."

She rushed over to me and gently took hold of the cloth, brows perked. "Please. Allow me."

I focused on the accent. Aside from the minor differences in language between the various parishes in Vonkovya, we mostly sounded the same. Her accent was rich and pleasing to the ear.

"Truly, it's no …" The look in her eyes begged me not to protest. "Of course. Thank you."

As she soaked the skirt of my dress in water, I stared at the scars on her hand.

"You're Lyverian?"

At that, she lowered her head.

"It's nice to meet you. I've never personally met someone from Lyveria before."

She offered a slight smile, still not bothering to lift her gaze to mine. Or speak again.

As she rinsed the cloth in the water, the tipping of her arm exposed a bruise so dark it appeared black. The shadowy shape of fingers told me she'd been handled roughly.

"He hurts you," I said before I could stop myself.

On a sharp inhale, she stepped back, dripping water onto the floor.

"I'm sorry. I …. Please tell me. Did Mr. Moros do this to you?"

Her brows came together, clearly not wanting to say.

I placed a gentle hand on her arm. "Please. I need to know."

Fidgeting with the cloth, she still seemed hesitant to say, but she eventually sighed and gave a solemn nod.

"He pretends to be kind, but he's cruel, isn't he?"

Another nod.

My stomach sank into itself, and I longed to wrap my arms around her. To let her know not every soul in Foxglove loathed the Lyverians.

A busty woman in an apron with graying hair appeared and hobbled over to us. "What is going on here?"

"Mr. Moros asked that I clean her dress. I … spilled tea on her."

"Red God in Heaven, Danyra, you mustn't be so clumsy!"

"I'm perfectly fine. I've got plenty of these godawful dresses to last me the year." I chuckled, catching the clipped smile Danyra tried to hide.

"Well, then, I've got a platter of desserts and hot tea on the way, Miss. If you'd like to return to the table."

I didn't, though. I'd have much preferred to stay in the kitchen with the two of them. How could I possibly entertain the man, or pretend to enjoy myself, knowing he'd hurt the poor woman that way? Perhaps worse.

When Danyra walked off, Shireen smiled at me in a way that had my skin crawling. "Say the word, Miss and she's gone."

"I'm sorry … what?" Gone? As in let go, or executed?

"You're to be the new madame of the house. If she displeases you, I'm happy to rid the house of her." Still wearing the smile, she casually set plates of dessert onto a brass serving platter.

"I do not live here as of yet."

"We're making preparations, Miss."

Preparations? My stomach twisted at the thought of marrying him. It was one thing when I thought of him as mildly decent, but knowing the abuse he'd inflicted changed the landscape of that. I doubted I'd have been any safer as his wife. "Do you …. Are you asking if I want you to let her go?"

"We do not let Lyverians go." Her spinechilling words held me speechless for a moment.

"She doesn't displease me." Eyes squinting at the confusion, I shook my head. "I want to keep her here. In the house. Alive." I spoke with as much clarity as I could muster, given the urgency I felt in my chest. "The spill was merely a mistake and nothing more. My fault, really. I distracted her."

"As you wish, Miss." A long nod, and she waved me toward the door. "Please."

I never wanted to leave a room so much in my life. At the same time, I didn't want to return to Moros, either.

CHAPTER THIRTEEN

MAEVYTH

"He's physically abusive. I've seen evidence."

Lolla brushed my hair as I sat on the edge of the bed staring out the window toward The Crone Witch's shack in a trance of thoughts.

"What evidence?" Lolla gently combed through a rough tangle, the twinges of pain hardly noticeable with my preoccupations.

"Bruises on his servants. The fact that he *has* Lyverian servants. I can't think of anything worse for her."

"And why are you so concerned about her welfare? It seems to me Mr. Moros's manor is far more civilized than here, and this girl undoubtedly comes from some unruly village, where she was likely forced to parade naked in front of grown men." Lolla had clearly taken up the same prejudices against Lyverians as everyone else in Foxglove.

"Men who probably don't leave bruises on her. I thought you were taking my side on this matter?"

She sighed and placed the brush on the dresser. "I don't love that you've been betrothed to the man, but the way he treats this

Lyverian girl and the way I suspect he'll treat you as his wife are vastly different."

I turned just enough to see her in my periphery. "And if they're not?"

"Then, you'll deal with matters when, and if, they even arise." She gathered my hair single-handedly, running her fingers through the locks to separate it into three chunks. "You're a strong girl, Maevyth. You've always been strong. And fiercely independent of mind. Too independent of mind, if you ask me."

"Can I tell you something, Lolla? Something I trust you won't repeat to anyone?" I stared off in the mirror, watching her reflection as she braided my hair with one hand, using her severed limb to hold one strand in place while she weaved the others together.

Her brows knitted together. "Of course."

I hesitated at first. Lolla had never betrayed my trust. Not even on the times I'd complained about Agatha. She'd never mentioned the day she'd caught me standing at the edge of the woods, nor the few times I'd snuck grandfather's remaining stash of morumberry wine from the cellar. While she seemed to have a good relationship with Agatha, she'd always remained loyal to me, as well. "His head servant asked me if I wanted to ... get rid of the Lyverian girl. And she didn't mean set her free."

"And how did you respond?" she asked, a mask of indifference on her face as she worked through the strands of my hair.

"I said I wanted to keep her, of course. What kind of question is that?"

"I like to think I've offered sound advice on social graces to you and your sister throughout the years. Allow me to impart this. Be careful in how you respond, Maevyth. Consider every word. Agatha can be cruel at times, but there is stark brutality in the world, and frighteningly enough, she is not the worst." She kissed the top of my head and, after securing the end of my braid with a ribbon, left the room, closing the door behind her.

I pondered her words only a moment more, then scrambled beneath the bed for the egg and held it up to the moon's light, catching only a tiny silhouette of the small creature it housed.

The sight of it brought a smile to my face, and I glanced around the room for some nesting material, opting for a small blanket at the foot of my bed. I lay the egg on the floor between my bed and the wall, where I hoped it would remain relatively concealed through the night. "I hope you don't require me to sit on you," I said, staring down from the edge of my bed. "I surely don't have the patience for that."

The click of the door had me turning over to see Aleysia stomping into the room, her jaw stiff, hands balled to fists at her side. She slammed the door, knocking a picture from the wall, and crossed the room to her bed. "That woman is a tyrant. A tyrant!" she screeched, and I pressed a finger to my lips to quiet her. "Do you know she arranged to have one of her warty-nosed witch friends attend an outing with Uncle Riftyn tomorrow? At the same time that I'll be forced to entertain that horrible bastard of a man she's chosen for me."

"Seems she's out to ruin everyone's lives."

"She is! And the fact that she's accepted money is repulsive! She should be locked in a cell with no window!"

Chuckling, I turned back to the egg, briefly considering how wonderful it would be to live in a place so isolated from this world. "Moros has a Lyverian girl as a servant."

"Oh, god. Poor thing." She yanked off her dress, exposing her bare breasts beneath—Aleysia rarely bothered with undergarments—and reached for the nightgown laid out on her bed. "No poorer than you'll be, though, I can assure you."

"I won't marry him. I can't."

"Beginning to sound like loony Aleysia now."

A slight smile graced my lips as I toyed with the hem of my own gown. "I don't disagree with you. I only disagree with your methods, at times."

Once dressed, Aleysia stared off, biting her nails. "This girl ... what if she's kind and good? And Uncle Riftyn falls madly in love with her?"

"I very much doubt the man seeks kindness and goodness, if he's taken by you," I joked, and she sailed a glare back at me. "If he falls for her, he was never in love with you to begin."

She winced as if I'd slapped her in the face. "I can't bear that thought."

"Then, don't think about it. I would venture to say you have enough on your plate with this Vonkovyan soldier. We have to figure a way out of this mess."

Plopping on her bed, she slouched on the edge of the mattress. "Did she hate our grandfather so much? Is that why she longs to make us suffer?"

"Perhaps he hated her." I turned down the light, as Aleysia crawled into bed, my thoughts winding back to the Lyverian girl and her burns and bruises. I tried to imagine myself in that position. So powerless against the man.

So small.

Every part of me wanted to run. Run away from it all.

Aleysia had convinced me to run away with her once, after grandfather had gone missing and father had left for the war, leaving us alone with Agatha. The Vonkovyan soldiers had tracked us down, of course, and I'd been forced to watch my sister suffer twenty lashes for it.

Running wasn't an option.

Instead, I closed my eyes and searched for solace in the black void.

CHAPTER FOURTEEN

MAEVYTH

"Help me! Please help me!"

The sound of screaming yanked me from sleep, and I jolted upright, searching the dark room. Across from me, Aleysia lay on her side, facing me, her arm hanging over the the edge of the bed. Quiet snores told me she was still sleeping peacefully.

Did she have a bad dream?

Or maybe I'd been the one dreaming. In the darkness of the room, a flash of the Banished Man slipped through my thoughts, and I screwed my eyes shut, pulling the blankets up to my chin.

When I opened them, he wasn't there.

"No! No, please!"

The voice again. From the vent. Just like nights ago, when I'd caught Aleysia with Uncle Riftyn. Except, clearly it wasn't Aleysia that time.

I ignored the tremble in my bones, the dark room devouring me, as I imagined that gaunt figure stumbling toward my bed.

"Someone, please! Make him stop! Please!"

I wanted to ignore those cries, as well, but what if someone was hurt? What if that were me, crying out for help, and I went ignored?

Frowning, I pushed out of bed and peered out the window, though I was certain the sound had come from within the house. I padded toward the staircase, avoiding the boards that I knew creaked, and descended the stairs to the second floor, where the corridor stood empty.

There, I waited, listening to see if it was coming from the bedrooms.

Nothing.

Ears perked, I descended the second staircase and swept through the parlor, the kitchen, the library, finding nothing in those rooms.

Resigned to going back to bed, I headed back toward the staircase, and heard the voice again, louder that time.

"Please! Oh, god, stop!"

Twisting around brought me standing before the door to the embalming rooms below. The place where Uncle Felix spent an exorbitant amount of time. What had once been a fun hiding spot, where Aleysia and I would play as children, was now a terrifying tomb, brimming with death. Before I could talk myself out of investigating, my feet carried me to the door, and as I took hold of the knob, I paused. I'd been down there once, or twice, but only whenever Agatha requested that I fetch something for Uncle Felix. The lowest level of the cottage, with its cold, stone walls, lack of windows, and bodies stored in that matrix of suffocating vaults, stirred the darkest corners of my imagination. Dread curled in my stomach like black snakes, at the thought of going down there now, particularly when my head so vividly toyed with me as of late. But after two nights of hearing those awful cries, I had to know.

"What are you doing there?" Agatha's voice struck my nerves, and muscles taut with the fear of having been caught, I turned to her.

"I ... thought I heard something."

"The house is old. There are many noises."

"Not a house sound. A cry for help."

Eyes narrowed on me, she hobbled closer. "Only your Uncle Felix is down there now, and I very much doubt he cried out for help. Which leaves me to wonder if you're hearing voices?"

In our world, hearing voices was a sign of demonic possession. An evil that the parish banished without question.

"How unfortunate that would be for you, if I were. With you having already sold me off."

Her lips stretched into something that looked more evil than amused. "I understand Mr. Moros has close ties to a surgeon. One who specializes in matters of the brain."

The very thought of what she was suggesting stirred a panic in my gut. "It could've been the wind I'd heard."

"Yes. I suspect it may have been the wind. Now, back to bed with you. A young woman should not be up and about at the witching hour without good cause."

Without another word, I hustled past her and up the staircase, but paused halfway to the top.

"Loathsome child," Agatha muttered, and the tapping of her cane across the floor alerted me to keep on.

Hidden behind the door to the attic stairwell, I peered through a small crack, watching her climb the stairs, passing the attic for her bedroom. At the click of her bedroom door, I stepped out of the stairwell. Curiosity chipped at my good sense, but I couldn't let it go. I had to know who was crying out for help.

On the tips of my toes, I slipped back down the stairs and, once again, found myself standing at that ominous entrance to the cellar. Slowly twisting the knob, I pushed open the door, careful not to creak the hinge by cracking it too far. Sticking close to the wall, I clung to the shadows as I rounded the spiral, stone stairwell. The sound of heavy breathing reached my ears, and I slowed my descent, my heart pounding against my ribs. Down a short corridor, I reached the door to Uncle Felix's examination room, where the breathing grew louder over the sounds of whimpering.

I peered around the corner, and the sight that greeted me sent a shock through my bones. I palmed my mouth, not daring to so much as a breath.

On the examination table, nothing more than a raised stone slab, lay a pale, naked girl, with long black hair spilling over the edges. From my angle, with her head turned away, I couldn't see her face, but her supine body lay motionless, as Uncle Felix caressed her breast. A look of adoration swirled in his eyes, something I didn't think the man capable of, while he ran his thumb over her exposed nipples. He bent forward, taking one into his mouth, and my lip curved in repulsion as he seemed to suckle her, his head slowly bobbing, mouth tugging at her flesh, like a nursing child.

"Help me!" The voice practically blared in my ears.

With his fervent suckling, he jostled her body, and her head lopped to the side until facing me.

A scream begged to escape my throat, as I stared into the milky-white eyes of the Lyverian girl from Moros's manor. Scattered across her face were the yellowing bruises of a beating. A cut slashed her cheek, and through her gaping mouth, I caught a glisten that left me wondering if her tongue had been cut.

"Maevyth!" she whisper-yelled, and I jumped, my foot knocking a bucket just outside the door.

Uncle Felix's head snapped in my direction.

I drew in a gasp and spun around for the staircase. Taking two steps at a time, I raced back to the first floor, up to the second, and toward the attic stairwell. On passing the vent, the sound of her screams had me covering my ears. When I finally reached the bedroom, I could scarcely draw in a breath, as I stood hunched over, wheezing.

Still, Aleysia lay sleeping. Oblivious.

Bones rattling with fear, I crossed the room for my bed and hid under the covers.

"Maevyth!" a raspy voice whispered, and I squeezed my eyes shut, refusing to uncover my face. "Maevyth!"

In the darkness, I whispered The Prayer of Caedes. I didn't know why. I didn't believe The Red God would've helped me then. I didn't believe in Him, at all.

"The dead don't pray!" The voice screamed its words louder that time, and a whimper escaped me, as I lay trembling.

"I'm sorry," I whispered back. "I'm so sorry."

The screams silenced.

Whispered breaths of my quiet sobbing bounced off the blanket. "I'm so sorry."

CHAPTER FIFTEEN

MAEVYTH

"All these leeks." Aleysia groaned from beside me. "Better than two winters ago. Remember all we ate was gruel? Gruel for breakfast, gruel for supper. If I never eat a bowl of that slop again, it'll be too soon. I feel nauseous just thinking about it," she said, and not even her imitation gagging managed to sever the menagerie of thoughts pouring through my mind right then.

I stared off to the sound of my own quiet chopping, until a sharp sting struck the tip of my finger. "Ouch!" The wooden board where I'd been slicing potatoes for stew was speckled with bits of blood that dotted the white flesh of the vegetables.

"Good grief, Maeve, pay attention." Aleysia had already gathered a cloth, and she dabbed away the blood before wrapping it up. While I stood entranced by the miniscule bit of blood soaking the cotton, she rinsed the bloody potatoes and threw them into the pot with the others.

"They killed her," I said quietly, not wanting to draw Lolla's attention, where she kneaded dough for bread across the kitchen, putting her whole body into the toil as she folded it one-handedly.

Two days had passed since I'd stumbled upon the Lyverian girl in the morgue, and yet, I couldn't get her out of my head. I'd thought about her all morning during bible study, during the afternoon while doing chores. Her face. That plea for help. "They killed her, anyway."

"Who?" Aleysia asked, taking over my half of the potatoes, while I stanched the blood.

"The servant girl. A Lyverian. Moros had killed her, I'm sure of it."

"He's evil, I'm telling you," she whispered. "Life isn't going to be grand, if you marry him."

I didn't want to imagine life with him. "They beat her to death. What could she have possibly done wrong to deserve that?"

"She lacked a cock. That's enough for them. But, regardless, this isn't your fault. Clearly, the man had ill intentions for the girl."

I knew that, but still, the guilt persisted.

"Lolla!" Agatha called from the other room, and the older woman dusted her hand across her apron and exited through the swinging door.

The moment she was gone, Aleysia gave a sly glance over her shoulder and stepped closer.

"I have to tell you something," she spoke even lower than before.

"What is it?"

Curling her lip between her teeth, she nibbled as she always did when she was nervous about something. "Promise you won't tell."

"I promise."

"I've not had menses in two months."

Frowning, I stared back at her. "Two months?"

She gave a solemn nod, chopping away at my share of the potatoes. "When it didn't come last month, I had to cut my finger and bleed into the menstrual cloth, just so Agatha wouldn't get suspicious. It still hasn't come."

"Is it …" I didn't want to say what I already suspected, and thankfully, she didn't bother to play ignorant that time.

She nodded, and tears formed in her eyes. "I don't know what to do."

"Have you told him?"

"Yes."

I inwardly groaned. "Why would you do that?"

"Because it's his baby, and I don't want to be tasked to figure this out alone."

"If they find out, Aleysia …"

"I know. It's a sin."

Worse than murder in the eyes of some.

"What are you thinking?"

She didn't answer, instead wiping tears from her eyes.

"You can't have this child here. Even if they don't send you to the woods, it will be shunned. Rejected. Agatha certainly won't care for it."

"She won't. But you would, wouldn't you, Maeve?"

I considered her question for a moment–caring for a child that the whole parish despised as much as they did me. "Of course I would. But a baby would fare better with its mother."

"It would. But I have no intentions of having this baby. The Crone Witch has been said to terminate unwanted pregnancy. She has herbs. Potent herbs." Had it only been a few days ago that she'd chided me for *talking* to the woman?

"And you intend to go to her?"

"Yes. I think so. I think it's for the best."

An ache throbbed in my chest. How terrifying it all must've been for her, having no one but Uncle Riftyn to help her navigate, and an entire parish against her–a whole flock of religious fanatics who would surely denounce her. And Agatha, of course, who'd make her life hell for the humiliation. "Whatever you decide, Aleysia, know that I'm with you. I will not leave you to figure this out alone."

She gave a tearful smile and nodded. "I love you, Sister. I love you more than any person in this world."

"And I love you."

With a loud groan, Lolla pushed through the kitchen door. "Girls, are you finished with those potatoes yet? Agatha is growing impatient for supper."

"Yes, Lolla," I answered for Aleysia, as I unspun the cloth from my wound. I stared down at the perfectly intact skin, where the slice of the blade had left a groove only moments ago. Frowning, I dabbed it with fresh water and returned to my chores.

CHAPTER SIXTEEN

ZEVANDER

Night had fallen, as Zevander rode up to the edge of Hagsmist forest, from where three of the king's calvary guarding it already galloped across the open field toward him. Thanks to his half-mask and hooded cowl making him look like a thief, they'd undoubtedly draw their weapons without bothering to ask his intentions.

They probably thought him mad, or drunk. After all, no one attempted to get so near to the forest, unless they'd completely lost their senses, which was why the guard was light.

While no one had ever endeavored to enter the disease-ridden mortal lands, if anyone were to be so ambitious, they'd be punished by execution per the king's decree.

On the mere threat of attack, the flames inked into Zevander's flesh stirred. Had he been any other Aethyrian, the calvary could apprehended him with ease, as their powers exceeded most and could've easily incapacitated any other trespasser.

Unfortunately for them, Zevander wasn't any other trespasser.

The men slowed as they approached, and before they could lift their hands to seize him with magic, his flames lashed out, winding around each of them. The searing sound of their burning flesh punctuated the awful stench of sizzling organs.

He fucking hated that smell.

Two of the men collapsed from their bucking horses that took off in the opposite direction. The guards convulsed on the ground, writhing and grunting, because the flame denied them a voice to scream. The third man tumbled from his horse, falling to the ground on a hard *thunk*, his body paralyzed with the pain that Zevander imagined felt like hot steel against the skin. While his comrades blackened, their bodies cooked alive from the inside out, his body merely blazed a swollen red.

Once the two had finally succumbed to the flame, Zevander picked through the soot for the bloodstones left behind. Death by magic often left a residue, an aura, easily identifiable by the most skilled forensic mage, and burning to ashes ensured no evidence. But the presence of bloodstones would hint at demutomancy, which would surely launch an extensive investigation. A potential headache if the king tasked him to assist in hunting down a culprit.

He strode back to where the third man lay squirming on the ground, attempting to cry out through clenched teeth, the flame only allowing for a quiet groan. "I've spared you in exchange for your silence. Do you understand?"

With what strength the guard could muster, he nodded. The flames receded, exiting through his skin, offering the man some relief. They took the form of black scorpions that circled him, hissing and clicking their pincers.

"Be very still," Zevander warned as he checked for the dagger at his hip. "They're not fond of fast movement." He stalked toward the adjacent woods, leaving the scorpions to watch the guard.

A shield of white mist rolled over the floor of the forest, Zevander's boots invisible in the thick vapor. At the back of his neck, he felt what was left of the moon sigil of his bloodline flare, when the cool silvery rays struck the marking, sending a tingle down his spine. The Solassions had attempted to cut it off during the years he'd been enslaved, in order to stunt his power, not knowing at the time that it'd already been stunted by his cursed blood. Burned away for the power of sablefyre that he hadn't even begun to scratch the surface of understanding.

They'd failed to remove it entirely, though. Even scarred and mutilated, it still absorbed the light.

Through the haze of fog, a high-pitched giggle zipped past his ear, and he turned in time to see the flutter of wings. His eyes adjusted in the darkness, and he could make out a small Spirityne—annoying little creatures often found in the woods. Small as a sparrow, they appeared harmless, but their vicious nature made them aggressive and dangerous, and their teeth carried an agonizing poison that was said to cause hallucinations. It was rare to see them when winter approached. Curiosity must've drawn it out of its hiding spot in the trees. Fortunately, it flew off, or he'd have skewered and charred it as a burnt snack for the catallys—nocturnal creatures that looked like a cross between a cat and a hawk and preyed on the Spiritynes.

An archway stood in the distance, its pale blue, glassy ward shimmering like liquid in its center. Only the blood of the seven, those he'd already killed for their bloodstones, could've passed through freely without a spell, as it was their ancestral blood magic that had crafted the Umbravale. Anyone else would've risked falling over the cliff that separated Hagsmist from the mortal lands. An abyssal trench between the two worlds, bridged only by the Umbravale. Some believed Nethyria resided at the bottom of the miles-deep crevice.

No one had ever been mad enough to confirm by venturing down there, though.

Zevander reached into the pocket of his leathers for the small scroll that Dolion had given him. He raised his palm to the ward and spoke the words inked on the small parchment.

"Zi da'dignio, septmiusz me liberih iteriusz." If I am worthy, the seven will grant me free passage.

The ward hummed and flickered, and he exhaled a breath, then pushed his hand past the watery barrier. A mild vibration shook his muscles as he stepped through the arch, and to his relief, instead of falling to his death, found himself in a small clearing encircled by thorny bushes. Keen eyes scanning over his surroundings, he strode toward the bushes, unbothered by the thorn-covered branches that scratched at his impenetrable leathers and crushed beneath his boots.

On the other side stood a forest that mirrored the one from which he'd come.

A howling sound echoed around him, and he clicked his tongue to zero in on the source of it. The image of a wolf took form in his mind, though the mortal variety seemed to be far smaller than what Zevander had come to know in his world. He kept on, senses alert.

The hum of wings buzzed past his ear, and he searched the darkness for the source.

It zipped past him again, and Zevander's black flame coiled and struck like a snake, holding the nefarious little beast captive, while it squealed and chirped and trilled, its teeth snapping at the vaporous flame. Spirityne. Strange to see one on that side of the Umbravale. He tipped his head, studying its trembling stick-like body that appeared like an actual twig, with a humanoid face and tattered black wings, making it almost entirely camouflaged in the surrounding wood. Had Zevander wanted, he could've breached the protective halo of magic that kept the creature from burning alive right then. Instead, he looked away, releasing the creature, and it flew off chirping, likely warning other Spiritynes.

Zevander strode on, and at the crunch of something beneath his boot, he paused and reached down into the mist. He lifted a broken and decayed human skull, his senses labelling it as at least a century old. Tossing it aside, he kept on, more crunching beneath his boots in what must've been a feeding ground.

He walked what he estimated to be two furlongs before noticing a structure ahead–another archway that shimmered like the first he'd passed through. This one made of bones and twisted wood. As Zevander made his way in that direction, a cold tingle brushed across the back of his neck, his instincts telling him there was something hidden amongst the trees. Watching him. A scan of the forest showed only the dark trees looming above the mist, and the dappled moonlight illuminating the bats flitting through their canopies.

He strode on, until he arrived at the ancient structure—the entrance from the forest to the mortal world.

Gaze trailing over the archway of bone and wood, he spied a spattering of black, as if it'd been burned into the structure, and ran his finger across it. The spatters sizzled and smoked and slid into his palm like black snakes. They gathered into small puddle, and the black faded for red. He closed his palm over it and opened it to a solid red stone. Skinny silver lines appeared as small cracks in the hard surface, a characteristic he hadn't seen before. His mind wound back to the conversation with Dolion at the tavern. *"A stone with silver markings."*

The clues leading to his quarry always revealed themselves, somehow, and Zevander trusted blood above everything else.

He lifted the tiny sphere up into the moon's light, examining the strange coloring and patterns, and felt a hum of energy vibrating across his palm as he held it. Sensing power in the blood was nothing new for the Letalisz, but the oddly pleasurable intensity that rippled beneath his skin, trembling across his bones like prey in a spider's web, struck him as foreign. Entirely unexpected.

Tongue wet with the urge to lick the salty stone, he screwed his eyes shut to the voice in his head that chimed *Taste.* Consuming blood was like playing with the devil's flame. A reckless indulgence that led to madness, as blood could be a very powerful aphrodisiac. He quickly tucked the stone away in his leathers.

A shimmer across his eye drew his hand to the ward. As he ran his finger across, tiny electrical impulses tickled his skin. He closed his eyes and imagined his hand passing through. When he opened them, the barrier enveloped at his wrist.

He stepped through.

Once on the other side, Zevander surveyed the open field of frost that glistened like diamonds, the scattered trees, and nocturnal animals scampering in the dark with eyes glowing. Clouds of white smoke drifting up from chimneys.

Life. So much unexpected life.

From a young age, he'd been taught the mortal world was a dead and barren wasteland. A place no Aethyrian would ever dare to venture. Above him, stars twinkled around a single crescent moon. The air, though crisp and cold, felt dry as it breezed over the exposed half of his face. Desiccated, like an aging world, but certainly not a dead one.

In the distance stood a dark cottage, and he spied a window near its roof.

An archway of bones seen through a window.

A glance back at the archway showed it to be in the path of the window's view.

He stuck out a hand, calling upon his powers, and across the frosty ground, a trail of fallen blood glowed red—the drops leading toward that same cottage across the dirt road. He strode toward it, following the blood path to the entrance, and through the door that creaked on worn hinges. The lower level stood empty and quiet. Up the staircase, he trod lightly, his boots making nary a sound over the aging wood. The blood trail stopped at what appeared to be a bathing suite—one far less elaborate than his own, back at the keep. It held a simple tub, and chamber pot with a pull string, the kind one would find in The

Hovel. He kept on down the corridor of closed doors, and halfway toward the end of it, he felt a vibration in his pocket as the stone radiated warmth across his thigh.

The strange sensation seemed to heighten, the deeper he ventured, until he stopped before a door at the end of the hallway. Opening it gave a light squeal of the hinges and revealed another staircase. When he reached the top, he found two beds across the room from one another. Mingled with a strong floral scent was something that hit the back of his throat, stiffening his jaw. Like sweet oranges.

A dizzying weakness swept over him, and he stumbled back a step, his senses overwhelmed.

Fucking hells .... What in the gods was wrong with him?

From the ceiling, dangled small white sachets decorated in flowers. Perhaps the source of the scent. He drew one to his face, nose crinkling at the strong, spicy herbs that didn't carry so much as a whiff of that orange scent.

As he set his sights on the bed directly across from him, the stone in his pocket flared with warmth. He shook his head of the strange vertigo and crossed the room, coming to a stop alongside his victim's bed. Nestled in the blankets, the creature slept soundly, its body rising and falling with easy breaths. Beneath the delicious orange scent that watered his mouth, something earthy loomed. A wicked odor, like brimstone, and he rounded the bed for the other side, nearest the window. On the floor, tucked halfway beneath the bed's frame, he found a black object and lifted it up to the light.

An egg, it seemed, but not one he recognized. The scales on the surface suggested some kind of raptor. He'd seen similar eggs in Draconysia in the north, when he'd crossed over from Solassios. When told they were drake eggs, Zevander had made the mistake of stealing three of them, not realizing he was committing himself to raising the damned things.

Resting another hand over the top of the egg sent the black

flame over the surface, which glowed a bright purple, and the silhouette of the tiny creature cocooned inside, squirming and writhing, confirmed that it was alive. He glanced down at the bundle of blankets below him, and back to the egg.

Zevander carefully placed the egg on the floor. He'd be sure to take it with him, as it'd certainly be worth quite a bit in the black markets of Costelwick.

He held out his hands toward the bundled mass beneath a flowered quilt, the stone in his pocket so hot against his thigh, he let out a grunt, adjusting its position in his leathers. Curls of black flame lifted from his skin and scaled down his arm, where it gathered in his palm. He directed the flame onto his victim, letting it wind around the blankets, and at the first movement, Zevander knew the flame was heating the pathetic creature's blood. Cooking it.

A soft but agonizing moan bled through the coverings, and Zevander frowned at the way the sound strummed his muscles. The bundle shifted, movement pulling the blankets away to reveal a face that snapped his spine straight.

Long, black hair lay strewn about her pillow and plastered to her sweaty brow. Porcelain skin that carried the soft pink of a fever. Full, bow-shaped lips, slightly parted.

Fucking beautiful.

As he pulled back the flames, he tipped his head, staring down at her. What a pity.

Like an enchanting goddess, she slept soundly, a fringe of long, black lashes fluttering against the top of her cheeks, while her body succumbed to his power. An ache stabbed his chest, as he marveled at those thick, pouty lips and gleaming skin that compelled him to touch her. That scent that clawed at his senses, urging him to put his mouth to her skin for a taste.

He'd never been so taken by one of his prey.

A sharp throb struck his groin, and he grunted, his cock pressed hard against his leathers as if it longed to climb out of his damn trousers. Frowning, he adjusted himself. Something about the girl stoked the fire in his veins, and were he not there to sear her blood to stone, he might've taken an interest in what she hid beneath that loose gown.

Instead, he raised his hand again, sending another blast of heat across her body, and just as before, she shifted again, raising her arm above her head to reveal a strange marking on her flesh. A feather-like scar with metallic silver accents.

As she squirmed with discomfort, her fever undoubtedly heightening, he felt a tickle at his brow. A bead of sweat dripping down his skin that, when he wiped it away, felt hot to the touch. So unusually hot, he broke concentration, and the flame in his palm fizzled.

He wiped his face across the sleeve of his tunic and held out a palm again. Focusing. Imagining the flame rushing through her veins like molten lava.

A flare of pain rippled through him, like tiny blades in his blood, and Zevander stumbled back a step.

Godspit!

Teeth grinding with frustration, he tried again, but again, he was struck with an agonizing burn beneath his skin that had him backing off.

The process normally took seconds. A quick and quiet kill, and he was ordinarily done before anyone even noticed him there. He lifted his palm yet again, eyes blazing with rage as he stared down at her sickeningly beautiful face.

An image of her head tipped back in ecstasy struck his skull, and he shook his head of the visual.

Fuck. Fuck!

His fist vibrated with the urge to punch a wall. To break him of whatever had hooked itself in his mind.

She let out another soft moan, and gods be damned, Zevander's ordinarily steady muscles shook. The sound rattled his concentration, and the flames retreated back across his skin.

Jaw clenched hard enough to crack his teeth, he tried for the half-dozenth time. Muscles steeled, he concentrated on the flames working their way through her veins. Boiling and hardening to stone.

Nothing came forth. As if his power refused to follow his command.

It'd never failed him before. Had never hesitated to take life, however brutally Zevander had willed it.

Staring down at her, his mind silently weaved the spell that he'd never had to speak aloud, and a streak of agonizing heat wound up through his forearm. He looked down to see one of his scorpions stinging *him*. Retaliating on him. The cursed flame attacking *him*, instead!

Enraged, he roughly brushed his knuckles against the scorpion, sending it off into a cloud of black smoke, and ground his teeth at the outrage. He would kill the ridiculous mortal if it took all the power he could summon, and gods help her then.

In his fury, he caught sight of her breast through the silky fabric of her sleeping gown. His hand itched with the momentary distraction of wondering if it'd fit in his palm as perfectly as he imagined right then. He ground his teeth harder, until a flash of pain struck his skull.

She held such a purity and innocence about her, a vibrancy that taunted the darkest corners of his soul. And seven hells, he wanted to tear his own eyeballs out for noticing.

Hand still hovering over top of her, he dared himself to touch her.

One touch.

He curled his hand into a fist.

No. If he had to fuck every sexsell from then until his death, so be it. *So be it!*

She stretched and shifted again, her body calling to him, and a stab of pain struck his groin.

On a grunt, he bent forward, his cock throbbing with an ache that would never be sated so long as she breathed. Zevander reached for the blade at his hip. Perhaps killing her first might allow him to concentrate on her blood. With trembling hands, he held the blade at her throat. One slice. That was all it'd take.

Hundreds, he'd killed before they could so much as draw in a breath, and yet, he loomed over her like a fledgling. Like a fucking newborn assassin terrified to follow through.

She opened her eyes to reveal beautiful, pale gray irises, the color of morning skies in Wyntertide, the left marred with a streak of silver that reminded him of the moon he'd seen earlier. Deep, intelligent eyes that gave an air of youth and mischief, their cat-like shape seductively sleepy.

As they sharpened into focus, he broke from his trance.

CHAPTER SEVENTEEN

MAEVYTH

The fog of sleep lifted, and I stared up at a cloaked, dark figure looming over me, the lower half of his face hidden beneath a black mask with silver embellishments that glinted in the moon's light. The upper half was barely discernible within the depths of his hood.

A stranger.

A stranger in my room.

A stranger in my room, staring down at me.

Reality struck like a zap of lightning across my skull, and I gasped, a scream cocked at the back of my throat ready to tear free.

A cold, sharp edge prodded my throat, the acute bite of a blade warning that, with one quick move, it would slice through my flesh like soft silk. Angry eyes lifted to mine. Even veiled by shadows, their irises blazed a golden yellow and orange, making the black pupils appear as eclipses that I feared looking at for too long. I'd never seen eyes so intense.

My body refused to move under a creeping paralysis that seemed to pin my limbs to the bed with invisible needles.

In a single breath, a swirling cloud of black surrounded the stranger.

I no more than blinked, and he disappeared.

As if he'd simply vanished.

The paralysis lifted, and shaken with nausea, I jolted upright, the scream I'd held withering to a terrified whimper. Tucking my knees close, I looked around the room.

Across from me, Aleysia quietly snored, entirely oblivious. The masked stranger was nowhere. A dream?

Another hallucination?

Clammy with sickness, I breathed hard through my nose, letting the rush of adrenaline settle inside me.

Hand trembling, I palpated my throat, and at the touch of damp skin, lifted it to find blood smeared over my fingertips. I practically leapt toward the window, peering down at the empty field and dirt road below. No sign of him there, either. As if I'd dreamed the whole thing.

The phantom sensation of that blade lingered across my neck, though.

A tapping sound steeled my muscles, and I spun around to the empty room, eyes searching for the source of the noise. I lowered my gaze to the floor, where the egg tottered from side to side. Moving on its own. As a twinge of excitement mingled with the fear still hammering through me, I crouched alongside the object, tracking the abrupt twitches.

A quiet crack announced a small fissure within the silvery lines of its surface, where a soft glow bled through. I watched in awe as the fissure widened, the crevice deepening, glowing brighter as it separated. Heart stammering in my chest, I reached out for the egg, running my fingertip through the soft radiance that heated my skin.

Another cracking sound. Another fissure.

A third crack sent another ray of light beaming toward the underside of my bed.

A tiny, silver claw slipped through the broader crevice, and I held my breath. Another followed. A chunk of the egg caved inward, creating a hole that grew bigger, as more chunks were broken away by those miniscule claws. A pointed maw, like a beak but lined with teeth, poked through, shifting and prodding, as though stuck. More of the egg cracked away, and a bony horn along the upper mandible lifted out of the destruction, giving way to a shiny, scaled, black creature with silvery eyes that matched its claws. Black wings lay tight against its body as it crawled out of the egg and stared up at me, drawing my attention to the small, silver crescents on either side of its face that glowed bright like the moon. Four taloned feet, each with three forward facing claws, and one hind claw left me questioning what kind of bird it could've been. Certainly nothing I'd ever seen before. The hind legs appeared thicker, stronger than those in the front, though all of them were equally vicious looking.

The little beast reminded me of a miniature dragon, like those that Grandfather Bronwick would tell me about from books he'd read to me as a child. It fluttered, spreading its wings outward to a span that defied its small size. Perhaps a foot in length on either side, before it tucked them back.

Beneath the small pulse of excitement racing through my blood, hummed fear. I'd never seen anything like it before. Had no idea if it was docile, or vicious.

Wide eyes gave it a cartoonish appearance, baby-like, and I reached out an open palm toward it, curious if it would jump there. It seemed to sniff my palm for a moment, running its beak over my skin. The dragon-bird stepped onto my palm, and I lifted it from the floor, into the light where I could study it closer.

"What are you?" I whispered in awe, noting the strange swirls embedded in its scaly flesh and over the long tail that, despite the creature appearing bird-like, seemed more akin to a lizard's with its small spikes along the surface. The curvature of them, like tiny hooked blades, left me imagining them getting lodged into flesh.

It made a tiny chuffing sound in its throat that had me smiling. "You are the most curious little thing I've ever seen."

It poked its beak at its claws, seeming to groom itself, and chuffed again.

A sharp sting bit into my palm, and I jerked my arm, knocking the creature from my hand. "Ouch!" I lifted my hand to find a tear across my palm, from where drops of blood leaked onto the floor.

It ran its claws over the pooled drops then brought them to its beak, but at a growling noise that I took as disappointment, it turned away from the blood.

Realization swept over me. "You're hungry."

Good grief, I hadn't a clue what it ate. Birds ate bread and berries. I knew that much, having fed them on occasion, and though it clearly wasn't like any bird I'd ever encountered, it did have bird features. With a glance toward Aleysia, who remained snoring away, I let out a huff. "I'm going to fetch you some food, okay? Stay here. Do not move."

It tipped its head as if trying to understand me.

I tapped a gentle finger against the floor. "Stay."

It mimicked the movement with its claws on a quiet tap, the sight of which made me chuckle. Smart little creature.

I hustled across the room, down the staircase, and out of the door, peering down the corridor for any sign of movement. At that hour, I suspected everyone would be asleep. Tiptoeing down the second flight of stairs, I examined the cut on my hand, noting it had completely sealed shut already, the skin left without so much as a scratch. The sight of it had me skidding to a halt, frowning.

How? I'd thought for certain I'd have to wrap it again.

How were these small cuts healing so quickly? It made no sense.

A cold tingle palmed the back of my neck, and I shook it off, not wanting to think too much on it because dwelling would've surely stirred my anxiety, and I didn't have the headspace to deal with that right then. Instead, I kept on toward the kitchen.

From the pantry, I grabbed a slice of bread from the bread box, and few of the berries from a basket beside it, popping a couple into my mouth. A rustling crinkle from behind jarred my muscles, and I turned to find a rat nibbling on a bag of seeds sat on the floor. I slapped a hand over my mouth, shielding the scream that begged to escape. A wild tremble moved through my bones, and I quietly scooted toward the door.

The rat paused its chewing and stared up at me, as if it just then noticed me, except the shells and crumbs lying about told me it'd been there a while.

A flash of black streaked across the floor.

The rat squealed, and I watched in horror as the creature from my bedroom wrangled it beneath its body and raked its sharp, front claws over the rat's fur, peeling away the animal's skin.

Mouth hanging open in shock, I stared at the glistening skinless rodent that, still alive, continued to twitch and snap its teeth. The creature pecked its beady eyes out next, tipping its head back to swallow them. Weakly, the rodent kicked at its captor, still fighting for its slowly fading life. It wasn't until the black, scaled beast began ripping bits of flesh away, that the animal finally stilled, its skin lying in a small heap beside them.

I glanced down at the berries and bread in my hands, acknowledging what a sorry substitute they would've made, and placed them back in their respective containers. Within seconds, the creature had cleaned every bit of flesh from the bones, which it discarded beside the rat's fur. Blood glistened over its mandibles as it teetered to the side, clearly flesh drunk, its belly rounded and full of rat meat. It stumbled toward me, and as it neared, with some hesitation, I knelt down to let it climb into my palm as before, where it curled into a ball.

Inhaling deep breaths to calm my racing heart, I forced myself not to look at the rat remains, and instead focused on the tiny little beast captured in my hand, who lay nuzzling my fingers.

"You may have repulsive eating habits, but I'll admit, you're terrifyingly cute," I spoke on the cusp of a whisper. "Adorrifying. And chaotic. I think I'll name you Raivox."

Raivox had been a fierce Vonkovyan, who'd plundered and raided in the age of old. History books had always described him as a contradiction of charmingly violent. It seemed fitting for the little monster.

Eyes on the discarded remnants of rat that I'd have to clean before anyone else happened upon it, I carried Raivox out of the pantry and back up to my room. Gathering the quilt from my mattress, I made a meager little nest under my bed, and placed the already-sleeping creature within. Once again, I hustled down the staircase, to the pantry where the fur and bones still lay in a heap. With a rag I swiped from the shelf beside me, I gathered the bits of rodent and tossed it into the trash, then wiped up the drops of blood. I shoved the rag deep into the trash so as not to draw attention, and washed my hands with far more soap than I'd ever used in my life. It was as I headed back up the stairs that I heard a voice from the vent crying out for help.

Not again.

Slapping my palms to my ears, I hustled up the staircase.

After a quick check of Raivox, sound asleep beneath my bed, I wrapped myself in the blankets, covering my ears so as not to hear the voice again.

My thoughts wound to earlier, when I'd woken to the man in the mask holding the knife to my throat. I suspected, by the way he'd vanished so quickly, that it was nothing more than an illusion, much like The Banished Man I'd seen before him, and Danyra, the Lyverian girl. And if that was the case, it could've only meant that I'd begun to lose my senses.

A gnawing thought chewed at my head as I lay there, willing myself to sleep–that perhaps something evil had infected me.

CHAPTER EIGHTEEN

ZEVANDER

Growling, Zevander neared the archway, his body wound tight with rage and an infuriating need to fuck something. Once beyond the barrier, he paced.

He had to go back. He had to finish the job.

You already tried, idiot. You failed!

He'd never failed to kill a target in his life. Not even the very first assassination he'd carried out for the king. Taking life had always come easy for him. The flame had never betrayed him that way.

Go back, his mind urged. *Finish.*

Going back would only make him look like an incompetent fool. Still pacing, he stared down at his hands, trying to wrap his head around what the fuck had happened back there. His own power had turned on him.

Snarling with rage, he kept on through the forest, and halfway to the Umbravale, the sense of something watching him tickled the back of Zevander's neck. He clicked his tongue, surveying the surroundings, listening. *Evanidusz*, the power he'd summoned to vanish into black smoke, had zapped him of energy, skewing his senses.

Yet, over the rustling of trees, he caught the quiet crunch of dried leaves.

He slipped behind a crooked oak beside him and, in the distance, watched a shadowy figure step into the moon's light. At first, it was difficult to discern if he was human, or animal, the way his torso was bent and long, branching horns stuck up from his head, but the more he stared, the more he realized it was no animal. It hobbled closer, and Zevander's tattoos lifted from his body, just as they had back in the girl's room, forming a black smoke that engulfed him, cloaking him in the darkness. Still, he could see the figure who dared to edge closer. Closer.

The burn across his skin warned that whatever approached was about to be reduced to ash, and Zevander breathed deeply, calming the power in him that itched to break free.

A crackling sound from behind seemed to capture the beast's attention, and it turned, lowered to all fours, and took off in the opposite direction.

Once it had dashed out of sight, Zevander stepped out of the black smoke and kept on through the woods, until he arrived at the Umbravale, where he'd first entered the mortal forest. He passed through, still cursing himself as he trekked the long stretch of Hagsmist forest. When he finally exited, he found the guard where he'd left him, guarded by the scorpions whose stingers remained pointed and ready to strike. On his approach, Zevander reached out his hand, drawing them back onto his flesh, except for one, and the guard collapsed to the ground, wheezing, as if he'd not taken a single breath the whole time.

Anger still rippled through him as, hands at his back, the Letalisz circled the man whose body trembled. With one hard flick of Zevander's hand, the scorpion shot out toward the man, too fast for its victim to react. The sound of its legs ticked against the guard's armor, as it climbed his body to his neck and slipped down into his arm. Before the guard could tear away the gauntlet and sleeve of his tunic, the scorpion had burrowed beneath the skin on his forearm, leaving what looked like a black searing burn on his flesh.

He twisted his arm to show the scorpion wriggling about, settling into its new home. "Ahhh, ahhhhhhh ..." His voice held an edge of terror and panic. "Ahhh, it's in my skin! It's in my fucking skin!"

"Yes. It is. Should you so much as utter the word *Letalisz*, or any mention of having seen me, it will be the last time you breathe. And I can't guarantee that it won't be the most excruciating death you could possibly suffer."

"I swear ... I won't say a thing. Just get it out of me! Please!" Arm outstretched and shaking, he collapsed in a pathetic sob that failed to move Zevander.

Particularly when his mind was still wound around that girl.

All he could summon was apathy and a sigh. "'Fraid I can't do that. He looks quite content. But I might think about it, if you remain loyal. Should anyone breach these woods from the other side, you'll tell me, yeah?"

"Yeah. I'll fucking tell you everything."

"Good. Good. You two will get along just fine, then." On those parting words, Zevander whistled, and his horse galloped toward him out of a cloud of black smoke.

CHAPTER NINETEEN

MAEVYTH

Wind bit my cheeks as I trudged along a dirt road with a basket full of figs that Lolla had requested I pick up from the village market. Prior to heading out, I'd tucked Raivox away into a moderately-sized crate of blankets, and stored him in the shed behind the Mortuary until my return. My hope was that he'd stay out of trouble, seeing as I'd be gone half the morning.

While in town, I'd visited Mrs. Chalmsley, offering the older woman, whose husband had been banished years ago, the usual bread and broth with a few berries, but saw no sign of the newly-homeless mother and her child from The Banishing.

The ominous border of The Eating Woods stood just off the road, stirring memories of The Banished Man's haunting face. The visual, so vivid in my head, raised the hairs on my flesh, and when I clamped my eyes to switch my focus to something else, I opened them to find the ghostly image of the Lyverian girl watching me from the trees. "Stop it, stop it!" I smacked at my head, desperate for distraction.

On passing the misty meadow, where the old hovel stood alongside the woods, I noticed The Crone Witch watching me, as she tossed what I presumed to be alfalfa and grain to a black goat penned in a wooden enclosure. Humiliation warmed my cheeks, imagining what I must've looked like just then, swatting at myself as if I'd lost my senses.

She waved me over, and without much command from my head, my feet carried me across the open field, toward her. "You got sick," she said, swapping one tin bucket for the next to feed her animals.

"For a bit. Fever. It passed after a few days."

"It didn't *pass*." Chickens clustered inside the coop where she tossed cracked corn. "It became a part of you."

"Part of me? What does that mean?"

Resting her hand atop the fence, she paused, watching them peck at the ground. "Your blood is their blood now."

"Whose blood?" Nothing she said was making sense.

"The dead, Girl." Huffing, she swapped the cracked corn for a bucket of water and filled a trough. "Blood given for blood taken. Can't be undone now." Blood taken. It was then I knew she'd seen me kill and bury the raven. "Your ties with the dead were eternal the moment you pricked yourself on the bone and sealed it with the blood." Nabbing her cane propped against the fence, she hobbled toward a small stable, and pondering her words, I followed after her.

"What do the dead have to do with the raven?"

"They guide the soul to the after, and you share its blood now," she explained, shoving barley straw into a netted bag. "You walk between realms of the dead and living. The world you've known, and the one that has remained hidden from you."

Walking between the living and dead? What a terrible existence that would be. Not to mention, such a thing would only further cement my place as the pariah of the parish.

She was wrong. I shook my head, refusing to believe such a thing. The hallucinations I'd suffered up until that point had merely been brought on by my illness. Perhaps a lingering effect of the infection. "What you speak of is blasphemy. The governor says only the cursed speak to the dead."

"Is it a curse, or a gift? Some believe communing with the dead is as much a blessing as a burden."

"How could speaking with the dead possibly be a blessing?"

"It is in what they tell you. What they know of the other side."

I chewed on those thoughts for a moment, trying to wrap my head around what The Banished Man, or Danyra, could've possibly tried to communicate to me. Were there secrets smuggled beyond the barrier of life? What would I have been tasked to do with such knowledge?

"And if I were … cursed. How do I rid myself of this affliction?"

"There is no ridding it. The gods chose, and you are their vessel." She swiped up a waterskin hanging just outside one of the stalls. After swallowing a large gulp, she wiped her mouth on the back of a wrinkled hand and held it up in offering.

With a raise of my palm, I politely declined. "I didn't ask for this. The bird was suffering. I only wanted to end its misery."

"Then, it seems you chose, as well." Brow quirked, she hobbled past me, and just as before, I fell into step after her. Around the other side of the shack, she led me to a garden of frost-weathered plants, their brown stems standing proud, from which she plucked the tips with her fingers. Some she pocketed, others she gathered in her palm. I recognized those as sickhash root, sometimes given to children before bed to make them sleep.

"This village … they already shun me." I lifted the skirt of my dress, where the dried remnants of saliva marked where a passerby in a carriage had spat on me coming home from town. "Visions of the dead will only further their suspicions of me."

"Yes. The poor little babe, left behind by her mother with a black rose laid upon her chest. The bassinet at the edge of The Eating Woods. You hardly cried that night." She hobbled back toward me and shoved the palmed pickings into my chest.

I mindlessly accepted her gift, but my focus snapped onto her words. "You saw me there? Did you see my mother?"

"No," she said, finally plopping down in a rocker on her porch. From beside her, she reached into a quilted bag and retrieved what looked to be a long pipe. She crushed the dried flowers from her pocket, and deposited the broken bits into the pipe's chamber, staring off for a moment. "But I felt the pain. Hands trembling against your cold, cherubic cheeks. I tasted those salty tears left behind."

"You were the one who found me."

Snapping a flint striker, she lit the contents of the pipe, her cheeks caving as she drew in the smoke and let it seep from the corners of her mouth. "I could've left you for the beast in the woods. Perhaps I should've."

"You know what lives in the woods? What eats the souls of sinners?"

She gave a mirthless chuckle and took another puff of her pipe. "I've seen more than that, Girl."

The scent of the weeds reminded me of chicklebane, a spicy flower Grandfather Bronwick added to his wine that was known to relax the muscles.

"What have you seen?" I asked, intrigued by her every word.

"Why should I say? Are you foolish enough to venture into those woods yourself?"

"Not with the monster."

"Ah, yes. The angel of judgment who punishes sins. Or is it the wrathavor? The soulless creature that feeds on the flesh of man."

"What do you believe?"

"Man feeds its cravings, but it longs for something else. Something that lies beyond the crooked trees and ravaged bones."

Beyond the crooked trees? "What is it? What lies there?"

"*What is it?*" she echoed. "You want to know what wicked diablerie lies beyond *The Eating Woods?*" The wood creaked as she slowly rocked in her chair, holding the bowl of the pipe in her palm. "A gateway to another world. I was no more than your age when I ventured into that dark forest."

Eyes wide, I lowered myself to one of the steps to her porch. "You breached the archway?"

"Had no choice. Winter was cold, and food was scarce." Another puff of her pipe, and she upped the pace of her rocking. "My brother and I had chased a rabbit deep into the trees before we came upon the beast. His skin like the bark of a tree. Eyes soulless pools of black." She stared off as if she were looking at the beast right then. "You see the dead, Girl. But have you ever stared death in the face yourself?"

Jaw slack with my absolute engrossment, I shook my head.

"As it consumed my brother, tearing the skin from his bones, I escaped. I ran until the air burned in my chest. And that's when I saw it. That shimmering veil. Like a wall of liquid glass." Her eyes held a spark of awe. "I dared myself to reach through."

"Did you?" I asked, rapt with fascination, having always wondered what existed beyond those crooked trees.

"No. An inexplicable fear came over me."

"More fearful than being consumed by the monster?"

"Yes." The enchantment in her eyes from a moment ago faded to a troubled expression. "I fled the forest and never returned."

"The governor said no one has ever returned from the woods." It wasn't that I meant to challenge her. On the contrary, I wanted to know he was wrong.

"Yes. And so he calls me The Crone Witch. He tells you that I lure children into the woods with fantastical stories, and share their flesh with the beast." Our own governor, whose son she'd saved from death, had branded her with that horrible rumor.

"If you found yourself stood before the archway now, would you still fear it?"

"Yes. You'd do well to stay away from the forest."

While it felt like an end to our conversation, I sat a moment longer, wanting so badly to ask her if my sister had sought her out, but I didn't. I certainly didn't want to be responsible for anyone having gotten a whiff of Aleysia's pregnancy.

"Did your egg hatch?" The witch asked, the question severing my thoughts.

"Yes. A baby ... bird."

"Is it now? Rather large egg for a bird, don't you think?"

"You've not seen large birds in these parts?"

"Not such that warrant an egg so large." She drew another puff of her pipe. "And what did you do with it?"

"I let it go," I lied. "Would've drawn too much attention."

She made a grunting sound in her throat and waved her hand. "Probably better off. That wretched grandmother of yours would've surely destroyed it."

I didn't say anything to that. Agatha *was* wretched—on that, the witch and I agreed.

"Go on now. I've much to do."

"Of course. I'm sorry to have kept you." I gathered my basket of figs, offering her a few of them, which she accepted with a nod, and headed in the direction of home.

CHAPTER TWENTY

ZEVANDER

Boots kicked up on the desk, Zevander held the small red stone in his fingers, studying the erratic silver veins, while forcing himself to ignore the vibration beneath his skin.

A mortal. A weak fucking mortal had sent him furiously trudging back through the woods without the stone. He'd never encountered a creature in his life that he couldn't turn to ash by summoning the flames, but somehow the girl managed to resist him.

How?

Was she *veniszka*?

He'd heard of the mortal witches, well-versed in alchemy and spellcasting, whose magic wasn't bloodborne, but potent just the same. The curiosity had gnawed at him for days, his thoughts becoming obtrusive.

Obsessive.

Who was the little mortal with raven hair and that silvery crescent in her eye that reminded him of a winter moon? And why had he not stopped seeing her in his mind since that night? Every detail of her face lingered so vividly in his thoughts, he wanted to carve them out with a blade. Visuals that sickened him as much as they intrigued him. After all, her blood was all that stood between ending the miserable curse that had destroyed his family.

Unfortunately, the small stone he had managed to acquire wasn't enough blood for Dolion's collection. Each of those stones had been roughly the same size, and by comparison, the one he held was a mere fraction. Which meant, he either had to track down another of her bloodline, or return to Mortasia.

"Cursed balls of Castero …" he muttered, rubbing a hand down his face.

He'd wanted to pass the news along to Dolion, who would've been exceptionally disappointed, except the shady bastard had disappeared—not seen for days at any of his usual haunts. Too bad, too, because Zevander had questions. Like, what in godswrath dwelled in those woods that didn't appear to be human. In fact, it reminded him very much of the deformities that his brother had suffered as a child.

A knock at the door prompted Zevander to tuck the stone away, before answering, "Come in."

Clad in the same black leathers Zevander wore, Kazhimyr strode into the room, fresh off his travels, it seemed, as a layer of dirt clung to his face. Like Zevander, he was a former Solassion prisoner and a member of King Sagaerin's Letalisz. He and two other members of the Letalisz, also former prisoners, lived in The Barracks, a separate building on the grounds of Eidolon Castle. Restoring Zevander's title as lord and allowing him to keep the castle, which had belonged to his family for centuries, was a small token of the king's gratitude for the assassinations he and his Letalisz brothers had carried out on behalf of the monarchy over the centuries.

"To what do I owe the honor."

"We've been summoned." Kazhimyr eased into the chair across from Zevander, adjusting the daggers at his hip. With his silvery hair, he could've been mistaken for Rykaia's brother, if not for the bright gold of his eyes.

Where Zevander could heat blood to stone, Kazhimyr held the power to freeze it into ice crystals that essentially lysed the veins of his victims. His was a blood-born magic, though, an inherited power shared by the kin who had rejected him years ago.

He leaned forward, passing along a scroll with its seal already broken.

Zevander unrolled the parchment and scanned over the summons. "And what great adventure has His Majesty bestowed upon us?"

"Former Magestrolian, who apparently thought it was a brilliant idea to hole himself up in the bowels of Corvus Keep."

Fuck me. Zevander slouched in his chair, just skimming over those very details contained in the letter.

"One Dolion Gevarys. Must be true what they say about him," Kazhimyr prattled on, as Zevander stared off.

Corvus Keep. The abandoned castle where the Carnificans were sent—Aethyrians poisoned with too much vivicantem, turning them stark raving mad. In the majority of cases, it was self-inflicted. Some took directly from a vein. Others, somehow developed a dangerous addiction. Once built up in the system, the vivicantem became toxic, altering the brain chemistry and turning them into dangerous venatics. Cannibals, if the rumors were true. On occasion, one would escape the keep and find itself in the small villages at the foot of the mountains, consuming mostly spindling children, as they were the easiest prey.

"Fucking seven hells." Zevander rubbed a hand across his skull and sank deeper into his seat. At least he knew where Dolion had skipped off to.

"Precisely my thoughts."

"And he's believed to be alive?"

"A mimicrow was sent to spy. Picked up on his voice. Ravings of Cadavros." Mimicrows were birds bred by the Magestroli to relay messages, or in many cases, serve as spies for the king. It was entirely possible King Sagaerin had come into possession of the blood stones, which would've implicated Dolion in the illegal practice of demutomancy.

While anyone could've tossed a body into one of the flaming veins and yielded a blood stone, the likelihood was slim, as heavily guarded as they were, and retrieving one from the flame would've been suicide. Only a few, mostly high mages, like Dolion had once been, were knowledgeable enough to wield sablefyre, which made him a highly plausible suspect.

Except that the resulting stones would've held imperfections. Flaws that might've very well affected the purity of the blood. Not even the most skilled mage possessed Zevander's efficiency at turning blood to stone.

Fortunately, no one had yet discovered his buried power, or he'd have surely been executed for it.

Because it was his black flame which had crafted the stones, he could easily destroy them with a single incantation. A last resort, seeing as the rogue mage still owed him the favor of breaking his curse. Besides, it hadn't been entirely easy gathering those damn stones, since each of the descendant bloodlines had been protected by a ward to hide their identity. Unfortunately for them, Dolion knew the spell to break the protective barrier and was able to track them down in his visions.

"Do any of the others know about this mission?" Zevander asked, entwining his fingers.

"Not yet. Torryn has been commissioned to another task by King Saegarin." Of the four Letalisz, Torryn's power was one of the most self-destructive, in that he possessed the ability to extract another's vivicantem, drawing it into himself, which rendered his opponents powerless. The king often liked to assign him to cases where interrogation preceded execution. "There's a flammellian creeping around The Hovel." The common term for those who abused flammapul. "Been slumming the brothels there. Killed two sexsells last week, but the Guard hasn't been able to track him."

"They don't give a damn about sexsells."

"Of course not. They take issue with the fact that he is using potions unauthorized by the magehood. And that he seems to know unreleased spells."

"Any idea who it is?"

"None. But I need not tell you how personal this one is."

Torryn had been in love with Zevander's sister since she'd first caught the eyes of many at her Becoming Ceremony–a sacred celebration, when girls transitioned to womanhood. Fortunately, he'd known better than to act on his growing obsession with her throughout the years, and instead, had taken it upon himself to be her quiet protector.

The fact that the flammellian targeted sexsells in particular would've made the job all too enticing for Torryn, seeing as he knew Rykaia liked to frequent the brothels.

"And may he find him before I do." Zevander didn't bother to tell his fellow Letalisz that Rykaia had been subjected to fire-bleeding. He'd also not bothered to mention the dealings he'd had with Dolion in trying to break the curse. Or the fact that he'd humiliated himself trying to retrieve the final stone.

He'd have preferred to forget everything all together, except that his dreams had become more vivid the last few nights since having laid eyes on that girl, and Zevander had grown weary of waking each morning with intense pain in his groin.

Over a mortal, no less.

Zevander reached for the glass of fervenszi he'd poured earlier and polished it off. "You and I can handle this assignment alone."

The idea was ludicrous, given what they'd be up against, and the cock of Kazhimyr's brows told Zevander his brother thought the same. Unfortunately, Zevander had no intentions of carrying out the king's order to assassinate Dolion, and the fewer who knew of this betrayal, the better.

"You and I take on the Carnificans alone? I don't know what's worse—your request, or the king's."

"If Dolion is alive, as you say, then he managed to get past the Carnificans himself. They're not a particularly docile lot."

Due to their high levels of vivicantem, they were known to have incredible strength and agility, their powers greater than a normal Mancer. Or Letalisz for that matter. Had they larger numbers, they could've probably wiped out the king's Imperial Guards fairly easily. Fortunately, most Aethyrians made a point to avoid vivicantem poisoning at all costs.

"Don't tell me you're less confident than a drunk old mage."

"Speaking of, mind if I have a drink?"

The question made Zevander smirk, but he passed over the decanter of liquor and a glass.

Kazhimyr tipped back the whole snifter of it, his nerves clearly rattled by the prospect of taking on the Carnificans alone. "And what happens if you're wrong? What happens when we're severely outnumbered by a whole colony of cannibals?"

"We send up a quick prayer before shitting ourselves."

"Doesn't sound like a stable backup plan."

"I never claimed to be much of a strategist."

Kazhimyr sighed and rubbed a hand down his face. "Fine. I'll keep it quiet. Getting eaten alive certainly isn't the worst way to die, I suppose."

"Care to enlighten me on what your opinion of the worst might be?"

"Cock in a meat grinder?"

Zevander frowned. "We'll do our best to avoid both."

With a nod, Kazhimyr pushed up from the chair. "When do we set out?"

"It'll take five days to arrive by horseback. Dusk."

CHAPTER TWENTY-ONE

MAEVYTH

On a quiet click, I opened the door to the shed and peered inside the open, dark space. A grotesque, squelching sound arose from somewhere toward the back, and I frowned, searching for Raivox in the dark. Padding quietly toward the center of the shed, I followed that horrible noise, peering through the dim light for anything that moved.

Along the east wall, a stack of pine boxes, built by Uncle Riftyn, sat waiting for the bodies stored in the morgue. How fortunate for Agatha, that both sons happened to be skilled in carpentry—one of wood, and the other of bodies.

The repulsive memory of Uncle Felix's lips on Danyra's breast sent a shiver spiraling down my back.

At the same time, a wet mass squished beneath my foot.

Lips twisted in a grimace, I lowered my gaze to the dirt floor, where a pink, fleshy mound enveloped my shoe. Tilting my head, I examined it, trying to imagine what I could've possibly been staring at, when a flash of black bolted in from the left and swiped up an end of it, before dashing back into the shadows. The pink mass trailed behind it. Long. Glistening.

Entrails.

I pressed the back of my hand to my mouth to stifle the acids burning the back of my throat, and tiptoed toward his hiding spot. Tucked in the corner of the shed, behind a stack of crates, Raivox sat hunched over himself, that disgusting sound louder than before. Movement flickered in my periphery, and I turned to see the stretch of intestines slithering across the ground into the little beast's mouth. A glance toward the carcass showed the striped head of what I was certain was Agatha's beloved tabby, Baxter.

Oh, no.

"What have you done?" I whispered, staring at the poor, unwitting thing. Not that I had much love for the feral little monster that tore up my legs with its claws, but if Agatha suspected I had any connection to its death, she'd probably tear me up with *her* claws. "Birds don't eat cats. It's the other way around."

After minutes of my listening to those wet, masticating sounds, the murdering little creature stumbled, clearly engorged, and I glanced back at the severed head.

"No, no. You can't leave that behind. You need to eat the whole thing and never eat a pet again, understand? Rats in the house are one thing, but we do not eat *pets*." With a shove of my boot, I guided the severed head over to him, the repulsion of it all winding my gut in knots. "Eat it."

Raivox hobbled over to the cat head and sank his teeth into the side of its face.

Instead of ripping away a chunk, he tottered to the side and let out a long, groaning sound, as if too full to take another bite.

"You must eat it! You can't just leave her cat's head lying about, or it'll be my head rolling on the floor next!" I pushed the head toward him again, but he swatted it away with a clawed foot.

Oh, no. I'd have to bury the damn thing, or risk her finding it. While Agatha wandering into the shed was rare, she had gone in on occasion, for God knew what.

Swallowing a hard gulp, I bent down to lift the head off the ground with the very tips of my fingers, avoiding the bloody threads of meat that hung beneath it, and padded toward the shed's door. The mere sight of it tugged a gag from my throat en route, but I swallowed back the urge to vomit.

Beyond the cracks in the wood, an obscure figure passed by, and on a quiet gasp, I froze.

If someone saw the severed head, I'd surely be punished. I winced at the last punishment to which Agatha had subjected me, when I'd been forced to clean out the abdominal cavity buckets for Uncle Felix. I swore I'd never do anything to earn that awful task again.

"Damned bird," I whispered through clenched teeth, desperately trying to swallow back the gurgling sickness climbing my throat as I clutched the head.

Once the figure had passed where the cracks in the door were widest, I couldn't discern whether, or not, they'd kept on, or still stood on the other side. With the cat's head precariously dangling at my side, I padded closer, listening. A chittering noise from behind steeled my muscles, and I turned to see Raivox hobbling toward me on all fours.

"No!" I whispered, waving him off with my hand. "Back to your corner."

He paused, head tilted as if confused.

A rattling of the door handle sent me spiraling into mindless panic, and I tossed the cat's head to my right, where it rolled beneath a dilapidated wagon used to transport bodies to the nearby graveyard.

As the door swung open, I held my breath, wiping the animal's blood on my dark skirt. Uncle Riftyn stood in the doorway, one of his hand-rolled cigarettes propped between his lips. As he removed it, he blew off the smoke, and his lips curved to a smile.

"What are you doing out here, Maevyth?"

I gave a furtive glance over my shoulder, and exhaled a breath of relief when I didn't see Raivox standing there. "I thought I might've heard something in here. An animal."

"An animal? I should check to make sure it isn't rabid." He stepped closer, farther into the shed, and my pulse hastened as I fought the urge to glance toward the discarded head.

"I searched. There was nothing. I was just leaving to head up for lunch."

With a smile, he tipped his head. "I've been meaning to talk to you, actually. Alone. About your sister."

Oh, no. Then wasn't the time for that conversation. Certainly not with him. "I'm actually really hungry."

"She's worried," he said, ignoring me. "You know Aleysia. Protective. She thinks a man like Moros will ruin a pretty innocent thing like yourself." I doubted that was the most pressing issue on my sister's mind, which left me wondering if she'd lied about telling him about the baby. Or maybe he just didn't give a damn.

He lifted a lock of my hair, letting it slip between his fingers. "She's sick, thinking about him forcing himself inside your tight, virgin cunt."

"I'd venture to say my sister doesn't think about those things." As I skirted him for the door, he grabbed my arm, sending off alarms inside my head.

"I could ease you into it." A wire of shock snapped my back straight, and as if sensing it, his grin widened, and he released me. "Only if you wanted me to, that is."

The urge to scream at him ripped at the back of my throat. That he could say these things to me, while my sister fretted over the child he shared inside of her. Even if she hadn't yet told him, what sickening audacity that he could proposition me so crudely. "You are my uncle."

"Step-uncle. We're not even blood related."

"It doesn't matter. I don't want anything to do with you."

His cheek twitched, like the comment had somehow wounded him. "See, I heard a rumor that Mr. Moros is into some strange things. A bit rough, as I understand. You might do well to loosen yourself up a bit."

"Excuse me, Uncle. I need to get back to the house."

"Yes, of course. Lunch." Tongue sweeping over his natural smirk, he tipped his head. "I understand Mr. Moros is due to be here at precisely noon."

"I have no interest in spending the afternoon with Mr. Moros."

"Doesn't matter what you want. Awful thing about these arrangements." Brows raised, he sighed. "Anyway, if you change your mind, let me know. I'll be happy to oblige. I'd hate to see an innocent young thing like yourself suffer more than necessary."

"I don't intend to suffer, at all."

His gaze lingered on my lips. "Well, wouldn't that be something. Young orphan girl standing up to a respected member of this fine parish." He let out a small chuckle and gave a curt nod. "I'll see you later. *Niece.*" On those parting words, he strode out of the shed, and I released a shaky breath, every cell in my body locked in a state of repulsion.

As I let the shock work its way through me, I hustled toward where I'd thrown the cat's head. I found it behind the wagon's wheel, and glanced around the shed for somewhere I could bury it quickly without being seen.

A small gap beneath Uncle Riftyn's carpentry bench.

Grabbing a spade from the benchtop, I fell to my knees and awkwardly hacked at the packed dirt of the shed's floor, my hand burning with a new blister as the wooden handle raked across my skin with each plunge.

Raivox hobbled up alongside me, his gaze flitting between my digging and what must've been an absolute look of disgust etched into my expression.

"I never want to clean up after one of your ... mishaps ... again." Air wheezed out of me with the toil of digging in such a confined space. Once the hole was big enough, I gently placed the cat's head into the grave and covered it with dirt, then pushed to my feet. Brushing away the sprinkling of soil on my dark dress, I pushed the thought of having to see Mr. Moros again out of my head and placed the overfed cat killer back inside his little nest. "No more pets, okay? We have to find something less traumatic for you to eat. If you insist on meat, perhaps I can see about getting some scraps from the butcher in town." I scratched the underside of his beak, and the small creature lifted his chin, letting out a purring sound that brought a reluctant smile to my face. "In spite of your macabre tendencies, you are ridiculously cute."

"Maevyth! Maevyth!"

The distant sound of Lolla calling for me had me groaning. Abandoning my murderous, little pet, I headed back toward the house, greeting her at the back entrance.

"Maevyth, come quickly."

"I know. Mr. Moros has asked me to lunch again. Has the man nothing better to do?" I prattled on. "I refuse to marry an abuser."

"It's your sister."

It was only then I noticed the pallor of her face. Completely drained of color.

"What about Aleysia?"

"She was found to be with child. Your *uncle's* child." Tears welled in Lolla's eyes.

The panic started small in my gut and curled its way with

metal talons up toward my throat, scratching inside my chest. "How ... how do they know?"

"She confessed."

The panic wriggled and lashed, slicing at my lungs. Lolla didn't have to say what I already knew. Aleysia's confession had branded her a sinner.

Sinners were fed to the forest.

CHAPTER TWENTY-TWO

ZEVANDER

Through a thick, white fog, Zevander and Kazhimyr peered across the mire of dead wood, where, in the distance, the dreaded Corvus Keep perched on a weathered, stone hill. Not much was known about the castle, abandoned long before Zevander's time. No scribe mage would've dared to scrounge the history of it, nor the small village within its crumbling walls that lined the perimeter, not with all the bloodthirsty Carnificans that'd made it their home.

"We'll continue on foot," Zevander said, dismounting Obsidyen. The thick muck served as a natural trap that the Carnificans would exploit to eat the horses alive. Not that it was any less treacherous for the two Letalisz, but at least they had the ability to defend themselves. Outside of snapping teeth, Obsidyen would have little at his disposal, while the Carnificans tore at his flesh with long, overgrown nails and teeth grounded to pointed tips.

"What do you say, nine furlongs?" Kazhimyr asked, as he tied his horse to a nearby tree, out of sight.

"I'd say so. We should make it just before nightfall."

The two set off down to the foot of the hill, where the dying grass met the foot-high deep, murky water. A white vapor hovered over the pygwog lilies gathered at the surface, while the stench of Aethyr and decaying foliage mingled with a foul odor that reminded Zevander of the sewers in The Hovel.

With the first step, his leather boots sank to his calf. Thankfully, caligosian leather didn't leak so much as a drop—although, it did have a tendency to shrink a bit when wet, squeezing his foot with each step.

"Well, this is going to be a fun nine furlongs." Kazhimyr's comment had Zevander smirking, as he trudged forward, the water climbing higher. "I hope you plan to make this one suffer."

Zevander exhaled a sigh, reminded that he hadn't yet clued in his fellow assassin. "We won't be killing this one."

"Pardon? Hard to hear over the sound of shit water splashing around me. It almost sounded like you said we're not killing him."

Zevander offered no more than a glance over his shoulder, catching sight of Kazhimyr tottering ungracefully in the soft muck. "I'm taking him to the dungeons of Eidolon."

"But the king has ordered his execution. That is how we get paid. That is how we keep from having our own heads severed."

"Yes, it's how we get paid. Indebted to a king for a crime we never committed."

"And how is sparing this mage going to change that?"

"He possesses the blood stones for the septomir." The knee-deep water slowed their pace, as the muck thickened, swallowing Zevander's boot with each step.

"The blood stones? The ones that are quite illegal to collect because they require a magic that is entirely forbidden by Imperial Law?"

"Those are the ones." Zevander's boot sank into a soft pit, and he hooked his hands beneath his knee to lift it from the suctioning soil. "He can break this wretched curse. The stones are far more powerful than the flame."

"Which will be fantastic, until the king finds out, and we're executed. And what about bringing him back to the very castle where you placed a ward to keep everyone out? Do you trust this rogue mage, known to be *mad*, I might add, around your sister?"

It was a question he'd pondered the whole ride to Corvus Keep. Zevander had made a point to keep his sister protected, his home guarded, but he'd be damned if he'd let the mage get off so easily, without having fulfilled his end of their bargain. "He'll reside in the dungeons. I'll shackle him with copper." The only element known to weaken a mage. "He's relatively harmless, but he'll be useless after."

"Harmless … *pfft*. He was a member of the Magestroli. The king's most powerful."

"Shhhh." Zevander came to an abrupt halt, ears perked, picking up on the faint sound of water moving. The moment he threw back his cape and reached for the sword at his back, swinging wide, a black serpent struck out of the water, fangs bared. Its fiery tongue merely kissed his cheek, before the blade struck its flesh, slicing through as easily as if its bones were liquid.

The upper half of the serpent fell into the bog, splashing the rotten concoction of blood and muck in his face. Wiping it away, he twisted around to find Kazhimyr sinking into the water that now reached his thighs. His hips.

Quicksand.

"Fuck!" Kazhimyr teetered and rocked in place, arms flailing, as the muck pulled him deeper. To his waist. His chest.

Zevander reached for his outstretched hand before the Letalisz could slip completely beneath the water. Forcing all of his strength into the toil, muscles shaking, he yanked Kazhimyr's arm with such violence, the other Letalisz shot up out of the water on a gasp.

Bending forward, he coughed, spitting murky swamp water out of his mouth.

He glanced up. "Behind you!"

Zevander swung around, sword still at the ready, as two Carnificans snarled and hopped their way through the water, toward them. The easy way they traversed over the bog indicated they'd hunted those grounds regularly.

Eyes blood red, wrinkled and weathered skin a pale white, with a flat nose, and lips that appeared to have been chewed away to expose pointed teeth—it was hard to believe they were once normal citizens going about their day. Any semblance of their former selves lay hidden beneath a mask of savagery.

Zevander raised his palm, mentally drawing the Aeryz glyph, and thrust his hand forward. A blast of air sent the Carnificans sailing backward, splashing into the muck. Two more advanced, but before Zevander had the chance to swing his sword, the scorpions etched into his flesh rose up in a black smoke, taking form as colossal-sized beasts. On the strike of the scorpion's stinger, one of the Carnificans reached out, grasping the thin, metallic tip of the stinger in his palm.

"'The fuck?" Zevander had never seen such a thing.

The Carnifican crushed it, sending the scorpion into a trembling, hissing fit, and it thrashed its tail, striking another Carnifican, who exploded on impact. The second scorpion struck, hitting the first Carnifican in the neck. He let out a high-pitched screech, one that Zevander silenced with a swing of his blade.

At a roar from behind, Zevander turned to see white smoke drifting upward from Kazhimyr's palm, his eyes an icy blue. He directed the mist toward the three approaching Carnificans, and all three of them skidded to a halt. Frozen. Skinny rivulets of red scattered beneath their skin as their veins lysed. Their flesh split open, tearing their bodies into small pieces that fell with a splash in the water.

The scorpion with the crushed stinger curled into black smoke, and from it emerged a new scorpion, its stinger glinting before driving through the abdomen of an oncoming Carnifican.

In the distance, Zevander caught sight of a dozen more, bounding toward them in their unsettling hops that made scarcely a splash across the water. Kazhimyr's mist sent another blast of white smoke over the bog's surface, which turned it to ice around their pale, bony legs. As the Carnificans wriggled and roared in a failed effort to get loose, Zevander's scorpions struck, the metal slicing through their bodies, severing them in half.

Within minutes, all the Carnificans lay in severed bits across the mire.

Reeling back their sigil powers, the two Letalisz stood breathing hard, Zevander's heart hammering in his chest. Calling on the powers of sablefyre expended his energy levels and had left him drained. Still, the two kept on, trudging through the remaining three furlongs of sludgy wetlands, without further incident, until they eventually reached the solid castle grounds.

Unfortunately, the few Carnificans they'd encountered in the bog were only a small fraction of the hundreds believed to inhabit Corvus Keep.

To the right lay what appeared to be the ravaged remains of a ribcage and leg bones, the size indicating the victim had been no more than ten. A spindling child, if Zevander had to guess. As they neared the castle, more bones lay in piles across the yard, their species indiscernible in the heap.

"I can't say I won't accidentally kill the crazy, old mage after that miserable fucking trek." Kazhimyr dislodged a chunk of muck that'd dried to his leather tunic.

"Aren't you the slightest bit impressed that he survived it?" How Dolion might've managed such a feat remained a mystery. While his power had been honed over a number of centuries, he lacked strength in his old age.

Kazhimyr groaned, knocking the heel of his boot against the dead grass, onto which more wet muck slipped away.

The scent of death and decomposition clung to the back of his throat, as Zevander crossed the yard toward the dilapidated door of the castle that stood cracked open.

The two pushed past the creaking iron doors into the grand entry hall, where a stone raven stood in the center, its wings broken and chipped with age. Tapestries, tattered and torn, dangled haphazardly over the water-stained, stone walls, and the portraits of royal lineage hung cocked and faded, punctured with violent destruction.

What was undoubtedly a once-grand foyer stood in decay, its remnants scavenged and destroyed.

"Whatever happened here … it must've been horrible. It's as if they left everything and fled."

Zevander scanned over the ruins, his thoughts darkening as he took in the state of the castle. "I'd venture to say they didn't flee. Not by choice, anyway."

"Who were they?"

"I don't know. There's nothing in the history books that speaks of anyone occupying this castle. Only that it belongs to Nyxteros."

The sound of crumbling stone alerted Zevander to the right, just as two Carnificans came charging on all fours, like animals. From his hip, Kazhimyr yanked a curved, double-bladed dagger that, under a glow of white light, extended to a spear.

Zevander unsheathed his black sword.

The Carnificans charged without hesitation, as was the state of their minds. They attacked relentlessly and without fear.

Zevander swung, just missing the Carnificans that ducked fast. As one of them scrambled toward him, he unsheathed his dagger and stabbed the ruthless creature in the throat. He twisted in time to slash another in the gut with his sword, slicing its stomach open with one hard yank of the blade. Another advanced, and he parried a jab to its skull, striking with unerring precision.

A half dozen more poured out of rooms, charging from the right and left. Dozens more after that, until Zevander and Kazhimyr stood back-to-back, fighting off the mob of berserkers. For every swing of Zevander's sword, Kazhimyr parried with a stab of his spear.

"Remind me ... again ... when we're supposed to start ... shitting ourselves?" Kazhimyr asked, jabbing his spear into the abdomen of his attacker. When he yanked it back out, a glob of jellied organs spilled onto the floor.

"Right about now, I'd say." Zevander swung wide, lopping off the head of a Carnifican that rolled across the cement.

Their sigils emerged, Zevander's scorpions and Kazhimyr's deadly mist of ice. Three Carnificans climbed the stinger of Zevander's scorpion, just before the appendage slammed into the cement, slicing one of them in half. The other two slipped off on impact and met the same fate.

A snowy blast of white mist hurled three other berserkers into the wall in a bloody explosion of limbs and bone. Zevander and Kazhimyr backed themselves up the crumbling staircase, until a tingle rushed over Zevander's skin, and he realized the Carnificans were no longer advancing.

They'd passed through a ward.

On the other side of a shimmering wall, his scorpions fought off the dozens more Carnificans that emerged to fill the great hall.

Zevander reached out to call them back, and the oversized arachnids faded to a cloud of black smoke that crawled beneath his sleeve.

Khazimyr bent forward, palms to his thighs, catching his breath. "Well, that was about as fun as stroking my cock with a gauntlet."

Carnificans charged after them, slamming into the invisible

force like a shield of liquid glass that stood between them and the two assassins.

"Judging by that ward, we must be close." Kazhimyr sheathed his spear back into its holster at his hip. "And I suppose that answers the question of *how*."

Wards expended incredible energy, so the likelihood of Dolion using his own blood magic was slim. Which meant the blood stones were with him.

The two Letalisz split up, Kazhimyr taking the west wing of the castle, while Zevander took the east. Room after room turned up nothing more than overturned and ravaged furniture speckled with blood, piles of bones and carcasses, and the stench of death everywhere he turned. Down a long corridor, he came upon a door that looked like it'd been pummeled with a battering ram, its surface marred in deep dents. The iron hinges had cracked, as though something had crashed into the unyielding barrier with no success.

One strong heave failed to move it. He took a step back and gave one forceful kick that swung the door so hard against the adjacent stone wall, it cracked down the center. Dagger at the ready, he climbed the winding staircase, catching the faint sound of whimpering from above. When he finally arrived at the topmost room of the turret, he stepped cautiously across the creaking wood and scanned the open space. In the upper rafters of the room, he spied the glow of yellow eyes staring down at him. The mimicrows, sent to spy.

"I've made a grave error," a weak voice said from behind, and Zevander swung around toward its source. In the shadowy corner, he found a glint of silver belonging to a shoe buckle, and an outstretched leg.

"How so?"

"To speak would be my demise." The scratchy nature of Dolion's voice suggested little water had been consumed, and probably little food, unless he'd managed to scrounge some vermin, though the Carnificans likely hunted anything with a pulse. On closer examination, Zevander noticed the disheveled state of the man–his white beard kinked and ungroomed, his hair standing about his head, clothes carrying more than a few days' grime.

Before the old man could answer further, Zevander unsheathed two blades at his hip. He spun around and hurled them toward the glowing eyes.

Two quiet thuds.

Two birds fell to the floor.

The third took flight before he could yank the next blade, zipping through the open window where the shutters had been torn away.

He threw out his arm, and a scorpion stinger impaled the bird in flight with one quick strike, then retracted just as fast. The growls from below indicated the Carnificans had scavenged it as a welcomed meal.

One more scan showed no other evidence of the mimicrows.

"Those gods damned birds. Always listening." He shifted on the floor, groaning when he stretched out another leg, as if he'd been sitting there for days. "The red stone. With the silver markings."

"Your vision was wrong?"

"Not wrong. Incomplete. After we met at the tavern, I dreamed again. Terrible things. War. Famine. The complete destruction of Aethyria."

"You've always raved of those things."

"My dreams never showed me *scorpions*."

Zevander let out a mirthless laugh. "Are you implying I'm your great villain now? That I will bring about this *end of days*? You *are* mad."

"You will join Cadavros in his destruction. This much I know for certain."

"Then, why not attempt to destroy me now?"

"Because I saw the Corvugon in this vision, also. And with you having fetched the final stone, I do not see how that is possible now." A dry cough jerked his body, and Zevander unclipped the waterskin he'd brought on his journey, handing it off to him. One exceptionally long swill later, and Dolion lowered the flask, wiping at his mouth. "Don't suppose you brought any ale."

"Unfortunately not."

The slight smile on his face sobered. "My visions, real as they may seem … perhaps they're *unreliable*."

"What is this Corvugon you mentioned?"

"They were messengers of the dead, believed to have been the beloved pets of the Death Goddess. Sizeable raptors with teeth and claws designed for tearing flesh. Centuries ago, they evoked as much fear as the dragon."

He considered for a moment that the egg tucked under the girl's bed could've very well been the creature Dolion described. "These raptors … they would bear eggs like a bird, or a dragon?"

"Yes. Large, black-scaled eggs, smelling of brimstone."

"And what does the stone with the silver marking have to do with this Corvugon? You once believed the stone was the end of this destruction. The end of Cadavros. The end of the fucking curse that supposedly makes me so much of a threat."

Hands clutching the top of his head, Dolion screwed his eyes shut. "I was wrong. My visions failed me."

Zevander ground his teeth, biting back the urge to punch his fist through a wall. "No. If your visions failed you, then I collected all those stones for nothing. And I surely did not collect those stones for nothing, old man."

Brows furrowed, he sat thoughtful. "No, I suppose you didn't."

When he didn't elaborate at first, Zevander said, "Speak freely. The mimicrows no longer report back to the king."

"The king didn't send those crows. It's the magehood that hunts me now. The very men who accused me of being a raving fool now covet those stones. They're the ones who drove me here."

"It makes sense that one person holding all of that power is a threat to them."

"Of course." He swallowed back another long gulp of water. "But they don't wish to destroy it, as they were ordered to destroy the first septomir, by our gracious king." Interesting, that the king had also outlawed demutomancy which would've ensured the power of the septomir would never return. "No ... they want to possess the weapon. And they want me to reveal where the seventh bloodstone lies."

"It seems you'd be more of an ally to them, with you and the magehood desiring the same thing."

Dolion scoffed and turned away. "Not in the least. As I said, I made a mistake, but my intentions were good. Who knows what they'd do with that kind of power." The focus in his eyes faded as he stared, perhaps imagining it then. "They will use any means of torture to extract the information from me. Then dispose of me for failing to remain quiet."

"Do you suspect they believe your visions? This famine and pestilence you fear?"

"I suspect they've always believed."

"If you're so foolish as to trap yourself in a castle with Carnificans, why not just give them what they want?"

He tipped his head back, resting it against the wall. "Do you know the history of Corvus Keep?"

"Outside of housing Carnificans, no."

"Strange, isn't it? This castle has existed for most of my life. Certainly, for all of yours. Yet, we know nothing about it. Why was it abandoned? Who occupied it before the Carnificans?"

"What is your point?"

"Prior to the Carnificans taking control of it, there existed an entire race. The Corvikae."

The name didn't strike a familiar chord, at all. Nothing he'd ever read in the history of Nyxteros had spoken of them.

"They were mortals who once occupied this land," Dolion prattled on. "Lived in this castle."

"Mortals haven't existed in Aethyria as long as the Umbravale has existed."

"You're wrong. History is *wrong*. Centuries ago, well before my time, they existed here. On these lands. Those with no power. No blood magic."

"So, what happened to them?"

"They were driven away. Forced beyond the reaches of civilization. To the deepest trenches, where no Mancer would dare to venture."

There was only one place Zevander had ever heard of, aside from the mortal land, that struck fear in the minds of all Aethyrians. "The Crussurian Trench ..." Beyond the reaches of civilization, in the dark and icy depths, where creatures more vicious than the Carnificans dwelled.

"Yes," Dolion answered in a sobering tone.

The sound of footsteps echoed from below, and eyes widening, Dolion swiped a blade from beside him up to the dusky light, his hands trembling. Kazhimyr appeared soon after, coming to a stop alongside Zevander, and on a relieved exhale, Dolion lowered his weapon.

"Who drove them away?" Zevander asked, returning to their conversation.

"This far north, I'd suspect Solassions. Mothers, children, warriors, even their sacred priestess, were marched from their burning village to the trench, and cast into the depths of Hell."

"How do you know this?" Zevander asked.

Dolion waved his hand over the stone walls, and the red glowing images and words of an ancient language appeared etched on their surface by blood ink. A binding spell that kept it preserved. While Zevander's Primyeria, the ancient tongue, was a bit rusty, he'd learned it from his mother as a child. What had been etched into the stone told the very story Dolion had just relayed. "There are books I found in the dungeons. Their scribes must've hidden them away during the siege, but these ... these are the last words of the only survivor."

Zevander dragged his attention back to Dolion. "I'll ask again, why the change of heart about the stones?"

He sat quietly for a moment. Thoughtful. "The seventh stone has always been a source of speculation, one the magehood has argued over since the Age of Renewal. For centuries, it remained a mystery." He tipped back another sip of the water-skin, polishing off the last of Zevander's supply, and handed him the empty vessel. "My apologies. I didn't want to consume all of it."

"Finish your explanation."

"The silver markings on that stone are unique to the Corvikae, who were known to worship the Goddess of Death. The very ichor that ran through her veins, ran through the veins of the Corvi people."

"And?"

"If my vision is correct, the mortal I sent you after may be the first, or the last, of the Corvikae bloodline. She may carry the blood of the death goddess. And while I may be many things to many people, I am not the vehicle for mortalicide." Lips pressed to a hard line, he shook his head. "I certainly don't want to fuck with the daughter of a death goddess."

A flash of the girl's goddess-like face slipped through Zevander's mind and tensed his muscles. "As young as she is, she hasn't had her powers long, then."

"I suspect not. But what do you mean, *hasn't*? Is she .... Is she alive?"

"The girl still resides in Mortasia," Zevander answered in a flat tone.

"Oh, thank the gods. Thank the ever-loving gods of mercy!"

"Mortasia?" Kazhimyr asked. "You ventured to the feared wastelands and never said a word about it?"

Zevander inwardly groaned. "It was uneventful."

"How is this possible?" Dolion interrupted. "How does she live?"

Zevander ground his teeth together, the question taking him back to that night, and the thousands of times since that he'd asked himself that very question.

The realization dawning across the old man's face only prodded his anger.

"You couldn't do it, could you? Something kept you from killing her."

Instead of answering, the Letalisz fought the urge to bite off his own tongue and said, "I have seen the egg of this Corvugon. It's with her."

"Then, it is true. It is true that they have returned!"

Wicked curls of anger snaked down Zevander's neck, as he set a hand to his hip, the other stroking his jaw. "The stones we've collected, the lives we've taken, they are useless, then."

"Those stones are holding back a castle full of Carnificans at the moment. While they are not powerful enough to prevent a pestilence, the six hold enough power to create a ward. And need I remind you that those you've killed were not exemplary citizens. They kept Nilivir as slaves, for fuck's sake."

"And need I remind you that I do not kill for charity, or to rid the world of fucking evil. I kill for purpose, and that purpose was the curse you promised to break. And, so, how do you intend to recompense? Before you answer, allow me to *advise* that we were sent by the king to execute you."

"I'm afraid I cannot break the curse without the blood stone of the Corvi daughter, and I will not be responsible for ending their bloodline twice. Kill me, if you must." The bastard had the audacity to tip up his chin, as if such a thing would offer him some dignity. "In fact, I insist. I've attempted it a number of days already. I'm a coward."

"Perhaps I'll just kill *her* and take those heavy stones off your hands."

"You've tried and failed. A war is on the horizon, Zevander. To rid yourself of the flame would leave you defenseless. Practically mortal." With a small bit of struggle, he pushed to his feet, stumbling backward a step. "Your curse, though a burden today, may prove useful tomorrow. It is an unrivaled power you possess."

Zevander unsheathed his blade. "Or you might just be a raving old man who needs to be silenced."

"Silence me, then." He tossed off his own weapon with a clang of metal and held his hands out to the side in surrender. "I'm begging you. It does not change your circumstances. Or your fate."

Jaw clenched, Zevander snarled at the old mage's stubborn refusal. His hands shook with the urge to throttle him, for daring to imagine the Letalisz would allow him to so easily dissolve the bargain they'd made.

"What do we do?" Kazhimyr asked, breaking him of his murderous thoughts. "I suspect the moment he's dead, that ward will fall."

"It most certainly will." Dolion jerked his head toward the staircase. "You better leave now while you have the chance."

"You're coming with us. You'll stay at Eidolon."

"I will be putting you at great risk, Zevander. And if I'm captured by the magehood, I could only hope for a swift execution. So, please. Do your king's bidding."

Zevander let out a spiteful chuckle, a mere fraction of his ire. "You owe me, old man. The magehood is the least of your worries now." If Dolion couldn't rid him of the curse, Zevander would force the old mage to figure out a way to slow the progression of its transformation in him. He didn't give a damn about

Dolion's shifty morals, or the fact the girl was the last of her kind. It enraged him that he hadn't been able to kill her.

"There's still the issue of getting back to our horses." Kazhimyr strode toward the window and peered out. "Much harder with an extra body."

"Should you choose to walk," Dolion countered.

"You've a better plan?"

Dolion cocked a brow and turned to the stone wall beside him. A glowing streak of light trailed his hand as he circled it against the wall. "*Accipezimu equivonis.*" The crumbling stone shimmered, opening up on the dark hill where their horses stood tied to the trees.

The view offered a glimpse of shadowy figures quickly bounding toward the helpless animals. Carnificans.

"What say you, Brother?"

Zevander let out a low growl and nabbed the collar of Dolion's cloak, yanking him to within punching distance. "Nothing tricky, or I'll burn you alive."

Nodding, the old man swiped up a leather bag from beside him, clanking whatever was inside, and they stepped through the shimmering circle.

Once on the other side, Kazhimyr loosed the horses, while Zevander yanked his sword for the oncoming Carnificans. No more than a few yards from having their hands severed, the berserkers froze, their eyes fixed on something behind Zevander. He turned in time to clock a mage stalking at his back, and when the stranger thrust his palm toward them, Zevander drew his cape, shielding him and Dolion from the flame that burst forth.

Intense heat beat against the cape, failing to break through the fireproof barrier, as Zevander protected his quarry from the blaze.

Dolion curled into a tight ball beside Zevander. "You should've pushed a blade through my heart back at the keep, you fool."

Zevander hardly flinched at the weaker flame that did little more than warm his cloak—nowhere near as intense as the sable-fyre that sizzled inside his own veins, desperate to lash out. "*He*'s the fool, for having picked an unfair fight."

The heat shifted to a frigid cold, and Zevander kept the shield in place a moment longer, to keep Kazhimyr's mist from touching Dolion. While the flame in his veins protected Zevander's blood from freezing, it certainly wouldn't have done much for the mage.

The cold lifted, and Zevander threw back the cape, sending forth three large scorpions. Two more mages had appeared, the first lying in chunks of split flesh, his veins having split open.

Zevander held his blade at the ready for the first who dared to charge. Unlike the Carnificans, completely devoid of magic, the mages moved swiftly and efficiently, avoiding the snapping strike of the scorpions' stingers.

Kazhimyr sent another blast of ice which the mages blocked with an invisible shield, deflecting the mist away from them.

"Keep it steady!" Zevander shouted.

Their powers could only hold the shield for so long. As the two assassins had learned in their training, the best weapon was exhausting the enemy. Using up whatever energy reserves they had and parrying with a counter attack. The scorpions waited, snapping their claws as Kazhimyr held a steady blast, forcing the mages to expend their magic to hold the shield. Both sides were undoubtedly growing weary as their power slowly depleted.

Zevander, on the other hand, patiently waited, mentally counting off the seconds that ticked by.

Until those shields finally fell.

All three of his scorpions struck fast into the hearts of the two mages. One of them split in half, as the metallic stinger swung out. Within minutes, all three mages lay mutilated on the grassy knoll.

Kazhimyr bent forward, wheezing as he fought to catch his breath. "For gods' sake ... I'm getting too old for this shit."

The scorpions skittered back to Zevander, and he glanced toward the Carnificans, who'd retreated back to Corvus Keep. As the remaining mage, who'd been stung in the heart, squirmed and writhed, Zevander drew his blade and stabbed him in the skull before he could call on a mimicrow to relay what had happened.

Dolion stood over the fallen mage and sighed. "This won't be the last we'll see of them."

"I suspect not," Zevander said, sheathing his sword.

CHAPTER TWENTY-THREE

MAEVYTH

"Aleysia! Aleysia! No!" I raced across the yard toward the Vonkovyan soldiers, who dragged my sister by the arms, while she kicked and screamed. "Leave her alone!"

Her dress had been torn at the sleeve with their rough handling, her hair falling out of the braid she'd worn earlier that morning. "Maevyth!" she cried out over a sob. "Please don't let them take me!"

As I came upon the first soldier, I swallowed back the fear climbing my throat and instinct took over. I swung out, my knuckles knocking into solid body, sending a shooting pain up through my joints. "Leave her alone! Leave her!" A hard shove to my chest sent me flying backward, and I tumbled onto my backside in a bruising hit.

Spears of icy adrenaline pulsed through me, and I scrambled over my skirts, pushing to my feet again, and charged toward him.

The moment I was upon him, he reached out and grabbed my throat, trapping the air. I clawed at his hand, eyes on the other guard, who shoved Aleysia into the carriage. Desperate, I yanked the paring knife from my dress pocket and, without aim, stabbed his forearm.

The guard let out a growl, and as soon as he released me, I bolted for the carriage. A fiery pain struck my scalp, and my body flew backward at a hard yank of my hair. The guard pulled me against him, his bloody arm pressed to my throat.

"Take me instead!" The sharp-edged words scraped across my dry throat, as I screamed them in desperation. "Please! I'll take her place! I'll take her place!" The view of Aleysia disappeared, as he spun me around and hauled me across the yard toward Agatha, Lolla, Uncle Felix, and Uncle Riftyn, who did nothing to save my sister. *Nothing.*

One, hard blow to my back, and I flew to the ground before them, the force of his fist knocking the wind out of me. Writhing against the cold dirt, I wheezed, failing to draw in enough air. Twinges of panic exploded through me, the view shrinking. Until, at last, the first small breath forced its way into my lungs. I coughed and retched, the vacuous hole in my chest slowly expanding on each breath. When I finally turned over to my side, the carriage had begun down the road.

"No!" I rasped, crawling, clawing at the dirt to get to my feet.

Still fighting for air, I gasped, tears blurring my eyes while I watched the carriage disappear over the hill.

Hands grabbed for me, and on a scream, I swatted them away, but they wrangled me into the tight grip of my two uncles.

Kicking and slamming my heels in the dirt, I fought to get loose, as they dragged me backward.

Agatha stepped toward me, and for one, brief moment, I caught a flash of what I mistook as sympathy in her eyes. I stilled for a moment, tears blurring her form. The moment the tears broke away, I realized it wasn't sympathy, at all.

A cold, sharp smack smarted my cheek. "You are an embarrassment. Both you and your whore of a sister."

Rage tore through me, and I spat in her face. Through a hard shake of my arm, I felt the bruising squeeze of Uncle Riftyn's grip.

"Do not make it worse!" He dug his fingers into my arm in warning.

I turned to him, teeth grinding. "You did nothing. You let them take her. And you did nothing!"

Another smack struck my jaw, that one all knuckles and bones, sending a flash of light to the backs of my eyes—not from Agatha, but Uncle Riftyn. A zap of pain shot to my sinuses, my jaw throbbing.

"Take her to Moros," Agatha said. "I've washed my hands of the both of them."

* * *

Hands and ankles bound in tight rope, I lay on the floor of the carriage, my head tormenting me with the visuals of Aleysia being dragged away. Tears streaked down my temples, pooling onto the floor beneath me. The copper scent of blood filled my nose, my cheekbone and split lip throbbing from the ache of Uncle Riftyn's hit.

I hadn't bothered to peer up at the window once on the ride over, but as the carriage rolled to a stop, I broke from the mire of thoughts at voices outside the carriage. Moros. And the head servant I'd met.

"Gather her bags and get her settled in her room," Moros said in a stiff and dispassionate tone.

The door swung open, and Uncle Riftyn appeared, his down-trodden expression telling me he might've felt a small bit of remorse for earlier. Beside him, Uncle Felix stood without a speck of emotion, his countenance as dead as those of the corpses he carved.

When Uncle Riftyn gripped my bound ankles, I kicked out at him, knocking him back a step. He growled and gathered my feet again, giving a hard yank. The wooden floorboards scraped over my skin with the sting of slivers, and he lifted me out of the carriage, throwing me over his shoulder like a lifeless sack of flour.

"Remove her binds," Moros ordered, and Uncle Riftyn halted, carefully setting me down on the gravelly path.

"She attacked the Vonkovyan soldiers. It's why we bound her up like this." Uncle Riftyn lowered to his knee and went to work on the knot at my ankle. By god, the moment he set me free, I'd give him a swift kick to the face.

"Wouldn't you, in her position?" Moros asked, and I glanced up, mildly surprised, his comment dragging my attention from the rope that'd bitten so hard into my ankles, I could hardly wiggle my toes. "Surely, you would have, given your responsibility in the matter."

Uncle Riftyn cleared his throat, and the second the rope slipped free, I hammered a kick to his chin that sent him flying back into the dirt.

A thrill of victory washed over me, watching him roll on the ground, cupping his mouth, from where blood trickled out.

"I bit my fucking tongue!" he rasped, and Uncle Felix snorted beside me.

I lurched for him again, but at a grip on my shoulder, I turned to see Moros standing beside me.

"That won't be necessary. Come with me, Girl. I'd like to show you something."

"I want to see my sister," I countered.

"See her, you shall, but first, follow me."

I lifted my bound hands for him, to which he offered a slight smile. "Perhaps we'll leave those bindings in place."

Whatever small bit of relief I'd felt a moment ago fizzled away.

He walked toward the manor, glancing over his shoulder. "Come on."

With another brief glimpse of Uncle Riftyn clambering to his feet, I followed after Moros, though not because I trusted him. After what had happened to the Lyverian girl, I'd neither forgive, nor trust him, at all. I followed only for the promise of seeing my sister.

Once inside the manor, he led me past the kitchen to a stairwell, beyond the mudroom and storage pantry. The sight of it stirred both curiosity and trepidation, but I followed him, anyway. We descended into an enormous, open space, like grandfather's wine cellar, but with higher ceilings and the glow of light. I turned to see a lamp blazing a bright blue.

"Azurmadine. Found in the caves of Sawtooth. When burned, it gives off a magnificent glow," he said, as we passed.

I'd never laid eyes on anything more compelling than that light, but I didn't bother to say anything in response, my mind anxious and desperate to see my sister.

I wanted to ask him why he'd killed the Lyverian girl. Why he'd beaten her so cruelly, as I was certain he'd been the one to put those bruises upon her, but I didn't dare say anything to offend him right then.

A wall to the left of me, made up of dozens of small niches, housed glass jars of varying sizes. A closer inspection on passing showed unusual creatures held within–a snake with two heads, a tiny octopus, strange looking wings, a brain, a skinned rat, and what looked like a fetus. Oddities I would've found disturbing, if not for the distraction of my sister.

She was all I could think about right then, and the brewing frustration of every wasted minute weighed heavily as he led me down the corridor.

We rounded a stone wall to another partition of the cellar, and once inside, my heart ground to a halt.

An impossibly bright light glowed from a glass enclosure that was filled with water and almost reached the ceiling. Within the tank, two figures swam about, their arms propelling them, giving the impression they were human, but their legs appeared bound together, as if attached. Bits of strange-looking cloth dangled from their feet like loose fins, their faces covered by masks attached to tubes.

The tubes connected to a box, where another glass enclosure held some sort of accordion structure that contracted and expanded, releasing a boisterous whoosh each time it collapsed. I studied it, my mind puzzling the scene. The accordion moved like a lung. Air. Air feeding the masks.

"What is this?" I asked, my chest tightening the more details I took in—the tiny stitching between their thighs and the shells that did an inadequate job of covering their private parts.

"A bit of a collection." Hands behind his back, he walked to the other side of the tank, facing me from that angle, his eyes beaming with a sickening fascination. "When I was a boy, my father took me to a fair, a traveling band of filthy nomads. I was intrigued by one of the exhibits, though. A collection of curiosities. Taxidermy, and jars filled with strange little specimens, like you saw on the wall a moment ago. There was also an exhibition of biological rarities they called *The Freak Show*. And that was the first time I laid eyes on the mermaids. Deliciously mysterious women said to inhabit the sea and attack ships." He ran his fingers over the glass, staring at the women as if mesmerized. "I was enamored with the idea of these dangerous, wild women. I wanted to capture one. Tame it into my own little pet. I was a little disappointed to learn that the women at the fair were nothing more than a parlor trick. So, I decided to make my own collection."

Nausea twisted inside of me like poisonous worms in my belly. In that moment, I decided Uncle Riftyn and even Agatha were far less terrifying.

"When I came across a Lyverian village, I took notice of two sisters, not much older than you. They ran half-naked with spears and rage. Wild as boars. My god, how I longed to *break* them. So, I made a deal with their father. I would spare their village. Their people. So long as he gave me his daughters. Of course, he refused, as any good father would. But he came around once we'd slaughtered his wife and two of his sons."

"You're a monster," I whispered. I lifted my gaze toward the women, whose palms were plastered against the glass, the strands of macerated skin that'd peeled from their raw hands floating around their fingers.

His dark chuckle echoed around me, sending a wave of terror down my spine. "Yes. I suppose, to some, I am a monster. Let your sister be a lesson. Wild and unruly women have no place in this world. You're meant to be tamed, or put down, if necessary."

"I want to see her. You told me I could see my sister."

"You will see her. At the toll of the bell, my dear, she will stand before The Eating Woods. And you will watch as her vibrant spirit is broken by fear. You will look upon her face and remember the remorse burning in her eyes."

Copper hit my tongue as I bit my cheek, desperate to hold back tears. I refused to let him see the effect his words had on me. How they stirred a cold and hollow panic in my gut. "You clearly do not know my sister."

"If only I'd had the ambition to take her, as well. I would have added her to my collection of magnificent creatures. Come. I have another to show you."

"I don't want to see it," I spat back.

"Oh, but you must! It is perhaps the most fascinating of my collection. And I suspect you'll appreciate this one." He lurched toward me, and I took a step back, but he swiped up my bound hands, giving a hard yank.

With reluctant steps, I followed after him, wriggling my wrists to get loose as I caught one more glimpse over my shoulder of those poor women.

He led me to another room, where snarls and growls bounced off the walls. From the shadowed corner, something watched us.

"You remember the good captain who sat next to you at brunch? The one who groped you under the table?"

A loud clank of chains answered in response, the sound of them scraping over the cement floor. A figure shot out from the shadows, and once in the flickering blue light, I took in its grotesque form. Fear knotted in my chest, squeezing my lungs, as I trailed my gaze over the terrifying deformity. It stood bent forward, its spine sticking up through the skin in spikes that reminded me of a lizard. Half its face had melted into a blank canvas of skin with no eyes, nose or teeth. The other half was a sunken eye socket, a deformed nose, and a skull jaw with teeth sharpened to points. Milky white skin served as a translucent barrier to the map of veins that pulsed with each pump of its heart, which protruded through its skin.

Jaw agape, I could scarcely breathe as I took in its monstrous form.

Moros held up the vial of stones he'd taken out at the brunch. The seemingly innocuous brunch that had given little insight into the horror I faced. "It seems, when consumed, the stones have the ability to alter bones and flesh. What was once the good and proper captain is now a flesh-eating animal."

Every nerve in my body flared with terror, as he rounded me.

"You see, I may be a monster, but I can also be quite protective of you, my delicate little rose." He brushed a lock of hair from my shoulder, my body so wound with shock, I hardly noticed the proximity of his lips to my neck, until he whispered, "Come. It's almost time for your sister's banishing."

CHAPTER TWENTY-FOUR

MAEVYTH

There were stages of trauma, as I'd come to learn, and I'd moved beyond anger to a feeling of utter hopelessness.

A bitter cold clenched my muscles, as I lay trembling on the bed in one of the rooms Mr. Moros had assigned to me. Lingering ripples of shock kept my body in a constant state of tension, and every time my mind wound back to visions of Aleysia getting dragged away, fresh panic bloomed in my chest. I taunted myself into imagining what they'd do to her. The fear and uncertainty she must've felt, facing those terrifying men alone, as they scrutinized and passed judgment on her. At the very least, I'd have held her hand through it all. Let her know that she was not alone.

Through the window, I watched the sun descend in a fiery blaze of pinks and oranges that, on any other day, I'd have found beautiful.

It wasn't long now.

While some banishings took place during the day, the majority happened at night.

Aleysia hated the dark.

The very thought of her wandering those woods at night had

my muscles bound in knots. My circumstances were no better, though. Moros had also proven to be just as much a monster as whatever dwelled in those woods.

An image of mermaids flashed through my head, and I winced, shuddering a breath. My thoughts pulled me into dark corners, where Moros's victims reached out at me, dragging me into the hell of their minds.

"He'll hurt you, too." A thick, accented voice sliced through my menagerie of thoughts, and I sucked in a sharp inhale, backing myself into the headboard of the bed.

A sweep of the surroundings showed Danyra, the Lyverian girl he'd killed, sitting in a rocking chair at the shadowy corner of the room. Her pale, naked skin illuminated the deep, blackened stitches of her embalming that ran just above her collarbone and below her bare breasts.

White, cloudy eyes stared off, unfocused, the sight of them sending a chill up the back of my neck. "You must escape. You and your sister."

Every muscle in my body quivered, my jaw stiff and aching. "Th-th-there's nowhere to r-r-r-un."

She stopped rocking in the chair. Eyes still fixed away from me, she pushed to her feet and padded slowly toward the bed, until standing at the foot of it. "Witch," she rasped. "Witch. Witch. Witch."

I pressed myself against the headboard, until my spine tingled with the pressure.

She held up her palm. As if carved by a blade, a symbol appeared to have been etched there. A vertical line with multiple intersecting lines that reminded me of a spine, behind which glowed a silvery light. "Witch. Witch. Witch." Her body twitched as she placed her palms against the bed and gave one last whispered, "Witch."

She scrambled toward me.

I jolted upright on a sharp breath, eyes scanning the darkened room. My muscles jerked as I took in the empty chair in the corner, where she'd sat a moment ago. Nothing but a towering armoire, a wash basin on a dresser, a nightstand and lamp beside the bed.

No sign of Danyra.

I released a shuddering breath, recalling the last few moments of what must've been a dream. The symbol on her hand had seared itself into my mind, though. What could it have possibly meant?

As I took a moment to ponder, reality poured in. My sister. The Banishing.

The doorknob clicked, and I lifted my hand to shield my eyes from the light spilling into the room. Shireen, Moros's servant, stood in the doorway. "It's time, Miss."

CHAPTER TWENTY-FIVE

MAEVYTH

Dusk had fallen, the dark blue sky lit by the many torches that flickered around the entrance of The Eating Woods. Tears slipped down my cheeks as I stood beside Moros, my mind spinning out a desperate plan for my and Aleysia's escape.

Even if we'd be hunted, it was better than what either of us faced otherwise. We could flee to the mountains. As far as Romisir in the north. Anywhere but here. Through a mess of red robes, four village men brought my sister before the archway, and on a breath of pure rage, I looked away from her. Stripped of all her clothes, she stood naked before the parish, her body bruised with beatings, her long blonde locks shorn away.

I wanted to charge forth and save her, but the Vonkovyan soldiers stood between the two of us, and without some sort of weapon, I'd be useless to defend her.

Instead, I kept my gaze turned from her, to collect myself, because it was up to me to figure this out. On the fringes of the crowd, I caught sight of The Crone Witch leaning into her cane, the hood of her cloak pulled up over her head. She tipped her chin up, and I followed the path of her gaze to find the bright, full moon overhead. Full moons on the night of the winter solstice were said to be rare.

An omen. A sign the villagers would see as justification for their cruelty.

I had to think logically. Wise. Haste would doom my sister and me.

"My fellow parishioners," Sacton Crain lifted his hands up. "On this eve of the winter solstice we bear witness to a most egregious crime against our beloved god. This young woman stands accused of fornicating with her uncle and sprouting the seed of this terrible iniquity. For, inside her belly lived the unholy beast, but by the Red God's grace, it has been destroyed!"

It was then I noticed the dried blood at her thighs that, in the dim light, I hadn't noticed before, and tears welled in my eyes as I choked back the urge to cry. Instead, I lifted my gaze to Aleysia, and where the spark of rebellion had once shined, nothing but a dull resignation remained.

No. I would not let them turn her into the monster. Not when I stood amongst so many of them in the crowd. Those who'd committed crimes far worse. Like Moros, and his repulsive collection.

"But she is not alone in this sin," Sacton Crain kept on, inciting a collective gasp from the crowd, and I listened intently to see if he'd dare to accuse Uncle Riftyn. "For the man who planted the seed is as much to blame!"

I scanned over the parishioners to find Agatha, Lolla, and Uncle Riftyn standing at the back. Even in the darkness, I could see Agatha's eyes widen with fear. Uncle Riftyn shook his head, backing up a step, but two brawny parishioners took hold of his arms.

"Tonight, we will bear witness to two banishings!" the governor announced from where he stood alongside Sacton Crain, while the men hauled Uncle Riftyn past me, toward the front of the crowd.

In one hard shove, they threw him to the ground before Aleysia, who stood trembling, undoubtedly chilled to the bone. Uncle Riftyn jumped to his feet and charged back toward the crowd. The Vonkovyan soldiers stepped in front of him, one of them knocking him backward.

"This good community has no tolerance for depravity and sexual perversion. Your bones, flesh, and blood will cleanse us of this offense!" Sacton Crain pointed to both of them, his teeth bared like a rabid dog ready to tear into them.

The soldiers prodded the two of them toward that dreaded archway.

Aleysia screamed, the sound rippling through my muscles like a battle cry.

Do something!

To my left, one of the parishioners stood holding a torch that blazed and wavered against the frigid wind. My mind swirled in chaos, my senses slipping into the depths of rage.

Without a lick of a plan, I reached for her torch, knocking embers onto her dress. She tugged for it, and in the struggle, it slipped just enough to catch on her cloak.

A hand gripped my arm, and I spun around to Moros, holding the flaming torch between us. The hood of my cloak fell back as I swiped out at him, and he jumped back a step. A Vonkovyan soldier took hold of my hood, yanking me backward, and I spun around, the fire catching on the cloth of his tunic.

He let out a cry and released me, frantically patting at the growing flame.

Another soldier lurched, but I swiped the torch at him and backed myself toward Aleysia and Uncle Riftyn.

Bayonet lifted and aimed at me, he prodded forward, and I found myself trapped between the crowd and the archway.

"Witch!" someone from the crowd shouted, and my blood turned to ice.

A hard object struck my hip on a blast of bruising pain, and I looked down to see a rock had been thrown at me. Another struck my arm.

"Witch!" another voice screeched.

Aleysia cried out, and I turned to see one had struck the side of her head, the blood trickling down her temple.

"Witch! Witch! Witch!" The crowd chanted in unison as they lurched forward, The Eating Woods at our backs.

An unbidden memory flashed through my mind out of nowhere. The dream I'd had of Danyra. The symbol on her hand that I saw clearly in my head–*the intersecting lines*.

One parishioner rushed toward the three of us, a pickaxe drawn back.

A rush of heat and adrenaline charged through me. As he neared, I threw out my hand on instinct, and a loud clattering sent me jumping back on a shocked breath. The man with the axe skidded to a halt. On the ground between us lay a pile of off-white and ivory-colored objects stained with rot and decay. Bones. Some splintered. Others were so intact, I could make out a long stretch of vertebrae.

Spine.

Short panting breaths beat out of me. I looked to the bones and up to the man who stared back at me, lip curled in repulsion, as if I were something dead that'd crawled out of a grave. The whole crowd had quieted, and I glanced over them to see their attention riveted on me. Torch still in hand, I waited, every muscle trembling and poised for their next move.

"Witch! Witch! Witch!" The crowd's chanting grew fevered.

"Evil!" Sacton Crain shouted over them. "The girl is an abomination!"

"No." I shook my head, backing farther away.

"Burn her!" someone from the crowd shouted.

"She's a death witch!" another cried out.

"She must be destroyed!" the governor finally shouted, and a roar of assent echoed around me.

"No! Stop this at once!" Moros yelled, pushing his way through the surrounding bodies. "Stop this now!"

The crack of a gun silenced the crowd, and with slow and careful steps, Moros approached me, lowering the gun he'd pointed skyward. He reached out a hand for me. "Come, dear. Do not fear, I will protect you."

"You are disgusting. What you've done to those poor women … is unspeakable evil. And I'd sooner face death than go anywhere with you."

His eye flickered with an unsettling amusement, and I could've only imagined the visuals racing through his mind—my legs sewn together, my skin peeling away as I floated in that tank.

I glanced over my shoulder and whispered to Aleysia, "Run."

My sister spun around on her heel and, to my horror, breached the archway into The Eating Woods.

"Do not follow her, Maevyth," Moros urged, his voice a distant sound to the clamor inside my head. "Do not go into those woods."

Frigid spikes of adrenaline rushed through my veins, and I dropped the torch as I chased after her, with the commotion of angry shouts at my back. A gun fired off behind me, but even if I'd been shot, I'd have refused to pause and look.

Passing over a fallen log, my cloak snagged on a branch. "Aleysia! Wait!" I called out, turning to yank myself free. Once loose, I shot forward after her, her pale form fading in the darkness of the trees. "Aleysia!" Cold air burned my lungs, but I pushed speed from my legs, ignoring the fatigue.

Dark trees loomed overhead, their gnarled branches reaching out for me as I ran deeper into the forest. Splintered branches tore at my calves and ankles, but I ignored them, keeping my eyes on her for as long as she remained in view—until I lost sight of her.

A crackling beneath my boot brought me to a halt, and I paused to catch my breath and bearings. Through a veil of white mist that blanketed the forest floor, I could just make out an object at my feet, the overall shape of it obscured, except for the dark hollow sockets that bled through the fog. A skull. Under the faint scent of pine needles and rich loam festered the sinister stench of rot and decay, the air thick with death's putrid breath. A graveyard of bones.

I snapped my gaze back to the surrounding trees, and fell into a jog, anxious to distance myself from this godless stretch of trees. "Aleysia!"

Something buzzed past my ear, and I swatted my hand, knocking an object bigger than a pesky bug. I slowed my jog to a brisk walk, looking around for it again.

Zzzzz. Zzzzzz.

I swatted again, its shadowy form slipping past me, the size of a sparrow.

A sharp sting struck my leg, and I looked down, lifting the hem of my dress to find some strange creature clung to my shin. Its stick-like body reminded me of a small twig, with translucent wings that fluttered against my skin. I reached down and smacked it away, knocking it backward from my limb, and it hovered in the air a moment, its face horrifically human-like and covered in my blood.

A wicken. My head slipped into stories of the small sprites that were said to attack unwitting foragers who got too close to the woods.

It snarled at me and charged again.

More buzzing alerted me to others. Flailing my hands about, I took off running, choking back a panicked sob as they caught up to me quickly. An eerie tittering at my ear urged me faster. Another sting pinched my arm. Another struck my neck. Teeth sank into my back in two spots.

I ground to a halt, twisting and swatting, to no avail. The wickens surrounded me, chittering and giggling and biting. The sound of tearing fabric drew my attention to one chewing away at my dress, just before its teeth lodged into my flesh.

"Get off me!" My slapping and flailing only seemed to goad them.

A flash of black swished past me.

The chattering sound turned to squealing.

Another flash of black, and I followed the path of it to where it landed on a branch overhead. Raivox sat perched with two of the wickens trapped in its front, clawed talons. Their tiny arms flailed just like mine had moments ago, and they screamed as the raptor lifted them to his salivating maw and tore away their heads, chomping on them like a snack, the bones crackling in the bird's mouth.

The other wickens buzzed off, squealing.

I reached out to Raivox, flicking my fingers. "C'mon, Raivox! Come here!"

He popped the last of the second wicken into his mouth and tipped his head, staring down at me.

"Come, Raivox. Come with me."

Another wicken shot past, and the bird took off after it, leaving me standing there in what I just then realized was a small clearing of the woods. I twisted around, found only a wall of trees everywhere I looked. The forest seemed never ending. A labyrinth of frost and moonlight. I'd lost sight of Aleysia so long ago, I didn't even know where to begin again.

Dizziness swept over me, my vision wide and blurry, and blinking hard, I shook my head. A burning sensation wormed beneath my skin like venomous snakes, and I frantically scratched at my arm where I'd been bitten. "Aleysia!" I called out, clawing at my skin. "Aleysia!" My surroundings bounced in and out of focus, as if something poisonous had worked its way into my blood.

Leaves crackled at my back, and I spun around.

A hand gripped my throat.

Moros stood before me, sharpening and blurring with my faulty vision, but I could see a blazing fury smoldering in his eyes. "Did you think I'd let you escape so freely?" He drew me in. "Tell me, how did you manage that little parlor trick back there, hmmm?"

"Let me go!"

"Let you go? You are mine! You will produce an heir for me, and I will add you to my curious little collection of freaks when I've no longer any use for you!"

"I will never give you an heir!"

A whack across my cheek left a bone-numbing sting, and I shook my head, my vision doubling and slinking back to a single image.

A low growl from my right caught my attention, and both of us turned toward a tall, shadowy figure in the distance, whose form wavered after that smack and whatever dizziness still persisted from earlier. Long, curled horns stuck up from its head, its body crooked where it stood on cloven feet. It reminded me of pictures I'd seen in the dark fairytales my grandfather had some-times read to Aleysia and me about the wrathavor.

Moros's hand fell away from my throat. "What in God's name …" The awe in his voice matched my own.

The figure hobbled closer, and while I couldn't summon a single muscle movement in my body, Moros turned to run in the opposite direction. The creature dropped to all fours and chased after him, swiping him up by his throat only a few yards from where I stood, paralyzed.

Was this the creature that hunted the woods? The one that stripped bodies of skin and devoured them? The one The Crone Witch had seen as a young girl?

Dangling in the air, Moros kicked his feet, while the beast sniffed him.

I quietly backed myself away, small steps at a time, so as to not rouse its attention.

With a grotesquely mutilated hand, the fingers of which reminded me of small branches, the creature reached into Moros's pocket and tore out the vial that held the white stone he'd given to the captain. As if mesmerized, its eyes widened, and it dropped Moros, who rolled and coughed on the ground. After popping the vial open, the creature dumped one of the stones into his palm and sniffed it again.

I'd finally hidden myself behind the twisted trunk of a thick tree, and something covered my mouth. A scream ripped through my throat, muffled by my captor's hand.

"Shhhh," Uncle Riftyn said, and I turned to see his eyes fixed on the creature that paused to scan the surroundings before setting its attention back on the stone in its palm.

"Where's Aleysia?" I whispered.

"I don't know."

The creature tossed the stone into its mouth, gulping it down, and let out a gravely moan that echoed through the woods. It tapped the vial against its palm, clearly wanting more.

Still on the ground, Moros stared up at it. "I … I know where to find more of it. I-i-if you want more … I can get it for you."

The creature tipped its head, as if it understood him.

"There's an entire chasm just outside of Sawtooth Mountain. I can take you there."

My heart hammered inside my chest, as I watched the creature hobble closer to Moros. Seconds ticked off in my head, wondering if it'd strip him of flesh. Instead, it opened its mouth. Wide. Wider—expanding its jaw to a cavern of sharp teeth, so impossibly stretched, it appeared unhinged. In one swift move, it clamped its mouth over Moros's head, while the man screamed and clawed at it.

It took both hands over my mouth to contain the scream that fought to tear out of me, while I watched the creature devour Moros whole.

"We have to go," Uncle Riftyn whispered, still standing behind me. "We have to get out of here. Now!"

As he tugged at my shoulders, I watched the last of Moros disappear inside the beast's mouth. Then, as it stood upright, swallowing the last of him, its form changed, its skin and bones shifting like marbles in a satchel. Until, at last, by some twisted evil, it had taken the appearance of Moros.

It held its hands up, as if marveling their human form, and it turned its head in our direction. It was Moros, but with grotesquely loose skin and protruding bones that looked like they hadn't quite settled beneath.

Black, beady eyes scanned over the forest, and I twisted around, chasing after Uncle Riftyn, who already had a good start ahead of me. Over snapping branches and twigs, and the crush of bones, I raced through the dark woods, goaded by the snarls that trailed after me. I leapt over a fallen log, and toppled to the ground, when something caught me from behind. I twisted to see my cloak snagged again. Tugging at the fabric, I tore it from the branch and felt arms hook beneath mine. Uncle Riftyn stood over me, lifting me to my feet.

As I turned to push on, a large palm gripped the top of his head and yanked him back.

"No!" I screamed, reaching out for Uncle Riftyn, as his body shot backward.

The creature held him by his skull, while Uncle Riftyn's legs dangled helplessly, and he let out a gut-wrenching scream.

In the next breath, the horrific deformity curled his fingers into Uncle Riftyn's cheek and tore his skin away on a wet meat sound that echoed inside my head. Uncle Riftyn's flayed skin dangled from the creature's fingers, his body convulsing as his exposed muscle and tendons glistened in the moonlight.

An insidious fear crawled down my spine, strangling my breath. My head couldn't process what I was seeing.

Run! Just like in nightmares, my legs wouldn't move at my

command, at first. Until, like trudging through quicksand, I turned to run, delirious with shock.

Instinct took over, the adrenaline commandeering my muscles, and I didn't look back. I ran until the air burned in my lungs. Until my legs flamed with fatigue. Until the trees blurred and my skin flushed and I stumbled in my steps. I ran until the prickles of a dead bramble bush prodded me out of my stupor, and I skidded to a halt in the thick of a thorny wall.

A pale blue light beamed from a clearing on the other side of it, and I stepped through, hypnotized by the soft glow behind a bony archway that appeared similar to the one I'd stepped through upon entering The Eating Woods. Thorns scratched at my skin with every step, until they cleared for a stony pathway.

Fireflies danced about the archway, the sight so beautiful after all the macabre I'd seen. Maybe Moros had caught up to me, after all, and this was the afterlife. As one of the fireflies neared, I raised my palm, letting it land there. On close examination, its tiny face appeared almost human-like, reminding me of the wickens, but not as malicious. It almost seemed docile with wide black eyes which tapered down to a small mouth—one that seemed to smile back at me—and instead of bristled legs, there were hands and feet with bitsy little fingers and toes. I studied its thorax, entirely translucent as if made of glass, with a magical blue light that pulsed slowly.

The sound of whimpers pulled my attention toward the edge of the thorn wall, where Aleysia sat crouched, bleeding and shivering.

"Aleysia!" I snapped out of my wonderment and abandoned the firefly for her.

One touch of her skin told me she was dangerously cold, and I yanked off my cloak to cover her.

Small teeth marks covered her body, not unlike the one at my shin, as if she'd encountered a swarm of wickens. "D-D-Did you … s-s-s-s-eeee it?"

"Yes. C'mon. Let's get out of here." It made no sense that she'd be so close to freedom, yet crouched there.

"I ... I couldn't leave you," she said, tears filling her eyes. "I wanted to run through, but I couldn't bear the thought that you were trapped with the monster."

"I'm here, Aleysia. Let's go. Let's run and never return to Foxglove."

With a nod, she pushed to her feet, and I wrapped my arms around her, guiding her toward the archway. A shimmering wall flickered as we approached, like a liquid mirror, reflecting our image so I couldn't see what was on the other side of it. I released her, padding carefully ahead of her.

Tiny silver sachets hung from the top of the archway, and I reached for one. An overwhelming warmth settled over me, followed by a wonderful, earthy scent so strong, it brought tears to my eyes. "It ... it smells like petrichor," I whispered. The inexplicable urge to pass through pulled at me, beckoning me beyond the archway. With an uncertain glance over my shoulder toward Aleysia, I drew in a deep breath and pushed my hand through the strange barrier, the prickly sensation scaring me into retracting my shaking limb.

Holding my cloak tight around her, Aleysia trembled, watching me.

A quick examination showed no damage to my hand, and I pushed it through again, pulling it back out with no resistance. I reached to push through again, and she gripped my arm.

"Wait!" The fear in her eyes darkened. "W-w-what if ... s-s-s-something bad is on the ... other s-s-s-side?" she asked.

"What if freedom lies on the other side, Aleysia? I'll go first. You follow, okay?"

She gave a tearful nod. "Okay."

"Promise me you'll follow."

"I promise."

I turned around and, in the reflection, caught sight of Moros standing in the thorn bushes behind us. Panic exploded inside of me. "C'mon!" Without hesitation, I jumped through the barrier to the other side, where I was greeted by what looked like the same forest. Only, when I twisted around, instead of a reflection, I could see Aleysia standing on the other side. I thrust out my hand to reach for her, and a hard surface smashed against my knuckles. The liquid barrier had hardened to an impenetrable wall.

"No. No!" I slammed my hands against the translucent surface. "Aleysia! Aleysia!"

Her lips trembled as she edged closer to the archway, but in the distance, the ruined version of Moros strode toward her.

"Aleysia! He's behind you! Aleysia!" I slammed on the clear surface again, desperate to break through, but it was as though she couldn't hear or see me. "Aleysia! Aleysia!"

"Turn around! Now!" a foreign voice shouted from behind, but I ignored it, watching Aleysia reach out for me.

"Come on, step through! He's coming!"

An arm banded around her throat, dragging her backward.

"No! Aleysia! No!"

At the same time, arms wrapped around my waist and neck, dragging me away from the archway.

I kicked and wriggled, fighting to get away, not yet having seen my captors.

A blast of light flickered around me, and a paralyzing rigidity gripped my muscles. The branches of trees slipped past my view, as I seemed to rise up into the air. Every muscle trembled, tight and burning, as if a bolt of lightning ran through me, locking up my limbs, my jaw. I could hardly draw in a breath as my body spun around, and I found myself facing a dark-haired man on horseback, decked out in steel and leather, his hand outstretched toward me.

Three other men stood on foot alongside him.

"What is that smell?" the blond, dressed in the same garb as Dark-Hair, asked. "I want to eat the fucking air, it's delicious."

"Is she mortal?" one with red, curly hair asked, and the man whose hand twisted slightly, turning me to the side, answered, "Yes."

Panic shook me, as I couldn't see Aleysia from this new angle, and my muscles refused to obey the command to turn around.

"Balls of Castero! A mortal! Has a mortal ever crossed over?" The blond stared up at me in awe.

"Not to my knowledge." The dark-haired one, who held me in some invisible grasp, tipped his head in curiosity. What I surmised to be guards, given that they all wore the same shiny metal and leather, with the same strange emblem, stared back at me, as I floated above them, completely helpless.

Let me go! my head screamed, but I couldn't summon a single word.

"How the fuck does she speak Nyxterosi if she's mortal, genius?" Redhead asked.

"Don't know. But Captain says that smell is distinct for mortals. That's how they lure ya." Eyes closed, the blond flared his nostrils with a deep breath. "I wonder what her cunt smells like?"

"Go on, then, taste it, if you're so curious," Red challenged, and I urged my muscles to wriggle free from whatever it was that held me. "My great-grandfather said they carry the nastiest blood diseases. Lost two of his brothers when they crossed the vale once. Came back sick as dogs. I heard, if they bite you, you can pretty much kiss your ass goodbye."

"That's a load of crap," the blond argued. "No one has ever crossed to the mortal lands. Your grandfather is a liar."

"He did! I swear it!"

"What do we do with her?" The blond licked his lips, and I didn't want to imagine the revolting thoughts running through his head right then. "You can't take her back to the castle dungeon. You'd be inviting a scourge, and the king would have your head. She smells so fucking delicious, though, I could piss myself. Like oranges, or something."

"No. We can't take her to the castle dungeons," Dark-Hair agreed. "The king would insist on her immediate execution, anyway. Seems a damn shame to waste such a monumental event as a mortal crossing over. I'm curious to see how they work."

One of the guards didn't speak, at all, but merely watched me in silence.

Aleysia. I had to focus on Aleysia. *Can you see her?* my head was desperate to ask the guards. *Is she alive?*

"What do you mean, how they *work*?"

The men prattled on, my impatience growing thinner by the second.

A toxic mixture of rage and terror clogged my throat, and I was on the verge of breaking, but only the silence persisted.

"I've never seen a mortal's cunt before, have you?" Dark-Hair asked over his shoulder toward the other men.

"No. Can't be any different than our women, eh?"

"Oh, I think you're wrong." The guard grabbed a stick from the ground and hooked it on the hem of my dress. "I heard their cunts have teeth. Bite your cock clean off." He lifted my skirt to my thigh, sparing me a wicked grin, then lifted it higher. "Does your cunt have teeth, pretty?"

My scream arrived as a muffled hum in my chest, unable to break past my clenched jaw.

All eyes remained rapt on my naked flesh beneath, but before he could expose my privates, the stick was somehow knocked out of his hands, though none of the other three were close enough to have touched it.

"Enough. Perhaps send her back through. No one has to know." It was the man who hadn't said a word up until then who'd spoken that time.

"You ever interrupt me again, I'll take your head clean off,"

Dark-Hair warned, snarling back at him. "She isn't going back through. The vale won't allow it."

"Then, offer her a mercy kill."

"I say we take her to Bonesguard and give her to the poor bastards due to be hanged." A wicked grin stretched across the redhead's lips. "They won't care about diseases, and we'll get a nice little show. From afar, of course."

Dark-Hair smirked and twisted his hand again, giving them a view of my backside. "I think that's a brilliant idea. She looks like a feisty one. Might put up a good fight."

Eyes straining, I peered out the corner for a single glimpse of the archway, still too far out of view.

He twisted me back around and dropped me just far and fast enough that my dress flew up, giving them a flash of my under-garments. "Ah, shame. Thought she'd be naked beneath."

The fourth guard turned silent again. With as much as I could muster, I focused my attention on him, my eyes pleading, begging him to speak up and let me go.

Warm fluids leaked down my leg, and tears filled my eyes.

"She fucking pissed herself!" One of them sneered, but I didn't care. The only thing that mattered to me was Aleysia.

My sister.

Who was probably dead.

CHAPTER TWENTY-SIX

ZEVANDER

A knock sounded at the door to Zevander's office, before Ravezio peered in. "You have company," he said. The fellow Letalisz stepped inside. The leather vest he wore, sans a tunic beneath, revealed his sigil that was inked in gold down his shoulder and bicep–the coiled body of a golden basilisk.

"Who is it?"

"A royal guard from the looks of it. Found him pacing outside the gates. Lucky for that ward, or I suspect the fyredrakes would've made a tasty meal of him."

Zevander frowned and pushed to his feet, following after Ravezio to the grand foyer, where a familiar face glanced around.

The guard at Hagsmist who he'd cursed with the scorpion. There was only one reason he'd have sought him out. "Someone crossed. A mortal, My Lord." Fear and urgency clung to his shaky voice.

"A mortal," Zevander echoed. "When?"

"This eve."

"Taken to the king's dungeons, I presume?"

"Bonesguard."

"Bonesguard?" Zevander frowned at that. Set apart from the main castle, Bonesguard Keep stood on the southern grounds of Costelwick, an impressive tower that hadn't been used for defense in centuries. Not since the Brumanox Solstice siege, during the coldest winter ever recorded in Aethyria. The Keep had remained empty of royalty since then, its dungeons mostly used to house the most violent of criminals, who weren't held for very long. Zevander knew firsthand of those cold, dank cells–he and his father had been guests there before Zevander had been sent off to work the mines in Solassia.

"Yes. Sometimes, female prisoners are … taken there." Brow furrowed, the guard looked away. "I have nothing to do with that. But they … the other guards … they find it entertaining to watch the lady prisoners with the more … violent criminals."

Zevander narrowed his eyes on the guard. "Are you telling me the mortal that crossed is a woman?"

"Well, yes."

"Describe her."

"Um. Long, black hair. Very slim. Petite. She smelled of oranges."

The mere description of that scent had his mouth watering again. "Any notable features?"

"Her eye … it was …. Well, it had a strange, silver marking."

Zevander growled. "Looks like I'll be heading to Bonesguard."

"Shall I accompany you?" Ravezio asked from where he leaned against the staircase, polishing his dagger. "You know how much I *adore* men in uniform." His eyes fell on the guard, who shifted on his feet, obviously uncomfortable in the presence of the Letalisz.

With his scaled, Eremician skin, mostly unnoticeable unless touched, Ravezio had suffered the most at the hands of the guards during imprisonment, as they'd sometimes enjoyed the torture of tearing away the scales on his body. Eremicians, in general, were looked down upon, particularly by the royal elite–

all deemed thieves and miscreants in the eyes of the king. But as an Eremician prisoner, Ravezio had been seen as nothing more than a caged animal to be poked and prodded.

"No. I'll do this alone. Keep an eye on this one for a moment, will you?"

"Of course." Ravezio's lips stretched to a grin, as he held the blade up, letting the light catch on the steel.

The guard's throat bobbed with a swallow. "Will you be long, Sir? I didn't announce that I'd left Costelwick."

"No. Not long." Zevander strode from the grand hall and down a corridor, to a stone anteroom that housed a steel door. He pushed through to a narrow, stone stairwell that curved with his descent toward the castle's crypts.

Centuries of family remains had been memorialized into stone statues, and as he passed his mother's he offered the sign of the gods, as was the respectable thing to do.

Beyond the memorials stood the dungeons, and Zevander stopped on reaching the cell that housed Dolion. Though the mage had been imprisoned, Zevander had made every effort to keep him comfortable, with fine silk and a plush feather bed. A tankard of ale sat out on the cell floor, along with a half-eaten grimshank pie and a loaf of bread.

"I must say, being your prisoner is not entirely a punishment," Dolion said, looking up from one of the scrolls he sat reading by firelamp.

"The girl crossed," Zevander said, ignoring his comment. "She's here, in Aethyria."

Frowning, he sat forward and twisted around in his chair. "She crossed? The mortal?"

"Yes. How is this possible? It was my understanding the Umbravale was designed to keep mortals out."

"Yes. However, this proves she is a descendant of the seven bloodlines. Only they would be permitted to cross so easily. Where is she now?"

"She was seized by The Imperial Guards."

"Oh, gods." He sank back in his chair and huffed. "The king will execute her. A mortal in Aethyria? Can you imagine the uproar?"

"She wasn't taken to the royal dungeons. She was taken to Bonesguard."

"*Bonesguard?*" Brows folded in confusion, he shook his head. "Whatever for?"

"I suspect the guards intend to dispose of her themselves. The question is, do we let them?" It would have been a shame, but Zevander didn't care to entangle himself with her if they weren't going to turn her blood to stone.

"*Let* them? Are you mad? Of course we don't let them! She is the last of her kind!"

"And she is a threat while living. Bringing her to Eidolon will only draw the magehood, and should they seek you out here, they will not only have you, but the final bloodline for the septomir." Zevander didn't bother to mention the fact that she'd seemed completely resistant to his power, somehow. That alone made her a threat to him.

"It is as I said, Zevander. She must be protected at all costs. If she should perish, we lose not just a bloodline but an entire ethnicity."

"I did not ask to take on a ward."

"Then you will be complicit in mortalicide."

The Letalisz ran his tongue across his back teeth. "You have a funny way with words, old man. I want proof that she is who you say."

"There is only one way to prove–"

Zevander held up the small sampling of blood he'd collected from the mortal world.

"How did you come about this?"

"It was all over the archway in the woods. It led me to her."

"Very well. Very well." He slid his magnifying lens over his eye and examined the small stone. "Far too small for the septomir, of course. But it might be enough to reveal her aura." He scrambled for his bag, rifling inside one-handedly before setting a crucible on his desk. "I'll need some supplies for the long term. A viewing scope and some potions."

"And where am I supposed to find these supplies?" Zevander asked, watching him place the small blood stone into the crucible.

"My old lab in The Citadel."

"Does the magehood not monitor your old lab?"

"They'd have already raided it and stolen anything of worth. I suspect the only items left behind will be my viewing scopes and what they'd consider useless potions that they could procure themselves." Nabbing one of the many colorful vials standing in a holder, he poured a purple fluid over the stone, and it sizzled on contact. Black smoke rose up from the crucible, and when the sizzling settled, only the silver from the blood stone remained. The smoke weaved itself together in the air, then fell into the crucible, somehow dragging the bits of metal around the surface, until it formed a shape that looked like a glyph. A sharp hook symbol, like a scythe, the blade of it serving as the bony upper ridge of what appeared to be a bird's eye. "The death glyph. The Corvikae worshipped the death goddess."

"That does not mean she possesses any great power."

"Bring her here. We'll see if she carries the sigil on her flesh. In the meantime, I promise you I am working on another means to temper your curse. Do me this favor, and I will put forth every effort to rid you of this insufferable sablefyre."

"If you don't, I will put forth every effort to see that you suffer for eternity."

CHAPTER TWENTY-SEVEN

MAEVYTH

A hard shove from behind sent me flying forward into a dark cell. Fire streaked across my knees and palms as the gravelly floor bit into my skin. I turned just as the iron door swung shut, and my captor peered in through a small hole carved into it.

Scrambling to my feet, I charged toward the door, slamming into the unyielding surface. "Let me out! Please! Let me out!"

"You aren't going anywhere, sweet girl," the dark-haired guard taunted.

"My sister ... she's .... I need to help her!"

"I'd say your sister's better off than you, at this point." He let out a cruel chuckle that goaded my anger.

Teeth grinding, I slammed my fist into the door, and a bright light flashed in my face on a blast of heat that shot me flying backward. Pain struck my spine as I crashed into the dirt floor, the air firing out of my lungs on impact. Every muscle trembled with whatever current ran through me. As it slowly subsided, I rolled to the side, groaning.

The guard chuckled again. "Smells like roasted oranges."

"What do you say? High moon?" the blond guard asked beside him.

"Yeah. Evening guard will take over, and we'll meet back here. Tell Ruvym and Stolyus."

I focused on breathing, as they prattled on about something sinister-sounding they had in mind.

"Stolyus?" The other guard groaned. "Bastard's about as fun as a dried up barnacle. I don't trust him. I think he'd rat us out, first chance he got."

"Give him a bit of baneberry, and he'll dive headfirst off Dandymir tower, if we tell him to."

Both guards chuckled.

"What I wouldn't give to see that," said the one whose voice I'd come to recognize as the blond. "The shady cunt has been acting weird lately. Always scratching at that arm."

"Probably has muripox. Maybe we throw him in with her."

Both guards laughed again, and I pushed to a sitting position, drawing in a deep breath.

"Go on now. I don't know how much longer I can stand this. My cock feels like it's about to break from its breeches. I'm dying to watch." Dark-Hair's words confirmed what I'd already dreaded.

At the sound of their retreating footsteps, I glanced around the cell. Only the flickering of the torch outside the door streamed in through that small window, provided a dim light. My muscles ached as, throat dry, I patted around on hands and knees, searching for a weapon, or, by some miracle, means of escape.

A wire of tension stiffened my limbs, my body growing weary from the stress of the evening. First, Aleysia's banishment, running through the woods from whatever creature inhabited it. Now *this*.

Aleysia. I hadn't even had time to mentally process the events from earlier. The very real possibility that Moros had slaughtered her.

Leave it, my brain urged. I couldn't afford the preoccupation right then. I had to secure a way out of the cell before they returned.

Then I'd find my way back to the woods. Back to her.

Even if it meant returning to nothing. I had to know if she was dead, or alive.

It was the unknown which clawed at me, perhaps worse than having seen Moros, or whatever he'd become, haul her off, because at least then, however devastating as that would be, I could've let go. I might not have cared what lay in store for me with these men, at that point, because without my sister, nothing mattered to me.

I hadn't seen her die, though.

And because of that, however small, there remained a sliver of hope. A reason.

The will to fight.

In the shadowed corner of the cell, I reached out and fingered a hard, stony object. Smiling, I took hold of it and scrambled back into the light to see what kind of weapon it'd make, but with it illuminated, I frowned on staring down at the strange, black object clutched in my palm.

Out of the top of it, two long, bristle-like structures unfurled, followed by dozens of hair-like fibers that tickled my skin. And pincers. Pincers that plucked at the fine layer of skin on my finger with the promise of a sharp bite.

I let out a piercing scream and dropped the object onto the floor, where it exploded into hundreds of small black bugs that scampered across the surface.

I shot to my feet and backed myself to the wall. At a tickle on my shin, I lifted my skirt just enough to see two crawling up my leg. A needling pain pierced my skin.

Screaming again, I kicked out, sending them flying, and stomped on the dozens more heading toward me. Crunchy carapaces crackled beneath my boots, the spray of guts wetting my exposed skin.

A much bigger bug skittered in my direction, snapping its pincers at me. A panicked gasp hitched my breath, and I stomped on it. Bright yellow guts shot up onto my skirt, oozing down the fabric.

A long hiss echoed through the cell, and all the tiny versions of the bug skittered toward the bigger one, as if sucked into it. Their shiny black shells crumpled into a pile of black ooze.

Blowing out a hard and shaky breath, I stared down at it all.

A tickling sensation at my arm threw me into another frenzy, as I yanked back the sleeve to find nothing there but a stray hair. Shivering, I slapped my hands over my arms and legs, completely rattled and shaken.

From the shadows, two more large bugs stepped into the light. One black like the other. The second, red with black markings.

"Oh, my god. Please."

The clanking of metal snapped my attention toward the door, where the dark-haired guard from before could be seen through the window.

"Ferrys gets first. He's due at the gallows first dawn," he said, my heart hammering at the click of the lock.

The bugs slinked back into the shadows as the light from the doorway spread over the dark cell, and two guards stepped inside. The third stood at the doorway.

"Jevhyr is after, then we set her loose in the pit."

I had no idea what the pit was, but the tone of his voice when he said it carried a harrowing edge of amusement.

A fourth guard stumbled alongside them, the one I recognized from the forest, who'd seemed against their ideas.

"Ah! Looks like someone changed his mind, after all." The redheaded guard patted him on the shoulder.

The quiet guard chuckled nervously. "Why should you cunts

249

get all the fun?" He cleared his throat and scratched at his arm, which appeared red and entirely inflamed.

Even if he might've once expressed opposition, there seemed to no longer be a chance to sway him. "Please," I begged. "Please help me out of here."

The guard cleared his throat again, turning his cheek as if refusing to look at me, and what little hope I had shriveled. "Quiet yourself. Mortal whore."

The men broke out in laughter. "Someone get Stolyus some baneberry! He'll go after Ferrys!"

"The hell I will," Stolyus countered. "She's …. She's a disgusting mortal! I'd rather watch."

One of the men chuckled, knocking him on the back as he handed him a bottle of what I presumed to be the liquor. "Well, let's get it on, then! No more dawdling about."

A man in tattered clothing was shoved into the room, his hair disheveled, eyes wild as they set on me. Markings and scars covered his skin, and on his wrists were copper-colored shackles. The guards unlocked the chain between them, but kept the shackles in place.

"No worries, he won't be using any magic," Dark-Hair said, as if that were the bulk of my concerns right then.

"For fuck sakes, at least arm the poor bastard. That cunt of hers might not let go!" One of the guards shoved a holstered blade into the disheveled man's pocket, and it was then I realized just how much of a threat they perceived me to be.

As the prisoner drew near, I backed myself to the wall. I'd be no match against whatever magic the guards had wielded back at those woods, but I'd be damned if I'd let any of the bastards get the best of me then. At his hip, I caught the glint of that knife, and he paused his approach, glancing down toward it and back to me, wearing a wicked grin.

"You like that blade, little one?" He removed it from the

holster, slowly drawing it out, and held it out to me, clutching the sharp end in his palm.

"'The fuck are you doing, man? You want to die! She's mortal!"

"Which means she's weak," the prisoner said over his shoulder, never taking those predatory eyes off me.

"Oh, this is going to be good." Redhead rubbed his hands together and shifted on his feet.

Body trembling, I looked down to the proffered weapon and back to the prisoner. In one quick lurch, I swiped it out of his hands, holding it out in front of me.

The sound of Red's chuckle was drowned by the other guards' boisterous laughter.

"Look at you tremble like a petal in the breeze. You think you can fight me, flower? No magic. Just fist to blade."

"I'd bet three quints she'd give you a run for it," the blond said behind Red.

"Three quints ..." Red snorted and glanced back. "Can't even buy a tankard of mors mead with that!"

"Mors mead? Only faeblood drink mors mead."

Eyes shifting between the two guards and the prisoner who circled me, I waited to see if they'd fight. Fighting would've offered a distraction. A distraction meant escape.

"Calling me faeblood now, are you?" The guard pushed the other in the chest, the clang of his steel breastplate echoing through the room.

The second guard socked his elbow into the first guard's nose, knocking him back against the wall.

As the man before me glanced back at them, I swung out, the blade slicing across his arm. I slipped past him and spun around, putting myself between him and the guards at the door.

"Fucking hells!" He growled, examining the wound. "Oh, you will pay for that, flower. Of all the foolish things!" Snarling, he lurched toward me, and I swiped out at him with the knife again.

He lost his footing and tumbled backward onto his butt in a clang of metal when the shackles hit the concrete.

"My blood? It's tainted all right. Nearly lost my eyesight from the sickness." I poked the tip of the blade into my finger, wincing at the slight sting there, and jabbed the knife toward him.

Eyes wide, he scrambled backward, and his body broke into tremors, his brow glistening with sweat.

Afraid? Of me?

A wild surge of victory swam through me, and I edged closer, jabbing the knife again. "C'mon, you boorish pig!" I shouted, taunting him like a madwoman, but I didn't care. I refused to be violated by the grotesque swine. "The germs in my blood will eat you alive!"

I was exhausted and furious.

And I still had the guards to contend with.

It was then it struck me. I hadn't heard the guards make a sound.

The prisoner's lips curved to a whimper as he raised his hands up in surrender. I slowly trailed my gaze to the stony wall at his back, where the flickering torches from the hallway showed my silhouette slowly getting swallowed by a monstrous shadow that blocked out the light.

A flash of black streaked over top of me on a quiet whoosh, and I watched in horror as an enormous silver object stabbed through the man's chest.

The prisoner's legs trembled, mouth fully agape, his arms outstretched, as if stunned by the strike. When the steel object recoiled, spilling blood and bits of organs onto the floor, I opened my mouth to scream, but could summon nothing more than fast, shaky breaths that sent puffs of cold air from my mouth.

Muscles board-stiff, I willed myself to look behind me, dizzy from panting. When I turned around, an impossibly giant scorpion stood in the doorway, its stinger stuck upright, hovering over top of me, pincers at the ready, big enough to lop off my head in one snap.

My body fell into hysterics, and I couldn't move. Couldn't breathe. Could only stare at the creature in mute horror.

Droplets fell onto my face, and choking for a breath of air, I lowered my gaze to blood spilling onto my open palms.

"Oh, god," I whispered. "Oh, miserable, wretched god, make it quick and painless."

The tick of insectile claws against the ground snapped my attention back to the terrifying creature stepping over the two guards lying disemboweled at either side of it.

A blackness settled over me.

And all went blissfully silent.

CHAPTER TWENTY-EIGHT

MAEVYTH

An earthy-root and leather scent invaded my nose, tugging me out of a black void. Something moved between my thighs in a steady cadence. Wet. Like something splashing water. *S-clop, s-clop, s-clop.*

A thick fog clung to my brain, and I could neither make sense of the sound, nor the sensation. I opened my eyes to … hair. Black hair. Draped across a wide, muscled black neck.

My mind puzzled the view and the sound. A horse.

A horse?

I lifted my head and double-blinked, the fog thinning as I took in the sight of jet-black ears, a flash of metal, and a set of reins.

What is this?

Images snapped through my mind in frustrating piecemeal.

Woods. A cell. An emblem. Bugs.

Scorpion.

Gasping, I jerked back into a hard surface, and something banded around my stomach. I kicked my legs, clawing at the limb restraining me. The scorpion?

No, that didn't make sense.

"Let me go! Let me go!"

"Still yourself, unless you'd like to be thrown into the black bog." The voice, deep and threatening, sent a shiver down the back of my neck.

I scanned over the surrounding shadowy landscape. Even in darkness, I could make out spikes of rotted trees sticking up from the mist-covered ground ahead, and walls of rock on either side that, when I tipped my head back, disappeared into the night sky overhead. Two moons shined against a star-speckled sky, offering an illuminated path through what appeared to be a wide gorge.

A void separated me from the last thing I remembered. What had happened between the scorpion attack and now?

"Who are you?" I asked. "What is this place?"

No response.

"Th-th-there was a scorpion. A big ... scorpion." I hated the way it sounded so ridiculous and unlikely in my head. Spoken in a weak voice, dry from thirst.

Still, he said nothing.

"I have to go back. My sister ... she's in trouble."

"She followed you into the woods?" he finally asked, and I focused on the voice, not recognizing it from any of the guards I'd encountered. It carried an ominous tone, every word like a warning spilling from his lips.

"Yes."

"She crossed through the archway?"

"No."

"Then, she's dead." Not a speck of emotion, or empathy, in his voice.

"She is not ... dead." In spite of the tears in my eyes, I choked back the urge to break. Not yet. I refused to break until I knew for certain what had happened to her. "Take me back."

Silence.

"I am asking you to take me back. I will return to where I

came from. I won't say a word. About this place. Or you. Just take me back."

Still nothing.

He tugged on the reins, bringing the horse to a stop and my attention zeroing in on the scorpion inked on the back of his hand.

"You can leave me here, and I'll …" The very thought of trudging back, of moving any part of my body that had become so laden with exhaustion, I could hardly keep my head upright, made me want to cry, but still, I said, "I can walk–" My words were cut short by the slap of his gloved hand over my mouth.

I clawed at the barrier, an angry retort pounding across my tongue.

From the quiet rose a squelching sound.

Through the darkness, I searched for the source, and found it crouched by a fallen log. A beast, the size of a fox, that reminded me of an oversized toad, with its stout, squatty body, big bulging eyes and flat snout. Long branching horns stuck out of its head, and when it lifted its nose up into the air, sniffing, I caught sight of fangs hanging down from its wide, upper jaw.

"It smells you," my captor said, and I noticed the creature's eyes were milky white, perhaps blind, the way it seemed to search the air with its flat nose. "Mortals make delicious little snacks. Much more exciting than its usual fare of snakes and swamp spiders."

"S-s-snakes and swamp spiders?" I trailed my gaze over the glassy, black surface of the water below me.

"They're all over this bog. Still up for a walk back to the woods?"

Before I could answer, the beast ahead let out a roar and opened its maw to show hundreds more teeth. It sniffed again, and lurched closer.

Closer.

"Shouldn't we be on our way?"

"Those things can outrun any horse. Their eyes aren't so keen, but their nose is spot on. And if they catch you? Well, imagine those teeth tearing across your delicate mortal skin?"

"So, what do we do?"

"I'm puzzling that very question as we speak."

I didn't dare turn to look at him. His voice was threatening enough, without needing a glimpse of his face. "Well, can you puzzle faster? It seems rather interested."

"Oh, to be sure. We don't get many mortals on this side. What luck that it stumbled upon you."

He shifted at my back, and I twisted just enough to see my captor slide from the saddle, his boots making only a minor splash as he landed in the water.

"What are you doing?" I whispered. As much as I didn't want anything to do with him, I also didn't want to be abandoned by him, either.

"Stay quiet." His voice held a strange, level tone that didn't match the frantic thrumming of my heart just then.

"How can you be so calm right now?"

"I'm not the one he wants to eat."

The hood of the cloak he wore covered his face, making him appear more shadow than a man, but I caught a flicker of black and metal at his mouth, as though covered by a mask. Before I could examine him too thoroughly, the beast roared again. I snapped my attention that way and nearly choked on the panic shooting up into my throat, as it lowered its maw and charged toward us.

The horse didn't rear up. Didn't whinny, or shift on its feet. It remained still, as if unmoved by the creature. I turned to find my captor had disappeared. Vanished, as if into thin air.

"What? Where'd … oh … dammit!" I kicked the horse's flank, hoping to stir it into motion, but the unflappable creature didn't move. "Move! Damnable beast! Gallop on!" Another kick, and the horse let out a deep, guttural growl.

A growl?

I'd never heard a horse growl in my life.

The toady beast splashed toward us, and my muscles locked up. I let out a scream as it leapt into the air for me.

A black object speared it mid-flight, plowing down through its head and out of its chest so fast, the beast still hovered in the air. The infernal toad cantered forward, sliding toward the water to reveal a shiny black blade that had impaled it, before it splashed into the bog beside the horse.

From a black curling smoke, my captor appeared, his gloved hand gripping the hilt of said sword.

Before I could process what had just happened, the horse bent forward and tore away a bite of the dead creature's flesh, chewing on it like it'd just innocently stuffed its head into a bucket of carrots.

Mouth hanging open, I silently sat, certain I must've been dreaming. Or worse.

Perhaps I'd died back in those woods. Maybe Moros had captured me, and this was some sort of strange purgatory.

My captor wiped his sword onto a white kerchief, leaving a green ooze across the fabric. "Well, you're free to go, if you'd like."

I was about to tell him he was free to go to hell, but he lifted his head, and I caught sight of his face for the first time. Moonlight struck him just enough that I could make out the features otherwise hidden by the hood of his cloak. A black mask with metallic embellishments covered the lower half of his face, but even with his disguise, I recognized him. I'd seen those unusual eyes before, in what had seemed like a dream. The burnt orange and bright gold that surrounded his pupil, like an explosion of light, nearly glowing from the depths of his hood.

"You," I whispered. "You …. I've seen you. You were in my room."

He didn't say anything as he shoved his sword into some unseen sheath at his back.

"I thought I'd imagined you, but … it's you! Why?"

Still not answering, he gathered the reins, and it was as he stood alongside the horse that I took in the size of him. Close to seven feet tall, by my estimates.

"I'll give you one of two choices. Get off this horse and find your own way back to the woods. Or stay quiet and don't ask another question."

"Can I at least ask your name? So that I'm not mentally calling you angry eyes?"

A sound of disapproval followed. "Zevander."

"Zevander," I echoed. "I'm Maevyth."

"I didn't ask." He waited a moment longer, and when I didn't move, he turned away and gave a slight tug of the reins, guiding the horse forward, on through the bog.

* * *

"I don't suppose you drink water here?" I dared to ask, after we'd gotten through that awful bog and he stopped to dry off his boots on a cushy, mushroomy object, just off the stone path.

He let out a huff and reached into a satchel behind me, pulling out the most elaborate-looking canteen I'd ever seen. What looked like moon phases, etched into the metal, loomed over the silhouette of a castle. Its back bore an inscription: *May you never go thirsty. Love, Rykaia.*

I didn't bother to ask who that was, figuring he wouldn't have told me, anyway. A lover, I guessed. Instead, I popped the cap open. Tipping it back sent a rush of cool fluids down my throat, practically sizzling as I gulped them back. Sweet mercy, had I ever tasted water so delicious? Unlike the well water back at the

KERI LAKE

cottage, which'd often had an eggy sulfur smell, this was clean and crystal-like. Ice cold, as if it'd sat out in the winter snow.

Once satisfied, I wiped my face with the back of my wrist and returned the canteen to him. He didn't bother to take a drink before tucking it back into the satchel. Pity. I'd hoped he'd remove that terrifying mask at some point, so I could catch a glimpse of more than just his eyes.

"What is this place?"

At first, he didn't answer, and I resigned myself to not knowing, because my guess was, the man couldn't be swayed.

"Aethyria. The world beyond the Umbravale."

"Umbravale?"

"The shiny barrier you passed through to get here."

The shiny barrier that'd also kept me from returning to my sister. "Another world," I said in disbelief. Complete disbelief. Surely, I'd hit my head too hard at some point. "One last question. Is it much farther? I'm only asking because … well, I'm not sure if Aethyrians relieve themselves, at all, but … that water only has one path to follow."

He groaned, adjusting the saddle on the horse. "Not much farther."

Another question bobbed at the tip of my tongue, begging to be asked. The same question that'd echoed over and over as he'd guided us through the bog, undoubtedly farther from the woods where I'd come through.

Where are you taking me?

I had every confidence the man would've probably thrown me off the horse if I'd asked aloud, though. And did it matter? I had no intentions of trudging through that bog again on my own.

Tingles of anxiety rushed over me, as he climbed onto the horse behind me, bringing to my awareness just how small I was compared to him, when his arms came around from behind, practically swallowing me as he took hold of the reins. With a light kick to the horse's flank, he set the animal into motion again.

I tried to not think about how broad and solid his chest felt against my back, or that he smelled of leather and tobacco mixed with a hint of something delicious I couldn't pinpoint. A scent that left me wondering when I'd last eaten.

The night seemed so long. Endless. My eyes burned with a longing for sleep, but I didn't dare close them. In the silence, I thought about my sister, lying naked and crouched, bleeding. How she'd waited there for me. How she could've easily stepped through that archway without me. And what? Would she have been safer, if she'd been found by those guards? Would they have captured her? Taken her to that cell so the prisoners could have their way with her before throwing her into whatever the pit was?

And if she had, would I have ever learned what'd happened to her?

"You're wrong about my sister," I said quietly, fighting to hold back tears. "She's alive."

"Then, I'm wrong," he said with little interest, sounding entirely unconvinced.

I ground my teeth in anger at his insouciance. "You're horrible for saying she was, in the first place."

"And you're a fool for crossing over."

"I had no choice. We were being chased by something in the woods. Something awful." My thoughts wound back to the strange beast-like version of Moros, and although it hadn't been the most terrifying creature I'd encountered tonight in its appearance, it was certainly one of the more sinister. "It tore the flesh off Uncle Riftyn …" I said mindlessly, lost to the memory.

"This creature in the woods. What did it look like?"

"My grandfather told me bedtime stories of a wrathavor. A beast half-man, half-stag. One that eats flesh voraciously. That's what it looked like to me. Anyway, it chased us to the archway. It was the only way out."

"It sounds like you're lucky to be alive."

"I'm tired, is what I am. I don't know what your intentions are, but I could really just use some rest." The guilt of having said that aloud crushed me, while not knowing if Aleysia was suffering at the hands of Moros and whatever had possessed him, or if he'd offered her a quick death and her body was lying on the cold ground. Having to imagine either, alongside my own survival, felt so heavy. Overwhelming. I had no idea what this Zevander had in mind for me. If he planned to do worse than the men who'd trapped me earlier. An edge of tension vibrated through me, while the pull to close my eyes and slip away from it all had me silently chiding myself to stay awake.

Until he said, "There, your wish has been granted."

Ahead of us stood a narrow path that wound up through the mountainside to a dark castle ahead, and while the sight of it, ominous and neglected, should've frightened me, it felt oddly safe. The kind of castle that scared even monsters away. Formidable enough to offer protection so I could close my eyes.

As the horse cantered up the path, I could make out flickering torches around the outside of it, illuminating its stony black and moss-covered walls.

"*Ith'tu somninis profundiet,*" Zevander's deep voice whispered in my ear.

The scene before me narrowed to a pinprick.

CHAPTER TWENTY-NINE

ZEVANDER

T he girl lay draped in Zevander's arms, as he carried her
up the staircase to Eidolon's entrance, her body limp
from the spell he'd cast. The scent of her, like mouthwatering oranges, sent a wild rush to his senses. He'd been gifted
some relief in the bog, when the odor of rot and sulfur had
masked it, but once past the swamp, it had commandeered his
every thought. Driving him mad with need. Not even the faint
whiff of piss on her detracted from the overpowering smell of
whatever the fuck that was.

Sickeningly sweet.

Through the castle's entrance, he strode past the staircase
toward the long corridor leading to the dungeon.

"What is this, Brother?" The air of intrigue in Rykaia's voice
grated on the Letalisz, as she descended the staircase and fell into
step alongside him.

"Mind your business."

"Your business is my business. That's how it works when you
force me to live in the same space as you."

While she'd weathered the worst of her withdrawals in the

last couple of days, confined to her room, she still bore the signs of exhaustion from long, sleepless nights. The red rims of her eyes and white pallor of her skin spoke of the hours she'd hung over the chamber pot, expelling the toxic remnants of the flammapul and tonics.

She followed after him, and at the grip of his arm, Zevander came to a halt. "That smell …" Gathering the girl's hair, she held it to her face and inhaled. "What is it? I want to eat it from the air."

He knew the feeling, unfortunately.

"She's mortal, isn't she? What in the gods are you doing with a mortal."

"Taking her to the dungeons."

Rykaia bristled at that. "The dungeons? Do you really think that's safe?"

"She'll be fine. Dolion's been down there for a few days now."

"Okay, but curiosity quite literally killed our cat, if you'll recall."

He did recall. He'd been the one to clean up its carcass all those years ago. "She'll be locked in. And if you touch the keys, I will know, so none of your tricks."

Scoffing, she crossed her arms. "I beg your pardon, they're not tricks. You're just mad that I happen to be one step ahead of you, sometimes." She toyed with the girl's long locks, running them through her fingers, which left Zevander curious to know how they'd feel tangled in his fist. "She's beautiful, and she smells delicious. How long do you think she'll be *safe* in a cell? Hmmm?"

"I said she'll be fine. Get some rest. I'll have some broth sent to your room."

Rykaia released her hair and chuckled. "If I relied on you to keep me fed, I'd be a rotting corpse by now. Thank the gods for Magdah, or I'd have withered away to nothing."

Instead of responding to that, Zevander grunted and kept on toward the south tower, away from his sister, who seemed far too interested in the girl. The fact was, the mortal was Dolion's problem, not his. Better to be with the old mage, than in any other part of the castle where she'd undoubtedly make trouble. He had his hands full with his sister. No need to stoke his headache with another young woman that he could already tell would get along swimmingly with Rykaia.

When he'd finally reached the castle's undercroft, he passed the memorial stones, shifting the weight of the girl to offer the sign of the gods for his mother, until he reached the cells.

Dolion stepped forward, pushing the door to his cell open, eyes wide with fascination. He didn't seem to pose much threat, so Zevander had granted him freedom to leave his cell. "It's her."

"It's her."

"You cast a sleeping spell over her?"

"She wouldn't stop talking."

"Such a brute," he muttered under his breath. "The daughter of the Corvikae." He stroked his hand down her hair, and tilted his head to admire her face. "She's quite filthy, isn't she? Smells delicious, but a bath would certainly be in her best interest."

"I did not agree to bathe her." Zevander hoisted her over his shoulder and opened the door to her cell, the same one he'd occasionally assigned to Rykaia as she went through withdrawals, seeing as his sister had found ways to escape her room every time. With silk sheets, a feather mattress and plush pillows, it was hardly a discomfort. He'd also had a private chamber pot installed for her many bouts of vomiting. Zevander lay the girl down on the bed, ignoring the way her dark tresses fell around her face in a way that made her almost angelic. Like a goddess.

"She must be exhausted from whatever hell she's suffered to look so … disheveled."

"She was chased in the woods by a figure. The same one I saw when I ventured to the mortal lands. A man that looked more beast, with his antlers and hooves."

"In the mortal lands, you say?" Dolion looked thoughtful for a moment. "I wonder if it's possible …"

The pensive expression on his face had Zevander's mind spinning. "You believe it's Cadavros." It wasn't a question.

"In my visions, I imagined him returning from the very flame said to have consumed him. Summoned from death. But what if he hasn't been consumed? What if he was simply denied his power? Stripped of it and banished to the lands where no vivicantem exists? What if he's been slumbering there all this time?"

"I'd say if he were going to make trouble, he'd have done it already. Centuries without vivicantem … he'd damn near be mortal."

"Yes, though the body can be nourished on blood and flesh." Dolion shook his head and waved a dismissive hand. "It can't be, though. I saw the Black Pestilence. Sablefyre and death and suffering."

"Is it possible, in his state, to cross back to Aethyria?"

"It would take tremendous power to shatter those wards. If he resides there—and I'm not entirely convinced of that—in his current state, without vivicantem? Certainly not. The question is … why? Why would the king have spared him? Why not destroy him?"

It seemed as if he'd been destroyed. A mage without power for centuries was essentially useless. "What kind of power would shatter the wards?"

"There are only two ways to shatter that ward. The blood of the seven, and a vein. Where there's a vein, there's penty of vivicantem and sablefyre, and Cadavros knows how to wield it."

"And you're certain there's no vein in Mortasia."

Brows raised, Dolion shrugged. "Mortals have no need for vivicantem. I don't see why one would exist there."

"Then, he's weak. I'll cross over, track him, and kill him."

His face pinched to a frown, and he cupped his jaw in his

palm. "Yes. But if he lives, I fear there's a reason for this. That is what is troubling me."

"He lives because no one killed him. I'm happy to solve that problem."

"Given the vision I had, I don't think that's wise. You, in particular, harbor the very power he seeks. The very power he is proficient in controlling. I'm admittedly not as versed as Cadavros in sablefyre, but what I do know about him is that he can be exceptionally manipulative. Who knows what control he could wield over you."

Zevander sneered. "What is essentially a mortal, wielding power over me? Not likely." As soon as he said the words, Zevander damn near choked on them. A mortal *had* wielded some kind of power over him. And it pissed him off. "So, we wait until he dies off? Or your vision comes to fruition?"

"There may be some … precautions we can take in the meantime."

"Perhaps gathering the final stone for the septomir, and ending my curse, while we're at it."

Dolion released a frustrated huff. "You asked for proof of her power. We'll see if she's worth sparing. Turn her on her side, if you will."

Reluctantly, Zevander obliged, turning her over as requested, the smooth curve of her hips not escaping his attention.

Dolion pushed her long locks of hair upward to reveal her nape, and ran his finger over her skin. "Poor girl is a bit cold. These dungeons are not the warmest."

Hand outstretched, Zevander groaned and sent a radiant heat over her that gave her otherwise pale skin a pink glow.

Dolion set his inner wrist against the crook of her neck and nodded. "Much better." From his coat, he yanked a quarter vial of vivicantem. "This will be the last of my supply. Let's keep our fingers crossed." He dropped the last bits across her nape and smoothed it into her skin before it could drip on the sheets.

She let out a quiet moan, and godsblood, the sound of it strummed his muscles like the quiver of a spider's web.

His hand curled into a fist at his side with whatever maddening effect the woman had on him. That he welcomed such sensations, when his entire bloodline hinged on breaking this curse, a curse that required her sacrifice, infuriated him.

Within seconds, a soft metallic glow appeared in the ancient death sigil he'd seen in the crucible. "Is that enough proof for you?" It was there. Her sigil. Her bloodline. "Come. Allow me to show you something."

* * *

Zevander stood over Dolion, who sat hunched over his desk. A firelamp beside him flickered over the strangest book Zevander had ever seen. One that appeared to be made of bone and feathers, carved in wood that smelled aged, and held strange carvings in its surface.

Dolion ran his fingers over the surface, as if it were a precious treasure. "In the scrolls I read, the priestess of the Corvikae spoke of a grimoire belonging to their people. In it, she explains how the old pass along their powers to the young. Baptized by death."

"And how are mortals baptized without blood magic?"

"In the age of the Corvugon, the blood of the raptor was used, which created a bond between the child and the beast. It served as a protector."

Zevander stroked his jaw in thought. "The Corvugon egg I saw hadn't hatched."

"Perhaps there was something else. I don't know her circumstances yet, but I look forward to picking her brain. And opening this blasted book that might offer even more insights."

"Why can't you open it?" It was then Zevander noticed the edges appeared sealed together, confirmed when Dolion gave a small tug of the cover.

"It's a puzzle book, meant only for the Corvikae. It's sealed by a spell, of some sort."

"So, in order for her to have acquired power, someone had to pass it down to her. Which means there may be another and killing her isn't ending her bloodline?"

"It is a cycle. If she dies before she can pass on her powers, then they are lost forever. And her gifts may prove more beneficial than her death."

Chuckling, Zevander shook his head and sneered. "Forgive my doubt. The girl nearly fell victim to a boggyr this evening. I'm finding it difficult to imagine her useful against the most dangerous power in Aethyria."

"We cannot be selfish about this, Zevander. It is a girl's life we're talking about here."

"Allow me to show you something, as well."

Frowning, Dolion rose up from his desk and followed Zevander from the cell, into the shadowy recesses at the end of the corridor. Zevander shot a blast of flame toward one of the sconce torches, illuminating the stone walls that surrounded them in an alcove and the iron door in the floor. A chain had since been placed over the handle of it, preventing escape.

"What is this?" Dolion asked, staring down at it.

The door thumped, rattling the chain.

Eyes on the mage, Zevander yanked a key hanging from a hook on the wall and knelt down to unlock the chain.

"Y-y-you're not going to open that, are you?"

Without answering, Zevander loosed the chain and stepped back.

Nothing stirred.

The door creaked slowly, and a black spider the size of a full-grown cat crawled out.

Dolion's eyes widened.

The spider lurched toward the old man, and Zevander sent a lash of black flame that coiled around its mid-section. The spider hissed, its legs still scrambling across the concrete. In one swift yank, it burst into black guts that spattered over Dolion. Grimacing, the old mage wiped the gore from his face.

Zevander swiped a mirror from the wall, along with a flaming sconce, which he lowered just inside the hole. The light illuminated a wall of webs, and in the corner crouched Branimir. Of course, he no longer looked like the brother Zevander had come to know. His face had hardened to a bark-like texture, his eyes black as onyx. Three horns had grown out the top of his head.

Dolion stared, seemingly entranced. "Dear gods of old ... what is this?"

"My brother. Cursed by the same sablefyre that resides in me."

The reflection of Branimir turned toward the mirror and hissed, showing a mouthful of sharpened teeth. Smaller black spiders rushed forward.

"Close it!" Dolion jumped back, as Zevander withdrew the mirror and flame, and slammed the door shut.

Boot braced on the surface of it, he felt a hard thump hit the other side, while he wound the chain back in place. "It is not a selfish pursuit that compels me to rid this curse. I have watched him evolve into this creature since I was a boy." He removed his mask, revealing the black veins over his face that had begun to branch out along his jaw. "Should that become my fate, I'd sooner plunge a dagger through my heart."

Dolion's brow flickered with the sort of empathy Zevander could no longer summon for his brother. He trailed his gaze toward the spider and Zevander sent a blast of flame over it, setting it ablaze. "Why not ..."

"Kill the spiders? I have. Each time I do, the nest grows bigger and bigger. I tried to kill him once, as well."

"You couldn't do it."

"He didn't ask for this. Neither of us asked for this."

Dolion nodded toward the pile of ash. "I suspect those spiders have the potential to infect. Crawling beneath the skin. In a baby whose magic hasn't matured, it presents less damage. In a mage like myself, the mutation would be catastrophic. Sablefyre is an exceptionally dangerous power."

"It is the will of the wielder. Branimir does not long for power. He longs to die."

"But his longing could change, and what then?"

"What then, indeed." Bracing one hand against the stone wall, Zevander rubbed the other hand down his face. "I'd hoped to cure him of this affliction. That is what you promised with the stones."

"This plague in my vision. It is not the first we've seen of its kind. The priestess spoke of one during the aegrogrian age. A wide-spread scourge of locusts that turned Mancers into flesh eating beasts."

"If you're asking me to kill my brother ..."

"The Corvi were the only ones to survive."

"How?" Zevander asked, intrigued.

"I don't know. We don't know the extent of their power. What this girl may offer *alive*."

"If the girl has any power, she certainly doesn't know a thing about it." Zevander stepped past him, heading back toward the cells, and Dolion followed after.

"She will need to learn how to tap into it. Which will require training." An irritating, expectant lift of his brows suggested he wanted Zevander to train her.

"No." Zevander snorted and shook his head. "I know nothing of the Corvi and their power."

"And I know very little. Only what I can scrounge from these few tomes. But there is someone who may be able to help. She's a bone scribe for The Citadel. Her uncle was renowned for his work."

"A historian." Zevander's tone couldn't have been any flatter. "How does that help, when there is no history of the Corvi to be found, aside from what you've already stolen?"

"*Borrowed*. As we do in libraries. And I don't know yet. At the very least, she can read bones. Perhaps there might be history buried beneath the girl's flesh. In the meantime, you can train her to call upon her power. That is a basic skill for any mage—whether born, or made."

"So, now I'm to seek out this bone scribe, as well." Zevander wanted to laugh at how ridiculous it was—opening the doors to the castle he'd spent years protecting, like a fucking inn and tavern. Instead, he snarled. "This sounds far more complicated than merely turning her blood to stone. It would take *seconds*. Educating and training her would take months. Years, even."

"Think of what we may stand to lose. Yes, we possess all seven stones of the septomir, but you said it yourself, that is too much power for one person."

"Enough of this feigned altruism, old man. Was it so long ago that you can't recall having ordered her death yourself?"

Chin tipped up, Dolion stared back at him in challenge. "And I'm curious, as well. Have you ever hesitated to kill anything?"

Zevander didn't bother to answer that. His reputation spoke for itself.

"Yet, you couldn't bring yourself to kill her. If only you could! Yes, I suppose these horrible visions would be laid to rest, and I might find peace in sleep. But the gods stepped in, and they demanded another path." The old mage shrugged. "Who am I to challenge them?"

"You said in your vision that I would join Cadavros in his destruction. Why would you trust me? If this power makes me such a threat, why not eliminate it now?"

"It's not you that I trust. It's the signs of the gods that I put my faith in."

"And I fear they will lead you astray." Zevander jerked his head toward the door in the floor. "You still wish to remain in the dungeon after having seen that?"

"I lived amongst the Carnificans in an abandoned castle. A

few spiders seems manageable. I'll put a ward to keep them out of both cells."

"Fine. Your choice." On those parting words, Zevander strode out of Dolion's cell. After pausing for one more glimpse of the girl, sleeping peacefully, he growled in frustration and kept on.

CHAPTER THIRTY

MAEVYTH

"Wake up, Maevyth," Aleysia whispered. *"You must wake up."*

I opened my eyes to find my sister standing over me, her closely-shorn hair a startling confusion in my half-awakened state. As I focused on her, scanning over the bruises and cuts and bites on her naked body, a niggling dread sat on the outskirts of my thoughts.

The Banishing Ceremony. Running through the woods. The archway.

Rapid images flashed through my mind like an all-too-vivid nightmare.

I trailed my gaze over my surroundings, visually swallowing the gray water-stained walls, stony dirt floor, bars that closed me in. A cage. Beside me stood a nightstand with a flickering lamp that illuminated the teary gaze of my sister.

"Come with me."

"How are you here?" I pushed to a sitting position, my mind hammering out the memories from the night before. The last detail I could recall was riding horseback toward a castle. An ominous castle. A man wearing a hooded cowl and leather mask.

"I crossed in the night. Come." She waved, urging me up out of bed. "He intends to kill you, Sister." She reached out her hand for me, and I glanced down, noticing the blood and gashes on her palm.

Something wasn't right, though, and as my mind untangled itself from sleep, it became clearer what failed to make sense. Aleysia couldn't have found me. The trek to the castle was long and rife with terrible creatures.

It was then the dread I'd feared moments ago rushed over me, settling deep into my bones. "I'm hallucinating you." Tears welled in my eyes, blurring her form. "Oh, god, Aleysia. He ... he ... killed you." Bottom lip quivering, I took her hand and, even through the numbing chill that wracked my own body, felt the icy-cold bite of her skin. "My poor sister."

Her grip tightened over mine, and I glanced up to see her eyes flip from their usual bright blue to orbs of black onyx. She gave a hard yank, pulling me into her, and opened her mouth to show sharpened teeth.

I kicked back on a scream, and she exploded into white vapor. When the shock finally faded, a suffocating ache settled in my chest, a wretched misery that longed to drown me. Tears wavered in my eyes as I forced myself to absorb the meaning of her visit. A soul-shattering grief withered the air, and I couldn't breathe. I couldn't draw in enough oxygen to banish the feeling of my lungs filling with a stifling anguish.

He killed her.

"Must've been quite a dream." The unfamiliar voice came from the left of me, and I startled, my spine hitting the stone wall as I jerked back.

Gathering myself, I crawled on hands and knees toward the end of the bed and found a young woman with long, silvery hair sitting on the floor across from the cell, her back pressed against the wall. Youth glowed in her alabaster skin tone that shimmered with a silvery overtone, and eyes like the shallow blue of the

Abyssius Sea. A long, burgundy, velvet dress pooled around her, the hem hiked up to her shins by her bent knees. In one hand she held a bright red apple, and a small paring knife in the other.

Blinking away tears, I studied her, trying to recall if I'd seen her at any point the night before. "Where am I? And who are you?" I couldn't help but stare at the apple. In spite of my confusion and heartbreak, the hunger in my belly refused to be ignored.

"You speak Nyxterosi." She carved a piece of the fruit and popped it into her mouth. "That's interesting," she said around a mouthful. "My name is Rykaia, and you're at the *luxurious* Castle Eidolon, home of pain, suffering, and utter decay."

"There was a man who brought me ... with a mask."

"Ah, yes, my brother. The feared Lord Rydainn—or tyrant beast, as I like to call him."

Her brother. I lurched forward, kicking my feet over the edge of the bed. "Can you get me out of this cell? I don't know why he brought me here, but I have to return to the woods."

"You are mortal, then. Balls of Castero ... I knew that smell was unusual. Quite delicious. Were I the cannibal type, I might be inclined to have a taste." She waved the knife in front of her. "Fortunately for you, I'm not that type. To answer your question, no. I'm afraid I can't help you."

My hope for escape withered, and I glanced around, noting a lock on the cage. "There isn't a key to unlock the cell?"

"Well, yes." She pointed, and I followed the path of her gaze to the stone wall, where a ring of keys hung from a nail. Completely out of reach.

"Won't you hand it to me? I can let myself out."

"I'm afraid not." She carved another slice of the apple and popped it into her mouth. "See, I've been sentenced to remain at this tomb of rot, and unfortunately for you, I'm thoroughly intrigued by your presence," she said, her words garbled in bits of apple. "Zevander doesn't bring women back to the castle. *Ever.*"

Brows raised, she sighed. "Besides that, the moment I put the key in that hole, my brother will be alerted, and seven hells will break. It's a terrible circumstance, I know. I've been in that very cell before."

"Your brother locked you in here?" Another sweep of the cell showed a box-like structure, like a standing closet, with a narrow door that had me questioning what might be inside. Granted, it was a bit fancier than most dungeons, definitely fancier than the one the guards had thrown me into, but it certainly wasn't where I'd have my sister sleep.

Aleysia.

I forced the image of her face out of my head. No time for tears or mourning when my escape took priority.

"I told you he was a tyrant beast." She crunched another bite of the apple, my stomach grumbling for a taste.

A chill spiraled through me, a slight mist expelling past my lips, and I wrapped my arms around my body, shivering. The lingering fright of my nightmare certainly didn't help my trembling.

"Gets a little cold down here. Worse in the dead of winter. Like an icebox."

"Who is Castero?" I asked, trying to distract myself from the pang in my stomach and the tremor in my bones. "You mentioned the name earlier."

She snorted and bit off the end of the apple—the bit that most tended to toss away—and took half the core, too. Seeds, and all. "Oh! Just a saying. He was an ancient warrior who, according to historians, slayed ten drakes at once." Pausing, she stared as if thoughtful for a moment. "I'm not sure if his balls were actually significant. I'd love to find a resource to confirm."

A long gargly noise echoed from the left, sounding like a snarling animal. "What is that awful sound?"

"Dolion. My brother's other prisoner. Snores like he's trying to inhale a small child, doesn't he?"

As much as I wanted to laugh at that, I could only muster a clipped smile.

Another bite of the apple, and she polished off the core, leaving only the tip that still carried the stem.

At that point, I'd have probably eaten the whole thing too, considering my stomach had begun to feel like it was consuming itself.

"Seems Zevander is racking them up these days. Ordinarily, these cells stand empty, aside from the times I'm locked in one."

"That must be incredibly terrifying and lonely down here."

"I'm not typically conscious." She gave a dismissive shrug. "So … the dream. Was it a good one, or a bad one?"

Her question sent me spiraling back to the last few minutes, just before Aleysia had tried to attack me, and I winced at the blackness of her eyes. How soulless she'd looked. "It was no dream. I apparently see the dead."

"Well, you weren't seeing much of anything with your eyes still closed, I'm sure."

I perked up at that. "My eyes were closed?"

"Up until you kicked out at the invisible air monster." She lifted her booted foot as if to demonstrate.

"Perhaps it *was* just a dream. An awful dream." Maybe Aleysia was still alive.

"Gods, what an awful thing that must be … seeing the dead. Are they intact when you see them? I mean, say someone was chopped entirely. Would you be visited by a pile of severed limbs? Or the person as a whole?"

As she asked the question, I found myself silently questioning the state of her mind. "I've … never encountered a pile of severed limbs."

Nodding, she smiled. "Makes sense. How could you have conversations with severed limbs, after all?"

"Did I speak aloud in my dreaming?"

"Yes. You dreamed of your sister."

I wouldn't have willingly offered up that detail, as I had no idea what her brother's intentions were with me. "I need to return to her. She's in trouble."

"Pity you found yourself trapped in here. My brother isn't known for being all that merciful." Eyes narrowed, she rested her elbows on her knees. "Which begs the question ... what *are* you doing here?"

"I don't know ... I was attacked and woke up on his horse. The last thing I remember before blacking out was an exceptionally ..." I hesitated to say for fear of sounding as ridiculous as it was in my head. "Large scorpion." The croaking howl of a dying animal erupted from the pit of my gut, echoing through the cell like a final war cry, and I threw my arms around my mid-section, cheeks burning. "Forgive me. I'm starving."

Rykaia chuckled, and the sound of scraping metal alerted me to a tray she dragged from the other side of her. "I brought some food. I hope you don't mind, but I stole the apple. Took forever for you to wake." She slid the tray beneath the narrow gap between the bars and the floor, and while I should've been more cautious taking food from a complete stranger, the much greater instinct to keep from starving to death wouldn't allow it.

I shamelessly dove for what looked like a hearty stew, the steam from which gave off a delicious savory scent, and fresh bread.

"You'll have to remind Zevander to feed you. He seems to forget that living creatures eat. It's why we don't have any plants, or animals, aside from the damn drakes that inhabit the grounds."

"You have drakes?" I said around an ungracious mouthful of food, some of which I accidentally spat, before swallowing it back. One bite warmed my insides, drowning the cold that vibrated my muscles. The savory flavor exploded on my tongue, and my eyes nearly rolled back at the heavenly taste. The thin stews back home had little meat, too much water, and a lot more onions. This was the most delicious meal I'd ever eaten in my life. "Like the lizard dragons without wings?"

"Yes, and they are vicious. Unless you're Zevander, or one of the other miscreants roaming the grounds."

"Miscreants?"

"Yes. The men my brother was imprisoned with."

"Imprisoned?" I gulped back a large bite of stew, nearly choking on the word. Had they broken out and taken me with them?

"Ah, you're awake!" A masculine voice drew my attention to a dark-skinned man, with white hair and a thick white beard, peeking in from outside the opposite end of my cell.

"And so are you," Rykaia said with little enthusiasm. "I thought it'd gotten rather quiet in here."

He dropped his gaze and cleared his throat. "My apologies for the snoring. It's an aging thing."

"Come now, Dolion. What are you? Four-hundred? Five?"

Surely, it couldn't have been age that they were discussing.

Hands clasped in front of him, he bowed. "Six-hundred-thirty. But thank you for the compliment."

"You're six-hundred-thirty years old." I couldn't hide the air of disbelief coloring my tone.

"Give, or take, yes."

"How?"

Brows raised, he shrugged. "Well, I'd like to think that I take good care of myself. For the most part. I do like a bit of mors mead, which is … punishing, I'm afraid. And ale. Can't seem to give up the ale."

"No. I mean how is it possible? We're lucky to live until the age of eighty, where I'm from."

"Eighty?" Rykaia snorted. "That's practically infantile."

"How old are you, if you don't mind me asking."

"Two-hundred-six."

Two-hundred-six? The girl looked like she couldn't have been much older than me. "You ... definitely do not look two-hundred-six years old."

"Ah, gods bless. You are a sweet thing, aren't you?"

"I'm no expert on the matter, a scholar would be much more informational, but as I understand, time moves a bit differently here than in Mortasia."

I sopped up some of the broth with a piece of bread and popped it into my mouth. "I thought you were a prisoner, as well?"

"Yes, well, I suppose, technically, I am. You're actually *not* a prisoner, Miss ..." His brows kicked up as if he wanted me to answer.

"Maevyth."

"Maevyth. And might I say, it is an absolute pleasure to meet you."

"If I'm no prisoner, then you'll let me go?"

"Oh, I didn't say that. It's complicated. Perhaps a bit over-whelming, if I tried to explain it all at once." Hands behind his back, he paced outside my cell. "I'm sure this is all very new and confusing."

"It's frustrating." I soaked up another bite of stew to stifle the anger stirring inside of me all over again. "Someone I care about is in grave danger as we speak."

"Her sister," Rykaia supplied, to which Dolion gave a sympathetic nod that pinched to a pensive expression.

"You've a sister?"

"Yes. Step-sister, but we may as well be blood. We tried to cross through an archway in the woods. I made it through, but ..." The quiver in my voice warned me to stop before I broke into tears. "She didn't."

"She attempted to step through?" he asked.

"No. She never had the chance."

Dolion huffed and lowered his gaze. "If it's any comfort to

you, had she tried, she'd have fallen to her death in the great chasm."

"That doesn't make sense. I made it through just fine."

"Her blood isn't your blood." Inhaling deeply, he frowned and paced again. "I can respect and sympathize with your worry, miss. But you are here, at Castle Eidolon, because you happen to be in grave danger yourself." Dolion cleared his throat and held up a finger, when I shot him a frown at his words. "If you'll excuse me one moment."

"Wait. How am I in danger?"

"I'll answer that in a moment," he said, and slipped away, as if it weren't the single most important thought in my head right then.

"Look," Rykaia said, pushing to her feet. "Those woods are guarded all hours of the day. There's no way you'd get past the cavalry, and if you did? You'd still have to get through the Umbravale, somehow. But before all of that, you'd have to get past my brother. He does *not*. Bring. Anyone. To Eidolon. The fact you're here does not bode well for your freedom."

"What could he possibly want from me?"

"That is a question I've mulled for hours now."

"Can I speak with him?"

Lips flattened, she shook her head. "Afraid not. The king has requested his presence this afternoon. He's on his way to Costelwick as we speak."

I had no idea what Costelwick was, or where it might be in relation to where I was right then.

Dolion appeared again, a brown bag clutched in his hand. "Suffice it to say, the Lord of Eidolon plans to keep you here for a bit. In the meantime, perhaps you might kill the hours with a book?"

A book? "I don't want to read. I can't read while the person I love may very well be suffering her last breaths. I want to go home."

"Perhaps you want a bath, too." Rykaia waved her hand in front of her face and pinched her nose. "No offense. The oranges are starting to smell a little *ripe*," she said in a nasally tone.

"I empathize with you." Dolion pressed his palms together. "Truly. And perhaps Lord Rydainn might be so kind as to track her down for you."

Rykaia snorted and shook her head. "Zevander is *not* a man of favors."

"No, I suppose he's not. But there are other ways." Staring off thoughtfully, he scratched at his beard. "Would you happen to have something belonging to your sister?"

"What kind of something?"

"Anything really. A lock of hair, a piece of clothing, jewelry. Anything you may have gotten a hold of."

I had none of those things, and the more I thought about that, the more my heart ached. Had she, in fact, perished, I had nothing by which to remember her. "No. I don't have anything."

"Ah, that is a shame. I can attempt with her name, but it's never accurate that way."

"What isn't accurate?"

"A scrying mirror. It's much better with something belonging to the person you seek to find."

Poking my spoon at the last couple of bites of stew, I shook my head. "So, I guess I'm stuck here. Reading books, while my sister's fate remains unknown."

"I wouldn't consider reading books in solitary the *worst* scenario." Rykaia tucked the small knife she'd used to carve the apple into the belt of her dress. "Well, I'm going to scrounge up a bit more to eat. I'll come back to check on you in a bit." With that, she set off down a long corridor that led to a shadowy end.

"The book in question is not just any book, miss." Dolion reached into the brown bag, before pushing an odd wooden book, with spindles that looked like bone along the spine, through the gap in the bars. The aged cover, garnished in black feathers, boasted one silvery pale eye set beneath a bony protruding ridge that gave it the fierce appearance of an angry dragon. Or bird. Yes, perhaps it looked more like a raven. It reminded me very much of Raivox, who I'd also lost in those woods.

The eye was divided by small diagonal slits that converged in the center at a pitch-black pupil. Along the edges, symbols had been carved in deep black grooves with small peg holes. Just outside of that, a strange pattern that reminded me of a maze lined either edge of the entire structure.

Book in hand, I sat on the edge of the bed and attempted to lift the cover, but it wouldn't budge. I turned the book over in my hands, examining the tightly sealed pages along the edge.

"It's a puzzle book," Dolion said. "Quite popular when I was a child. Every winter solstice, my grandmother would gift one to me. Each page, including the cover, is a mechanical puzzle fused with magic. You solve a puzzle, you unlock a page."

"Is it a story?" I asked, and pried at the cover, to no avail.

"Yes. A very compelling one, I'm sure. Though, I've not personally been successful at opening it."

Huffing, I set the book on the table beside me, no longer interested. "What makes you think I'd fare any better?"

"Oh, I'm certain if you worked with it, you'd be successful in opening it. Again, just a means of passing the time, until this confusion over your circumstances is cleared with Lord Rydainn."

I very much doubted there was any confusion on Lord Rydainn's part. In fact, my kidnapping seemed very intentional. "You said I was in grave danger. Why? From whom?"

A look of uncertainty crossed his face, as if he didn't want to tell me. "There are mages looking for you. Powerful mages."

"Why? Because I crossed?"

"At the moment, they're not aware of your presence here," he said, pacing again. "But when they do become aware, and I suspect they will, you can be sure they will go to every effort to hunt you down."

Hunt me? "Why? What did I do?"

"It isn't what you did, but what you possess, Maevyth." He paused his pacing. "They believe in a prophesy. Well, one I may have started …" Brows furrowed, he rubbed a finger across his lips. "I don't want to frighten you, but you happen to possess extraordinary abilities. Is it possible you've stumbled upon oddities about yourself? Things you can't explain?"

The first to come to mind had happened just before Aleysia had taken off into the woods. "I …" I hesitated, because admitting such a thing back in Foxglove would've stirred suspicions of witchcraft.

"Do not fear to say. We've been anxious to know what wonderful gifts you possess."

"The villagers … they wanted to hurt my sister. They approached, and the moment I threw out my hands, a pile of bones lay on the ground."

The concern etched into Dolion's face softened to a beaming smile. With a flick of his fingers, he urged me to the bars of the cage. "Come. I must see your palm."

I flipped my hand over and frowned down on seeing the same strange symbol I'd seen in the sky just before The Banishing etched as a faint scar on my skin. With everything that'd happened, I hadn't noticed it at all until right then. Rubbing my thumb over the scar failed to erase it, and I pushed to my feet. Still staring down at the marking, I crossed the cell and, with a small bit of reluctance, pushed my hand between the bars.

Dolion smiled, running his thumb over the symbol that flickered under his gentle caress. *"Osflagulle.* My gods, I've never seen this particular magic before."

"Magic?"

"You possess incredible power, Maevyth. This one, in particular, has not been seen in centuries."

The excitement in his voice contrasted with the growing fear inside of me. The very real possibility that I'd lost my senses completely and was hallucinating everything.

"Who knows what others are tied to your bloodline."

My head remained in a state of disbelief when I asked, "So, these mages that are hunting me, as you say—they want me because of these abilities?"

"They want your blood, I'm afraid."

I'd definitely lost my mind. The more farfetched the story, the more questions I asked, because at that point, I couldn't stop myself. "My blood? As a bat *consumes* blood." It wasn't a question on my part, it was a refusal to accept his explanation.

"No. To rebirth an ancient weapon."

What started as a small chuckle in my throat grew to a full-blown laugh. I laughed so hard, tears welled in my eyes.

Dolion lowered his gaze and nodded. "For you, I imagine this all sounds quite unlikely." His comment made me laugh harder, and I wiped the tears from my eyes, only then realizing how sore and aching they felt. It very much sounded ridiculous. Impossible.

"I can assure you, it's all true."

The laughter died in my chest, and the intense urge to break into tears stung the rims of my eyes, but just as before, I choked them back. "You can assure me," I said in a flat tone. "So, how am I safe in this cell? It seems I should return before they discover I'm here."

"Should they learn who you are, I'm afraid they won't hesitate to seek you out, no matter which side of the vale you're on. Here, the castle is guarded by a very powerful ward. There are also four of the king's best assassins prepared to protect you. Tell me, do you have that level of protection back at home?"

I couldn't even say I still had a home, let alone anyone willing to protect me there, besides Aleysia.

Aleysia.

While I sat entertaining these outrageous explanations, the likelihood of her being alive withered, because even if Moros hadn't killed her that night, the governor and Sacton Crain would've surely seen to her execution. "Why would I possibly believe any of this?"

"Because I'm very invested in watching you live a long and prosperous life, Maevyth. If you believe nothing else, believe that."

"I don't even know you, nor do you know me."

"I know more than you think."

CHAPTER THIRTY-ONE

ZEVANDER

Obsidyen cantered beneath Zevander, up to the fork in the road. One path led toward The Citadel's House of Sages, an academy dedicated to science and medicine, along with history and ancestry. A number of mages taught there, as well, but most were eager young scribes, with no other ambition than to read and study.

The other path led toward Costelwick Castle.

Kazhimyr slowed his horse alongside Zevander. "What is the name of this bone scribe you've asked me to seek out?"

"Allura Marabe." Zevander stared out at the long road ahead of him. "Her uncle is Odion. As I understand, he's well known amongst scholars. You shouldn't have trouble finding her. But it is imperative that you not draw too much attention to yourself."

"Of course. Do I take her by force?" Kazhimyr asked, smoothing his hand over his leather glove.

"Ask her to accompany you first. If she refuses, then yes."

"And I'm to tell her we happened upon some scrolls for her to assist in interpreting."

"Yes, but keep it discreet. I suspect the mere mention of the castle will spark her interest."

"I hope so. It'd be a shame to get forceful when I'm known for my charm." Stroking his jaw, he chuckled. "As for the items Dolion requested …"

Zevander handed off a scroll to his fellow Letalisz. "He wrote a list. While he claims no one is watching his lab, I'd advise you seek the supplies out elsewhere. Perhaps from another lab."

"Are you asking me to *steal*, Brother?" Amusement colored his tone. Stealing happened to have been the reason the Solassions had imprisoned Kazhimyr all those years ago. His skills in thievery had gone unmatched, up until he'd gotten caught.

"I'm asking you to *borrow*. I'll see you back at Eidolon."

"Yes, give King Sagaerin a kiss for me."

Zevander snorted and shook his head, then kept on toward the king's palace. As the leader of the Letalisz, he met with the king far more frequently than the other three, and had built more of a rapport with him. Still, Zevander wasn't looking forward to what would've undoubtedly made for a long afternoon.

Once inside The Citadel gates, the villagers offered a wide berth, as he guided his horse over the cobblestones, past merchants, blacksmiths and taverns, up through the narrow winding streets, lined with tall buildings whose pointed spires reached toward the sky, all the way to the gates of the castle grounds. The savory scent of smoking meat, exotic spices and burning incense muted the occasional waft of damp stones and wood. Purple and forest green sails stretched across the crowded alleyways, shielding the carts overflowing with grim-looking fruits and vegetables from the overcast sky, where dark clouds swallowed the sun. Hardly ever shined bright in Nyxteros, thanks to the positioning of the moons. Unlike in Solassia, where produce required sunlight, it was the prilunar light that helped food grow in the southern continent.

Merchants shouted from their wooden stands, offering fine silks and leather, fancy pottery, smoking pipes, and jewelry. Others wearing muted cloaks and talismans, selling arcane artifacts—enchanted tomes and crystal orbs, dowsing pendulums and ritual daggers—watched him warily as he passed.

In a clearing, a large crowd gathered around a theater platform where actors and actresses put on a play. Their laughter carried over the music that weaved through the streets, adding a festive ambience, as the minstrels played their instruments and sang.

The Citadel, with its bustling alleyways and eclectic fashion allowed him to blend in easier than the outskirts where the citizens there knew his name and curse. As it was daylight, he wore a linen tunic and leathers with a hooded cloak. The mask, which he'd mostly worn to conceal his identifiable scars, provided a bit more anonymity.

Once he arrived at the palace gates, The Imperial Guards allowed him passage. Inside the walls, to them, Zevander was nothing more than a combat tutor and guard to the king's son, Prince Dorjan. A guise that allowed him to walk freely with his weapons, without suspicion. They had no idea the miles he'd traveled, the years he'd trained in secret, honing the skills to kill in the name of their king. No one did, as the king had gone out of his way to conceal that part of Zevander's duties. Though they loathed the Letalisz for the way the king had always favored him, the fact was, it'd never made sense to Zevander, either—particularly as King Sagaerin had never been known as a benevolent man. Even without his curse, the Rydainn name had never been noble enough to warrant his favor. It was only his mother who'd afforded him a small bit of status.

Once inside the barbican, Obsidyen trotted toward the second gatehouse, and there, Zevander dismounted his horse, handing the reins off to one of the awaiting stable boys. As at the outer gate, he was granted permission to cross the stony bridge that hovered over Blackwater Moat, and as he made his way across, he glanced over the edge, catching the scaled spine of a water serpent, the length of which measured six meters, at least.

Koryn, they were called. Vicious, flesh-eating monsters that wouldn't hesitate to devour him whole, regardless of his stature with the king.

Beyond the bridge, he passed through yet another gate, to the castle's much smaller courtyard, that one teeming with well-groomed shrubs and gardens, weathered fountains and monstrous statues. Few had the opportunity to pass through these gardens, as entry tended to be exceptionally strict. Mostly officers, mages, and the occasional royal–the king's most trusted.

While most kings tended to keep themselves insulated from the public for their own protection, King Sagaerin was most strict about it.

Zevander climbed the stone stairs lined with grotesques and unlit torches, up to the stately entrance of the castle that was nearly hidden by the encroaching moss and vines which covered its towering gray walls. Gargoyle waterspouts peered down between flying buttresses, drawing attention to the castle's elaborately carved stonework. The iron doors creaked open with his approach, flanked on either side by more guards who offered him no passing gestures, or acknowledgment, which suited Zevander just fine, as he hadn't come for niceties.

En route to Hemwell Tower, where the king often held meetings with his advisors, a familiar face strode up alongside him. Garbed in a fine silk tunic, and brocade surcoat decorated with the Sagaerin heraldry, he was only a decade, or so, younger than Zevander, but carried himself with the kind of regal grace that the Letalisz clearly lacked.

"Prince Dorjan," Zevander said with a respectful nod, not bothering to slow his strides as the prince kept up with him.

"I understand my father called on you for a meeting."

"Will you be in attendance?"

"I'd much prefer to pluck my own eyeballs from their sockets and toss them to the Koryn."

Zevander smirked behind his mask. "Then, to what do I owe the honor of your company?"

Still keeping the pace, the prince leaned to the side. "I understand you traveled to Corvus Keep recently," he said in a lowered voice. "What were they like?"

"The Carnificans? Vicious, pale as the fallen snow, emaciated, precisely your type."

The prince chuckled, knocking Zevander in the arm. "Your reputation as a brute rears its ugly head once again." Few knew of the prince's penchant for men, aside from Zevander, who'd sometimes escorted his lovers safely to and from the castle. His father, the king, turned a blind eye, so long as Dorjan agreed to fulfill his duty by producing an heir. "I understand they sometimes toy with their prey before feasting on their flesh."

"You sound exceptionally intrigued by this."

"I'm intrigued by the state of mind that would compel someone to consume flesh." Prince Dorjan possessed the rare power of reading thoughts, though in his case, it required some form of contact with the other person.

"If you value your hand, I don't advise touching one to find out."

"I've no intentions, but can you imagine the utter chaos? To desire the flesh and blood of another so … violently? It's almost macabrely romantic."

Zevander shot him a frown. "I can assure you, there is not one romantic thought in their minds when they're gnawing the flesh from your bones."

"Well, speaking of gnawing flesh from bones, enjoy your meeting." Chuckling, the prince patted him on the back. "I'm off to paint in the gardens."

"Enjoy," Zevander grumbled, as he kept on down the corridor toward the two Imperial Guards who stood posted outside the king's meeting chambers..

One held out his hand as Zevander approached. With a sigh,

he removed his baldric and sword, the two daggers at his thigh, the small dagger strapped to his arm, and the fragor from the pocket of his leathers. Zevander smirked behind the mask, as the guard regarded the stone with trepidation and plucked it from his palm as if he were offering up a venomous snake. One chant was all it would have taken to activate the rock, which could've easily leveled all of Hemwell Tower in one blow. The sight of them tended to make most want to shit their trousers.

The long table within was often crowded with all variety of disciplines—war general, the silver master for the treasury, the king's cohort, which included his advisors for both tactical and social affairs. On that occasion, it sat only Akmyrios—the Magelord, or Mage Superior—the Imperial Captain, and a woman Zevander didn't recognize. Behind the king stood his cup bearer, a boy no more than sixteen, by Zevander's estimates.

A thread of tension wound in the Letalisz's muscles, as he contemplated the possibility that the king might've been privy to the bloodstones, and that the otherwise casual meeting might've been called as a pretense to an inquisition and arrest.

King Sagaerin sat at the head of the table, sipping out of a silver goblet that he lifted when the Letalisz approached. "Ah, Zevander. Always a pleasure." The mention of his name struck him as odd, considering the king took measures to ensure Zevander's anonymity. In fact, Zevander only knew who was in attendance during the usual meetings because he hid in the shadows as an unseen guard for the king. Any meetings he openly attended were strictly between him and the king—not even his cup bearer was allowed entry.

Wordlessly, Zevander took his seat two down from the king. "I was under the impression this was a private meeting."

"It was, but we've encountered a bit of a problem." King Sagaerin gulped back his wine, holding the goblet out for the boy, who promptly filled it. "A number of guards from the Imperial Army have gone missing. Captain Zivant has scoured the city in search of not only his men, but whomever may be responsible for their disappearances."

"And, so, why am I here?"

"Your name was mentioned. By one of the guards," Captain Zivant said, glaring at him from across the table where he sat. The animosity in his eyes surged with his accusation. "We asked him if he'd seen anything unusual. He only got so far as saying your name before he suffered an attack, of some sort."

The scorpion. It would've stung him to death for having said Zevander's name.

"We had one of our physicians examine him afterward," the Magelord said from beside the captain. "All his organs had completely liquefied, somehow."

"So, perhaps you might tell us who murdered my men?"

"Murder? How do you know they didn't abandon their duty and leave The Citadel?" A stupid question, but Zevander certainly had no intentions of confessing he'd burnt them to a pile of dust.

"For what?" Captain Zivant spat the words like a sour taste in his mouth. "What could possibly exist outside the walls that would interest a highly decorated soldier?" It was true that soldiers to the king were afforded a life of privilege not granted to most. They were also loathed beyond the walls of The Citadel.

"Then, what leads you to the conclusion that something happened to them?"

"An aura was left behind," the Magelord answered.

Impossible. Zevander had trained for centuries, to learn how to avoid leaving the trace bits of magic. It came down to burning efficiently and hot enough that the aura was singed and incomplete. Undetectable, even by the most skilled forenzycaris, whose magic picked up on the faintest element. Hence, the liquefied organs. After stinging the guard, the scorpion would've burst into black flame inside of him.

"We've determined the aura is Corvikae," the woman beside the Magelord said.

"Zevander, this is Melantha, apprentice to the Magelord." With a small bit of apathy in his voice, King Sagaerin waved his hand toward the woman with auburn hair.

Apprentice? As far as Zevander knew, women had historically been denied positions in the Magestroli.

"It's a pleasure to meet you. His majesty speaks highly of you."

Something about the woman struck him as untrustworthy, and as subtly as he could muster, he removed his glove beneath the table and pushed an invisible veil of protection around him, in the event she attempted to scour his memories. Without responding to her comment, Zevander turned his attention back to Captain Zivant. "I'm afraid I know nothing of these missing soldiers. Or whatever a Corvikae might be."

The Magelord cleared his throat, shifting in his chair. "The Corvikae are an ancient civilization that existed centuries ago. A very hostile people. They raided villages, plundered, and raped. Spread diseases throughout all of Nyxteros."

Lies, of course. What fuckery, to falsify the history of a people that was nearly extinct.

Magic pulsed around Zevander as something prodded to get past his defenses. A glance toward Melantha showed her staring back at him, unabashed.

"An ancient civilization. As in, no longer existing?" Zevander asked.

"Yes," Magelord Akmyrios answered. "Though, it is our understanding that one of our colleagues, a rogue mage, had spent some time in Corvus Keep. We think it might be possible that he acquired scrolls and may have practiced a bit of demutomancy."

It was then Zevander knew for certain that they had knowledge of the stones and reminded himself to tread lightly. "What does demutomancy have to do with the missing guards? Or my quarry, for that matter, seeing as I've already disposed of him."

"Precisely as I said," King Sagaerin sat forward, placing his palms on the tabletop. "Zevander is my best Letalisz. He does not fail."

"Still, we'd like to confirm," the Captain chimed.

The king sighed and drummed his fingers. "Zevander, the captain and Magelord Akmyrios have asked that you take Nilmirth. I'd personally like to lay this matter to rest and begin searching for our missing men."

Nilmirth was a known toxin that, when ingested, assured only truth was spoken. If a lie happened to slip past the offender's lips, he'd spend the next hour in excruciating pain while the poison worked its way through the system. If the offense was serious enough, he'd be swiftly executed after. Lying to the king and his advisors would've certainly added Zevander to the list of upcoming executions scheduled.

Fortunately, he'd also trained to tolerate Nilmirth. While it did nauseate him, it would fail to elicit pain, no matter how many lies he might tell them.

"If it pleases Your Majesty, I'm happy to oblige."

"It would, and I thank you for your cooperation."

"Very well." The Magelord reached into a satchel clipped at his side and retrieved a vial of black liquid. The very sight of it churned Zevander's stomach, but he schooled his expression and reached out for the proffered toxin. "If you'd be so kind as to consume the entirety of it."

It'd taken small increments over the course of a century to build up the tolerance to an entire vial, and Zevander had suffered his share of agonizing pain in the process. He certainly wasn't looking forward to swallowing it right then. After popping the cork, he tipped back the fluid, and it assaulted his tongue with the horrific flavor of charred wood and ashes. Left an unbearable aftertaste in his mouth that had him yearning for a sip of ale to wash it down.

"Now, let us begin …" the woman said, her lips curved to a smile. "State your full name."

"Zevander Rydainn."

"And where were you born, Zevander Rydainn?"

"Castle Eidolon, north of the Aeramere River."

"And what is your sigil?" She continued to pry, much to his irritation.

"May I ask why all the banal questions?"

"To establish that the toxin is working, Your Lordship." She turned toward the king, who gave Zevander a subtle nod.

Huffing, the Letalisz swung his gaze back toward the woman. "The Scorpion."

"Ah. The sigil of pain and fear. You are said to be cursed."

"Yes." He clenched his jaw, growing more impatient with her questions.

"Who laid this curse upon you?"

"The king's former Magelord. Cadavros."

The way she shifted in her seat left Zevander wondering if the name made her uncomfortable. "And you were enslaved because of this curse, is that correct?"

"Yes."

"It was the good King Sagaerin who freed you and made you one of his *elite* Letalisz."

Zevander had spent years ensuring that only those who were seconds from death at his hands were privy to that information. And no one else, no matter their station. Again, he shot a glance toward the king, who nodded back at him. "Yes."

"He commissioned you to kill Dolion Gevarys?"

"He did."

"And did you carry out this request?"

"I did." The poison bubbled in his stomach, churning like it wanted out through his mouth, but Zevander swallowed it back.

"You're absolutely certain that Dolion is dead."

"I am." Another gurgling that rose up into his chest that time, and the Letalisz breathed through his nose to hold it down.

"How did you dispose of him?"

"My sword."

A cold sweat came over him, his hands trembling against his thigh where he rested them under the table.

"Were you aware that he attempted to collect bloodstones?"

"No."

A tightening in his chest expanded behind his ribs, and Zevander took deep breaths through his nose.

"You've absolutely no awareness of these stones?"

"None." Acids rushed up his throat, and Zevander gripped the chair, swallowing the toxin back down.

"The guard who mentioned your name ... do you know him?"

"Yes." Zevander answered honestly that time, not wanting to risk vomiting what he fought so hard to choke back right then.

"How?"

"Seen him at the tavern a time, or two." A deep, aching cramp twisted his insides, his hands trembling while his guts churned in chaos.

Still, the insufferable shrew kept on with her questions. "And why do you think he would mention your name with regard to the missing guards?"

"Don't think he much cared for me." Nothing that time, and Zevander was grateful for that.

"Did you kill the guards?"

Fuck.

"No." A sharp stabbing ache sent another round of acids shooting up his throat. Zevander tensed and clawed the arms of the chair, his eyes damn near watering. Surely, his face must have gone pale. Thankfully, that wasn't entirely unusual with Nilmirth–not even for those who told the truth.

"Interesting." She sat back in her chair, tongue sweeping across her lips as she tapped her fingernail against the tabletop.

"Would you be privy to what may have left the aura back at Bonesguard?"

"Enough of this. He's not a seer, by the gods. What kind of question is that?" The king tipped back another sip of his wine and slammed the goblet onto the table, clearly vexed. "He's answered your inquiries quite sufficiently. Dolion is dead. Perhaps your skills at identifying auras could use some sharpening."

Magelord Akmyrios straightened in his chair, and even after the king's insult, the woman's gaze didn't waver once, as she continued to stare back at Zevander. "I beg your pardon, My Lordship, but Melantha's skills are unparalleled. She is exceptional."

"Good. Perhaps she can put them to use and track down the real culprit in all of this. You put Zevander at great risk by requesting this meeting. By the gods, should any one of you divulge that he is a member of my Letalisz, I will see to it that you're thoroughly interrogated in the dungeons. Am I clear?"

"Yes, Your Grace," all three answered in unison.

"Good. I'll ask you to give me the room."

The three of them stood and bowed respectfully toward the king, Zevander bracing his hand on the table to keep from toppling over as he joined them.

"Not you, Zevander. I'd like you to stay a moment."

"As you wish." The thought of a longer meeting would've ordinarily left the Letalisz inwardly groaning, but Zevander was grateful to sit and breathe a moment more.

When the others finally filed out of the room, the king shook his head. "My sincere apologies. I did not mean to offend your loyalty. I simply wanted to establish your integrity, particularly with this new apprentice. As I understand, she's to take over as Magelord at some point."

"Where does she come from?"

"The north, apparently. I'd never be inclined to allow a

woman to attend my council meetings, as you know, but Akmyrios speaks very highly of her. Though, I must say, I'm not impressed," the king said, running his finger over the rim of the goblet, before taking another sip.

Zevander swallowed back another round of acids and cleared his throat.

Waving his hand in dismissal, King Sagaerin rose up from his chair. "Princess Calisza's Becoming Ceremony is a fortnight away and I will be expected to open the castle to a number of guests. I do loathe these social affairs, but what kind of king would I be, to deny my daughter her Becoming?"

When girls reached the age of fertility, roughly seventeen years old, or so, a Becoming Ceremony was thrown, and young men would fight for the right to claim her virginity. At times, the coupling resulted in marriage, but most often, it was simply a rite of passage to celebrate the fertility goddess, who'd ironically been raped and plundered at a young age. Zevander had long thought it a vicious custom, particularly when Rykaia had gone through it. She'd cried for days after, but it was believed that a virgin was bad luck and would result in the decline of a bloodline.

"I'd like all of the Letalisz in attendance. The Solassions are expected. Such a brutal lot, all of them."

The very mention of them ground at his nerves. "You're inviting the Solassions?"

"Not by choice. I find them repulsive, but it is a matter of social graces." He waved the cup bearer over, and when the boy placed a second cup down in front of Zevander, he politely declined. "I attended their princess's Becoming years ago, and it would serve as an insult if I were to deny King Jeret a returned invitation. I would like you and your men to watch over both Dorjan *and* Calisza. Ensure that there are no complications." He leveled his gaze on Zevander. "But watch Dorjan closest of all."

"Of course."

"I've appreciated your loyalty. As I hope you've appreciated my hospitality. When I heard those ruthless Solassions were holding such a brilliantly talented young boy all those years ago, I knew I needed to bring you back here to Costelwick. My hope is, when General Loyce sets eyes on you again, she'll be reminded of their foolish attempt to murder a highly skilled Lunasier."

A pulsing tension hammered at his muscles. "Loyce is expected to attend, as well?"

"Yes, she is Jeret's highest in command. She'll be heading the Solassion guards that accompany the king. Will that be difficult for you?"

The very name sent a bolt of rage through Zevander's blood.

"On your knees, Boy."

"Now, swallow."

"Not at all," he answered, and let out a quiet grunt when a cramping ache writhed in his stomach. *Fucking Nilmirth.*

"Good. Your sister is welcome to attend, as well, if you'd like."

The king's words were nothing but a distant sound to the thoughts clamoring through his mind. "I'm afraid Rykaia has not been feeling herself lately."

"Of course." The king pushed up from his chair, stealing another sip of wine. "If you wouldn't mind removing your mask so that I might see the progression."

Swallowing back his reluctance, Zevander lowered the mask from his face and allowed the king to examine him, as he sometimes requested.

A look of concern furrowed the king's brow. "It's gotten worse."

"Every day."

"What is this beast that longs to consume?" King Sagaerin strode toward a box set out on a chest and, with a small key, opened it. He retrieved a bag of coin and something else from inside, and locked it again before returning to the table. "I've consulted with every mage and priestess from every corner of Aethyria. Not one of them have offered any insight for a cure." As kind as the gesture was, Zevander was already well aware. For centuries, he'd searched every corner of Nyxteros–the deserts of Eremicia, and the farthest reaches of Solassia, consulting with priestesses, healers, and holy men. It wasn't until Dolion had suggested the bloodstones that Zevander had felt even the slightest shred of hope for a cure.

Placing one hand on Zevander's shoulder, he handed him the coin and a small vial of white liquid. "The vivicantem slows it a bit?"

"Seems to." Zevander knew it slowed the spread, as he'd already watched his brother suffer the course of it during a time when his family couldn't afford vivicantem. "I appreciate it."

"A small show of gratitude for taking care of that noisy and obnoxious mage."

Zevander wanted to laugh at the image of Dolion lounging in his cell, eating, drinking his ale as he studied the forbidden scrolls of Corvus Keep.

"The absolute lunacy is what I find most difficult to understand. Dolion was a very dear friend before he began all that ranting and raving of Cadavros. Can you imagine? Why on earth would he dream that the beast would rise from the dead?"

"Before I slid my blade across his throat, he spoke of an entity in the mortal lands." A fresh gurgling stirred in Zevander's stomach, and acids prickled in his chest with the lie. "He believed Cadavros resides there. That he was banished."

With a calm smile, the king shook his head. "I feel compelled to show you something, my friend." The smile on his face faded as he pulled an object from beneath the high neck of his brocade jerkin. A black amulet, or so it appeared, given the small dragon's claw dangling alongside it that was thought to secure an incantation. Attached to a small black chain, the shiny stone bore a spider etched into whatever metal made up the amulet. "Do you know what this is?"

"An ominous charm of some sort."

"Ominous, indeed." He chuckled, holding it in his palm. "It is chaos contained. A veritable Pandora's box. Sorrow. Disease. Violence. Madness. Death." In a manner that seemed more admirable than fearsome, he caressed the object with his thumb. "I had it made the day Dorjan was born. I distinctly remember holding him in my arms and feeling this overwhelming emotion to protect him. Furious at the thought of someone ever hurting him, or taking him from me." Beneath the sadness of his gaze flickered a spark of rage. "What would I do, if someone took my son from me ..." His jaw shifted, lips curving to a snarl. "His blood is linked to this amulet. If something should happen to him, a plague will be unleashed, and all of Nyxteros will be destroyed by it. Nothing would survive." A quiet tension rippled through Zevander as he silently absorbed the information. "I've not told anyone of this. My conscience has urged me to destroy it a number of times throughout the years, but you cannot destroy magic like this. Not even destroying the claw which binds it. I've tried." He stroked a thumb over the severed appendage. "It is a magic that comes from the darkest depths, where fear and vengeance reside." Tucking the amulet back into his tunic, he stood, thoughtful, for a moment. "It was Cadavros who bound the amulet to my newborn son. He was the only one who knew that it carried Dorjan's blood and not mine. Not even Captain Zivant is privy to this binding. A king is nothing without his legacy, after all. Do you understand why Cadavros had to die? Why it's absurd to imagine that I would let him live?"

"Yes," Zevander answered. Though, it made sense that the king would've had him killed for such a thing, he didn't bother to dispute him with the speculations he had about Cadavros in the mortal lands. Doing so would've been a slap in the face. Of what little the Letalisz had come to know of Sagaerin over the years, one thing was certain—the king did not like to be challenged. It would've had him investigating matters that would've unveiled secrets.

"This is why it is imperative that you watch Dorjan closely, in particular."

"And what of Calisza?"

With a dolorous expression, he gripped the back of his chair and sighed. "I would sooner see my beloved daughter consumed by insects and famine, than to watch her suffer at the hands of my enemies who would surely do worse. It brings me tremendous grief to imagine such a thing." He set his goblet down and patted Zevander on the shoulder. "All the more reason I'm grateful you've taken care of this rogue mage. One less preoccupation as Calisza's Becoming draws closer. In the meantime, keep your eyes and ears sharp for any mention of what may have happened to those missing guards. While I never once doubted that you took care of the mage, it is a curious coincidence that the aura at Bonesguard turned out to be Corvikae."

"Dolion might've been working with someone."

"Perhaps. I'd like you to be involved in finding out. Keep it between us. I don't want Magelord Akmyrios thinking I'm undermining his efforts."

"Of course."

He waved Zevander toward the door. "That is all. Safe travels back to Eidolon."

Zevander gave a courteous nod and pushed up from the chair, the nausea from before tugging at his throat again.

* * *

Leaning into the post beneath the bridge, Zevander expelled what he hoped was the last of the toxin into the moat. Squeezing his eyes shut, he shook his head and wiped his mouth on the back of his arm. "Fuck," he muttered, his guts finally settling down. It'd been years since he'd had to take in that much Nilmirth, and his body had surely reminded him how much it remembered its distaste. He stuffed the vial of vivicantem back inside his leathers—the catalyst for having expelled the last of it—and covered his face with the mask.

"How long have you been immune to Nilmirth?" The feminine voice came from behind, and he turned to see Melantha emerge from behind one of the posts, her head covered beneath the purple, velvet cloak that all of the king's mages wore.

"A bad batch, I suspect."

"Not likely. I made it myself."

In as subtle a movement as he could muster, he twisted his hand, palm up to summon his shield.

"No need. I've no intentions of probing you. Not now, anyway. I suspect your mind is a complicated labyrinth just waiting to be explored. Perhaps some other time."

"Perhaps you might consider a swim with the Koryn in the meantime."

Arms crossed, she sauntered closer, her lips clinging to a smile. "Is it that I'm a woman seated at the council or you truly do not care for me?"

"I care more for the vomit I just expelled than I do the members of the king's council."

Her smile widened and she tipped her head. "I'm offended that you have no interest in knowing who I am, when I've taken great care to study you, Zevander Rydainn. The Scorpion of Nyxteros. Lord of Eidolon. How has no one caught on that you're one of the king's infamous Letalisz?"

"I've made a point to draw little attention. Until today."

She chuckled, her flirtatious eyes doing nothing for him. "I find that hard to believe. A man as fierce looking as you must draw quite a bit of attention."

He didn't bother to respond to that, watching her make her way toward the edge of the moat, not far from where he'd just thrown up.

"The king isn't aware of your little secret, is he?" She held out her hand, agitating the water with whatever power she cast toward it. "He believes your sigil, the scorpion, to be the curse itself. A mere *affliction* propagated by Cadavros. He has no idea of its derivation, does he?"

Zevander kept his thoughts narrowed and focused, refusing to confirm.

"He has no idea the ancient power that resides in you. The mystical black flame that could wreak havoc on his kingdom, with no more than a wave of your hand."

A bold accusation, given the belief held by the highest mages, that no one had ever successfully undergone the Emberforge ritual without losing their powers. Still, he held his tongue, rejecting her manipulative provocations.

The Koryn rose up out of the water, eyes glowing with menace.

Zevander's scorpions stirred at the sight of the beast looming over him, primed to strike at any moment. Melantha reached out a hand and petted the serpent's scaly snout, then turned around to face Zevander, putting her back to the creature that slowly retreated into the moat. "My apologies for the inquisition earlier. On one hand, I wanted to clear the air. On the other, I hoped for an opportunity to meet the skilled man cursed by sablefyre."

Eyes narrowed, Zevander studied her, trying to discern if she had, in fact, scanned his thoughts.

"We've mutual acquaintances in the Solassions. I once suffered the very mines that held you prisoner." It didn't surprise Zevander. The Solassions were ruthless cunts, and would've had no qualms about keeping a woman as prisoner.

"Look at you now. Apprentice to the Magelord."

"Yes. I've lived an interesting life." Hands behind her back, she sauntered toward him. "Not without suffering, though. Perhaps we can exchange stories sometime."

"I don't think so." Zevander strode past her toward the hill.

"Zevander," she said, bringing him to a reluctant halt. "I failed to mention in the meeting that three of the Magestroli have also gone missing."

"Strange that you wouldn't mention that in front of the king."

"He has enough on his plate, what with his soldiers missing and his daughter's Becoming. Word is, the mages were headed to Corvus Keep."

He didn't give her the satisfaction of a reaction, instead keeping his expression stoic. "Did they have such little confidence that I would take care of the mage myself?"

"They were under the impression that Dolion had taken the bloodstones there. I don't suppose you retrieved them before killing him?"

"I've answered all of your questions. I have no awareness of the stones." A thousand tiny needles surged across his abdomen, proving that he hadn't expelled all of the Nilmirth.

"Pity. It's said the stones are the only thing that can destroy sablefyre."

"Interesting."

"It is. Exceptionally interesting. I shall see you at the Becoming, then." With that, she sauntered past him, her fingers brushing over his chest, and Zevander's flame reached out, as if drawn to her somehow.

Snarling, he pulled it back into himself.

* * *

Darkness had fallen by the time Zevander reached Eidolon, and every muscle in his body ached from the residual toxin still circulating in his blood. He'd expelled twice more on the ride back, and was ready to sleep it off. The moment he entered the castle, he found Rykaia sitting on stairs, a glass of wine dangling from her fingertips.

"Why keep the mortal in the dungeons?" she asked as he approached.

"I am in no mood tonight."

"You'd prefer to be fetching me from The Hovel again, is that it? Because this is what being off elixirs is like, Brother. I have to distract myself with life."

He halted and sighed, pinching the bridge of his nose. "She is of interest. That is all."

"Oh, clearly she is of interest. I cannot summon a single memory of when you brought another woman back to the castle. I find that intriguing."

"I'm happy to oblige your curiosity."

"Women do not belong in cages, Brother. Perhaps you might offer better accommodations to our guest."

"She's not our guest."

Brows raised, she tipped her head. "Is she your prisoner, then?"

"I've no idea what she is. I'm not interested in this discussion. I've had a long journey." He strode past her, up the staircase.

"Yes, you look a little peaked."

"Nilmirth," he threw over his shoulder.

The clack of her heeled boots had him inwardly groaning, as she followed after him. "Who forced you to drink Nilmirth?"

"The new apprentice to the Magelord."

"New apprentice? Is he handsome?"

"*She* is going to be a headache for me."

"She?" Rykaia frowned. "I'm sorry, did you just say *she*? As in, next in line for Magelord?"

"If she backs off, I suppose. Otherwise, she'll be next in line for my blade."

She finally caught up to him, her wine sloshing around in the glass as she walked briskly at his side. "If you didn't go through so much trouble on my behalf, I'd almost think you loathed women altogether."

"I loathe the torment your kind puts me through." Zevander pushed through the door of his office, desperate for a drink.

"At least let Maevyth take a bath." Rykaia entered after him, and as he rounded his desk, she plopped herself into one of the chairs across from him. "She smells awful. And you have to get better about feeding your prisoners. I'm not your kennel keeper. In fact, she'll need supper soon. I'll leave that to you."

"Fine." He quietly growled to himself. "She can take a bath. But I'm putting you on watch duty to make sure she doesn't try anything tricky."

"She's worried about her sister. She may be in danger."

"I don't give a damn about her sister." He poured a drink and tipped it back, the burn of the liquor warming his tense muscles. "She should be grateful I bothered to bring her here, at all. When I found her, she had three Imperial Guards and a prisoner ready to tear into her."

Rykaia slid her wine onto the desk, as though no longer interested in it. "Tell me you punished them for that."

"Every one of them burned."

"Good." She nodded and rolled her shoulders back. "She gets a bath. And time out of that godforsaken cell."

"A bath? Yes. Time out of the cell? No." Zevander still didn't trust the mortal to be freely wandering about the castle.

"She asked to speak with you. If you're going to keep her locked away down there, the least you can do is give her your ear for a moment."

"I've no interest."

"Then, why keep her?"

He'd asked himself the same question numerous times. The girl was the closest he'd come to a cure, and the fact that he couldn't kill her only added to his intrigue. "I have my reasons."

"You have your reasons," she echoed in a mocking tone. "Is this not my home, as well, Zevander? Or am I one of your guests?" When he didn't bother to answer, she swiped up her wine and gulped the whole thing back. "At least tell me this ... are you planning to kill her? I'd like to know, so I don't get too attached to the prey."

"Stay away from her, Rykaia," was all he said, as he pushed up from his desk, abandoning his drink. Too many conflicts muddled his brain, and he didn't need his sister stirring the chaos. He exited the office, and instead of heading toward his chambers, he kept on, following the clanking of metal as he approached the sparring room.

Ravezio and Torryn swung swords at each other–both equal in speed and skill, but as Torryn had been born without a sigil, he'd honed the strength of his body, which made him undefeated with a sword. Even without a sigil, he possessed one of the most dangerous powers of the four Letalisz–the ability to absorb large amounts of vivicantem from others, which made him twice as strong as any of the Letalisz, but also twice as unstable. Mentally, Torryn was a mess, his mind in constant chaos, always battling the effects of vivicantem toxicity that, in any other, would've turned him Carnifican.

In one swift move, Torryn swiped Ravezio's feet out from under him, knocking the graces out of his opponent.

Ravezio lay on the ground, coughing and wheezing, as Zevander entered the room, chuckling. "Is it the golden basilisk that supplies your wits?" Zevander asked.

Ravezio shot him a disgruntled look and pushed to his feet. "It is my basilisk that would've poisoned his blood." While Ravezio didn't have the power to summon an actual basilisk, like with Zevander's scorpions, his blood carried a potent venom. A bite, scratch, or prick from one of the spikes that protruded through his scales when threatened rendered his enemy dead within seconds.

"Not before he'd have depleted all of your vivicantem." It only took one touch from Torryn, as simple as a handshake, to weaken his opponent. But the magic always came at a cost. Depleting more than one person at a time sent him into delirium.

Torryn adjusted the wrappings he wore on his hands during sparring matches to avoid inadvertently sapping his opponent. "Did you come looking for a match?"

"Perhaps some other time. I came to tell you I have a woman in the dungeon."

Ravezio's brows kicked up with nauseating interest. "A woman, you say? Here?"

A scratch of annoyance jabbed at Zevander, curling his lip. "You will not lay your hands on her," he said, more gruffly than intended, and cleared his throat of whatever green-eyed monstrum had spoken for him. "She's a prisoner. The mortal who crossed the Umbravale."

"Ah, yes. Is that why you're keeping her locked in a cage?" Ravezio teased, stoking Zevander's frustration.

"It isn't a damned cage." Again, Zevander had to force his anger away. "Have you forgotten what a true cage looks like?"

"I've not. Which is why I certainly wouldn't wish one upon a frightened young mortal who probably has no idea why she's been brought here."

"Why is she here?" Torryn asked, getting to the point of the interruption.

"She's to be trained," Zevander grumbled, still bitter about it.

"Trained? What would a mortal need training for?" If only Torryn had seen how easily she'd resisted Zevander's flame, he might not have found the question so perplexing.

"According to Dolion, she harbors a unique power."

Torryn sneered. "How does a mortal possess any power? They're brittle and weak."

"She's apparently Corvikae."

"What is—"

Before Torryn could finish, Zevander shook his head. "I'll fill you in later," he said, too damned tired to give a history lesson right then. "The point is, she may very well offer something unique. But she has absolutely no awareness of it, nor understanding of how to use it."

Torryn snorted. "I feel for the bastard who has to train with her."

"Funny you should say …. That bastard will be you."

"What?" The amusement in his expression faded to a frown. "Why?"

"You're the most skilled at defense. If she begins with something natural, like fighting, it may help her tap into her powers, just as yours manifested."

Torryn frowned harder. "I'm not certain that I'm right for this." Except that he'd given Rykaia lessons years ago at Zevander's request, and she'd come to be quite proficient at defending herself.

"You are most skilled with a blade," Ravezio added. "Even if you move like cattle."

"I should've stabbed you earlier."

"What of the flammelian in The Hovel?" Zevander nodded toward Torryn, interrupting their banter.

"Hasn't attacked in days. No leads, as of yet. I'm chasing a fucking ghost."

"I'll join the hunt." Zevander's plan was to plant a rumor in The Hovel of a possible killer, to keep Melantha off his back and skew her investigation into the missing guardsmen whose bodies had long scattered into the wind.

"And what of this woman you want me to train? Does she have any fighting skill, at all?" Once again Zevander was reminded of her resistance to his flame.

"Very little. But I wouldn't call her weak. She did attempt to take on three Imperial Guards."

Torryn raised a brow. "I like her already."

"You intend to train a girl to fight and wield magic, you may want to consider nicer accommodations. Don't want her coming after you for a shit night's sleep, now, do we?" Chuckling,

Ravezio yanked his blade out and chucked it across the room toward a log of wood that held a half-dozen other throwing knives.

"She may try to flee. Her sister is apparently in danger."

"You of all people should relate to such a thing," Ravezio said, and strode off after his blade.

Groaning, Zevander turned for the door. "I relate to nothing with a mortal."

"You did remember to feed the little mortal supper, though, didn't you?" Ravezio called out after him.

Zevander squeezed his eyes shut and quietly growled as he strode from the room.

CHAPTER THIRTY-TWO

MAEVYTH

K nees pulled into my chest, I watched through the small window of my cell, as the moon rose and darkness swallowed daylight like a fading flame. Another day my sister might've been suffering alone, cold and terrified.

I hated that I was grateful to be safe and sheltered, even if the lingering chill of the dungeons still nipped at my bones. But most of all, I hated that even if I wanted to help her, I wouldn't have known where to begin.

My stomach gurgled with new hunger, and I rested my head against my knees, breathing through my nose to stifle the gnawing ache of starvation. Much as my heart wanted to mourn my sister's circumstances, my body reminded me there was never time to focus solely on someone else's pain.

Heavy boots thudded against the concrete, unlike Rykaia's delicate steps of earlier, alerting me of someone's approach. On instinct, I backed myself to the wall. The echoing fear from the guards attacking me still rattled my nerves. I held my breath as a shadowy form strode into the light of the flickering sconces and revealed himself to be Zevander.

Why I still held my breath at the sight of him was a mystery.

Although he wore the same mask as he had the last time I'd seen him, the hood of his cloak had been lowered away from his face, showing hair as black as mine curled at the nape of his neck. Finger-raked back from his face, with a few strands reaching his brow, it gave him a rugged, disheveled appearance.

He carried two wooden bowls and strode past my cell with both of them. The lingering scent of meat prickled my tongue. Seconds later, he appeared before my cell, still holding one of the bowls, but instead of shoving it under the bars, as Rykaia had earlier, he opened the door to my cell.

My whole body remained on guard as I watched him step inside, his massive size devouring the small space. I imagined my height, though not entirely petite, would've brought me to about his mid-chest.

Without a word, he handed me the bowl, which I scrambled toward with a level of gratitude I'd never felt at the sight of food before. The delicious scent of the chicken pottage filled my nose, and I sat back on the edge of the bed with the bowl, surprised when my captor didn't leave right away. Instead, he grabbed the wooden chair propped at the corner of my cell, which looked exceptionally small, more like a stool—even more so when he sat down on it.

Not daring to look at him, I sprinkled the pottage with a bit of purslane that was draped over the bowl's edge, sparing one of the succulent leaves to nibble. A delicious, tart lemon flavor puckered my tongue, and I spooned a bite of the warm soup. And another. Another warmed my belly, the meat not quite filling the vacuous hole of my appetite. While the breakfast had certainly taken off the edge of starvation, it hadn't completely sated the hunger that continued to gnaw at me.

Guilt knotted the pangs in my stomach. Had my sister eaten a single bite in the time I'd been offered two meals?

"You asked to speak to me," he said, breaking my thoughts.

I'd forgotten how deep that voice was, or how easily it sent a shiver over my skin. I swallowed back another bite of food and cleared my throat. "I wondered … how long you intend to keep me here. And *why* you're keeping me here."

"Has Dolion not offered any insights?"

"Um … well, I thought I'd introduce things slowly on that front."

Both of us turned to find Dolion peeking in on the cell.

"Perhaps you might sup somewhere else," Zevander said in an annoyed tone. "I need to speak with you, as well."

"Of course, of course." Bowl in hand, Dolion scrambled past the cell and disappeared down the same corridor from which Zevander had arrived.

"He's not your prisoner, yet you keep him down here. Why?"

"He enjoys the solitude."

"And, so, what are these insights you mentioned?" Picking at my food, I stole brief glances of my captor while he sat across from me, those few fleeting glimpses highlighting the differences in appearance between him and the sister that I'd met earlier. The way his black hair and light bronze skin bore a stark contrast to her silvery hair and pale complexion. An observation that left me wondering if they were related by blood.

"Why aren't you eating?"

"Why is every question I ask met with another question?" The ire in my voice was a mere spark of the anger stirring in my gut. Not so much that I was confined to a cell, but that even if granted my freedom, I'd have no idea how to navigate back to my sister, or what vicious things I might encounter along the way. When he didn't answer, I lowered my gaze and stirred the pottage with my spoon. "I find it difficult to eat when my sister might be starving."

"And if she's not, you're the fool who starves for nothing." The flat tone of his voice ground at my nerves.

"It's called empathy. Something you lack entirely."

He leaned forward, resting his elbows against his muscled thighs. "Perhaps you've forgotten the three men who tried to violate you. I'm the fucking *empath* who killed those men. For *you*."

I snorted at that and shook my head. "How was it you who killed them, when I specifically recall a scorpion the size of a small village doing the job?"

Zevander flipped his hand over, palm up, and a cloud of black smoke seeped up from his skin, morphing into the shape of a scorpion that sat in his palm as a living creature.

A sharp breath escaped me, and as I took in the oddity, every hair on the back of my neck stood on end. "What is this?"

"This? It's magic." He flipped his hand over, the scorpion following the movement, scampering over his knuckles, and I watched in horror as it burrowed itself beneath the skin on the back of his palm, leaving behind a small imprint of itself on the surface that mingled with the dark flames. The ink looked as if it'd been burned into his flesh. "And this is my curse."

"You …. You killed them?" I shook my head harder, still trying to puzzle how any of it was possible. It wasn't possible. "I didn't ask you to kill anyone."

His gaze lowered, presumably to the choker at my throat. "No. You pray to a god that doesn't listen, and you're shocked when he doesn't come to save you."

"And what are you? The good and benevolent passerby who stalks the night for rapists and murderers? What were *you* doing there?"

"Good and benevolent." He sneered. "I have little care for others in general, but less so for mortals."

I ran my tongue across the back of my teeth. "Why is that?"

"You're pests," he said, his voice thick with repulsion. "Weak little rodents that infest and spread disease."

"Then, why did you save me, if I'm so loathsome? Why bring me back to your home?"

The mask he wore made it impossible to tell if I'd angered him more. It seemed his eyes perpetually carried an edge of malice. "You serve a purpose. That is the only reason you're still alive."

"What purpose?" I'd heard of girls outside of Foxglove getting swept up to serve abhorrent purposes. Shackled to beds and forced to lie with countless men for coin. "What is it you want from me?"

"What I'm certain you won't give freely."

For the second time since I'd arrived in this place, I found myself wondering if I'd be brutishly violated by night's end. My lip curled at the possibility of it, but before I could tell him that I'd sooner die than entertain such a thing, he spoke.

"You're going to begin training in the morning."

Senses slapped into a stupor, I double blinked. "I'm sorry, what? Did you say *training*?"

"Yes."

"What kind of training?"

"We'll begin with the basics. Focus. Calling upon simple glyphs."

"Glyphs? As in symbols?" With the bowl resting in my lap, I rubbed my fingertips over the strange scar I'd shown Dolion earlier.

"Yes. It's how magic works."

Except I hadn't come any closer to accepting the idea that I possessed magic since my conversation with Dolion earlier that morning.

"I am ... thoroughly confused. You killed three men who tried to ... harm me. Brought me all the way here, to your castle, imprisoned me, all so you could turn around and train me to learn glyphs?"

"You can blame Dolion for the illogics."

"Why do I need to learn the glyphs? Will that help against the supposed mages who are after me?"

"Seems you've chatted with Dolion, after all."

"And none of this makes any sense." I still wasn't convinced that I hadn't died back in those woods, and that this wasn't some strange version of purgatory. "Why would you go through the trouble of training your prisoner?"

"Because you're weak—"

"And repulsive, yes, we've established this," I snipped back, impatiently. "I believe you likened me to a rat."

"Rodent."

"Semantics." Eyes narrowed, I stared back at him, tapping my spoon against the bowl, my appetite nowhere near as ravenous as before. "What are you not telling me?"

He sat upright in his chair again. "I'll leave the details to Dolion. In the meantime, I suggest you get some rest. And eat. Training begins at dawn, and I can assure you, you will need your strength. It can be quite physical."

"Physical? I'm to train in this?" I stared down at myself and the grimy, torn dress I'd worn for two days, which still carried the dried guts of the bug I'd squashed. "A tattered dress?"

"I'll leave your attire to Rykaia." He pushed to his feet, clearly finished with the conversation.

But I wasn't.

"Well, it seems you've delegated just about everything."

"I like efficiency."

"And I like freedom. Take me back to those woods, and I promise you will never hear from me again. No need for any delegation. No headache for you."

He let out a sound of disapproval. "You are relentless."

"Were it your sister, wouldn't you do the same?"

"Do not attempt to appeal to my good nature. We've established that I don't have one."

The creeping sensation of hopelessness crawled over me again. "Then, I will beg. If that's what it takes. I will beg that you take me back."

"Beg all you like." He let out a sardonic chuckle. "I'd quite like to see you on your knees."

With absolutely no forethought, I shot up from the bed and threw the pottage at him. The bowl hit his chest on a thump, and the pottage oozed down his leathers.

For the briefest moment, a zap of panic shot through me. Had I done the same to anyone back home, I'd have been slapped across the face—or worse. Vonkovyan soldiers would've added to the collection of scars on my back and legs.

"Your sister was right. You are a tyrant beast!"

He snarled as he wiped chunks of grain from his face. "And you are vexatious, yet by some mystery of the gods, you still have your tongue."

A whim of madness surged through me, and I darted for the open cell door. A blast of air shot from my mouth, as something banded around my stomach. With little effort, I was hoisted up into the air. My spine sank against the billowy mattress on an explosion of feathers that drifted around me.

Massive arms plowed into the soft mattress at either side of my head, as he caged me beneath him, and to my horror, he gathered my flailing limbs, pinning my wrists above my head. His intimidating form swallowed me as he loomed like a black squall, his infernal eyes glowing with annoyance. "Perhaps I should free you. See how you fare on your own, with all the creatures and beasts that would sniff you out and hunt you all the way to those woods."

"Yes! Please!" I shouted through tightly clenched teeth. "I can't think of anything worse than being your captive!"

"Clearly, you've not considered my point of view. You think I want you here? You think I asked to be your fucking keeper?" Even the bed trembled with the flexing of his muscles. Or maybe that was me and the fury he'd stirred inside of me. "I'd sooner toss you to the fyredrakes!"

"Then, do it!" Wriggling to free myself, I jerked my knee and struck him hard in the groin.

Perhaps too hard.

His brawny body recoiled, muscles contracted. A furious growl rumbled out of him, and a tight grip at my throat sent an explosion of stars across my vision. "Don't fuck with me, mortal. There are far too many painful ways to die." His patience unraveled in loose stitches with the angry veins that protruded from his neck, his black pupils swallowing the fiery gold and orange, and the ease of his grasp confirmed how effortlessly he could snap my windpipe.

I glanced to his cheek above the mask, where the grain had dried against his skin. "Perhaps you might wipe my dinner off your face before making serious threats against me." Teeth grinding, I forced myself not to spit at him right then.

On another growl he released me, and when he spun around, I caught the subtle swipe at his cheek as he strode toward the cell door. "Get your rest. Training begins at dawn."

With that, he exited my cell, locking the door as before.

CHAPTER THIRTY-THREE

ZEVANDER

Muscles wound tight, Zevander ground his teeth and made his way up the stone staircase, brushing his hand across his face again. He snarled when another bit of dried grain flecked off.

On the upper level, he found Dolion staring at a painting on the wall while spooning a bite of his pottage into his mouth.

"I need to speak with you," Zevander grumbled as he passed. "In my office. Now."

"Of course." The sound of his trailing footsteps followed after Zevander, through the Great Hall and up another staircase.

Past the solar room, Zevander led Dolion to an office with a wide Eremician redwood desk, where Rykaia still sat with her feet propped on it. Her lips pulled to a smile when he entered, stirring the ire already pulsing through his blood. "Who pissed in your pottage, Brother?" She chuckled, setting down the book she'd been reading.

A growl rumbled in Zevander's throat. "Give us the room."

"Of course. I was on my way to the dungeons to assist Maevyth with a bath."

He ground his teeth harder at the mention of her name,

loathing the way it stirred a deep and pleasurable surge of blood to his cock. "Good. Her scent has become absolutely repulsive."

Acids shot up into his throat, and Zevander realized the Nilmirth still hadn't entirely left his system. Palms to his desk, he took a moment to swallow it back, eyes watering from the burn in his nose.

"Everything okay?" Dolion asked, falling into one of the chairs set out before the desk.

"Fine." Zevander stumbled once on his way to the chair and fell into the already warmed leather seat. "I met with King Sagaerin this afternoon." He removed his mask, breathing through his nose while the last remnants of acid slipped back down his throat. "It seems the Magelord has a new apprentice. A young woman."

"Woman? What in the gods ..." Dolion looked thoughtful for a moment, lowering his bowl to his lap. "Did you catch her name?"

"Melantha."

A contemplative look crossed Dolion's face, and he shook his head. "I'm not familiar with her. This is quite strange."

"Well, she is determined to prove that you're alive. And she apparently reads auras, as well."

He winced, catching onto the implication. "She detected the Corvikae."

"Yes, and I entertained quite a few of her inquiries," Zevander gritted.

Eyes wide, Dolion rested a hand against his chest. "Nilmirth?"

"I told them nothing."

"Nothing? Do you have some sort of an immunity to *Nilmirth*?" The mage chuckled with an air of disbelief.

"A tolerance."

"My gods ... I didn't think that was possible. How?"

"That's unimportant. I learned something today that has me wondering if it may be the root of these visions you've been having." Zevander eased back into his chair. "King Sagaerin made me privy to an amulet he wears. Crafted by Cadavros. Should anything happen to Prince Dorjan, it will unleash a deadly plague on Nyxteros."

"You saw this amulet?" Before Zevander could answer, Dolion leaned forward, eyes brimming with intrigue. "What did it look like?"

"Black with a black chain and a spider etched into its surface. Dragon's claw to seal it."

"A soulbinder." Brows pinched together, he stroked his long, white beard. "It can't be, though ... I ... saw Cadavros in this vision. Clearly. He sat on the throne!"

"Perhaps your vision is a bit more abstract."

"Perhaps." He blew a resigned breath and slumped back into his chair. "Though, they've always been rather straightforward." Exhaling a breath, the mage shook his head. "If the plague is unleashed, then that means ..."

"Someone, or something, will kill the prince. My question is ... how many of your visions actually come to pass?"

The old mage pressed his lips to a flat line. "All of them. So far. I've a couple in the works."

"What are the others?"

Dolion waved his hand in dismissal. "Certainly not a plague. So, the prince must be protected at all costs," he said, changing the subject.

"Yes. In a fortnight, Princess Calisza's Becoming is going to bring nobility from all over Aethyria. Including the Solassions."

"Gods' teeth, whyever would he risk that his daughter would end up with one of the brutal beasts for the evening?" It wasn't that the Solassions looked like actual beasts. On the contrary, with their blond hair, bronzed skin, and blue eyes, they were considered exceptionally attractive by most.

Zevander wasn't most.

"Social graces," Zevander muttered. "In the meantime, you will continue to lay low and keep the bloodstones hidden."

"Of course. Though, it might be considered wise to hide the bloodstones somewhere else."

Zevander snorted and reached for his empty glass from earlier and filled it again, before kicking back a long swill. "Surely, you're not considering the mortal lands."

"Of course not. If Cadavros resides there, we'd be handing him six of the seven stones. I was thinking the home of my birth. Calyxar."

An island of predominantly Elvynira in the south. A world of mountains and ice. If Zevander thought Nyxteros winters were cold, they were nothing in comparison.

"Cleaving?" Zevander asked.

"Too far, I'm afraid. But even if I could, the Elvynira take great care in making sure no one enters their domain without their knowledge. I'd find myself in chunks of meat on the floor, if I attempted such a thing. Which, again, speaks of its level of safety for the stones. In fact, the first septomir resided for a millennia amongst the Elvynira, until it was stolen by the former king."

"Then, just how do you intend to stay concealed on this trek to Calyxar, seeing as it's my head the king would demand for lying to his face?" Zevander fought to tamp down the ire burning through him at the mere prospect that Dolion would risk such a thing.

"I've become privy to a very effective cloaking spell. It would require a decent amount of vivicantem. If you can procure that, I can assure safe travel."

With both the Magelord and Captain Zivant a little too focused on him, it made sense to get rid of the stones. Zevander reached into his pocket for the remaining vivicantem the king had given him earlier and passed it to the mage, who examined its contents.

"Should get us to Wyntertide," Dolion said, stuffing the vial into a pocket of his robe.

"You intend to journey by foot."

"Well, by steed, if you'd be so kind. I'll board a ship in Wyntertide."

"And what of breaking this curse?"

"Calyxar is home to the most brilliant minds in our world. I will consult with them and return."

Zevander sneered before taking another sip of liquor. "I thought you were one of the most brilliant."

"Certainly not. In fact, I'm beginning to question my visions, as of late." He nodded toward Zevander's drink. "Might I trouble you for some of that?"

The Letalisz opened a small cabinet beside him, retrieving a glass that he filled with the fiery, orange liquor. "I want a guarantee that you'll return."

Dolion sipped the liquor, his brows raised. "It's quite potent, isn't it?" When Zevander didn't bother to answer, still waiting for a response to his demand, the old mage lifted the sleeve of his robe to reveal three gold bands wrapped tightly around his bicep. Family relics that served as a source of protection for the Elvynira. In Dolion's world, there was nothing more valuable. "I've worn these bands since I was a boy. My own father placed them upon my arm." He unwound the bands from his bicep and handed them to Zevander. "Please take care of them. They are all I have left of my bloodline."

"You are the last?"

"I am. All my power dies with me."

It suddenly made sense why he was so against killing the girl. "And if you encounter trouble on the way?"

"I have six stones of the septomir. Surely, that should be enough to ward off trouble."

"Who will train the girl while you're gone?"

He stared back at him over the rim of his glass before taking a sip. "I trust you've sent for Allura from The Citadel?"

"Yes. Kazhimyr is expected to return with her."

"I'll educate her on the basics and leave my codex for the

glyphs. I suspect she'll need tremendous practice with the first few." Dolion huffed, swirling the drink in his glass. "Or I could take her with me. She would be safer in Calyxar than here."

"If I didn't have some level of trust in you, I'd say that's a fucking shady plan. You with all seven bloodlines at your fingertips."

"I've made my position clear. The girl will live so long as I draw breath."

Zevander mentally chewed on the idea of sending her away. It certainly would've made his life easier, a thought he held onto as he fought to ignore an intrusive sliver of disappointment that he wanted to stab with a blade. "I suspect the king will have his mages in attendance at The Becoming Ceremony as a means of protection. Consider leaving that night, and the two of you may have less to contend with on the road."

He gave an assenting nod, steepling his fingers. "A wise idea. Unless, of course, you'd prefer the girl stays with you. I'm certain you'd make a fine preceptor."

"I've no interest in playing school with an unfledged mortal." Another twist of his gut had Zevander's hands curled to tight fists, as the Nilmirth made itself known once again.

Dolion laughed at that. "She's lost her family and her home, Zevander. Whatever must this poor girl do before you'll warm up to her?"

"Sew her lips shut. That's a start." Zevander tipped back another gulp of his drink, letting the burn distract his mind from the many things he'd have enjoyed about those lips.

"You are perhaps the most irascible creature I've ever met. I pity the girl, truly." Dolion pushed to his feet, grabbing his empty bowl from the desk. "And, so, we shall begin training in the morning."

"I've assigned Torryn to work with the two of you."

"Excuse my Elvynese but Torryn knows fuck all about glyphs. You are the one person most equipped to train her, as you did not acquire the powers of sablefyre by blood." It was true that, unlike most Lunasier, who typically acquired the power of their parents and could anticipate which glyphs they would inherit, he'd had to learn on his own. And because most mages either didn't know much about sablefyre, or feared it all together, he hadn't had a mentor. "Even Torryn, though he doesn't have a sigil, knows what powers he wields. But you, Zevander, are as much a curiosity as she is."

"And why the fuck should I care? I learned on my own. She can, as well."

"Aren't you the least bit curious? You couldn't kill her. Why?" When Zevander didn't answer, Dolion continued, "Her powers may have some answers for your curse."

"I've conceded time and time again for you, old man. I will not bow to your request again."

"Yes, you have. And you are not a man who entertains the requests of others, so I have to believe it is not for myself that you have made these concessions, but out of your own curiosity."

Again, Dolion's words rang true. Since the night he'd snuck into the girl's room with every intent to kill her, she'd roused a maddening plague on his mind. Why *couldn't* he kill her? Why had the flame that he'd known his whole life turned on him?

"Training her could take years," Zevander groused. "That is not a burden I long to carry."

"Two weeks. Train her for the two weeks so she has some skill in defending herself before I leave with her to Calyxar. You may glean something in that time, or nothing, at all, but it may also satisfy your curiosity."

"Every day, this curse threatens to consume me, the way it has consumed my brother, and he has little time left before I'll be forced to entertain his only request." Killing him was the only way for Branimir, as the spiders would never have allowed him to take his own life. "I have moments myself, where I can't control it. As if it longs to break free."

"It is a power forged by the gods. It wasn't meant to be controlled, or wielded by mancers, but still, I know nothing of the septomir's power. If you killed the girl today, it would take countless days for me to understand a magic so ancient that it's not even written in scrolls. And, what then? What if I can't help you, and she dies for nothing?"

"You've lost your confidence." Zevander stared into his drink, the conflict burning in his own mind.

"If you saw what I've seen in my visions, there would be no question. Two weeks, Zevander."

It was bad enough that he'd agreed to save the girl and shelter her from the mages, but to ask him to train her felt like a fucking slap to his pride. "No. I'm done pandering to you. I spared her life and gave up the only hope I had for finding a cure for Branimir and me. Brought her here, gave her shelter. She's your problem, not mine," he snarled.

A troubled expression crossed his face. "Please, Zevander. I'm begging you. I'm an old mage whose mind is slipping. I cannot be tasked to train her myself. I've no knowledge of defensive magic, I'm merely a scholar. And she *needs* protection. You are the girl's only chance of survival."

Gnashing his molars, Zevander curled his hand to a tight fist. It was only his burning curiosity about the girl that had him considering it. Resisting the flame might've been a gateway to controlling it. Controlling it might've meant slowing its faulty side effects. "I will give you two weeks. And you will take her away. Far away. She must never return, do you understand?"

"I do. Two weeks."

CHAPTER THIRTY-FOUR

MAEVYTH

"Idiot." Still sat on the bed, I held my face in my palms, chiding myself for the ridiculous outburst from earlier. While I had been known to spout off at the mouth on occasion, I'd never lost my temper quite so abruptly as I had with Zevander. What a complete fool. If there was an inkling of hope that he might've returned me to Aleysia, my little tantrum had certainly crushed any chance of it.

The weight of everything had pressed down on me, and in that moment, I'd crumbled. Of course, his comment certainly hadn't helped.

Freedom seemed twice as far as before.

At a clanking sound, I looked up to find Rykaia at the door of my cell, holding up a key. I hadn't even heard her approach. "You're letting me go?"

"Not exactly." She opened the cell door on a click and waved me out.

Frowning, I pushed to my feet, padding toward her with cautious steps. "What's going on?"

"A bath. A bath is what's going on."

As guilt-ridden as I may have felt accepting food and comfort while tormented by thoughts of my sister, a bath sounded heavenly right then. I followed after her, down a dark corridor and up a stone stairwell that spat us out into yet another corridor, and on into a massive room with ornate stone floors and tapestries that hung from stone walls. A staircase, illuminated by the warm flicker of sconces, led to an upper level.

I'd never been inside a castle before.

In Vonkovya, King Alaric served as the monarch, but was nothing more than a face of tradition. Most of the country was ruled by the Lord of Parliament and his Vonkovyan Army in the capital. A place I'd never visited but had heard was opulent and brimming with modern amenities not found in the rural parts, where I'd lived my whole life. As we made our way through what appeared to be a grand foyer, I caught sight of the towering entry doors to the right of me, not remembering a single moment of having been brought through them when I'd first arrived.

Rykaia led me up the staircase and down another hallway, to a room with a heavy wooden door and black, iron hinges. The moment she pushed it open, a familiar masculine scent hit me, and I glanced around a vast room with beautiful stone archways and gorgeous stained glass. Multiple candelabras flickered from the mantle over a stone hearth, the cozy warmth of which sent a shiver across my bones. Across from it was a black, velvet settee cluttered with books. The biggest, most elaborate bed I'd ever seen stood within an alcove of bowed lancet windows that reached the ceiling, offering a gorgeous view of a vast darkness beyond, where faint white spires in the distance hinted at mountains.

I ran my hand over the ebony wood and black silk sheets, so soft they felt like warm liquid beneath my fingertips. Paintings of ghostly, white animals in dark woods hung about the room. Black armor and leather lay draped over a metal contraption at the foot of the bed, and I frowned, recognizing the garments.

"The bed was a gift from King Sagaerin. All those years of

forcing my brother to sleep on a stone floor must've left him with a sour conscience," Rykaia said from behind.

"You brought me to *his* bedroom ..." I retracted my hand, suddenly aware that I was touching the very place where Zevander slept. A prickling suspicion coiled around my thoughts. "Why would you bring me to *his* bedroom?"

"Because *his* bathing room is the best in the castle. And, I say, our guests deserve the best." Smiling, she turned toward a set of double doors twice my height and pushed them open into another dome-ceilinged room with towering stony lancet windows that looked out on the same gorgeous view as the bedroom. An image of ethereal beings adorned the ceiling, like angels, with strange silver markings on their skin that glowed against the backdrop of two bright moons and stars. The enthrallment must've been clear on my face, as Rykaia smiled and looked upward.

"The Lunadei. Moon gods." She knelt beside a stone structure that was as big as my room back in Vonkovya and filled with crystal water, and ran her hand through the surface. "The temperature is perfect."

I glanced over my shoulder and back. "What if he returns?"

"My brother spends the hours away in his meeting chamber, drinking his liquor and reading."

"He reads?" I did a poor job of hiding the surprise from my voice.

"Nothing thrilling, believe me. Mostly scrolls on history and glyphs. I'm certain he's read everything in Eidolon's library, yet he is forever enraptured in some arcane codex."

I found that to be an interesting contradiction to the man who'd come off as such a brute.

"So, I will grab a warm towel and some nightclothes. There's a sponge on the edge of the bath with some sickleberry soap and jasmine oil." She pointed to where she'd already set out the items for me.

"Why are you doing this?" I mentally chided myself for asking the question. For the unfounded discomfort I felt having someone pamper me that way. Possibly because, aside from my sister, no one had ever gone out of their way to do things for me.

"Why would you ask that?"

I lowered my gaze. "I'm sorry. I didn't mean anything by it."

As if sensing my sudden unease, she clasped her hands together and crossed the room toward a cupboard, grabbing a towel from a folded stack in there. "This place ... it can be so heavy at times. It's nice to have something to care about."

"I appreciate your kind hospitality."

"Right, so, I'll leave you to it."

"Thank you, Rykaia."

She turned toward the door, but swung back around. "Why are you here?"

Dumbstruck by her question, I pondered it for a moment.

"What drove you beyond the Umbravale?" she clarified.

"I told you, my sister and I were chased through the woods."

Crossing her arms, she shifted on her feet. "And, so, if you were to go back, if you found your sister, would you stay in your world?"

It was a good question. Would I? What was there for me? Certainly no family, nor home, nor the village I'd grown up in. None of them wanted me.

"I don't know. In my world, I was considered cursed. An outsider."

"Did your family curse you?"

"The villagers. I was found by the woods as a baby. The governor thought it was an act of mercy, but the villagers thought me an aberration. And then, of course, there was the accident." I lowered my gaze to my fidgeting hands.

"What accident?" she asked.

While it was a stain on my conscience, even after all these

years, I hadn't decided how much I should've shouldered the blame for it.

Remorse bit into my words with jagged teeth, as I relived that day, telling her the story of how Lilleven and her brother had taunted me, picking at my clothes and calling me Lorn. I didn't know why I bothered to detail it all. Maybe because I'd listened to everyone else's versions of the story my whole life, and it felt good to put the truth out into the universe. Or maybe I needed to remind myself of the truth. Either way, I kept on, "She told me she longed to see me burn at the stake, so in retaliation, I told her I longed to see her trampled by horses." Even then, I still winced at the harsh words I'd spoken. Didn't matter that she'd threatened me, too. What had bothered me most was that I'd let her words crawl beneath my skin. "As she was crossing the road, a carriage barreled into her. I should've been burned, or banished for her death, but I suppose the village saw fit to punish me in other ways."

"I find it interesting that any time a girl is unusual, or dare I say, unique, she's deemed evil, or cursed." From the ledge beside the basin, she lifted one of the bottles there, uncorking it for a sniff. "I've also learned to survive on the mere crumbs of social graces. Like you, I've grown thin and weary from it," Rykaia said with an unexpected doleful expression, setting the bottle back down. "I'm sorry, Maevyth. I'm sorry they treated you so horribly. But I'm not sorry she's dead." With that, she left the room, closing the door behind her, and for a moment, I pondered her cold words. How easily she'd spoken them.

Distracting myself, I glanced around again, marveling at the gorgeous detail in the glass above me, the frescoes painted on the outside of the windows and down the walls, the absolute luxury that I had never known myself. Grandfather's winery had allowed us to live comfortably, but never royally.

The door flew open, and I startled, nearly tumbling backward into the water. Rykaia strode in, carrying a white garment. "I nearly forgot your nightclothes." She slipped past me and plopped it down with the towel.

I only managed a quick, "Thanks," before she slipped out of the room again, closing the door behind her.

Pausing for another potential interruption, I stared at the door a moment, then undressed quickly, discarding my black dress and choker alongside the stone basin. The wavering light from the candles offered a small bit of illumination, as I carefully stepped down into the warm water that gathered around my legs like a hearth-heated blanket. A stone ledge beneath the water served as a place to sit, and I closed my eyes as I breathed in the steam rising from the surface. How the water remained warm was a mystery I didn't have the energy, or care, to untangle. But I was grateful for that magnificent heat that soothed the ache in my muscles.

Candles flickered around me, the water dark and depthless as I peered down at my submerged hands. Aleysia would've hated bathing with candles. My sister had always feared the dark, but I was the opposite. I'd always found the light far too scrutinizing.

On a long exhale, I rested my head against the edge of the basin and closed my eyes for a moment. In the quiet of my mind, I saw my sister–cold, bruised and beaten.

The pressure in my sinuses had me sitting upright, and I pulled my knees into my chest. For the first time since having separated from her, I finally broke. Every horrible thing from that night sank its teeth into my conscience and tore away at my heart. I wanted to reach into the void and pull my sister from whatever misery she suffered, to divide the burden so that she might have a moment to breathe. While we may not have been blood, I loved her as a second half of myself. A twin.

My mind tormented me with the fateful moment when I'd jumped through that archway. A hasty act of stupidity. "I'm sorry," I whispered. "I should not have left you, my sweet sister."

I cried for what seemed like an eternity in the span of mere minutes. All the agony and pain poured out of me in hot tears that fell into the water like poison rain. I let the misery I'd tucked away ravage me, pulling me into the depths of possibilities I didn't want to imagine, the worst being her death. Until I had no more tears. Nothing left in me.

I stared out at the mountains in the distance, where the moon appeared as a downturned crescent. I'd never seen such a thing. Most of the second moon remained off to the side, out of the window's view. I wondered if the two ever crossed, what it'd look like.

The distraction dulled the pain and guilt that my head refused to relinquish.

A voice inside my mind told me that every decision Aleysia had made, had been her own, and that I was not responsible for what might have happened to her. That voice carried the distinct tone of Zevander, mirroring what he'd said to me earlier about refusing to eat. While I loathed my irascible captor, in spite of his grumpy demeanor, he'd spoken some measure of truth.

I lifted my head from my knees and glanced around at this sacred space that belonged to him. A space that I had invaded with my anguish and tears.

From the ledge beside me, I grabbed the bar of soap and sniffed it, greeted by the mouthwatering aroma of warm vanilla, and a spicy berry with a hint of cinnamon. An intricately embellished brass flask that reminded me of an anointing bottle sat off to the side of the soaps Rykaia had provided, and I lifted it and unclasped the small chain connected to the cork top. A delicious scent emanated from the bottle—one I knew distinctly. The woodsy, amber scent that roused my senses.

Foregoing the berry soap, I lathered the other onto the sponge and washed myself of the grime and dirt I'd collected over the last few days.

Once coated in the musky-smelling soap, I stepped off from the ledge where I sat, surprised to find the bottom was much deeper than it appeared, as the water rose up to my neck. I dunked my head below the surface, the vastness of the bath reminding me of the times Aleysia and I would bathe in the river, though the river water was nowhere near as warm and comforting.

After washing my hair and rinsing away the soap, I treaded back toward the edge of the basin and grabbed the towel that Rykaia had set out for me.

The door swung open again, and I scrambled to wrap the towel around my body, covering as much of myself as I could.

I expected to chide Rykaia for her rudeness.

Instead, I found a tall, brawny figure standing in the doorway, his body completely filling the frame of it. One hand covered the lower part of his face, the other clenched at his side.

"What are you doing in here?" he asked, his voice gruff and deep, its rough timber strumming my heart into a flutter, as I stood naked beneath the towel.

"Rykaia … she …. I'm sorry. I didn't mean to invade your space."

"Rykaia …" he grumbled, his fist tighter than before. Still, he held his hand over his jaw, as if to hide his face, and I realized he was as flustered as I was right then.

Strange. Based on what little I knew of him at that point, he didn't seem capable of being caught off guard. In fact, on the ride to the castle, I recalled having been impressed by how very aware and vigilant he'd been of his surroundings. Like a hunter.

Yet, there he stood, refusing to look at me.

"I'll leave." I gathered up the clothes Rykaia had offered me, only then noticing what I thought to be a white shift was actually a man's tunic.

He seemed to take notice, as well, frowning down at the garment dangling from my fingertips that matched the half-tied tunic he wore tucked into his black, leather trousers. A sight I would've stolen a moment to appreciate, had I not felt like what little I'd eaten was about to make an appearance on the floor right then.

"I'll wear what I arrived–"

"No," he said abruptly. "I'll see to it that your dress is properly washed and returned to you."

"I don't want to impose."

"No imposition." His clipped and grumpy responses hinted at irritation, though.

Why he refused to lower his hand from his face had me searching for the source of his apparent insecurity, but I could hardly see anything in the dim light of the room.

A strange detail caught my attention, though. The scorpion that'd burrowed into his palm suddenly wasn't there, but instead, appeared at his forearm just below his rolled-up sleeve. To be sure, I glanced down to the back of his other hand, which bore no scorpion tattoo there, either. Had it moved?

"You used my soap." The comment yanked me from my thoughts to see his gaze shifted, presumably to the unused bar that Rykaia had supplied, and back to me.

"My apologies if that wasn't okay. The berry soap is lovely, but I ... I just happen to like that particular scent." The lack of response that followed left me thinking he was annoyed that I'd dipped into his personal things. "I'm sorry for earlier, too. I lost my temper, and I didn't mean to .... I sometimes act before thinking."

Again, he didn't say anything in return, only peered back at me over the top of his hand, his eyes a turbulent mix of scrutiny and curiosity. Unless I was misled by the fickle lighting, they seemed more golden, less angry. The more he stared at me, the more aware I became of my body's reaction–the twitch in my inner thighs and the soft tickle in my belly. My pulse trembled, waiting for him to say, or do, something. A maddening silence hovered between us, the tension so thick, it swallowed the air.

"I'd like to get dressed, if that's all right," I finally said.

His eyes sharpened when he seemed to snap out of his silent musing. He turned as if to leave, but paused and kicked his head to the side, revealing a profile as handsome as I'd have imagined. Angular and chiseled jawline, with a day's worth of stubble, the intense slope of his brows, and an elegantly shaped nose, all of which, gave him a commanding appearance. The lethal features of a man who could have any woman he wanted. "I did not mean to put my hand to your throat," he said, the calm in his voice catching me off guard.

Leaving me as the one not knowing what to say, while I stood fumbling for thought. The pause stretched longer, stoking the awkward exchange between us. *Say something.* In the absolute absence of thought, I found myself staring at his broad shoulders, my mind wandering to what he must've looked like without his shirt. "You have a nice back." The words tumbled haphazardly from my lips, and I slapped my hand to my mouth far too late to contain them.

I turned away, covering my eyes and the humiliating blush that crawled over my face. "Bath. I meant you have a nice bath."

Before he wordlessly strode from the room, closing the door behind him, I caught a distinct dimple in his cheek.

"You insufferable fool." I hid my face behind my hands, the mortification unrelenting as it pounded through my head. What was it about the man that turned me into a blundering idiot?

I dressed quickly, hating that I didn't have a clean cammyk to wear underneath. Staring down at my cloth bodysuit that typically covered all of my private parts, I pondered wearing it unlaundered, then remembered I'd pissed myself back at the woods.

God. It felt so unnatural walking around without it. Aleysia had always refused to wear one, calling them restrictive torture devices. While my breasts felt heavy and exposed without the support, it was certainly a relief to be able to breathe easier than before.

Piled atop the bodysuit sat the cross choker, and while I was inclined to simply toss the cursed thing, I somehow felt naked without it. All my life I'd been forced to wear it, but here, it didn't feel so much as a punishment anymore. In spite of its negative implications, it felt like a link to home. To my sister. Sighing, I clipped it back on.

When I exited the bathing room, I found Zevander standing alongside the alcove of windows, his face covered by the mask he always wore. It didn't make sense, given that mesmerizing profile I'd seen moments ago. His gaze trailed over me, and whatever thoughts passed through his mind had his hands balled into tight fists again. Anger? Disgust? I couldn't tell with that damned mask covering half his face.

Every inch of my body tingled, the awareness of my naked form beneath the shirt only a mild distraction from how utterly attractive he looked in his casual clothes. The way his chest muscles peeked through the open neckline of his tunic and the fabric bunched around his bulging biceps. His midnight-toned hair stood tousled about his face in lazy wisps that refused to flatten. I'd never stood before a man so virile, so wildly masculine, in my life. There was something dangerously seductive about him, leaving me feeling too warm beneath the tunic. A deadly allure, fitting for the kind of man who could whisper honeyed words in your ear as he ran a blade through your heart.

"I'll escort you to your room," he said, but as he took a step in my direction, I shook my head.

"No, it's all right. I can return on my own." The last thing I wanted was to walk all the way to the dungeon alongside him, flustered like some silly little girl.

"You can't return to the dungeon dressed like that. You'll take one of the rooms on the upper floor. The door will be locked, of course."

"For my privacy? Or because I'm your prisoner?"

Something flickered in his eyes, and I dared to think he

would've loved to call me as such. "I don't house prisoners, *Lunamiszka*." The unspoken implication in his voice told me what he didn't bother to say. He killed them. "Would you prefer to sleep in the dungeon?"

"I prefer to be entrusted with my freedom, no matter where I sleep. As I understand, there are fyredrakes on the premises that you'd happily toss me to. So, how could I possibly escape?"

"As relentless as you are, I'm sure you'd find a way."

"I hardly know you, but I'm certain you'd do the same in my position. And what in seven hells is *Lunamiszka*?"

He snorted. "A language you apparently don't speak, for once."

For once? "I'm speaking as I've spoken my entire life, which means we must share the same language."

"And what do you call your language?"

"Vonkovyan."

"I am familiar with Vonkovyan. It is one of our many *dead* languages." He crossed his arms, drawing my eyes to the deep groove in his chest visible through the laces of his tunic. "You are not speaking Vonkovyan. You are speaking perfect Nyxterosi. How? Answer that question, and I'd be more inclined to let you roam free."

A dead language? "That doesn't make any sense. I've never learned a language outside of Vonkovyan." Not even Lyverian.

"Then, your door will remain locked." Clearly, he thought I was something far more interesting. Like a spy—or worse, a threat. It was almost laughable, so unimaginably far from reality.

"You never answered my question. What does *Lunamiszka* mean?"

He leaned back against the stony wall behind him, his stance more relaxed. Casual. Devastating, how brutal and aristocratic he could look at the same time. "It means you're persistently frustrating and you ask too many questions."

"All that in a single word?"

"We like brevity. And silence."

"Are you speaking for all of your personalities?"

The way his mask moved, I could tell he was grinding his jaw.

"If I'm going to be locked away all day, I'd prefer to have company, at least. I'll remain in the dungeons with Dolion." I wanted to ask the elder man more about glyphs and the symbol he'd examined on my hand. At least he seemed willing to entertain my questions. I couldn't stand the thought of being locked in a room by myself all day long. Even if the view was beautiful, the thought of being alone for hours on end terrified me.

"Then, you will be escorted without argument."

"Fine."

He strode toward me, setting my nerves ablaze as he came to a stop not quite a foot from where I stood, his height and size apparent when I stared at the middle of his broad and muscled chest. His body reminded me of the solid oak in front of the cottage back at Foxglove, and the way it shaded the entire yard when the sun was high.

A flick of his fingers dragged my attention to his rough and scarred hand outstretched toward me. Markings on his skin held the faint outline of strange shapes, and I wondered if they were the glyphs. "I'll pass your clothes off to Magdah for laundering."

I clutched them tighter, remembering my undergarments were buried in the pile. "Magdah?"

"Yes. She makes the food that you enjoy flinging," he said, his voice sharp with sarcasm.

Clearing my throat, I balled the pile tighter, ensuring my dirty undergarments were tucked deep into the mound, and handed them off.

He jerked his head for me to follow after him, and as we exited his room for the corridor, I tried not to study the way his broad shoulders tapered down to a narrow waist and muscled backside that moved in perfect cadence as he walked. I'd never paid much attention to a man's haunches before, but for reasons that frustrated me, I couldn't stop myself. It seemed every inch of him had been carved by God–even his damned ass. He possessed an effortless sensuality about him that Aleysia would've surely fawned over. The thought left me wondering what my wily sister would've done, had she found herself in my position.

Undoubtedly, she'd have seduced him, and not necessarily for her freedom.

I'd seen her do it a few times in the village, with the Vonkovyan guards who enjoyed random interrogations of young girls. It came natural to her, with her golden hair and bright eyes that she made a point to bat with her flirtations. Without a doubt, Zevander would've had her loins stirring like a tempest.

He glanced over his shoulder, and I jerked my head up so fast, I nearly toppled backward. "Perhaps you should walk alongside me, unless you insist on staring at my ass the whole way."

A scorching heat warmed my cheeks, cooled only by the icy anger of having been humiliated. "Perhaps you shouldn't walk like you've got two snapping turtles attached to your *ass*."

I winced at the slippery insult.

Another glance showed a slight squint of his eyes, and I wondered if he'd smiled, or sneered beneath that mask. Not likely a smile. I doubted the man's lips ever stretched beyond a snarl. Yet, his voice held a small bit of amusement when he asked, "What are the odds that I'd stumble upon someone brassier than my own sister."

I wasn't usually, that was the oddity of it. Something about him brought out a side of me I mostly kept subdued, for fear of the consequences. I'd always had a sharp tongue, but men, in particular, had always found a way of silencing it, either by a slap to the face, or flogging.

As imposing and threatening as Zevander was, I didn't feel the same fear in his presence. If anything, I felt emboldened. While he was doubtlessly capable of it, he didn't strike me as a man who enjoyed unnecessary violence.

Past the Great Hall, and down another corridor, he led me to a kitchen twice the size of the one I'd seen at Mr. Moros's manor. Candelabras hung from high, vaulted ceilings with thick wooden trusses that buttressed the walls. Lancet windows, with beautifully carved iron grilles, made up the far wall, and black wooden counters and larders stood laden with age and wear.

A figure manned an elaborately carved, iron stove, stirring a steaming pot. A brown, linen dress with a hood hid their face and hugged the curves of a plump body. At our approach, they turned, revealing an older woman with gray hair. Two black horns stood out from the top of her head and curled back inside the hood.

I turned away to keep from staring at them.

"Magdah, I have some garments that need laundering."

"Yes, My Lord, of course." Her accent held a pronounced rhoticity, as she reached for them with long, bony fingers, two of which were missing.

Again, I watched to make sure my dirty undergarments didn't make an unwelcomed exit onto the floor.

While she offered a bright smile for Zevander, it quickly faded when she set her eyes upon me.

"Thank you for the pottage," I said, the guilt of having wasted it gnawing at me.

"Oh, the two bites you managed to eat before casting it across the room?" As much as the humiliation of what she'd said snaked beneath my skin, I found myself fascinated, almost lured by her accent. The way *two* sounded like *chew*, and the roll of her tongue when she'd said *room*. "Thank you, dear. I'm thrilled to have obliged your temper."

Zevander leaned into me. "Magdah sees everything in this house."

I swallowed a gulp, the urge to crawl into myself and scream beating at my ribs. The awareness of being naked and wearing his tunic only made it worse. "It was impulsive. My apologies."

She made a sound of disapproval and turned back to her pot,

giving it another stir. "I'll get to the stinkin' clothes after I finish this stew."

Clearly, she didn't like me.

After an uncomfortable moment longer, one I was certain Zevander reveled in, he led me out of the kitchen and back to the corridor. Down the staircase, I followed him. While I'd grown used to being loathed by most, for some reason, it bothered me that Magdah didn't care for me.

"I suppose that was on purpose," I said, ignoring the way the air rushed between my thighs as we walked briskly along. "I'll have you know, it was your comment which inspired my reaction."

"Comment?"

"Seeing me on my knees." The reminder of it still needled me.

"That bothered you."

"I imagine it'd bother most women. It implies …"

"Yes?" he asked, and I wanted to swat the amusement from his voice.

"It implies dominance over me. Which you do not possess."

He snorted and kept on down the corridor. "Yet, you follow after me to your cell. Wearing my tunic."

"I chose this cell, did I not? And as for your tunic, I'd have sooner slept in a potato sack, had I been given the choice."

"You're welcome to remove it, if you'd like."

His comment slapped me silly, sending a twitch to my cold thighs, and I cleared my throat. "My point is, I will never fall to my knees for you, or any man, in case that was your expectation."

"Never said it was." He gave a quick glance over his shoulder. "I simply said I'd like to see it."

"Well, I'm sorry to disappoint." Movement flickered out of the corner of my eye, and I turned to see a shadowy figure disappear into the stone, as if it'd been sucked inside. Halting my steps seemed to catch Zevander's attention, as he turned around.

"I saw something just now. A shadow slipping into the wall."

"Deimosi," he said, unconcerned, and kept on.

I stared a moment longer, and at no further movement, I shuffled after him to catch up. "What are they?"

"Fears left behind from those who've died. There's no place for them in Nethyria."

"Nethyria?"

"Death. When someone passes, their fears have nowhere to go. They embed themselves."

Swallowing hard, I glanced back to see the shadows zipping in and out of the stones after us. "Do they ... embed themselves in other beings?"

"Only if invited. I suggest you don't invite them. Some fears are paralyzing."

The way they moved so fluidly reminded me of snakes, the sight of them setting my nerves on edge. "How do you invite them?"

"By staring too long."

I snapped my attention forward, refusing to entertain the niggling urge to look again. "They just stay around forever?"

"Not as a general rule, no. They seem content to stay in this castle, though."

Once we reached the dungeons, Zevander swiped up the key and opened the door to my cage. "You're certain you'd prefer to sleep down here?"

"As opposed to what? Pacing an empty room with only shadows to keep me company? Yes. If I'm going to be a prisoner, might as well sleep in the dungeons."

He groaned, stepping aside so I could enter the small cell. "Enjoy, then." The moment I entered, he closed the door behind me.

"Don't you feel just a small bit of guilt locking me in?"

"No." The obnoxious turn of the key emphasized his point.

"Your heart must be the smallest organ you possess."

"And your mouth must be the largest."

Oooh, what I wouldn't have given to smack him across the face!

He hung the key onto the hook across from me. The way he lingered for a moment, staring back at me, left me feeling the need to climb beneath the blankets. I'd never met a man whose stare was more unreadable. In fairness, I'd also never met a man who wore a mask more hours of the day than not.

Without another word, he strode off, back up the staircase.

With a huff, I placed my hands on my hips, looking around the cramped place that I'd chosen to return to. "You're a fool."

CHAPTER THIRTY-FIVE

MAEVYTH

Stars twinkled, as I lay curled on my side, staring through the barred window. In the muck of memories I wanted to forget from home, the ones I most loved were of the nights I would sing to Aleysia while staring out at the stars. Tears formed in my eyes, and closing my lids over them, I hummed her favorite song, fighting to hold back the trapped tears as my voice hardly carried over Dolion's snores in the next cell. Covering my ears to drown the noise, I raised the pitch, and for the briefest moment, I was back in my own bed, with my sister lying beside me.

When the song ended, I opened my eyes, and caught a flicker of movement from the shadows, only noticeable beneath the sconces burning outside my cell. Frowning, I sat up, trying to discern what it was I'd seen.

Quietly, I waited.

Was it a mouse? A mouse I could've dealt with. Even a rat, as awful as the thought might've been.

Not daring to step off the bed, I watched that corner of the cell for what seemed like minutes. Still, nothing appeared.

I exhaled a sigh and fell back against the pillow.

Perhaps I'd imagined it.

I went back to humming the song, and as I prepared to close my eyes, something shifted in my periphery again. My first thought was of the Deimosi that Zevander had told me about, and I hesitated to look for a moment. Then I turned my head, and the breath deflated from my lungs. A black spider, perhaps the size of a cob loaf, stared at me from the other side of the bars, the sight of its long, hairy legs casting a shiver down my spine. I let out a shaky breath, my eyes scanning for something to throw at it, but all I had at my disposal was the book Dolion had given me and the firelamp on the table beside my bed.

My thoughts wound back to the cell with the guards and the bug that had multiplied into hundreds of smaller bugs, and another shiver rippled through me. In as subtle a gesture as I could muster, I reached for the book, knowing hundreds of little beady eyes were watching my every movement.

Just as I raised the book, the spider slipped back into the shadows.

"Oh, shoot!" I shifted on the bed, scrambling to the foot of it for a glimpse of where it might've scampered off to. When nothing moved again, I hummed again in hopes of drawing it out, assuming that had been what'd drawn it both times before.

The spider skittered to the side out of the shadows again and, unless I was imagining it, seemed to sway with my singing.

Frowning, I lifted the book as I kept on with my humming, ready to throw the damn thing if it attempted to come inside the cell.

Instead, it remained where it was, staring, seemingly lulled into a trance.

The book slipped in my hands and something sharp bit into my finger. All I imagined were spider fangs piercing my skin, and my head spiraled into a panic "Ouch! Damn it!" I dropped the book to search for the culprit, and glanced back to see the spider scampering off again.

Scrambling for the firelamp, I turned it up to full flame, but found nothing in that corner of the room. Exhaling a breath, I turned to my finger to where a tiny drop of blood slid over my skin, falling onto the cover's maze. The blood slipped through the maze quickly, like a bead of mercury moving of its own will, until it filled what looked like a skinny vial, no bigger than a grain of rice. A click echoed through the cell, and I flinched, my muscles still on edge as I glanced back toward where the spider had stood moments before. Thankfully, it hadn't bothered to return.

The machinations of the book quickly became clear, as small gears wound on their own and the bird's eye opened over a lever. I stared at it a moment, attempting to puzzle its purpose, then reached into the eye and turned the lever with a click.

The cover popped open.

Why I hesitated, I couldn't say, but after a moment, I flipped the cover open to an elaborately illustrated image of people and bird-like creatures and dragons that spanned across two pages. One so rich with detail, my eyes could scarcely focus. At the center of the image stood an impressive castle with stone walls and creeping vines. Silver, embossed markings beside it appeared illegible, but when I ran my finger over them, they shifted on the page.

My breath hitched with a gasp, and I snapped my hand back, watching the word fade to its original form. Hesitating, I touched it again, and the markings shifted to the word a second time, in a stretch of letters I understood. *Corvus Keep.* A breath of a laughter escaped me as I tried it two more times, marveling at mystical movement on the page.

I studied the illustrations of the people in the image, who wore thick furs, their hair pulled back in tight braids. Painted over their eyes was a shadowy depiction of a black bird. A raven. Each carried a crude weapon that looked like a handheld scythe, while some wore quivers strapped to their backs.

More markings lined the bottom of the image, and I ran my

finger over them, somehow changing their shape with the contact, just like the first.

The ashes of our dead protect us in battle, the goddess, in death.

Tracking to the right showed a woman with long, black hair, surrounded by a white mist and black birds flying around her. I thumbed the strange symbols beside her, revealing the word *Morsana*.

"Morsana," I whispered, noting the striking silver of her eyes that seized my attention.

Above her flew bird-like dragons, colossal-sized beasts that made the humans look small by comparison. Some flew in the sky, breathing a silvery flame as they circled overhead, while others attacked armored figures, whose severed heads and limbs lay scattered about in pools of red. Each creature carried a silver marking, like the one I'd seen on Raivox—a crescent moon.

The same mark that marred my eye.

I dragged a finger over the peculiar symbols beside the creatures, like the ones before, which reminded me of etched runes.

Corvugon appeared.

"Corvugon." Fascinated, I caressed my fingertip over the bird, and it flapped its wings.

Another gasp locked my lungs, and I stared as the bird sprang to life on the page, attacking an armored man with its beak and horns that sliced through the metal with ease. A strange, moving picture that animated the attack, as if I were standing there in the thick of it.

I touched the lower part of the image, and one of the warriors with the raven makeup lurched into motion, running toward an armored figure who sat perched on a horse. The armored figure raised his hand, and the warrior shot backward to his original position as if by some invisible force.

How? How was this possible? Pictures didn't move that way; they captured a single moment in time.

A tingling sensation prickled my fingertips, and with both

hands, I smoothed them over the image, and the entire scene came to life, as if I were watching it firsthand. A battle.

The cluster of markings to the right flickered to words I understood.

The men with yellow hair and steel weapons came upon us in the night. They sought the vein. But we did not relent. For this land is ours. By the strength of Morsana, we defend it.

I watched in horror, as the raven people fought with lesser weapons and were slaughtered by the armored men. A violet glow drew my eyes to a crevice that ran along the castle, and when I glided my finger over it, a white-hot sting pricked my fingertips.

"Ouch!" I drew back my hand, frowning.

Within the dark and scorching chasm, black fire flickered and moved, and a figure rose up, as if some being had been swallowed by the flame. Had become part of it. It lashed out at the armored men and turned them to ash. Careful not to touch the flame, I slipped my thumb across the symbols beside it, and *Deimos* appeared.

Something about the name sent a shiver down my spine. I studied the figure in the flame a moment longer, and for reasons I couldn't explain, my heart clenched.

Feathered dragons in the sky battled with golden scaled beasts that breathed fire, but they were no match for the raptors who flew right through those flames. The two beasts clashed, claws tearing flesh. The silvery flames of the black dragon birds sent the golden dragon riders plunging toward the ground in a fiery ball of death.

All at once, everything stilled, and the image flickered. In the next breath, all the figures returned to their original positions, like when I first opened the book.

Yet, the questions lingered in my head. Who were the armored men? What had happened to the raven warriors? Had they survived? What was trapped inside that black flame?

And how in god's eyes had the image come to life that way?

Again, I stared at my fingertips where a tingle still hummed beneath my skin.

I turned the page to a new puzzle–a raised wooden circle with symbols etched both within and outside of its edges. Other strange symbols adorned the edge in deep, black carvings, the arrangement of it reminding me of a multi-faceted clock. I ran my fingers over the symbols, thinking they might change, as the other markings had, but they remained. And for the life of me, I could not begin to imagine what they meant individually.

Eyes burning, I sighed and double blinked to stave off the exhaustion tugging at my eyelids. I needed sleep. I'd have to save the next puzzle for the morrow.

As I closed the cover of the book, the wooden circle slid down into a depression, flattening itself so the cover would close again. A genius design. Something one might find marveled by scholars at a university, and it left me wondering how Dolion had acquired such a thing.

Before lying back on the pillow, I glanced over to where I'd last seen the spider and performed a quick visual sweep of my room. While I may not have minded the presence of mice, spiders, on the other hand, terrified me.

When I finally lay back on the pillow, I forced my mind to think of something else. Something that would chase away the image of that spider sinking its fangs into my flesh.

The first and only thought I could summon was Zevander.

CHAPTER THIRTY-SIX

MAEVYTH

The clank of metal reached through the void, and I opened my eyes to a mantle of dim light that blanketed the cell. Groaning, I shielded my eyes and lifted my head from the pillow.

"Wake up, *Bellitula!*"

The fog in my eyes sharpened on Rykaia swinging the door open, carrying a tray of something that smelled delicious.

I groaned and shook my head of the last remnants of sleep. "What is *Bellitula?*"

"A classic story my mother told me when I was little." She placed the tray on the table beside me, the savory scent taunting my tastebuds, and it was then I noticed clothes folded on the chair. "Bellitula was a dancer who longed to be the best in all of Aethyria. So, she made a pact with a malevol–"

"A malevol?"

"Uhhhh ... a bad spirit?"

"A demon?" At her confused expression, I described, "Horns, cloven feet, collects souls."

"Ah, yes. A *demon.* Anyway, she wanted all eyes on her for the upcoming *Grandetalar,* which featured the most exquisite dance

354

ever performed by a single being. She wanted to dance so beautifully that the audience would weep."

As she told her story, I sat up in bed to reach for a slice of thick bread, and spooned a strange, pink-colored jam onto it. With a dip of my pinky, I sampled the jam. A delicious floral flavor of rose hips delighted my tongue, with a splash of honey and summerberry. I had yet to try something in this place that my palate didn't relish. Still half asleep, I devoured the bread and jam as Rykaia prattled on.

"The malevol—er, *demon*, promised that men would weep and women would swoon, and the world would forever know her name. In exchange, she would agree to give him her heart." She placed her hand over her own heart, dramatizing the story. "She agreed, thinking he meant love. Malevols are sneaky that way, though. On the night of her performance, it was said that she danced with such grace, not a sound could be heard but the swift movement of her feet and the rippling of her dress." Rykaia spun around awkwardly in her boots, her dress, with black laces at the corset, an even deeper burgundy than the last I'd seen her wear. "She danced so beautifully, the men wept and women fainted. And at the end of the dance, she lay on the floor as if to rest. And she never woke again. Her chest bore a gaping hole where it appeared her heart had been mysteriously torn out by an unseen force."

"That's a terrible story," I said around a mouthful of bread that I swallowed back with a chug of water.

"Well, I called your name three times and you didn't wake. Anyway, it's time to train." She tossed garments onto the bed, and placed a set of black boots by the chair

Leather. Lots of leather.

I lifted one of the garments that unraveled into long legs. "What is this?"

"Your training gear."

"Leather trousers?" They reminded me of riding breeches worn by the wealthier in Vonkovya.

"You expected a ballgown?"

"Of course not. But leather clings. To everything." The image of the material clinging to my breasts and hips made me wince. "I can't."

"You have to. That's what makes it perfect for training. Doesn't catch on swords and daggers."

"What do swords and daggers have to do with glyphs?" I swiped up the cup of water beside me to wash back the panic rising into my throat.

Arms crossed, she shrugged. "Sometimes, the best way to summon your power is when you fear for your life."

"Wait." My heart ground to a stop, and I coughed out water. "Are you saying ... I'm expected to *fight*?" I didn't know the first thing about fighting. I'd stabbed the guard who'd taken Aleysia in the forearm, of all places. "What am I fighting?"

"Torryn. He's the best at physical fighting out of all the Letalisz."

"Letalisz? What is that?"

"The king's trained assassins. Centuries ago, Torryn, along with my brother and two others were pulled from the Solassion prison to carry out secret murders for the king." The casual tone of her voice, as if secret king assassins were a perfectly normal occupation, rendered me momentarily speechless.

"Brilliant. That's absolutely brilliant. I'd make the perfect match for him, then." Snorting a laugh, I shook my head. "This is a ridiculous idea."

"You can thank my brother for that. Now, get dressed."

I glanced toward the outside of my cell. "What about Dolion?"

"What *about* Dolion?"

"I don't care to change in front of him."

"Trust me, he has no interest in you. You have no cock."

"He's ..."

Brow quirked, she tipped her head. "Into fucking men? Yes. Now, change. Quickly. Torryn has a bad temper."

Wonderful. I very much looked forward to meeting the bad-tempered man I was expected to fight.

Frowning, I threw another glance past her, to make sure Dolion wasn't there. It wasn't just that he was a man, I really wasn't comfortable dressing in front of anyone, including Rykaia. Unfortunately, I'd made the decision to forego my privacy when I'd chosen the cells over one of the rooms Zevander had offered.

At no sign of the older mage, I tossed back the blanket and pushed to my feet, lifting the pants from the bed and staring at the garment as it dangled from my finger.

"What is it?" Rykaia asked, watching me. "Afraid it won't fit?"

"No ... I've never worn trousers before."

"Ever?"

"Ever."

Her brows furrowed. "You're telling me you've only ever worn dresses." She gave me a quick onceover. "And tunics?"

"Yes. And thank you for that, your brother did not appreciate finding me in his bath, nor wearing his tunic."

Her expression twisted to an evil grin that had me grinding my teeth. "Oh, he actually returned to his room?"

"Yes. He looked angry."

"*Angry*? Or *angrier* than usual?"

"Angrier than usual."

Wearing a thoughtful expression, she stroked her thumb across her bottom lip. "That could've been my fault, I suppose. I told him I'd seen something unusual in his bathing room."

My spine snapped straight. "*You* sent him to his room?"

"You make it sound like a punishment."

"I was naked, Rykaia!"

"Yes, which confuses me on the angrier than usual point," she said, tapping a finger to her chin. "Are you sure about it? It's hard to tell with that mask he constantly wears."

"Why would you send him there, when I asked for privacy?"

"Because I'm horrible at following orders. You should know that going forward. If you tell me to do something, chances are, I'm going to fail somehow." Sighing, she plopped down into the chair my clothes had occupied. "Now that we got that out of the way, I'm still having trouble wrapping my head around the idea that you've never worn trousers."

"Where I come from, the only women who wear trousers are the ones who live on the streets."

"Have you ever trained in your life?" It occurred to me that her question only seemed ridiculous because I'd been taught my whole life that women were weak and incapable of fighting. That only wild women, tainted by the devil, longed for skills such as hunting and fighting.

Troubled by that, I shook my head.

"Oh, gods. Torryn is going to crush you." She rubbed her brow, and suddenly the food I'd eaten stirred in my gut.

"Wonderful. Thank you. That makes me want to hustle to get dressed for it."

"Okay." Hands atop her thighs, she huffed and pushed to her feet. "I'm going to teach you a very basic glyph, one every woman should know. This might help you, going in."

Kneeling to the floor, she yanked a dagger from the wide, leather belt cinched at her waist, and carved three wiggly lines onto the gravelly floor that appeared as white scratches in the packed dirt. "Aeryz." Holstering the dagger, she pushed to her feet and held out her palm at me, as if she were halting my approach. After breathing in through her nose, she closed her eyes and let out an easy exhale.

What sounded like wind being sucked into something had me glancing around—before a force plowed into me, like getting kicked in the chest by a horse, and knocked me backward onto the mattress.

Objects floated before my eyes, as I lay coughing, my chest

throbbing for a sip of air, and I sat up, frowning back at her as I took in one long inhale. "A warning would've been nice," I grumbled.

Unfazed by my irritation, she said, "Now, you try. Close your eyes and imagine the glyph. Then hold out your palm and push it into the universe."

Curiosity urged me out of the bed, and I jumped to my feet. I took a deep breath and closed my eyes, imagining the squiggly lines. As I'd seen her do, I held out my palm.

A faint gust of wind tickled the ends of her hair, but failed to move her.

"That was weak. Try again."

Once more, I shuttered my eyes, imagining the lines she'd drawn. When I held out my palm again, nothing happened, except for the strange deflating sound that reminded me of a cat being smothered. "Well, at least it made a sound that time."

"That was my stomach." Rykaia rested her hand over her belly. "I'm starving."

Rolling my shoulders back, I cleared my throat. "Fine." I squeezed my eyes shut, growing frustrated by the repetition. I thrusted my hand out that time, and my body flew backward just like before, landing on the bed.

Rykaia snorted a laugh and covered her face. "Never saw that happen before."

"Forget it, then. I'm not meant to wield magic."

"I'm beginning to think that myself."

"Then, perhaps you should just let me go back to where I came from, just as I've been requesting since I got here."

"Or maybe you should try a little harder, mortal. You're weak. You need to build up those muscles."

"I'm not weak!" Hands balled to tight fists, I let the frustration and relentless exhaustion swallow me. "Forgive me for not being interested in playing with symbols, when my sister might very well be dead!"

"If she's dead, why the hell do you want to go back to her so bad! You said it yourself, you're *unwanted*!" Her words slapped me across the face, the sting burning my cheeks.

"You wouldn't understand. You're a heartless immortal, like your brother!"

Eyes bright and flickering, she glowered back at me. "If I were my brother, I'd have fed you to the fyredrakes by now!"

I jumped to my feet and waved a hand at her. "Then, do it!"

Rykaia flew backward into the bars. She flinched on impact, before sliding to the floor.

"Oh, my God." I rushed toward her, falling to my knees at her side. "I'm so sorry. Are you okay?"

She chuckled, rubbing the back of her head. "Finally. You see? Sometimes, it can be physical learning glyphs."

"What happened?" A burning sensation flared across my palm. I turned my hand over and found the three squiggly lines had appeared like three open cuts carved into my flesh.

"Congratulations, mortal. You've earned a new glyph."

I ran my finger over the wounds, smearing the blood over my palm. "Is that how it works?"

"Yes. The first time you use a glyph successfully, it remains permanently etched on your palm." She held up her own palms to show seven symbols–four on her left and three on her right. "These are the powers I wield."

"Seven?"

"You can only summon a glyph based on your bloodline. Hence the training. You need to figure out what your powers are. Some are basic, and they're known as the minor glyphs. All manceborn master them because they're easy." She wriggled her fingers on her left hand. "Some are much harder to summon and require intense concentration. Those are the major glyphs."

"May I ask what that one is?" I pointed to a scar, a complex symbol of curls and lines and dots contained within a circle.

"I'm an empath. My mother had the same glyph."

"You feel the emotions of others?" I asked, studying the symbol.

"I absorb the emotions. But only when I want to. It's a curse, really." She sneered, curling her fingers over it.

I thought back to Zevander's horrifically scarred hands. "Your brother …. He has so many."

"Yes, well, he's a bit of an anomaly. Most Lunasier only have about one, or two, major glyphs. Sometimes, three, like me. I could learn more, but it takes years, and only those who study at the House of Sages are given access to the other glyphs."

"What is a Lunasier?"

"Oh … a history lesson." She raked her hands through her long, silvery locks. "Lunasier is our race of people. So mancers are like humans, in some ways, but immortal, and … quite frankly, more interesting. We're divided into the Lunasier and the Solassions. The Lunasier get their powers from the moons. The Solassions, from the sun."

Rubbing a hand across my forehead failed to declutter my head of all the information she'd just offered up. "I thought you got your power from blood."

"We do, but it requires nutrients and energy. Without the moon, my powers are weak."

"I see. Is Dolion Lunasier?"

"No. He's Elvynira. Their power is a bit mysterious, but most can command glyphs, like mancers. It isn't based on blood for them, but understanding, and *nexumis*, which is a spiritual connection that the Elvynira have with the glyph. Dolion is a high mage, which means he's mastered many glyphs." She pushed to her feet and brushed the dust from her skirt, then offered her hand to help me up. "Our Magelord for the king can wield nearly every glyph, though they're not as powerful as those who wield by blood. Take my brother, for instance. His power was given by sablefyre. The Magelord can certainly wield sablefyre, but not as *proficiently* as Zevander."

"What is sablefyre?"

"It is a black flame, so hot, it can disintegrate a body in seconds."

My mouth turned dry at the visual of that. It brought to mind the black markings on his skin. "I see. Sablefyre is your bloodline?"

"No. My brother is cursed with it."

"And the scorpions?"

"They're his *prodozja*," she said, grabbing a slice of the bread still sat out on the table. Instead of opting for the jam, she opened a second jar of a thick black substance that she smeared over the bread before taking a bite. "Mmmm. Magdah makes the best beetlejam."

My stomach lurched. "Beetle jam? As in, bugs?"

"It's good." She raised the bread up and took another bite. "Crunchy is my favorite."

I swallowed past the lump in my throat. "And the pink jam?"

"The innards."

Acids shot up my throat, and my face must've blanched three shades whiter.

She snorted a laugh. "I'm kidding. Yours is bitterberry." She chomped another bite of the bread. "Gods, Maeve, you looked like you were about to vomit just now."

Though I smiled, my mind lingered on the name. "You called me Maeve."

"Oh, you don't like diminutives?"

"No, it's fine. Aleysia always called me Maeve." A wave of emotion swept over me, and I cleared my throat. "Anyway, *pro ... doh ... sah*. What is that?"

"*Pro-doh*-ja. It's the protective form of blood magic. A creature that unfailingly manifests in the form of whatever magic a person wields."

"What is your *prodozja*?" I asked.

She shrugged. "Don't have one. Never manifests for some of

us. Zevander was lucky to learn his early on." She stared off as though there was something more to the story. Instead of elaborating, though, she shook her head. "Anyway, now you have something to fight back with. So, get dressed."

I glanced at the clothing again, noting the absence of a cammyck. "By chance, has Magdah finished laundering my clothes?"

"Laundering? I saw her flinging your old dress into a fire."

"Fire? She really doesn't like me, that one."

Rykaia popped the last of the bread into her mouth. "Just needs to warm up to you is all. To be fair, it reeked of more than just your mortal scent."

While her comment should've been humiliating, a much greater concern occupied my mind. "Do you happen to have cammyck's here?"

"Cammyck?" Her face scrunched to a frown. "What in the gods is that?"

"It's a body-fitting suit that you wear under dresses, and the sort."

"You mean undergarments?"

"Well, I suppose it could be called that."

"Yes. Did I not give you any last night?"

"No?"

"Oh. Terribly sorry." She strode out of the cell and headed toward the stone wall just outside of it. It was only when she knelt down that I noticed a small door in one of the stones, essentially invisible in the way it blended so seamlessly with the water-stained rock. After knocking three times, she crossed her arms and huffed. The door swung open, and a hairless rat-like humanoid appeared, slightly taller than the length of my hand, with pink wrinkled skin and beady black eyes. Yet, he wore clothes—tattered pants and a ragged, green vest, with a laced-up brown tunic beneath that clung to his slender body.

I could feel my jaw slowly coming unhinged.

"I need a favor, dear. In my room, there are two brand spanking new undergarments laid out on the dresser. Can you fetch them for me?"

"Of course." The ratman nodded and, unless I was imagining it, wore a slight bit of blush on his pink, skin-like cheek.

Rykaia pointed a finger at him. "And no rummaging through my lingerie. I mean it." She booped the little creature on the snout.

"I would not, Mistress."

"Good. Now, run along."

The door slammed shut after him, but she remained there.

"What is … was …"

"A golvyn. You don't have one? Wonderful creatures, but they can be tricky. He likes to sniff undergarments. But no worries, I've never worn the ones I intend to let you borrow."

I began untying my borrowed tunic, to get started on the leather garments, and she held up a finger. "If you're squirrely about others seeing you dress, you may want to wait just one moment. He'll return any second."

"That quickly?"

No sooner had I spoken the words than the door flew open again. The ratman handed over two black garments, far too small to be cammycks, to Rykaia.

"Thank you, love." She planted a kiss to the top of his head, and his cheeks seemed to redden again, before he slipped back through the door, closing it behind him. "You see? Wonderfully useful creatures." Rykaia sauntered toward me.

Taking the proffered garments, I couldn't help but note how *small* they were—they'd hardly cover much of anything, at all. Whereas the cammyck had reached the middle of my thighs, these looked like nothing more than a small patch of fabric connected by strings. "I hardly think this will keep me from chafing."

"You'd be surprised how soft caligosian leather is. Particularly between the thighs. Now, hurry along. I'll wait for you at the top of the staircase."

"And if nothing fits?"

"Why wouldn't it?"

"We may not be the exact size."

She held out her hand toward the clothing laid out on the bed and jerked her head. "Put the undergarments with the others."

I did as she commanded, setting them on top of the pile.

"*Fitilia quantya.*" Without another word, she turned and exited the cell.

I glanced back at the garments, trying to comprehend what had just happened. Curious, I swiped up the clothes and backed myself to the shadowy corner of the room, where I dressed quickly, sliding on the undergarment that clung to my hips for dear life. While the fit seemed good, I tugged at the edges of the fabric on the backside, but they didn't budge from where they covered my two fleshy cheeks. How desperately I longed for my cammyck.

Next, I slipped my leg into the trousers and yanked it up over my calf, confused by the sensation. Warm and fitting, it clung to my skin like stockings, and I couldn't deny, it felt … nice. I yanked the other leg up and tied the string, pulling the waistband in to a perfect fit. Staring down at myself, I smoothed a hand over my leg and smiled. No wonder Ms. Chalmsley had always opted for trousers. Far less chilly than an open-hemmed dress.

Turning away from the cell bars, I removed the tunic, the air against my bare breasts sending a jolt of urgency through me. I pulled on the long sleeve of the hooded leather tunic that fit snugly over my arms, then I fastened the many laces on the front, pulling it tight against my breasts. As close fitting as it was, I was glad not to be wearing a cammyck, which would've only suffocated me. A black, leather corset fit just below my breasts, and held small loops and pockets that I imagined housed daggers, though mine were empty.

KERI LAKE

After tugging on the leather boots, I examined myself, running my hands over the soft leather of the pants and jacket.

"Oh! You're … dressed." At the sound of Dolion's voice, I turned around, not sure if I felt clothed, or fully exposed, the way the garments emphasized every curve of my body.

"Training clothes. For … training. Against a king's assassin." Saying it aloud sounded worse than in my head, and I let out a nervous laugh.

"Yes. You'll be grateful for those." He nodded at my clothes. "I remember my first day learning glyphs back at the House of Sages. My mentor had asked me to perform the *intorquiusz* command, and I managed to become completely entangled in my robes. I suspect it was intentional on his part." He let out a chuckle that brought a smile to my face.

"It's strange. I've worn the same style of dress my entire life."

"The black dress you arrived in?"

"Yes. I was forced to wear it. And the choker," I said, running my hand over my neck and realizing I hadn't bothered to take it off while dressing.

"Whatever for?"

"All cursed women wear them."

"It seems you and Lord Rydainn have something in common, then."

His handsome profile came to mind. "The mask."

"Yes. While he's required to wear it in public, I think he chooses to wear it most other times."

"Why?"

"That would be a question for him, I suppose."

"I don't think he likes my questions very much."

"It's true, he is quite abrasive. I suspect he'll warm to you in time." Dolion widened the door and waved me out of the cell. "Now, shall we begin training?"

"You'll be training me, as well?"

"Yes. Well, I wouldn't leave you to contend with Lord Rydainn yourself."

My stomach lurched. "Lord Rydainn? I was under the understanding I'd be training with Torryn."

"Change of plans. Lord Rydainn has expressed interest in training you himself."

Somehow, I found that hard to believe. Lord Rydainn regarded me like a mole on his ass that he hoped to burn off at some point.

"I'm afraid I can only serve as a scribe in this case. These glyphs are uncharted territory for me. Zevander is better equipped to physically train you."

Whatever knots had already wound in my stomach cinched tighter. "Dolion, I don't think this is a good idea. I appreciate the opportunity to—"

"A fortnight. Learn the glyphs. Earn your power, and in a fortnight, I will take you away from this place."

"Two weeks? I don't have two weeks!"

"The alternative is that you don't leave, at all. I'll not dump you in that forest with nothing to defend yourself. The mages who seek you are quite vicious, Maevyth. You've no idea what they're capable of, and they *will* find you. Whether here, or in your world. They have powers you cannot begin to comprehend. Do you want your sister endangered?"

Of course I didn't. "Two weeks will drive me mad."

Huffing, he nodded. "I will attempt to scry. Perhaps that will give you piece of mind, seeing her."

Hope bloomed in my chest. "I would very much appreciate that. Thank you."

"Very good." He jerked his head toward my cell. "Tell me, have you made any headway on the book?"

I glanced over my shoulder to where the puzzle book sat on the table beside my bed. "I managed to open the cover. There was an image on the inside." I didn't bother to mention the way the figures moved on the page, seeing as I hadn't opened it again since the night before to confirm whether, or not, I'd hallucinated that bit.

"Excellent! I'd love to learn how you figured out the mechanisms of it. After training?"

"Sure." I said, though a nagging curiosity lingered in the air. Although Dolion had told me it was a means to pass the time, I believed it was more intentional than that. "What is this book and why exactly am I being tasked to solve these puzzles?"

"You are the only one qualified to do so."

"Why?"

Lips pressed together, he seemed to chew on the question a moment, as if he hesitated to tell me. "I have reason to believe the book is one of few relics left behind by your people."

"*My* people? I'm Vonkovyan. Born in Vonkovya."

"That may be true. But your blood may very well be Corvikae."

The word brought to mind the Corvus Keep and the Corvugon I'd seen in the book the night before. "What is Corvikae?"

"They are a race of mortals who existed here centuries ago."

"Existed? As in, they're no longer?"

Brows lowering, he gave a solemn shake of his head. "They were slaughtered. Cast into the Crussurian Trench."

"Then, how is it possible that I, a human from the mortal world, could be a descendent?"

He huffed. "Admittedly, I'm not entirely sure yet. It's why you're here. So that we may learn more about your bloodline, your abilities."

I took a deep breath to calm the brewing frustration prodding at me. "I appreciate that. And under any other circumstances I'd be a willing participant, but I am severely distracted by the well-being of my sister. I have neither the time, nor mental capacity, for your studies and experimentation, when she is my priority."

"And I can assure you, we will try to reach out to her. Safely, through a scrying mirror with no harm to you." He rested a hand on my shoulder and with raised brows, he tipped his head, although I hesitated to agree. "Now, if you don't mind, I'm going to take a look at the image you mentioned, and I'll meet you in the training room."

"Of course," I said, and with a nod, he patted me on the shoulder, as I headed down the corridor to my impending doom.

CHAPTER THIRTY-SEVEN

MAEVYTH

I arrived at the top of the stone staircase, to find Rykaia talking to a man dressed similarly to me, in all black leather. Down his left thigh hung a series of daggers holstered in leather straps. Dark brown, not quite black hair reached his shoulders, straggly strands framing each edge of intense burgundy-colored eyes. His expression held a contradictory mix of dark amusement. I presumed him to be Torryn, but Rykaia turned toward me and said, "Maevyth, this is Ravezio."

While I gave a polite nod, he reached for my hand, lifting it to his face. I'd expected him to kiss the back of my hand, the way he held my knuckles close enough to his lips that I could feel his warm breath on my skin. Instead, he took in a long inhale and shuttered his eyes.

"Didn't I tell you?" Rykaia said with an air of amusement. "Her scent is a weapon itself. Utterly distracting."

"Indeed." He lowered my hand and tipped his head, studying me. He had a feral quality about him, something that prowled within, like a black cat. At the base of his neck, just above his collarbone, I noticed hash marks, scars in intricately designed patterns that looked like connecting suns, which seemed impossible to have been made by hand. He tipped his head further, undoubtedly noticing my staring, and I cleared my throat, snapping my attention away.

He smiled, and the expression completely changed his face. Stark white teeth, eyes brimming with amusement. He was darkly handsome. The kind who'd have been sought by the women in Foxglove while accused of sorcery by the men there. He reminded me of the transient wanderers who slipped through towns like shadows, never staying in one place too long.

Movement at the corner of my eye dragged my attention away to Zevander, who slowly descended the stairs toward us. Over the top of the mask covering his face, his eyes appeared to be fixed on me, and suddenly, I felt as naked as I'd been in the bathing room the night before.

"And where are you fine gents off to today?" Rykaia asked, her question failing to break his staring.

"The Hovel. Seems someone likes playing with flammapul." Ravezio bent forward to adjust a dagger just inside his boot, and I caught sight of black arrows protruding from a black leather quiver strapped to his back.

"Torryn will be going to The Hovel with you. I'll be training today." Zevander's attention shifted from Ravezio to me, and my pulse thrummed at the thought of fighting against him.

"*You're* training Maevyth?" Rykaia asked, her eyes flitting between Zevander and me. "And you're siccing your dogs after the flammellian?"

"I take offense to that," Ravezio said, but Rykaia didn't bother to acknowledge him.

Crossing her arms over her chest, she rolled her eyes. "For gods' sakes, Zevander, leave it alone. You're only going to stir trouble."

"You didn't think I'd let him get away with what he did, did you?" Zevander finally spoke, the sound of malice in his voice sending a strange vibration beneath my skin. He turned toward Ravezio. "When you find him, bring him here. To me."

"Of course."

"And you're bringing him *here*? Which means whoever it is, isn't walking out of here." Rykaia shifted on her feet. "You know, you don't need to kill every soul that's wronged me."

"And you don't need to fret. His murder was commissioned by the king."

She let out a bitter laugh. "If King Sagaerin thinks he's going to put an end to every mage who dabbles in demutomancy, he's wrong. They'll find a way. They always do."

His gaze fell on me again, but with half his face covered in a mask, it was hard to guess what thoughts occupied his mind. "I do not care about every other mage." That questionable gaze lingered a moment longer before he turned back to his sister. "He hurt you. End of story. For him." He gave a nod toward Ravezio. "A quick word."

The two stepped off to the side, their voices low and indiscernible over the sound of Rykaia huffing and mumbling beside me.

After a quick pat to Ravezio's shoulder, Zevander strode past the two of us, but paused to look over his shoulder in my direction. "Are you coming?"

The question somehow shifted the air around me, my pulse hammering a steady beat of anxiety, and for a moment I felt like I was suffocating.

With a glance at Rykaia, who frowned back at her brother, I followed after him.

Once out of earshot from Rykaia, I asked, "What's a flammellian?"

He threw a quick glance over his shoulder. "One who is intensely aroused by control. The name comes from the substance they use to inject into their victims. Flammapul. It's a poison that renders you useless, so your abuser, or *flammellian*, can do whatever they wish."

"That sounds … horrifying. Someone did this to Rykaia?"

"Yes."

The mere thought sent a bolt of rage through me and Rykaia wasn't even my sister. "I don't blame you for wanting to hurt him. In fact, I feel compelled to do the same to whatever took Aleysia."

"Have you fought before?"

"No." I'd always wanted some form of training, or defense. Mostly for use against the boys in our parish, who touched without asking. But Grandfather Bronwick had thought it unladylike. He'd always worried that such a graceless past time would've only fueled more rumors and scorn. "I stabbed the guard who tried taking her, though."

"Dare I ask what you stabbed him with?"

"A knife I used to carry. For carving and fruit, mostly. I sort of fought the prisoner who tried to attack me before your scorpion showed up."

"You fought a prisoner of Bonesguard, as well? How?"

"A knife." I hastened my steps to keep up with him.

"How did you manage to acquire a knife at the prison?"

"Well, he gave it to me. I think he was toying with me."

"Or he underestimated you." The subtle compliment had me hiding a smile.

"I don't exactly look all that threatening."

"You don't have to look threatening to *be* threatening. Perceived weakness is your most vicious weapon. Remember that, as it will serve as an advantage. You're small, but your power can make up for your stature, if you learn to wield it well." He finally led me to an expansive room the size of the cottage back home.

An entire wall of arched windows looked out over an impressive scene of trees and a wintery sky. Candelabras, like those I'd seen in the kitchen, hung from the arched ceiling, and the wall opposite the windows held all variety of weapons. Swords, daggers, and other terrifying items I couldn't identify, along with armor, gauntlets and shields. At the far end of the room, a painting of a black, scaled dragon spanned the width of the wall, illuminated by sconces that blazed below it.

The image mesmerized me. "Are there winged dragons in Aethyria?"

"Fewer these days. They're mostly found in Draconysia. Except when they decide to feed on local villagers."

"They're aggressive?"

"Extremely." Zevander led me to the center of the room and removed his jacket, tossing it onto a nearby chair and leaving him in a black leather vest with no tunic beneath.

Carved, muscled arms displayed inky black images of scorpions and black fire that stretched from the top of his hands to his bicep. The honey tones in his skin and the jet black of his hair starkly contrasted his sister's silvery hair and ivory complexion. Black metal cuffs, with intricately carved designs that had been hidden by the long sleeves of his tunic, banded around both wrists.

Brutal and fierce were the only words that came to mind while I stared back at him.

He was a man who commanded attention, and I found it nearly impossible to avert my gaze. As he strode toward me, my heart drummed a frantic rhythm against my ribs, like the erratic creature might break right out of its cage. The mask he wore only enhanced the strange curiosities tickling my thoughts. It irritated me, the way he consumed my attention. I didn't even have to be skilled in fighting to know it was already a weakness.

Stay focused, my head warned.

"We'll start with a basic glyph. Aeryz."

"Rykaia taught me that one." I held up my hand to show the healing marks on my palm.

"Show me."

A gurgling in my stomach warned me against it. What if I ended up flying backward, as I had in the cell? For reasons I couldn't explain, the prospect of humiliating myself in front of Zevander felt worse than it had with Rykaia.

With an expectant arch of his brow, he tipped his head. "Now."

I took a deep breath and held up a shaky palm. Closing my eyes brought to mind the squiggly lines Rykaia had drawn, and I prepared to exhale and push that image into the space between us, but at the last second, it flashed to another.

The intersecting crosses I'd seen in my dream.

"Oh, no!" Before I could stop it, a pile of bones flew forth, and I watched as they pummeled Zevander in the chest, before falling into an ungracious pile at his feet. Humiliation burned my cheeks as I held my hands to my face.

Lips tight, he looked down at the collection of spines on the floor. "Well, that was something."

"That was *Osflagulle!*" Dolion smiled as he strode into the room carrying books and rolled parchment, like ancient scrolls, he'd tucked under his arm. "No mage in all of Aethyria, not even the Magelord himself, possesses that particular glyph."

"What exactly is it supposed to do?" I asked, staring down at the bones.

"It's a bone whip. A very powerful one, if the scrolls I've been reading are anything to go by. One strike could shatter the bones of your opponents."

Shatter bones? "And if I don't want to shatter anyone's bones?"

"Not even the bones of the creature that took your sister?" Zevander crossed his arms, and I had to look away. I'd never seen so many muscles flex at once, and the urge to ogle him only infuriated me, especially after I'd made a fool out of myself a moment ago. "We'll start with easy defensive glyphs. Then we'll see if we can fix whatever that was."

"Ah, good plan," Dolion agreed.

"Show me Aeryz again." He kicked the pile of bones to the side, reminding me of my blunder.

"You should know I'm a bit nervous," I admitted, my voice quiet and tight.

"You should be. Who knows what in seven hells will fly out next?" His comment had me biting back a chuckle, given the dry, humorous tone of it. Completely unfitting. And yet, a welcomed side to him.

I raised my hand that bore the glyph, shakier than before. *Inhale.* On the exhale, I pushed outward, the glyph clear in my mind, and Zevander slid back, the soles of his boots scraping against the marble floor.

I bit my lip in an effort to control the inward squealing of a victory.

With a nod of approval, he straightened himself and strode back to me. "Try again."

"Did I do it wrong?"

"Do you know what Aeryz means?" At the shake of my head, he continued, "In the ancient language it means wind's vengeance. Tell me, did that seem like a vengeful gust of wind to you?"

I shook my head again.

"Try again."

Once again, I held up my palm, imagined the glyph, and exhaled. On a faint squeal, a gust shot out from my palm with a force that felt like a rock hitting the surface, beating against my bones.

Zevander flew back faster than the first time, but still kept his feet planted on the floor. Again, he strode toward me, sighing. "Imagine for a moment that you're stood before the thing that took your sister."

A memory flashed inside my head. *Aleysia standing on the other side of the archway. Moros grabbing her from behind. Her screams echoing all around me.*

Grinding my teeth, I shot my palm out without warning. The blast thumped against my hand, vibrating my bones, and Zevander shot backward, but still, he maintained his unyielding stance. "Again."

"Again?" I echoed.

"You will repeat this move until I find it satisfactory. Now, raise your palm." He commanded the same move three more times. Each time, he landed on his feet, despite the power growing stronger. My palm ached with the force, my body growing warm in my gear. Yet, he never tired. Never smiled, nor praised, nor gave any indication that I'd improved from my first attempt.

Dolion's words of encouragement filled the obvious absence of Zevander's.

A dozen more times, I fulfilled the command, and dozens more after that, growing weaker as the afternoon wore on.

Every mistake seemed to frustrate him, and his impatience chipped away at my confidence. Hours passed, my palm sore, muscles weak. I felt as if I'd run circles around a village a dozen times over.

"Focus!" Zevander barked, and I bit back the urge to tell him to go to hell.

"What is it I'm trying to accomplish with this glyph?" I asked, catching my breath, confused by my lack of energy. All I'd really done was stand and order a command, yet I felt like my bones were melting.

"It is meant to disarm, or stun, your opponent."

"Wouldn't the bones be more effective for that?"

"Do not question my teaching."

"It's not your teaching I question," I volleyed back, "but your relentless pursuit of some invisible goal I've yet to understand."

"Then perhaps you should remain quiet. Now, try again."

I steeled my nerves, glaring back at him. "No. I'm tired. I haven't had water all afternoon and I'm practically sliding in this damned suit from all the perspiration I've worked up."

"Again! Now!"

Ice rushed through my veins. "I will not!"

"Then, I am wasting my time with you!" His intimidating voice thundered around me, and I winced at the harshness. Lips gnarled, he stared back at me, his eyes smoldering orbs of ire.

"Zevander, let the poor girl take a break." Dolion's voice, calmer by comparison, came as a relief. He waved me over for a pitcher of water he'd fetched for me an hour ago, and poured a glass. "Magic is exhausting, isn't it?"

"Yes." It was as I lifted the glass to my lips that I noticed my hands were trembling. Not from fear but adrenaline. I glanced back to Zevander, who rubbed the back of his neck, pacing like an angry wolf. "I think he's getting frustrated with me."

Dolion chuckled and nodded toward him. "I knew the man who trained him, after he was released by the Solassions. His name was Solvyn. He was the master of magical warfare for the Imperial Army while I worked as a Magestroli." He lowered his gaze, and the way his lips twitched, as if to hide a smile, made me suspect he and Solvyn might've known each other intimately. "I used to pass the training yard on my way to the library when I lived in The Citadel. Hours, the two of them would be out there. Well into the night, when I'd return from my studies, I'd still catch Zevander training alone." As he spoke, I sipped my water, watching the devil himself trace his palm with his thumb, his muscles less bunched than before. "I asked Solvyn one day, why do you torture this poor boy, forcing him to train so many hours in the day?" When I glanced back at the older man, he smiled, a nostalgic expression in his eyes. "He said to me, it's not me who requests long hours of training, but the boy."

It was strange to think of him that way—a boy so eager to learn. It made me wonder what drove him then.

Dolion tipped back a sip of his own glass. "I suspect he trains this way because he refuses to watch you fail. In his mind, such a thing would be his own failure."

I sighed and took a long swill of the water, then returned to the floor, standing before Zevander.

"We can stop for the afternoon." The calm in his voice didn't match his brutal form and the effortless intimidation he radiated. "It wasn't my intent—"

"No. I'm okay now. I just needed some fluids in me."

He cleared his throat and rolled his shoulders back. "Yes, well. Let's pick up where we left off."

His sudden flustering had me puzzled, but I drew in an inhale and forced my head to focus. The moment he lowered his arm, I exhaled, and the force that hit my palm sent me flying backward. The marble floor crashed into my spine and stars burst before my eyes. With a quiet moan, I sat up, double blinking, and noticed Zevander across the room, lying flat on his back. A jolting alarm wound through me, as I forced myself to my feet and stumbled toward him. When I reached him, his eyes were closed, his chest wasn't moving.

Panic flared inside of me. "Dolion! I don't think he's breathing!" A shift in my periphery drew my eyes to the shadows frantically weaving in and out of the walls. Deimosi. I snapped my focus back to Zevander.

The older mage scrambled to his feet and shuffled across the room toward us. By the time he reached my side, Zevander gasped a breath that left a concave dip in his mask. He turned to his side, away from me, and unfastened the covering.

I could only just make out what looked like black veins across the part of his cheek I could see. The half of his profile that he'd tried to hide.

He coughed and wheezed, until, at last, he seemed to breathe easy. "Now, that is wind's vengeance."

Relieved, I sat back on my heels and huffed. "I thought ... for a second …" I stared down at my palm to find the Aeryz glyph glowing a bright silvery blue. "What is this?"

He slipped his mask back over his face and his gaze fell to the glyph on my palm.

"Interesting. I've never seen Aeryz as a major glyph before." Dolion bent forward, reaching out for my hand. "May I?"

I held it up to him, catching a glimpse of Zevander staring back at me, before he shifted his attention toward the mage. "A Corvikae glyph?" I asked.

"Perhaps. It's always been a minor glyph, a very simple command. But it seems it certainly packed a punch this time."

"So, the major glyphs glow that way?" I examined the way the silvery blue illuminated the shape of the glyph.

"They are your most powerful, yes." Dolion released my hand, and the glow faded, leaving only the faint white lines in my palm. "I must record this in the annals. Excuse me."

The mage jogged back toward the books that lay in a pile on the floor, and I turned my attention back to Zevander. "I'm sorry. I didn't mean to … whatever that was."

"Never apologize for incapacitating your enemy."

"You're not my enemy, though."

"Aren't I?"

"I mean, you are rude, sometimes. And grouchy. And extremely impatient." I smiled when he frowned back at me. "But you're a good teacher. I'll give you that."

"Yes, well, we'll stop for the evening." He groaned as he pushed to his feet and reached out a hand to help me to mine.

When I stood before him, he continued to hold my hand, staring down at it.

I glanced down to our clasped hands and, for the first time, noticed the thick scars beneath the bands that circled his wrists. Horrific scars, as though something had seared itself into his flesh. "What are they?"

Instead of answering, he slipped his hand from mine, making me immediately regret the inquiry.

"I shouldn't have asked. I'm sorry."

"I'll see you first thing in the morning." Ignoring my comment, he strode off, back toward Dolion. After a few words exchanged that I couldn't hear from where I stood, he glanced back at me and exited the room.

Exhaling a sigh, I made my way over to Dolion and helped him gather his books and scrolls. "You mentioned the Solassions earlier."

"Did I? Oh! Yes, when they imprisoned Zevander." He hobbled over to the pile of bones that I'd thrown at Zevander earlier, examining each one as he gathered them in his robe.

"For what?" I swiped up a couple of them, curious as to why he'd keep them, but much more interested in Zevander's story to ask.

"All followers of Cadavros and those who'd struck bargains with him were swiftly executed by King Sagaerin. However, due to her bloodline, Lady Rydainn had always had a good relationship with the king, and as such, he spared Zevander's and his father's life, by imprisoning them instead." He held up a connected vertebrae, brushing his thumb over a marking etched into the bone, and frantically grabbed another. "But Lord Rydainn had many enemies. The most notable being the captain of the Solassion Army, who demanded our king hand both father and son over to them. And, well, King Sagaerin didn't want any bad blood, so he did as they asked."

"And the Solassions let Zevander go?"

"Not exactly. For reasons that don't entirely make sense to me, King Sagaerin *himself* bought Zevander and three other Solassion prisoners. I believe you met Ravezio earlier. There's also Torryn and Kazhimyr. He had them trained to be his personal assassins."

After all the bones were gathered, I pushed to my feet, carrying about a half-dozen in the crook of my arm. "So, you're saying the king imprisoned him and his father, then handed them over to the Solassions, who then sold Zevander back to the king?"

Carrying the bones in his robe, Dolion walked alongside me as we exited the training room for the corridor. "Yes. The Solassions are a brutal lot. They executed his father in front of him, as I understand, and sent young Zevander to work the mines."

"In front of him?" I knew that my adopted father had been executed on his mission to Lyveria, but I couldn't imagine having to watch it happen firsthand. It tore at my heart to think of a young boy witnessing something so cruel and traumatic. "That's horrible. What happened to his mother?"

"That is a terrible story. The Solassions returned to Eidolon. As further punishment to Lord Rydainn, they … did terrible things to Lady Rydainn." Inhaling deeply, he closed his eyes and shook his head, and the expression on his face told me I didn't want to know the details of it.

"And Rykaia?"

"They intended to harm her, as well, but she was spared, somehow."

Again, I didn't bother to ask for the details. The look on Dolion's face told me everything I needed to know. "No wonder he's so angry."

"Yes. Life has not been easy or fair for the Rydainns." We arrived in the Great Hall, and Dolion came to a stop. "Zevander carries tremendous guilt. What happened to their family is a horrible tragedy, and I believe he blames himself for it."

"But he was just a boy."

"Yes. We are quite vicious to our younger selves, aren't we?" Dolion's question echoed my own guilt, and I stood pondering how many times I'd blamed myself for something I was too young to understand.

A thunderous click echoed around me, and I turned in time to see the enormous entry door swing open. A man dressed in black leathers, with silvery hair, like Rykaia's strode through, and beside him came a woman, with warm umber-toned skin, long white hair similar in shade to Dolion's, and eyes like glowing amethysts. When she seemed to catch sight of us, those bright violet orbs widened.

"Dolion Gevarys!" She shoved back the hood of her royal blue cloak and scurried across the foyer toward us. Like Dolion's, her ears were pointed, sticking up through her long, curled tresses. There was a beautiful grace about her that made me think she was royalty. Or perhaps it was the silver leaf circlet she wore across her forehead, which reminded me of a crown. She wrapped her arms around Dolion, releasing a happy chuckle. "I was told you were dead! My gods, it is good to see you!" Stepping back, she looked him up and down. "I cannot believe it!" Unlike Magdah's accent, hers was heavy on every syllable, very articulate.

"You have grown into the lovely image of your mother, gods rest her soul." Dolion laid a gentle hand against her cheek and smiled. "So. Is it Praeceptress Makabe?"

"Ah, not yet. One compelling research paper away from that." Her gaze fell upon me, and the smile on her face lit her eyes. "And you must be Maevyth."

"Yes," I said with an uncertain glance toward Dolion, surprised that she knew my name. I held out my hand to shake hers and the moment she clutched my palm, the smile faded for intense concentration. "You came from Mortasia. Through the Umbravale."

"Do you read palms?"

"No. Mortal bones tend to be smaller. Much more fragile." She flipped my arm over and stared down at where the scar marred my forearm, as if she could see it through the leather sleeve it hid beneath.

I lifted the sleeve, showing her the contracted skin there that looked like a feather.

Cold fingers drifted over the grooves and bumps. "You cut yourself on the bone."

The accuracy of her observations chilled my blood. "How do you know this?"

"Allura is a bone scribe. She has the power of sight from merely touching them." Dolion rattled the robe full of bones he carried. "We have much to study, my dear! Look at all these incredible specimens!"

Allura lifted one of the vertebrae from the pile and closed her eyes. Not a second later, her eyes shot open. "This bone is two thousand years old. It belonged to a woman named Verena."

"What? How in heavens would I ..." I didn't bother to finish. How in heavens would I have cast bones from my hands in the first place? As obvious as it was, I didn't particularly want to know that they *actually belonged* to another being. "None of this makes any sense to me."

"Well, that is why I sent for Allura. She can help us better understand."

The silver-haired man with eyes of molten gold strode up to us, carrying a brown bag that he started to hand off to Dolion, before seeming to take notice of the books, scrolls and bones in his arms. "Where would you like these?" he asked with a groan, his golden eyes locked on me.

"Are they the items I requested from my lab?"

"The items I was charged with gathering from The Citadel."

"Oh, um. In my room. In the dungeon."

Allura frowned back at him. "The dungeon?"

"It's by choice," he assured with a smile. "I struggle with heights, and I fear the views from this castle will stir my anxiety."

"Are there no drapes you can close?" she asked.

"I have a very keen awareness of heights. Even without the visual confirmation."

"I see …. Then, I will stay in the dungeons, as well."

"No, no, dear." Dolion patted her arm. "Zevander offered a room in the tower to me, perhaps you could take that one." He nodded toward me. "And you, Maevyth, I'm certain he'd provide much better accommodations now that he's a bit more comfortable with you."

"I'm fine where I'm at." Though, I hoped never to see that spider again.

"Very good. Well, what do you say we go and read some bones!" Again, he shook them, stirring a peculiar feeling about the fact that they had once belonged to actual beings.

"Dolion … will you still try to reach my sister?"

The excitement in his expression from moments before darkened to something more earnest. "Of course. But, Maevyth … understand, without a personal object, it's far more difficult to reach the other person." His lips thinned. "Try not to get your hopes too high."

"I won't." Any semblance of hope had already faded, the moment I'd watched Moros grab Aleysia.

CHAPTER THIRTY-EIGHT

MAEVYTH

I stared down at the shadowy mirror, the reflection of myself a haunting, ghostly appearance, in spite of the fire-lamp that illuminated Dolion's cell. Allura, Dolion, and I sat around a small wooden table in the center of the cramped space, as Dolion burned a savory smelling herb in a black crucible, its white smoke drifting over the top as he wafted it over the mirror.

"*Vetusza deosium invocasteus visionestaz.*" He repeated the phrase a half-dozen times, only pausing to blow the white smoke over the top of the scrying mirror.

A strange, anxious sensation curled in my stomach, and my pulse hastened, as if I were nervous. Or antsy. It made sense, I supposed. He was calling on a vision of my sister, and the possibility of seeing her dead sat heavy in my heart.

Breathing through my nose, I pushed the sensation away, but it lingered, scratching at my chest like something inside of me trying to get out.

"*Vetusza deosium invocasteus visionestaz e sapientaz.*"

Ancient gods, we call upon your vision and wisdom, a feminine voice whispered in my head.

I frowned, my heart pounding in my chest, and I looked

around, searching for who'd said it. Allura sat beside me, her eyes closed, as she rolled her head on her shoulders. As if drawn by my staring, she opened her eyes, flashing me a quick smile.

"Did you say something to me?" I whispered in a volume faint enough to keep from disturbing Dolion.

A look of confusion crossed her face, and she shook her head.

What was it, then? I surely wouldn't have understood those words, spoken in a language I'd never heard.

As Dolion kept on with the smoke and the chanting, I caught the trembling of my hands against the table.

"Vetusza deosium invocasteus visionestaz e sapientaz." His voice morphed into a deep, terrifying tone, as if he spoke from inside the chasm of a monster's belly. *"Vetusza deosium invocasteus visionestaz e sapientaz."*

Panic gripped my lungs, my breaths shaky and uneven. My head commanded me to say something, to make him stop, but my lips refused to obey.

My muscles jolted, locked up into a tight knot, and I kicked my head back. The ceiling faded beneath a bright flash of light. Through it, I could see Aleysia, her closely-shorn hair, the cuts and nicks above her ear. Bruised, pale skin. A fire burning in a hearth behind her. Whether she was alive, or dead, I couldn't tell, until she shifted beneath the blanket that covered her body.

The vision snapped to blackness, and my body jostled with a rough shake of my arm.

"Maevyth!"

I snapped my eyes open to two figures standing over me, a blur at first, but they sharpened into the concerned expressions of Dolion and Allura.

My mind scrambled to make sense of the view, my thoughts spinning, winding, tumbling out of control. Behind them were the table and chairs where I'd sat moments before. A sharp pain hammered at my skull, and had me wincing and rubbing the most painful side of my head. "What happened?"

Dolion hooked his arm in mine, lifting me up from where I'd apparently crashed to the floor. "I was summoning the aid of the gods, and all of a sudden, your eyes rolled back into your head and you fell from the chair."

Once upright, I climbed back into my seat and noticed the glass on the mirror had cracked. "Did you see anything about my sister?"

"Unfortunately, no. The summoning stopped before it even began."

"You asked for the vision and wisdom of the ancient gods. I understood the words." I rubbed my brow and shook my head, forcing myself to remember the details of what felt like a dream.

Dolion's brows winged up. "You must have an impressive education system in Mortasia to know Primyria."

"I never learned it. Where is it from?"

"It's believed to have been spoken by the gods, thousands of years ago."

An ache throbbed at my temples, and I pressed my fingers there. "How would I know that? In fact, how would I know Nyxterosi, which I swear is Vonkovyan, a language I've spoken my entire life!"

"It is quite a mystery, I'll admit. Primyria is said to be one of the most difficult to learn."

Allura added, "I've studied Vonkovyan, and you are definitely not speaking the dead language now."

I let out a strained chuckle. "I'm beginning to wonder if I've lost my mind. Or maybe … maybe I've hit my head so incredibly hard back in those woods that I don't remember and I'm lying unconscious. And this? This is just my head trying to reconcile the pain."

"You certainly have a vivid imagination, if that's the case, because I feel quite alive." Dolion sighed. "And quite old."

Palms pressed to my face, I took three deep breaths. "I saw my sister."

"Just now?"

"When I apparently lost my senses and fell from the chair. I saw her lying beneath a pile of blankets. There was a fire burning."

"Did she look to be in pain?" Dolion asked.

"Not at all." Staring off brought the image to mind again. "She looked to be at peace."

"Then, the gods shared their vision, after all."

Snapping out of my trance, I shook my head and frowned. "How can I trust that? You said the image would be in the mirror, not in my head."

"The gods do not abide by the rules of what should be, Maevyth."

"Is it possible, then? Is it possible that she's alive?" I wanted to believe with every fiber of my being that Aleysia had found safety somehow.

"If her spirit is as stubborn as yours? I would say so."

Eyes screwed shut, I willed my head to accept the vision, to convince my mind that what I'd seen just now wasn't made up. "I saw her, though. Moros, he …. He dragged her away."

"Perhaps she escaped." Dolion offered, but he hadn't seen the way that creature had hunted both Moros and Uncle Riftyn. He hadn't watched how easily it had torn the flesh from Uncle Riftyn's body. Even then, I had to shake my head of the horror, the efficiency in which it had killed. What reason would it have had to spare her?

"I can't begin to express how badly I want to believe that."

A hand gripped my shoulder, and when I looked up, it was Allura staring down at me. "Then, believe it."

* * *

Allura sat beside me, as I opened the puzzle book to the first page I'd unveiled. Across from us, Dolion sat scribbling in a leather-bound journal, the bones that Allura had analyzed earlier strewn about the table. She'd determined that each had belonged to a different person at some point. Which meant the bones of at least a dozen deceased individuals had shot from my hand, and I still struggled to wrap my head around that.

He lifted one of the specimens, studying it before placing it back down and scribbling again.

"It appears to be the story of Deimos and Morsana," Allura said, yanking my attention back to the book.

I ran my fingers over the figures, spurring them into motion again, just as before. "Who are they?"

"Morsana was a death goddess. It was said that her eyes were so strikingly silver, no mortal creature dared to look at her. Except for Deimos." Her amethyst eyes dulled with concentration as she stared down at the page. "He was a feared warrior for an ancient tribe who conquered lands and killed without remorse. Some believed the God of Chaos inhabited him, and Morsana was said to have sought him so relentlessly, she followed him into every battle, disguised as a flock of ravens. With every victory, her endeavors to claim his soul withered. And soon, she fell in love with the brave mortal who did not so much as flinch in her presence." She peered down at the painting, her hand hovering over the shadowy figure trapped in flames. For her, the images didn't move, but remained static. "He offered his kills as a gift to her, and his people worshipped the once-feared goddess. But Magekae, the God of Dark Alchemy, was obsessed with her. Had been since the dawn of time. And he was furious over her love for a mortal. So, he took matters into his own hands. He armed the enemies of Deimos with a powerful magic that turned them immortal. Strengthened them by daylight, which made them undefeatable for the mortals. And so, the Solassions came to be.

And they conquered the lands that Deimos had claimed for his people."

She shifted her focus to the woman bathed in a silver glowing light. "Unfortunately, Magekae and his immortals prevailed. They cast Deimos into sablefyre, to burn for eternity, and slaughtered his people. Magekae imprisoned Morsana for many years. Determined never to marry the corrupt god, Morsana took the form of a raven and escaped. That is why it is believed the raven carries the souls of the dead to Nethyria."

Still staring down at the page, she placed her palm over the bones on the spine of the book. "We were never taught about the Corvikae people. All of these stories were nothing but fables of gods and mortals." Shifting her attention to me, she smiled. "But they're not, are they? If you exist, they must be real."

"They are very real." Dolion looked up from his studies. "We have so much to learn from you, Maevyth."

I sank back into my chair, trying to absorb everything. "I feel as if I've so much to learn of myself."

"And you will." Allura gave a reassuring smile.

"Yes, but perhaps in the morning." Dolion yawned and stretched his arms. "I'm growing quite weary of studying bones."

"It has been a long day of travel." Allura sighed.

At a knock that echoed through the dungeon, the three of us looked up to find Rykaia standing outside of Dolion's cell with her arms crossed. "So ... I'm supposed to show our new guest to her room." Her eyes fell on Allura in a way that seemed appraising. "That must be you."

"I'm happy to sleep down here, if–"

"Sorry. There are only two cells with beds. If you took one of the others, you'd be sleeping on a concrete floor." Gone was the warmth that Rykaia had shown me when I'd first arrived, and I frowned, wondering what it was about the woman she seemed to not like very much.

"Very well. I will bid the two of you goodnight." Allura gave a nod and pushed up from the table, gracefully making her way toward Rykaia, who glared at the woman as if she'd done something to offend her.

Rykaia looked back to me. "And you. I suspect you'll want another bath and a change of clothes."

"A basin and a sponge is fine. Maybe a change of clothes. I'm guessing Zevander will want his tunic returned."

Her lips pulled to a smirk. "He hasn't requested that I retrieve it from you."

"In that case, just a sponge and basin."

"Very well." With that, the two of them set off down the corridor.

CHAPTER THIRTY-NINE

MAEVYTH

As I waited for Rykaia to bring me the basin and sponge, I flipped open the puzzle book to the next mechanism–the clock-like box with all of the various symbols. Eyes sweeping over each one, I twisted the book around, and paused on one I'd seen before–the spiny glyph that'd shot forth bones from my hand. Frowning, I studied it closer and, on the clock's edge, noticed the three squiggly lines Rykaia had taught me for Aeryz.

Glyphs. The symbols were glyphs.

I turned the top of the box until it clicked into place, and discovered that each glyph on top lined up with the glyphs on the side somehow, though they were not the same symbol. They also aligned with what looked to be the different phases of each moon, carved on the outer edge of the top just outside of the clockface.

The question was, how did each glyph on top link to those on the side?

I would've asked Dolion, but I could already hear his snores through the wall.

A tiny hole in the center of the clockface caught my attention.

Flipping back a page, I plucked out the lever that I'd used to open the book, and stuffed one end into the small hole. The other end of it stuck up like a crank, and when I turned it, something plinked inside. I turned it again to more plinking, a beautiful song with the impossibly rich melody of a harp. Turning and turning, I kept the song going, until it stopped and the box clicked louder than before. I looked at the arrangement of glyphs. The spine lined up to a scorpion. Aeryz to flame. The two halves of the moons united at the top and bottom of the clockface to form one full moon. With ease, I lifted the top of the box. Inside, lay a black rose, perfectly intact, as if it'd recently been picked. I plucked it from the box, noting the beautiful, metallic silver edges along every petal. After inspecting the flower, I turned the page for the next part of the story.

What looked to be Morsana, as she appeared on the first page of the puzzle book, stood over a baby lying in a bassinet, holding a rose similar to the one I clutched right then. When I ran my fingers over the page, the scene came to life. Morsana placed the rose on the baby's chest, and ravens flocked around the bassinet.

Another brush of my finger unveiled words below the scene. *From death, we rose. A new generation was born.*

I thought back to the conversation I'd had with The Crone Witch, when she'd told me she had been the one to find me. That she hadn't seen who'd left me there. Had she left the rose? What did it mean?

I turned the page again to yet another puzzle. A circular object, with various lines and a peg at the center. Beneath it appeared to be some kind of maze made of deep grooves, but too weary to decipher it right then, I lay the book down with a sigh. Between my earlier training and studying bones, my head was spinning.

The stars through the window captured my attention as I curled up in my blankets. As it had on previous nights, my mind drifted to Aleysia. I thought back to the vision I'd seen of her earlier in the day, lying calm and alive beside a warm hearth. Had someone found her and taken her in? I couldn't imagine who, in Foxglove, would've done such a thing after her banishment.

Except for one.

The Crone Witch.

She was the only one who wouldn't have been troubled by rumor, or the supposed evil that my sister represented. Yes, I prayed that she'd found Aleysia, and that my sister was safe with her.

My eyes prickled with tears.

Something moved in my periphery, and I jolted upright.

Long, spindly legs stepped into view.

The spider I'd seen the night before, just outside my cell.

The quickening of my pulse accompanied the rough pounding of my heart as, again, I searched for something to throw at it. Unless I imagined it, the spider seemed to have grown since its previous visit, and it was then I considered that I may have been hallucinating the damned thing.

It didn't advance closer, as if it couldn't for some reason.

"Shoo!" I waved it off, not daring to step down from the bed.

From its furry back, it tugged an object that its long skinny leg placed on the stony floor on the other side of the bars. Frowning, I leaned forward, trying to make out what it'd placed there.

The spider skittered to the side, out of view, and I pushed to my feet, eyes glued to the object it'd left behind. A mirror, from what I could see of the shiny surface.

With no sign of the spider, I padded cautiously toward the cell door, eyes sweeping from one corner to the other. A thread of tension wound inside my stomach as I opened the door it seemed no one had bothered to lock, scanning for that damned spider.

My reflection stared back at me in the mirror, when I lifted it from the floor, and on lowering it, I caught the shine of something else ahead of me. I padded carefully toward it, eyes peeled for the slightest movement.

Dolion's snores reverberated off the walls of his cell as I passed, and I kept on, toward the dark end of the corridor. Until I came upon the second object. A key.

In the distance, a sconce flared to life, startling me at first. And yet another object caught my attention.

On the floor.

A lock and chain.

I glanced down at the key in my hand and back to the door. Still no sign of the spider I'd seen. The logical side of my brain told me to leave it alone and return to my cell, because nothing good ever came from chasing after enormous spiders. As a child, I'd once tracked a tarantula along the edge of the woods and ended up getting bitten, leaving quite a knot on my leg.

The illogical and maddeningly curious half of my brain needed to know what was locked away, though. Surely, Dolion and I wouldn't have been expected to sleep near something capable of harming us. It could've very well have been nothing more than more spiders.

A thought that squeezed my spine.

Questioning my sanity, I tiptoed closer, and the gravity of my decision to open the door left my hands trembling as I shoved the key into the lock. On a click, the lock opened, and I loosened the chain from the anchors that held the door closed. Every muscle shook, as I lifted the door on a creak of old wood and rusted hinges. Grabbing the sconce from the wall, I held it over the open door to peer inside. Nothing but darkness, and a ladder that disappeared into shadows.

I shifted the sconce to the other side of the door, the light illuminating a horrifically colossal spider web that took up the entirety of the wall.

A crashing sound snapped my attention away from the hole. "Maevyth! What are you doing!" At the end of the corridor, just outside of my cell, Rykaia stood over broken porcelain, her eyes wide with fear. "Get away from there! Now!"

A force banded around my waist, yanking me through the hole. On impact, zaps of pain shot up my spine, jagged flashes of light behind my eyes converging into an explosion of agony at the back of my skull. The door overhead slammed shut.

On the gravelly dirt beside me, the sconce burned, and I trembled as I turned over onto my stomach. Above me, I could hear Rykaia and Dolion pounding against the door.

"Branimir!" Rykaia's muffled scream bled through the barrier, and I reached out for the sconce, lifting it into the air.

In the dark corner, something shifted. What little I could make of its shape told me it wasn't a spider, though I felt like eyes were watching my every move from every corner of that small space. The putrid odor of rot and mold assaulted my nose, and I coughed and gagged, swallowing back the acids in my throat. I pushed onto my knees, trailing the flaming torch back and forth.

"Hello?"

A deep, guttural growl answered, and it was then I realized I'd made a grave mistake in opening that door.

Slowly, I backed myself away toward the ladder, but a tickle on the back of my calf brought me to a halt, and I slowly turned my head.

Looming over me were the largest set of fangs I'd ever seen, and above them, hundreds of beady eyes watching me.

I let out a scream and scampered away on all fours, dropping the sconce. "Somebody, help me!"

"Maevyth!" Dolion's voice carried an edge of panic.

"Quiet," a deep, raspy voice spoke from behind.

I turned to the corner where I'd seen movement only a moment ago. "Is someone there?"

"They don't like screams," it answered.

I didn't dare to look back at the gargantuan beast blocking my escape. "Wh-wh-who are you?"

"Sing. It will calm them."

Sing? Had he lost his senses? How in seven hells could I be expected to sing anything, under the circumstances. "I … I don't know if I can. I'm … shaking."

"I won't let them hurt you." Though hoarse and terrifying, his voice held a certain sincerity.

"O-o-okay." I inhaled a long, shaky breath, and exhaled one equally as shaky. *Don't think about the spiders.*

Closing my eyes, I imagined my sister, and the nights she'd ask me to sing to her. I imagined the stars and my bed, and all the things that brought me comfort. I hummed at first, to see if I was even capable of forming a single note with my throat tight and my muscles locked. Fortunately, my body didn't fail me, and I sang the song I knew best. The one that reminded me of watching my father mourn.

So wrapped up in the song and the memories playing inside my head, I didn't notice the figure moving closer.

Until I opened my eyes.

Before me, a beastly creature crouched, his skin like bark and covered in black veins, his eyes two black and soulless orbs that stared back at me. Crooked horns protruded from his head, his lips peeled back over sharpened teeth.

A scream blasted out of me, as I kicked myself backward. The fear inside bore teeth that hooked into my stomach and chest, paralyzing me as the beast prowled closer.

The wrathavor from The Eating Woods!

"Please. Sing," he said, lifting a bony finger to his lips that reminded me of a tree branch.

Every cell in my body shook and bounced, wild with the fear that cinched my lungs. My bottom lip quivered with the urge to cry, but I swallowed it back and nodded. Because I was trapped, and I had no intention of having my skin ripped from my flesh. Closing my eyes again, I forced myself to another place. Anywhere but there.

Something scratched my thighs, and I opened my eyes to find the humanoid creature resting his head in my lap, his thin, pale body curled into himself.

I could scarcely draw in a breath as I watched him. Waiting for the moment when he'd snap and dangle me from those bony hands, while he clawed away my skin.

He didn't, though.

Instead, he merely lay across my legs, and I felt a bead of moisture slip over my shin.

Tears. His tears. Weeping, as I sang to him.

My pulse slowed. My breaths calmed.

He no longer looked terrifying to me.

In that moment, he reminded me of a child. A sad and desperate child who longed for contact.

As I sang, I lowered my hand toward his face, hesitating a moment. I stroked a gentle finger across his shoulder, and he startled, but didn't move. I kept on singing as I rested my hand against him, and I felt him shake with a sob. Tears formed in my eyes. My heart clenched and broke for this poor, helpless creature, who seemed to want nothing more than a gentle touch.

I was no longer afraid.

I was furious at whoever had hurt him.

CHAPTER FORTY

ZEVANDER

The potent liquor failed to numb the frustration pounding through Zevander, as he sat back in his chair, staring through the window over the vast valley of trees, to the mountains in the distance.

Hours, he'd spent training Maevyth on a single glyph. It'd take years to train her on the more powerful ones, and he didn't have that kind of time. Who in seven hells knew when Branimir would finally snap and he'd have to take a blade to his own brother.

Or worse.

Still, Zevander couldn't deny the joy he'd gleaned in watching her. The unwavering determination in her eyes that hardened his body in the most infuriating ways.

The door crashed open on an obnoxious clatter, and he turned to find Rykaia standing in the doorway, out of breath.

"Zevander! Come! It's Maevyth!"

"What's wrong?" Strange, the way every muscle locked up right then.

"Branimir has her!" Sheer terror clung to Rykaia's voice.

Placing his drink on the desk, Zevander pushed to his feet and strode across the room. He hustled down the corridor and the staircase, to the Great Hall, and down another corridor to the dungeon staircase.

All along the way, Rykaia relayed what she'd seen, her voice growing more hysterical with every step. "I was bringing her a basin and sponge to wash, and I saw one of his spiders pull her in! Do you think he'll hurt her?"

Zevander dared himself to imagine such a thing, the visual sending hot spears of rage through him. "No," he said, for his sister's sake. Once in the dungeons, he strode toward where Dolion hunched over the door.

"I attempted a paralysis spell, but he seems resistant."

Ignoring the older man, Zevander took hold of the door handle and forced all of his muscles into the effort of lifting it. It wouldn't budge. On a growl, he took a step back and summoned the black flame to his palm. He threw his hand out, sending the flame toward the door like a lasso that hooked onto the anchor. Against the resistance, it threw open the door on a crack of its hinges, and Zevander swiped up the mirror as he stalked toward the hole.

He lowered the mirror into Branimir's cell, spinning it around, past the flaming sconce—to two figures sitting against the far wall. And the sound that rose up from below pierced him in the heart. A song he remembered from some distant memory he couldn't place. An angelic voice that strummed his soul. The most beautiful sound he'd ever heard.

In the mirror's reflection, Branimir lay in Maevyth's lap, as she gently stroked his face. For the first time in centuries, his brother looked completely at peace. The sight of them together stirred a deep sorrow, and something else. Jealousy? He couldn't place the emotions. Branimir had only ever made him feel pity.

His brother tilted his head back, and on catching sight of the mirror, he let out a hiss and backed himself away from the girl.

"No, wait!" Maevyth reached out for him, as he retreated to the shadows.

Setting the mirror aside, Zevander climbed down the stairs, and when she turned toward him, he flicked his fingers. "Come."

"No," she said, and damn her stubborn nature and the challenge in her voice that spiked his blood. "Why is he locked down here?"

"It is his choice."

"You're lying."

"No," Branimir spoke in a raspy voice. "It is true. Go with him."

Confused, she shifted her attention from one brother to the other. "Come with me. You don't need to lock yourself away."

"Maevyth," Zevander warned. "Come. Now."

When she didn't move at his command, Zevander sent forth a blast of power that lifted her from the ground.

Branimir snarled from the corner where he cowered.

"Stay," Zevander growled back. "Or I will send a thousand poisonous shocks to your heart." The moment the words slipped from his lips, he regretted them. It'd been a long time since he'd threatened his brother that way.

He placed Maevyth carefully to her feet and urged her to come to him.

She gave one glance back to Branimir then made her way toward the ladder, not bothering to spare Zevander a glance as she climbed up.

Sighing, Zevander followed after her and, once out of the cell, closed the door, replacing the chain. "You will sleep in one of the rooms in the tower."

"Who is he?"

"Our brother," Rykaia answered for him. "Branimir."

"Why would you …. Why would you lock him down there? That's … cruel."

"You don't know him, or what he's capable of," Rykaia snapped.

"Rykaia, perhaps you might give us a minute and clean up the shattered porcelain." Zevander's voice remained calm, in spite of the rage and adrenaline coursing through him. It was then it occurred to him that something else pulsed through his veins, though he couldn't pinpoint exactly what had him feeling so unsettled. Beyond jealousy. Something deeper. Darker.

Possessive.

Seeing Branimir lying in her lap had scrambled his thoughts to an irritating muddle of anger and resentment.

"Fine. I told you this wasn't a good idea, having her down here." Rykaia spun back down the corridor, to where the broken basin lay shattered in front of Maevyth's cell.

Dolion followed after her, leaving Zevander and Maevyth standing over the locked door.

"What happened to him?" she asked.

Zevander hung the mirror back on the hook. "We share the same curse." He caught his reflection in the mirror, realizing in his rush to the dungeon, he hadn't bothered to cover his face.

"But you … you don't look like him."

"Branimir went through the ritual when he was much older. I was a baby and didn't suffer as many side effects."

"But you have some," she said, having clearly noticed the gash across his face and the grotesque veins pouring out of it.

"Yes. It's possible his fate will be my own."

"Why keep him down there?" Her voice held an accusing tone, and though he couldn't blame her for it, it nettled him just the same.

He hesitated to entertain her questions. It was none of her business, after all. She had been the one to venture where she hadn't been invited. But for reasons he couldn't explain, he didn't like her seeing him in that light. It troubled him. "He wishes to hide himself away. It's not my choice."

"How does he eat? How does he live down there?"

"His creatures provide for him."

She huffed, glancing back toward the door. "I think I'd lose my senses, if I were trapped in that dark place every day. But if it's his choice …"

"Why did you go down there?" he asked through clenched teeth, a fresh anger pulsing through him.

"I was led … by a huge spider who left a trail of trinkets, including the key."

The spiders had grown clever, it seemed. Luring her either independently, or by Branimir's command, he couldn't say. For what, though? "The desire to find a cure and let him live out his remaining years in peace is fading on the horizon."

"You're saying it isn't possible to cure him?"

Zevander wanted to laugh at the irony of her question, that the cure to his affliction was standing there, inquiring about it. He didn't bother to voice that, though, for fear that she might've offered herself up right then.

"I'm sorry if I sounded like I was accusing." Gaze lowered, she nibbled on her bottom lip, insufferably beautiful with her annoying little habits that seized his attention and left him wondering what she tasted like. If her lips were sweet, like berries, or bitter, like his liquor. "I thought–"

"I know what you thought. As I said, you'll sleep in the upper level from now on. And you will leave him be."

"Is he dangerous?"

"He's killed before."

"Innocents?"

The visual Zevander had been given many years ago slipped through his thoughts, of his brother ripping apart the Solassion marauders who'd come for his mother and sister, the blood and gore of their bodies torn into like a wild animal had ravaged them. "No."

"Then, that would make him far less dangerous than you, by my calculations."

"I suppose."

She wasn't wrong in her assumptions. Zevander had killed many times without question, or remorse. Didn't matter who, or why. If the king had ordered it, he'd carried out those orders efficiently and swiftly. He'd even tried to kill her once and perhaps that made Branimir less of a threat.

"So, how am I safer being closer to you than here?"

"Because I'm no longer asking. Now, if you'd prefer to sleep outside with–"

She set her hands to her hips, her frown deepening to something she probably hoped was vicious and terrifying. He found her oddly arousing and adorable at the same time. "Are you ever going to stop using the *vicious* fyredrakes against me?" she asked.

"No."

"Fine. I'll sleep in the upper level. On the condition that you let me bring him food and sing to him."

Who was this strange creature?

As much as it had always hurt Rykaia to stay away, she'd avoided Branimir out of fear. Though, in fairness, she'd also seen him at his most violent. "You're not the least bit frightened of him?"

"Well, yes. Of course. But that's not his fault."

He didn't like her being alone with him, and while part of him wanted to chide the ridiculous thoughts in his head, the other insisted on refusing her request. Regardless of his mostly gentle nature, the fact was, Branimir possessed a violent strength that made him a threat. "You'd need to be accompanied."

"Is it possible Rykaia–"

"Not Rykaia. Nor Dolion." He jerked his head for her to follow after him, and as they passed her cell, she scampered inside for a book lying out on the bed. The one Dolion had showed him days ago, with the bony spine and silvery dragon's eye.

"What about you?"

Zevander groaned. "You must think I have all the time in the world for you," he grumbled. "Training and babysitting you."

"This isn't for me, this is for your brother. Surely, you'd make time for him."

He ground his jaw and narrowed his eyes.

"You're thinking about feeding me to the fyredrakes again, aren't you? Perhaps I should meet these terrible beasts, so I can truly appreciate your threat without rolling my eyes."

"One song," he said in a flat tone, ignoring the way his cock lurched at her brassy comment. "That's it." He jerked his head and led her up the staircase to the upper level, away from his brother.

"And food ... what does he like?" she asked after him.

"Meat. Raw." He glanced over his shoulder in time to see her lips twisted in disgust, and smirked when he turned back around.

"Any chance you might have a steak on hand?"

Instead of answering, Zevander opened the door to her room.

She hesitated a moment before turning, and her eyes lit up as she took in the room that once belonged to his mother. Across the ample space stood a four-post bed, the points of which had been carved to look like spires. The inner dome of the wooden canopy held a delicate candelabra that gave off a soft glow when the curtains were drawn. Burgundy velvet covered the bed, with black silk sheets beneath. Dozens of candles stood about the room that his mother had always called dark and brimming with gloom.

Tall lancet windows overlooked the expanse of woods–the same view as that from his own chambers, seeing as he'd put her in the room just down the hall.

"This is where I will sleep?" Her voice held an air of disbelief.

"Do you find it too morose?"

"No. Not at all." Just inside the room stood a beautifully

carved wooden table with a vase full of asphodels that Magdah saw fit to change out every so often in remembrance of his mother. Maevyth caressed her thumb over one of the delicate petals. "I thought asphodels were springtime flowers."

"Magdah keeps them in a greenhouse on the castle grounds."

"Flowers of the afterlife." Wearing a slight smile, she sauntered toward the window, and something about her dark figure set against the misty, aphotic view, and the candles flickering around her, as if the light longed to touch her, made his chest clench. She was beautiful.

No, beautiful was too weak a word.

She was intoxicating. Exquisitely divine.

Once again, his thoughts wound back to the moment he'd found her cradling his brother's head, giving him the gentle caresses he'd been denied most of his life. Hands balled to tight fists, he fought the tugging in his chest. The urge to carve the image from his skull and set it aflame.

Frustrated by the peculiar reaction, he turned to leave.

"Zevander," she said, and the sound of his name rolling off her tongue sent a chill down his spine.

He turned his head to the side, refusing to let her see the yearning that was damned near beaming in his eyes. How ridiculous he must've looked, a man of his strict training and discipline, pining after her like a fucking prepubescent schoolboy.

"Goodnight."

"Goodnight, *Lunamiszka*."

"Do I still annoy you?" she asked.

"Endlessly."

CHAPTER FORTY-ONE

MAEVYTH

J ust as I had the previous day, I met Zevander and Dolion in the training room, escorted by Rykaia—who'd made a point to chide me for having opened the door to her brother's cellar the night before.

"It isn't that he's a danger to you, per se," she'd said, as I'd scarfed down the milky oats and apples she'd brought me. "It's just that he's ... well, worse than before. And he can't really control his emotions, sometimes. I visited him once without bothering to tell Zevander. He ended up nearly strangling me to death. It was Aeryz that saved me."

Up until we'd reached the training room, I'd promised at least three times not to venture down there alone again. Yet, while the bed in my new chambers was far more comfortable than the one in my cell, I hadn't slept much at all the night before, my mind not only questioning the vision I'd seen of Aleysia, but what I'd learned of Branimir, as well.

Standing at the center of the training room, Zevander once more wore the mask he seemed insistent on wearing, despite my having already seen what hid beneath. With, or without it, he still looked as exceptionally fierce and handsome as the day before.

And just as I had then, I found myself equally annoyed by that observation.

Far from being in no mood to train, I found myself curious for what the day's lesson would bring. While the method may have been exhausting, my reluctant intrigue with the glyphs compelled me past the ache in my eyeballs.

Rykaia fell into step alongside me.

"You're staying for this one?" I asked, glad for her presence.

"I've been tasked to help train." The lack of enthusiasm in her voice made it clear that said task held little interest for her. She hadn't even opted for training clothes, and instead, wore an emerald-green dress.

"Another grueling day of wind's vengeance?" I asked, strolling up to Zevander.

"No. I'm going to show you a new glyph today, with Rykaia's help. Another defense mechanism, one that might be most handy to you, and fairly easy to learn."

"Thank god for that."

When he opened his palm, a glyph glowed across his skin. *"Propulszir. To repel."*

I rounded myself to his point of view until standing beside him and studied the glyph. A small square set inside a larger one, its points touching the sides of the bigger shape, and small lines sticking out from each of the bigger square's sides.

"Propulszir," I whispered, committing as much of the shape to memory as I could. "This one seems a bit complex." The other glyphs I'd learned seemed to have simple shapes that I'd found easier to recall.

"The more powerful glyphs are the most complex. Some mages never learn their intricacies." Unless I was overanalyzing, his voice seemed calmer today, less irritated.

Having committed the glyph to memory, I returned to my original spot across from him, and it was from there that I happened to glance downward, catching sight of the massive bulge in his leathers.

Dear god.

I'd only seen one in my lifetime, belonging to the son of the miner who'd shown me how to touch him there, and it had been nowhere near as big.

"You do not push this glyph," Zevander prattled on, completely unaware of the intrusive visual swallowing my attention. "You clutch." He lifted his hand, curling it into a fist. The sight of his muscled arm had me stifling a shiver, as I imagined his hand curled around his massive length. "It's useful against those who wish to read your mind, or probe your power. We'll test with Rykaia."

Tendrils of horror curled down my spine. I swallowed a gulp and turned to Rykaia. "You can read minds?"

"Unfortunately, yes," Zevander answered for her. "In her case, she has to be physically touching you."

I forced all thoughts of him and his bulge out of my head as best I could, as I stared down at the marble floor, desperate for something else to focus on.

Do not think about him.

"Think of a word," he said, that deep voice bringing the image forth again. "Any word. And Rykaia will say it aloud."

A word. A word. What word? My head frantically scrambled for a word, as she took hold of my arm.

The moment her lips curved to a smile, I knew she knew.

"My, my, Maevyth. You are a naughty girl," she said with an edge of amusement.

A flare of heat warmed my cheeks, my head a dizzying maze of humiliation, as I scrambled to think of something else. I did not dare glance at Zevander.

"Speak the word," Zevander commanded, and Rykaia's lips curved higher.

Eyes pleading, I silently begged her not to say the word aloud. *Please.*

"Oranges," she said, licking her lips.

Breathing a sigh of relief, I nodded. "Oranges."

"Good. Now close your eyes and imagine the glyph in your mind. See it clearly. Every detail." When I nodded, he kept on. "Think of another word. Remember to make a fist." He lifted his hand again to a fist, and once again, my head betrayed me.

Gnawing the inside of my cheek, I fought to come up with another word. At the first taste of copper on my tongue, she took hold of my arm.

"Blood," she said.

"Blood," I agreed.

"Try again."

Again, she released me.

Focus, Maevyth.

I closed my eyes and squeezed my fist so hard, the bite of my nails left a sting across my palm. My head apparently decided there was no other thought more important, and my muscles tensed with my rising frustration.

Focus. Focus!

Show me something else! My head screamed. The glow of light through my shuttered lids turned pitch black.

All went silent.

"Hello, Maevyth," a feminine voice said, and I turned around to find a willowy figure sauntering toward me, her silhouette illuminated by some obscure light source behind her.

As she neared, her features sharpened into view—long, raven-black hair and silvery eyes.

In the distance, I heard Rykaia call out for me, and the woman turned, as if she'd heard it too.

She smiled back at me. "Don't worry, she can't hear us here."

"Who are you?"

"Who do you think I am?"

All of her features matched those of the death goddess I'd recently learned about. "Morsana. Am I dead?"

"No, sweet girl. You have much to do before you die. But should you ever need me, I am here. You can find me in this dark space."

"Maevyth!" The fierce tone of Zevander's voice thundered around us, and she glanced around, smiling again.

"He is irresistibly provocative, isn't he?" Her eyes flickered, as though excited by his intensity. "There's something you should know about him, Maevyth."

"What?"

"Maevyth!" One hard shake snapped me out of the visual, and I opened my eyes to Zevander, Dolion, and Rykaia standing over me. A quick sweep of my surroundings showed I was lying on the floor.

"Again?" An ache flared at the back of my head, where I'd apparently struck it again, and a bitter taste flooded my mouth, like a chalky coating on my tongue.

"It seems you have a nasty little habit of this." Dolion stepped back, as Zevander held out a hand, pulling me to my feet. "Had to use the rousing spell. My apologies for the aftertaste."

"I ... slipped into a blackness. Like a dream."

Zevander and Dolion exchanged a glance, and Dolion knelt down to me, handing me a glass of water that I sipped with fervor. "You fell into caligorya. The darkspace. Interesting. Some never reach that state of mind."

"It's there you'll learn the glyphs that are unique to your bloodline," Zevander added. "That's where I discovered mine. But I suggest you work your way to that. Caligorya is dangerous."

"How so?"

"In that space, resides the dark side of you." It was Dolion who answered. "The creature that feeds on rage, vengeance, apathy. Every living thing possesses this darkness, whether they care to admit it, or not, but we are taught from a young age to suppress it. By going there, you are opening a door, of sorts, and if you're not careful, it may be quite difficult to close it."

Dark side of myself? Creature? "I saw the death goddess there."

"Morsana?" Dolion asked, brows pinched together.

"Yes."

He shrugged and shook his head. "It's possible that might be unique to the Corvikae. They are tied to her, after all. All the more reason to heed caution. She is a powerful goddess and leans a bit on the darker side of the moral compass." He scratched at his beard, eyes lost to thought, as usual. "For now, we'll stick to the easier glyphs. Try to avoid overcompensating. Propulszir should be effortless and natural."

"Effortless and natural. Got it." I pushed to my feet and gave one more rub to the back of my neck.

Rykaia stood across from me and mouthed, *Are you all right?*

I nodded and cleared my throat. "Right, so. New word." Closing my eyes, I imagined a new word. One that Morsana had said about Zevander.

Provocative.

The word was swallowed by the image of the symbol I'd seen on Zevander's hand. So clear in my head, I almost didn't notice Rykaia's grip on my wrist, until I felt her squeeze harder.

Harder.

She released me on a groan. "Nothing."

Smiling, I opened my eyes and glanced down at a sharp burn on my palm, where and the soft glow of the new glyph had permanently etched into my skin.

"Again," Zevander said in an unimpressed tone.

"Does he ever celebrate a victory?" I grumbled, lowering my hand and frowning after him, as he strode off for one of the weapons hung on the wall.

Rykaia snorted. "Only when he's killed something."

Zevander stood off from us, holding a long stick with two

pointed ends. In wide circles, he twirled it like a wheel at his side. Then, like the snap of a whip, he flipped it around his body, over his head, behind his back, and at his sides. The staff moved so fast, it formed a perfect circle.

Mouth hung wide, I watched in awe as he manipulated the stick with ease, pausing to toss it in the air then catch it in perfect cadence.

"Keep practicing," he said, never breaking his rhythm.

"How am I supposed to concentrate with that going on?"

"I think that's the point," Rykaia answered, picking at her own palm. "You don't always get perfect, quiet conditions to repel someone. It has to be something you can do simultaneously to other things going on about you. That's the beauty of it. No one knows you're repelling."

With a nod, I stared at Zevander, watching him wield his staff around, watching the muscles in his arms flex and the sweat bead across his skin. How gracefully ruthless he must've looked against an opponent. I closed my fingers over my palm, giving a brief thought to the glyph there.

My head wandered into a different space this time. An image of two nights before, when he'd stood before me in his loose tunic and leathers, the deep grooves of muscle in his chest. I imagined him pulling me in for a kiss, his rough lips across mine, his strong hands at the small of my back.

"You like my brother, don't you?"

A panicked breath shot out of me. I swallowed hard and stepped back, releasing her hold of my arm.

"Don't worry, I didn't see anything." Rykaia chuckled and glanced toward her brother and back. "It's written all over your face."

"I was just ... looking for distraction, is all."

"It seems you found it." She offered a wink and a smile, before turning her attention to Zevander. "Brother, I am tired. She has effectively kept me from reading her thoughts. Can we move on?"

At that, Zevander finally lowered the staff. "Go. Rest," he said to Rykaia, before leaning against the staff, looking painfully, irritatingly delicious. "Would you like to practice Aeryz again? Or should we move on to a new glyph?"

"What's the glyph?" I asked, and Rykaia patted me on the shoulder as she strode off toward Dolion, who sat with his usual pile of books and scrolls.

"*Erigorisz*. Lifting objects with your mind. It requires intense concentration, though."

The very thought of doing something else with my mind was completely unappealing, though I didn't feel exhausted, as Rykaia had claimed to be.

"How about you teach me to flip that staff the way you did earlier."

He arched a brow. "You wish to learn fighting techniques?"

"Is this when you tell me girls shouldn't possess such skills?"

Leaning against the pole, he shrugged. "Not at all. I'm merely surprised you're interested."

"If I plan to return for my sister, and I do, I'll need some skills to defend myself." I said, with an upward tip of my chin, daring him to dispute me.

"You'll soon have a very powerful magic to call upon."

"The bone whip?"

"Yes. It sounds quite unappealing from an enemy standpoint."

"Are you my enemy?"

With an introspective tension etched into his brow, he lowered his gaze. "I'm everyone's enemy. There's nothing virtuous about the magic I wield."

"And if mine is associated with death, maybe I'm everyone's enemy, as well."

Those mercurial eyes found me again, brimming with dark

amusement. "Aren't we a pair …" He jerked his head. "Come, *Lunamiszka*."

"I'm beginning to question your interpretation of that word. It seems luna should have something to do with the moon."

"It seems you're right," he said over his shoulder, as he led me to the center of the room again.

"So, what do I have to do with the moon?"

He pointed to the corner of his own eye and realization dawned on me.

"The silver mark in my eye. And miszka?"

"Witch."

"Moon Witch, you're calling me. I suppose it would be fitting now that I've learned magic. Which, by the way, would be grounds for burning me at the stake, where I come from."

"Mortals fear what they don't understand." He flicked his wrist, calling me to stand in front of him.

I nervously positioned myself where he directed me, which put my back against the breadth of his solid chest. Unlike the night on the horse, when encumbered by layers of clothes and the cold, the thin layer of soft leather allowed me to feel him as if we were skin to skin. "Do you think Rykaia was bored with training?" I asked, desperate for distraction.

"No. She tires quickly. Her power requires quite a bit of vivicantem." He brought his muscled arms around me, the inked flames and scorpions a contrast to my smaller leather clad arms that he positioned out in front of me.

God, the smell of him–that delicious mixture of leather and cloves, but there was something else I hadn't been able to pinpoint. A sweet, amber musk that watered my mouth.

"What's vivicantem?" I mindlessly asked, trying not to lose myself in that exceptionally distracting smell.

"It's an element." As if oblivious to my struggles right then, he placed the stick into my opened palm. "Much like humans require certain nutrients for their bodies—iron, calcium, potas-sium—we require vivicantem for our blood magic."

"But you don't seem to tire."

"I require less."

"Will I require it, too?"

"It seems you don't, if you're willing to try physical training after learning glyphs." He placed his scarred and calloused hand over mine. "Grip the stick here," he said, sliding my hand down to the middle of it. "We're going to start with a warmup spin."

As he twisted the stick with one hand, he took hold of my other and positioned it to continue the full arc. "Then come under it again, grip, and over." His arms flexed around me as he guided my hands over the staff.

Once I seemed to catch on to the rhythm, he released me and circled around to the front, watching.

"How long did it take you? Learning to fight?" I asked, awkwardly spinning the stick.

"Most of my life. I'm still learning."

"So, it'll be a while before I'm flipping this around my head?" I focused on my hand placement, determined to keep the staff in motion.

"Up the speed a little," he ordered, ignoring my question.

I did as he asked, and with a slip of my grip, the staff tumbled out of my hands onto the floor. Both of us reached down to pick it up, our cheeks practically touching.

He stepped back and allowed me to retrieve it. Once the stick was back in hand, I resumed my twirling, faster and faster.

His palm smacked against the stick, bringing it to an abrupt halt. "Now the opposite direction."

Irritated by his interruption of my perfect twirls, I frowned and set the stick into motion the other way.

"Keep it smooth."

In the blur of motion, I fell into a trance.

"*Faster.*"

I upped the pace.

"Keep it smooth. Faster."

I found myself focusing on him instead of the staff, taking in the way he concentrated on my hand placement. Through the winding stick, his eyes found me. And there we stood, in a face off, separated by the fast-twirling staff between us.

"Faster."

I did as he commanded, twirling the staff faster, so fast, it was nothing but a blur passing before me.

He circled me, prowling. Hands gripped my waist, firmly. His broad chest pressed against my back. "Faster," he whispered in my ear, and I felt his fingers curl into my sides. A rising heat warmed my blood, and I flushed at the thought of what I wanted him to do with those fingers.

I didn't know what happened in that moment, but my heart pounded a steady thump, and something tugged at my belly. The urge to cross my thighs twitched my muscles. Every breath arrived shaky and fast.

"Let go, *Lunamiszka*."

Let go? Of the staff?

The second I let go, it started to fall, but he quickly pressed his palms to the tops of my hands, and an intense heat pulsed through my wrists. Black smoke drifted upward from our joined hands while the stick remained spinning in the air by itself.

A breath of a laugh escaped me, as it hovered in front of me, spinning faster and faster.

"Is it me doing this, or you?"

"I'm supplying the power, but it's you who commands it."

Me commanding his power.

I closed my eyes, focusing on the heat in my palm, hardly noticing he slid his hand to my hip, until his fingers gripped my bones. The winding, searing tendrils of black flame curled through me, stretching and coiling around my muscles. The heat intensified, rippling through my hand, throbbing between my thighs, and in that moment, I had the strongest, most infuriating inclination to reach down into my leather trousers.

In the darkness of my mind, I saw black swirls dancing around me, billowing through my veins like hot ribbons that throbbed in my muscles.

"What are you doing?" he whispered in a shaky voice.

The question severed my thoughts. The stick flew out of my hands, spinning in the air to the left of me, where it crashed to the floor in a clatter.

Zevander released me at the same time Dolion's head snapped up from his reading.

Breaths heaving, I stood trying to decipher what I was feeling right then.

"We'll stop for today." He strode past me, not bothering to say anything to Dolion as he exited the training room.

Having caught my breath, I crossed the room for the staff and hung it back on the wall. As I approached, Dolion held out a glass of water, a puzzled look on his face.

"What happened?"

I stared down into the water, noting the agitated surface, bubbling as if over a hot flame. "One minute I was innocently channeling his power, and the next, I felt like I was somehow siphoning it into myself." A burn at my palm drew my attention to a glowing symbol etched into my skin, the blood trickling out of the tiny cuts.

I held out my hand to him. "What is this?"

Raising his spectacles to his eyes, he took hold of my hand, tilting it in his palm. "I'm not familiar with this one, at all."

He scrambled for his paper and inkwell, and made quick sketches of the glyph, his hands trembling with what I imagined was far more excitement than I could summon. "This is incredible, indeed! Tell me, what were you doing just now?"

"Spinning a staff in the air. Zevander told me to let go of it, and he channeled his power through me."

As I spoke, Dolion hastily jotted notes, dipping his quill in between. "And did you feel something?"

I had no intention of telling him what I felt in that moment. "Well, yes. I felt like … like I was in control."

His scribbling paused, and he lifted his gaze to me. "You felt as if his power became yours?"

"Yes. But it's rather hard to describe. I felt like …"

"Yes?"

My cheeks burned, but the concerned face he'd made moments ago had me feeling like I should say something. "I felt like it was seducing me. The flame itself was pulling me toward something."

Dolion's eyes widened, and he stroked his beard. "I'm afraid I'm a bit out of my league on that one. Perhaps I'll observe a bit closer next time."

"Out of curiosity, what would it mean if I were to control his power?"

"It would make your newest glyph quite dangerous. And should the magehood become privy, they would surely see you destroyed for it."

Lips flat, I nodded. "Perfect."

CHAPTER FORTY-TWO

ZEVANDER

Zevander stared down at his trembling hands, trying to wrap his head around what, in godsblood, had happened just then. It wasn't the first time he'd channeled his power–when Rykaia was first coming into her own blood magic, he'd sometimes used the technique to help her, as well. It was common practice, and for the most part, harmless.

Never in his life had he felt such a loss of control. As if she were commanding the flame herself.

And never had he felt the hum of excitement vibrating through his blood, as he had in that training room. Every nerve ending had sprung to life, desperate and eager to connect with every inch of her skin. The very thought of it, of her, had him breaking into a sweat all over again. Whatever poisonous spell she'd cast over him had stirred a dark and dangerous craving for more.

At the same time, it enraged him.

Zevander had spent centuries learning to control the flame. Had trained for hours upon hours, forcing himself to command the very part of him he feared. And there, a mortal with no formal training, had commandeered it as if it had always been a part of her.

As if it longed to be inside of her.

An unrelenting ache throbbed in his groin, and Zevander clutched the arms of the chair, teeth grinding. He refused to fuck his hand at the visual of what her tight body would feel like wrapped around his starving cock.

Instead, he reached for his glass of liquor, swallowed back a long swill, and forced himself to imagine something else. Something that didn't have every muscle in his body locked and ready to tear into something.

At a knock on the door, Zevander shook his mind free of those thoughts.

"Yes," he said, and Ravezio stepped inside.

"We've got him. In the dungeons."

The flammellian.

Finally, a means to exercise the pent-up aggression that had him desperate to rip something to shreds.

Better the man who'd harmed his sister.

* * *

Zevander stood flanked by Ravezio and Torryn, a flaming sconce in hand as he stared through the bars of the cell, beyond which a pale-skinned man crouched in the corner. Unlike the furnished cells, where Dolion and Maevyth had slept, this one held no bed, no windows and no light. "Where did you find him?"

"Asked around. Found him holed up in one of the tunnels beneath Costelwick." Torryn tapped his finger on the hilt of his blade, his jaw clenched. "It's only out of respect for you that I didn't kill him on the spot."

The emaciated bastard wore a smug grin that Zevander wanted more than anything to rip clean off his face. Hard to believe Rykaia would've had anything to do with him, as gaunt and unkempt as he appeared to be, but perhaps she'd been too far gone on whatever elixirs she'd taken to care. "And the flammapul?"

Ravezio handed off an ampoule of red liquid, the tiny floating bubbles that appeared as negative space confirming its contents.

"Who are you?" Zevander tucked the ampoule away into the pocket of his tunic.

The stranger tipped his chin up, the smile never leaving his face. "I could've killed her, if I wanted. But I didn't."

"If you think I'll spare you for that, you've overestimated my merciful nature."

"I *wanted* to kill her. That is *my* nature. I wanted to watch life fade from her eyes while I strangled her. I wanted to feel her pain seeping into my skin, tickling me with delicious delight." A realization dawned on Zevander right then. "You're a painkeeper."

His magic was extracting pain from his victims. While some struggled with the power, others found it thrilling. A means of sexual gratification.

The visual he'd planted in Zevander's head stirred the flames inside of him. A thick, black smoke curled up from his flesh and took the form of a scorpion in his palm. Zevander knelt, allowing the scorpion to enter the man's cell, and once past the threshold, it grew larger, until it was about the size of a cat, prowling inside the small space.

While the man kept his eyes on the scorpion, the smile on his face still failed to disappear, even in the presence of a threat.

"Who supplied the flammapul?" Torryn asked in his usual gruff voice.

The man chuckled, his eyes shifting between the scorpion and Zevander. "You think your scorpion will frighten me into telling you all I know?"

The scorpion's size expanded to that of a dog.

"There's enough venom in that stinger to paralyze you while

his pincers rip your flesh to small pieces. You see, I want to kill you, too. It would bring me tremendous joy to hear your suffering."

This prisoner twitched and scratched at his arm. "Is it so inconceivable that I might've made the flammapul myself?"

With a flick of his hand, Zevander's scorpion lifted its tail, primed to strike at the first command.

"I have a secret," the man whispered, and the disturbing giggle that followed echoed through the dungeon. "I fucked your sister with the hilt of my blade while she was under. Did she tell you that? She wanted to scream, but couldn't." He lifted his nose in the air and sniffed. "I smell her here. Perhaps when I'm finished with you, I'll find her for one more fuck before I leave."

Snarling, Zevander ordered the scorpion to strike with a clench of his fist, and the moment the stinger swung down, it dissipated into black smoke.

The man let out a boisterous laugh that had Zevander grinding his jaw. "Someone smarter than you put an enchantment on me. I can't be killed by any Letalisz. Regardless of power."

"Who?" Zevander asked, teeth clenched.

A grin stretched the stranger's lips, and he rolled his head against the wall. "Are you so mad as to think I would tell you such a secret?"

"I think you fear whoever it is."

The flammelian's eyes held a glint of derangement. "Where is your sister, Letalisz? I want to tear into that pretty little flower of hers."

Torryn lurched on a growl and Zevander gripped his arm to stop him from carrying what he, himself, longed to do right then: flay that smug grin right off his face.

"Do you like riddles?" When Zevander didn't answer, the flammelian kept on, "What is something that all men yearn for in life but doesn't begin until the last dying breath?"

"Afterlife," Ravezio answered beside Zevander.

"I confess." He scratched at his arm again, and Zevander noticed a marking there. A black snake from what he could make out. "Even if you answer correctly, it's merely a sense of direction. You won't glean the answer. But sadly, you are wrong."

Zevander let out a dark chuckle as he stared back at his prey. When he opened the cell door, the man's eyes widened, but still, he maintained his smugness, which only goaded Zevander's rage. The Letalisz lifted him by the collar of his tunic and dragged him out of the cell, then down the corridor between where sconces flickered around the stony alcove.

"Should you attempt to torture me, it'll only prove fruitless for you. For all of your Letalisz."

"Do not fear. I am not going to torture you." Zevander gestured toward Ravezio to grab the key from the wall and unlock the cellar door.

"I cannot be starved, either, for the enchantment grants me a bounty if you should try."

Still holding the man by his shirt, Zevander bent just enough to throw the door open. "I will not starve you, nor torture you, nor attempt to kill you by my own hands."

"Then, perhaps it's best to let me go. Your sister would love a visit, I suspect."

"Perhaps." Had he not been granted protection, Zevander would've carved out the bastard's tongue for speaking of Rykaia again. "But whoever enchanted you failed to consider one thing." He pushed the man down into the hole, where he fell to the ground on a hard thunk. "I have an older brother."

The stranger groaned and coughed, as the air must've exited his lungs on impact. He turned onto his side and gasped, scrambling backward as he undoubtedly caught sight of Branimir and his pets.

Zevander watched the man lurch for the ladder and climb a

half dozen rungs, before he slammed the door over top of him and linked the chain back into place.

His screams bled through the wood and iron, until they finally silenced, and the wet squelch of tearing flesh echoed from below.

"Probably should've tried to get the answer to the riddle out of him," Torryn said beside him.

"I already know the answer. It doesn't bring us any closer to identifying his supplier."

Ravezio scratched at the back of his head. "Just out of curiosity, what is it?"

"Legacy."

CHAPTER FORTY-THREE

MAEVYTH

The bath suite in my room wasn't quite as big as the one in Zevander's, but it was just as beautiful. A circular, marble and stone basin, with lit candles at its base, frescos on the ceiling, and an entire wall of lancet windows that bowed outward toward a stunning view. Although it was mid-afternoon, the gray snow clouds and perpetual mist cast a gloom that darkened the room, despite the multitude of candles that added a soft glow.

On the ledge was a brass flask I recognized—the one I'd seen in Zevander's bathing room that'd reminded me of an anointing bottle. Smiling, I uncorked the top for a sniff, confirming the delicious scent. A gift, I presumed.

As I sponged the amber soap onto my shoulder, I stared down at my opened palm, where the glyphs I'd earned had scarred into faint white symbols.

"What a strange dream," I whispered, still not entirely convinced that any of this was real. My thoughts wound back to training earlier, when I'd channeled Zevander's power. How utterly consumed I'd felt in the moment.

The bathwater swallowed me in warmth as I recalled his

massive arms around me, his hands guiding mine. The way I'd felt small beside him, but powerful. Eyes closed, I summoned the image of the two of us, and a dizzying heat swept through me while I sponged myself, dragging the foamy soap across my skin and imagining the soft caress of fingertips. The phantom brush of his lips tingled at my throat, and at the first prickle of teeth, I opened my eyes on a sharp inhale.

Stop. If I planned to keep training with the man, I'd need to shake the ungodly thoughts he roused.

I set the sponge at the edge of the basin and lathered the soap into my hair, pausing when my finger caught on something at the back of my neck. A series of bumps arranged in a strange pattern that didn't feel like a scab, or a cut. I gently ran my finger over them, and in the water's reflection, noticed a scintillating silver glow on my back at my shoulder.

Frowning, I twisted to the side to get a good look at it, my reflection in the dark windows across from me lit up by whatever it was. A shape that I couldn't quite make out in the brightness. A glyph, maybe. Strange, that it was on my back and not my hand like the others.

I ran my finger over the symbol, feeling a slight vibration beneath my skin. *What is this?* Had I been back home, I'd have been poked and prodded, banished, or burned, because the governor didn't always trust The Eating Woods to eliminate the worst cases of evil. Even I found myself to be shaken by the presence of whatever these strange markings meant, but while I couldn't make out a thing from the angle at which I stood, at least I felt no pain from whatever they were. More concern over the odd little changes happening to me.

I hadn't even taken a moment to breathe in the time I'd been there, to reflect on how much had changed since leaving my world. How, even as limited as this world had become while confined to the castle—and, at times, to my own room—it still felt bigger than Mortasia. Intriguing, in spite of its strange and dangerous creatures. It saddened me to think that Aleysia was the only reason I'd consider returning to the place I'd lived my whole life.

Once I'd rinsed the soap away and rung the water out of my hair, I made quick work of toweling off and dressed in one of the outfits that Rykaia had supplied in the armoire for me. A long, black velvet, hooded dress, with a lace-up corset and low cut bodice that lifted my breasts. Something urged me to take it off and find something a bit more modest, but I paused, trying to discern whose voice had demanded such a thing.

Certainly not mine.

Agatha would've called me a whore, had I worn anything like it back home. *A wicked little harlot*, as I'd heard her call other women of the parish. I smiled at the thought and decided the dress was perfect, even if it did add more black to my wardrobe. I'd grown to hate the color less since my time here. In fact, I felt a sense of pride, as if I'd finally embraced my aberrant nature.

I padded quietly toward the door, surprised when the knob turned with ease. While I'd returned to my room on my own after training, I'd wondered if Zevander had bothered to lock me in while I bathed.

Seemed he hadn't.

Peering out into the hallway showed a long, empty corridor in both directions, and I stepped out of the room, walking briskly toward the staircase ahead. Down the stairs, I followed the same path Zevander had led me along two nights ago, but paused when I reached the Great Hall, only to find no one there. Just the entry doors standing unguarded.

Fyredrakes, my head warned, but what if that was merely a tactic to scare me? A story to keep me from trying to escape.

It didn't matter. I had no idea where I was, or where to go, and after my experience with the guards, I didn't trust to ask any strangers I might've encountered, should I have decided to run.

Instead, I kept on, toward the kitchen. Once there, I found Magdah chopping vegetables.

Not bothering to spare me a glance, she asked, "What do you want?"

"I'd like to help."

She made a disapproving sound in her throat, but I stepped closer.

"Please? I'm happy to chop those potatoes for you."

"Potatoes?" She scoffed. "These aren't potatoes, Girl. They're called pahzatsz. It's a root."

"Pah-zahts," I mimicked, minus the thick accent she'd spoken in. "May I?" I held out my hand for the knife, which earned me a suspicious look.

"Just know, you try anything tricky with the blade, and we'll be having mortal girl stew for supper." She certainly wasn't reserved when it came to her threats.

"That sounds like a horrible meal to me."

Her lips curved to a smile, and she slapped the broad side of the knife into my palm. "You cut the pahzatsz, I'll cut the meat."

With a nod, I placed the knife on the wooden surface and turned to the sink—an elaborately carved metal spigot attached to a black porcelain basin filled with water. I washed my hands then returned to my station, where I chopped the roots, while Magdah quietly cut the meat that I eyed from where I stood.

"Magdah, may I take some of the meat to Branimir?"

Her brows came together as though his very name made her sad. She gave a silent nod and divided some of the pieces she'd cut onto a separate plate. After having cut all the pahzatsz, I moved on to chopping onions, carrots, and some other strange vegetable I couldn't pronounce.

Magdah then handed me the plate of meat. "Thank you," she said, as I took the plate from her. "Appreciate the help."

I gave a slight smile and scampered off for the dungeons with

Branimir's loathsome supper in hand. Down the staircase and corridor, I carried the plate. Along the way, I passed beautifully carved statues of angels, and on rounding the corner for the cells, I noted Dolion's stood empty–probably off studying bones and scrolls with Allura. In my staring, I slammed headfirst into an unyielding wall of muscle, and while I succeeded in keeping the plate clutched in my hands, some of the meat fell onto the floor with a splat.

I glanced up to find Zevander's angry eyes staring down at me. Without the mask covering his face, I finally managed to absorb the severity of his scar up close, which looked like a poorly healed gash, with tiny cracks out of which dark veins branched across his lips and down his chin. Against his honey-toned skin and rough-hewn face, it had a ghastly beauty about it, giving him a fierce appearance, with his scintillating eyes that reminded me of a blazing fire. My fingertips itched to do something bold, like touch him.

"What do you think you're doing? Did I not make it clear that you're not to visit Branimir on your own?" A furious tension sharpened his tone.

I stepped back, clearing my throat. "I didn't think you'd want to accompany me, after what happened this afternoon. I figured you might be angry with me." By comparison, my voice was softer, almost too soft.

His gaze fell to the plate. "You're too late. He's already had supper."

"Oh." I lowered to the ground, gathering up the fallen chunks of meat onto the plate. "Well, it would be a waste to toss this. Perhaps the fyredrakes might eat it?" I held the plate out to him, noticing the trembling of my hand.

He wordlessly accepted the pile of meat without bothering to look down at it, his steely gaze unwavering.

"May I sing to him, at least?"

"He's occupied at the moment."

Frustrated, I set my hands on my hips. "*Are* you mad at me? Is that why you won't let me see him?"

"Why do you care?" He dropped the plate onto an adjacent stone ledge and lurched toward me, backing me up a step.

"Why *don't* you?" I countered, frowning up at him.

"You know nothing of me." He advanced again, forcing me backward.

"And you know nothing of me." A pathetic retort, but the fury in his eyes and his intimidating stature dulled my wit. My spine hit the stone wall behind me, warning me there was nowhere else to go.

He raised a muscled arm, blocking me from my path, and I didn't even have to look at the massive limb in my periphery to know he could've crushed my skull in the crook of his elbow like a walnut, if he were ambitious enough. That intoxicating mix of spice and amber pervaded my senses. "Perhaps you can enlighten me. What was that in the training room?"

"I haven't a clue. All of this is foreign to me. Magic, power. I don't know what happened."

His jaw ticced, and he planted his other arm against the wall, effectively caging me in, bringing his face mere inches from mine. "You felt nothing."

My blood vibrated with his proximity, the heat of his body swallowing the chilly air. It was then I remembered the dress I'd worn, with its busty corset, but he didn't so much as glance at my breasts. Not that he'd have had to go out of his way when they were so blatantly in his face. "I didn't say that."

"What did you feel? Tell me." His gaze fell to my lips.

Drowning in humiliation, I turned away from him. "I'd rather not say."

He hooked a finger beneath my chin and drew my attention back to him. "Tell me."

Something about what had happened troubled him. Perhaps he thought I was trying to steal his power, as Dolion had mentioned, which hadn't been the case, at all. I wouldn't have had a clue what to do with that flame—or his scorpions, for that matter. Or maybe he'd felt the same thing I had.

As mortifying as the confession was, maybe it was better to face the possibility of embarrassment than hostility. "I felt … aroused." I didn't bother to look up at him, but focused on the steady rise and fall of his chest and the pounding of my heart, while his massive body trapped me like a bird caught between a wolf's teeth.

He didn't move at first, and I wondered if I should've kept the confession to myself. Maybe he didn't like that I'd felt that way in the thick of training that he took so seriously. "You can sing to him later this evening. I'll accompany you then. Now, please return to your room." He pushed off the wall and stepped back.

Nodding, I spun around for the direction from which I'd come, but paused at a grip on my arm, the strength of it nearly crushing my bones.

"And if you wander down here alone again, I'll be sure to lock your door next time."

* * *

Sitting on my bed, my belly warm and full of Magdah's delicious meat pie, I stared down at the next puzzle in the book, but just as I twisted the top dial around, lining it up with one of the grooves in the maze below it, a knock sounded on my door. I padded across the room and opened it to find Zevander standing in the doorway, his head nearly touching the top frame. Following a shameless sweep of his gaze over my too-tight bodice, he jerked his head for me to follow after him. I did, all the way to the dungeons, where a chair waited beside Branimir's open cellar door.

"One song," he said, leaning against the adjacent wall, as I lowered into the seat and peered down to find one of the spiders staring up at me with its hundreds of beady eyes. Stifling a shiver, I cleared my throat and began to sing a darkly humorous song about a governor's daughter who fell in love with a demon.

As I arrived at the lively chorus, clapping my hands against my knees, I caught a glimpse of Branimir staring up at me, his ruined lips stretched to a smile. The speed of the song heightened, and I fought to keep the lyrics straight in my head, which had me chuckling between verses. The fast song along with my laughter sapped me of breath by the time I finished.

I glanced over to see Zevander staring at me in a way that left me wondering what thoughts spun inside that head of his. Was he angry that I'd found his brother? Frustrated that I'd insisted on singing to him? Or was it something else that I mistook?

Branimir slinked back into the shadows, as Zevander closed the lid on him and replaced the chains.

"I understand it's his choice to be down there, but is it also his choice to be chained?"

"Yes." With no additional explanation, Zevander hung up the key and waved for me to follow him.

We walked halfway down the long corridor in silence, before he asked, "Who taught you to sing?"

Smiling, I shrugged. "Myself, I suppose. Who taught you to frown?" I asked with an air of amusement.

His lips twitched, as if he might smile but refused. "Quite the opportunist, aren't you?"

"I'm just not familiar with your other talents, besides fighting and growling and snarling."

Again, his jaw shifted, and he cleared his throat. The man could not bring himself to cut loose and smile for anything.

"So, what is it?" I toyed with one of the laces on my corset. "You read all evening. Surely, you enjoy other pastimes."

"I do. Tracking and hunting."

"Those you're ordered to kill."

"Sometimes, yes."

"Do you *enjoy* killing?"

"Sometimes, yes."

"Do you ever think you'd kill me?"

"Sometimes, yes."

I elbowed him in the arm and let loose a chuckle, turning in time to catch the elusive smile on his face. How handsome, with his bright white teeth and the dimple in his unscarred cheek.

When the humor died out, he lowered his gaze. "I think the world would be far duller, though."

I was the one who turned away from him that time, hiding my smile. "It seems you can be charming, after all, Lord Rydainn."

"I suppose I have my moments. Between bouts of rationality."

I chuckled again, slowing my pace as we approached the stairwell to the upper floor. "Do you regret any kills?"

"Perhaps it's best for your innocent perceptions that I don't answer that."

The smile on my face faded. "I'm not as innocent as you might imagine."

"I'm certain our definitions of innocence are not the same."

Although I shouldn't have thought of his words as a challenge, I also didn't want him thinking that I lived so purely as to be naïve. "I crafted poisons back in Mortasia. I told myself that they were for pests and rodents, but after a while ..." I hesitated to say at first. Speaking my thoughts aloud felt too much like a confession, but Sacton Crain had always said confession cleansed the soul. "I wondered if I even cared that they weren't."

"The *ability* to kill doesn't make you a killer."

"These were fairly deadly concoctions."

"Everything is poison with the proper dose. Even you."

I bit my lip to stifle a smile. "I'm not sure if that's an insult, or compliment," I said, keeping my gaze from his, despite knowing the answer to that was probably written in his expression right then. "You're implying too much of me is deadly?"

He shrugged. "Depends on one's tolerance for poison."

Linking my fingers behind my back I nodded. "Hmmm. It seems most would choose to avoid the risk all together. How unfortunate for me."

"I wouldn't call it misfortune, but rather, a means of weeding out weaker prospects. There are those who fear flirting with death, while some of us find it utterly enthralling."

We arrived at my bedroom door, and I still couldn't bring myself to look up at him, my thoughts winding around the meaning of his words that seemed uncharacteristically flirtatious, unless he was being literal. "So, if not death, then what does a dangerous scorpion killer fear?" I asked, with a hint of amusement, and daring to lift my gaze, I found his eyes riveted on my lips.

"You first," he volleyed back. "You don't seem to fear the things you should. The darkness, impossibly large spiders, things that long to take your life. What in seven hells *do* you fear?"

Schooling a smile, I opened my mouth to answer, but the words caught at the back of my throat, my hesitation strangling them. Answering felt too vulnerable. Too intimate. And yet, for some strange reason, I was compelled to tell him, anyway. "Being alone." The truth in those words burned inside my mouth. "I'm afraid of being completely alone in the world." I urged myself not to think of Aleysia, but at a flash of her face, the first tingle of tears hit the rims of my eyes, and I cleared my throat, desperate for distraction. "Now you."

He toyed with one of my loose curls, running it through his thumb and forefinger. "I fear the unknown," he said, his brows flickering with a troubled expression. "The uncalculated fragments of time that are left to fate."

"I wouldn't have guessed a man like you believed in fate."

The gentle caress of his thumb across my throat stifled my breath. "I don't. That's what troubles me. I require both precision and predictability." The way he stared at my lips stirred a restless and wanton ache that had me clenching my thighs. "The whims of fate are an irksome intrusion, and yet ..." He canted toward me, as if to kiss me, his lips mere inches from mine. "Who could've predicted that one touch of your pounding pulse would be so *disarming*." Warm breath scattered across my skin, and my heart stuttered with anticipation as he thumbed the curve of my neck. "What wicked spells you weave, little witch."

I'd never longed for a kiss so much in my life. The dizzying aroma of leather and spice watered my tongue for one taste of him. "And still, you're not inclined to act impulsively," I said a little too boldly, given my complete lack of experience with a man like him. The kind who surely took pleasure with the same dauntless tenacity that he undoubtedly took life.

His lips pulled to a devilish smirk. "Consider that a kindness. My *inclination* is to break whatever stirs my impulsive nature." His thumb lingered at my throat a moment longer, then without another word, he released me and strode off.

CHAPTER FORTY-FOUR

ZEVANDER

Ablack bird perched itself on a weathered branch of a tree just outside of Eidolon's gates, as Zevander strode up to Ravezio, whose arrow was nocked and aimed at the small creature.

A mimicrow, no doubt.

The bird hopped along the branch, closer to the gates, but quickly jumped back when he seemed to hit the ward that shimmered on impact. It let out a caw and fluttered its wings. "I bring a message from the king."

Zevander crossed his arms. "What is your message?"

"He requests your presence this afternoon. Urgently."

Stifling a groan, or any sound of disapproval that the bird would've undoubtedly carried back to Sagaerin, Zevander rolled his shoulders back. "Did he say what for?"

"Did he say what for?" the bird echoed, and the Letalisz did groan that time, as the bird seemed to be out of further instruction.

"I will set out at once."

"I will set out at once," the bird reverberated and flapped its wings again. "Did he say what for? I will set out at once." With that, the bird took flight, and Ravezio lowered his arrow.

The two of them started back toward Eidolon, careful not to say another word, in case another mimicrow might've been within earshot. Once safely out of range, Zevander asked, "When you visited The Hovel, you did as I asked?"

"The rumor about a stranger attacking the guards? Yes. Seems to have stirred some commotion. I overheard someone talking about it in the market square. It's taken on a life of its own." Ravezio chuckled, slipping the arrow he'd aimed at the mimicrow back into its quiver at his back. "They're claiming he's a dangerous nomad from the Eremician Deadlands. One of the merchants even said he'd seen him arguing with a guard days before their disappearances."

"Good." As they neared the castle, one of the fyredrakes, Zelos, prowled toward the two. Careful not to startle him, Zevander held out his hand, and the drake lowered its gargantuan maw that could've swallowed both Letalisz in one gulp, allowing him to pet the top of its head. Rough scales scraped across Zevander's palm and the glyphs carved into his flesh tingled with the drakon's power. He'd managed to keep the oversized beasts sufficiently fed on wild animals that roamed nearby. Bears and moose, mostly, and so far, they hadn't yet eaten a person, to Zevander's knowledge.

Seemingly bored with his affection, the drakon offered a gratified chuff and lumbered off.

The feeling of someone watching crawled over the back of his neck, and Zevander trailed his gaze toward the tower, where Maevyth stared down at him from her bedroom window. Long, lazy curls spilled over her slender shoulders, her lips curved to a bitable pout that accentuated her dolorously beautiful face. The soft glow of her pale skin gave her an ethereal and ghostly aura.

Delicate. Breakable.

An ache throbbed in his chest at the sight of her, his every thought plagued by her haunting allure. Damn him for not seizing the opportunity that night and ending this maddening curiosity. She'd laid down the gauntlet with that dress, daring him to indulge, but kissing her would've been the sweetest poison. An intoxicating elixir, as deadly as it was addicting.

Night after night, he'd watched her sing to his brother, laugh with his sister, and infuse life back into Eidolon. He'd secretly observed as she'd studied with Dolion and Allura, and exchanged lighthearted insults with Magdah while cooking. And those gods-forsaken weavers she left hanging around served as a constant reminder of her presence, even when he wasn't watching her. Yet, in spite of her infectious draw, he'd chosen to distance himself from her over the last week. A decision that burned in his chest every time he'd heard her voice carry from another room, or caught her staring at him, as she was right then.

"Heard her asking about you," Ravezio said beside him.

After a moment's pause, Zevander huffed and glanced back at his friend. "Are you going to leave me in utter suspense?" he asked sarcastically.

The Letalisz chuckled. "Asked your sister if you were angry with her."

Instead of answering, Zevander stole another glance of her and whistled for Obsidyen. Moments later, the pound of hooves drew his attention to where the horse rounded the castle toward them.

"You wouldn't happen to have thoughts about this mortal, would you?" Ravezio pried.

Zevander snorted, adjusting the saddle he'd strapped to the beast earlier in the morning when they'd gone out to patrol the castle's perimeter—another poor attempt to distract himself from the girl. "I've plenty of thoughts," he grumbled, not bothering to tell him most happened at night as he lay in his bed.

"You just seem rather eager to leave."

"Simply heeding to my king's request."

"I'm sure. As is your usual inclination." Ravezio rolled his eyes and patted Obsidyen's flank, and as the horse trotted toward the gate, he called out, "I'll be sure to pass along a goodbye kiss to her for you."

"Only if you intend to spend eternity in the Shadow Realm," Zevander said over his shoulder, gnashing his molars at the thought of Ravezio's lips pressed to hers. He shot one more glance toward her, noting she hadn't moved from that window, as she watched him ride off.

* * *

The road to Costelwick seemed longer than usual, and as Zevander guided Obsidyen through the village streets, he took note of the preparations that'd begun for the princess's Becoming. Purple and silver streamers that matched Sagaerin's heraldry. Banners and firelights strung between buildings. Merchant carts, spilling over with goods, lined the thoroughfare toward the castle.

Once inside the gates, Zevander found himself caught up in the hustle and bustle of guards and servants rushing to prepare for the many guests that were due to arrive from all corners of Aethyria over the next few days.

He made his way to the king's meeting chambers, where he found Sagaerin pacing, his shoulders bunched with tension.

"You called on me, Your Grace." Zevander said, as he strode toward the long conference table.

"Yes, yes." He gestured to his cup bearer, who scrambled to fill two goblets. "Please sit," he said, and Zevander settled into the nearest chair.

"There are rumblings of discontent." Hands rubbing together, Sagaerin kept on with his pacing, looking more unsettled than ever before. "The public is insisting that Dorjan perform the Initios." The Initios signaled the beginning of the festivities and blessings for the tournament, which gathered formidable contenders from all over Aethyria, who fought for the glory of claiming the princess's womanhood. All major ceremonies typically began with the formality, which involved lighting a swirling wheel aflame. "They fear that his absence in the last few years indicates a weakness in the monarchy. That we're hiding something." He paused to swipe up his goblet of wine, spilling it en route to his mouth. "He'll be exposed to all of the public, if I send him! A fucking walking target!"

"You're asking me to escort him."

He slammed his goblet down, the wine splashing onto the table. "I'm asking you to defend his life as if it were your own, or it'll be everyone's lives at stake!" With deep breaths, and a face as red as beets, he lowered his gaze. "I am beside myself over this nonsense." He patted Zevander on the shoulder. "I trust you. I know you'll do your best, but balls of Castero! Why can't these godsforsaken people be satisfied with their king's blessing! Why must they insist on putting Dorjan's life at risk!"

Another gulp of wine, and he held out the goblet for the steward, then nodded toward Zevander's. "Drink up. I don't like drinking alone."

Reluctantly, Zevander lifted the goblet and unfastened his mask to take a sip. Though he didn't detest wine, it certainly wasn't his drink of choice. "When does the ceremony begin?"

"Dusk. And I appreciate your timely arrival, Zevander. You are, as always, a most reliable and loyal subject."

Loyalty had nothing to do with it. Zevander simply appreciated the time away from the castle, the distraction of the royal minutiae, instead of stalking the girl's every movement. Had he been there right at that moment, he'd have probably been overly occupied with her interactions with Ravezio. Still, he acknowledged the king's compliment with a nod.

"I'll have Dorjan's carriage inspected and prepared right away."

"I'll inspect it myself."

"Truly, I am grateful for you." With another nervous pat to Zevander's shoulder, he gulped back his wine.

Zevander finished his, while the king sent his cup bearer to summon the carriage, then he pushed to his feet and exited the chambers. He made his way down to the front of the castle, where the carriage awaited and three footmen carefully scanned over its every inch. Zevander joined them, looking for any evidence of tampering, whether it be an explosive fragor, or cursed malustone, hidden somewhere on the body of it.

After a thorough scouring, he found nothing.

From there, he made his way to the armory for a suit that would allow him to blend in with the other guards. While he loathed the cumbersome weight of the armor, the way it slowed and restricted his movements, it kept his identity hidden while allowing him to remain in close proximity to the prince. Once fully garbed in the armor, he returned to the carriage.

Prince Dorjan strode up, donned in fine silks of purple and silver, with newly shined leather shoes. "I understand you're to escort me to my doom, according to my father." The prince straightened his cuff and smiled.

"Strange, I was under the impression I was escorting you to the nearest cliff to practice your diving skills."

The prince chuckled, and waited as the coachman opened the door for him. "Honestly, Zevander, you're the only one I'd permit to speak to me that way. And only because I fear you could pummel me into dust, if you were ambitious enough."

"Pummeling is for brutes." Zevander climbed into the carriage and took a seat across from the prince. "Poison is far more elegant."

"Quite. Thankfully, your alchemy is shit, as I understand." The comment brought a slight smile to Zevander's face, even though his mind remained entangled in his infuriating preoccupations with a mortal beauty.

The door slammed, and the carriage set into motion.

Dusk mantled the village, and the festive firelights that'd been strung overhead glowed in the waning light. Through the window of the carriage, Zevander watched as an older villager climbed a wooden ladder and, with a strike of flint, lit the first bulb. The flame caught the second bulb and the third, lighting each bulb in its path. The village enlivened as the moon rose into the sky and a crowd gathered around a platform set in Hemlock Square.

The arena where the fighting would soon take place stood off in the distance, the stony pillars of its entrance adorned with flowers and lights, along with the purple and silver banners boasting the king's heraldry and bloodline.

The carriage rolled to a stop beside where The Imperial Guard had gathered, and they shielded the prince as he strode up the stairs to the center of the platform, which held the elaborate wheel of silver filigree.

Dorjan stood before his audience and bowed. "My good people," he began. "On this night, when the moons are nearly one, we honor my sister with three nights of tournaments and festivities."

Zevander scanned over the crowd from his position beside the prince, his gaze not missing a single body in the throng as he searched for any sign of hostility. The Imperial Guard lined the perimeter of the platform, and a second line formed a barrier between the prince and the crowd. The mere gesture itself implied a lack of trust, but the king had spared no cost, nor measure, to keep his son safe.

Another sweep of the crowd, and Zevander's gaze landed on a man toward the back, whose hooded cloak hid most of his face. He lifted a crossbow, aiming it square at the prince.

"Dorjan! Move!" Zevander shouted, and the prince flinched, ducking to the side.

The thunk of an arrow pierced the wheel's wooden frame no more than a mere inch from Prince Dorjan's face.

Zevander lurched forward, shielding the prince. He drew his Venetox sword from its scabbard, eyes scanning for the man who'd disappeared.

Vibrations against the wooden platform drew his attention to a raw, pale pink mass quivering there. Pig's fat. A gesture of greed.

An outcry from the far reaches of the crowd rose into an angry chant, and as Zevander listened, he could make out the incredulous name on their lips.

"Cadavros lives! Cadavros lives! The king will die! The king will die!"

A group of hooded villagers rushed forward while drawing weapons and attacked the front line of Imperial Guards.

"Get the prince to the carriage!" Zevander called to the men near the staircase, and they gathered around Dorjan as he descended the platform. A flaming arrow hit the wheel, igniting the kindling that set it in motion.

The chants grew louder.

A villager slipped through the guard and rushed toward the prince, swinging a flail over his head.

Zevander jumped off the platform and hammered a powerful kick to his chest that sent the pale, skinny man flying backward.

Nilivir.

A larger crowd pushed toward the guard, forcing them back into a circle around the carriage. The prince's protectors were severely outnumbered by the otherwise powerless citizens of the city.

One of the guards maintained a halo, a ward that kept the insurgent villagers back, while two other guards used Aeryz to keep those who charged forward from breaching it. Zevander climbed into the carriage after the prince, annoyed by the bulky weight of his suit. "Back to the castle! Now!" he ordered, and the carriage lurched forward.

The guard followed after, as they wound through the streets of Costelwick. At a screeching halt, Zevander peered out of the window to see another crowd of villagers blocking their path.

"Fucking godsblood!" he muttered and stepped out of the carriage.

Pig's fat splattered across the cobblestones, the crowd keeping their distance at first, until one of them jumped forward, flinging brown clumps of what Zevander presumed was pig shit at the carriage. They closed in on them, chanting as they circled with their torches and weapons.

Frustrated and out of patience, Zevander summoned his scorpion to his palm and set it on the cobblestones. The creature grew and expanded, the crowd gasping as it towered over them, snapping its pincers. Some screamed and scattered. One bold bastard had the nerve to lift his sword and charge toward them, but before Zevander had the opportunity to swing out and lop his head off, the scorpion struck first with its metallic stinger and sliced the attacker in half.

The villagers backed away as the scorpion led the carriage along the path to the castle, until they fell back entirely, and he retracted his magic.

Returning to the carriage, he took a seat across from Dorjan, who stared out the window, shaking his head.

"This is my father's doing." Jaw clenched, he breathed hard through his nose, his anger apparent in the red flush of his face. "He starves them and then expects them to bow? What logic is there in such a thing?"

Zevander couldn't argue with him. He'd always been put off by the king's greed. How the wealthy were supplied with much needed vivicantem, while the poor withered, their bloodlines dying off like a frosted vine.

Tears formed in Dorjan's eyes. "They hate me as much as they hate him."

"They've no idea you're not like your father."

"I hate him for this." Tears fell down his cheek. "I hate him."

Zevander remained silent as the carriage rolled to a stop inside the gates, and the guards awaiting his return escorted the prince to the castle. King Sagaerin stood on the stairs of the entryway, and as he reached for his son, Dorjan knocked his hand away and kept on.

Consternation wrinkled the king's brow, when Zevander reached him. "Attacked by my own people." He shook his head. "How can I fix this? How can I possibly fix this mess?"

"I'm no advisor. But a gesture of charity seems wise."

"Vivicantem."

"They're starving. Weak. Angry."

"I've only got enough to make it to one more moon cycle, and with Calisza's Becoming Ceremony, I'll need my reserves." For his wealthy guests, of course. He winced. "The humiliation. The last thing I need right now is an uprising. Dear gods, what will the Solassions think, when they see I can't even walk through the streets of my own city!"

That his only concern was the humiliation he faced eroded what little respect Zevander had for the man.

"I thank you for being there. Again." From his pocket, he pulled a bag of coin and vial of liquid vivicantem, a slap in the face, if Zevander thought about it. "You're welcome to stay for the night. Eidolon is quite a journey this late at night."

"I'll be fine." Without another word, he headed toward the armory to doff the suffocating and exceptionally miserable suit. Once free of it, he strode toward the outer courtyard and whistled for Obsidyen. Watchful and cautious, he rode through the gates, back out into the streets of Costelwick. Without the presence of the prince, nor the armor that identified him as an Imperial Guardsman, he slipped by unbothered. The village had settled into festivities, drinking and eating and singing. Aside from the spatters of blood on the cobblestone, there was little evidence that they'd gotten unruly at any point.

Zevander kept on, beyond the center of the village to the outskirts, where he arrived at Black Salt Tavern.

After dismounting his horse, he strode into the small and quiet hostelrie that offered rooms on the top floor, if he felt like staying for the night. Sitting at the back of the tavern was a familiar face, an old blacksmith who'd since retired from his lifelong work. Hunched over a tankard of ale, he didn't bother to look up as Zevander approached, until the Letalisz stood alongside the booth.

The old man, with graying red hair and a silver eye where his natural one had been popped out by a hot fleck of metal, snorted. "Well, look what the wind blew in."

Zevander removed his baldric and slid into the booth. Not a minute later, two tankards hit the table, before the barmaid who'd set them there sauntered off.

Hiking a brawny arm onto the back of the booth, Oswin tipped his head. "What brings you out of your crypt of a castle?"

"The Initios."

His brows kicked up. "Ah, you were there, eh? Quite a spectacle."

"I heard them chanting Cadavros's name." Zevander lifted the tankard, unclasping his mask for a gulp.

"There are rumblings in The Hovel that Cadavros will return. The Nilivir believe he's going to deliver them from their miserable lives."

"How so?"

Oswin took another long sip of his ale and wiped the back of his hand across his mouth. "By giving them the power of sablefyre."

Frowning, Zevander drowned his thoughts in another swill of his drink. "Sablefyre is dangerous. It causes horrible deformities."

"In those with magic. Nilivir have no magic. They have no control over it, either, so it doesn't bode well, anyway. Not when there are mages who know how to wield the flame. And Cadavros was the worst of them." Oswin would've been alive during the years when Cadavros posed a threat to the crown.

"Any idea who's behind the uprising?"

"I thought it to be The Mad Mage, but as I understand, he was put down like a lame dog."

Not exactly, but Zevander didn't bother to correct him. "And when do they believe he's due to return?"

"I don't even think they know." Shaking his head, he tipped back his tankard for a guzzle. "Costelwick is going to shit. Between the uprising and the murder of sexsells."

Zevander's eye twitched with the stupifying news. "There's been another murder?"

"Earlier tonight, yep."

"What happened?"

Oswin shrugged and shook his head. "Don't know the details. I only know that the brothels have become mighty stingy about time. No more than a quick fuck is all you get these days." He gestured to himself. "A virile stallion like me needs a good hour. Maybe two."

Zevander snorted, and when he glanced away, he noticed a pale, skinny boy hiding beneath one of the adjacent tables. As the man sitting there flirted with the barmaid, the boy reached a bony arm around the edge of the table, dumping a crystalline powder into the man's tankard. When the kid crawled out, he and Zevander made eye contact.

Gavroche.

Frowning, Zevander plopped down a coin for his ale and, after saying a quick goodbye to Oswin, followed the kid, who scampered out of the tavern.

"Hey!" Zevander called out to him. "Gavroche!" When the boy

didn't bother to stop, he added, "Is that how you treat those who save your scrawny hide?"

The boy slowed his steps and huffed, allowing Zevander to catch up.

"What is the powder?"

Gavroche glanced toward the tavern and back. "Dindleweed."

Dindleweed? It was given to the poor old bastards who could no longer get a proper erection. A powerful aphrodisiac that gave men, in particular, certain urges.

"What are you doing with Dindleweed?"

"Bringing business to Madame Lazarine."

Zevander crossed his arms. "You're still staying at the brothel?"

The boy nodded. "I take care of the linens and draw in the patrons, and she lets me stay in the cellar."

"Does she now." A loud clatter from behind had Zevander turning.

The man who'd been flirting with the barmaid spilled outside, cupping his groin as he strode quickly for his horse tied up out front. Once astride the beast, he cantered in the direction of The Hovel.

Zevander snorted. "You know anything about the sexsell that was murdered earlier? How she may have died?"

Gavroche shrugged. "Flammapul, I think. Madame Lazarine is pretty flustered over it."

"I want you to do something for me, Gavroche." The Letalisz unclasped a satchel at his hip and pulled out the vial of vivicantem the king had just given him. When he held it in front of Gavroche, the boy's eyes widened. "I want you to be eyes and ears for me. In the tavern and brothel. You hear anything about the sexsells and who might be hurting them, you don't tell anyone but me. Can you do that?"

The boy gave a frantic nod, his long skinny fingers reaching up for the vial that Zevander yanked back.

"You know not take it all at once, yeah?"

"I know. One drop."

"One drop," Zevander echoed, handing it off to him. "Don't need you joining the carnificans."

With trembling hands, the boy popped open the vial and squeezed a drop of the nutrient onto his tongue. Eyes closed, he smiled and shivered. "It's tingly." The red in his eyes sparkled and dulled to a pink. By the end of the week, if he'd taken the whole vial, they might've returned to their natural appearance. Unfortunately, his bloodline magic was gone for good. It would've taken centuries of consistent consumption to restore his power, and unfortunately for Gavroche, he'd probably never have access to pure vivicantem again. He'd also not likely live that long, either. While the lifespan of spindling children was far longer than humans, it was nowhere near as long as a healthy Mancer, who might live to be nearly a thousand years. At the very least, it made them feel energetic and whole again.

"You know anything about Cadavros?"

The boy shrugged. "Some folks call him a god. Say he's due to return."

"Any idea who's spreading that around?"

He shook his head, stuffing the vial into the pocket of his trousers that fit better than the last pair he'd worn. "I only hear folks talking about the black flame. How it's supposed to save the Nilivir and restore our power."

Zevander huffed. "Take it from me, kid. Sablefyre isn't going to save anyone." He patted the boy on the shoulder. "Give Madame Lazarine my best."

CHAPTER FORTY-FIVE

MAEVYTH

F reshly bathed, I grabbed the warm mug of tea that Magdah had brought to my room–an herbal concoction she'd wanted me to try after I'd told her of my trouble sleeping. Mug in hand, I padded toward the thick, mahogany door adorned with dragon carvings and ornate hinges, which led out onto a stone balcony that arced outward from the castle. Crisp air had me wrapping myself tighter in the heavy robe I'd found in my armoire. Made of black velvet, with intricately embroidered deep crimson roses and black fur trim, I trusted it to keep me warm.

Flickering torches that seemed to light up on their own cast shadows over the balustrade. I peered over the edge, below which I found gargoyles and grotesques perched on jutting ledges, and beyond those was the dizzying height to the ground beneath, barely visible through the thick fog. The two moons shone high above, their crescent shapes inverted across from one another, and illuminated the dark silhouettes of the distant mountains. I wondered what Aleysia was doing right then, assuming the vision I'd had was true, and she was still alive. I had to believe so, because believing anything else would've destroyed me.

A cluster of tiny, glowing specks fluttered in the air around me, and I held out my palm, allowing one to land there. The moment it made contact with my palm, the glyphs on my hand let off a silvery glow. The insect reminded me of the small fireflies I'd seen in The Eating Woods, with its long thorax and human-like face that smiled at me, before taking flight again.

"It's said to be good luck to catch one."

At the sound of the deep voice, I turned to see Zevander standing out on the balcony next to mine. He peered upward as the cluster of fireflies danced toward him.

"What are they?"

"Celaestrioz. Some believe they harbor the essence of the gods." He reached out his palm, allowing one to land there. "As a young boy, I used to feed them to my pet scorpions."

Horror stricken by the visual, I shook my head. "Why would you do that?"

"The Celaestrioz are known to invade the nests of Noxidae birds. While some consider them a nuisance, the birds are harmless. However, the Celaestrioz swarm the mother and her young, devouring them alive." He turned his hand over, allowing the insect to crawl over it. "I watched them once. When threatened, the mother bird sings a song to her young to calm them. It's called *Le'Susszia*. Death's Song." He lifted his palm, and the insect took flight, the swarm dancing around him a moment longer before flying off into the night. "The scorpion is the only known predator that can withstand their venomous bite."

"They bite?"

"Yes," he said, staring after the luminescent plume that faded in the distance. "Most die from the venom. They detect hostility and attack on instinct. Which is why it's considered good luck to successfully catch one."

"And they didn't detect any hostility when they allowed you to feed them to your scorpions?"

His lips twitched with a smirk. "I suppose my intentions have always been obscure." It somehow seemed fitting that even as a child he'd been an enigma.

"I'd have never guessed something so beautiful and enchanting could be so awful."

"I rarely trust the enchanting." A fleeting look at me, and he sipped his drink. "Particularly something so beautiful."

"I'd be inclined to think a man like you rarely trusts anything. Or any*one* for that matter." I took a sip of the warm and soothing tea, staring at him over the rim of the mug. How darkly tantalizing he looked in his black tunic and leathers.

"Yet, there you are, standing on a balcony not far from where I sleep."

"Yes, given how *dangerous* I am, it was probably foolish to assign me this room. I might just be ambitious enough to leap over to your balcony one night and hold a blade to your throat while you sleep." The sliver of humor in my voice withered on a dry gulp when I peered over the edge of the balcony, to the sloping yard a disorienting forty meters, or more, below us.

Not a chance.

He turned away, but I managed to catch a glimpse of the dimple in his cheek. "Perhaps I should lock my door. I wouldn't want you thinking I was eager to test your stalking skills."

"Nor would I want to give you the impression my visit was anything but lethal." I buried a smile into my mug and took another sip of my tea.

"Careful now," he said, looking out over the dark landscape. "I consider threats to my life an invitation."

I chuckled at that. "For what? Retaliation?"

Brow cocked, he set his drink down and, without warning, sprang up onto the balustrade, balancing himself on the stony rail with an uncanny agility, given his size.

Gasping a breath, I lurched forward, nearly dropping my mug. "What are you doing?"

Air blasted out of me when he leapt to my balcony, over the

perilous drop that would've surely crushed the life out of him with one misstep. He landed without so much as a sound, a deadly quiet to his every move that left me wondering if his victims ever saw, or heard, him coming. If they stared into the devil's eyes before he claimed their souls, or if the world flicked to blackness with no explanation. Neither sound, nor warning.

Eyes on me, he climbed down from the railing, and as he prowled toward me, I backed up a step. Another. Then another. The wall behind me pressed into my spine, while he drew closer and yanked a blade from its holster at his thigh. "As I said, I consider threats to my life an invitation." The broad side of the blade scratched over the fabric of my robe when he gently dragged it across my tightly contracted stomach. "You ought to be careful how you wield them," he warned in that rich, baritone voice.

My spine stiffened at the awareness of the blade between us and the errant splashes of tea across my hand alerted me to the tremble in my body. Not from fear, though. I knew he wouldn't hurt me.

An inexplicable thrill wound through me, while his eyes, ravishingly intense, seemed captivated by my lips. Far too riveted for me to mistake his thoughts right then. The indisputable longing to devour them.

He relieved me of the mug, setting it on the railing beside us, then placed the blade into my palm, curling my fingers around the hilt. With a sweep of his fingertip, he brushed the hair from my shoulders, and warm breath, scented with smoldering spice and caramel, scattered across my skin when he angled his mouth toward my neck.

My thighs clenched and shallow breaths stuttered out of me. I was all too aware that beneath his deadly charm and mesmerizing gaze hid a skilled and clever predator. And while instinct had me tightening my grip on the blade, my skin prickled, desperate for a single brush of his lips.

Instead, he whispered, "Should you decide to carry through with your threat, I'll leave my balcony door unlocked."

Bitter cold filled the space between us when he pulled away from me, and with a cocky smirk, he turned for the door.

The tremble in my muscles persisted as I stared down at the ornate dagger in my palm, the pommel of it shaped like a scorpion's tail.

Much as I fought to deny it, the man captivated me. That spellbinding, defiant nature of his roused a dark and lecherous craving that refused to be smothered.

* * *

The dagger rested on the bed, and legs crossed, I stared down at it, forcing myself to imagine the lives he may have taken with its blade. *He's a bad man*, I told myself, because I needed something to pull me from the lustful thoughts he'd stirred. Thoughts that I'd long been taught were the devil's seeds of iniquity.

He's a killer. He has taken lives for coin.

Possibly innocent lives. A fact that I should've found revolting. Still, my head refused to accept the immorality, because he'd *saved* my life back at that prison, and as selfish a thought as that may have been, I couldn't ignore it. Nor could I deny his impressive skills that must've made him exceptionally dangerous to his prey. All I could summon to mind was the visual of him leaping from his balcony to mine. The lethal grace and stealthy flexibility of his muscled body.

Sighing, I placed the blade on the table beside my bed and lay back against the pillow, where I curled onto my side, staring at it.

Shadows passed in my periphery, and I sat back up. Only the crackling fire of the hearth lit the room, but grew dim with unstoked logs. A figure in the corner caught my eye, its dark form blending into the shadows. It sat hunched over itself, the bony protrusions of its pale spine reminding me of thorny lizard scutes. Dark wisps danced in and out of its spectral form. Deimosi.

My heart thrummed a beat of terror as it turned toward me, staring back at me through black, soulless eyes. Long white hair hung in straggled sheaves about her gray, sunken face.

It was only then that it occurred to me I hadn't seen visions of the dead since the nightmare of Aleysia I had when I'd first arrived.

"*Nonei le confidezsa.*" A raspy voice carried across the room, the sound of it sending a chill down my spine. "*Mortiz a dae et punire.*"

"I don't understand."

With a deep gnarl, she scrambled on all fours toward me, and I swiped up the blade, screwing my eyes shut as I held it outward with a trembling hand.

The raspy voice softened to one I'd heard before inside my head. "Do not put your trust in him. The Goddess of Death will punish."

My eyes shot open on a gasp of breath. "Who? Do not trust who?"

The ghost had disappeared, though. All that remained were the shadows cast by the fire. Still clutching Zevander's dagger, I sank down into the covers of the bed, breathing in through my nose to calm the shaky breaths that sawed in and out of me.

Who? my head echoed. *Zevander?* Had the ghost been warning me against him? Or someone else?

And who was the woman I'd seen just now? No one I recognized.

I slid the blade beneath the pillow, but held tight to the hilt as I closed my eyes, praying for sleep.

CHAPTER FORTY-SIX

MAEVYTH

A bright haze of light blanketed my face, and I squinted past the luminosity to the clock on the mantel of the hearth.

Just past noon.

What?

I shot up out of bed, my hand tightly clutching an object. The dagger.

"Oh, no!" I darted across the room to the armoire, and swiped my training clothes from their hangers. Nearly five hours late, I very much doubted I'd find Zevander waiting for me in the training room. Nonetheless, I didn't plan to scamper down there in my nightclothes to check. Once dressed, I slid the dagger into one of the otherwise weaponless loops on my breeches and hustled down the corridor, passing the butler along the way.

"Vendryck, have you seen Zevander?" I asked.

Chin tipped up, he stared down the long bridge of his nose. "Lord Rydainn is in his study, I believe."

"Can you point me in that direction?

He extended a lengthy, slender finger toward the main hallway, which curved around a tower to another long corridor. "Fourth door on the right."

"Thank you." Despite the intense pangs of hunger gnawing at my stomach, I darted down the hallway until I came upon the fourth door.

The frantic thudding of my racing pulse had my hands trembling, made obvious as I held up my fist to knock twice against the wooden panel.

"Yes." The irritation in his voice bled through the door, and I winced as I opened it to find him hunched over a desk, sifting through pages of a book. He made a disapproving growl in his throat, as I stepped inside the room.

Rain tapped against the wide arched windows behind him, the gloom of clouds casting a dim light across the room. Candles stood in clusters on the fireplace mantle and a small table, wavering as I passed. The room held a hauntingly beautiful ambience, but with a moody undercurrent, and I could easily have imagined hours spent reading in peace. "I'm sorry. I don't know how I overslept." I slid into the seat across from him, clutching the arms of the chair to calm myself.

Another grumbling sound in his throat while he kept on with his reading. Ignoring me.

A minute passed in what felt like the span of a century.

Then another.

Finally, I peered across the desk for a peek of his book. "May I ask what you're studying?"

He flipped the book closed on his finger, allowing me to read the title on the faded, leather cover. *Aethyrian Alchemical Codex.*

"That must be quite old. The leather looks like it's about to peel right off."

"It isn't leather. It's human skin."

"Oh." A grimace pulled at my lips, and I cleared my throat. "Is that some sort of medical reference?" It must've been the thickest book I'd ever seen.

"Some sort." He didn't even bother to look up at me as he turned the page.

Knee bouncing, I bit the inside of my cheek, the irritation of his clipped responses grinding on me. "If you must know, it's partially your fault that I woke up late."

That earned me a scowl. He sat back in his chair and tipped his head. "And just how am I responsible?"

"The dagger." I slipped it from the holster at my hip and laid it carefully on the desk. "I've not slept well in days. Between Magdah's tea and the comfort of the dagger at my bedside, I slept like the dead." Sans the moments beforehand, when I'd actually been visited by the dead.

His gaze shifted to the blade and back to me, but he made no effort to retrieve it. "What about the dagger made you sleep well?"

"I don't know. I've always felt somewhat vulnerable in my sleep."

He exhaled a long sigh and pushed the weapon back toward me. "Keep it."

"You trust me roaming about with a blade?"

"Possessing a blade doesn't make you a threat. It's the mind which governs the weapon."

"The mind can be capricious," I countered. "One moment it's content, the next, it's spoiling for violence."

His eyes darkened, and my skin prickled. "Is that another threat?"

"If I didn't know better, I'd think you enjoyed the challenge."

While his lips twitched, his expression remained as impassive as ever. "Depends on who's holding the dagger." His gaze dipped to the blade in my hand. "We'll skip training today. Perhaps you can help me understand something."

"Me?" Frowning, I slid the blade back at my hip. "How?"

"The day in the training room when you spun the staff ... you mentioned you felt a sense of arousal. But tell me exactly what you saw in your *mind*."

The request had me shifting in my seat, recalling the sensations I'd felt that day. Arousal was the simplest of terms. "I actually felt a complete loss of control. It wasn't so much that I was controlling the staff. It felt more so that the staff was controlling me. Or ... something inside of me."

"What was it inside of you that felt affected?"

I shrugged. "I don't know, but there was a sense of ... familiarity. Protection. Like a warm blanket."

His brows pinched with a frown. "A warm blanket."

"I just mean I felt comforted. I trusted it. In my mind it appeared as gentle ribbons of fire. Calming."

He cleared his throat and rubbed his hand across his jaw, his eyes studying me, as usual. "The amount of magic that you pulled from me would've killed anyone else. Burned them from the inside out. Had my own sister attempted such a thing, she would've been vomiting liquid organs." His words snapped me out of my musings, and a sobering realization washed over me. "You have a very dangerous gift, Maevyth. Were you anyone else, you'd be considered a threat, and I eliminate threats without question."

"I swear to you, none of this makes any sense to me. I would not lie to you."

Easing back into his chair, he sighed. "I believe you. Even if it makes me a fool."

"I promise I won't do it again."

"Oh, you'll do it again. Because I want to know the mechanics behind it."

"Right now?"

"Right now." He pushed up from his chair and rounded his desk, looming over me as he came to a stop alongside my chair. With a flick of his fingers, he urged me to stand, and I did, staring square at his muscled chest while I fought to look him in the eye. He raised his palm. "Place your hand against mine."

Without hesitation, I did as he commanded, noting how much longer and stronger his fingers were compared to mine. How easily he could crush my bones, had he the notion to do so.

"I'm going to channel the flame into you. As much as you can take. However, if it becomes too much, I want you to tell me."

"Okay."

"Promise you'll tell me, Maevyth."

I nodded. "I promise."

His tongue swept across his lips, and God help me, I had to look away at the twinge of curiosity rippling through me, taunting me with phantom sensations of how they'd feel across my throat. "We'll go slow."

Another nod, and I stifled a shiver at the anticipation.

Heat hit the center of my palm, a pulsing radiance that beat into my wrist, my forearm and elbow, to my shoulder and across my chest. I closed my eyes as the heat warmed my insides, the way Grandfather's wine had felt whenever I'd had too much to drink. A pleasant buzz of energy that toasted my cheeks.

"Tell me how it feels, Maevyth." His voice. God, his voice tickled my imagination, while that glorious sensation snaked through my blood.

"It feels … good." The brevity of my words was the only shield to the carnal thoughts that corrupted my imagination.

"I'm going to give you a little more."

"Yes. Please." I opened my eyes to see his rapt gaze, the fascination in his intense stare.

Heat simmered and heightened, my muscles trembling, softening, yielding to the power that throbbed in my blood and muscles in erotic waves of pleasure. Lips parted, I tipped my head back as the ribbons of flame weaved in and out of my veins, as if it longed to touch every corner of me. Squeezing and releasing in slow and sensual contractions.

"A little more, okay?" His voice held a deep, husky timber, as if he were restraining himself, holding his power back.

Again, I nodded, my lids lowering once more. "Yes. It's okay. Give me more."

Another rush of burning heat flooded my body, like scorching lava, but god, it felt good. So good. Like the times I'd touched myself in the quiet darkness and my muscles had begun to lock up, trembling and warming with the promise of climax.

"Maevyth, are you okay?"

"Yes. Please. Don't stop."

His fingers curled into mine, and another round of fire blazed through me. "What are you feeling?"

The feverish tension between us turned ravenous and exhilarating, raking through me with sharp claws.

"Chaos," I said on a choked breath. "It feels like chaos." I clenched my teeth, my muscles taut and trembling as I clutched his hand, letting the power surge through me. A moan leaked past my lips, and I felt his fingers tighten on mine, crushing my hand.

When I opened my eyes, his hair clung to his damp forehead, where beads of sweat had gathered. The veins in his neck protruded, and he licked his lips, eyes intently focused on me.

I slowly dragged my tongue across my lips, and he raised his other hand, which I didn't hesitate to clutch. "More," I rasped.

The intensity of heat pouring through me had me tipping my head back, and I cried out, nails digging into his hands. "Don't stop. Please. Please don't stop!"

The heat snapped to cold as he released my hands.

I opened my eyes to see him stumble back a step, sweat pouring down his temples. Shallow panting breaths fluttered out of me, as I stared back at him, feeling as if we'd just gone to battle.

"What the seven hells are you?" he rasped through labored breaths. "Anyone privy to this loathsome curse would fear the flame, but you ... " Brow furrowed, he shook his head. "You revel in it like a drunken spirityne." The trace contempt in his voice took me by surprise.

"I don't know what happened. I was just—"

He lurched toward me, clamped his hand around my nape, and crushed his lips to mine.

A shocked breath escaped me, captured by his commanding mouth and those full lips that consumed me with the delicious flavor of toffee, undertones of smoldering embers, and a hint of something warm and spicy, like cinnamon. Beneath those, the lingering traces of his liquor. A taste that brought to mind images of long, languid nights beside a slowly fading fire. An engulfing heat and damp skin. Wandering fingertips and wet tongues.

Whatever disdain he'd felt moments ago melted in the heat of his kiss.

I stood dumbfounded, lips parted, allowing him to exert his control as he devoured the air in my lungs between stinging nips of his teeth. A raw, aching need weakened my knees, while he kissed me with the assertion of a man who'd never been refused by a woman. One whose catalogue of dark pleasures rivaled the thickness of the book he'd studied moments ago. The way his tongue masterfully swept through my mouth and across my lips, teasing and taunting me, warned of dangerous passion. A man who could easily ruin me in one night.

"You are a fucking torment, *Lunamiszka*," he said through clenched teeth, as if he were angry. With me? Before I could voice the question, he dug his fingers into my nape and dragged me in for another kiss, growling against my lips.

A peculiar sensation wound inside my chest, like strings pulling me inside of him. Stomach fluttering. Thighs trembling. A greedy hunger pulsed and throbbed between my legs on a rush of liquid heat. An intensity that stirred my nerves to life, quickly severed when his hand pressed against my throat, breaking the kiss.

I opened my eyes to find his chest heaving, a guarded expression on his face, like that of a cornered animal.

My lips burned with his assault, tingling with a craving for more of his kiss.

"What is this?" he asked, his ragged voice carrying a hint of bewilderment. Dilated pupils swallowed the gold of his irises, and his brows furrowed deeper than before as he thumbed his lip. "It can't ..." His voice drifted off, eyes losing focus as he seemed to slip into thoughts.

"It's okay. I want this."

"You don't know what *this* is."

I reached out for him, and he nearly tripped over himself to back away. Pangs of humiliation coiled in my stomach and burned in my already heated cheeks. "Did I .... Did I do something wrong?"

"I need you to leave. Now."

"Not until you tell me if I did something wrong."

"You did nothing wrong. Now, go."

Without another word, I made my way to the door, his warm, spicy flavor still burning my lips.

"Maevyth," he called out for me, and I paused, with my hand on the lever. "We can never do this again."

Without another word, I slipped out of his office.

* * *

Small, white sachets sat stacked on the settee, alongside a wooden bowl of mixed herbs that I'd gathered from the kitchen. Lavender and chamomile, star anise and thyme, mugwort and peppermint. A separate bowl held dried asphodels that Magdah kept on hand as protection against the Deimosi.

I slid the stems of dried baby's breath and lady's mantle through the fabric of the sachet, my head tormenting me with thoughts. Thoughts of strong hands across my skin, fingertips rubbing and caressing warm and swollen flesh, salt on my tongue and teeth at my throat. His lips, and that delicious flavor lingering on my palate like an unforgotten delight. How badly I wanted to feel it again, to savor it.

On a sharp exhale, I forced myself to focus on the task, to banish the visuals of that kiss which had clearly troubled him for reasons I still puzzled.

Focus.

I filled the sachet with the herbs, then strung it with twine from the canopy of my bed.

A knock at the door jerked my muscles that were still jittery and warm. The door cracked open, and Rykaia peered in, before crossing the room and taking a seat on the other end of the settee, her confused gaze sweeping over my mess.

"What is this?"

"We call them weavers back at home. The combination of herbs and spices induce sleep and ward off nightmares."

She twisted toward my bed, where a half-dozen already hung. "Can I make one?"

I nodded and handed her a sachet, along with the bowl of herbs.

"What is that bowl?" she asked, pointing to the asphodels.

"That one is for the dead."

"You see the dead here? In this castle?" She eyed me, as I weaved the dried flowers through the fabric and carefully poked a stem of baby's breath through hers.

"I haven't until last night. It's strange, I was seeing them frequently back in Mortasia." I kept on with my weaving, doing my best to mentally ward off the image of the ghostly woman that'd plagued my mind the night before, until I'd finally fallen asleep.

"Do you burn your dead?"

"No. Not unless they're diseased, or believed to harbor demons."

She snorted. "Harbor demons? Malevol inside a *mortal* body? I can't think of anything worse. Mortals are essentially powerless, you being the exception, and you don't live long."

"I suppose, when you put it that way, it is silly that they'd choose to inhabit us."

Quiet lingered between us, before she paused her weaving, the lack of movement dragging my attention to her. "But you saw one last night. In this room."

"Yes. A woman."

She nibbled on her bottom lip. "What did she look like?"

I sighed, recalling the features that had imprinted themselves in my nightmares, alongside The Banishing Man and the Lyverian girl. And Aleysia. "White hair, pale skin. Black eyes."

Her eyes flickered in a way that left me wondering if she knew the woman. "Did she say anything to you?"

"She told me not to trust *him*."

"Who?"

Shaking my head, I shrugged. "I don't know. I only saw her briefly. Why did you ask if we burn our dead?"

"All our dead are burned. Their bodies create bloodstones, which eventually become vivicantem. I just wondered if perhaps that's why you're not seeing them as much here."

"Maybe. But then, why would I have been visited last night?"

She snapped her gaze from mine and looped the stems faster, sloppier, as she shoved stems haphazardly through the fabric. "Some aren't burned. Some die in awful ways."

"You knew the woman."

Her jaw shifted, and she nodded. "Pain and grief are entwined in every stone of this castle."

"May I ask who she was?"

Brows pinched, she ignored my question and kept on with her weaving. When she finished, she held it up between us. "How's this?"

Not wanting to prod her any further, I glanced toward the sachet and smiled. "Perfect. It's absolutely perfect."

CHAPTER FORTY-SEVEN

MAEVYTH

Somehow, eleven days managed to slip by.

I spent most of the time studying bones and scrolls with Dolion and Allura, cooking dinner with Magdah, teaching Rykaia how to make weavers–a skill she didn't entirely have the patience for. And on the very few days when Zevander hadn't been summoned to some obscure location that he never bothered to disclose, I trained with him. In the evenings, he'd take me down to the dungeon to feed and sing to Branimir. A few times, Rykaia had joined us, and the two of us sang silly songs, while Zevander watched from the shadows. As I'd become more familiar with his family, though, he seemed to grow more reticent. I'd caught him staring at me a few times. Long, unabashed stares that'd stirred thoughts of that day in his office. Nothing had ever come of those stares, though.

The other Letalisz, who I'd learned also lived on the grounds of Eidolon, kept to themselves, for the most part. I'd only caught glimpses of the one named Kazhimyr on occasion, and still hadn't yet met Torryn. I'd learned through Rykaia that he'd long been in love with her and apparently had an inclination to kill anything that so much as looked at her sideways.

With a sigh of boredom, I opened the puzzle book that Dolion had given to me. It happened to be one of the days Zevander had gotten called away, so I decided to pass the time figuring out the maze puzzle that I still hadn't solved. At the very least, it helped settle my anxiety, the antsy feeling in my gut that needled me any time I thought about my sister and returning to Vonkovya. While Aleysia remained at the forefront of my mind, the prospect of seeing her again felt unlikely. Hopeless.

Dolion had tried scrying for her a second time, but the attempt had produced nothing. Nothing but a question mark that loomed over me. Haunting me, day in and day out.

At a knock on my bedroom door, I pushed up from the puzzle book and padded across the room. Allura stood in the doorway, holding two mugs of steaming tea, one of which she passed to me. "Thought you might want something warm to drink."

Temperatures had cooled over the last few days, and though I hadn't spent much time outside, I felt it in the walls of the castle, through the stones and cracks that had me sitting closer to the hearth in the evenings.

"Thank you," I said with a smile, and she peered past me.

"Are you still working on the last puzzle?"

Smiling, I nodded. Allura and I had spent a good couple of hours on it the day before, a challenge I think she'd enjoyed, more so than me. "Would you like to help?"

Brows raised, she nodded, and I stepped aside, allowing her entry into the room. "I thought about it a bit last night. Have you learned mind projection yet?"

"No."

"Come. I'll show you how it works."

"Is this another glyph?"

"No, no. It harnesses the power you've already gleaned." She placed her mug of tea on the bedside table and took a seat on the bed opposite to where I'd sat moments before. Once I'd settled across from her, she placed her hand over top of the puzzle and closed her eyes. Clicking her tongue, she remained in place for a moment, then slid her hand over a small bit and clicked her tongue again. Sighing, she shook her head. "Well, I can't see it."

"What is it that you're trying to see?"

"The image on the other side. The peg in the center seems to follow a distinct pattern. If we could visualize the image, we'd know where to move the pegs. My guess, given the complexity of the grooves, is that it forms something. All I see is blackness, but you try." She took my hand, gently resting it against the top of the puzzle. "Now click your tongue."

"What does my tongue have to do with my hand?"

"Clicking it creates a benign noise that bounces off the surrounding objects. Like echolocation. If you focus on the sound, really focus, it should project the image against your hand. The power in the glyphs will then communicate that image to your mind."

"That sounds exceptionally complicated."

She chuckled. "It isn't, I promise. Be sure to close your eyes."

Eyes shuttered, I clicked my tongue as she had.

Nothing but darkness persisted.

I tried again, and still, nothing came to mind. Shrugging, I opened my eyes. "Must not work for me, either."

"Try one more time. This time, use only your fingertips to concentrate the vibrations."

Once again, I closed my eyes, and when I clicked my tongue as before, a flash of an image came to mind. "Oh! I saw something!"

A spark of excitement had me shifting on the bed, and I adjusted my hand just enough to ensure a better image next time. I clicked my tongue again and the image lingered in my head that time. Brighter. Clearer.

"It's a … tree? A massive tree, with curled branches and old bark."

"Good. Hold that image in your mind. Don't let it slip. And try to trace it."

Using the same hand I'd placed on the puzzle, I twisted the dial of the top puzzle, as I'd done dozens of times before, and pushed it along the groove of the bottom maze, beginning at the top of the tree. Something clicked that time, and goaded by my success, I twisted the dial again, moving the peg downward into another groove. Another click. Another turn of the dial, another slide of the peg, another click.

I followed the same pattern, repeatedly, along every branch, until I pushed past what felt like a lump in the bottom of the tree, just before the roots.

Something popped against my palm, and I opened my eyes to see the top of the dial opened.

"You did it! It's open!" Allura gave a small and frantic clap.

The peg in the center of it served as something of a doorknob, which I pulled open to show an image carved in wood. The tree I'd seen in my mind—only the carving held a more haunting depiction of it, with a woman's face etched into the bark and the limbs made to look like arms reaching over top of her.

"The Grymswood." The excitement in Allura's voice from moments ago had sobered. "It is the cursed tree that lies at the bottom of the Crussurian Trench. The forest of the dead. They say the tree houses the soul of a powerful priestess."

"Crussurian Trench. Dolion told me that's where the Corvikae were sent to die."

Lips pressed tight, she nodded. "He told me that as well."

The more I stared at the woman's face in the bark, the more I longed to free her.

"She's in pain," I said, tracing a finger over the ridges that felt like rough bark.

"It would seem, yes."

I lifted the carved image and found a small depression beneath, inside of which sat a fancy silver whistle.

I held it up to the light, where I could study the gorgeous etched filigree designs in the metal. Turning the page showed no story, nor explanation, for what it was meant to do. Only another puzzle to solve.

A flat end made up the mouthpiece, which I stared at for a moment, before looking back at Allura, who nodded, urging me to try. I placed the mouthpiece between my lips and blew hard. Not a single sound came forth.

Frowning, I studied the whistle and, thinking it might've been broken, blew it again.

Still nothing.

"Well, it seems to be broken, whatever it's fo–"

A distant rumble reached my ears, like rolling thunder. Light flickered in my periphery, and I turned toward the window, where an indistinct black mass flew toward the castle.

My and Allura's gazes locked, the look of confusion on her face mirroring what I felt right then.

I slowly rose up from the bed and padded toward the window, watching the blackness move closer. Closer.

"It's coming toward us, but what *is it?*" Allura asked from behind.

I shook my head, watching as a massive shadow moved across the yard below.

The rumbling sound grew louder. Louder.

The object didn't stop, it advanced toward the window like it might crash right through the glass. Both Allura and I flinched as the black swarm fell upon us. Hundreds of ravens outside the window, their wings beating against the glass, claws scraping the surface. Another massive shadow zipped overhead, and the ravens all shot up into the sky, where they hovered, making way for something enormous that perched itself against the castle wall.

I drew in a shaky breath and leaned forward, staring through one of the lancet windows. An enormous, feathered dragon, whose claws scraped against the stones of the castle wall, hopped his way over to the balcony.

"Dear gods." Awe livened Allura's voice as she crept toward the window with slow and careful steps. "Is that ... what I think it is?"

I studied the silvery eyes that were all too familiar to me. "Raivox?" Scrambling for the balcony door, I fumbled with the lever for a moment, my hands shaking.

"Maevyth, wait! We don't .... What if he's dangerous."

"I know him." I swung the door open and stepped out onto the balcony where he perched on the balustrade, his massive body taking up the whole opening of the arched stone. At least eight meters tall, his claws alone were half the length of my body.

In awe, I took in the size of him. *Was* it Raivox? It had to be. Even if nothing else appeared to be the same, I recognized those tiny crescent markings on him. "How .... How are you ... so *grown*? And how in the world did you ever find me?" No sooner had I asked the question, I glanced down at the whistle in my hands and back to him. His claws slid over the stone, leaving long white scratch marks. Behind him, the birds dove and flew about, drawing the attention of the fyredrakes who prowled below my balcony. The vicious-looking beasts that I'd seen Zevander *petting.*

Raivox hopped toward the castle wall, where he scaled the side of it before taking flight. Hovering in front of my balcony, his wings must've stretched at least twenty meters in each direction. The sheer size of him sent a cold rush of adrenaline through me, the clash of excitement and fear squeezing my chest.

"Am I dreaming?" Allura said as she padded to my side. "Did I hit my head at any point?"

"No. It's not a dream." I stuffed the whistle into the pocket of my dress and smiled, relieved to see him. "He's real."

"In all my life, I've never seen one. They're said to be mythical, like unicorns."

An obnoxious pounding at my bedroom door startled me, and I snapped my attention in that direction only a moment. By the time I looked back, Raivox was no longer there. I leaned over the balcony railing, searching the sky for him.

"Maevyth! Don't do it!"

A grip took hold of me, yanking me back from the window, and my spine crashed into the stony floor of the balcony. A shock of pain spiraled up the back of my neck, and I winced.

"Have you lost your senses? And, you!" Rykaia glared back at Allura, pointing a finger in the other woman's face. "You just stand there and watch her do it."

"I beg your pardon." Though polite, Allura's voice held a sharpness to it.

"I wasn't going to jump. I saw something fly over the castle."

Rykaia peered over the balcony, though nothing remained to be seen. "What was it?"

"Just a bird." While I wanted to tell her the truth, even Allura had questioned whether, or not, Raivox had been real. A creature she'd called mythical, like unicorns.

Shaking her head, Rykaia stepped back from the railing. "All that for a bird?"

"It was an exceptionally large bird."

"Yes, well. I'm going to go," Allura said. "Thank you for having tea with me, Maevyth. We'll meet up for some history discussion later this afternoon." She gave a knowing smile and winked.

"Of course," I said, nodding as she left the balcony.

Rykaia swung her gaze back to me. "You had tea with her?"

"Yes. She was helping me with a puzzle."

"*And* you worked on a puzzle together. Are you friends?"

"I ... suppose. We're pleasant toward one another. What constitutes friends, exactly?"

"No matter. Grab your cloak. Quickly."

"Why?"

She groaned, scampering toward the armoire, where she

threw open the doors and yanked my black cloak from one of the hangers. "No time for questions," she said, tossing the garment to me. "Or whatever thoughts are swirling in that head of yours. Now, come." With a yank of my arm, she dragged me to the door, pausing to look down the hallway, then tugged me toward the staircase.

"Where are we going?" I whisper-yelled.

"You'll see. It's a surprise."

Down corridors and stairs, we finally arrived in the dungeons, and Rykaia pulled me into the cell where I'd once slept.

A mischievous smile curved her lips as she came to a stop before the wall. "We're going on a little adventure."

"Adventure?" Confused, I watched her draw a vertical line on the wall with her index finger. When the line glowed a bright blue, my eyes widened, and I peered into the slit at what looked like the outdoors on the other side. "How is this possible?"

She pushed her hand through the illuminated seam in the wall, and my jaw slackened for the second time. "It's called cleaving."

"Is this how you get from place to place here?"

She snorted. "This is how *I* get from place to place with a tyrant brother who watches my every move. Fortunately, not everyone can do it, Zevander being one of them. It's like rolling the tongue. Some can, some can't."

As she spoke, I silently rolled my tongue in my mouth. "What about Dolion?"

"He's in the library. No doubt that ... *intruder* Kazhimyr brought back here went looking for him after she left your room, so I'm certain he's occupied." Clearly, she had a distaste for Allura. "All they ever do is study those bones. For hours."

"Allura is not a bad person."

"No. She's a scholar." Rykaia crossed her arms, her top lip peeled back. "A highbred. Haughty, if you ask me."

"Well, I didn't."

"Fine. Would you prefer to sit over piles of bones, marveling at their history and taking notes for hours, *days,* on end?"

Eyes narrowed on her, I held back a smile. "You sound like you've watched them for an awful long time. Were you spying?"

"Of course not." She gave a dismissive wave of her hand. "I find that woman absolutely insufferable." Given the fact that Rykaia couldn't look at me as she said that, I didn't believe her. In fact, I'd have bet she rather liked the woman. Quite a bit.

"What about your brother? He'll be furious. Dolion said someone is actively looking for me right now. Going on an adventure seems unwise."

"Ah. Yes, I almost forgot. We have to do something about your smell."

"What?" I lifted my arm, taking in a subtle sniff of what smelled like the soap I'd used. "I just bathed."

"Yes, but every soul in Nyxteros is going to know you're mortal with that scent you carry." From inside her cloak, she produced a small vial of purple fluid and popped the cork. As she poured it over top of my head, I flinched on instinct, anticipating the liquid to pour down my face, but instead, it evaporated into a mist that fell around me. "That's better."

I scented myself again, not picking up on any difference. "What's better?"

"You no longer smell like oranges that everyone wants to eat. And believe me, there are those in Aethyria who would eat you. Orgoths, for example."

"Orgoths?"

"Big ogre-like beasts. Fortunately, they stick to the southern part of the continent. Though, they have been known to raid a village, or two."

"So, if I don't smell like oranges, what do I smell like?"

She shrugged. "Pig shit."

Eyes bulging, I sniffed myself again. "Are you serious?"

"Trust me, it's better. One more detail before we head out." She raised her hand, placing her palm against my face, and a radiant heat warmed my cheeks. Hotter.

"Ouch!" I backed away, palpating my face to make sure there were no raw burn marks left behind. Except, my nose didn't feel like my nose. It was bigger, rounder and rougher. My face also had a rough texture, and when I lifted a lock of my hair, it was no longer black, but gray. Gasping, I looked back at her, as lowering her palm from her face revealed an entirely different person—a woman with dark brown hair coiffed at the top of her head, and hazel eyes. Her nose was thinner, her face gaunter than before. The sight of her was so ridiculously not Rykaia, that I blurted a laugh.

She laughed, too.

Both of us broke into hysterical laughter, pointing at each other.

"What did you do?" I asked, falling into another laughing spell.

"I can't … I'm laughing … too hard!" Her response had me gasping for breath between obnoxious bouts of laughter, and I fell back against the bed.

Which made us laugh more.

The two of us must've looked and sounded absolutely juvenile.

But it felt good to laugh.

At the distant sound of approaching steps and Dolion's voice prattling on, Rykaia yanked me into the glowing seam with her, and in the next breath, we were standing in an alley on wet cobblestones, with the overpowering scent of sewage clogging my foreign nose.

"Do not tell my brother that I know how to do this. He will have my head and likely my hands."

I glanced around at the tall, stone buildings at either side of us, and above them, the gloomy dusk sky that promised darkness soon. "Where are we?" I asked, my voice sketched in awe.

"Costelwick. The main street." She gave me a tug. "Come. It smells awful in this alley."

"Is it the alley, or the scent of pig shit?" I asked, unamused.

"Bit of both." She pressed her lips together, clearly trying to stifle a laugh.

We exited the narrow passage onto a bustling road, with sleek, black, horse-drawn carriages embellished with beautiful black filigree design and far fancier than those in Foxglove. Women, men, and children of all shapes, skin tones and ages filled the busy sidewalks. Some had long, pointed ears, others rounded. Some wore cloaks and long dresses, others wore chiffon pants and corset tops, as if the cold didn't bother them.

In the crowd, I spied Elvynira, though some had ghostly white skin, and others blue.

Carts lined the road, overflowing with fruits, vegetable and flowers.

Stone bridges crossed over foggy canals, lit by flickering torches that dotted the thick mist. In the far distance overlooking the city stood a magnificent castle with a dozen pointed spires and towers.

"It's so beautiful," I said, drinking in as many details as my eyes could capture.

"If you think that's beautiful, you should see Wyntertide." She jerked her head for me to follow, and led the way down the cobblestones to a stretch of small shops. "It's where my mother grew up, in the lower half of Vespyria. A stunning snowy village with mountains, crystal forests, and delightful califonsz."

"Califonsz?"

"Little aquifers in the snow that sit over top of active veins, hundreds of feet below the surface. Zevander and I used to love playing in them when we were young."

"I somehow can't imagine your brother as a carefree child."

"I don't think he's ever been entirely carefree. Just less stern. But let's not speak of him anymore. I'm angry at him."

Leaning against the edge of a building two young children sat—a boy, and a girl who looked slightly younger than him—dressed in threadbare clothes, faces covered in grime. Their long, skinny arms hugged their chests as they crouched, shivering. A tin cup on the ground in front of them held a single coin. *Homeless*. By the looks of their pale, thin bodies, they hadn't eaten in a while, and I wished I had some bread, or broth, to offer.

I unclasped my cloak and walked up to the children, careful not to frighten them. Lifting the garment in offering, I silently asked permission to cover them with it, to which they both nodded. The heavy velvet cloak swallowed both of their small bodies, and I tucked it around them, earning a smile from the little girl, who hid her face in the fabric. It hurt my heart to see them that way, particularly when so many passed by them in luxurious clothes that spoke of wealth. With nothing else to offer, I pushed to my feet and met Rykaia, who waited a few steps ahead of me.

"Spindlings," she said, nodding toward them. "Their families can't afford vivicantem, so they have no magic. Without power, they live in poverty."

"Power determines wealth?" My cheeks blushed with the silly question. Power had always equated to wealth. I knew that first-hand, having watched the governor rule over Foxglove from the comfort of his sprawling manor.

"Unfortunately, yes. And the more useful your skills, the more wealth you acquire."

"That's terrible. They don't really have a chance at all, then."

"Nope. Not with the greedy elite who squander the vivicantem. You and my brother seem to have a soft spot for Spindlings. He spared one a short while back." She skidded to a halt and smacked her own face, the odd behavior catching me off guard. "Damn it. I just said I didn't want to talk about him, and here I am talking about him."

"Why are you mad at him?"

"Do you know the princess is celebrating her Becoming, and he said nothing of it? Not a single word! I had to find out on my own that he planned to go without me."

"What is a Becoming?"

"It's a crude celebration of womanhood." She kept on, leading me down the road, closer to the shops. "Horrible for the princess, really."

"How so?"

"Well, she's expected to offer up her virginity."

"In front of everyone?"

The question was something of a joke, and I was horror-stricken when she answered, "Well, sort of, yes. It happens in a private room, usually. In the castle, it'd be the King's coupling room."

"Coupling room?"

"The room where he takes his mistresses, separate from the royal chambers. As the queen passed not long ago, the king hasn't yet filled her seat, so to speak, so nothing entirely scandalous going on there."

"That's awful. Why would anyone want to celebrate that?"

"Because not celebrating it is bad luck for her. The king doesn't want to do anything that might negatively impact his sovereignty. However, you and I can find something else to keep us occupied while that goes on." Her words didn't fully absorb at first.

"You and I? What do you mean you and I?"

"We are going. This will be the biggest celebration in all of Nyxteros. Everyone will be there."

"Yes, which makes this a very bad idea."

"Look around, Maevyth. Not one person has batted an eye at you. You don't even look like you." Clutching my wrist, she dragged me to one of the storefronts, where I caught my reflection in the window. I looked exactly as I imagined when I'd palpated my face back at Eidolon castle. The gray hair. The bulbous nose and age lines that put me at about sixty years old. In disbelief, I touched my cheeks, my nose, and turned to Rykaia. "Whose face is this?" I whispered.

"So, you know that I can read minds, yeah?"

"Uh-huh," I said, impatiently.

"Well, I'm an empath. I also extract emotions, and in doing so, I have a bit of a collection of faces."

"These are actual people?"

"Well, yes. But I'm afraid it doesn't last long, so we're going to need to hustle it along." Still gripping my arm, she hurried me down the street, passing a variety of shops–bakeries, florist, clockmakers, and an apothecary. Until we eventually came upon a dress shop, through the door of which she hauled me.

Racks of elegant gowns lined the walls. I'd never been in a such a place where one could choose a dress of their liking. Back in Foxglove, the dressmakers took our orders and delivered four to five of the same dresses at a time. Enough to last a year, or two.

"What color would you like?" she asked, perusing through the gowns.

"I really don't think I should attend this thing. I just have a bad feeling."

Groaning, she rolled her eyes and turned toward me. "What is the most exciting thing you've done in your life?"

"Crossing over. Coming here."

"You need to enjoy life." She lifted a long, golden dress from the rack and held it up to me. "This is stunning."

"Not gold."

"Red? Green? Yellow? Blue?"

"Your brother has been exceptionally accommodating, and I just feel like I should–"

"Stop. He kept you in a dungeon."

"Probably the most luxurious dungeon I've ever seen," I countered.

"Regardless. You owe him nothing. Eidolon belongs to me, as well."

"Women can own property here? *Without* being married?"

"Yes. Of course." She looked repulsed, as if the question was the most ridiculous inquiry she'd ever heard. "A number of castles are owned by women. Obscenely wealthy women. In fact, you're wearing the face of one right now. So, embody her, or someone is going to get suspicious." She jerked her head toward the woman at the front of the shop, who stood bent over a counter, writing with a quill.

It still seemed reckless to me, but clearly Rykaia had no intentions of letting me walk out of here without a dress. Besides that, a ceremony would mean leaving Eidolon. Leaving Eidolon might present an opportunity. For escape? It seemed irresponsible at that point, but on the other hand, I refused to give up on my sister.

"Black," I said.

"What?"

"I'll wear black." I sifted through the dresses and yanked one out. A beautiful, black rose jacquard gown with long, draping sleeves.

"And I'll wear red," she said, holding up another gown.

From the dress racks, Rykaia scampered toward the jewelry set out in glass cases, and asked the attendant there to retrieve a beautiful moon and star necklace that rested across the chest like a sky full of constellations.

I scanned over the options, and my gaze fell on a long, black chain with a scorpion. "I'd like that one," I said, and the woman lifted it from the case and handed it to me. The attached tag read three hundred keltzig. Leaning into Rykaia, I whispered, "How do we pay?"

"Like nobility," she said, leading me toward the woman at the front of the shop. "I'd like both dresses added to my tab."

Eyes wide, the woman looked up and scrambled to grab the dresses from our hands. "Oh, my, yes, Lady Gwyeth." She turned to me and gave a small nod. "My apologies, Lady Festwyn, I didn't see that you had an appointment with us until this evening."

"I needed these in a hurry. The Becoming, you know." I gave a nervous chuckle.

"Oh, of course. We've been quite busy." She stuffed both dresses into long bags and handed them to us, then placed the jewelry in boxes. "Do you need a fitting for the dress?"

"Uh, no," Rykaia answered for me. "We have a personal seamstress."

"Very good."

Something moved in my periphery, and I glanced down to see that the ends of my hair had begun to turn black.

I twisted toward Rykaia and lowered my voice, "We need to hurry."

Rykaia cleared her throat. "If you could bag those quickly, I would appreciate it, dear."

"Of course, of course. Shall I schedule your next appointment while you're here?"

"No, thank you."

"Very well, then." She handed off another small satchel with the jewelry, and both of us hustled toward the exit. On the way out, we passed a woman who looked frighteningly similar to the face Rykaia wore.

Rykaia lifted her gaze to the woman, who stared back at her, frowning. As if on cue, both of us sprinted out of the store and down the street, to the alley where we'd first arrived. By the time we reached the center of the alley, both of us were laughing hysterically again.

When the laughter had died down, though, I sighed. "I feel bad."

"Don't. Lady Gyweth wears vivicantem as jewels, while the spindlings and Nilivir starve. She makes a point to wear that necklace everywhere she goes, and it makes me sick."

"Jewelry?" I remembered Zevander telling me vivicantem was necessary for Rykaia. "Why?"

"Because they can. Never show pity on them. They don't give a damn about anyone but themselves."

"So, why mingle with them at this celebration?"

"Because *we* can." She drew a line in the wall of the building, which, as before, glowed a bright blue.

"Do you think this is going to be a good idea at The Becoming Ceremony? I was nearly recognized."

"No need to worry about that at the ceremony. Everyone wears a mask." She stepped through the glowing seam, and I followed after, but instead of stepping back into the dungeon, we found ourselves on a misty patch of an upward sloping yard, with decaying grass and the monstrous black stone castle in the distance. Too far of a distance.

"Oh, no," Rykaia said beside me. "Run." She darted toward the castle, and on a gulp of panic, I gathered up my dress bag and took off after her. The upward trek had my lungs burning, my thighs weak with exhaustion.

A strange, guttural growl rose up from the side of me, and I turned to see three black scaled creatures with spikes along their spines bounding toward us on all fours, their long tails whipping behind them. The fyredrakes I'd seen from the balcony. Instinct told me to drop the dress, but I didn't. I clutched the damned thing and ran like a madwoman.

"Faster, Maevyth!" Rykaia shouted over her shoulder on a wheeze of breath. "If they ... catch us ... they'll ... eat us!"

Eat us? I didn't know what I'd imagined they'd do if they'd caught us, but eating hadn't been a thought, for some reason. "Can't you ... blast them ... with something?" The waning air in my lungs thinned, the faster we ran uphill, a burning agony that clamped over my ribs.

"I don't ... have that ... kind of magic! I'm an empath!"

One of the drakes leapt out in front of her, and on a scream, she skidded to a stop. I plowed into her from behind, nearly knocking her forward, and the other two caught up to us, prowling and pacing, as if waiting for the order from the bigger animal to dive in and feast. Long, black claws pierced the ground with every step, the spikes on their backs sticking straight up.

"We're too far from the castle to call on Zevander." Rykaia's voice shook with fear, but something kept me from believing this moment was the end. Denial. Ignorance.

I couldn't place what in seven hells was keeping my hysterics at bay.

I twisted around, standing back-to-back with Rykaia, watching the two beasts that prowled closer. "Can you cleave?"

"I need a surface to cleave. I can't just cleave into the air."

"So, what do we do!"

"I don't know! This has never happened to me."

"Ever?"

"Well, no. But to be fair, I don't typically cleave back. Zevander usually comes and fetches me."

The beasts, tall as a carriage, loomed over us, like giant, black-scaled lizards. Starving lizards, I'd bet.

"They're getting closer, so we need to do something." I could hardly speak, my jaw so tight with tension.

"If you .... If you show dominance, they'll back off. But you have to challenge the alpha." She roared at one that stepped a little too close, and it backed away, snarling at her. Still, they prowled, their teeth sharp and dripping with saliva. "I'm sorry, Maevyth. I'm sorry I dragged you into this. Literally."

"Are you toying with me, Rykaia? Because if you are, this really isn't funny."

"How could I possibly toy about this! I learned to cleave *because* of these awful beasts!"

The bigger one lurched forward and roared, and while the urge to scream and cower rattled me to the core, I swallowed back the fear, eyes blurred with the threat of tears. My muscles turned weak, the air heavy and suffocating with terror.

"This was so stupid." Rykaia smacked her head. "Stupid!"

The drake tipped its head, backing up a step, as if confused.

"Hit yourself," I whispered to her. "A lot. And give yourself an extra for me."

I growled at the beast and smacked my face. Hard. The sting of the strike brought more tears to my eyes, but I didn't care. The act seemed to confuse them. I struck again and bared my teeth.

The drakes grunted and paced, still closing the circle around us.

"It's not working!" The panic in her voice didn't help my quickening pulse.

One lurched for me again, and I grabbed Rykaia's hand. The gravity of the situation finally weighed down on me, as the two of us remained back-to-back, circling to keep the beasts in front of us at all times.

"How does Zevander not get eaten?" I asked, eyeing the saliva stringing from the maw of the beast that watched me intently.

"He has them trained. They follow his command."

Like trained dogs. Trained. An idea sprang to mind.

I tugged the whistle from my pocket. Not that I'd effectively trained anything with it, but just in case it had worked the last time, I gave one hard blow.

Rykaia kicked her head to the side. "What are you doing?"

"Calling my own little pet."

The distant echo of a roar came from overhead, and both Rykaia and I froze.

"What was that?" she asked, her hands shaking in mine.

Even the drakes seemed curious to know, as they continued their prowling with the occasional upward glance.

Another roar from overhead.

That time, the drakes halted, their attention fixed toward the sky.

A flash of black was the only warning before a treachery of ravens swooped and cawed at the drakes, while they flinched and snapped their enormous jaws at them in return.

"There's an opening between them," Rykaia whispered. "We can run." She tugged my arm, and we sprinted in the direction of the castle, though we were still too far for me to feel any relief.

Growls reached us from behind once again, and we ground to a stop as the drakes caught up with us, abandoning their earlier preoccupation with the birds.

One of them lunged at me and took hold of the dress bag, thrashing it so hard, the beast ripped it from my hands. Teeth bared, it stared at me with eyes that looked too human.

A thud beside me shook the ground beneath my feet, jerking my muscles.

Rykaia screamed.

Raivox stood beside me, his colossal size twice that of the fyredrakes.

"What in the name of the gods!" Rykaia tugged my arm, urging me away from it. "Run, Maevyth! Run!"

As I reached out to pet him, the raptor roared, sending a blast of glowing silver from its mouth over the three cowering drakes. One of them yelped and hobbled away. The raptor lunged forward, and all three scattered off.

Feathers ruffling with a shake of his head, Raivox hobbled his way back toward us.

"What is this?" Rykaia asked, keeping her distance from him.

"He's a Corvugon, from what I've gathered." I ran my hand over his rough scales, careful of the long, curled horn that stuck out from the top of his head, sharp enough to stab right through me. "His name is Raivox. He hatched in my bedroom back home."

"I've never heard of a *Corvugon*."

"They went extinct, according to Allura and Dolion." As I continued petting him, he let out a purring sound that brought a smile to my face. "He's grown so quickly! He was no bigger than a hawk when I left Mortasia."

Rykaia took a careful step forward, eyes on Raivox. "It is strange. Dragons tend to grow quite slowly." She didn't seem interested in petting him, but kept her hands clutched tightly to her new dress.

"He's come to my rescue twice now." The raptor bowed his head toward me, allowing me to scratch his crown. "It's almost as if he senses when I'm in danger."

"Well, I'm grateful for it." She gave a nod of her head toward him. "Thank you, Raivox." The moment she stepped closer, Raivox bared his teeth and lurched toward her, and Rykaia jumped backward with a gasp.

"Hey! Hey," I said, pressing against his feathery scaled chest. "She's a friend."

As if the raptor understood, it sniffed and chuffed at her, closing its mandible over those vicious teeth. With one fast flap of its wings, I jumped back as he took flight. Sighing, I watched him climb higher until he disappeared behind the white clouds overhead. "He never seems to stay." Still shaken, I turned in time to expel whatever was left of my last meal onto the ground. "That was horrible."

"Part of your sickness might've been from the cleaving. It tends to make one a bit nauseous." She rounded me, careful not to step in the mess, and swiped up my dress. "Hopefully, the beast didn't tear anything." Handing it over, she gave another glance toward the sky. "I think I could use a drink."

"Will they come back? The drakes?"

"I'm fairly certain your little dragonbird established your dominance."

"I don't understand why in seven hells your brother would keep such dangerous animals on the premises?"

She huffed and stepped past me in the direction of the castle. "Because you haven't seen the kind of animals that sometimes want to get in."

CHAPTER FORTY-EIGHT

MAEVYTH

Having snuck back into my room with the dress, I hung the garment in the armoire. Thankfully, the drake's efforts hadn't torn the actual dress, but only the bag. I held the scorpion on the chain up to my neck and stared at myself in the mirror on the inside of the armoire.

"It goes on the back." At the sound of Allura's voice, I nearly dropped the jewelry, as I scrambled to hide it away. "I missed you for afternoon study." She sauntered into the room, her hands behind her back.

"Yes, I'm sorry. I …. Well, Rykaia had something to show me. I should've informed you of my absence, and for that, I apologize."

"I don't have a lot of time to dedicate to these sessions, Maevyth, but I want to help you while I'm here. I have put my research, my studies, on pause. Willingly," she said, lifting her hand in assurance. "I do want to be here, I promise you. This is an extraordinary discovery. *You* are extraordinary. And you have a duty, to the generations before you, who gifted you these incredible powers."

A horrible guilt trampled me. "I promise I will not miss another session."

"I appreciate that." She nodded toward the armoire. "The jewelry. Is it for a special occasion?"

I didn't want to lie, but I also didn't want to get Rykaia in trouble for having taken me out of the castle. "Just something I found."

She smiled and gave a nod. "This place is brimming with treasures. My goodness, the library has so many books and scrolls. I could get lost in them."

"I was never allowed to read anything outside of our Bible." I made my way toward the bed and sat down on the edge of the mattress. "Grandfather Bronwick would tell us stories sometimes, but we'd have to sneak books."

Her brows tightened with a frown. "How awful. I couldn't imagine a world so ... small."

"That's the perfect description for my world. And this one feels so big, it's overwhelming at times."

"I understand. It can be overwhelming for me, as well. It's best to take it in little doses." Wearing a troubled expression, she clasped her hands together. "And Maevyth, forgive me if I sounded like I was chiding you. Sometimes, I can be so caught up in the joy and excitement of new discoveries that I lose sight."

"Of what?"

"Of the fact that everything I take for granted is completely new to you. You have so much to discover here. Enjoy it."

I smiled again. "Thank you, Allura."

As she turned to leave, I stepped toward her. "Oh! Allura ... I wanted to ask you about the Corvugon. What is known about them?"

"Very little, I'm afraid." She crossed the room and took a seat beside me on the bed. "Years ago, I accompanied my uncle on an archeology expedition in the Veritian Mountains." She sighed. "We found bones in a cave that I identified as bird-like. A very *large* bird. Unfortunately, the entire expedition was discredited and dismissed." Her lips pulled to a sullen expression. "But Dolion tells me you hatched the egg."

My mind puzzled over when I would've told him that, or how he might've known. In all our interactions, I couldn't recall having mentioned the Corvugon egg. "I did." The hesitation in my voice echoed the confusion still muddling my head. "Do you know if their growth rate tends to be rapid?"

"From what I have studied of the metaphysis of these bones, yes. Unlike the dragon, whose collagenous matrix shows a number of LAG's, or lines of arrested growth, the bone that I recovered, which I believed to be that of the Corvugon, indicated almost continuous growth."

I stared off, struggling to grasp what she'd just said. "I'm sorry, I have no idea what any of that means."

"It just means that they are very much different from their dragon cousins. Yes, they grow very fast from, what I have gleaned."

"Interesting. Would you happen to know if they're capable of … well, if they have some sort of bond to those who hatch them?"

"It wouldn't be unusual. I read of a woman who found a dragon egg while hiking in the Veritian Mountains. She hatched it herself and raised a dragon that, to this day, as I understand, visits her and allows her to hand feed it. And, of course, the drakes seem very bonded to Lord Rydainn. They're very intelligent creatures. Some believe they're even capable of communication." With a raised brow, she shrugged. "The Corvugon is a bit of a mystery, but it would stand to reason. And in that case, you'd be very lucky. From what I've read, the Corvugon was fiercely protective of the Corvikae people." Her comment brought to mind the stories Grandfather Bronwick had told me as a child about warriors who rode astride the beasts.

"Has anyone attempted to mount a dragon?"

Lips pressed together, she shook her head. "I don't know why anyone *would* attempt such a thing. Unless they'd lost their senses. Dragons are exceptionally wild and unpredictable. And stubborn, as I understand."

Rykaia strode into the room, coming to a stop just past the doorway as if catching sight of Allura. "Oh. I didn't know you were busy. *Again*. Pardon."

"No, it's all right. I was just chatting with Maevyth. I should actually retire to my chambers." Allura stood from the bed. "She's all yours."

Rykaia gave what I determined to be an insincere smile as the woman passed her. It was when she turned to close the door that I noticed she was carrying a dark bottle and two goblets at her back. One-handedly. An observation I'd have told her I found impressive, except that she swung around, eyes narrowed.

"The woman smells like jasmine all the time. What woman goes around smelling like jasmine all day long."

"You do have jasmine oil in the bathing suites."

"Yes. We do. But you know, at some point, women stink. It's perfectly natural. Body odor, you know." She padded toward the dresser, placing the goblets and bottle down there.

"What is your fascination with smells?"

"It's what happens when you're forced back into reality after years of blissful unawareness. Everything smells different. Everything sounds different." She tugged on the bottle's cork, failing to loosen it. "Everything feels different. I'm losing my mind over it, to be honest."

I watched her struggle with the bottle, distracted by her comment. "What made you so unaware before?"

"I happened to be quite fond of tonics. Sleep elixirs, in particular."

"Fond? As in, consuming them at bedtime every night?"

"Fond as in consuming them for breakfast, lunch and dinner." Her face scrunched as she held the bottle between her legs and tugged harder.

"God ... you must've been asleep all day long?"

"Well, see that's the … unfortunate thing … about taking them all day." Voice strained and muscles trembling, she held the bottle in a way that would surely send it crashing to the floor, the moment the cork loosened. "The body … yearns for waking hours … so they become less effective over time."

"You must've been pretty unhappy to want to sleep all the time."

She paused in her struggling and frowned back at me, as if I'd said something strange. "Well, that's new."

"I'm sorry if I said something wrong, I'm not the best with words."

"You didn't. Most people assume that I *enjoy* sleeping all the time. They never consider that I *don't* enjoy being sad." She took hold of the cork once again, and the wrangling ensued. "So, going back to all the things that I'm now flagrantly aware of … yes … I am bothered by her smell in particular. I think she does it on purpose."

It was almost humorous listening to her attempt to deny her attraction toward Allura. "To bother you?"

"Why else would she meander around the castle smelling so fucking … delicious. It's unnerving." She threw her head back, groaning. "My gods! I want to strangle whoever corked this thing."

"You like her."

"What?" She scoffed and shook her head. "I just said the woman is unnerving. Have you been listening, or are your ears still clogged from all the noise your dragon made. You know, Kazhimyr asked if I'd heard something strange earlier. I had to lie to his face. Granted, I'm a beautiful liar, but … he's so good at making me feel like I've done something wrong."

"May I ask what you're struggling with?"

"This damned cork! Remember I said I wanted a drink? What I meant to say is *we* need a drink. Because two is better than one." She put the cork between her teeth, and I winced, watching her tug at it. "Who in the gods … I'll bet it was Zevander. He enchanted the damned thing so I wouldn't open it. You know what, though? I've learned to corrupt his silly spells." She lifted her hand with the bottle outstretched, her eyes focused on the cork. *"What binding on this cork was placed, shall be removed and now erased."* A squealing sound followed, and in the next second, the cork popped off the bottle, plinking against the ceiling. "Haha! Success!"

"So, you have spells, too?"

"Yes. It's considered archaic magic. Powerless. The Nilivir, or those not born with blood magic, tend to use it most. They have rituals with candles and herbs. It's very involved."

"Where I come from, that's called witchcraft." I stared off, thinking how strange that it'd become such a normal part of my life since crossing. How ignorant Governor Grimsby had been for trying to banish witchcraft when it'd proven to be useful in Aethyria. "Women and men were burned and banished to The Eating Woods for casting spells."

As she filled the goblets with the crystal blue liquid from the bottle, Rykaia shot me a frown over her shoulder. "Banished? What in the gods is *The Eating Woods?*"

"A place where sinners die. Those who cast spells—heretics. They're sent to the woods, and the creature that lives there eats them."

"Gods, Maeve. Your world sounds positively awful." After a quick swirl, she crossed the room, carrying one goblet while sipping the other. "Mmmmm. So good."

"What is it?" I asked, as she handed one of the goblets to me.

"You are going to love this."

With a small bit of hesitation, I accepted the proffered drink, giving it a quick sniff. A spicy fruity scent, like blueberries and cinnamon with a hint of nutmeg, hit the back of my throat and watered my tongue. A glimpse of Rykaia showed her polishing off her glass and pouring another.

I sipped my own, just a small taste, and the tart flavor hit my tastebuds with a slight fizz that tickled my tongue and warmed my throat. I'd tried Grandfather's morumberry wine a number of times, the bitter bite and alcohol always limiting how much I could tolerate. This was so crisp and piquant, I wanted to gulp it down.

As I reached the bottom of my goblet, Rykaia filled it and while I was inclined to stop her, I couldn't. I *wanted* more.

She topped off her goblet, and as she crossed the room, she moved with grace and poise, dancing her way to the dresser. "Do you know how to dance, Maevyth?"

"Not particularly well."

With the goblet in one hand, she reached for me with the other. "Come. Let me show you."

"I ... try not to dance in front of anyone."

"Oh, but you will! At The Becoming Ceremony."

"There's dancing? You never said–"

"What did you think we bought ball gowns for?" She chuckled, pulling me by my arm. "Come."

Reluctantly, I stood, and the moment I did, a dizziness swept over me. Not in a nauseating sense. On the contrary, I felt warm and carefree.

She swallowed another gulp of her drink and placed both goblets down on the trunk at the foot of the bed. "Have you ever danced with a *man* before?"

"No." Blush crept over my face with the admission, but it was true.

"He, whomever the lucky gentleman might be, will hold you here." She rested one palm against my hip. "And he'll take your hand, like this," she said, lifting our clasped hands to the side. "Now, this is just a simple waltz. They may get fancy at the ceremony and perform The Virgin Hunt, but we'll start with this."

"The Virgin Hunt?" I grimaced at the implication in the words. "That's a horrible name for a dance."

"Agreed, though the dance itself is quite seductive. But that's a whole other lesson for another time. The waltz ... you'll take three steps, and curtsy on four. Understand?" At my nod, she stepped into motion. "So, one, two, three, four."

I curtsied late and awkwardly scrambled to catch up, smiling at my mistake. "One, two, three, four."

That time, I did it right.

"Good. One, two, three, four." That time, she bowed, instead of curtsying. "This is what the man will do, unless you choose a woman. Then she will curtsy."

"There is no punishment for choosing women here?"

"What? No, of course not. Unless you're royalty. But even royals are allowed their mistresses. Or gentlemen fucks."

Again, I blushed. I blamed the drink, because in the time since we'd begun to dance, I could feel my body flush with a thrum of euphoria. "Where I come from, it's a sin. Cause for banishment."

"But, how? Some are simply born to love one or the other, or both."

I shrugged and hiccupped. "They don't believe that way."

"We don't choose our mates, so they could be a man, a woman .... Sometimes, if two are bonded and one dies, they might bond again with the opposite sex."

"You have mates?" I finally fell into the rhythm of the dance, moving fluidly with her.

"Yes. It is a very strong bond."

"How do you know who your mate is?"

"You don't until you kiss them. Or so I've been told." She bowed and stepped into the first count again.

"You've never had a mate before?"

"Nope."

"And Zevander? Has he ever ... had a mate?"

"Someone tried once. It was forced through enchantment. A horrible ordeal that was for him." The troubled expression on her face pulled to a wily grin. "Perhaps he's interested in the mortal variety."

I bit the inside of my cheek, stifling the urge to smile. "Your brother is far too serious for that."

"He definitely is. In fact, I've never seen him with another woman. Ever. Until you came here."

The heat in my cheeks flared, and the dizziness had me breaking away from her to sit for a moment.

She carried the bottle over to the bedside table and filled our goblets again.

After a few long gulps, my drink was gone. "I have to admit, I'm feeling ... very warm. And a little dizzy."

"I have to admit something, too."

"What?"

Lips flat, she cleared her throat. "You may want to lock your doors tonight. The liquor is a bit of an aphrodisiac."

"What?" My voice was far less amused that time. "What does .... Why lock the door?"

"Because you are probably going to need to fuck something, and there are too many men in this castle who would happily oblige. You'll probably have your fingers down your undergarments most of the night."

"Rykaia ..." Dear God, I wanted to cry. Everything she did arrived with some evil plot twist. "Why would you .... What were you thinking, giving .... Why didn't you tell me?"

"Would you have tried it, if I'd told you that it'd make you horny as a spring rabbit?"

"No. Absolutely not."

"Well, that's why I didn't tell you." She shrugged, then polished off the last of her drink before setting the goblet down. "It's delicious and it's fun. The best fucking orgasm you'll ever have by yourself."

"I don't feel fun right now. I feel very worried."

"It's only really a problem if you drink too much."

"How much is *too* much?"

"One cup will give you a fairly good jolt. Two is a bit much."

"I had three."

Eyes wide, she scratched the back of her neck. "I gave you three? Balls of Castero, I must've lost count."

"How long before it sets in?"

"Usually about an hour. Maybe less."

"Oh, my god."

"Relax. We just need to burn it off a bit." The mattress dipped, as she climbed onto the bed and gave my elbow a tap. "Come on. On the bed."

Frowning, I glanced back at her, the fast movement spinning in my periphery. "I'm not burning it off with you in the bed."

Rykaia chuckled. "You're not even close to being my type. Now, up with you. Quickly."

Clutching my head, I clambered onto the mattress until standing beside her. "Now what?"

"Now, jump!"

"I'm not a toddler. I'm not jumping on the bed."

"Okay, then, you can sit and be dizzy and be miserable." She started in with her jumping, the commotion knocking me off balance.

"Will you stop? I can hardly stand upright."

"You're not supposed to stand upright, silly. You're supposed to jump! Whoo! Whoo!"

I watched her for a moment, shaking my head at how utterly ridiculous she looked. A giggle escaped me. And another.

Choking back the urges, I cleared my throat. "You know, I always had to be the sensible one with Aleysia, too. It's exhausting."

"If it's exhausting, then stop being sensible and have some fun!"

Crossing my arms only left me stumbling around on the mattress. I found myself slow bouncing, not quite a jump, but certainly better than trying to keep upright while standing still. "I can't do this. I feel too …"

"Old? I'm over a century and a half older than you." Higher and higher, she jumped, and I couldn't help but chuckle at the sight of her coming so close to the candelabra. "C'mon, old woman! Get those legs up off the mattress! It's liberating!"

"You're going to hit your head on the candelabra, you fool."

"I'm not even close!" She took my hands, in spite of my attempt to keep them tight to my body, and it was a battle I quickly lost when I nearly toppled into her.

"Why are you doing this?"

She finally stopped, and the elation on her face sobered to something serious. "I have slept for a very long time. But since you arrived, I don't want to sleep. I want to jump and dance and *breathe* again."

I didn't know why that brought tears to my eyes, and I turned away to keep her from seeing the strange emotion breaking over me. Perhaps because she reminded me so much of Aleysia right then. "Then, let's jump." Still clutching her hands, I hopped low and easy at first, and her smile returned as she urged me higher.

"Just promise me your fragile, mortal heart won't give out on me."

Chuckling harder, I jumped higher. Higher. My chuckles turned to laughter.

Rykaia grabbed a pillow and smacked me over the head, the uncontrollable weakness making me laugh even harder. Between jumps, I nabbed a pillow and swatted her back on an explosion of feathers.

She screamed and laughed and struck me again.

I screamed and laughed.

The fight intensified, while feathers flew around us to cover the burgundy, velvet blankets. They were in our hair, and the sight of it only made us laugh harder.

In that moment, I let go of everything, and I jumped like Aleysia and I used to do when we were children.

CHAPTER FORTY-NINE

ZEVANDER

In the Great Hall, Zevander patted Ravezio on the shoulder, as the other Letalisz headed toward the door to leave, but when the distant clamor of screams reached his ear, both of them froze and gave a quick glance to one another, before racing up the staircase.

They followed the sound down the corridor, coming to a stop before Maevyth's room.

Zevander listened for a moment, and at the sound of another scream, he opened the door, just as Rykaia swung a pillow at Maevyth. She failed to connect, and Rykaia tottered backward before falling over the edge of the bed with a hard *thunk*.

His muscles lurched, but both women let out a laugh so intense, they wheezed.

"What in the gods' shriveled balls is this?" Ravezio chuckled beside him, not bothering to hide his amusement when Zevander glanced his way.

Frowning, Zevander stepped inside the room. Objects drifted in front of his face, and he held out his hand to catch them in his palm. Feathers.

Maevyth fell to her knees on the mattress and peered over the edge at Rykaia. "Are you okay down there?"

Both girls screamed with laughter again and lazily rolled around, seemingly unaware of them standing at the doorway.

"Seems somebody got into something." Ravezio pointed to the dresser, where a bottle of liquor sat.

Zevander strode toward it, swiped it up, and one sniff confirmed it was Ambrozhyr. The gods' nectar. He dragged a hand down his face as he held it up to the light. The bottle was completely empty. "Fuck." He'd enchanted the cork to keep Rykaia, in particular, away from the potent liquor that had a tendency to make her sneak away to the brothel.

Rykaia craned her neck back, and the moment she seemed to notice him, she snorted another obnoxious laugh. "We're doomed, Maevyth. The fun governor has arrived, and he is *not* happy."

Across from him, Ravezio snorted, then quickly cleared his throat, clearly desperate to keep from laughing. Thankfully, Zevander wore his mask to hide the biting of his tongue.

"I'm so tired now, Ry." Maevyth squirmed and writhed on the bed. "These sheets are so … soft." She lifted the hem of her dress, exposing long, slender legs that she rubbed against the sheets.

Fucking hells, the sight of her and that natural scent which drifted across the room tightened his muscles.

"She is going to be hurting soon," Ravezio said. "If she's never had Ambrozhyr, the first time is always the worst, and who in fucking hells knows what it'll be like for a mortal. Someone will have to stay with her. Perhaps give her relief."

The drink was known for its very enticing flavor, but that enticing flavor happened to be a powerful herb and aphrodisiac. For most Aethyrians, it elicited a strong attraction toward someone, or an urge to touch, or fuck, something. In a mortal? Zevander couldn't even imagine what it'd do to her.

"She just needs sleep," he said, wondering if her skin felt as soft and smooth as it looked, like the dreamy silk of the sheets crumpled around her legs. "She'll be fine."

Higher, her dress lifted, until her bare thighs were exposed, and Zevander felt the first twinge of need shoot straight to his groin.

Alongside him, Ravezio licked his lips, and the sight of his arousal for her had Zevander's hands curling into tight fists at his sides. "Merciful gods, let me give her relief, if you refuse."

"She's mortal. Aren't you afraid of whatever diseases she harbors?" he asked in a mocking tone.

"No."

Zevander frowned back at him. "You so much as breathe across her neck, and I will take pleasure in skewering your skull before I set it aflame."

Brows tight, Ravezio gave him a sidelong glance. "Easy, there. You skewer my skull, and you will suffer tremendous guilt for having murdered your only *loyal* friend."

"That is a pathetic assumption."

"If only it weren't true."

Rykaia let out a moan, and Zevander jerked his head toward her. "Help her to her room, and so help me gods, if you touch her–"

"You'll skewer me. Yes, I'm aware." The other Letalisz strode across the room and lifted Zevander's sister into his arms. Despite the threat, Zevander knew Ravezio wouldn't dare touch Rykaia, because if Zevander didn't kill him, Torryn surely would.

Rykaia wrapped her arms around Ravezio's neck and moaned again. "I think ... I drank too much."

"I think you're right." Ravezio said, as he carried her out of the room.

Zevander took in the state of the room. The feathers everywhere, the bed in total disarray. It occurred to him then that he couldn't remember the last time he'd heard his sister laugh. A true laugh. Not in mocking, or anger, but genuine.

His gaze fell on Maevyth.

She rubbed the silky sheets against her thigh, her senses probably so intensely chaotic right then. He could feel the hunger, craving and desperation rolling off her like a wild tempest. A beautiful and dangerous storm that he longed to wind himself inside.

Eyes riveted on her, he closed the door and strode past the bed for the chair in the corner of the room, where he planned to sit and keep an eye on her. For selfish reasons, of course.

Still lost to her body's needs, she didn't seem to notice him at first, until her gaze lifted to his, and beneath the carnal lust swirled a pained plea. A cry for help.

His knees damned near buckled from that look.

He sank into the plush chair, his cock pushing against his trousers, as her long, slender legs tangled in the folds of black silk. Zevander gripped the arms of the chair, his body hard as iron, muscles tight and aching. Desperate to give her the release that would have her sleeping like a milk-glutted kitten through the night.

"Zevander?" The sound of his name on her lips in that pained, breathy tone had his fingers gouging the arms of the chair. "Please. Something's wrong."

Entirely wrong.

"It aches." She swiped one of the pillows and pushed it between her legs. "It aches so badly."

"It'll pass," he pathetically assuaged. It'd take hours to pass, unless she gave in to what her body wanted most right then.

She let out another moan, that needy, mewling sound slowly chipping away at his restraint.

A long, slumbering hunger stirred to life inside of him, a clawing in his guts that rejoiced in her suffering. The same vile creature that yearned to tie her to the bed, to deny her any relief, just as he'd been made to suffer. To show her just how utterly depraved he could be.

Take her. She belongs to no one else.

"Zevander?" Her voice, that sweet, angelic tone strummed the nerves in his brain, and he squeezed his eyes shut, forcing the unbidden thoughts back into their shadowy corner. "Please."

A sweat had broken across her body, and she tugged at her bottom lip with her teeth.

He could've helped her. Could've easily made her climax, and some of the pain would've subsided as a result, but he refused to touch her in that state. He'd have much preferred her lucid and sober, hating him for the agony he longed to inflict on her. The sweet torment that would have her nails digging into his back, her teeth sinking into his flesh.

Enough of this, you masochistic bastard.

Still, his head tormented him with the visuals. Relentless images of her obnoxiously wet cunt welcoming every rung of his piercings. Warm and tight, squeezing them with each lazy thrust. The scratching and biting and pulling his hair. The greedy appetite for blood and sweat and the salt of her skin.

Fucking hell, the mere fantasy was enough to break him.

It was going to be a long and painful night. For both of them.

She rolled her hips against the padding wedged between her thighs, and gods be damned, Zevander had to look away. His body was so tight and coiled, it felt like he'd snap any moment. Damn Rykaia. *Damn her for doing this.*

Even with his head turned from her, he could hear Maevyth shifting against the sheets, the quiet agony vibrating in her throat. The need. So much need, his cock damned near punched through the laces of his trousers.

The first time he'd been given the liquor, during his first moon cycle, he was sixteen and at the mercy of General Loyce. He recalled the deep, cramping ache, and the intense need to fuck something. She'd bound his hands and legs, then tortured him for hours, teasing him while he writhed in pain. He'd have taken a whipping to his back over the agony of too much Ambrozhyr.

He screwed his eyes shut and willed those thoughts away, for fear of what they'd dredge inside him, before opening them on the girl.

In brisk and jerky snaps of movement, entirely unnatural, she managed to turn herself on the bed until her head was at the headboard. In the supine position, her body rose up from the mattress, somehow lifted into the air, and the sheets that covered her fell away, onto the bed below her.

Frowning, Zevander pushed up from his chair and slowly stalked toward the edge of the bed to find her eyes had rolled back, her body stiff as a plank and trembling, as if every muscle were contracted. Possessed by something. He circled around her, curious as to what powers had caused her to levitate. Certainly nothing he'd yet taught her.

At the foot of the bed, he watched her toes twitch, her thighs shiver. Her arms shook, stiff at her side, fingers curled and twisted, as if in pain. Soft whispers carried on the air, spoken in a language he recognized, one she'd claimed not to speak.

"*Da'haj mihirit voluptasz.*" *Give me pleasure.*

Eyes still an unsettling white, she sat up while remaining elevated above the mattress, and she crawled toward him across the air. "*Da'haj mihirit voluptasz.*" The soft kitten voice from before had grown husky, raspy. Enrapturing.

What was this exquisite creature? This peculiar little enchantress who stirred his soul?

He stared in awe, mesmerized by her bewitching darkness. *Magnificent.*

"*Da'haj mihirit voluptasz.*"

The request sent a shiver coiling down his spine, his body wanting nothing more than to appease it. Lazy, black curls that he so badly wanted to capture in his fist, spilled over her shoulders and lay plastered to her forehead against the dewy shine of her skin. Her body writhed with a hypnotic sensuality that had

Zevander grinding his teeth, desperate to keep from tearing into her.

"Da'haj mihirit voluptasz," she beseeched.

Body lowering back to the mattress, she squirmed and writhed and mindlessly pulled down her undergarments. The sight of them banded at her thighs watered his mouth for what he knew hid beneath her skirt.

Thighs apart, she arched her back. *"Da'haj mihirit voluptasz."*

He reached down and stroked her hair, his appetite stirred at the mere touch of her. Gods, he'd have sacrificed his next breath to be the bastard who made her scream in ecstasy right then.

He raised his hand to a black flame that hovered above his palm. *"Revelah'ret te mej."* *Reveal yourself to me.*

Her eyes rolled forward, but the black of her pupils swallowed the usual foggy gray irises, indicating something still possessed her. She giggled and lifted the hem of her skirt higher, not yet exposing herself.

"Revelah'ret te mej," he repeated.

She licked her lips and raised her hand. The flame shot from his palm to hers without his command. As if she'd summoned it herself.

He watched in rapt fascination as the flame dissipated to smoke and traveled across her arm as a pulsing onyx vein to her hands, turning her fingertips black. No one had ever been capable enough to snatch his power that way and Zevander couldn't tell if he was troubled or turned on by it.

"Da'haj mihirit voluptasz et da'minha vitatej." *Give me pleasure and I will give you life.* Eyes shuttering, she tipped her head back at the same time she reached beneath the hiked hem of her skirt, and the moment her fingertips made contact, Zevander felt the glide of warm silk across his own fingertips, as if he were touching her himself.

His body shuddered. *Spread your legs.*

Her legs parted for him, and the tight seam widened for what he imagined to be a deliciously pink shell within. Gods' teeth, what he wouldn't have given to yank back her coverings and behold what was doubtlessly the most revoltingly beautiful flesh he'd ever lay eyes on. In a feather-light stroke, she slid her middle finger down between her lips, and he took in the warm silky folds that enveloped the digit.

Mouth parted, she let out a shaky breath, and he could feel the flinch of her stomach muscles. Her thighs that shook at either side, while she toyed with her seam. When she drew her finger back upward, she found the small bundle of nerves and brought her thighs together on a moan.

Fuck me.

Zevander planted a fist against the bed, his muscles weak.

She circled her clit that, had he been pleasuring her himself, would've suffered the torment of his tongue, but he didn't dare lower his face there. Every fiber of his willpower resisted.

When she slid her fingers back down, over her mound, and found the small entrance, slick with her arousal, he let out a groan. The sticky juices coated her fingers, and damn her to Nethyria, she had the fucking audacity to shove her fingers into her mouth, her tongue enveloping the flesh, sucking it away.

His tongue prickled with her sweet flavor.

She lay back on the pillow and closed her eyes, curving her fingers up inside her again.

Zevander fell to his knees beside the bed, the height of it at his chest, offering a view so intimate, he could smell that delectable orange flavor mingling with the heady scent of arousal. Mouth watering, he gnashed his teeth, as the need inside him clawed at his spine.

Touch her. Taste her. Fuck her.

Soft moans leaked past her lips, as she plunged wet fingers in and out of her tight cunt, titillating that electric ball of nerves up inside of her. The wet squelch of her fingers working up her arousal goaded him to reach down into his trousers and take hold of the beast that begged to plow into her. To spear through that swollen flesh without mercy.

Her body twitched, her other hand curled into a fist, as if she felt him, as well. Breaths turned staccato, she plunged faster, soaking her fingers, moaning and writhing in pleasure. Muscles tight, he could feel the climax building inside of her.

"*Veni'adj meh, Lunamiszka.*" *Come for me, my little moon witch.*

Thighs shaking, she convulsed, breath held as her body climbed. Higher. Higher.

A distant growl echoed in his ear, and he glanced around to see shadows slipping in and out of the walls. The curtains across the room shivered, as if a gust of wind had ruffled them, though the windows remained locked. A rattling sound drew his attention to the candelabra overhead that trembled, the flames flickering, casting shadows across the underside of the canopy. At a cracking sound, he turned to where the mirror on the wall fractured, splitting down the middle—one half showing her lying on the bed, the other showing him at her side, his hands shoved down his trousers. He stared at the obscure reflection of her, only making out the pale silhouette of her hand furiously driving in and out of her. The tension in her muscles mirrored his own, winding like a band stretched too tight.

Zevander marveled at her unfurling darkness, like peeling back the petals of a black rose.

She let out a tearful sob of release at the same time the walls of her cunt pulsed around her fingers. Another spasm, and her walls clamped harder—a second orgasm.

Jaw tight, he let out a moan, his fist banded around his rigid cock, pinching the metal along the pierced underside. He bent forward, his stomach flexed with a cramping ache that tightened his balls. "Fuck!" Warm jets of cum sprang forth, coating the top of his hand. Pulse after pulse had him clenching his teeth with how fucking *good* it felt.

Without so much as a single stroke of his flesh. It'd been years since he'd felt that level of release.

She arched upward on an outcry that sent another surge of his release across her thighs.

The black smoke drifted upward, rising up from her hand, and slipped back beneath his skin on a pleasurable jolt that had him groaning.

Her hand fell to her side.

Her eyes rolled back to white again, then shuttered closed.

She turned limp.

His muscles lurched, and he lowered his head to her face. On feeling the faint panting breaths against his cheek, he let out a sigh of relief and stroked his clean hand down her face, brushing away the damp hair that clung to her skin. A slight vibration hummed across his fingertips and shot straight to his groin as a satisfying throb. He stared at her lips, wanting so badly to kiss them.

She was a vision of perfection.

How greedily he desired her. His little moon witch.

Tomorrow, she would travel with Dolion to Calyxar with the stones, where she would be safe and protected. Far from the mages who hunted her.

Away from harm.

And most importantly, away from him.

CHAPTER FIFTY

MAEVYTH

An ache pulsed in my temple, and I winced, digging my fingers into the pain. With a yawn and a cat-like stretch, my bones popped, and I rolled onto my back. Pain bit into my thighs, and I lifted my head to find my undergarments stretched between them, as if I'd pulled them down at some point in the night.

A dampness beneath me had me patting the bed, and I gasped. Had I pissed myself in the night? I yanked up the undergarments and sniffed my hand, not catching the faintest whiff of piss, but instead, a sweet, heady scent. One I knew intimately from the nights I'd touched myself.

My mind wound back to the night before. The last thing I remembered was jumping on the bed with Aleysia, followed by an intense feeling of exhaustion. Had I fainted, or fallen asleep? Surely, I wouldn't have *touched* myself while completely unconscious ... but I couldn't recall a single moment.

A thought crossed my mind, something Rykaia had said about locking my door, so as not to rouse any of the men in the house. I focused on any pain between my thighs that might've indicated that I'd been violated in any way, but there was nothing. No ache.

No pain. Nothing but an overwhelming sense of relaxation, as if I'd slept for two days straight.

I sat up from the bed, noting the mirror across from me that'd cracked as though something had been thrown at it. Candles lay toppled on the table beside my bed, the dried wax spilling over the edge while not quite touching the floor. Feathers lay strewn about the room … and I did vaguely recall swinging pillows at Rykaia.

God, what had we done?

I pushed out of bed and straightened the candles upright. Gathering the feathers on the floor felt like chasing after a gust of wind, as they blew around my hands with every movement I made, but I managed to wrangle most of the mess into a pile that I gathered into a wicker basket beside the settee. Pausing in front of the mirror, I ran my finger down the ominous crack and wondered how it'd gotten there.

In the bathing room, I made my way to the elaborate chamber pot, the narrow walls closing me in as I shut the door behind me. For all the ancient details that Eidolon held, I was impressed by the modern plumbing. In place of the chain I'd typically have to pull to flush back home, this one had an ornate brass lever that hardly made a sound when depressed.

Once finished relieving myself, I undressed and bathed, then donned my training gear. And after a quick breakfast of milky oats, I made my way to the training room, only to find Zevander wasn't there.

Again.

Disappointed, I headed toward the castle's library and, along the way, found Rykaia sprawled out on a velvet couch in one of the parlors, eating an apple. The moment her eyes found me, a wily smile lit her face.

"How did you sleep, *Bellitula?*" she asked, clearly amused with herself.

"Fairly well, though I don't remember most of the night."

"You're kidding. You didn't touch yourself, at all?"

An unbidden visual of writhing on the bed to the sound of Zevander's voice in my ear flashed through my head. "If I did, I don't remember."

"Gods, what a waste. That's the whole point of Ambrozhyr. *Memorable* orgasms."

"Well, maybe it's different for mortals. Have you seen Zevander?"

"He rode to Costelwick early this morning with the other Letalisz. Tonight is Princess Calisza's Becoming, if you'll recall." She raised her brow, clearly anticipating an argument from me.

Tension wound in my stomach at the thought of betraying Zevander, sneaking behind his back. "About that ... I don't know–"

"Stop. You have a dress. You're going."

"We were nearly discovered the last time you tried to hide my face in public."

She tore off another bite of the apple, staring back at me as she crunched it between her teeth and swallowed it back. "As I already told you, I don't have to disguise you that way this time. Everyone will be wearing a mask."

"What if *he* sees me there? He won't be happy."

She snorted and rolled her eyes. "In that dress? I think he'll be quite happy to see you, no matter what he tells himself."

"What are you saying?"

"I'm saying, I think my brother is smitten with you." She'd made a similar comment the night before, and still, my skin flushed anew as if it were the first mention.

"You're wrong. He's been avoiding me all week."

"Exactly. Zevander doesn't avoid any*thing* unless he's frustrated by said *thing*."

"That doesn't sound like attraction to me. It sounds like annoyance."

She sat upright and chomped into the end of the apple,

forcing me to wait until she swallowed it. "Right, so, normal individuals fawn and flirt when they like someone. My brother, on the other hand, acts as if he's positively repelled."

Frowning, I shook my head. "That makes no sense."

"Well, given that he kills people for a living, has enemies all over Aethyria, and was trained to shun affection from women, it stands to reason, I think."

When she put it that way, I supposed it did.

"I don't think he knows what to do with you, Maevyth." She sighed. "Which is why I think you should go tonight. It'll force him to decide if he's your protector, or your enemy."

"I don't want to force him to decide anything."

"Then, go for me? I don't want to be alone in that crowd. The wealthy give me hives."

"So, why go? What could possibly be so important about this ceremony that you'd risk being seen there?"

Her eyes lit up. "Because Circ'Lunae will be there, and I haven't seen them since I was a young girl."

"What is that?"

"You'll see. When you accompany me in your scintillating black dress. Now run along, little mouse, and examine your dull pile of bones with Dolion and the intruder." She waved me on. "I shall find you later this evening."

* * *

In the library, I found Dolion and Allura hunched over piles of scrolls and books, as usual. The bones sat in two mounds, one of which was separated further into sets that Allura had determined belonged to different people.

As I approached, Dolion removed his spectacles. "Good morning. You're a bit early today."

"Zevander missed training again." I cringed at the somber tone of my voice.

"Hmm. That makes four times in the last week. Has he taught you anything new?"

"Nothing as of late."

"I suspect he's distancing himself a bit." Dolion's puzzling words stuck in my head, as he waved to the seat across from him. "Sit. I need to speak with you about something."

For the briefest moment, I thought he planned to chide me for drinking with Rykaia the night before, until I remembered it wasn't Foxglove, nor Grandfather Bronwick's waning supply of morumberry wine. Nor Aleysia. The rules I'd grown up with didn't exist here, and I wouldn't be subjected to punishment simply for being silly. I sat down as he'd asked, entwining my fingers.

"I'm leaving for Calyxar this evening. And ... you'll be coming with me."

"Calyxar? Is that a village?"

"It's an island, in the south." He nodded toward Allura. "The land of our people."

Wariness settled over me at the thought of traveling to somewhere I presumed to be even farther away from my sister. "And what about Zevander?"

"He agreed to let me take you. A precaution, as there seems to be quite a bit of unrest in Costelwick. Although, that also makes it the perfect opportunity to slip away unnoticed."

"He agreed to this?" It felt like a betrayal that he'd gone behind my back to discuss these plans.

"Very much. He longs to do what's best for you."

"I see." I turned my attention to Allura. "And will you accompany us?"

Lips tight, she shook her head. "I'm afraid not. I must return to the House of Sages to continue my studies."

"So ... it'll just be the two of us."

"Yes. Which is best. We'll draw less attention that way."

"And … what about my sister? What about returning to Mortasia?"

Dolion scratched the back of his neck. "I don't think that's wise, Maevyth."

"But … you promised. You promised that, if I learned how to use my powers, you would personally escort me back to the woods." With a quickening anger, I clenched my fists. "You lied to me."

"I did not lie. You haven't even begun to learn your major glyphs. There are scholars in Calyxar, the most brilliant minds in Aethyria, who may be able to shed light on some of these."

"I don't care about glyphs!" I slammed my fist against the table, knocking the bones out of their piles. "I don't care about anything but my sister right now. She is the only family I have, Dolion. The only piece of my world that I care to keep."

"Forgive me, but I will not escort you into danger. There are ruthless mages that long to turn your blood to stone, Maevyth. Should they find you–"

"I'm not going to Calyxar. I'm not giving up on my sister." I pushed to my feet and stormed out of the library, my blood seething with anger. While the rational half of me understood Dolion's intentions, or at least thought I did, the other side couldn't allow him to sweep me away to an island in the middle of nowhere. Studying the glyphs and old bones and learning my powers meant little to me while the fate of my sister remained unknown.

Up the staircase and down the corridor, I found myself standing before Rykaia's room.

I knocked on the door.

With a goblet in hand, she smiled. "Change your mind about going?"

My muscles still shook with anger. "Will there be mages there?"

"Yes. Of course. The king's mages are expected to be in attendance."

"And just how do you plan to fool the king's mages? What tricks do you have that will keep me veiled from those who want to turn my blood to stone?"

She leaned against the doorframe, her expression more serious than before. "You'll be masked. Your scent. Your face. Your aura. They won't know you from any other Lunasier."

"You promise. This is entirely foolproof."

"Well, nothing's entirely foolproof, but I would not endeavor to put you in danger."

It was a foolish plan, but I had other motives driving my thoughts. Motives that were worth the risk. If I stayed, I'd be shipped off to an island, farther away from my sister. "I'll go with you on one condition."

"Yes?"

"You help me get back to the woods."

She huffed. "No deal." Sipping her drink, she sauntered off into her room, taking a seat in front of the burning hearth.

"What do you mean, no deal?" I asked, following after her. "I'm offering to go with you. I'll stay with you. And then you'll cleave me to the woods."

"Are you serious? You can just ... leave? Everything?" Her eyes flickered, as if wounded by the suggestion.

"I've told you from the start what was important to me."

"Yes, you did, Maevyth. You've absolutely made that clear." Jaw set to a stubborn angle, she pressed her lips together. "I'm not taking you."

Vision wobbling with tears, I sat down in the chair across from her, both of us watching the fire. "I can't give up on her, Rykaia. I won't. I have this strange and nagging sense that she's still alive. It's difficult to explain, but ... I need to return to her."

Jaw tight, she kept her eyes fixed on the flame, not bothering to respond.

I sighed, hands fidgeting in my lap. "You don't want me to leave. I know that's why you've been playing matchmaker with Zevander and me."

"Do not ask me to do this, Maevyth. Do not ask *me* to do this."

"I have no one else to ask. Everyone seems to have some reason to keep me here, but you're all forgetting this isn't my home."

"This *is* your home!" she snapped, quickly looking away. "You've said it before, your home is cruel and punishing. You came here for a reason, Maevyth. It's your fate. There's a plan for you."

"It's *not* my fate!" That time, I was the one who snapped. "I don't believe in fate. It's done nothing but curse me my entire life. So, forgive me if I don't give a damn about what it has planned for me."

"I have a million reasons, myself, but I believe. And if you think I'm letting you saunter off and risk that you'll never come back, you've underestimated just how much of a bitch I can be." Eyes watering, lips peeled back into a snarl, she looked away.

"Once I find my sister, I promise you, I'll return."

"That is a promise you cannot keep. And what if your *gut feeling* is wrong?"

"Rykaia, look. I understand—"

"You don't understand. You will never understand. Because you can't." She swiped at her cheek, as though embarrassed by her tears. "I have the power to take every sad day you've ever had and turn them into nothing more than a distant dream for you. Yet, I cannot share my pain with you. I cannot show you what horrible things live inside me. Things I have to live with—" Lips slammed shut, she swallowed hard, but the quiver in her chin belied her efforts to fight back the emotions. "But since you've been here, I feel less burdened by them. So, do not ask *me* to do this. I cannot be the one to see you off, because the moment you leave is when my hell begins again." She shook her head. "And I don't care if that's selfish of me to say."

An ache bloomed in my chest. I knew the loneliness, the panic of losing someone in the darkness. I'd felt it in a literal sense as I'd chased after Aleysia that night in the woods, and again when I'd crossed over without her. Like a chunk of my heart had been torn away.

Across the gap that separated us, I reached for her hand. "Tell me what horrible things you've suffered. And I will do my best to take some of the pain."

Her face twisted in anguish, and she lowered her gaze. The heartrending sound of her weeping pulled at my ribs. I slid from my chair and fell to my knees in front of her, drawing her in as I wrapped my arms around her. At first, she didn't move, but then I felt her clutch my arms as if she were clinging to a lifeline.

"Every night I close my eyes, all I see …" She choked on a sob, her fingers digging into me as she pulled me tighter.

"Tell me, Rykaia."

"I see … the horrible things they did to her. My beautiful mother. They forced me to hold her hand through it all. And I felt everything she felt. The fear. The humiliation. The hopelessness." Her body shook against me, and I blinked back my own tears, refusing to let her go. "I tried to block it out, but I couldn't. It was all I could feel." Another sob wracked her body, her tears wet on my shoulder. "I felt the apology. She apologized to me while they destroyed her. While they tore into her without a shred of remorse. Until I finally felt her life fade. I was holding her hand when she died."

Tears streamed down my cheeks as she told me her story. Although I didn't have the power to absorb pain and suffering, like Rykaia, I felt her anguish pulsing through me in the tremble of her muscles, the tightness of her clutch, and the suffering of every word. I held her through the tears—the hot, angry tears, and the quietly soft ones too.

When she finally loosened her grip, she sat back, her eyes red and lost, as if she were trapped in another time. "It was Branimir who kept them from hurting me, too. They tore away my clothes, and they promised worse than what my mother suffered." She spoke in a flat tone, as if relaying someone else's experience. Completely devoid of emotion. "Have you ever been afraid of monsters?"

"Sometimes, yes."

"I had no idea the kind of monster that lived inside my brother, until I watched him and his spiders feast on those soldiers alive."

My blood turned cold. "He consumed them? Alive?"

"He made sport of it first. His … creatures formed webs around them so there was no escape. It was well into the night by the time the last one stopped screaming. There was so much blood. Rivers of blood that crawled toward me as I lay hidden beneath the bed. I don't want to fear my brother, but … what he did was—"

"Terrible and frightening." I squeezed her hand, emphasizing my point. "But what they had planned for you was so much worse. He protected you, Rykaia."

"At what cost?" Lips quivering, she shook her head, and I realized her torment was thinking she'd turned him into what he was. "I avoided touching him afterward because I knew there was nothing there to absorb. An empty shell whose insides had turned to rot. Because of me."

"Not because of you. And there's still something good in Branimir."

She stared off for a moment and wiped at her eyes again. "As I understand, it was a Solassion who won the tournament. A soldier who'll take Calisza's innocence at the ceremony." Wincing, she shook her head. "Perhaps that's why Zevander felt the need to keep me away, but he doesn't understand. He's never known the feeling of being in a room full of complete strangers who are all imagining you entangled with some beastly creature that happened to win the right. It's terrifying and lonely and Calisza doesn't have a mother to calm her. She has nothing but the men who are relying on her to fulfill her duty without question." Her brow twitched as if she might break into more tears. "I'm well acquainted with the brutal nature of Solassion soldiers. They'll carouse and laugh, like everything is sport. They'll be far gentler and respectful than they were with my mother, of course, but in the end, they'll still take." She paused for a moment, brows pinched to a frown. "You asked why it's so important for me to be there. This is why. I want her to know I'm there and that she's not alone. But I don't want to go alone, either."

I pushed to my feet, my head wound up chaos as I sat back in the chair across from her. In the silence, I felt her rest her hand atop of mine and I turned to see her eyes brimming with tears again.

"I promise. I'll take you to the woods after."

CHAPTER FIFTY-ONE

MAEVYTH

Rykaia clipped the silver chain to my neck, letting the cold metal rest against my spine where it reached to the center of my back. "Dear gods, Maeve. You better pray my brother doesn't see you …. This …." She lifted the scorpion charm and let it fall against my back again, reminding me of its presence. "Well, I'll just apologize now for any indecency on his part."

I stared at myself in her mirror, the black roses etched in gorgeous, silk jacquard, the bodice cinched at the waist. Off-the-shoulder sleeves elegantly framed my collarbone and shoulders, cut low enough that the whole of my back was left exposed. "You're sure this isn't too much? I feel like I'm hardly dressed."

"That's the point!" Rykaia stood beside me in her blood-red gown, the bust of which was cut just as low, but at least her sleeves covered her shoulders. Regardless, Rykaia looked effortlessly stunning, as usual. "You look good enough to eat."

Pulling my hair to the side, I turned to see if I could get a glimpse of the glyph that'd glowed when I'd taken a bath. Only bare skin, from what I could make out.

"What is it?" Rykaia tipped her head, staring back at me in the mirror.

"There was something on my left shoulder I noticed while taking a bath." I awkwardly pointed to where I'd seen it. "It looked like a glyph, the way it glowed."

"Your sigil."

"Sigil?"

"The symbol of your bloodline. It can be anywhere on the body. Mine is at my ribcage, but also at the nape of my neck." She dragged her hair to the side, rubbing her finger over the spot.

"Why would it have glowed the way it did?"

Shrugging, she turned toward her bed and lifted a silver and black jeweled mask with glittering black wings that faced downward. "Mine glows when the moon hits it. Or when I'm mad, or scared. Or uncomfortable. You say you were in the bath when it happened? Do you recall any particular thoughts you were having at the time?"

My cheeks burned at the memory of fantasizing Zevander's hands and lips on my skin. "Nothing unusual."

"Maybe the heat of the water, then." When she placed the mask on my face, the wings covered my eyes and stuck outward at either side of my head, but I could still see out. The jeweled thorax of the insect covered the bridge of my nose, and its antennae pointed upward like two crooked horns.

"What is this?" I ran my fingers over the horns that stood above my head.

"This is the grotesque representation of the cicada who climbed out of the underworld with a message for the stag, convincing him to rape the Goddess of Fertility."

"Why on earth would I ever dream of representing that?"

"Because we are a loathsome society. And technically, it also represents the dawn of mankind. The goddess gave birth to the sun and moon. The Solassions and Lunasier." She placed a similar glittery black and silver mask with wings over her face, also covering her eyes. The only part of our faces showing were our lips and jaw. "The women wear the cicada masks, the men wear the stag masks."

"I still think it's a vile story."

"Agreed. But I can assure you, the festivities will be marvelous. And tomorrow, I will cleave you to the woods, as promised."

"So, what exactly happens at this Becoming Ceremony?" I ran my finger over the delicate flounced sleeves of my dress, so long, they nearly touched the floor.

"The king chooses a formidable group of men and women to fight for her virginity, essentially. The one who lives gets to claim her for the night. The fighting already took place, and unfortunately, as I mentioned, a Solassion won, so we're just attending the reception."

"Like a wedding?"

"Well, no. There is no marriage between the two."

As revolting as I considered the ritual, I had no place to comment, having come from a world that burned men and women for who they chose to love.

Rykaia lifted a purple vial from her dresser and held it up. "This is to mask your scent," she said, and poured it over me. Like before, it fell as a white vapor around my body. "I promise no pig shit this time, but it's strong enough to mask your aura, as well. So long as you don't murder anyone, you'll be fine."

"Strong enough to fool your brother?"

A sheepish grin stretched her lips. "We'd best keep our distance from him. He's exceptionally good at seeing through my tricks, but only because he's lived with me for centuries. And he happens to be a trained killer, of course."

The humor withered inside of me. "Has he taken a lot of lives?"

"Do you want the truth?" In the mirror's reflection, she

dabbed a berry coloring onto her lips. "I don't even know. He says nothing to me."

How cold that must've felt.

When the girl from my village had gotten trampled in front of me, it'd taken years for me to process it, to reconcile the thoughts in my head, and I hadn't even deliberately gone out of my way to take a life. Zevander must've suffered constant torment.

Unless he didn't. I couldn't fathom the kind of man who thought nothing at all about his kills.

At a knock at the door, both of us turned toward it.

"Rykaia? Is Maevyth with you?" Dolion's voice bled through the wood. "I'd like to speak with her for a moment."

"Sorry! I've not seen her!" Rykaia called out, before turning to cut loose a quiet snort.

"I've searched the entire castle, and I haven't been able to find her."

"Ah, perhaps she's napping? Or bathing, as some of us do without wanting to be disturbed."

Dolion cleared his throat. "Of course, my apologies. If you see her, please let her know I'm looking for her."

At the sound of his retreating footsteps, I slapped her on the arm. "You're terrible. I feel bad lying to him that way."

"You didn't lie. I did. And are you forgetting he lied to you first?"

I'd filled her in on Dolion's plan to take me to Calyxar, while we were getting dressed.

"And his lie was far more terrible than that."

True. Dolion hadn't only lied, he'd left me feeling hopeless as a result.

"C'mon. It's time to put all this misery behind us and have some fun." Just as she had the day before, Rykaia drew a line on the wall to create a glowing seam.

"No fyredrakes this time," I said as she pushed her arm through.

"We can only pray. What shit that would be trying to run in this monstrous dress. They'd have me by the ass before I knew what hit me."

Just in case, I'd worn the whistle, the one that'd summoned Raivox. Rykaia had tried arguing that it took away from the simplicity of the scorpion chain, but I'd insisted. I liked having a link to him.

She stepped through first, I followed after, and the two of us found ourselves in a small copse of trees just outside of a stony wall, where a half-dozen guards stood before a gate. Another half-dozen flanked either side of them.

Brushing the dried leaves from my skirt, I asked, "Why not just cleave into the ballroom and avoid the guards all together?"

She snorted. "Are you familiar with wards? There is no cleaving into the ballroom. We're lucky to have gotten as close as we did."

We stepped over the bracken and sauntered up to the gate.

"Name," the guard said in a flat tone, eyeing the two of us up and down.

With a giggle, Rykaia set her hand against the moody guard's arm, as he peered down at the names. "Lady Anadara and Lady Sivarekis," she said as easily and fluidly as if they were our real names.

He waved a hand over the back of hers, and a glowing heraldry appeared. With a flick of his fingers, he urged me to lift my hand, and when I did, he left the same mark.

Without a word, he stepped aside and gave a respectful bow. "Ladies."

She must've read his mind as he'd skimmed over the names.

I studied the strange marking that didn't fade when I rubbed my finger across it, and Rykaia placed a hand over mine, stopping the action. "It'll be gone by evening's end," she assured.

The two of us entered what seemed to have been the outer court, given the stables that stood off to the side. The walled enclosure was filled with elegantly dressed guests, all of whom wore cicada and stag masks, and I searched what little I could see of their faces for Zevander. Not likely that he'd have exposed the lower half of his face, though. My guess was, he'd be the only one not wearing the blind masks.

Tiny flames flickered in glass bulbs strung across the courtyard, with purple and silver banners strewn between them and matching streamers that fell from the sky. A massive purple, black, and silver striped tent stood off to the side of it, flanked by two smaller tents on either side, from where the sound of music drifted out over the crowd. I visually devoured the mystically enchanting ambience, eyes feasting on every beguiling detail. So enthralled, I hardly noticed the masked faces that turned toward us as we passed.

The delicate shoes I wore clacked against the stones of the bridge, when we crossed the moat. I peered over the edge to see a black serpent beast slithering beneath the walkway. Gasping, I tensed at its size, and Rykaia grabbed my arm.

"It's a Koryn. Stay away from the edge," she warned.

Another stony wall stood guarded by soldiers. Rykaia lifted her hand with the glowing mark, and I did the same. The two guards nodded, allowing us passage.

We finally reached the inner courtyard, where more guests mingled about, and I scanned over the gorgeously kempt gardens, stark white statues set among the tall bushes like ghostly animals, and a beautiful fountain. Another purple and black tent stood propped open, and I could just make out bodies within, donned in elaborately colorful, tight-fitting suits, performing mesmerizing acrobatics. There were flame-throwers, and those dressed as puppets on strings, magicians, and men on stilts that walked among the crowd. The air was rich with the scent of mors mead and ginger pops, roasted nutkerns, and savory meat pies— foods I recognized from the few fairs and festivals that would pass through Foxglove Parish. An entrancing flurry of activity that ravished my senses, as Rykaia led me up a stone staircase, lined with flickering torches and snarling gargoyles, to a set of colossal-sized doors propped open either side of three guardsmen.

"Lady Anadara and Lady Sivarekis," Rykaia said with a curtsy.

A man in a silver, brocade jacket and trousers, wearing a white stag mask shuffled us inside. "I present Lady Anadara and Lady Sivarekis!"

A few heads turned, setting my nerves aflame, but most remained engaged in conversation. Descending the staircase into the ballroom, I leaned into Rykaia and whispered, "What happens when those two guests turn up?"

A smile curved her lips. "It will be a most unfortunate situation for them."

My conscience withered, as she took my hand and led me to a dimly-lit grand room, with stone pillars and another fountain. Vines hung from the ceiling, draped around candelabras, from which beautiful, white streamers dangled alongside diamonds. White roses decorated the room, along with sparkling white branches in vases that stood like eidolic silhouettes in the shadowy corners.

Masked women dressed in shimmering chiffon fabrics, their breasts clearly seen through the thin material, and men clad in only masks and silver loincloths danced sensually around the guests. A few of them danced with each other, in the motions that reminded me of the night I'd found Uncle Riftyn and Aleysia together, their hips thrusting against one another, hands groping. My breath caught in my throat, and a tingle of arousal stirred in my belly as I watched them.

The room seemed divided into groups, with those bearing blond hair and bronze skin on one side, those with dark hair and pale skin on the other.

"Solassions and Lunasier," Rykaia said, as if reading my thoughts.

Perhaps she was.

I had to remember that annoying ability of hers.

She chuckled, releasing my arm. "You're worried I'll know what you're thinking when you see my brother."

"I'm thinking no such thing."

As she reached for my arm, I yanked it quickly away, and she laughed harder.

"Well, then, I won't bother to tell you that I've already spotted the tyrant."

"Where?" I asked, not wanting to sound too eager, but my voice betrayed me in that respect.

"The only splotch of black in the back corner."

I scanned the crowd, and though there were a few clad in black, my eyes fell on the tall figure standing alongside a regally dressed man wearing purple and silver. Zevander wore a black brocade jacket and trousers, the fine clothes making him look every bit a noble instead of an assassin. A full-sized stag mask with horns completely covered his face—as expected, no part of his jaw exposed. Strange that, for as much of him that was covered, I could still tell that it was him, just based on his rigid stance and the way he stood off from the crowd. Watching. Always watching. An unsettling worry left me wondering if he'd recognize me, as well. Perhaps more of a preoccupation than the mages hunting me.

"Beside him is Prince Dorjan. Keep track of the prince, and you'll always know where Zevander is."

I'd always know where he was anyway, as wickedly distracting as he looked in his suit and mask. "He's going to be furious if he sees that I'm here."

"It so happens I have a spell that can make him forget his anger," she said with a smile. "If you were to get close, just whisper the words in his ear and all will be forgotten, I promise."

"You've got a spell for everything." I rolled my eyes. "Well, what is it?"

"*Rapiuza'mej et rapellah'mej.* Forgive and forget."

"*Rapi-oo-zah-meh. A. Rapell-ah-meh,*" I sounded it out in a far less elegant accent.

"Close enough. You whisper that and I promise, he won't remember a damn thing."

"Got it. Hopefully I won't have to use it." I needed to tear my gaze away or risk that he'd sense me ogling him. "And which is the princess?" I asked.

She pointed across the room, to where a young girl stood, wearing a long, hooded, stark white gown, her hair coiled in soft brown curls. Hers was the only face not covered in a sea of masks, and I could see that she only looked to be about fifteen years old, at most. A somber preoccupation claimed her expression, and the way she fidgeted told me she was nervous.

"She's so young," I whispered.

"Yes. As was the goddess."

"This feels so wrong."

"Having gone through it myself, I can agree with that. However, if you gave her a choice right now, she'd undoubtedly continue with it."

"Why?"

Rykaia sighed. "Because men decided that the future of the bloodline was solely a woman's burden to carry. If she refuses, she will bring both shame and misfortune to her family. And, of course, the entire city of Costelwick will see that as a problem."

A masked man carrying a tray of champagne flutes strode up to the two of us. Rykaia lifted two from the tray and gave me a nod.

With a small bit of hesitation, I grabbed one of the drinks, as well. "After last night, I'm not entirely sure this is wise."

"The liquor I gave you last night is far worse. This is practically water by comparison."

After a quick sniff, I sipped the sparkly fluid, which sent a rush of deliciously crisp apples and a hint of cinnamon across my tongue. "Mmmm," I said, swallowing it back.

Mixed within the crowd were those wearing long purple robes and black masks, making them all look similar, as their hoods concealed their hair.

One of them passed, and I glanced over, noticing whoever it was looking back at me.

"Who are they?" I whispered to Rykaia.

"The Magestroli. The king's mages," she answered casually.

Studying their robes, which set them apart from others in the room, I nodded. "And you're certain these mages, I'm guessing the most brilliant mages in your world, would have no clue that the one they're hunting is right in front of their faces?"

"You'd be surprised. The most brilliant minds can be incredibly imperceptive. Come, I'll show you." She took my arm, tugging me after her toward one of the robed guests, who stood with their back to us.

Wriggling from her grasp, I ground to a halt. "This is foolish. If I'm going to be here, I'd rather not make that known to everyone."

"I'm attempting to put your mind at ease so you can enjoy the evening. Your scent is what identifies you as human," she said in a quiet voice. "They *will not* detect it."

"Wouldn't they be *expecting* trickery to hide it, though?"

"Perhaps. But unfortunately for them, there's no antidote for this potion. No way to undo or breach its cloaking effect. Now come." As I drew back my arm, she swiped it up again, giving an impressive tug that splashed some of my drink across my hand. Without slowing her pace, she leaned into my ear. "You remember Propulszir?"

At my nod, she added, "Good. Use it. An added layer of protection."

For god's sake, this was reckless. A thought that urged me to run in the opposite direction as we neared the mage, who stood before a painting of an ethereal figure holding two orbs of light in his palms. I summoned the glyph to mind, focusing on its distinct details as hard as I could, but a strange sense of familiarity washed over me as I studied the image on the wall, a feeling of dread heavy in the pit of my stomach.

The moment the mage turned to face us, the drink in my hand slipped, nearly falling to the floor. If not for Rykaia's quick reflexes, it would've made a clamor that surely would've drawn attention to us. Instead, there was only a minor spill.

The unmasked mage looked to Rykaia and back. "Excellent catch," he said, his smile too familiar.

The scribe from Foxglove. The one who'd pried into Grandfather's business and who I'd seen again at brunch with Moros, when he'd asked about the white stones.

Fortunately, the mask seemed to do a decent job hiding my identity and the shocked expression on my face.

"Are you ladies enjoying your evening?" he asked.

"Absolutely. The entertainment is top notch!" Rykaia sipped her drink, nudging me in the arm.

"Absolutely." While I held a vague awareness of their conversation, my mind had wound itself around the possibility that he might've known what'd happened to my sister. The scribe would've surely been present for her Banishing. Asking outright would've been foolish, though. Clearly, he was one of those hunting me, based on the robe he wore. Perhaps he'd been hunting me all along.

Rykaia tilted her head back toward the painting. "Magekae, the God of Alchemy and Father of Immortality."

"Yes. The embodiment of eternal life." The mage glanced back at the painting. "Our most blessed savior."

"As I understand, he was entirely obsessed with the Goddess of Death. Did he not imprison and rape her?"

At the mention of the goddess, I snapped out of my thoughts. "Morsana?"

"Yes." He smiled back at me and turned to Rykaia. "Some believe as much. Radicals, mostly. Others believe it was he who saved her. Her true lover was said to be the God of Fear and Destruction. Deimos."

"Was he not a mortal?" I asked, recalling the story Allura had told me.

"Prior to being cast into sablefyre, yes." His gaze swept over me again, lingering at the whistle around my neck, then trailing downward. "Your masks are superb." Except that his eyes weren't on my mask, nor Rykaia's.

I cleared my throat, trying to imagine something clever I could say to get him to tell me about what'd happened after I'd fled to the woods, the night of The Banishing. Anything I said would've revealed my identity, though. Instead, I bit the inside of my lip, the desperation clawing through me. An opportunity. A perfect opportunity to know if anyone had seen her afterward.

Except, I refused to do something foolish. More foolish than having walked up to one of the mages, anyway.

A second mage strolled up, that one wearing the hood and mask, making it impossible to see their face. Panic gurgled at the back of my throat, with two of them in close proximity, and I glanced away, focusing exceptionally hard on the Propulszir glyph.

"I see you've made friends, Anatolis." The deep, articulate voice of the masked man, along with the respectful bow of the other mage, hinted at his stature.

"I'm afraid I didn't catch your names." Anatolis tipped his head, expectantly.

"Lady Anadara and Lady Sivarekis," the other mage answered. His lips, exposed by the mask, stretched to a smile. "Did you miss their introduction entirely?" He chuckled, patting Anatolis on the hand, and I glanced down to see an onyx ring on his finger, his nails long and black to match.

"And this is our most esteemed Magelord, Akmyrios," the lesser mage said.

"What a lovely charm, my dear." Akmyrios reached out for my neck, but paused when I clasped my hand over the whistle.

"It's a family heirloom." I gave a feigned smile. "My apologies. I'm very protective of it."

"As you should be." The Magelord spun the ring on his finger. "Mine is an heirloom, as well."

A third man strode up, in a white tunic and black surcoat, with embellishments of purple heraldry. The regal angle of his chin and thrust of his chest told me he was an authority figure. A disciplined man, the way he carried himself, perhaps military, given the weapons strapped to him.

"Captain Zivant, have you had the pleasure of meeting *Lady Anadara* and *Lady Sivarekis*?" The way he emphasized the names struck me as odd.

"No." In a clipped tone, the captain turned dismissively, but I caught his pale blue eyes staring out at me from the holes in his mask. He turned to the scribe beside him. "You wanted to speak with me about something?"

"Yes. Both you and Akmyrios. Privately, if possible."

Anatolis bowed and smiled, before slipping away with the Magelord and captain down one of the nearby corridors.

Instincts told me to follow after them, for the possibility that he might divulge something to them about my world. Instead, Rykaia squealed beside me, snapping me of the temptation.

"It's them! Circ'Lunae!" Again, one hard yank of my arm had me following after her, as she weaved through the crowd before coming to an abrupt stop.

A dark figure blocked our path, and a tremor of fear shook me as I peered up at angry eyes staring down at us through a full-sized mask, before said eyes slowly trailed up and down as he seemed to take in what I was wearing. He gripped both our arms, pulling us toward a corner of the room. "What in seven hells are you two doing here?" Fury burned in Zevander's voice, and while it should've terrified me, I felt oddly titillated by it.

Rykaia sighed. "It was her idea."

I snapped my gaze toward her, the mask nearly flying off my face.

"You know me, Brother. I'd have much preferred being locked away in that lifeless tomb of a castle all night. But she insisted."

I scowled back at her, but Zevander clearly wasn't convinced, as he released me to pull his sister further away.

"Have you lost your senses?" Though fainter than before, I could still make out their conversation over the hum of voices at my back. He glanced toward me, his gaze lingering a moment, before he turned back to her. "The Magestroli are looking for her, and worse, you waltzed her right up to the captain of the fucking Imperial Guard! What were you thinking, Rykaia!"

"They have no idea who she is! The captain held conversation with us, without a single interest in Maevyth."

"They don't play a game of the obvious." The muffle of his deep, angry breaths bled through the mask on his face. "You will take her back to Eidolon now."

"You know we can't leave before the ceremony, Brother. Don't be silly. The guards are watching everyone who comes and goes. It'll draw more attention than if we stayed. No one leaves before The Becoming."

He gripped her harder. "Then, you will leave after. And you will not go near another mage. Is that clear?"

With as furious as he seemed to be, I didn't understand why Rykaia didn't use the spell she'd taught me moments before.

"Yes. No more mingling with mages. Leave after the ceremony. Spend another wretchedly uneventful night at home. Got it."

The spell, I mouthed, leaning to the side to get her attention, but she didn't so much as spare me a glance, her angry eyes focused on her brother.

"If anything should happen to her, by gods, Rykaia ..."

"Shouldn't you be with the prince?"

He let out a growl and threw off her arm.

Anxious, I strode up to him, gathering my dress to keep from tripping with my brisk steps, and placed my hand on his shoulder, as I rose up to my toes.

His muscles tightened beneath my palm.

Rykaia lurched for me. "Maevyth, wait—"

"*Rapiuza'mej et rapellah'mej,*" I whispered in his ear, as close as our masks would allow, and stepped back to observe, hoping I'd pronounced it correctly.

He shuddered and rolled his shoulders back. When he turned toward me, I glanced at Rykaia, who stood with her fingers pressed to her lips, as though trying to contain a smile. "Have you been drinking?" he asked, the question leaving me to wonder if I'd spoken the wrong words or forgotten them, entirely.

The heat of humiliation crawled over my cheeks, and I cleared my throat, taking another step back. "Nevermind."

Not sparing him another minute, Rykaia sauntered toward me, swiping up my hand along the way, and tugged me to follow. Keeping my gaze on Zevander, who stared back at me, I turned to follow her, and noticed the bunching of his shoulders easing, his clenched hands loosening, his rage from moments ago unfurling.

Almost as if he'd caught sight of the scorpion dangling at my back. Or maybe I *had* spoken the words correctly, after all.

"I swear he gleans sadistic pleasure in making me miserable." It was interesting, the way she constantly perceived him as a threat to her recklessness, much the way Aleysia probably perceived me.

"Or maybe he cares about you quite a bit."

"If he cared so much, he wouldn't lock me away in that horrible place."

"And you still see fit to pair us together?" I wondered if our commonalities were obvious to her.

"It's diverting to see him so *provoked*. And you, dear Maevyth, provoke him." Through the crowd, she led me toward a man with black hair pulled back from a face that was painted in silver and purple. He also wore a skintight suit of black, purple and silver. Guests had gathered in a circle around him, as he performed strange contortions of his body, bending and stretching into positions that seemed impossible.

Light throughout the ballroom dimmed, and the guests gasped in unison, as something moved overhead. I glanced up to see ribbons falling from the domed ceiling, where they hovered just above the floor. Two men in skintight suits—one the pattern of a snow leopard, the other like iridescent green scales—dangled from the ropes at the top. Both of them dropped down the threads, and I held my breath. A few screams from the audience echoed in the otherwise quiet room. The men caught themselves about six meters from the ground, where they hung suspended in the purple and black threads. The green-scaled man held a glass globe of fire, which he kept undisturbed while balanced on his palm, as he flipped and twirled in the long ribbons. The leopard-skinned man spun impossibly fast in the ribbons, the speed of which left me dizzy as I stared, mesmerized.

The man in the circle below them bent backward, which thrusted his groin upward, drawing attention to a massive bulge between his slender thighs. Some of the guests whispered and giggled amongst themselves.

"Oh, my," Rykaia said beside me, clearly enraptured by it, as she also stared.

While they ogled his anatomy, I found myself looking around in search of Zevander, and felt a slight tug of my arm. When I turned back toward the circle, the contortionist stood before me, twisting his body in a way that had me wincing. In his painfully disfigured form, he somehow managed to slide his hand down into the tight neck of his shirt and pulled out a black rose with silver edges.

Frowning, I stared back at the flower, which matched the one I'd discovered in the book Dolion had given me.

Straightening himself upright again, he stood and bowed as he handed it off to me, which I reluctantly accepted.

The crowd clapped, and the contortionist slid his palm across my stomach, his gaze lingering as he sauntered away.

"Well, you seem to be hard to ignore." Rykaia chuckled, and when another servant passed by, she traded the empty goblets for two more, freshly poured drinks, one of which she handed to me.

Music rose above the babbling voices, and Rykaia darted forward, waving me after her toward a massive clearing. For a moment, my stomach gurgled, thinking we were about to witness The Becoming Ceremony, as Princess Calisza stepped into the center of the clearing. Her brother strode up to her, lifting his palm to hers, and the two engaged in a dance.

"As he represents the future, Dorjan will be the one to give her away," Rykaia whispered beside me.

Others from the crowd joined the prince and his sister, forming a line of synchronized movements that complimented the music. In the dimness of the light that persisted after the acrobatic act, an enchanting seductive ambience blanketed the room. The more people joined, the more the clearing filled, until I could hardly make out the other side where Zevander stood. The line broke off into couples, performing the dance with each other.

Through gaps in the crowd, I saw the prince wave to the grump, who raised his hand to decline at first, but the prince seemed insistent, calling him into the circle. My heart shivered at the sight of him in his black jacket and breeches–a shadow in the crowd. A wolf in the birch.

A new song played, one whose drums pounded through my

chest with a sensual rhythm, the beat so powerful, it vibrated my lungs.

Zevander's gaze fell on me, and he flicked his fingers, calling me toward him.

"Do you know how the scorpion chooses his mate?" Rykaia whispered in my ear. "*Promenade à deux*. By asking her to dance."

My muscles trembled as I handed her the rose and stepped through the crowd toward him. On one hand, I was surprised he'd called me over, placing me in the center of the room with everyone. On the other hand, it made sense. Fewer were standing on the outskirts, as more guests joined in the dance, which would've eventually drawn attention to me.

"I'm not familiar with this dance," I whispered, glancing around for some instruction by watching the others. Rykaia had only shown me the waltz, and this was far more seductive.

"Follow my lead." With that, he banded his arm around my waist, his other palm against mine.

I managed to step on his boots a few times, and nearly tumbled backward before he tightened his grip around me, but his hands guided me with gentle force.

"I understand you intended to send me off to Calyxar." I kept my voice low and between us, glancing around at the others, whose movements reminded me of a battle between the couples, circling, pulling, pushing.

"You'd have been safer there. Far safer than you are now."

"What could be safer than dancing with a king's assassin?" My whispered voice held a small bit of amusement, but he had no reaction. "You gave your blessings to see me go. You must truly want me out of Eidolon."

"I don't." He dipped me backward, his masked face low to my throat. "But you clearly have no idea what hunts you here," he said, guiding me upright again. "Otherwise, you wouldn't have been so foolish to come."

"I'm sorry. I didn't mean to sneak behind your back."

"It isn't you who should apologize."

"But you're angry with me." Palm to palm, we circled each other, and he paused to dip me again. "I can feel it."

"Have you learned a new glyph to sense that?" He twirled me around, and we switched palms.

"I've not learned anything since you've decided to ignore me." I dragged my finger across his chest as I circled him, like the other women with their partners. Stealing a moment to observe one of the chiffon dancers performing the moves in a much more sensuous way, I added a bit more sway and saunter in my steps.

When I came back around front, he dragged me into him, just as the other men did. Unlike the others, he dug his fingers into me, pressing me hard against his solid chest. "I am angry at you." The deep timber of his voice rumbled in my ear, and he spun me around, keeping in time with the other couples. "For wearing this dress. For looking so painfully exquisite, you've managed to draw everyone's attention. Including mine." Still clutching one hand at my waist, we held the other above our heads, staring at each other as we turned.

A strange, magnetic energy simmered between us. With our gazes locked, his intensely evocative eyes seen through the holes in his mask somehow stripped me bare. As if I were the only person in the room. The sole object of his focus.

The unspoken desire that lurked on the fringes thickened the air and stirred my pulse, forcing me to look away. "I told Rykaia it was too much. But she swore I'd blend in. She masked my scent and aura."

"Yes, she did. I can hardly smell you, and yet, I still knew it was you." He gripped me with both hands that time and dipped his head to the crook of my neck. "You're incapable of blending, Maevyth." Again, we found ourselves palm to palm, repeating the same steps as before. "And the scorpion?"

"I like the way it feels against my spine."

He slid his hand to the small of my back, and my stomach

fluttered at the gentle touch of his fingers there. "I curse Rykaia for bringing you here. And yet, the thought of never seeing you in this dress is a torment in itself."

As before, I dragged my hand across his chest, circling him. "Then, you forgive me?"

He wound my body into his, my back to his chest, his arms tight around me. "So long as you do not speak to another soul while you're here, yes."

"There is one I'm dying to speak with, though. The unmasked mage we were talking to earlier. Anatolis. I know him."

Still keeping up with the steps, he made a quick visual sweep of the room. "Did he recognize you?"

"No. I don't think so."

"Then, why are you so *interested* in him?" Hands clasped above our heads, I felt the tight squeeze of his grip nearly crushing mine.

"Were I more astute, I'd imagine that troubles you." I twisted into him, then unraveled outward, palms clutched, and I smiled while imagining the ire in his expression right then. It wasn't my nature to flirt, but Zevander made it nearly effortless with his obvious annoyance. I only wished I could've seen his face. "He's handsome without being grumpy."

"If you like *boys* who can barely lift their own swords," he grumbled. "The words you whispered to me earlier. Where do you learn to say that?"

Lowering my gaze, I pressed my lips together, refusing to implicate her.

"Rykaia, no doubt," he said humorlessly, and we switched palms, stepping in the opposite direction. "You've not spoken them to anyone else, have you?"

Confused, I frowned. "Why would I?"

The corner of his lips curved, as if he wanted to smile and pulled me closer, the possession in his grasp becoming ever apparent as he held me against him with both hands. "This juvenile mage you mentioned earlier. What is it that interests you?"

I chuckled and circled around him. "He's a scribe in Foxglove. I attended a brunch with Mr. Moros, and he was there."

His head tracked to the side as I came around him again. "Who is Moros?"

"He's the one I was betrothed to. The one my step-grandmother sold me off to."

He made a growling sound in his throat, wrapping me in his embrace. "You're mated?"

"*Mated*?" Acids shot to my throat at the thought of being a mate to Moros. "No. I ran away. Into the woods. But Moros, he has mines in Lyveria, and he claimed to have come upon a chasm filled with white stones."

Zevander froze. Clutching my arm, he dragged me away from the dance floor, and against the wall. Not far from us, two of the scantily clad dancers seemed to be caught up in themselves, their bodies moving to the motions of sex, as Zevander caged me against the wall.

"What did the stones look like?" he asked, his voice urgent but low, clearly not wanting anyone to hear us. "Did you see them?"

"Yes. They were white and glittery. He had two of them, but he gave one to the captain, and it turned him into a horrible looking creature. The other, he gave to the monster in the woods."

His muscles tensed around me. "It was Anatolis you recognized?"

"Yes."

"Then, I will speak with him."

"I'm coming with you."

"You will do no such thing," he gritted, and even through the mask, I could tell his teeth were clenched. "Stay with Rykaia until The Becoming has commenced, then slip away. No one will notice the two of you have left."

I tipped my head to the side, looking past his massive body, to see Rykaia dancing with a man. "Wouldn't I be safest with you?"

In my periphery, the erotic dancers moved faster, and I turned to see the man's loincloth was flipped up. I quickly looked away, realizing they were actually engaged in the act not far from where we stood. A hot blush crept over my face, and as though he'd noticed it, Zevander stared down at me for a moment, his chest rising and falling. "Fine. You'll come with me, but do not say a word."

"I will not say a word, so long as you inquire about Aleysia."

"Doing so would mean I'd have to kill him."

"What? Why?"

"Because asking him about her would inspire him to think of you."

"Neither of us know his motivations. *Thinking* is not *speaking*."

"Thoughts can be extracted by a skilled mage."

"Even past thoughts?"

"Even past thoughts. But I suspect he hasn't stopped thinking of you since he saw you in this dress. Pairing you with Mortasia creates too much of a link."

I sighed. While his reasoning made sense, I certainly had no intentions of having the man killed. "I have to know, Zevander. It's killing *me*."

He traced his thumb over my lips and across my jaw in a way that felt intimate, affectionate. "The prince will be escorted to his chambers soon. I'll have the opportunity to slip away then."

"You make it sound scandalous."

He lowered his hand from my face, only to take hold of my waist with a possessive grip. "Return to Rykaia until then," he commanded, ignoring my comment. "I'll have Torryn keep watch of both of you."

The moans from beside us begged me to peek, but I refused.

As if sensing my temptation, he glanced toward them and back. "They make you uncomfortable?"

"I wouldn't call it discomfort, per se." I swallowed past the lump in my throat. "How are you so unaffected?"

"I wouldn't call myself unaffected." A downward sweep of his gaze, and he pushed away, releasing me from his muscled cage and his greedy clutch. "I'll find you after the ceremony."

As Zevander strode off, a woman dressed in gold armor, shorter, but equally muscled, stepped into his path. Clearly a Solassion, given her long, sunny locks and bronze skin.

His back rippled with tension, seen even through the tight jacket.

The woman's lips stretched to a smile, and Zevander strode past her. When her gaze lifted to mine, I scampered toward Rykaia, who stood talking to the princess.

"Ah, Princess, this is Lady Anadara." Rykaia took hold of my arm, and I schooled my face to avoid reacting to the fact that she'd introduced me with the wrong name.

I'd never formally met royalty before, had no idea how to greet her, but I curtsied, bowing my head, to which she offered a kind smile.

"It's a pleasure to meet you. Rykaia has spoken very highly of you, Lady Anadara." The delicate tone of her voice hardly carried over the obnoxious conversations around us, further reminding me of her innocence.

Clearly, she had a much closer relationship with Rykaia than I had originally imagined, using her first name to address her. In my world, the princess was untouchable and rarely seen by the public. It made more sense why Rykaia would want to be present at the ceremony.

"The pleasure is mine." I smiled, my nerves slightly on edge after the encounter with Zevander. "I had no idea you and Rykaia were close friends."

"She was designated to watch over me when we were younger. Something of a nursemaid, but horrible." Princess

Calisza giggled. "I think I was the one watching over her most times."

Rykaia elbowed her and smiled. "Tell me we didn't have the best adventures, and you'll be lying."

"I miss those innocent adventures." The smile on her face faded, and once again, I was reminded of the impending ritual. "Will you be here for the ceremony?"

"Of course. I wouldn't miss it," Rykaia lied.

Or perhaps she'd lied to me.

"Good. I'll feel better knowing there's a familiar face." She kissed the back of Rykaia's hands. "I'm afraid I must make the rounds and mingle." On those parting words, she padded off.

"We'll leave before it begins." Rykaia leaned into me and spoke low. "Just let me show myself, so she knows I'm there." The solemnity in her tone told me that she felt uneasy about the ceremony, too. "Once it begins, I doubt she'll care to look at anyone in the crowd."

"I still cannot believe that poor girl will be forced to do that as a spectacle."

"How was your first?"

I snapped my attention from hers and cleared my throat.

"You've not had a *first*, have you? Perhaps my brother isn't the best match for you, then. I understand, from the others at the brothel, he can be a bit on the rough side."

"Perhaps we can change the subject?" Glancing around the room, I fought the curiosity that her comment had just stirred. "He visits brothels?" Not that there was anything wrong with that. Zevander just didn't strike me as someone who got lost in the frivolities of sex.

She shrugged and looked out over the crowd. "Mostly during his moon cycle. Hasn't been in a while, as I understand."

"Moon cycle?"

She groaned and shook her head. "That's the time to stay

away from him. If you think he's grumpy now, you've not seen him when both moons cross."

Still without a clue as to what she was talking about, I frowned. "Why would he be cranky?"

"Imagine your body insisting on fucking more hours of the day than not. All Lunasier men suffer the dreaded moon cycle, which is why we have such a bountiful population and far more Nilivir than any other country." She raised her goblet up. "Nature's finest plan," she said, and sipped her drink. "Would you like a first?"

I recoiled at the question. "What? Absolutely not. What does that mean?"

"The men in loincloths make themselves available to anyone who might become ... aroused."

"Aroused by a young girl forced to bed a man in front of hundreds of people? That's repulsive."

"People are repulsive. But your reasoning would be different."

"I don't feel the need, but thank you for your concern."

Rykaia chuckled and sipped from her goblet. "I saw him corner you. What for?"

"The mage we spoke with earlier. Anatolis. I've seen him. In Mortasia."

"Are you serious?"

"Very. Your brother is going to speak with him."

"My brother is going to *kill* him. Mark my words."

"What for?" He'd certainly threatened as much, but I was curious to know why she thought so.

"For having looked at you the way he did."

"How could he have possibly–" But it occurred to me, it was entirely possible. In fact, it was quite possible Zevander had spotted us the moment we walked in.

"Nothing slips past my brother. Believe me."

"Then, by that logic, you knew he'd find us here, and this was all a game of resentment?"

She chuckled. "You give me too much credit, but you're not entirely wrong. He did insist that my name be removed from the guestlist," she grumbled.

"Well, it was just a look. Harmless."

"That was not a harmless look, Maeve. That was an *I-want-to-rip-that-dress-off-and-fuck-you-silly* expression. If I noticed it, you can be sure Zevander noticed."

"I should hope he wouldn't kill someone just for looking at me."

Rykaia snorted and turned back toward the crowd. "Be grateful he didn't inherit our mother's gift for reading minds. I suspect half the guests here would be lying in a pool of blood."

"What makes you so certain your brother thinks of me that way?"

"I've known him my whole life, and while plenty of women have taken to him, I've never seen him behave the way he does around you. Zevander is known for being abrasive and cold and positively heartless. Yet, since you've arrived, I've seen a side to him that I didn't know existed."

"I believe that's *aversion*. Disgust. *Loathing*."

She sighed and hooked her arm into mine. "I believe it's called lust and a severely besetting attraction, but what do I know? I'm just his annoying little sister who's lived with him for nearly two centuries."

CHAPTER FIFTY-TWO

ZEVANDER

U sually determined to keep his senses sharp, it was rare that Zevander drank while guarding the prince, but turmoil consumed both his mind and body. Between seeing Maevyth in that dangerously tempting dress, to his appetite quickly souring when he ran into General Loyce, he needed something to relax the fiery clash of tension blazing through him.

He tipped back the first goblet, finishing it off entirely, then filled it with wine from the elaborate fountain--the sculpture of a white rose--and swallowed back another. Dancing with Maevyth might've been foolish, given the eyes that watched him, but fortunately, everyone had seen the prince urge him onto the dance floor. Declining would've looked suspicious, and watching Maevyth dance with another would've had him gnawing off his own fist to keep from burying it in someone's face.

"Was that any way to greet an old friend?" Even the sound of the woman's voice stirred a dark violence inside of him.

"Who said we were friends?" Zevander didn't bother to look at her as he filled a third goblet.

General Loyce chuckled, the sound of it twisting his lips with disgust. "You were just a scrawny boy when I saw you last. Look at you now. A beast of a *man*."

Zevander had been young, only just having stepped into adulthood, when she'd made him her toy. He hadn't had a clue about his power then, nor did he have the training to fight. When she'd seen him last, he truly was a pathetic and scrawny boy, starving and afraid. Plagued by an unbridled rage that General Loyce had sought to smother and control.

"You clean up nicely, too. Are those the fine silks of a *high-blood*?" When he didn't answer, she leaned in. "If I didn't know better, I'd say you were attempting to blend in. Unfortunately for you, love, I could find you with a blindfold."

"If you value your spine and internal organs, I suggest you keep your distance tonight, General."

She threw her head back on a laugh. "I wish I could say that your threats enrage me, but they merely turn me on." With a lazy saunter, she closed the space, holding her goblet up, as if to assure she was only intending to fill it. "Would you believe me, if I told you that I think about you nearly every hour of every day?"

"You'll be disappointed to know I haven't thought about you, at all."

"Oh, I doubt that." Tipping back a sip, she stepped closer, her proximity sending alarms through him.

His palm itched to yank his blade and silence her.

Doing so would've started a war right then.

Instead, he ground his teeth and finished off another goblet.

"I think you hear my voice every time you take hold of your cock. I think you smell my cunt every time you come. And I think, somewhere deep down inside, you enjoy the torment I put you through."

A spasm of pain struck his skull as he gnashed his molars, wanting nothing more than to strangle the life right out of her. To set her aflame and watch her scream as her insides burned to liquid. He quietly set his goblet down on the nearby table to curb the temptation of using it as a weapon.

"I'm certain your little beauty over there finds pleasure in those delicious piercings. She has the most exquisite little body I've seen in a while. Perhaps I'll ask her back to my room for a bit of play tonight. It would be fun to watch her delicate little body ravaged by a pack of hungry Solassion men."

In a wisp of a breath, Zevander yanked his blade and held it at her throat, fury tearing through him in pulsing waves of violence. "You fucking look at her, and I'll carve your eyes from their sockets then cram them down your gullet."

"Bold words." The clank of metal from behind warned other Solassion guards had closed in on him. She swallowed, and the blade nicked her skin, leaking a skinny drop of blood down her throat. "One word, and they'll attack like a pack of dogs."

A split-second glance showed Ravezio and Kazhimyr stealthily approaching her guards from behind, lending no warning to the danger the Solassions faced right then. While the armored men were formidable, they hadn't been trained like the Letalisz in *mageduell*, a fighting technique that incorporated eldritch glyphs and blood spells. Solassions were nothing more than grunts who followed her command.

Zevander slid his tongue across his teeth, the enjoyment of her obvious humiliation exhilarating him. While the rest of the guests hadn't yet taken notice, it would only be a matter of time before the king caught him threatening the general, and then all hell would break loose.

He released her and stepped back.

Clearing her throat, she waved off her men. "Right. Then, perhaps you might accompany me to my chambers. For old times' sake."

"I'd sooner flay my cock with a dull blade than let you within arms reach of it."

"What a shame that would be."

"Keep your distance, General. Or, mark my word, you will be dead by morning."

Her lips stretched to an evil grin. "While I miss the scrawny boy from long ago, I must say, you have certainly not lost your fuck appeal, Zevander Rydainn. I'll be thinking of you this eve, while your lowly replacement does a poor job of pleasuring me. I've not had a proper climax since you left."

Without another word, Zevander strode off, feeling as if he'd sloughed a massive leech off of him. Had she not been the general of the Solassion army, he'd have gladly turned her blood to stone.

Tray in hand and dressed as a servant in a simple tunic and trousers, Kazhimyr strode up, as if to offer a drink, and Zevander plucked one of the proffered goblets. "Rekindling old friendships, I see."

"If she's breathing by night's end, it'll be by the grace of the gods, not me."

"She could only hope the gods would spare her a merciful thought." Kazhimyr gave him a subtle pat on the shoulder. "Do not let her rattle you, Brother. That is her favored torment, after all."

Zevander gave a nod, and Kazhimyr weaved on through the crowd, playing the role of watchful servant.

At the far end of the room stood a platform, upon which King Sagaerin stood, waiting for the room to settle to quiet.

Eyeing Dorjan standing behind the platform, Zevander made his way there. En route to the prince, he spied Torryn, who was assigned to watching the crowd, and came to a stop alongside him. "Perhaps you might keep an eye on my sister and Maevyth."

"I've been watching them since the moment they arrived." It seemed their disguise had failed to fool him, also.

Zevander gave a nod and kept on, until he reached Dorjan, who swayed on his feet, clearly having had far too much wine. An inevitable outcome, really. The prince rarely managed an entire night of festivities without getting drunk, and what'd happened in the village had only seemed to spur more resentment and anger.

More drinking.

"Zev'der ... p'haps y'might fetch m'friend." He wanted Zevander to inform his lover that he was ready for bed.

Having already anticipated the events of the evening, Zevander had requested that the young man head to his chambers early on, to avoid any suspicion. "He's waiting for you now."

"Ah, goo'man." He patted Zevander on the back and started in the direction of his chambers.

Zevander followed, scanning the corridors for any sign of attack along the way.

The prince stumbled, running into the walls, until they eventually arrived at the door of his chambers. Dorjan pushed it open, and within his lover lay naked on the bed, stroking his cock. As the prince peeled away his clothes, Zevander closed them inside.

While he should've posted himself outside the door, Zevander refused to listen to the prince fucking all hours of the night when he could've been keeping an eye on Maevyth and Rykaia. Instead, he summoned his scorpion and placed it on the floor in front of the door. Should anyone attempt to come after the prince, the scorpion would attack.

When Zevander returned to the ballroom, the king was addressing his subjects.

"My most honored guests, it is with great pleasure that I invite you to witness my beautiful daughter's Becoming Ceremony." The waver of his smile hinted at his disappointment. "The winner of this afternoon's match has been determined. Princess Calisza will be paired with Captain Avith of the Solassion Army."

A raucous of obnoxious cheering from the back of the room came from the Solassions, and a brute of a man stepped forward. The Imperial Guards maintained the perimeter, ready to act in the event the captain was anything but gentle with the princess.

Zevander scanned over the king's audience in search of

Rykaia and Maevyth, and found the two on the opposite side of the platform.

Gods blood, the dress that Maevyth wore stirred something dark inside of him. The way she so innocently swept through a room, not even realizing the yearning that trailed in her wake. The eyes that watched her every move because looking away would've been a godsdamn tragedy.

She was chaos wrapped in fine silk. The embodiment of trouble that'd nearly brought him to his fucking knees when he'd first laid eyes on her across the ballroom. So achingly beautiful, his chest hurt.

He thought back to the night before, when she'd lay writhing and moaning. The memory of her satin flesh clenched tight with her climax cast a shiver down his spine. His body had hardened to stone by the time he'd stumbled his way back to his own room. It'd taken three doses of his poisoned blade to calm him–three angry cuts that still burned beneath his trousers even as he stared back at her then.

And those words she'd whispered earlier ... asking him to take her and essentially ravish her, though the Primyrian word didn't translate quite the same. Clearly, she hadn't known what she was saying or asking of him, and her accent was a bit rough, which had struck him as odd, given the ease with which she'd spoken the language the night before. But that certainly didn't stop him from wanting to throw her over his shoulder and find the nearest bed. Sure as seven hells didn't relieve his already-engorged cock.

The blare of horns broke his musings as the ceremony began with Princess Calisza being escorted up the winding staircase to the balcony, where the coupling room awaited her. Goaded by obnoxious cheering from the Solassions, Captain Avith followed, his armor peeled away by his fellow soldiers as he climbed the stairs after her.

"Make her bleed!" one of the men called out.

The comment curled Zevander's lip. Cocky bastards. He'd have loved to silence every one of them with a quick cut to the throat.

Zevander looked away, his gaze landing on Maevyth, who stared down at her hands. When he scanned over the crowd again, he found the mage she'd talked to earlier in the evening, Anatolis, making his way toward the exit.

While the audience watched the princess and captain entering the chamber with rapt fascination, Zevander weaved his way through the crowd, toward Maevyth. The subtle brush of his hand against hers was the cue to follow him. As if trying not to look suspicious, she didn't fall immediately into step, but, instead, waited until he was through the crowd.

Smart girl.

Some of the crowd had begun to disperse. Others who longed for proof often chose to remain until the end.

Rykaia headed toward the wine fountain with Torryn trailing after her.

The guards at the door stepped aside, as Zevander slipped out into the courtyard, tracking after Anatolis. The mage rounded the corner, and Zevander silently ordered Maevyth into a shadowy recess. He tossed off the stag mask, replacing it with his usual leather mask, and yanked the hood of his cloak up over his head, before heading after the mage.

With his back to Zevander, Anatolis stood hunched over, and the sound of a snort alerted the Letalisz to what he was doing. Some of the highbloods mixed vivicantem with other stimulants and ground them into a fine powder snuff, which was said to enhance arousal.

On Zevander's approach, he swung back around and flinched, wiping his nose.

"Godsblood, you frightened the balls off me with that mask."

"Anatolis, is it?" Zevander didn't know all the mages by

name—only those who met with the king. He'd only recognized him as the bastard who'd ogled Maevyth.

"Yes, and you are?"

"Curious, is all. Why are you not wearing a mask?"

"I ... simply have an aversion to them."

Zevander nodded and, in the next breath, propped a blade at his throat. "I have an aversion, as well. To liars."

Chin tipped high, the mage stared up at him, his bottom lip quivering. "What makes you think I'm lying?"

"Aside from the princess, you're the only one who's chosen not to cover his face."

A knowing smile slid across the mage's lips. "They watched you follow me out."

"I'm certain of it." Keeping his eyes on Anatolis, he turned his head to the side. "Maevyth." The mere fact that Zevander had said her name aloud in front of him assured the mage would not be breathing by the end of their meeting.

She peeked around the corner, and as Anatolis attempted to turn his head, Zevander pressed the blade harder.

"Keep your fucking eyes off her."

Once she stood at his side, he summoned a black fog around them.

Zevander remained silent, staring back at the mage, a knowing smile on his own face as he imagined how he'd ultimately kill him. By plucking out those wandering eyes, to start.

Moments later, two mages peered around the corner, wearing confused expressions on their unmasked faces. They walked aimlessly for a moment, no doubt wondering where the mage had gone. One of them treaded impossibly close, and as Anatolis drew in a breath as if to call out to them, Zevander slid the blade's edge across his throat just enough to leave a burn there.

The two mages strode back toward the ballroom, and once he'd determined they weren't coming back, Zevander lifted the fog.

"You were in Mortasia. A scribe."

The mage's gaze flicked to Maevyth and back, but he didn't bother to answer.

"I can do this the easy way, or the hard way." Lifting his palm, he summoned a scorpion and let it crawl onto the mage's robe.

The man trembled, his eyes tracking the scorpion as it wandered over his robe to his tunic. When it scampered down his neckline, he let out a whimper.

Zevander smashed his hand over the mage's mouth, muffling a scream as the scorpion burrowed itself into his flesh. "Now, as I was saying. You were in Mortasia. A scribe."

He gave a frantic nod, and Zevander released his mouth. "It burns, please. It burns," he whispered on a shaky breath.

"Yes. It will burn an awful lot, if you fail to answer my questions. Why were you in Mortasia?"

His lower lip quivered to a pout, clearly not wanting to divulge the information. "The mages. They sent me there."

"Why?"

Lips pressed together, he shook his head. At what must've been an excruciating pinch from the scorpion, he clenched his teeth, tears leaking out of the corners of his eyes. "A vein. The Mortasians found a vein. I was sent to confirm and report back."

"And Cadavros? He lives?"

His nostrils flared with his heavy breathing. "You're asking me very confidential information. I don't even know who you are."

"My name is irrelevant. Answer the question."

"Yes. Cadavros lives. And he knows of the vein."

"The Magestroli lied about his death. Why?"

"I can't answer that." He whimpered, and at another pinch of the scorpion, he let out a scream that Zevander muffled with his hand.

"I have no reservations about gutting you open right here."

The mage's cries died down to sniffles. "The Magestroli were simply following orders."

"From whom?"

"Akmyrios."

"Was he aware of the vein when they banished Cadavros?"

"No. The scouts who were sent to Mortasia reported no vein. It's been dead for millennia. Buried beneath the Lyverian mountains." His body trembled, and Zevander glanced down to see the mage's hand shaking wildly at his side. "A man by the name of Moros discovered it."

The mention of his name stirred a rumble of tension, as Zevander recalled Maevyth's betrothal to the man. "And what is the state of Mortasia now?"

"I don't know. I left soon after finding out about the vein. There were … rumors of … mutations." His face ashened, a sweat breaking over his brow. "Horribly deformed creatures."

"Were you there for the banishing of a young girl? Aleysia?"

His gaze shifted toward Maevyth, who still wore her mask. "Yes."

"And did you see what happened to her after The Banishing?"

"I know … she emerged with Moros." His body jerked, and he let out a grunt. "I don't know if she is alive."

"But you saw her!" Maevyth lurched toward him, and Zevander let out a groan.

"I did see her. But I don't know her fate."

"And what is the Magestroli's plan?"

Again, his gaze fell on Maevyth, and he let out a shaky breath.

"Keep your eyes off her," Zevander warned again, and the mage's eyes snapped back to his. "Answer the question."

"To destroy Cadavros and strengthen the Umbravale." The only way to accomplish such a thing was securing the septomir.

"You wanted her to recognize you. What made you think she'd come tonight?"

For the third time, the mage's gaze fell on Maevyth and

lingered there too long for Zevander's taste. His rage quickened, and he flipped the knife in his hand, holding the blade to Anatolis's eyeball. "One more time." Fingers pressed into his socket, he pinned the man's eyelid open, watching his pupils dilate with fear. "Look at her one more time, and from this night forward, the only thing you'll be staring at is the endless, black void of remorse." His muscles shook as he delivered the threat, and though it wasn't like him to lose his composure, something in Anatolis's gaze had troubled Zevander from the moment he'd first noticed him watching her.

"I wasn't certain, at all. I didn't believe she'd actually crossed before tonight."

"But you knew when she arrived here."

The mage clamped his eyes, breathing hard through his nose, the sickly pallor of his skin turning whiter by the second. "Your sister …. They set her up."

A frenzied rage vibrated through Zevander's muscles, the urge to slice out his tongue taunting him. "How?"

"The names. There is no Lady Anadara or Sivarekis. They knew Rykaia could read minds."

Meaning, the guards had informed them the moment Rykaia had spoken the names.

"Why didn't the king kill Cadavros?"

Anatolis's eyes watered as he shook his head. He flinched and let out a gut-wrenching scream behind Zevander's palm. His body shook, convulsing with agony. The screaming continued, and Zevander clamped his mouth harder.

"Tell me, and it will stop!" he growled.

It didn't, though. Zevander drew back his scorpion that crawled out of the mage's robe, and still, Anatolis screamed. Eyes rolled back into his head, he collapsed to his knees. A red, gelatinous chunk stuck out of his mouth as he gagged, and it poured out, landing on the ground.

On a gasp, Maevyth jumped back.

Another meaty chunk followed the first, splatting across the wet stones.

Organs. Something was attacking his organs. A spell to keep him from talking.

Anatolis collapsed to the ground face first, blood oozing past his lips.

"The scorpion killed him?" Maevyth's voice held a shaky panic.

"No. But no matter. I planned to kill him, anyway." Zevander knelt beside the mage and rifled through his pocket for the powdered vivicantem.

A thunderous pounding echoed in the distance, and he froze, swinging his gaze toward the clamor.

He grabbed Maevyth's hand, leading her back to the front of the castle, where Imperial Guards rushed toward the gates. Flames hurled over the stony barrier, catching on the tents and straw scattered about the courtyard.

"The villagers!" one of the guards shouted. "They're attacking!"

The uprising.

"What is it? What's going on?" Maevyth said, and Zevander glanced back to see bodies scurrying around her, as she raised her hands to shield herself from their armor and jostling weapons. Solassion soldiers alongside The Imperial Guard headed toward the gate, while guests of The Becoming rushed into the castle for cover.

A chaotic bustling of the crowd.

Zevander scooped her up into his arms and carried her into the castle that'd grown crowded with guests pouring in from the courtyard. While she clung to his neck, he scanned for Rykaia and Torryn, finding them barricaded in the corner.

With quick strides, Zevander pushed through bodies, holding Maevyth in his arms as he made his way to them. "Take the corridor to the west tower and cleave yourselves back to

Eidolon." Over the din of screams behind them, his voice hardly carried. He carefully set Maevyth to her feet.

"What about you!" Rykaia shouted back.

"I have to find Dorjan. Stay with Torryn. Now, go!"

The three of them took off down the corridor as he instructed, Maevyth looking back at him as Rykaia dragged her along.

Zevander exhaled an exasperated sigh as he turned toward the unruly crowd. "Fuck."

CHAPTER FIFTY-THREE

MAEVYTH

Rykaia pulled me along, as I watched Zevander disappear into the melee. A voice inside my head told me to stay with him. That I was safest with him. Instead, I scurried after Rykaia and Torryn as they searched for a quiet place to cleave, away from anyone who might try to follow after us.

Rykaia darted toward a shadowy corner, and the moment she put her finger to the stone, the sound of approaching footsteps alerted us that someone was coming from the other direction. Four figures in gold armor stalked toward us–Solassion guards.

"Go," Torryn said, stepping around her in the direction of the footsteps. "I'll deal with them." Striding toward them, he removed his gloves, tossed them aside, and yanked away his cloak for a short, but vicious looking, cutlass strapped to his back. It'd managed to stay concealed beneath his cloak, somehow, and it was as he reached for the hilt that it lengthened to its full size toward his hand.

Hand trembling, Rykaia drew a shimmering line down the wall and stepped through.

As I lifted my leg to follow after her, something gripped my arm. Before I had the chance to identify what had clutched me, a hand banded across my mouth and yanked me backward, away from it. I sank my teeth into my captor's flesh, and they growled, releasing me. Once free, I jolted for that glowing seam with a single-minded determination to get back to Eidolon.

A weakness claimed my legs, like running through thick muck, and I fell to my knees just short of the cleave, watching the glow fade. My pulse raced as the terrifying sensation climbed up my thighs to my stomach. Reaching out for the slowly sealing exit, I opened my mouth for a scream that died to a choke.

The distant sound of Rykaia calling out to me faded beneath a piercing static in my ears. My hands fell at my side, my body shutting down on me without will.

The stone floor crashed into my cheekbone, and a shock of pain exploded across my jaw. I let out a grunt as I watched a black boot step into my view, the purple hem of a robe hovering just above it. The figure reached down and took hold of the whistle at my neck. In one rough yank, he tore it away.

Blackness swallowed my vision.

* * *

The scent of burning herbs invaded my nose and I opened my eyes to the lambent glow of candles. Hundreds of candles that illuminated a domed, white ceiling above me. The hum of quiet chanting dragged my attention to the right, where robed figures, in black and gold masks, stood in rows. At pressure across my wrists, I looked down to see my arms shackled in copper, the chain attached to a cement slab beneath me. I tugged at it in a frenzy of confusion, and when I kicked my feet, they too failed to move freely.

A cold, branching panic crawled over my chest, squeezing my lungs, allowing only a whimper to escape me.

I rolled my head to the left and found a gold brazier, from where a rich, black flame writhed and quivered in a hypnotic dance. Starved and restless for kindling, it seemed to reach out for anything to consume.

Beside the brazier stood another figure, wearing the telling purple and black robes of a mage, his face concealed by a black mask.

He held out his hands to either side of him. "Behold the last daughter of the Corvikae! A contradiction to all we represent." He held up one palm. "The father of alchemy. Of life, magic and creation." He raised his other hand. "And the daughter of death and decay. Her blood, when turned to stone, will bring forth the truest alchemical transformation. Through her death, we shall live. By her essence, we shall fortify the Umbravale to protect against our enemies. To drive out disease and famine, as is prophesied by the divine Goddess of Foresight. Together, with the six stones we've yet to reclaim, we will not fall prey to the Black Pestilence."

"Let me go! Please! I'm not what you think I am!" I wriggled and squirmed in the cuffs. "Please! I'm begging you! Don't do this!"

He lifted the thurible from his side, wafting the scent of dried herbs I'd smelled earlier, and dangled it over me in circles to form puffs of white smoke. "Magekae, lord of alchemy and knowledge, we call upon your wisdom and skill to tame the sablefyre, the force you created, so that we might carry forth your incorporeal spirit." Lowering the thurible, he tilted his head back. "*Egrezeder deosz! Da'haj'mihirit teviras!*"

A feminine voice that wasn't my own spoke inside my head. *Come forth, God of Alchemy! Give me your strength!*

Eyes on the black flame, I tugged at my binds, desperate to get loose, and glanced around for any familiar faces. Only a sea of emotionless masks stared back at me. A number of them wore purple cloaks like that of the mage standing over me.

From the brazier, the mage lit a small bundle of kindling, which he placed in a porcelain crucible. As he held it over my body, I stared up at the black onyx ring on his finger. The Magelord I'd met earlier. "She will burn in sablefyre. And her blood shall turn to stone. And the stone shall grant us immunity from the blight!"

"Covis honet et obedisz, petimirsj ze noz eripeh," the crowd chanted, their voices harsh and staccato, terrifying.

With honor and obedience, we ask that you deliver us, the voice in my mind translated.

"No, please! Don't do this!" My muscles shook with the futile effort of trying to free myself from the chains.

Wordlessly, he passed his hand through the flame, wincing as he scooped the fire into his palm. Without warning, he slapped his hand over my mouth, forcing the fire down my throat.

I kicked and struggled, the air in my lungs crackling with each gasp through my nose. A silvery glow in my periphery cast a haze over my eyes, the room closing in on the fringes.

"Stop!" My head screamed in agony, the words trapped behind fire. "Please stop!" Shackles bit into my wrists as I shook and wriggled for freedom.

A searing burn marked the flame's path, as it crawled down my throat into my chest, and I arched my back, a scream tearing out of me while the fire scorched my insides. Tremors shook my muscles, the darkness on the edge of my vision pulling me deeper.

It's all right, Maevyth. Come to me. Do not let them see your fear, the comforting voice said.

The room shrank smaller. Smaller, still. Until I stood in complete blackness.

A radiant light shone from behind, and I turned to face it. Squinting against the painful luminosity, I found the willowy figure I'd seen before. Morsana.

"He searches for me." She lifted her gaze, as if something hovered above us, but when I looked, there was only the fading rays of light and blackness beyond them. "He wants to destroy you."

"What do I do?"

"You command the flame. Remember that."

A searing heat danced over my skin, but when I looked down at myself, I saw nothing. No evidence of pain, or flame.

"Let the flame do your bidding. Now, go. Go before it's too late."

The darkness faded, fizzling away to that silvery glow from before, and I stared up at the mage who'd removed his mask, his face twisted in fear and confusion.

"Who are you?" he asked on the cusp of a whimper.

Something dark and scaly moved through me, stirring inside my chest. A white haze slipped across my eyes, as a cold and numb sensation burrowed into my skin and bones. I pursed my lips and blew a torrent of black flame at the Magelord's face.

The mages at my back let out a collective scream that reverberated through the room. As the Magelord raised his hands to shield himself, another searing flame burst from my lips, and the scent of cooked meat wafted through the air.

He stumbled backward. The skin on the back of his hands slid away to leave only raw glistening flesh, and when he lowered them from his face, I watched as two milky white masses slid from his eye sockets, plopping onto the floor with a splat. The mage dropped to his knees, then fell backward, convulsing.

Screams heightened to a pitch of terror from the crowd, and when I turned toward them, one of the masked figures raised his palm, his glyph glowing bright. Shocks of blinding pain curled through me, and I cried out, my body arched against the slab. Another mage raised his hand, and an invisible force garroted my throat, the pressure springing tears to my eyes. I shook against my binds, desperate to make it stop. The light waned, the view darkening, shrinking smaller and smaller.

Let the flame do your bidding, the voice chimed inside my head.

Overhead, I watched the black move across the ceiling, like shadows swallowing me. Tears streaked down my temples. The pain in my body tore at my muscles with hooked claws, while the pressure at my throat siphoned the air from my lungs.

Everything turned to darkness.

In the quiet of my mind, I saw a vision of myself dancing in a meadow of white mist and asphodels, my long, dark locks bouncing around my shoulders. How peculiar and unsettling to see myself, as if I were looking through the eyes of someone else. The distant echo of my twin's laughter brought a smile to my face. She twirled amongst the tall, white flowers, before she paused to look back at me, the mirth on her face sobering to fear. *"What did you do?"* The horror in her expression darkened, and a cold, branching dread crawled over my spine. *"What did you do!"*

I snapped my eyes open to screams. Loud, throaty screams of intense fear. Turning my head to the side, I watched bodies running into one another, a commotion of alarm. The mages gathered near the exit, but something kept them from leaving. A wall of black flame. I clocked the way it entirely circled the room, as if it'd caught on a path of kindling and formed a barricade around us, corralling us.

I stared down at myself to the metallic cuffs that'd melted away from my wrists and ankles, setting me free. As I lifted my hands, I examined the red bands across my skin, burn marks left there. The mages huddled into a tight group, their eyes brimming with horror as they stared my way. *Afraid* of me?

On the stone floor lay two piles of ash, where the two mages had stood before, the ones who'd inflicted pain. Confused, I raised my hand to my throat, the phantom sensation of pressure still lingering. What had happened?

Behind me and across the room stood multiple stone arches, and beyond them, dark corridors blocked by the black flame. No way out.

A bleak panic settled over me.

What did you do?

The black flame refused to die, as it burned with fervor in a circle around us, trapping us in the room. Shallow breaths sawed in and out of me, and I slid off the altar and looked around for a means of escape.

There was nothing. The relentless fire blocked every possible passage out of the room and the unbearable heat had me feeling dizzy, in spite of the hollow cold in my chest.

One of the mages darted for the flame, the gasps and screams from the other mages failing to mask the revolting sound of sizzling meat, the moment he made contact with the fire. Something thudded against the floor and rolled toward me, coming to a stop at my feet. A crimson-colored stone. *Bloodstone.*

Muscles trembling, I backed myself away from it, around the altar, and my heel caught on something behind me. I fell backward, the floor crashing into my flailing hands as I tumbled onto my backside over a mass beneath me. A body, lying on the floor, the sight of his empty eye sockets twisting my stomach. A tearless sob shook out of me, and I kicked myself away from him, curling my knees into my chest.

Oh, god, what have I done? What have I done!

A silvery, blue light glimmered over top of the altar, where I'd lay moments before, and I whimpered in horror when a hand shot upward from the center of it. Another hand followed.

I moved farther away, my pulse hammering as I watched a figure crawl out of the altar.

A head popped through, and at the sight of Rykaia's face, I wheezed a tearful laugh, the relief sagging my muscles as I tried to push to my feet.

She slid over the side of the altar, and another dark-skinned hand pushed through after her.

"Maevyth!" Rykaia rushed toward me, enveloping me in a hug that I so desperately needed right then. "I thought …. Oh, gods, I thought …"

"I'm okay," I said in a shaky voice.

Behind her, Dolion tumbled onto the floor and clambered to his feet, straightening his robes. He raised the hood of his cloak to cover his head. Frowning, he glanced around the room. "What in the gods ..."

"We have to get back to Eidolon. There's no way out." As I broke from Rykaia's embrace and lurched for the seam, she gripped my arm.

"No. You *never* cleave down." Her voice held a grim warning.

"What?" Tone muddled in distress, I searched her face for any sign that she might've been joking.

"You can cleave up and through walls, but never down. It's the gateway to Nethyria. The underworld."

"Then, there's no escape. The flame is blocking every wall and passage out of this room."

Dolion stepped toward me, eyes earnest as he took hold of my arm. "You control the flame, Maevyth. It follows your command."

I shook my head, distinctly recalling the invisible force that had commandeered my body when I'd blown the flames in the Magelord's face. The blackness that'd consumed me afterward, when I'd somehow gotten myself free. All of it out of my control. "It's not me that controls it."

"It *is* you. You possess the ability to control sablefyre." With a gentle nudge, he urged me toward the fire behind us, but I resisted him, refusing so much as a step closer.

"I just watched someone turn to ash trying to touch that flame. I want nothing to do with it!"

His grip tightened. "They did not have the power that you possess, Maevyth. Now, raise your hand and command the flame to allow you passage."

"How?"

"Raise your hand."

I lifted my hand, as directed, my palm held out to the flame.

"Close your eyes and imagine the flame parting way for you."

Breath trembling, I shuttered my eyes and brought to mind a visual of the black flame parting like a curtain. Heat blazed across my palm, and I jerked my hand back, opening my eyes to a gap in the flame and the dark corridor beyond it.

Elation bloomed inside me, and I let out a chuckle, only for it to be quickly smothered, when Solassion guards appeared from the dark depths of the passage—a half-dozen, or more, storming toward us. Dolion and I backed away, toward the altar, as they stepped through the gap in the flames.

Before they could reach us, Dolion thrusted his hand forth, and a shimmering wall materialized, like puzzle pieces clicking into place, climbing toward the ceiling and separating us from the soldiers, who pounded their fists against it. "Let's go! Quickly!"

I twisted around and knelt beside the Magelord, rifling through his pockets while desperate not to look at him.

"What are you doing, Maevyth! We have to go! Now!" Rykaia's voice brimmed with panic.

"I need my whistle!" I frantically searched his robe for it, shoving my trembling hand into whatever pockets I could find.

"There's no time!" Dolion took hold of my arm, and with reluctance, I let him pull me to my feet, and the three of us darted toward another arched pillar at the opposite side of the room.

I closed my eyes and held out my hand like before, except that time, I imagined a much wider curtain across the room, opening the exit further, allowing the other mages to escape through. Instead of following them, the three of us jogged through one of the arched pillars to a corridor within.

"The further I distance myself from that ward, the faster it will fall. We have to cleave back to Eidolon immediately." Dolion ground to a halt and pressed his fingertip to the adjacent stone wall. Before he could draw a line, his chin tipped up, and he stumbled backward.

A woman stood on the other side of him, garbed in the telling black and purple mage robe of the Magestroli, holding a blade at his throat.

"Hello, Dolion Gevarys. So nice to finally make your acquaintance," she said, her voice laced with amusement.

"And you must be Melantha."

"I'm flattered you know my name."

"You." The confusion in Rykaia's voice had me turning to see a troubled expression slinking across her face. "I remember you." Rykaia's brows lowered to a frown. "I remember everything."

"Yes, well, this isn't the time for that." Melantha raised her hand, but not before I lifted mine and closed my eyes to the image of Aeryz. When I pushed it toward her, she flew backward just far enough that the three of us could run in the opposite direction. Halfway down the corridor, we froze in place, our bodies lifted off the ground with ease, to a height that I could kick my feet.

Somehow, Rykaia managed to get loose and dropped to the floor, but before she could scramble away, she collapsed to the side.

"Rykaia!" I screamed. "Rykaia!"

"She's all right. It's just a sleeping spell." Melantha padded toward her, wearing a smile of satisfaction.

"Leave her alone!"

She swung her attention back toward me. "I've no interest in *her*."

"You're making a grave mistake, Melantha. Turning her blood to stone will not prevent the inevitable," Dolion warned, his voice strained as if pained by the spell that held us paralyzed.

"Yet, it was you who raved about it for years. It was you who led the charge to turn her blood to stone, was it not? You sent Zevander to kill her."

Frowning, I turned to Dolion as much as my movement would allow. "Is this true?"

Melantha chuckled. "You didn't tell her? Oh, you are a despicable man."

A remorseful expression twisted his face, stirring the ache in my chest. The betrayal left me biting back tears. "I was wrong. Very wrong. Maevyth has more to offer alive than dead."

"Of course she does. I've no intentions of turning her blood to stone. Not like the piggish men who dream of power they can't control." Her comment dragged my attention away from Dolion.

"Then, what do you want with me?"

"I want to return you to Mortasia. To your sister."

"What?" The unexpected response slapped me upside the head.

"She waits for you at the archway."

"Do not believe her," Dolion beseeched. "Believe me, Maevyth."

Do not believe him. The echoed words of the ghost I'd seen back at Eidolon chimed in my head.

"If I go with you, you'll promise to let them cleave back." It wasn't a request, but a demand.

Melantha gave a dismissive wave of her hand. "I have no business with these two. No interest in the stones."

"She's lying!"

Her viperous eyes snapped to Dolion. "You are the one who lied to her, Dolion. I speak the truth. Come with me Maevyth. Aleysia is very anxious to see you again."

I wanted to believe it, but I'd grown weary of being tricked. I had no idea who to believe. Who to trust. "What do you want from me? Why would you help me? I don't even know you."

"I understand you have absolutely no reason to believe, or trust, me. But your choices are diminishing by the minute." She drew her finger down the wall and pulled at either side of the seam, widening the view that showed the archway on the other side. Beyond it, my sister paced back and forth.

"Aleysia!" I called out to her, and she skidded to a halt, turning to me as if she'd heard me.

Confusion twisted her face. "Maevyth?"

"It isn't real, Maevyth!" Dolion urged.

"It is real," the woman assured.

The sound of approaching footsteps and the clank of armor alerted me to the guards that had gotten past the ward and were heading toward us.

"Go to your sister. Or stay and risk capture by the Solassions. Your choice."

A chaotic mess of thoughts spun in my head. Dolion. Rykaia. Eidolon. And Zevander. Would leaving mean I'd never see him again? Yet, staying ensured that I'd put all of them in danger. I didn't know the right answer. I lifted my gaze to Aleysia. My sister. Alive. "I'll go. Just remove the spell on Rykaia."

Eyes locked on me, she waved her hand toward her, and Rykaia let out a grunt, rolling on the ground, released from the spell.

"Maevyth! Don't do this! Don't trust her!" Dolion's kicking and squirming beside me was only a minor distraction from where my attention remained anchored.

Through the seam, Aleysia continued to pace, biting her nails, as always. I still didn't bother to look at Dolion when I said, "Please get Rykaia back to Eidolon. Promise me you will."

"Of course I will, but you cannot trust this woman!"

Even if that was true, I needed an escape. Fast.

CHAPTER FIFTY-FOUR

ZEVANDER

An hour earlier ...

Through the restive crowd, Zevander spied Kazhimyr and Ravezio, who'd originally been assigned to watch the Solassions—in particular, the unruly guards—but were now guarding the king and Princess Calisza amid the panic.

When Zevander finally reached Dorjan's chambers, he called back the scorpion he'd left standing guard and slammed through the door, finding Dorjan naked and passed out beside his lover, the heady stench of sex in the air. With quick strides, he came up alongside the bed and tugged the vivicantem powder he'd stolen from Anatolis from his pocket. Zevander poured a small bit on his finger and placed his hand over the prince's mouth. One abrupt inhale through his nose, and he snorted the powder, jerking his head back. The vivicantem served as a powerful sobering agent, even when mixed with other stimulants.

"What in gods!" Dorjan triple blinked, staring up at Zevander. "What is it?"

"The villagers are attacking. I'm taking you to the undercroft. Now."

Dorjan scrambled out of bed and gave his bedmate a shove. "Time for you to leave. Quickly."

The other man groaned, but Zevander had no intention of waiting on him. The moment the prince was dressed, he guided him out of the room, toward the west tower. Through the tower's narrow window, Zevander could make out Solassions in their gold armor, and The Imperial Guard in their silver, fending off the villagers who charged toward them in droves. They'd broken past the palisade the king had ordered after Dorjan's attack, and wreaked havoc on the gates of the outer courtyard. Destructive flames licked the night sky in thick plumes of ash and ember, from the fires set to homes and shops.

"My father once told me we need the Nilivir to remind ourselves of the gods' cruelty." Dorjan peered out of the window, the fury in his eyes from moments ago dulling to grief. "It isn't the gods who are cruel."

"C'mon," Zevander commanded, his only thought to get Dorjan to safety, or risk an invasion far worse than the Nilivir.

Dorjan followed after him, down flights of stone stairs, until they reached the undercroft–a vast space lit by flaming sconces and braziers, with arched, stone ceilings and pillars that stretched ten meters in height. An intricate network of tunnels spanned beneath all of Costelwick, an escape route in the event of a siege.

They passed stone statues and fountains, until they finally reached the hallway to the Validyne Holdfast, which housed the royal apartments. Imperial Guards stood posted outside the door and down the corridor, offering safe passage for the prince.

Still, in the interest of ensuring his safety, Zevander followed the prince to the door, his formal clothes serving as a disguise for the Solassion guards who stood amongst King Sagaerin's men.

Zevander bit back the urge to punch one of the guards who eyed him up and down, undoubtedly criticizing the ridiculous garments that had him feeling like a frilly boar on a meat platter.

He and the prince made their way to the entrance of the apartments, where just inside the threshold, Ravezio and Kazhimyr upheld their disguises as servants. He offered a nod on passing, then turned his attention to King Sagaerin, who paced back and forth. Standing off from him, sipping from goblets, was King Jeret and his wife, Queen Sonnehild. Princess Calisza sat with Captain Avith on the couch, while a quick scan showed two more Solassion guards and a few additional servants. Without a doubt, King Sagaerin would be shitting himself, having the Solassions so close to his son in their forced proximity to one another. Unfortunately, it was the proper courtesy to have his guest take shelter alongside him.

On seeing his son, King Sagaerin's eyes widened, and he lurched toward him, arms outstretched. "Oh, thank the gods!"

Dorjan swatted his father's hands away, his jaw steeled. "You did this! This is your fault!"

The king's face reddened with humiliation. "Careful, my son. I would hate to think you do not stand with your father on these matters."

"I do not. You've fattened the wealthy, while the Nilivir starve. It was only a matter of time."

"Guards," the king said through clenched teeth. "Please show Prince Dorjan to his chambers." Straightening his robes, the king took long breaths between sips of wine. "Thank you for escorting him to safety," he said, lifting his gaze to Zevander.

"Is it common to task your noble guests with *errands*?" King Jeret padded toward them, sailing a suspicious glance toward Zevander. While he hadn't seen him since he was a boy, Zevander didn't doubt that his general may have informed the king of his identity.

"Leoric has been a family friend and combat tutor for Prince Dorjan for a number of years." How easily the false name slipped from the king's mouth.

"Combat tutor?" His gaze cruised over the Letalisz, and on instinct, Zevander made a mental note of every Solassion in the room, just in case. "Perhaps you might remove your mask. It's rude in the presence of royalty."

"Leoric is the exception to formalities," the king answered for him. "He suffers from a rare condition. Quite contagious. You may want to step back."

Frowning, the other king did step back. "And are you a native of Costelwick?" he prodded, doing his best to whittle Zevander's false identity.

"I am. My father was a blacksmith." Not entirely untrue. If not for the shady dealings he'd had with the Solassions, Zevander's father very likely would've followed in his grandfather's footsteps and taken over the blacksmith trade."

"Blacksmith," he echoed. "An important skill in times of war. Is it one you acquired yourself?"

"Unfortunately, no. I chose to play with the swords as a child, as opposed to forging them." Charm had become a learned skill for Zevander. A means of concealing himself under the scrutinizing stares, though he'd have gladly ripped away the mask and showed King Jeret the brutal side of his nature.

"Of course. It would be interesting to see how a skilled combat tutor might fare against our own General Loyce."

Zevander bristled at the sound of her name, but bit back his repulsion. "Perhaps when the castle isn't under attack."

"Of course. Silly notions to pass the time."

"You are dismissed, Leoric. Thank you." King Sagaerin gave a knowing nod, a silent directive to keep watch.

Zevander returned the nod and exited the apartments.

Guards sneered at his back as he passed. Bold, given the fact he could've singed every one of them to ash in the time it'd take them to draw their weapons. He turned down an adjacent corridor, and at the sound of distant voices, he flattened himself against the wall, hiding in the dark shadows. Drawing a thick fog around himself, he masked his presence as he slid closer to where two figures stood within a narrow alcove. The one facing him was Captain Zivant of the king's guard, but the other remained unseen from his angle.

"I must have a guarantee, bound in blood, that you will not betray me." A tremble in the captain's voice stirred Zevander's curiosity.

"Bound in blood. Don't be ridiculous." The sound of General Loyce skated over his skin like razor blades, distracting him from the strangeness of the two rivals meeting in secret. "There are no blood oaths in betrayal."

"Should the king find out, I will be skinned alive. No doubt, by the scurvy assassin he's kept hidden all this time." The malice in the captain's voice confirmed what Zevander had known all along—he surely didn't like him.

The feeling was mutual.

"You leave Rydainn to me. As for the king finding out, it doesn't matter. King Jeret has promised a pardon for anyone who claims fealty to him."

"A promise isn't good enough!" Zivant growled. "I do not trust the motives of *any* ambitious king. Particularly now, when we've no idea what Cadavros intends. We lost the only mage willing to cross the Umbravale and spy on the mortals!"

"You lost a traitor. And good riddance. He spilled too much! Fortunately for you, we were able to snatch the girl away before she cleaved."

Zevander's blood iced at the mention of what he was certain was Maevyth.

"You have her, then," Zivant said.

"Yes, preparations are being made. You're certain of your Magelord's skills to manipulate the flame?"

"Yes. But what of the other stones? They're still missing."

"They're not missing. Zevander knows where they are. Your fool king believed him, but I have personal experience with how deviant his mind can be. And how ... *loyal.*" Her comment would've had Zevander laughing, if he weren't so enraged right then. "Which is why we took his sister, as well. He'll have to choose between her and his affections for his little whore."

An icy rage crawled through Zevander's veins, and his hands shook with the effort of keeping his scorpion from tearing out of him.

"It is not my intention to betray my king, but he is a fool to rely on the Umbravale to protect us. Anatolis has confirmed— there is a vein in Mortasia."

"Your king brought this upon himself, when he chose not to destroy Cadavros all those centuries ago. King Jeret isn't willing to risk the lives of his people, as Sagaerin has chosen to do."

How many years had King Sagaerin led him to believe Cadavros had been executed like every other mage and civilian who'd followed him? Why? Why had he kept him alive?

"I warned him this would happen. Even without a vein in Mortasia, that lunatic would've found a way to destroy us." Zivant rubbed a hand down his face. "And now he has access to sablefyre. Who knows how much vivicantem it holds."

She reached a hand to his cheek. "Be patient. We will secure all seven stones and possess a power greater than any other. Including the flame."

"And what if the annals are right about the Corvikae? What if they are immune to the pestilence? What if an elixir can be made to prevent the spread?"

"Are you willing to make the same foolish mistake your king made? To squander lives on the promise of a long-forgotten fairytale?"

"Of course not."

"Of course not." She gave a playful slap to his cheek. "Stick to the plan."

"And the uprising?"

"While I certainly loathe a mutiny, this may work in our favor.

Sagaerin's attention will be divided. He'll be forced to address his people. And his son's opposition." She leaned forward and kissed him. "Now, let us simplify Zevander's decision by turning the girl's blood to stone. He'll supply the other stones for his sister's life, and all will be well."

"And what happens to him after?"

"I have my own plans for Zevander Rydainn." Had he not been curious to know where they'd taken Maevyth, he'd have pissed on her plans by slicing his blade across her throat.

"You still have affections for him."

"Affections isn't quite the word to describe what I feel. Now, go. We've much to do."

With another kiss, Captain Zivant scurried out of the alcove. While Zevander wanted nothing more than to run his blade through the general, he followed after the captain instead, keeping himself cloaked by the fog.

Three of The Imperial Guard approached en route, and Zivant signaled for them to follow after him. The soldiers fell into step behind Zevander.

Violence churned in his blood as he stared at the captain's back. They marched down a maze of tunnels that seemed to go on forever, until they came upon an ominous door at the end of a dark, cavernous passageway. A sculpted, arched lintel above it carved a scene of a hooded mage holding a scepter. The wear and chipping over the surface made it appear centuries old.

Zivant pounded his fist against the door, the sound echoing down the hallway.

Zevander strode up close. So close he could see the tiny hairs on the back of the captain's neck stand upright.

The captain turned his head, as though sensing him there, and once again, Zevander had to restrain himself as the urge to smash his head into the stone wall prickled his fingers.

A small wicket door swung outward, revealing a hooded figure whose face was cloaked by darkness.

"Pre dominisz nozi Magekae, da'haj mihirit liberih iteriusz." By our lord Magekae, grant me free passage.

The wicket door slammed shut and, on a click of locks, the larger door swung open. Zivant urged his guards through first, then strode through the door after them. As the hooded figure attempted to close it, the door struck Zevander's concealed boot. He peered up at the door, and in his distraction, Zevander slipped through as an invisible darkness following after Zivant.

In what felt like an endless trek through a dimly-lit passage, Zevander's mind churned a violent storm of thoughts—how complicated things had gotten with Maevyth. Having to tear Rykaia from General Loyce's clutches was bad enough, but the idea of being forced to choose between Maevyth and Rykaia enraged him. It was precisely the reason he'd longed to stay away from her. In his world, the slightest show of affection for someone served as a dangerous bargaining chip, and the less Zevander had to barter for, the better.

The high pitch of distant screams echoed down the corridor, the sound of it curdling his blood. More screams and shouts erupted.

The captain upped his pace, the soldiers jogging after him. A crowd of robed figures raced toward them, nearly trampling them as they passed. Most wore the purple and black robes of King Sagaerin's Magestroli, but there were others in various colored robes with heraldry from all over Aethyria. A gathering of mages, it seemed.

"What's going on!" Zivant shouted back at them.

"The flame!" someone from the crowd shouted back, without bothering to stop. "It came after them!"

"Came after them?" Zivant echoed, frowning to himself.

They kept on, until they arrived at the entrance of a massive room with vaulted ceilings and pillars. Still cloaked, Zevander placed his hand through the flickering sablefyre that flanked the entryway and stepped into the room.

Remnants of the black flame blocked a few of the corridors, as he trailed his gaze over the destruction. At the center of the room, black smoke drifted upward, and Zevander came upon two piles of ash that'd begun to merge with each other, half scattered across the floor. He knelt down for the small bloodstones lying in the ash, and held one of them up to the light, relieved to see no silver markings in its surface that would indicate it was Maevyth's.

An altar of sorts stood at the front of the room, and he made his way toward the stone slab there, finding drops of blood scattered over its surface. On the other side of the altar lay what appeared to be Magelord Akmyrios, though his lack of eyeballs made it difficult to know for certain. Angry red flesh lined two empty sockets, and beside him lay the milky white remnants of his eyeballs. Tucked just under the Magelord's robe lay an object Zevander recognized—the whistle that Maevyth had worn earlier in the night. He knelt down and pocketed it, scanning for any other evidence of her.

Black steam rose up from the Magelord's skin, and Zevander turned toward the brazier behind him, where the flame contained within reached out for him. A quick palpation of Akmyrios's pulse, and the Magelord gasped, convulsing on the floor.

"Who is it? Who's there?"

Instead of answering, Zevander stepped past him, toward the brazier.

"What happened here? Where's the girl?" Captain Zivant rushed toward the Magelord, falling at his side.

"She … she escaped! She is … the purest of evil!" the Magelord said in a dry, raspy voice. "Might you have … some water?"

"No." Captain Zivant said coldly. "Where did she go?"

"I do not know! I can't see, you fool! Please! Take me to a healer."

Lips peeled to a snarl, Zivant nodded toward his men. "Get him out of here."

Zevander scanned over the room and, at the opposite corner, noticed an unusual gap in the flame. A quick glance toward Zivant showed him heading toward the corridor behind the altar with three of his men.

Zevander strode in the opposite direction, toward the gap, and as he neared it, he noticed the shimmering wall across the entrance. A ward. His skin tingled as he stepped through it, and once cloaked by the darkness of the corridor, the fog lifted from around him.

It wasn't until he'd breached the ward that he noticed a figure lying on the ground up ahead, clothed in a burgundy dress. Rykaia. Groaning, she rolled on the floor, clutching her head. Next to her lay three Solassion soldiers in their gold armor.

He hastened his steps toward her, and as he drew near, the pools of blood surrounding the guards came into view, their armor crushed at the chest.

Before he could reach them, something gripped his arm.

Snapping around, he drew his dagger, holding it to Dolion's throat.

"I promise you she's fine. She's just coming out of a sleeping spell. Go. Find Maevyth. I'll take your sister back to Eidolon."

Zevander snarled and sheathed his blade. "What happened here?"

"Solassion guards came for us. I couldn't move at first. When the paralysis lifted, I was able to fight them off."

Not wasting another moment, Zevander lurched in the direction of his sister, but Dolion took hold of him again. Growling, he spun around. "Unhand me now, old man, or you will be handless."

"Zevander! You must go after her!"

"They intend to torture Rykaia to find *you* and the bloodstones." Zevander snarled and yanked his arm free. "I'm not leaving her until I know she's safe."

"I will hand *myself* over to the Solassions, if it means sparing your sister."

He lifted his gaze toward Rykaia, his mind drawn back to General Loyce's words from earlier, forcing him to choose between his sister and Maevyth. Keeping Rykaia safe had been his priority since the day he'd returned from that fucking Solassion prison. He'd turned himself into a killer for her. As much as he'd grown to care for Maevyth, as much as he craved her, he couldn't abandon Rykaia. Not now. Not when he knew both the Solassions and The Imperial Guard were searching for her. "The mortal is your problem. Not mine." Damn the sharp stab in his chest as his cold words betrayed his heart. The urge to rip out his own tongue had his hands curled into tight fists at his side.

"Oh, she is very much your problem."

Zevander ignored him and kept on toward Rykaia.

"Fuck it all, you stubborn bastard. She's your mate, Zevander!"

Dolion's words brought him to a grinding halt, and eyes narrowed, Zevander turned to face him. "What did you just say?"

"I said she is your mate. I saw it in a vision. She wore your sigil, the mark of your scorpion. As did your son."

The words snaked through his blood with a burning veracity he refused to accept. Shaking his head, Zevander let out a dark and humorless chuckle. "That is a new low for you, old man. That, or you really are as mad as they say."

"I am entirely serious. Tell me you feel nothing for the girl and see how the lies burn your tongue."

Zevander gnashed his molars, daring himself to admit such a thing. As much as a small part of him might've loathed the truth, everything about her had felt different from the moment he'd first laid eyes on her. "This is why you changed your mind about the bloodstones, isn't it? This was never about sparing the last daughter of the Corvikae."

"I wish it were. At least then, I might be redeemable." He lowered his gaze and sighed. "I saw it before I sent you to kill her. I knew all along she was your mate. What was one mortal, after all, when the lives of millions were at stake?" He exhaled a humorless laugh. "I hadn't calculated the possibility of you being a much bigger threat as a result. The vision of you joining Cadavros arrived after I'd sent you to retrieve the stone, and it was then I realized killing her gave you nothing to live for. Nothing to fight for. And such a thing would put every one of us in peril. I made a grave error."

Nostrils flaring, Zevander flexed his hands at his side, desperate to keep from punching something. "You're a lying cunt that I should've left to rot in Corvus Keep."

"Yes. You should've." The arrogant bastard had the fucking gall to tip his chin up. "I practically begged you. But I am no liar. She is your mate. It's why you couldn't kill her, and why the black flame refuses to take her life."

"What does sablefyre have to do with this?"

"Everything. But there's no time for that. Go. Find her."

"I told you before. I'm not leaving Rykaia here with you. I'm not leaving until she's back at Eidolon."

Dolion nodded. "I understand. Might you have some vivi-cantem to help revive her?"

Lips tight, he strode toward her, tugging the powdered vivi-cantem from his pocket. Yes, it was laced with stimulants, but only a small bit would be needed rouse her from the sleeping spell. He knelt alongside her and poured a few grains onto his finger. In the same manner he'd administered it to Dorjan, he placed his hand over her mouth and Rykaia inhaled sharply.

Her eyes shot open, and she blinked, coming out of her sleep. "Zevander!" Rykaia jolted forward, wrapping her arms around him. Voice trembling with tears, she buried her face in his shoulder. "It's her, Zevander. It's her!"

"Who?"

"The flammellian from The Hovel. Melantha is the flammellian who hurt me. I wouldn't doubt she's been killing the sexsells," she prattled in a frantic string of words. "She took Maevyth. You have to find Maevyth. Find her!"

Frowning, Zevander stared off, his mind doing a shit job of absorbing what she'd just said. The flammellian? Melantha?

"You're certain of this." It wasn't a question, and he didn't doubt Rykaia's accusation. He simply couldn't fathom a motive, unless she'd tried to get to him.

"I am. And I don't know what she wants with Maevyth, but it can't be good."

"Staying with me isn't good for her, either. She isn't safe with me. Particularly now that General Loyce has taken notice of her."

"She isn't safe with you? Or you aren't safe with her?" Her brows lowered with the unyielding look Rykaia always gave him when she was about to be fucking stubborn about something. The gentle caress of her hand to the ruined half of his face caught him off guard. Even masked, he flinched at the thought of her touching it, but in that moment, she looked like their mother staring back at him. "Some women are fire in your veins and hell between your teeth, Brother. Accept that Maevyth will never be safe. And no one will be safe from you because of it. Now, go find her, or by gods, I will make every day of your life a tribulation."

Movement in the distance caught his attention, distracting his thoughts. Imperial Guards stood at the ward, running their hands over it. They slammed their fists against it, the barrier shimmering with each strike.

"Go. With Dolion. Return to Eidolon immediately." Without another word, he unlatched her arms from him.

Dolion stepped forward and gently assisted her to her feet.

The moment she was upright, she stumbled back a step and groaned. "Come, dear. We must get you home at once."

Rykaia clung to Dolion as he helped her toward the stony wall, where he drew a line down its center. On the other side, Zevander could see the Great Hall of Eidolon awaiting them. Once Rykaia stepped through, he let out an easy breath.

"Find her, Zevander," Dolion said, not yet having followed after Rykaia.

"Where?"

"You know where." Dolion cleaved a second portal into the wall, this one looking in on the woods. "Melantha promised to return her to her sister."

Exhaling a forced breath, Zevander rubbed a hand down his face. "You will take Rykaia and flee to Calyxar tonight. Swear to me."

"I will. I will take her with me tonight. She will be protected by the stones."

"Torryn will accompany you."

"Allura will also accompany us. It seems it is not safe for her to return to her studies in this climate. She's chosen to return to her family."

"Go. And, by the gods, if any harm should come to my sister, I will burn you to the ground."

"She will be safe with me." Without another word, Dolion stepped through the same seam that Rykaia had moments before.

The ward at the end of the hall dissolved, and The Imperial Guards rushed toward him. "You! Halt there!" Captain Zivant shouted.

He ignored them, the echo of Dolion's words sinking beneath his muscles and bones, stirring the beast that longed to claw out of him. A possessive, vengeful creature that urged him to stake his claim. Dozens of arrowheads clanked around him, one of them lodging into his calf, and Zevander turned to see one of the guards advancing toward him, the glyph on his palm glowing bright. Snarling, Zevander yanked the arrowhead free and, on a blast of flames, sailed it back at the guard, who exploded into ash on impact. Startled, the other guards hesitated, then charged toward him. With a sweep of his hand, Zevander drew two more of the fallen arrowheads to his palm and hurled them at his attackers on a lash of black flame.

His aim proved true as two more guards collapsed into ash.

The others slowed their approach as he stepped through the portal.

After his mate.

PART

3

CHAPTER FIFTY-FIVE

MAEVYTH

The silvery-blue glow beckoned me, as I stood before the archway.

Not even the distant sounds of trampling twigs and branches failed to break my attention from my sister, who paced on the other side of it as if she'd been waiting for me this whole time.

Fireflies danced around her, and I took in the state of her appearance—the length of her hair that'd begun to grow back. Bruises that'd long since faded. Her face bright and illuminated by the glowing reflection of the archway, and the spark of life that relit her eyes. The freshly tailored dress she wore proved she'd found refuge somewhere.

It seemed unreal.

Too unreal.

Heavy footfalls through the bracken grew louder.

"Solassion soldiers," Melantha warned from where she stood beside me. "They've followed us."

A threat that should've goaded me to step through to where my sister waited for me, but I couldn't shake the feeling of suspicion writhing at the pit of my stomach. The oily sense of betrayal and skepticism that'd begun to simmer, the moment I saw her through that portal. Was she even real? At the same time, I couldn't turn back. Not when there was the slightest chance that I might embrace her again. Not when the possibility of reuniting with her was literally within arm's reach.

"Aleysia!" I called out to her, and she glanced around, as if she couldn't discern where the sound had come from. "Aleysia! I'm here!"

She ran in the opposite direction, toward the woods on her side.

"No!" I slammed my hands against the surface, the watery barrier of the archway as impenetrable as the day I'd arrived and tried to step back through. "Aleysia!"

"This way!" the soldiers shouted in the distance, as if alerted by my racket.

"Place your hand on the ward, Maevyth. And repeat my words." From my periphery, Melantha canted her head, clearly trying to grab my attention, but I couldn't break from my thoughts.

Anxiety thrummed through me while I stared at the empty woods on the other side. Did I trust this woman? I didn't know who I could trust anymore. What if she'd led me there, only to throw me into the chasm under the guise of helping me? Through a murk of thoughts, I tried to tease a motive.

"Maevyth, please. We don't have time," she urged, and mindlessly, I did as she instructed, placing my palm against the strange watery shield. *"Zi da'dignio, septimiusz me liberih iteriusz."*

"Zi da'dignio, septimiusz me liberih iteriusz," I muttered quietly, the uncertainty clawing at my conscience. Not a moment later, my hand slipped through the barrier.

"Go. Find your sister."

Frowning, I stared at my half-breached arm. *No.* Something didn't feel right.

Run.

An arrow speared the ground only inches from where I stood, and I jumped back, retracting my hand. In the short distance, soldiers marched through the trees toward us, one of them nocking another arrow, while the others drew their weapons.

"Go now!"

A powerful force struck my back, knocking me through the glimmering archway to the other side, where the cold forest bed slammed into my palms as I tumbled to the ground.

The atmosphere instantly changed.

The glow from the other side had dimmed to a brute darkness, the surrounding trees illuminated only by the full moon overhead. Eerie silence hung in the air and felt thick and suffocating. No light from the archway. No fireflies dancing about. Only the frigid cold that chewed at my bones as I pushed to my feet.

I'd passed through, back to Mortasia.

A glance back at the archway showed nothing more than my reflection against the blackness of the forest—an unnerving sight that had me looking away.

Shivering, I scanned the thorn bushes for any sign of my sister. "Aleysia," I said, quieter than before, only to be met by silence.

The creeping realization that she might've been nothing more than an illusion, a trickery, crawled over the back of my neck. And still, beneath that treachery festered an unfounded sliver of possibility. A sixth sense, of sorts, which kept me from turning back.

I started off in the direction I'd seen her run, stepping cautiously through the briars. The darkness itself was a predator, watching me with its endless eyes, its cold breath across my neck a constant reminder of its presence. Images of Uncle Riftyn having been flayed taunted my thoughts, as I searched the trees for the creature I'd seen that night.

Hairs on the back of my neck stood on end, the forest

completely devoid of any life. No wickens, birds, bats, or any sign of predators lurking amongst the trees. And yet, I felt eyes watching me as I plodded over bracken and dead vegetation, which pummeled the soles of my feet. The slippers I'd worn for The Becoming ceremony were useless against the rough terrain. An unsettling fear crawled beneath my skin, made ever more aware, the deeper I ventured with no sign of Aleysia.

As if I *had* been tricked.

The moon watched me from overhead, its luminous eye the only beacon I had to guide me.

"Maevyth!" Aleysia called out to me in a voice that held far too much whimsy to belong to my sister.

The moment I opened my mouth to answer, the rule of the forest sprang to mind and the words withered on my tongue. *Never answer to the sound of your own name.* Instead, I kept on, eyes cautiously scanning the trees.

After what felt like an hour, or more, had passed, I finally spied the second archway ahead of me.

An overwhelming relief bloomed in my chest, the closer I padded toward it. No matter the terms upon which I'd left Agatha, so long as Aleysia was alive, I'd forgive. As I neared the entryway to home, I promised myself that I'd harbor no grudge against my step-grandmother. After all, it'd been Uncle Riftyn who'd helped me escape that night. Without him, I couldn't begin to imagine what would've happened to me.

At the threshold, I pushed my hand through, noting the stark difference in temperature, colder outside of the woods. With careful steps, I passed through and found myself on familiar ground, absent of warm welcome.

Winter had arrived, the ground a blanket of white, as I stared across the yard to the cottage. No smoke from the chimney. No lights through the windows. Nothing but a dark stillness that left me wondering if anyone still lived there.

I glanced back toward the forest.

Could I turn back if I wanted, or was it too late?

"Maevyth!" Aleysia's voice called out to me, and I snapped my attention in the direction of the cottage. Without much direction from my head, I jogged across the dirt road, eyes on the windows for any sign of movement, until I reached the entry door and pushed through to the dark parlor within. A stark cold nipped at my skin, and I crossed my arms over my chest, glancing around at the signs of abandonment. Agatha's teacup sat out on a coffee table, mold crawling over the rim of it, onto the saucer. Her beloved reading chair tipped on its side. Tattered curtains danced in the breeze blowing in through the cracked window.

I didn't dare call out for Aleysia, for fear that only silence would answer.

Or something else.

Having swept through the lower level to find no sign of her, I made my way up the staircase to the upper level, peering into the rooms for Agatha, or Uncle Felix. I didn't care who I encountered, so long as they had a pulse. When those rooms showed no sign of life, I climbed the staircase to the attic.

My old room was probably the warmest, but cold enough to stoke the shivers wracking my bones. Standing in the remnants of what I remembered, I suddenly yearned for the warm bed back at Eidolon, the hearth, and Magdah's tea. A glance around the small space showed no evidence that anyone had been there since that fateful day Aleysia had been dragged away. The beds stood undisturbed and neatly made, my slippers tucked beneath. Weavers hung unmoving from the ceilings overhead, and I wondered if their herbal bellies were full of nightmares witnessed in my absence.

What had happened here?

Where had everyone gone?

I crossed the room to the dresser and dragged my finger over a thick layer of dust. Far too thick for the couple of weeks I'd gone missing. It coated my finger, and I frowned, rubbing it away. Lifting my gaze showed opaque tangles of cobwebs at the ceiling, as if no one had lived there in quite some time.

What had happened after the night of The Banishing?

A soft tapping snagged my attention, and I spun around, searching the dark room for the source .

An unbidden image of The Banishing Man flashed through my mind, casting a chill down my spine. Eyes clamped, I willed it away, for fear my mind might easily materialize the terrifying visual in my head. When I opened them again, a mouse scampered from beneath my bed to Aleysia's, and I breathed a sigh of relief.

Even so, I hurried out of the room and back down the staircase to the first floor. The door to the cellar stood open, and I shook my head, refusing to investigate there. *Don't be a fool.* Instead, I headed in the direction of the entry door.

Something struck the back of my head on an explosion of stars and a jarring shockwave of pain. Pressure swelled in my skull and sinuses, my vision blurring in and out of focus. I swayed on my feet, desperate to keep upright, and as the room spun around, I searched for something to anchor myself, to catch my bearings again.

In the center of the nauseating whirlwind, a tall, shadowy figure watched me crash to the floor.

CHAPTER FIFTY-SIX

MAEVYTH

rip. Drip. Drip.

Sharp pain throbbed in my skull. I groaned and winced at the ache there. *Cold. So cold.* A relentless tremble vibrated across my bones, my body failing to find warmth. The gnawing cold locked every muscle into an endless shiver. A horrible stench assaulted my nose, like that of a rotting animal, and I opened my eyes to a glass shield, beyond which I could see wooden rafters and shadows flickering across them. Surrounding walls closed in on me in a suffocating clutch.

Drip. Drip. Drip.

The ice box. What Aleysia and I used to call the ice casket that Uncle Felix used for showing and storing bodies before embalming them.

A gnawing cold chewed deeper into my flesh.

Above me sat about thirty pounds of ice scattered over a metal lid, with an opening through which to see. Enclosing the ice to keep it chilled was the wooden lid with a glass shield over the face–often locked in place.

I gasped a breath and pushed against the metal panel on top of me. "Help me! Help!" A numbing ache swelled in my fingers and toes. Worse than that, though, I had an intense fear of confined spaces, and I could feel the prickles across my chest, as panic burrowed its way into my head.

Fire zapped up my wrist when I banged harder against the lid of the coffin. "Help me!"

A shadow slipped past, and I quieted, breaths shaky as I peered through the glass in search of whatever it was. "Uncle Felix?"

The figure slowly stepped into view of the glass shield, and my heart caught in my throat. Half of his face looked as if it'd been melted away, just like that of the captain's whom Moros had chained in his basement. Nothing but a blank canvas of pale skin. His neck had shortened, his head merged with his shoulders, and I could just make out what reminded me of long, spindly spider legs sticking out from his back, shadowy limbs seen over the top of his head. Macerated lips looked to have been chewed away by something, his skeletal teeth bared. He tapped a finger to the glass, the bone exposed as though something had chomped the skin and flesh there, too.

I let out a gut-wrenching scream, and twitching, he slammed his fist against the box, releasing a grunt. Shallow, panted breaths escaped me when he stepped out of view again, and my mind spun in chaos, trying to imagine how I might escape.

At the click of what I presumed was the lock, the wooden lid flew back, and my stomach curled with tension and terror. "No," I whimpered. I fought to hold the metal lining closed, as a force tugged hard against me. Using every ounce of my strength, I clutched the ice-laden lid, so cold a white-hot pain streaked across my hand.

Uncle Felix snarled and pounded his fist against my fingers.

I let out a scream when the crushing pain radiated across my hand, and I curled my fingers into my chest. The ice clattered to the floor as he tore back the metallic lid, and I stared up in horror, taking in the whole of his deformities. The exposed ribs on half his chest, the pale and bony state of his body, as though he'd starved for months. And his exposed genitals that hung between his thighs.

He leaned over me and ran his chewed-up finger down my cheek in a gentle caress, but my whole body quaked with cold and fear. His hand drifted further down, to the bodice of my dress.

Tears sprang to my eyes, my thoughts spinning back to the night I found him fondling the Lyverian girl's corpse. He ran his mutated palm over my breast, and I clenched my teeth.

"No!" I slapped his hand away.

A terrifying roar ripped out of him, vibrating his bony ribs, the sound skating down my spine. He gripped my hair, and a blistery pain licked my scalp.

One hard yank nearly threw me out of the casket, but I clung to the edge of it, fighting him. I punched at his arms, trying to loosen his grip, which only seemed to enrage him, as he snarled and snapped his teeth at me.

"Uncle Felix! Stop!" I screamed, wrestling with him until I tumbled out of the casket onto the floor. The impact dislodged his grip of my hair, and I scrambled backward, noting the state of his legs, the bones sticking out in odd places, as if they'd been busted.

He lurched toward me, and on instinct, I held up my hand, imagining the spine glyph. Nothing but a pile of bones spewed forth, clacking against the floor.

Uncle Felix stared down at them for a moment, and in his distraction, I pushed to my feet, backing myself away. He staggered closer. Closer.

Desperate for escape, I trailed my gaze over the room in search of somewhere I could run. Nothing but walls of specimens and strange fluids, and his grotesque tools that I imagined he'd planned to use on me. The only exit was beyond him.

I had to get past him, somehow.

He lurched again, and I lifted my palm for the Aeryz glyph. An invisible force blasted him backward, slamming him against the adjacent wall.

Seizing the opportunity, I darted for the door, leaping over him.

A tight yank of my throat thew me backward, as the scorpion necklace bit hard into my flesh. I dropped to the floor, smacking my tailbone against the concrete. A jagged flash of light spiraled up the back of my neck, and stars exploded in my eyes for a second time, the pain rippling through my spine. On a groan, I turned in time to see him scramble over top of me.

A scream ripped past the dryness of my throat, and I kicked back. Bony hands clawed at my legs, and with a tight grip, he pried them open, pushing the skirt of my dress aside. His manhood dangled perilously close to me, and in a panic, I glanced around for something to use as a weapon. Suspended above me was the embalming needle, set beside the edge of the casket. In my struggle, I reached up for it, knocking it away, as he wrenched my body closer to him, wedging himself between my knees. A burning tension surged through me, and I reached again, the tip of the needle dancing around my jerking fingers.

The sound of tearing fabric hurtled me into hysterics, as he ripped away my undergarments. "Please!" I choked back a sob. At last, I took hold of the needle and, with a quick strike, jabbed it into his ear, lodging it deep and yanking its curved tip downward.

He let out another roar that shattered my courage, but as he pushed up from me, I gripped the handheld pump and squeezed the fluids. He screeched again, tugging at the needle ordinarily meant to pierce the carotid artery. I kicked myself away, watching him tear it from his ear on the sound of squelching meat.

He swiped out for me, just missing my leg, and fell forward.

Urgency pounded through my muscles, and I pushed to my

feet and dashed out of the room, down the long, dark corridor. I could hear him chasing after me, the heavy thud of his footfalls closing in.

To my horror, he crawled over the walls beside me with the ease of an enormous spider, the legs protruding from his spine a vision of absolute terror, and I came to a skidding halt as he leaped in front of me, once again blocking my exit.

Tears formed in my eyes, exhaustion weighing heavy on my muscles.

His lips stretched to a smile, his ear oozing a black liquid that dripped down his face. He hobbled toward me again, but there was no exit at the opposite end of the corridor.

I was trapped.

For the second time tonight.

Let me help you, the familiar voice inside my head chimed, and I closed my eyes to the blackness. In that space, I heard the heavy clunk of his footfalls advancing toward me.

When I lifted my lids, through the haze of white that clouded my vision, the spinal glyph burned in my mind. I threw out my hand, and a long, bony whip lashed out on a wicked snap, just missing his skull.

In absolute bewilderment, I stared down at the stretch of bones that must've reached five meters in length, the end of it captured in my trembling palm. I drew back my arm, and the bones scraped over the concrete floor, retracting back into my hand.

Uncle Felix paused only a second before hobbling for me again.

Again, I threw out my hand, and the bones unfurled toward him at lightning speed, snapping against his chest.

He froze in place, trembling. Not a breath later, a loud splintering sound crackled down the corridor, and his body slumped into a pile of loose skin, his head landing on top of it. The haze over my eyes lifted, and I yanked at the bone whip, drawing it back. It retracted into my hand on an aching throb, the spinal glyph glowing impossibly bright in the dim surroundings. A frigid tendril of disbelief crawled over the back of my neck, and I lifted my gaze to where Uncle Felix lay snarling, nothing but a pile of broken bones and flesh.

Tears slipped down my cheeks, the cold spreading across my chest in frosty tingles as I stumbled toward him. Only his eye and mouth moved, absent of teeth that lay scattered around him.

Breathing hard through my nose, I made my way to the staircase, but halfway there, a hard pounding caught my attention, bringing me to a halt once again.

I desperately wanted to ignore it and escape the house, but all I could imagine was Aleysia, trapped inside another ice box, begging for escape. I followed the sound to the main morgue, where Uncle Felix used to store the embalmed bodies in the small compartments that lined the walls. Those ready to be buried.

Still trembling, I padded carefully toward them. "Aleysia?"

"Maeve?" she answered, and with a blossom of hope stirring in my chest, I yanked open the doors of the narrow-bodied cabinets in search of her.

One of the doors beside me flew open on its own, and I backed myself away, frowning. A body crawled out, its pale white skin stretched over sharp, spiny bones. Silvery gray hair lay straggled over its shoulders as it climbed down the wall of compartments. Clutched in its arm was the decaying remains of what appeared to be a severed head. Only the few features that remained intact–the teeth, nose and small patches of fur—told me it belonged to a cat.

I backed away to the door, as the body crawled toward me, and when it finally lifted its head, I held my breath.

Agatha.

A spine-tingling yowl rattled past her lips that were carved with long black cracks.

She scuttled toward me on all fours, and I threw out my palm toward her. The bone whip wrapped around her neck, and before she could reach out for it, I retracted, tearing her head from her body in a spray of viscous, black fluid. At the same time I pulled back the whip, her head rolled across the floor toward me, the rest of her body collapsing.

My muscles locked up as I stared down at her mangled face, and something black crawled over her milky white eyeballs. With long, black legs, it stepped out onto the bridge of her nose, revealing itself to be a black spider.

As I backed myself toward the door, it slowly crawled over her nose to the floor. More black spiders erupted from her nose, her eyes, her mouth. They poured out of the neck of her headless torso.

I spun on my heel and dashed down the hallway toward the staircase. As I clutched the rail, I looked back and wheezed a breath on seeing hundreds of spiders scuttling toward me. I jogged up the staircase, slamming the door shut behind me.

Backing away, I took long, heaving breaths, and to my horror, the spiders slipped beneath the crack of the door.

"No!" Sapped of energy, I raced out of the house, into the darkness, but managed only a few short feet before I felt something crawl up the hem of my skirt and across my ankle.

A scream ripped out of me, and I stomped the ground and lifted my skirt to swat the spider off of me. Eyes wide, I nearly choked when a glance upward showed hundreds more scampering toward me in a horde of black against the white snow. Before I could so much raise my hand for the aeryz glyph, they leapt onto my dress, skittering up to my bodice. Through hoarse screams, I swatted and flailed, feeling their tiny legs and bulbous bodies scuttling across my skin.

"Maevyth!" the voice inside my head called out, but it was futile. Any glyph I might've used in defense was smothered by the cluster of spiders that scurried up my arms.

At the first prod of a spider leg against my lips, I clamped my mouth shut, as my body erupted into a wild frenzy. I swatted at my face and arms, and fell to the ground, kicking and rolling. The more I fought to dislodge them, the more they swarmed me.

So lost in panic, I didn't even notice the moment that they'd finally stopped moving.

Not until every one of the spiders shot upward, into the air and I stilled, gasping for breath when they no longer covered my face. My head fought to make sense of what I was seeing.

Above me loomed a hideous cloud of black carapaces, as if suspended by an invisible force. I didn't bother to investigate why, or how, but just scrambled to my feet and blindly ran in the opposite direction. When I glanced back, I plowed into something hard and unyielding.

A scream rattled out of me, and on instinct, I pounded my fists against the wall of a body. "Let me go! Let me go!" I looked up to see Zevander staring down at me, and in that instant, my muscles sagged in relief. A heavy sob wracked my body, and I wrapped my arms around him. It only lasted a moment, though, before another wave of panic washed over me.

Before I even spoke a word of the ensuing spiders, a blast of heat warmed my back, and I turned in time to see Zevander send a torrent of black flames over the floating cluster of arachnids, which he must've been holding suspended the whole time.

They let out a hiss as their bodies burned, and he directed the flame onto the cottage, which caught like dried kindling.

As I watched, the home I'd grown up in blazed in flickering waves of black and violet, a mesmerizing pyre that turned it into crumbling ash as it devoured the structure in seconds.

"Are you hurt, at all?" His question prompted me to focus on any part of my body that the spiders might've bitten. All I could feel was a numbing cold that spread across my limbs and into my chest.

Seeming to sense my distress, he ran his hands over my

exposed skin, purposely palpating, as if for any sign of injury. As he checked me over, he paused on a cut I'd sustained when Uncle Felix had dragged me out of the ice box.

I could feel the faint burn on my scalp where my uncle had pulled my hair and the bruising on my thighs where he'd pried them open. Scratches on my back flared with the memory of struggling to fight him off with the gritty floor tearing across my skin. Wincing, I forced those thoughts away by focusing on the gentle sweep of Zevander's palms.

Once finished, he hooked my chin with his finger, drawing my eyes to his, and as if he could see right through the shadows of my thoughts, he asked, "Maevyth, are you *okay*?"

Emotions snapped inside of me when I nodded, and choked back a sob, while my head tormented me with visuals of those spiders swarming me, ready to finish me off. Strong arms enveloped me, and I melted into the warmth and safety of his embrace. Fighting to calm my breaths, I trembled against him, clutching him so tightly, I refused to let go. "I was so scared."

He removed his cloak, wrapping it around my shivering body, and the comfort of his scent radiated a calming balm to my fear. "Come on. Let's go back."

I wanted to. Every part of me wanted to return to Eidolon with him, but I shook my head and stepped back. "I can't. I'm sorry. I have to find her, Zevander. She's here. I can feel it." I couldn't bring myself to look at him. Perhaps he thought I'd lost my senses to cling so tightly to the belief that I'd see her again, but I didn't care. All I could imagine was Aleysia in the same place I'd been moments before, but without the power to fight back. "I'm sorry. I know you must think I'm … ridiculous for such a thing."

He pushed a wavy strand of hair behind my ear. "I think you're the bravest mortal I've ever met. And perhaps the most fucking stubborn, as well." His comment brought a tearful smile to my face. "Regardless, I'll stay and help you find her."

The relief of his words left me weak in the knees, but through a mist of tears, I shook my head. "I can't ask you to do that. Not when Rykaia needs you."

"Rykaia will always need me." He rubbed his thumb across my cheek, capturing the fallen tear. "This is about you."

The unspoken words lingered between us, and something electric moved through me when he removed his mask and lowered his face to mine. Butterflies took flight in my stomach as his hands gripped either side of my face, and he paused a moment, as if to ask permission.

I tilted my head back, and a flickering in my periphery caught my eye. Distracted, I turned away from him, focusing on the wavering light from the cottage across the field and puffs of white smoke drifting upward from the chimney. "The Crone Witch," I whispered, instantly regretting the diversion when he released me and stepped back.

Turning toward the cottage, he nodded. "We'll need shelter for the night."

Disappointment filled the cold space between us, but he jerked his head and took the lead toward the cottage.

CHAPTER FIFTY-SEVEN

MAEVYTH

A rms wrapped around my body to stave off the cold, I followed Zevander toward The Crone Witch's cottage, gaze trailing over the empty pen that had once housed a number of animals. We padded quietly toward the front door, not wanting to startle her, if she happened to be inside. Zevander peered through the windows, at the darker end of the cabin, while I looked in on the hearth that blazed a glowing orange. The mere sight of it cast a shiver down my spine, my toes numb and throbbing in my meager shoes. No one seemed to be inside, at all, though.

While Zevander rounded the house, I quietly tiptoed to the door, noticing long lines of symbols that'd been carved into the wood. Frowning, I ran my finger over them. The moment my hand touched the knob, a sharp pointed object prodded my back.

"I'd think twice, Girl."

I raised my hands to either side. "It's me. Maevyth."

"Don't care who you are. Folks ain't what they were before. Turn around and let me see your face."

Before I had the chance, she gasped, and I twisted to see

Zevander materialize out of nowhere, a monstrous shadow behind the old woman, holding a blade to her throat.

"I'd be careful about threatening her," he said, and the moment she dropped her weapon, letting it clang against the porch, he released her.

"I know it's been a couple of weeks, but do you remember me?" I asked.

Her brows came together in a frown. "A couple weeks? The Banishing of your sister was months ago."

I blinked at that, my gaze flicking to Zevander, who sheathed his blade. "Months ago? That can't be. I was only gone for ... well, two weeks."

She gave an uncertain look, eyeing me up and down. "Since you don't seem to be infected, I suppose you might as well come inside and warm yourselves." She hobbled past me for the door, and when she opened it, a wave of heat washed over me.

Zevander raised his brow, and I gave a nod, following after the witch. He lowered his head, forced to duck inside the archway as he trailed after me.

A blanket of heat nuzzled into my bones when I stepped into the room.

The Crone Witch grabbed a ladle, stirring a pot of stew she had on the flame. The savory scent of meat and spices watered my tongue.

"I don't believe I ever asked your name."

"Afraid you might call me Crone Witch?" She snorted, tapping the ladle on the edge of the pot. "It's Elowen."

"Elowen," I echoed, glancing around her small but clean space. By the hearth stood two chairs, and adjacent to them, a wooden table with an additional two chairs, where Zevander sat. The wood creaked with his weight and looked almost comical beneath his big bulky form.

"What happened after The Banishing?"

"Hmmm," she said, scratching her face, her long, yellowing nails digging into the wrinkles of her skin. "The fighting eventually stopped. Some suggested going after you in the woods, to be sure you'd died. They didn't, though. Too fearful. But Moros followed you, seemed like he'd been in there for hours. Most left to go home after, figuring he'd died. Not me, I waited. Needed to see if anyone emerged from those woods." She sat down in a chair and, from the small table beside her, lifted her pipe, already full of whatever she'd crushed into it. She leaned forward lighting a skinny wooden twig from the hearth and puffed her cheeks, burning the herbs. Leaning back in her chair, she stared off at the fire. "Moros did emerge."

"Did he have Aleysia with him?"

"He did. Took her with him."

I shot Zevander a worried look. "Then, she could be at Moros's now."

"She could be anywhere now. Moros didn't stay long. He left town for a week, or so. It was when he returned that folks started getting sick. Complaining of spider bites." Another puff of her pipe, and she frowned. "Then they started changing. Like those spiders burrowed right into their bones. Wasn't long before the whole damn village went raving mad, killing and eating the living."

"How did you survive?"

"Doing what I've always done. Kept to myself. Kept quiet. They don't care for the noise much. Hurts their brains, or something. That's when they get violent."

My thoughts wound back to earlier, when I'd screamed for help and Uncle Felix had attacked. "The villagers, where are they now?"

"They slumber." She sniffed and eased back in her chair. "In their homes. In the village. Almost like they're waitin' for something."

"And Moros?"

"Can't say. Haven't seen him. Haven't been to the village." She nodded toward the pot of stew. "Couldn't scrounge any meat from the woods, so I had to slaughter my goat. No matter, though. If I hadn't done it, they'd have gotten him." Another long puff, and she lowered her pipe. "Don't know how much longer I can stay here. Don't know how far the sickness has spread."

Another glance toward Zevander showed him watching her closely, clearly not trusting the old woman.

"Where you been, Girl, that you think only two weeks have passed?" Elowen asked.

"In the woods," I lied.

"Hmph." She waved a hand and shook her head. "Nothing living in those woods. Not even the creature that once dwelled there." A quick once over, and she added, "Certainly not you."

I didn't want to say where I'd been, for fear she might've questioned my state of mind. Even I still questioned it. "I watched that creature swallow Moros on the night of The Banishing."

Eyes narrowed on mine, she ran her tongue across her teeth. "Then, what emerged wasn't Moros."

"I don't think it was."

Lips pursed, she nodded slowly, and I wondered if she suspected there to be more beyond those woods. If she could possibly fathom a whole other world. "What do you say we share some stew? Been a long time since I had any company. After supper, I'll fix you a bed." She raised a brow, staring out of the corner of her eye toward Zevander. "If that's sufficient for you."

I swallowed a gulp at the idea sharing a bed with him. "We'd be grateful." A quick glance toward Zevander showed him staring back at me, a hint of amusement behind his otherwise dark gaze.

With a nod, she pushed from her chair and hobbled across the small space toward a cupboard, which held only a few bowls and mugs. When she returned to the hearth, she ladled the stew into all three bowls, handing one off to me, and one off to Zevander. "Would you like some water to go with it?"

"Yes, please," I said, noticing the dryness in my throat.

Twisting to Zevander, she cocked a brow. "And you?"

"Got anything a little harder than that?"

Lips stretched to a smile, she nodded. "Depends on your preference for hard. Most can't handle my home brew."

"I'll take that."

After another trip to the cupboards, she returned to the hearth with two cups, one sloshing water onto the floor, as she limped her way back. The other, she set in front of Zevander, along with a dark, corked bottle. After placing my water onto the floor beside my chair, she took her seat, and as she poked at her stew a moment, I waited to see her take a bite.

As if sensing my stare, her gaze lifted to mine, and I cleared my throat, mixing the stew around with my spoon. "It smells delicious."

"The poisoner worried that I poisoned *her*?" She let out a dark chuckle and spooned a bite into her mouth. "Doesn't bother *me* so much these days. Not even your Snake Tooth."

I raised a brow at that. "You've consumed poison?"

"In one form, or another. But the stew is clean of it." She spooned another bite into her mouth, and I turned to Zevander, who sniffed it, crinkling his nose before taking a bite. In his world, stews were hearty, filled with fresh vegetables and meat. Winter stews were always thin in Foxglove, with no more than the roots of whatever had been harvested and saved from the prior summer.

On seeing him, I spooned a bite, as well. Even the savory flavor of it warmed my belly. "So, my sister—you haven't seen her, at all, then?"

"Not at all." Another slurp of her stew, and she lowered the bowl to her lap. "Where might you have met your traveling companion? Seems rather brawny for these parts." Though she didn't bother to look at him, it was clear she was talking about Zevander. "Doesn't say much, does he? Except when he's giving threats."

Zevander lifted the bottle of liquor and popped the cork, giving it a sniff, just as he had the stew. Seemingly satisfied, he poured some into the cup beside him. "Perhaps you might tell me how you knew to speak Nyxterosi," he said, tipping back the cup without so much as a wince, before he setting it back down and pouring another round.

Before I could argue the point on her behalf, as I still swore that I'd been speaking Vonkovyan the whole time, a smile crept over Elowen's face.

"One might imagine that centuries of living here might've caused me to forget my native tongue."

My jaw unhinged, and I curled my fingers around my bowl to keep from dropping it.

"Lunasier?" Zevander asked, taking another sip of his drink.

"Nilivir. I was rejected by the Lunasier," she said with a bitter bite. "So, I left my home and traveled north." After spooning another bite, she chewed the meat slowly, and slid her gaze toward me. "It was the Corvikae who took me in."

"That would've been nearly a millennia ago, given how long Corvus Keep has stood abandoned. That makes you the oldest Nilivir I've ever met." Zevander sat forward, the intrigue in his expression unmistakable. "You knew the Corvikae."

"I did. Lived with them a good portion of my life. They didn't care about power, or status. They accepted me for what I was. A living, breathing Aethyrian."

Zevander rested his elbows on his knees. "Were you there when they abandoned the castle?"

On a mirthless chuckle, she shook her head. "Is that what your history tells you, young man? That they so easily gave up their land?"

"My history tells me they never existed," Zevander countered. "I've been to Corvus Keep. I've seen the writing on the wall."

Her brow lifted, and she twisted around in her chair. "Then, you know the truth. Those words were my own. Written in blood ink." She stared off, lost in thought. "They were forced from their home and marched to the Crussurian Trench."

"That's where the Grymswood lies, isn't it?" I asked, recalling the story Allura had told me.

"It is." Her eyes narrowed on me. "The priestess. Made to watch her people die, before she was turned into a tree in the middle of hell. Consumed by the horrible creatures that dwell at the bottom of that trench."

"By whom?" Zevander's question seemed to repulse her, as her lips twisted with disgust.

"The ones in the golden armor. Greedy beasts who longed to claim the vein that ran alongside Corvus Keep."

"Solassions. And how did you survive the attack?" he prodded.

"I fled. The priestess gave me the last rose of Morsana. The gift of the goddess herself." She sailed a smile at me. "They only bloom in Nethyria. The priestess told me to flee to the mortal lands. That she had seen a vision of a child who would one day avenge our people and lead a new generation of Corvikae."

A cold sensation moved through me as I listened to her story, wondering if she was referring to me. If I had somehow been the vision of a thousand years ago.

"I didn't believe her, but I fled, anyway. Passed through the Umbravale, where I waited for this child. And waited. Centuries, I watched the mortals in their banal lives, warring with each other and fighting for their single god, waiting for the day I might return home." A sadness claimed her expression. "Oh, I longed for it." The wistfulness in her voice sharpened to gravity when she said, "Then another creature crossed over. This one, vicious and vengeful."

"The creature in the woods," I clarified.

"Cadavros, he calls himself, former mage to the king." She snorted and shook her head. "A ruse for what lies within him."

"And what is that?" Zevander intoned, clearly unimpressed with the woman and her cryptic words.

"Pestilios, the God of Disease and Famine. Uncle to the goddess, Morsana."

Zevander frowned. "It is a masochistic god who would choose to reside inside a mere mage."

With a long, overgrown nail, she crudely dug at something lodged in her teeth. "The belief in the gods is not what it was, you know. Belief is power. Without it, the gods do not truly exist. Therefore, some have chosen a more corporeal presence."

"If he's a god, how were mere Aethyrians able to banish him?" Voice thick with skepticism, Zevander shook his head. "Not even the septomir possesses the power to rival a god."

"Even a god is only as powerful as the body it inhabits." She leaned forward, grabbing the poker from beside the hearth, and stoked the flames. "Once he's acquired enough power, there's little your ward can do to keep him from crossing back to Aethyria."

In all of her explanations, there was a detail, an inconsistency, that nagged at me. "You told me that you had a brother. That the two of you ventured into the woods together for food."

"I did tell you that, didn't I?" She smiled, rubbing her hands together, then held them out for the heat. "Not entirely true, dear." Brow raised, she sighed. "As I said, I longed to return home. So, I plucked that boy from the village in exchange for free passage to the archway."

As I absorbed what she was saying, an unsettling horror crept over me. "You sacrificed a child?"

"Oh, fret not. The gods have seen fit to punish me well for it." She lifted her arm to show a strange marking that appeared to be the scar of a horrific burn. "I offered that boy to Cadavros, and he allowed me passage. Unharmed. Except, when I arrived at the archway, I had a terrible feeling that I was no longer worthy to cross back. I'm sure you know what happens to those who are unworthy."

Dolion had once told me that Aleysia wouldn't have been permitted to pass through the archway. That she would've fallen to her death because we didn't share the same blood.

"When I pushed my hand through, something gripped my arm to pull me in with hands that burned like fire. So, I returned here. And I waited to fulfill my promise."

"You left me the rose." It wasn't a question at that point. "I'll ask again, did you see my mother that night?"

"No." She pushed up from her chair and gathered up our bowls, but mine was only half eaten, and she seemed to take notice, staring down at the remains. "What I saw was the sign the priestess had promised. A babe in a basket. Ravens in a flock. Eyes of silver." After collecting Zevander's bowl, she hobbled back over to the pot on the hearth and scraped the bits from each bowl into it.

I'd have been disgusted, if not for the distraction of her comment. "My eyes are gray."

"Couldn't have a silver-eyed child walking around these parts, could we? Imagine what vicious rumors such a thing would stir." Twisting to face me, she seemed to stare at the corner of my eye, presumably to the small crescent there. "My attempt to mask your true nature wasn't entirely foolproof. Then again, I've always been shit at spells. Had I known they'd make such a fuss over you, anyway, I'd have left them be."

I raised my hand toward my eye, imagining them silver. "Can I see them? How they look?"

She shrugged. "Spell's binding. Only death will reveal their true form. I don't suppose you want to see them that bad, hmmm?" At the shake of my head, she sighed and nodded toward Zevander. "Perhaps I should show you to your bed."

The older woman waved us after her, swiping up a ceramic

pitcher of water along the way, as she led us to a door at the back of the cottage. She opened it onto a small room, with a bed that wouldn't leave much space between Zevander and me, and limped her way to a basin set out on a washstand.

"Try to get some rest," she said, making her way back toward the door. "It's around the witching hour those things wake from their slumber to feed." On those parting words, she closed the door after her.

CHAPTER FIFTY-EIGHT

MAEVYTH

My pulse hastened as I watched Zevander doff the jacket he'd worn to The Becoming Ceremony, leaving him in the black tunic and trousers. I'd never slept beside a man in my life.

Keeping my eyes from him, I removed the cloak he'd loaned me, draping it over a wooden chair by the window. A firelamp flickered on the table beside the bed, casting shadows of our bodies against the wall, and as I looked up to Zevander's, I watched him slide off his boots.

"I'll sleep on the floor," he said.

With a slight smile, I turned to face him, watching him unlace his trousers. Clearing my throat, I turned away, eyes wide with distress. "Don't be silly. The floor is hard planks. I'm sure it's entirely uncomfortable."

"I've slept on worse."

"When you were … prisoner to the Solassions?" I recalled the story Dolion had told me.

"Yes." The clipped tone of his voice told me not to prod any further.

"Still, I insist on sharing. It would trouble me to have the whole bed to myself." I unclasped the scorpion necklace and stared down at the long, elegant gown that would surely take up most of the room on the bed. As if reading my thoughts, he hooked his fingers beneath the hem of his tunic and yanked it over his head. My heart shot to my throat on seeing his brutally muscled form, each groove carved to perfection. A warrior's body, his skin slashed by the scars of what I imagined were weapons that'd been used against him.

I begged myself to look away, but it was the other scars that prodded my gaze to linger. The ones that suggested a darker intention. Malicious scars that criss-crossed over each other, as if he'd been violently struck.

He handed off the tunic and turned around, perhaps offering me privacy while he unstrapped the weapons down his thigh and across his waist, unbuckling the holster that held them.

I glanced away only a moment, before my eyes were once again drawn to his body. Stretched from one shoulder to the other was an enormous, inked scorpion that failed to cover the multitude of scars carved into his back, as well. As he moved, his muscles flexed, and my fingers tingled with the urge to touch his skin.

Swallowing a gulp, I turned my back to him and tugged my arms from the wretched dress that held me trapped in the fabric. It fell to my mid-section, caught by the narrow bodice that cinched my waist. Stealing a moment to clean the black ooze that'd trickled out of Uncle Felix from my skin, I dipped one of the cloths into the basin and washed my shoulders and chest. When I dragged the rag over my arms, I noticed the cut from earlier, the one Zevander had palpated, had already healed, leaving only a small sealed mark on my skin. No bites from the spiders, thank goodness. Arms crossed over my breasts, a quick glance over my shoulder showed him quickly looking away, and in his profile, I watched his brows lower with a scowl.

It was then I remembered my own scars.

"Someone struck you," he said, his jagged voice brimming with tension.

"When I was young. Soldiers from my village. Seemed my mouth got me in trouble again."

He made a gruff sound of disapproval in his throat, but said nothing more, and I slipped into the oversized tunic that reached my knees.

Pushing the bodice over my hips, I let the dress fall beneath the cover of the tunic, the stark cold reminding me I wasn't wearing undergarments after Uncle Felix had torn them away. I yanked the quilt from the bed and climbed onto the thin mattress, scooting myself as close to the wall as I could, to allow him room. Once settled under the covers, I faced the wall and dared to point out the obvious. "Someone struck you, as well."

"Solassion soldiers." He climbed onto the bed beside me, his massive presence, at close proximity, prickling every nerve across my skin.

When he turned off the firelamp, the light in the room died down to nothing more than the silvery bands of moonlight shining in through the window.

The room fell to quietness, with only the sound of my unsteady breaths.

"Seemed they didn't like the mouth I had on me, as well," he said, breaking the lingering silence between us.

In the darkness, I smiled. "Well, imagine that. We have something in common."

"Perhaps. Though, I dare say, your tongue is sharper than mine." His comment made me chuckle.

Another bout of silence between us.

"Am I making you nervous lying here?"

The pleasurable tone of his deep voice certainly didn't calm the roistering flock of butterflies in my stomach. "No," I lied.

"Have you lain with a man before?"

The question sent a hot flush to my cheeks, stirring an irritation. "If you *must* know, no. I have not."

"Good."

Frowning, I turned my head. "Good?"

"Yes," he said, casually, and as he shifted on the bed, his massive leg brushed mine.

I turned back over, puzzling his words for far longer than I should have. Nearly two minutes must've passed before curiosity drove me mad enough to ask, "Why is that good?"

He groaned. "Must you always prod for an explanation?"

"Yes. I like to have clarity of thought. Why are you so hesitant to say?"

"I'm not hesitant."

"Well, you're not saying."

A growl rumbled from his chest. "Because I'm a jealous cunt who refuses to entertain thoughts of you lying next to another man. Is that explanation enough?"

I hardly imagined he'd come forth with anything even remotely close to that. Pinching my lips failed to contain the smile tugging at my mouth. Because, as pathetic as I may have been for it, I happened to enjoy the game of push and pull between us. The tension that left me constantly guessing.

I cleared my throat, banishing my amusement. "So jealous, you tried to *assassinate* me that night you came to my room while I slept."

He exhaled a forced breath. "I did."

"And why didn't you carry through with it?"

"Am I to believe you're disappointed that I didn't kill you?"

"I'm simply curious as to why."

"You want the truth?"

"Always, yes."

"Your snoring."

"What?" Heat flared in my cheeks. "I don't …. I don't *snore*."

"You do. Was awful that night. Scared me shitless."

I pressed my lips together, half burying my face into the pillow to hide a giggle at the visual of that.

"You're laughing. I can feel the bed shaking." His comment made me laugh more, and the more I tried to hide it, the more my body shook with the effort.

"I do ... not snore." My tone refused to be serious, no matter how much I fought to reel in the laughter.

"Honestly, I wouldn't have been surprised to see fire coming out of your nostrils."

A wheeze of laughter had me turning into the pillow, and tears sprang to my eyes.

"I believe it when you say you see the dead. That racket was enough to wake them for sure."

Not even the pillow could entirely subdue the howl of laughter that tore out of me.

He let out a chuckle, and it was then I realized that it was the first time I'd really heard him laugh. The sound, so deep and unexpected, distracted me from my own.

The laughter died down to quiet again. How strange to find even a small measure of mirth when the world felt like it was crumbling around us. My thoughts spun back to the conversation with Elowen earlier, and the possibility that Aleysia was very likely dead. "Zevander?"

"Yeah."

"Perhaps we should return to Nyxteros tomorrow. I'm .... Given the state of things. I just don't imagine Aleysia would ..." I couldn't say it. Of course, I knew she was strong, but I just couldn't imagine her surviving such a world. "I don't want to give up–" My voice cracked and I cleared my throat.

"If she's alive, Maevyth, it's by the grace of the gods. No mortal stands a chance against Cadavros."

"But if there's a chance?"

"Wait until morning to decide. Assuming all hell doesn't break loose tonight."

I blinked to hold back tears and nodded. "Okay, we'll wait until morning, then." Turning back over, I let out a sigh of relief. "Thank you for coming after me." The thought of being there alone brought more tears to my eyes.

A long pause followed. "You're welcome."

The room fell to a deafening quiet once again, as I lay staring at the cob walls that gave off an earthen odor.

Zevander shifted behind me, his bulky body jostling me around. I tilted back toward him, and when something brushed my backside, my body tautened. I jolted forward, kicking my leg out against his thigh.

"Oh! I'm sorry," I said, scooting myself closer to the wall.

"Are you not wearing undergarments?"

Brows pinched to a frown, I turned to the side. "Did you *intentionally* touch me there?"

"Not intentionally." In my periphery, I saw him slide his arm beneath his head. "Can't say I regret it, though."

I ran my tongue across my back teeth, slightly irritated and wholly embarrassed. "Well, I didn't *intentionally* not wear them."

"You unintentionally didn't wear them?"

"They were ... torn away by the creature that used to be my step-uncle. He was trying to–" I choked off the last bit, refusing to put myself back in that nightmarish moment. Acids shot to my throat at the visual of his manhood dangling over me.

Zevander made another sound of disapproval in his throat. "And did he *burn* with the house?" he asked through clenched teeth.

"Yes."

"Pity. I'd have liked to divest him of his hands."

"Well, you'd have had to piece them back together first."

I heard him shift behind me. "Oh?"

"It seems I learned the spinal whip rather quickly while my virtue was in jeopardy." When I glanced over my shoulder, I caught the dimple in his cheek, as if the thought of that pleased him. Strange, how much I liked the idea of pleasing him.

"How did it feel?"

"I don't know. I was terrified at the time. Relieved, but also … confused." Lying as far away from him as I was, I could feel the air leaking through the walls, and I wasn't entirely certain whether it was the bitter chill, or the memory of that moment, that left me shivering right then.

"You're cold," he said.

"A little."

The bed jostled again with his movement, and a radiant heat enveloped me as he wrapped his arm around me, drawing me back into his body.

"What are you doing?" I asked, startled by his hard chest pressed into my back and the bulge in his trousers that I could feel against my backside.

"Body heat. Best way to stay warm."

Pride urged me to fight his embrace, but it felt too good. Far too intimate, yet still, I didn't protest. Eyes glued to the wall, I took in the feel of his arm banded around my stomach, his broad chest at my back like a shield. How small and safe I felt beside him, like nothing and no one could possibly touch me.

While I no longer felt cold, my body continued to shiver. Much as I tried to calm myself, I couldn't help but imagine his hands slipping up the hem of the shirt, the thought of which had me trembling harder.

"You're worried I'm going to touch you." The lazy baritone of his voice, when he said it, sent another ripple down my spine, and I shuttered my eyes, imagining darkly wicked words spoken in that timbre. "I promise to be a gentleman, in spite of the fact that you unintentionally have no undergarments on."

"Do you find it difficult, lying beside a woman this way?"

"As a general rule? No. But when that woman is you? Yes."

Like the strike of a match, his words set me aflame. The

knot in my belly wound tighter, and I crossed my legs over one another, the ache to be touched, the curiosity of what his fingertips would feel like against my flesh, unbearable. I needed something. Distraction. Anger. Anything to keep me from imagining his fingers languorously exploring my body in the dark.

I exhaled a shaky breath. "Surely you've enjoyed the pleasures of other women," I said, squeezing my legs tighter when a visual of him in the throes of sex came to mind. How utterly delicious he must've looked, with his muscles coated in sweat and those fiery eyes fixated.

"I have," he answered, the frustration of his aloof response cooling the fire inside of me.

"How many?" The more he irritated me with his answers, the faster this longing would fizzle away.

"Not enough to drown the urges I'm feeling now."

A greedy desire pulsed through me, and I gripped the pillow to keep from doing something foolish, like reaching back to feel just how big that bulge was. "Perhaps you should take care of that then."

He let out a dark chuckle, and god, the sound of it failed to abate whatever clawed inside of me right then. "Are you suggesting that I relieve myself here, beside you?"

"Of course not," I answered quickly, though the visual of that nearly broke me. "I'm merely suggesting that if you're *uncomfortable* lying next to me, perhaps you should do whatever it is men do for that."

"You've never seen it done before." The air of amusement in his voice gnawed at me.

"Do you enjoy making me uncomfortable?"

"If I'm being honest, yes. Blush looks good on you."

Gnashing my teeth, the unbearable tension, coupled with embarrassment, had my cheeks burning, and I pushed at his steely arm still banded around me. "Fine. I'll sleep by the hearth.

At least it won't find amusement at my naiveté, or whatever it is you think is so entertaining."

As I pushed myself up to crawl out of bed, he tightened his hold and threw me back down against the mattress on a blast of air from my lungs. The gesture triggered my defenses, and I squirmed to get loose, scratching at his arm that held me imprisoned.

"Let me go!" I snarled, but he wrapped his muscled leg over mine, trapping me beneath him. The way he so effortlessly held me down, as if I were nothing but a weak child, only fueled my irritation. Temper ignited, I kicked upward, accidentally hitting him in what I estimated to be his groin, and he let out a quiet growl. Whatever small bit of remorse I felt for that was quickly smothered when he pressed into my body, caging me in his brawny arms.

Squirming for freedom, my legs rubbed against his, and the shirt inched its way up my thighs. "Release me now!"

The struggle ensued, and I ground my teeth, arching my back to break his grip, but it was futile and I'd grown tired.

"Shhhh," he whispered in my ear, wrangling me closer, and buried his face in my hair. "I didn't mean to upset you."

I stilled at the hypnotically calm tone of his voice, the breath sawing in and out of me as I abandoned my fight.

His chest rose and fell with his heaving breaths, and he let out a wry chuckle. "Fucking hell, you are a vicious little rosebud. One minute, you're soft and inviting, the next, you're thorns and blood."

"What blood?"

He lifted his arm where I'd scratched him, tiny red rivulets trickling down his skin over the scorpion and flames. Once again, I felt a small bit of remorse.

"Had you not taunted me with your ..." I clamped the spicy words on my tongue that begged to be cut loose. "I'm not as naive as you think. I'm well aware you've got all this ... *experience* with women. And that you think I'm just this stupid little mortal who–"

His lips seized mine, silencing me.

Stunned, I lay paralyzed in his grip, the argument dying in my throat. While my stubborn temper begged me to push him off, screamed at me to smack his annoyingly handsome face for daring to quiet me that way, the battle in my head was quickly lost in one bitter swallow. My bones melted, softening, as he pushed up onto his elbow and threaded his fingers through my hair. Slow and lazy, he ran his tongue over my lips, licking, tasting, exploring.

I savored the flavor of whatever bitter liquor Elowen had given him that lingered on his lips. That sensuously delicious spice and flame, which mingled with the musk and ambery clove of his skin. An intoxicating medley that consumed me.

His hands drifted to the small of my back, and I gripped his thick biceps as he dragged me even closer. With a sweep of his tongue, he deepened the kiss and groaned against my mouth. Even while lying down, dizziness swept over me, and I opened my eyes, worried that I might faint. Shadowy wisps danced around us, burrowing in and out of my flesh in pleasurable bursts, and I moaned, the sound vibrating against our joined lips.

His fingers tightened around me, and he kissed me harder, sealing off the oxygen. Calloused palms slid down to the hem of the tunic he'd let me borrow, and never breaking the kiss, he grabbed my thigh in a bruising grip, letting out a grunt when he pressed his groin against me.

Heat surged beneath my skin and across my palms. My heart beat a strange rhythm that sent a wave of panic through me. I pushed against his chest to sever the kiss, and in resting my hand there, felt the rhythm of his heart, beating in time to mine. As if in perfect sync with one another. The cadence of it calmed me, and I could feel myself growing weak, drifting, floating, lifting out of my body. What was this strange sensation?

I surrendered myself to it. To him.

His hand slid higher. Higher. Until he found the fleshy cheeks of my naked bottom and squeezed. The bulge in his trousers pressed hard against the very spot where I ached to be touched.

As if he'd heard my thoughts, his palm glided across my hip, dancing over bones and curves with maddening patience.

I looked up to see him staring down at me, and my heart ratcheted in my chest as his fingertips drifted lower, until he found the apex of my thighs. Breath caught in my throat, I spread my legs apart, an invitation, one I desperately hoped he'd accept.

He licked his lips, and the moment his fingers found the bare seam of my flesh, his eyes shuttered closed. A deep, guttural sound rumbled out of him, like that of a dangerous animal, rousing an obscene need to be ravaged.

Clutching his biceps, I exhaled a shaky breath, my thighs trembling, as I held them apart for him. Prickles of excitement and fear clashed inside my head, my arms shaking while I gripped him tightly, allowing him to explore my flesh.

In long, lazy strokes, he ran his finger up and down my wet slit, his dangerously expert touch sending my muscles into a frenzy, until clenching and shaking with his fondling. As if he knew what I needed, possessed some intimate knowledge of my body that I didn't. His other hand found my breast, and through the thin tunic, he rubbed tiny circles over my nipple, bringing it to a hardened peak. The maddening combination consumed my senses, swallowed me in a wave of pure ecstasy.

A mewling sound leaked from my mouth, as he worked me into a knot of tension, and he pressed his lips to mine. "Shhh. I wouldn't want the old woman to think I'm hurting you."

I smiled and nodded, my hips shamelessly circling against him, desperate for his fingers, his tongue. Anything to relieve the unrelenting ache he'd stirred. The feral longing that writhed in my chest, climbing the bones of my ribcage, like an ensnared animal. Lip caught between my teeth, I pressed the crown of my head into the pillow, the urge to bite something curling through my muscles.

He pushed up inside of me, curving that wicked digit back, and touched a sensitive spot that had me arching into him. "Gods be damned. So wet and needy." His teeth found the ticklish crook of my neck, and as he added more pressure, I arched higher, dragging my heels over the mattress.

Through the fabric of the shirt, he pulled on my nipple and plunged his fingers in and out of me in long, slickening strokes. "Should I stop, *Lunamiszka?*"

I frantically shook my head. "No, please. Don't stop."

He dragged his nose along my throat and licked my hammering pulse. "Your scent is stirring my appetite." The moment his fingers slid out of me, my muscles sagged with disappointment.

I opened my eyes to see him shove his fingers into his mouth, sucking away the shine of my arousal, and god, the sight of him sent a deep, cramping need between my thighs.

He climbed over top of me, his body a massive shadow that eclipsed the moon's light, and he licked his lips before canting his head just enough to kiss me. The bed creaked as he sat back and tugged my legs, pulling me onto his lap with ease, his hard and massive bulge pressed into my aching core.

"Your beauty is unrivaled, Maevyth." Hands gripping my bottom, he buried his face in my neck, planting kisses across my throat and collarbone. Goosebumps scattered across my flesh as he ran his tongue along the column of my neck. Lost to the sensation, I let him lure me into euphoria, until, like a zap of lightning, teeth sank into the base of my throat, not hard enough to draw blood, but enough that my whole body tensed around him. The bliss from moments ago spiraled into something darker. Something raw and primal that burned in my blood. A wicked and hungry desire swelling inside of me, begging to be fed.

Legs wrapped around his back, I gripped his shoulders as he kissed and nipped my throat.

His hand slid down between my thighs again, and as I sat straddling him, he pushed two fingers inside of me.

The monstrous agony pulsing in my belly awakened again and welcomed the intrusion with overwhelming relief. I tipped my head back, mouth agape, the air stuttering in my lungs as I surrendered to it.

He knew exactly where to touch me. How to touch me. Slow and languid, he braced one hand on the mattress and let his hips follow each plunge of his fingers, as if his cock were thrusting inside of me, while his sturdy thighs held me open, while his eyes remained riveted on me. Watching me. His muscles flexed against my palms, and I wanted to capture the moment and mentally frame it in my mind forever. How ravishing and powerful he looked right then. Elegantly brutal, but with a gleam of boyish fascination.

He upped the pace, and I circled my hips, grinding my bottom against his thighs, the ache only relieved when he thrusted into me. Harder.

A moan escaped me, and I dug my nails into his biceps, scratching and clawing, starving for whatever it was that twisted in my stomach. The need he stirred inside of me stretched and writhed, tightening my muscles. "Please," I rasped, though I didn't have a clue what I was begging for, what lurked on the other side of this delicious tension. Agony and pleasure curled through me, the desperation so overwhelming, I bit down on his shoulder with a shuddering breath and whimpered.

"Cursed gods, you are a ferociously breathtaking creature when you're ravenous." The dark amusement in his voice mirrored the devilish glint in his eyes. "I wonder what sounds will spill from your lips when your thighs are trembling against my palms and your sweet nectar wets my tongue." His words wrenched a tearless sob from my chest as my blood burned hotter, this merciless craving unbearable.

Spinning our positions, he lay me back against the pillow again, bracing his body over mine, his greedy fingers plundering in time to the wet sounds that would've had me blushing had I not been so lust-drunk.

I arched into him, taking in the feel of his solid chest against my breasts, his body hard and unyielding—a prison, from which I never wanted to escape.

A searing heat snaked beneath my skin, and I turned to find black flames dancing on the perimeter of the bed.

The rational side of my brain urged me to scramble away or risk burning alive, but I was too intoxicated, too far gone to care. Whatever magic Zevander wielded between my thighs right then left me both pliant and weak with pleasure.

The frail and tired wood of the bed's frame remained intact, sturdy, as it quietly squealed with his movements, the flame merely dancing across its surface as though reveling in the sight of us. One jolting curve of Zevander's finger hit a sensitive ball of nerves deep inside of me and I mindlessly rolled my head against the pillow, the pleasure burning low in my belly. Winding and tightening as he toyed with it, mercilessly rubbing and tickling me to a fevered state. Before I could release the scream cocked at the back of my throat, he covered my mouth with his hand, trapping the sound against his palm.

The torment fizzled when he removed his fingers from inside me, and as he lifted the tunic's hem, baring my flesh, he sat back, releasing a long exhale, his gaze never wavering from between my thighs. "Fuck," he said, the awe in his voice lessening the anxious thoughts swirling in my head. He ran his hand through his hair and down his face. "A thousand times I've fantasized this moment, and still, I failed to imagine you'd be this perfect."

With little effort, he banded his arms around my thighs and lifted my sex to his face, hiking my legs over his shoulders as he sat back on his heels. My body slid closer, the back of my head pressed into the mattress. From that angle, I could see up the length of my torso to where he stared down at me. Eyes on me, he dipped his head, and when he dragged the broad width of his tongue across my flesh, my stomach and toes curled. A coppery taste prickled my tongue as I bit my lip hard, fighting the urge to cry out while watching him watch me, as he voraciously devoured me. I didn't need experience to know the man was a master at his skill. Every drag and flick of his tongue arrived in perfect timing and cadence, building and climbing.

He moaned and grunted, fingers digging into my thighs as he held me to his face, feasting on me like a starved animal. The sight of him made me ravenous, as he'd said, and I clutched the blankets, desperate to dig my nails into something as the tension heightened inside of me.

"Oh, god please," I whispered and I grabbed the pillow from beneath me, smashing it over my face to smother a long, droning moan that I breathed into the damp cotton.

Ribbons of heat weaved through my muscles, and eyes shuttered, I surrendered to the chaos that burrowed into my bones. Weightlessness settled over me, and lowering the pillow away, I opened my eyes. The ceiling above was closer than before and craning my neck showed the bed below where I hovered. I gasped with a jolt on realizing I was suspended in the air, the flickering black flames crackling around me. When I swung my undoubtedly shocked gaze back to Zevander, a smirk curved his lips, those knowing, devilish eyes studying my reaction.

He held his palms up and with one flick of his fingers, my body floated toward him until I was straddling his face in the air. "Erigorisz," he said and swept his tongue across his lips. "Perhaps one of the more useful glyphs." Strong hands gripped my thighs, as he resumed his torment and my preoccupations, every silent speculation, burned and fizzled away with the delicious sweep of his unforgiving tongue. His mouth consumed my mind with the same voracious appetite that he devoured my swollen flesh.

Writhing and moaning, I hugged the pillow against my chest, my body stiffening, tightening as the heat intensified and my muscles twisted in pleasure. Winding tighter and tighter. My thighs shook around him, my toes curled, digging into his muscled shoulders, while a need that bordered on pain throbbed with each lazy stroke of his tongue.

Every thought in my head spiraled into focus—the unyielding grip of his palms, the stubble on his cheek and wet fullness of his lips when he sucked at my tender folds.

The world faded around me, the quiet sounds of sucking and moaning and kissing drawing me into a dark hypnotic space where only he and I existed.

Tension beating through my veins heightened, then snapped inside of me, and holding the pillow to my face, I jerked my hips forward on a scream that drowned in the plush, feathery barrier.

A distant cracking sound, like a fracture, hardly registered over the pulsing waves of pleasure that burst across my thighs and shot to my limbs in warm tingles, and I circled my hips in the air, grinding out the last bits of release.

As my body settled, he lowered me to the bed and tore the pillow from my face, staring down at me with a reverent gleam in his eyes, a glint of adoration that knotted my stomach.

"I dare you to look her in the eyes!" Unbidden voices bubbled from the darkest corner of my memories. *"Look the lorn in the eye and every one you love will die!"* The taunting rhymes from other children, and the scorn of their parents who quietly laughed along with them. Years of rejection and ostracism carved into my thoughts with sharp-edged tongues.

Zevander looked at me as if I were something more than the disparaging word that'd been hammered into me since I was found by the edge of the woods: *unwanted. Lorn.* He looked at me as if I was worthy of being seen.

The emotion sank its teeth into me, and I turned away from him, willing myself to hold back the tears that would surely destroy this moment between us.

"You look like a goddess right now," he whispered, burying his face in my neck, kissing me. He ghosted his mouth over my jaw, my cheek, until he finally crushed his lips to mine. "And you taste as divine."

Poisonous thoughts stabbed my mind, urging me not to trust his words. *He's lying.* A quiet fear crawled beneath my skin, winding itself in my bones. Zevander had somehow managed to dig his fingers past sharp ribs and into the stoniest corner of my heart. A place so few had ever tenanted. I didn't trust its walls, nor its strength. Not when every person I'd grown to love had been torn away from me. What would having breached that fragile boundary into something more intimate mean for us?

Eyes screwed shut, I pushed those thoughts away. Because even if he was lying, even if this was nothing more than temporary, it didn't matter. Nothing mattered in this place where death loomed beyond the walls. We were sketching an illusion of normalcy in a world too dark to imagine. A place that longed to devour us. Here, in this little hovel, with our bodies entwined and our hearts beating in sync, we transcended death, existing on our own plane.

Our own uncharted terrain.

The magic and heat between us warned of something explosive. Something I'd never find in another so long as I lived. A sensation that would inevitably consume me like those wicked black flames he wielded. Better to have experienced that passion and watched it fade like a dying star than to have never known it at all.

"You are destructive in the throes of climax."

Still ruminating in the aftermath, I smiled through my preoccupations. "How so?"

He jerked his head back, and I pushed up onto my elbows to

find the flames had retreated, allowing a perfect view of a long crack in the window's pane across the room.

"I did that?"

"When you screamed." He pulled me into him and kissed my forehead. "Not that I'm complaining. That is a sound I'll never tire of hearing."

"You've heard it before, have you?" I teased.

To my horror, he said, "I have." An unflinching gaze met mine. "The night you drank too much Ambrozhyr," he added with a shameless air of amusement. A smile tugged at the corner of his mouth, as though recalling that night held some humor, the thought, once again, stirring an unsettling mortification in the pit of my gut.

"Did we ..."

"No. As open as you seemed to be to the idea of that, I wouldn't touch a woman in such a state." He let out a sigh. "But I surely enjoyed watching you."

"Watching me do what?" No sooner had I said the words, I recalled my undergarments having been slung mid-thigh and the wetness of my sheets. Humiliation flared in my cheeks while flickers of memory flashed through my mind. Whispered words and heavy breaths. The decadent sound of his voice in my ear. An exhilarating sensation that stirred between my thighs all over again.

My slack jaw clenched with embarrassment, as I imagined how I must've looked that night. "So happy to have entertained you," I spat.

"I was only there to make sure you didn't hurt yourself. Seems I was the only one left in pain."

I winced at that, reminded that the only reason he'd need to have been concerned was because I had consumed far too much Ambrozhyr that night. "I'm sorry. However I might've been the cause of it."

He tucked his bent arm beneath his head. "It's a pain I'm quite familiar with, unfortunately."

In a subtle a gesture as I could muster, I glanced down to the massive bulge tenting his trousers and back. "This pain is of a sexual nature?"

His lip twitched. "It is."

I rested my hand against his chest and traced a small scar below his collarbone. While I knew very little of a man's body, I wondered how I might ease him of this ache. On a whim of madness, I skated my hand down his chest, to the deep grooves of his muscled stomach that twitched with my caress. The hem of his trousers tickled the bottom of my palm, and I dared myself to reach inside. To lay my unrelenting curiosities to rest.

He stilled, his body rigid, as he seemed to realize my intent.

I reached lower, only nudging his tip.

All at once, Zevander broke away, turning his face from mine, and took long, heaving breaths. He unthreaded his hands from my hair and fell to the side of me. At first, I thought he'd sought a better angle to reach down inside his pants, but when I attempted to resume my explorations, he took hold of my wrist. "Please," he said through clenched teeth.

The poisonous thoughts from moments ago bubbled like a cauldron inside my head, and with a nod, I pulled my hand away from him. "If you do not want me to touch you, I will respect your wishes."

He quickly captured my retreating hand and held it to his chest, as if to assure me it wasn't rejection. "I want you. I want you so desperately that I'd kill anything with a pulse just to have you for one night. This insatiable craving I feel …" A muscle in his jaw twitched with the tension in his words and he squeezed my hand. "I can't fucking breathe. I ache for you, Maevyth. Believe me when I say this."

But he didn't bother to say why he hesitated.

And I didn't bother to ask.

CHAPTER FIFTY-NINE

ZEVANDER

In the darkness, Zevander lay staring at Maevyth. Her quiet snores confirmed she'd fallen asleep, and with her back to him, he ran his fingertips over her long, soft curls. His mind spun back to earlier, when she'd lay spread out before him, trembling and needy. Perfect. He could still hear the echo of her moans in his head. A sound that called to his instincts to claim her.

His gaze fell to the small of her back, where he'd seen the faint scars of a whipping. He'd refused to examine them too closely, because, by the gods, he'd have torn through the folds of time to punish whoever had laid hands on her. Instead, he made a silent vow that he'd viciously strike down anything that touched her from that day forward.

His mate.

He couldn't wrap his head around it. Mates were for those who believed in fate, who gazed at the stars with a longing to capture them. He'd lived too long with the practicality of knowing the stars were too far out of reach, and yet, in his arms lay the brightest of them all.

The girl with the moon in her eyes and fire in her soul.

Damn the gods for sending him one so beautiful, with a heart so pure. So fragile.

In sleep, she rolled onto her back, her head still turned away from him, but her snores died away to long, peaceful breaths.

Touch her. She's yours.

He screwed his eyes shut and shook his head. What had he ever done in his ruthless life to deserve something so innocent and good? The world had never given him anything so freely. Everything he'd ever given a damn about had come at a tragic cost, so why would he trust that fate wouldn't stab him in the back?

At the same time, while every dark corner of his mind resisted the possibility of it, the fact was, Dolion's vision was indisputable. Seers did not possess the power to dream of mating bonds on their own. Regardless of whatever visions the old mage might've had over the years that'd turned out to be false, mates were always true. Particularly when, at the time he'd dreamed it, Dolion hadn't yet met Maevyth. And even if Zevander had the audacity to question a vision from the gods, that first kiss in his office had certainly laid all doubt to rest. It was then he'd felt the first tug of his bond. The shaking of his bones that'd awakened the possessive beast inside of him.

The first sputtering beat of his dead heart.

What a cruel destiny she'd been given, though. And, to some extent, him, as well. Having a mortal for a mate would mean suffering the agony of watching her die too soon.

But perhaps that was fitting. The final punishment of the gods, because an eternity with her seemed as unreachable as the stars. The blackness on his horizon, that colorless stretch of nothingness, had always left him wondering if anything existed beyond it. Or maybe it was the same empty void that called to him on the nights he'd held that poison-tipped blade to his own throat.

Yet, knowing her life would be cut short, could he sacrifice even a fractional moment with her? To spare her from the possibility that he would turn out like Branimir? That she'd be forced to watch his mind deteriorate and spiral into madness?

He gnashed his teeth as the truth pummeled his conscience.

No. He couldn't spare so much as a minute. That sort of altruism was reserved for better men. Not those whose souls were desiccated and thirsting for one drop of life.

Zevander's withering heart had been caged for far too long to so selflessly let her go. As much as he loathed his greedy, self-indulgence, the mere thought of setting her free was a kindness he refused to entertain.

It was true what Rykaia had said—she was the fire in his veins. A torment, for which he vilified the gods.

For centuries, he'd roamed as nothing more than a shadow, a cursed son of sablefyre. Maevyth radiated an irresistible warmth that he voraciously craved in his cold and calculated existence. Like scattered rays of sunlight reaching down to the darkest depths of the sea. The promise of redemption for all the vile things he'd done. Lives he'd taken.

So many lives.

Claiming her, though, meant offering up another target for his adversaries, and a mate was far more dangerous than a sister. She was a weakness, a pawn they could use to make him heel like a dog. Because losing a mate was said to be more painful than burning alive.

One of few tortures he'd managed to evade up until that point.

He rubbed a hand down his face, his head a relentless mess of thoughts that hammered at his skull. A turbulent gale of confusion over what he wanted and what he'd have sooner carved his own heart out to avoid. And in the center of that storm was Maevyth. The only constant. A beacon in a dark, black sea. A light too bright for his eyes, but damn the gods, even if he had to maim and kill for all eternity to keep her safe from his enemies, one fact remained true.

She was his. *Lunamiszka. My little moon witch.*

A cold and selfish pursuit, but he didn't care. When the gods offered atonement for a life of hell, best to grab it by the fucking teeth. He slid a hand over her, dragging her sleeping body closer.

She moaned and shifted, but didn't resist him, nor did she wake. With her back to his chest and his face buried in her hair, Zevander inhaled deeply, wanting to devour her all over again. One taste hadn't been enough. He could've easily spent the night exploring every inch of her body. Learning her pleasures and fears. Acquainting himself with his mate's darkest fantasies. He wouldn't take her yet, though. Not here, where he had nothing at his disposal to temper his appetite. Because once he plunged himself into that heavenly abyss, he knew damned well he'd never want to stop. Zevander had been trained by that cursed wretch, General Loyce, to take like a vicious dog. To ravage and plunder the brutal Bellatryx who enjoyed rough and oftentimes painful sex. Without some measure of restraint, he'd fuck Maevyth against every wall and surface to get his fill, and even then, he'd spoil for more. The same way he'd been conditioned to go for hours while feeding the depraved hunger of the Bellatryx.

He winced at the thought of subjecting Maevyth to such a thing.

No. Not her. If it took every ounce of power in his body or the deadliest tinctures of poison to quell his urges, he'd be gentle. For her.

No matter how much he craved being inside her, how obsessively he fantasized about her, he would wait for a time and place better suited for a claiming. A place he could reach for his noxious blade if needed—a safeguard he didn't happen to include in the arsenal of weapons he'd brought across the vale.

A creaking sound had him swinging his attention toward the window behind him. He silently watched the fluctuating light, indicating a presence outside. Unraveling himself from Maevyth, he sat up in the bed, careful not to disturb her, and quietly clicked his tongue. An image materialized in his mind–the window and the porch.

And a figure standing just out of the window's view.

Not entirely clear, but Zevander could make out long, branching antlers, a hunched body, and hooves.

He stalked toward the window, not making a sound over the aged floorboards, and pressed his back to the wall, opposite to where he'd seen the figure. From that angle, he caught a glimpse of it slipping past–a creature with bark-like skin and long, branching arms, sniffing the air.

"I see you watching me," a voice in his head said, and Zevander frowned, backing himself into the shadows. *"Come. I wish to speak with you.*

Then speak, Zevander thought to himself.

"Have you no idea that I could drag you from that hovel with nothing more than my mind?"

And you will be met with my blade. Reveal yourself and tell me what you want.

The thud of hooves on the weathered porch revealed movement, and he stepped before the window. Just as Zevander had seen in the obscure image from earlier, the creature's long, branching horns stood up from his head, scraping over the glass. His eyes glowed like that of an animal's in the dark, and rough, tessellated skin, with deep grooves like the bark of a tree, covered his body. Though he appeared more animal than man, he stood on hind legs, slightly hunched.

The same beastly form he'd seen in the woods when he'd first ventured to Mortasia.

"Cadavros," Zevander spoke low and stepped in front of him, the two face-to-face, separated only by the glass between them. "The creature I saw in the woods that night. It was you."

"Yes. I've since taken a more acceptable appearance as a mortal, but

I thought you might appreciate the familiarity. A ghastliness I shared with your brother." He waved toward Zevander through the window, his branch-like fingers scraping the glass. *"You've taken to the black flame rather well over the years. Far better than I."*

Zevander didn't bother to respond to that, and instead took note of what appeared to be blood smeared at his chin.

"I've been forced to consume mortal flesh to keep my strength." He tipped his head to the side, presumably toward Maevyth. *"It seems you've also consumed your share of flesh."* Even in thoughts, his voice held amusement, and his attention on Maevyth stoked a dark ire in Zevander.

In as subtle a movement as he could muster, Zevander forced his shield to block his mind, as he recalled his blades sat out on the table beside him.

"It's futile. I cursed you, and therefore, you cannot hide your thoughts from me." Those black, beady eyes tracked to the left, toward the table. *"Not even your longing to kill me. And what for, really? I've no inclination to kill you."*

"Then, why are you here?"

"To propose a bargain of sorts. As the Black Pestilence spreads, my power grows. Give me your loyalty, your fealty, and you will rule Mortasia alongside me."

Zevander sneered. *"And become one of your faceless creatures. Your grotesque mutilations?"*

Lips gnarled, he hissed, as though offended. *"They are the ones who refused fealty to me. Who chose their pride above all else."*

"I've already sworn fealty."

"Your king has already betrayed you. In fact, if he knew you were here now, he'd have you locked away in his dungeons for regicide."

Regicide?

"You're aware that if Prince Dorjan dies, a black plague will be unleashed, and all of Aethyria will be at my mercy. But the prince and I are also linked by blood magic," he went on. *"Should I die, he will surely die, also."*

Zevander's blood iced. It was then he realized why Sagaerin had chosen to banish Cadavros instead of killing him. Why he'd forbade anyone crossing the Umbravale. His son's life had been soulbound. Not only to the amulet, but to Cadavros himself.

"Or you can join me. At my side, you'll have more power than you imagined. Everything you desire most."

Zevander snarled. "I desire nothing from you."

"Don't you?"

An unbidden image glimmered in his head. Maevyth's naked form on top of him, her head tipped back in ecstasy.

Waves of pleasure pulsed through him, his body hardening.

Out of his control.

"Imagine you could have her freely. Without those meddling memories clouding your mind." Cadavros continued to taunt. *"Imagine you could have her, take her, as you've dreamed. Imagine her touch without the pain."*

Zevander clamped his eyes to banish the thought, but it rooted itself in his mind so deeply, he could feel his engorged cock buried inside of her then, every metal rung sliding in and out of her. The rapacity burning in his muscles as he plundered her tight little body. When he opened his eyes, she was there, her bare, wet flesh slickening his skin as she ground her hips against his stomach.

Fuck.

He took hold of her hips, guiding her lower, desperate to sink into that tight warmth, the swollen, weeping entrance which begged to be filled. A ravenous hunger hooked itself in his bones, thinning his restraint. Gods, he wanted her more than his next breath.

Waves of black curls spilled over her slender shoulders, her pouty lips parted around shallow flutters of breath as she closed her eyes, smearing her arousal over him. Stirring his predatory instincts like blood in shark-infested waters. Sharp nails scored his chest, as she circled her hips against his groin and let out a dulcet little moan so fucking pleasing to his ears, he wanted to swallow it. The heady scent of sex in the air watered his tongue.

He reached out for her breasts, ignoring the niggling thought in his mind, the warning that told him something about this wasn't right. His hands longed to touch her skin, and he took hold of her flesh, lifting his head to suck at her nipple. Feral hunger writhed inside of him. He wanted more. All of her.

A carnal madness burned hot in his veins, and on a growl, he bit down into the softness of her breast. She let out a yelp, and Zevander cuffed her throat to silence her, gripping tight and marveling at the way her pulse hammered against his palm. Her life in his hand. At his mercy. Teeth clenched, he dug his fingers into her hips, forcing them to move faster. Harder.

The pleasure in her eyes darkened to fear and she clawed at his hand still cuffing her throat, releasing a raspy choke of air.

He gripped tighter. Tighter.

"Kill her," the voice commanded.

"No!" Zevander snarled, willing his hand away from her throat, but it wouldn't move.

"Zevander!" Maevyth's screams echoed in his head. *"Zevander!"*

The sound of a dark chuckle skated down his spine. *"You will give me your loyalty. Or I will take everything that matters to you away."*

CHAPTER SIXTY

MAEVYTH

Light danced across my eyelids, and I winced at the brightness, stretching and yawning. A strange vibration shook the bed, the sound of grunting from behind me. I opened my eyes and turned to find Zevander lying beside me, his entire body convulsing. A thick sheen of sweat dampened his skin, his hair plastered to his face. His arms flexed at his side, fists clenched tight.

Frowning, I pushed up from the bed, staring down at his eyes —as black as coal, with tiny black veins branching out from his sockets. A numbing cold tingled across my chest at the sight, the ghostly caress of terror springing goosebumps across my skin.

"Zevander?" I dared myself to touch him, and when I did, a searing heat scorched my fingertips. "Ouch!" I retracted my hand, curling my fingers. Panic rose into my throat. I scrambled out of the bed, careful not to disturb him, and swung the door open. On the other side, Elowen wore a curious expression on her face. "I don't know what's wrong with him! I woke up, and he …. He's not responding to me. He's burning up."

She tipped her head and hobbled past me into the room,

coming to a stop alongside the bed. Without laying her hands on him, she held her palm over his trembling body and shuttered her eyes. "Abyssal binding."

"What is that?"

"Something has gripped his mind and refuses to release him. Can happen when you slip into a state of caligorya."

Caligorya. I remembered the term Dolion had mentioned, the day in the training room when I'd passed out. He'd called it the dark side of the mind.

I glanced to Zevander, whose muscles clenched so tight, it was a wonder they didn't split right through his skin. "How can we stop it?"

"No way to stop it. That's why it's called abyssal. No way to reach him. But we need to bring his fever down."

"His power is a black flame. Might that have anything to do with it?"

She shrugged and hobbled past me again. "Might. It'd certainly explain his eyes."

"I … I've controlled the black flame before." I twisted around after her, following her as she made her way to a bowl on the countertop in the kitchen.

"You." She snorted and headed for the door.

Wearing nothing but Zevander's tunic, I darted across the room for the cloak he let me borrow, pausing to stare down at his suffering form. An ache wrenched my heart, and careful not to touch his skin, I pushed a strand of his hair from his brow.

"Stay with me," I whispered and threw the cloak around me.

Instead of opting for the flat slippers I'd worn with my dress, I shoved my feet into his oversized boots that reached to my thighs. With clunky steps, I chased after her into the snow, shivering at the icy cold that bit my exposed skin. A clanking sound drew my attention to the other side of The Hovel, and I jogged as fast as the boots would allow.

I found her beside a well pump, filling the bowl and a pitcher with water. "I'm telling you the truth. I've controlled his flame before," I said, watching her swap the pitcher for the bowl, which she shoved into my chest, sloshing some of it onto my arm.

"No one controls sablefyre. It's wild and chaotic and does what it wants." A few pumps of the well filled the pitcher, and she carried it past me.

"Well, whatever is inside of me does a fine job of it."

The old woman swung around. "And what is inside of you?"

I had no idea how to answer that, and the longer I argued with the woman, the longer Zevander suffered. "Nothing."

She *hmphed* and turned back in the direction of the cottage. Once inside, she gathered some apothecary jars from the cupboard—herbs, I guessed—and the two of us returned to Zevander's side.

There, she worked to unlace the trousers he'd loosened the night before, but never removed. As she gave them a hard yank down his hips, I threw my arm across hers.

"What are you doing?"

"Removing as much of his clothing as possible." Her bushy brows practically creaked when she raised them. "Have you never brought down a fever, girl?"

I stepped back and turned away, as another hard yank sent his trousers halfway down his thighs, springing his manhood free.

"Dear gods …" The disturbance in Elowen's voice had me turning back toward him, and my heart shriveled inside my chest.

As Zevander lay convulsing, his length remained stiff against his stomach at full mast. The underside had been crudely pierced with metal bars that ran the exceptional length of it. Scars marred his thighs and groin, as if he'd suffered unimaginable abuse at one time. Skinny white lines that stretched hip to hip, leaving me to imagine he'd taken a whip against his groin. Some carried a deeper scarring, though, as if he'd been cut by a blade.

Elowen ran her finger along one at his thigh. "Poison. Can tell by the thread of violet flesh there," she said, pointing to the crooked cicatrix where the flesh had sealed together.

Tears wobbled in my eyes, and I turned away, swallowing hard.

"What horrible creature did this?" Elowen shook her head, staring down at him. "Such pain, this young man has suffered."

"The Solassions did this to him," I said, teeth clenched to hold back my emotion. The mere sight of his abuse left me wanting to tear every one of them apart. "They enslaved him." Blinking, I cleared my throat. "Might we offer him some dignity?"

Elowen gave a nod, and I grasped the other side of his trousers, helping her carefully push them back up onto his hips, covering him as before.

She handed me a washcloth, which I dipped into the cold water she'd collected. "Try to cool him down a bit. I'll see if I've a spell somewhere to stop the convulsions," she said, making her way to the door.

Nodding, I placed the cloth against his skin, and his muscles jerked on contact. With gentle pressure, I dabbed the cloth across his throat and up along his jaw. Another dunk in the water, and I squeezed the excess into the bowl and dabbed the cloth over his cheeks and brow.

Still, he shook beneath me, every muscle seemingly locked tight.

"Zevander," I whispered. "If you can hear me, please come back."

I continued to dunk the cloth, adding fresh, cool water to his skin. When I reached his chest, I winced at the rigid state of his muscles, how painful it must've been to have them endlessly taut. My own chest ached just looking at him.

"What happened to you?" I dabbed the cloth up by his hair-line, careful to avoid his eyes. On closer examination, I couldn't even see his irises—the entire surface of his eyeball had blackened. I gently placed my hand over his lids to shutter them closed.

Elowen appeared in the doorway. "Gotta grab some herbs from the forest. Shadowroot and foxfell."

"Should I go with you?"

"No. You stay with him. I shouldn't be long."

I turned back to Zevander and continued to dab him, wondering what had hooked its talons inside his mind after I'd fallen asleep.

* * *

An hour must have passed, and I ran the cloth for the hundredth time over his body, listening for Elowen. How difficult must it have been to find the herbs and roots she required?

Zevander still convulsed, his muscles still flinching, but I was able to touch his skin without the burn, at least.

I pushed to my feet and huffed, peering through the window. With no sign of Elowen, I exited the room in search of something I could wear out in the cold to look for her. The room across from ours was neat and clean, the bed made, blankets folded, with a small dresser against the wall. The first three drawers held nothing. It wasn't until I opened the fourth that I found a pair of old trousers with holes and thinning patches. I slipped them on, the waistband double my size, and I wrapped the laces around me twice to tighten them. Beneath the bed, I spied a pair of leather boots. While still bigger than my feet, they fit snugger than Zevander's had, so I made the switch before grabbing the cloak.

After checking on Zevander one more time, I headed out the door in search of her.

The temperature must have dropped about ten degrees from

when I'd first ventured out that morning. Vonkovya had always been known for some pretty harsh winters, but I couldn't recall one so bitterly cold.

After a long trek through the snow, I found myself standing before the dreaded archway. Strange that, even after having passed through once, I still hesitated to step into those woods.

A mental image sprang to mind, of Zevander on the bed, and I hustled past the barrier, eyes searching for the older woman. The overcast against the snow reflected a bright light that had my vision blurring.

Not daring to call out to her, I trekked deeper, keeping the archway in sight at all times.

In the distance, I sighted a dark figure in the snow. Careful steps brought me closer, and I kept to the trees, just in case. As I drew nearer, I could make out the pudgy form of Elowen lying on the ground, and with a gasp, I rushed toward her. "Elowen?"

She didn't move, her eyes closed as if sleeping. Beside her on the ground lay a basket of herbs and roots, and the telling red drops of blood scattered across the snow.

I lifted my gaze to the surrounding forest, performing a quick sweep to make sure there were no animals, or creatures, hidden in the trees. On seeing nothing there, I shook her shoulders. "Elowen?"

She didn't move, nor so much as flinch.

I yanked up her sleeves and tugged down the scarf at her throat in search of the wound that'd bled. Nothing there. Nothing on her face. Her skirt didn't carry any evidence of blood. Eyes trailing over the fallen drops of blood, I visually followed the path of it to the back of her neck. With a heave, I pushed her just enough to totter her to the side and found a good chunk of her flesh torn away. Realizing they might've been bite marks, I scanned the trees again, and when I lowered her back to the ground her eyes shot open.

Shiny black orbs stared back at me, and as I watched in horror, her forehead swelled, bigger and bigger, her bones creaking as they shifted, swallowing her eyes.

A cold pulse of shock left me paralyzed, while I stared at her slowly lengthening teeth.

Move! Now!

I gathered my feet beneath me to dart away, but her hand shot out, gripping my arm. A wheeze of panic tore out of me, and I clawed at her fingers to loosen them. A rough jerk of my arm sent me flying face first into the snow. I scrambled onto my back, and as I kicked away from her, she scampered toward me on all fours, her mouth the only thing left visible on her face. She let out a terrifying screech that echoed through the forest and climbed over top of me, her impossible strength pinning me beneath her. A snap of her teeth nearly reached my cheek, but I shot out my right hand, grabbing her by the neck.

"Elowen! Please!"

Drool dripped from her teeth onto my chin, and I turned away, straining to hold her from my face. It was as I craned my neck that I noticed an image carved in the bark of a tree a short distance away. It reminded me of two bird's eyes, opposite of each other and inverted like a mirrored image of one another. So wildly out of place, I couldn't help but stare. Couldn't look away, as some invisible force seemed to anchor my attention there. I stared at it, studying it. Time slowed. The muscles in my arms shook, threatening to give beneath her weight pressing down on them.

Heat burned across my palm, and a flash of bright light struck my eyes, nearly blinding. I blinked away the floating objects, and when I turned back to Elowen, time leapt into motion again.

A blackness crawled from my knuckles to the tips of my fingers wrapped tight at her throat. Elowen's spine snapped straight, her head tipped back, and the pressure weighing down on me lessened. Tiny black veins pulsed beneath her pale white skin, thickening and thickening. The veins stretched and reached across her face, swallowing the alabaster white, until, at last, she crumbled to black dust that fell upon me.

Coughing, I kicked myself backward until my spine hit something hard, and I let out a scream, twisting to see a tree trunk at my back. Snapping my attention back to Elowen showed nothing but her threadbare clothes lying in a pile over scattered black dust that'd blown across the snow.

I looked down to the tips of my fingers, which remained black as onyx, and when I turned my palm up, the image I'd seen carved in the tree glowed on my right hand. A new glyph. Up close, I could see it was two vertically inverted eyes, but the ridge of each eye actually made up a scythe. Two inverted scythes.

Another glance at Elowen.

Death.

A deep growl had me glancing up again to see two pale-skinned creatures skulking toward me through the trees. I pushed to my feet and ran back toward the archway.

The trailing growls told me they chased after me, but I didn't stop, nor turn, to see how closely. Through the snow, I booked it back toward the cottage, a suffocating fear robbing me of air as I wheezed and coughed. My boot struck a log, and I tumbled forward, the ground smashing into my chest. A quick glance showed the creatures bounding after me on all fours, and I jumped to my feet, dashing forward once more.

The archway stood just ahead of me. The air burned in my lungs, and my muscles shook as I sprinted past it to the open field, toward the cottage in the distance. The faster I raced toward it, the closer the growls seemed to chase after me.

A tearless sob tugged at my throat, but I clamped my lips to keep it in check. Zevander needed me to return. He needed me. I refused to die. I refused to leave him vulnerable and alone.

I will not die in this wretched world.

My lungs pounded at my chest for a sip of oxygen by the time

I reached the porch. Weak with exhaustion, I slammed through the front door of the cottage and closed it behind me, switching the lock into place. With my back against the door, I panted, waiting for those creatures to slam through after me. Growls and snarls bled through the door. A hard thud jerked me forward. Another clanked the metal locks.

"Stop!" I screamed as they rammed into the barrier a third time.

Their growls heightened, and I slapped my hands to my ears, screwing my eyes shut. "Go away, go away, go away!"

A cold gust swirled around me, and for the briefest moment, I wondered if they'd gotten through somehow.

The beating against the door stopped, and I opened my eyes to an eerie stillness that settled through the room.

Nothing but the quiet grunts from the bedroom that told me Zevander still lay there.

Stepping cautiously over the floorboards, I padded toward the window beside the door and peered out. My heart pounded in my throat. Dozens of the creatures paced in the yard, snarling and snapping their teeth, but none of them approached the door. As if they couldn't.

As if my presence stirred them into a frenzy, one of them rushed toward the porch. An invisible force threw it backward across the yard.

"A ward," I whispered. It was then I remembered the symbols carved into the wood on the door.

Backing away from the window, I looked around in search of a rag and found one on a countertop. I tore it into small strips, wrapping each small section around my fingers, all the way to their blackened tips, until they were completely covered. My whole body trembled as I limped my way to the bedroom, and after sliding off the boots, I crawled into bed next to Zevander. Even unconscious, he calmed me, his massive body like an iron shield that I hid behind while the monsters paced outside the window.

If only he'd wake.

While his body continued to tremble, I buried my face in his damp skin that'd begun to heat again. "Please wake up," I whispered. "Please don't leave me here alone."

CHAPTER SIXTY-ONE

ZEVANDER

With his hand gripped tight to her throat, Zevander slammed Maevyth into the wall and drove himself so deep inside her, she whimpered. Drenched in sweat, he'd fucked her for hours, his body never tiring. The weariness in her eyes and laxity in her muscles told him she was growing weaker by the second. He couldn't stop, though. Something drove him, urging him to keep going.

A foreign sensation hooked into his veins, feeding him an unbridled craving to ravage her. A vicious and violent need chewing at his mind.

"You can have everything you want. Go anywhere you want," the voice came from behind, as if Cadavros stood at his back. Watching him plunder her with greed.

Teeth clenched, Zevander growled, staring back at Maevyth and her sickeningly sweet pouty lips. "I don't want anything else but her." Blood pumped furiously in his veins, his appetite amped for an endless night. He drove his hips harder and tipped her head just enough to sink his teeth into her neck. A weak cry escaped her, but Zevander didn't care. The sound of her mewling voice sent a thrill down his spine.

He wanted to devour her. Every fiber of his being called him to finish inside of her, to fill her, and he wouldn't stop until then.

"General Loyce robbed you of this pleasure. She made you this way." His words snaked themselves beneath Zevander's skin, rousing a savage fury that vibrated his muscles. *"Even now you can't properly enjoy her, can you?"*

Maevyth's face morphed into the bronze skin and yellow-blonde hair of the woman who'd torn through his nightmares when he was just a boy. She tipped her head back and laughed, her fingers tight in his hair.

"I love a good hate fuck," she said, and Zevander pressed into her throat harder, wanting nothing more than to choke the life out of her. To fill her with the black flame and watch her crumble to ash in his hands.

His body begged to disentangle from her, but he couldn't. He couldn't stop himself. An insatiable need to keep going tore through his resistance. The loathing he felt, like an oily black sludge, burned in the pit of his stomach.

"Please wake up," Maevyth whispered. "Please don't leave me here alone." The sound of her voice disarmed him, and Zevander looked around. Shame spiraled through him at the thought of her watching him fuck Loyce. He turned back to the repulsive woman, only to find Maevyth propped against the wall, her head lolling to the side.

Confused, he shook his head, and a dark possession surged through his blood all over again.

He resumed his thrusts, the sweat dripping down their bodies in rivulets. He dragged a wet line with his tongue over the crook of her neck, gathering the salty flavor of her skin.

"You fuck like a corpse." The merging of Maevyth's voice and General Loyce's sent a ripple of disgust through him, and he stared back at her, watching Maevyth's hair fade to blonde. *"Fuck me proper, or there will be punishment after."*

Eyes screwed shut, he turned away, still driving his hips into her.

"*Harder,*" the merged voices said.

"*Harder.*" General Loyce's voice stood out that time.

Zevander growled and slid his hand to her mouth. "Enough!"

"*If you didn't enjoy what I did to you, then why did you give me your seed?*" Loyce taunted.

He slammed her harder into the wall, and the wretched woman laughed, the sound bouncing off his skull in a maddening clamor. There was no climax in sight. No end to the torment.

"Can you hear me, Zevander?" Maevyth asked, her voice severing his thoughts.

He glanced around in search of her.

"*Is she not everything you wanted?*" Cadavros interrupted, and a cold gust brushed across the back of his neck. "*Take her. Make her yours. You can have her this way for eternity.*"

Again, he looked up to find he was thrusting into Maevyth, her eyes shuttered, as if she were completely unconscious.

Yes. Eternity. A darkness clawed at his brain, and Zevander carried her to the bed, throwing her down onto the mattress. Her limp body failed to protest, as he turned her over onto her stomach, and as he lined his tip to her entrance, he paused at the sound of her voice again.

"I'm going to help you."

He frowned, her voice so angelic and pure, the euphony of it had his stomach knotted in shame. "Maevyth?" Eyes clamped shut, he shook his head, and when he opened them, he raised his hands to find them covered in a shiny black fluid.

He lowered his gaze to her naked form, and the blood across her thighs and at her throat where he'd bitten her before. From the wound, tiny black veins crawled over her pale skin, pulsing like a heartbeat.

A stab of pain pierced his chest, and he stumbled backward, his body cold with shock. "Maevyth?"

Tears sprang to his eyes as he turned her over to find the bite mark at her throat oozing an oily black substance. "No, no, no. What did I do? What the fuck did I do!" He lifted her into his arms, cradling her body. "Wake up, Maevyth."

A dark chuckle echoed around him, the sound rattling inside his skull. *"As I said, I can take everything away from you."*

"Even your favorite toy," Loyce added.

He buried his face in Maevyth's hair, but the delicious scent he craved was no longer there. Only the cold stench of rot and disease burned in his nose. A searing heat blasted across his chest in a flare of black fire. Adrenaline shot through his veins, as he scrambled to hold onto her, while the flame devoured her limp body. "No! No, no, no!" In seconds, she disintegrated in his arms, until all that remained was a small red bloodstone with silver markings caught in his palm.

"No! Maevyth, please. *No!*" he roared, the molten fury slinking through his blood like lava.

"Zevander?"

At the sound of her voice, he looked around for her.

"Can you hear me? Come back to me."

"Where are you? Tell me where you are!"

"Open your eyes, Zevander. Open them!"

His eyes were open, though. They'd been open the whole time.

"Look at me," she whispered. "Please."

The violence in him calmed, and the beast tearing through his chest finally stilled. He exhaled a long breath and closed his eyes. When he opened them again, Maevyth stared down at him, their palms pressed against one another.

Her eyes, a glowing silver.

CHAPTER SIXTY-TWO

MAEVYTH

I breathed a tearful chuckle, staring down at the beautiful eclipse of Zevander's eyes. "Hi."

I hadn't imagined that merely pressing my palms to his would've incited the flame, but I could feel it drawing into me, that delicious heat warming my bones as I commanded it.

His body had stopped convulsing, and while his pupils remained dilated, the sliver of gold and orange had begun to widen, replacing the eerie blackness from before.

Confusion slid over his bewildered expression, and he jolted upright, turning away from me as he swung his legs over the edge of the bed. The muscles in his back twitched, and he bent forward, cupping his head in his hands.

"Zevander?" I asked with caution, not entirely certain if he was lucid.

"What did I do?" He ran his hands back and forth over his skull, mussing his hair.

Frowning at his back, I shook my head. "What do you mean? You did nothing."

"Your eyes ... they're more silver than before."

Touching a finger to my cheek, I glanced around the room for a mirror, but there was nothing to see my reflection. "I'm not sure why." Elowen had said that only death could break the spell. Perhaps *her* death? Eyes clamped, I shook my head, banishing the creeping visuals of her exploding to dust at my hand. *Not now.*

"I hurt you," he said, his voice hoarse.

"You never touched me, Zevander. Not once." The way his body trembled, his muscles tense and distressed, I wanted to touch *him*. Comfort him. I reached out to him, but paused. Unwilling to chance his rejection right then, I pushed to my hands and knees instead. "I'm going to get you some water."

He neither moved, nor acknowledged me, as I slid off the bed and made my way to the other room. Rifling through cupboards, I found a cup, a clean rag, and from the counter I took the pitcher of water that Elowen had filled earlier. I carried the supplies back to the room to find he hadn't moved at all, still cradling his head in his hands. After setting everything down on the table beside his weapons, I poured the sulfur-smelling contents of the pitcher into the cup.

"You must be horribly dehydrated." Holding it out to him, I watched his chest expand and contract with deep breaths, as if he were trying to calm himself. I desperately wanted to ask him what had him so rattled, but I decided to wait until he'd had a chance to catch his breath.

He reached for the cup and sniffed it, crinkling his nose. Well water. Nothing like the crisp, clean water I'd had in Aethyria. He tipped it back and wiped his mouth with the back of his hand. "I'll take the liquor, instead."

With a nod, I padded out of the room and returned with the bottle of liquor Elowen had given him the night before.

Hand trembling, he poured it into the cup and swallowed it all in one gulp.

The wash basin still sat at the bedside, and I dipped the cloth into the water, squeezing off the excess. "May I?" I asked, holding it up to him.

Gaze trailing to mine, he sat upright, and I pressed the cloth to his face. He kept his eyes on me all the while, as I dabbed the cool cloth over his forehead, to his cheek and neck.

In the quiet between us, my thoughts got the best of me, and I imagined him never waking from that spell. Being alone in this cottage, day after day, with those creatures pacing in the yard. Waiting for the opportunity to get inside. The rims of my eyes stung with the threat of tears, and I quickly looked away, dipping the cloth for fresh water. I cleared my throat, "I didn't know if you ..." The words refused to come forth, as I fought to hold back my emotions.

Massive arms wrapped around me, dragging me down to the bed beside him. His body still shook as he held me against him. He didn't move, just breathed, and I didn't fight his suffocating grip, but let him hold onto me. Quiet tears of relief spilled down my temples.

"I thought you'd left me. For good." My voice cracked on the last two words, and I blinked back more tears. "Where did you go?"

He didn't answer immediately, but curled his fingers into me, as if I might try to get away from him. "Hell," he finally rasped, his voice painfully dry. "I was in Hell."

I raised my unwrapped hand to softly caress his unmarred cheek, tears forming again. "I was so scared."

He pushed my hair away from my face, staring down at me. Without warning, he slanted his lips over mine, and I shuttered my eyes when he kissed me. A comforting warmth surged through me, the overwhelming sense of calm and safety melting my bones. He threaded his fingers through my hair. Breaths hastened. With a grip of my thigh, he pulled me against him, caging me in his merciless and rigid embrace.

Lungs begging for air, I turned to break the kiss, but he tightened his hold, keeping us locked together. The need for air pounded against my chest, drowned by the relief that he was here. Alive and awake and kissing me.

When he finally broke away, he held my face in his palms, both of us fighting to catch our breath. "Even now, I question what is real."

"I'm here. I'm real." I gripped his arms, and his fingers curled into my hair.

He crushed his lips to mine again, in a more fervent kiss than the last, his hands fisting my hair. He kissed me with ruthless possession, plundering my mouth with his tongue. Angry and violent, as if he didn't believe me. As though he were searching for clarity in our joined lips. His leg muscles flexed over my hip, drawing me into him, pressing his groin against me.

So caught up in a tempest of conflicting emotions, I mindlessly reached down to his unlaced trousers, slinking my hand to the tip of his erection.

A tight grip held me in place, and he broke from the kiss. "Don't."

Humiliation burned hot across my face, and I drew my hand back, remembering the scars there. "Oh, god, I'm sorry."

As difficult as it was to move in his steely embrace, I turned away from him, the loathing I felt for myself thick in my throat.

What was I thinking?

Hands banded around me, drawing me back, as he crushed me against his chest. For a moment, he did nothing more than breathe against the back of my neck, while my head punished me for my thoughtless stupidity. "Forgive me," he said, and I frowned.

"Forgive *you?*" Tears wobbled in my eyes. "I'm the one who touched you without asking."

"And I am yours to touch, Maevyth. I crave your touch more than my next breath." His fingers dug into my belly as he held me tight to him. "I saw visions, though … fucking horrible things.

Things I can't get out of my head. Even now, I see and feel everything. As if it lives inside of me."

"What kinds of things?" I whispered, trying to imagine what could possibly be worse than what Elowen and I had uncovered when she'd drawn back his trousers.

He shook his head. "I will never speak them aloud."

A needling guilt scratched at my thoughts. "I saw the scars. The metal piercings." I swallowed back the humiliation in my throat and turned to face him. "We tried to bring your fever down. To undress you and … I saw. You've suffered."

"I was young. Defenseless. I'm no longer that boy," he said roughly, as if I thought him weak for what had happened to him.

It crushed my heart to imagine what he'd been forced to endure. The gut-wrenching stories those scars told. No, I didn't think him weak. On the contrary.

"You must have been exceptionally strong." I ran the pad of my thumb across his lips. "And in so much pain."

He kicked his head to the side, rejecting my caress. "Do not pity me."

"I can assure you, it isn't pity that I feel for you, Zevander. I feel many things right now, but pity isn't one of them."

The cutting anger in his eyes dulled when he turned back to me. "What do you feel?"

I thought about it for a moment, the words messy and scattered in my head. I stared at his chest, the scars and muscles and sweat that stirred a yearning and curiosity inside me. A craving for things I shouldn't have wanted from a man who'd suffered so much. This virile creature who made me feel safe. Who made me feel like I was home, even as we lay in a cold, dark hovel in the thick of hell. One who'd clearly been mistreated and abused.

Even if the nature of my attraction wasn't rooted in selfish desires, but a longing to steal away his pain and give *him* pleasure, to make him feel good and worthy, a prickling shame persisted, strangling my words. "I don't want to say for fear that I'll sound like everyone who's ever harmed you." I lowered my gaze, not wanting to look at him.

His finger hooked my chin, forcing my eyes to his. "You will never be them." His brows pinched to a frown, and he ran his fingers through my hair, before clenching his fist around the strands. "But I do not trust myself with you. Something took over my mind with the kind of ease that troubles me."

"Elowen said you'd fallen into the dark space. Caligorya."

"I've slipped into Caligorya before in training. This was different. This was, perhaps, the first time I've felt … trapped there." The shadows in his eyes flickered and he winced, as if he were living that moment all over again. "My head is not a safe place, Maevyth. I'm losing my senses, just like Branimir. You'd do well to keep your distance." Untangling his fingers from my hair, he turned away, but I gripped his arm.

"No." Nails digging into his biceps, I shook my head of any meek inclinations there. My stubborn tenacity refused to accept his rejection. "I will not. You're not leaving me alone in this place. I won't allow it and I won't allow you to drift off into your head again."

A muscle in his jaw ticced with the tight clenching of his teeth. "I had no control over myself. I could've easily stayed in that state of mind. The things I saw … and did … I couldn't escape it."

"But you did. By the grace of gods or forces or fate, you escaped."

"The gods did nothing. It was you, Maevyth. By the grace of a flitting rope that you managed to tug hard enough."

With a hand against his cheek, I guided his anguished eyes to mine. "Should you slip into that state again, I will grab that rope with both hands and pull you back."

The furrow in his brow deepened. "And if it doesn't work next time?"

"I won't let go. I promise." I scarcely drew a breath before his lips were on mine again, stealing my breath with a kiss that sent a shock of relief through me.

Hands gripped my face as he held me imprisoned in that breathless moment, then pressed his forehead to mine. "I'll never know what in seven hells inspired the universe to send you to me, Maevyth."

"Some might call it a punishment," I said, smiling.

"If this is punishment, then I welcome an eternity of suffering." The kiss that followed was gentle and teasing in the way he merely brushed his lips across mine. "You consume me entirely, little moon witch."

I lifted my hand to trace my fingers over his jaw, realizing they were still wrapped.

As if he'd just noticed then, he gripped my hand and frowned. "What is this?"

"I'm afraid to touch you."

"Why?"

I glanced away, shame and guilt, once again, rising up from the murky depth of my conscience. "I took life with this hand."

"Elowen?"

Lips pressed together, I nodded, pushing away the emotion that threatened to pull me under. How silly I must've looked to him. A man who took life easily. Who killed without hesitation, or remorse. "She turned into one of them, attacked me, and I grabbed her throat. The next thing I knew ... my fingers blackened and ... she turned to dust." The devastation of that moment wound itself around my heart, and tears sprang to my eyes. "I'm sorry. I know I must sound foolish to you, but ... killing her with my bare hands ... I felt like a ... monster."

"You're no monster." He gripped my hand and unraveled the rag from my fingers, lifting them toward his lips as if to kiss them.

Dread tautened my muscles, and I curled my hand into a tight fist. "No. Don't. I don't want to hurt you."

"The will of the wielder, Maevyth. Magic only works at your will. Remember that." He unfurled them and kissed the tips of my fingers.

I sucked in a breath, waiting for that horrible pulsing blackness to crawl over him, just as it had in the woods. A hysterical panic churned in my stomach when the image of the inverted bird's eyes came to mind, and I tugged at my hands to get loose. "No! Wait! Please!"

He paused, staring back at me. "You will not harm me." Eyes on me, he shoved my fingers into his mouth, and I watched in rapt fascination as he sucked the tip of one. "Magic requires your command."

"But I have such ... intrusive thoughts. Thoughts I can't help sometimes."

"They're thoughts. Not will." He dragged my finger over the sharp edge of his teeth. "I can imagine biting into your flesh, can practically taste the blood on my tongue, but I'd sooner rip my own heart out than hurt you that way. Do you understand the difference?"

Enthralled by him, I nodded.

"Never fear your power." He ran his thumb over my cheek, staring back at me. "Your eyes are mesmerizing."

While part of me was curious to see them, I couldn't bear the thought of what their change meant. "I can't help but wonder if her death broke the spell to hide them."

"Could have." The way he looked at me left me struggling for breath. "You are dangerously stunning." Still clutching my face, he seized my mouth with another kiss, and I melted into him. He skimmed his lips over my jaw to my neck and guided my murdering hand downward, inside of his trousers.

I felt his breath catch against my throat, the moment my hand made contact with his stiff length. At first, he held me there, and rested his forehead against my shoulder, his body trembling against mine.

My heart pounded, anxious and unsteady, like a planchette awaiting its possessor's command. "Is this okay?" I asked.

He nodded against me. "I didn't know it would feel like this."

Knots wound in my stomach, and the niggling remorse from before crept over me, but then I felt him smile against the crook of my neck, and he squeezed his hand around mine, his muscles flexing around me as he banded his arm tight across my back, pressing me close. He let out a grunt and shifted his hips, exhaling a shaky breath against my neck. Heat pulsed against my palm where I held him, and though I hadn't yet given a single stroke, he let out a deep, masculine moan.

A downward glance showed a silvery band of light where my hand met his flesh. A brief panic shook my nerves at the visual of hurting him, but the heat spiraled up my wrist into the familiar black ribbons of flame, as his power pulled into me, drawing me like tiny threads, tugging at my womb. A delicious sensation that had me squirming beside him.

His hand gripped mine tighter, the length and girth making it difficult to wrap my fingers around. "I've not allowed a woman to touch me like this in centuries."

I silently chided myself for taking pleasure in that, wanting to slap the satisfaction right out of me after the scars I'd seen.

He finally released my hand and shoved his trousers down his thighs, guiding my palm to him once again. With his forehead pressed to mine, he stared down between us, as though enraptured by the sight of his cock in my hand.

The metal rods pressed into my palm, stirring my imagination. What they must've felt like inside a woman. My belly coiled at the visual of them rubbing across my most sensitive flesh. "May I touch them?" I asked, and at his nod, I let my fingers explore his swollen flesh. The smooth, blunt ends of the rods that tickled my fingertips, the soft skin that pulsed with thick veins as I skimmed them to the curved ridge of his tip.

Both hands tangled in my hair, he clutched either side of my face and kissed my forehead. "You're driving me mad, woman." He let out a groan, and an exhilarating weakness rippled down my spine.

His words goaded me to keep going, gently circling my finger over the tip that wept a sticky fluid. I spread it over his skin, recalling the night before when he'd sucked my arousal from his fingers. The curiosity to know what he tasted like watered my mouth.

Lost to my musings, I raised my hand to my lips, and closed my eyes, sucking away the salty flavor that coated my fingers. Opening my eyes showed him staring back at me, and I quickly lowered my hand from my face.

He seized my wrist, his gaze never veering from mine. Though he didn't say a word, his expression was clear. Focused.

Intrigued.

The moment he released me, I slipped them into my mouth again and sucked them clean, savoring the taste that time. As I licked the last of him from my lips, I watched the satisfaction and lust darken his eyes. I reached down again, running my fingers across those rods, and he licked his own lips, staring down at me.

"I don't want to hurt you," he said, and curled his fist into my hair. "I don't ever want to hurt you, Maevyth."

"You won't." I leaned forward and kissed his neck, while my fingers caressed his flesh and he shuddered. Even the smallest touch seemed to affect him so profoundly. "Can I …" A flare of humiliation swelled inside of me, and I shook my head. "Never mind."

"Can you what?"

"I want to feel them against my tongue."

He chuckled. "These curiosities will be the death of me." Again, he kissed my forehead. "My body belongs to you, Maevyth. It is yours."

A thrill wound through me, as I stared at his massive, muscled form and slid my free hand over the deep ridges and hard planes of his chest. *Mine.* Like a vast night sky claimed by a single star. A fierce and beautiful darkness that I had neither the right nor business to call my own.

I imagined him as a grand feast spread out before me, one I selfishly wanted to consume without leaving a single crumb.

I straddled his legs and ran my fingertip over one of the piercings. "Do they hurt?"

His tongue swept over his lips and he shook his head.

Planting my palms against the mattress, I leaned forward, giving one more upward glance, to see him staring down at me. The sight of him watching me, the hunger in his eyes, had my stomach flipping over on itself. I lowered myself to his groin, breathing in his delectably masculine scent, and ran my tongue over one of the piercings. The same, salty flavor as the liquid that leaked from his tip watered my mouth, as I wrapped my lips around the end of a rung.

His thighs flexed beneath me, and he hissed, the back of his head pressed hard into the pillow, the veins in his neck pulsing to the surface.

A metallic bite lingered on my tongue, as I dragged it over the thick vein of skin that ran the center of each rung and along the velvety length of his shaft.

He moaned and writhed, but didn't push me away. As I made my way to the tip of his cock, I circled my tongue over the small slit there and sucked the fluids away.

"Maevyth, what are you doing to me?" Threading his fingers through my hair, he slowly thrusted his hips forward and let out a grunt, as the tip breached my lips.

An ache struck my jaw when I widened my mouth to accommodate his girth and I lifted my gaze in search of his approval.

Staring down at me, he ran his thumb along my cheek, a look of pained ecstasy creasing his brows as I slid my lips further, over the thick ridge of his tip. "Godsteeth," he said, his jaw clenched tight. "Seeing you like this …" He threw his head back, stretching the wires of tension in his neck. "Fuck."

The sight of his rapture goaded me to take more of him, deeper, until the tip hit the back of my throat, and I gagged against him, quickly dislodging myself. Pressing the back of my hand to my mouth, I fought to swallow down the acids that shot up into my nose.

"I'm sorry," I said in a choked voice. "It's so big."

He tugged at my arm. "Come here."

Abandoning my exploration, I slithered up the length of his body and lay beside him, where he wound me in a tight embrace. "I wish I was a bit more experienced with these things."

"Whether you're experienced, or not, makes no difference. You're the only one who makes me feel something." He threaded his fingers in mine and kissed the back of my hand. "Your scent, your lips, your touch. It's all I think about. *Incessantly*." A kiss to my jaw. "The way you've crawled inside my head …" Fist tangled in my hair, he tugged my head back and dragged his teeth across my throat, the threat of a bite quickening my pulse. "I crave every part of you with an ungodly voracity."

I smiled as he planted kisses along my neck. "It seems such an appetite would make you a dangerous predator."

"It seems it would." The devilish amusement in his voice roused a flare of goosebumps across my skin.

"Show me how to reciprocate," I whispered. "I want to give you pleasure."

He stilled and lifted his head, wearing a guarded expression. "To what end?"

"What do you mean? Your pleasure, and nothing more."

The furrow in his brow deepened as he stared back at me, not saying a word, as though my response had jarred him into silence.

I rested my hand against his cheek. "I want to show you the way you make *me* feel."

Keeping his eyes on me, he turned just enough to kiss my palm. "A man should not long for madness with such enthusiasm as I feel right now."

"You're calling me mad now?" I asked with a smile.

"I'm calling you mine." His lips found the curve of my neck, and he crawled over me, taking hold of what must've been a painfully stiff erection, given the hardness I'd felt. "Lift your shirt," he commanded, and with a nervous nod, I slowly raised it up, until my breasts lay bared to him. Eyes shimmering with gratitude, he fell back on his heels, staring at me in a way that had my stomach fluttering. "By gods, you will be my undoing." He leaned forward, laying a gentle kiss to my stomach. "Put your hands above your head. Grip the headboard."

Without question, I curled my fingers around the wooden spindles of the headboard. A thrilling sense of vulnerability moved through me, as his big body loomed over mine, every inch of him a threat—from his broad muscled shoulders to his powerful legs that could crush me in one hard flex of his thighs. I surrendered myself as his prisoner, completely at his mercy.

He gave a lazy stroke of his cock, and his eyes shuttered closed, teeth clenched.

I lifted my head to watch him, never breaking my grip of the headboard.

His powerful and scarred body, inked in dark magic, virile and damp with sweat, roused a wanton craving to be ravaged by him. To hear the sounds of my clothes being torn by his strong hands, to feel the weight of being pinned beneath him.

Another stroke sent more fluids leaking from his tip, and in rapt fascination, I watched as it dripped onto my exposed belly. He upped the pace of his strokes, his fist planted beside my head, and he bent low, sucking one of my nipples into his mouth.

Like strings pulling at my core, every suck had me arched into him. The sound of pounding flesh beat a rhythm of need into my muscles, so raw and aching, I writhed in the agony of it. A sharp sting zipped across my breast, as he nipped me and groaned, panting through his nose. He stroked himself so fast, it shook the bed.

Switching breasts, he lavished the same attention to my other nipple—licking, sucking, stirring a maddening craving inside of me, but for what? I didn't know. I ground my bottom into the mattress. Desperate. Needy. My fingers gripped the wooden spindles, so tight, they creaked, as if they'd break.

The tattooed flames across his arms and shoulders shifted and flickered, rousing to life. Black ribbons of fire lashed out at the air, like a serpent's tongue. The flames danced across the space between us, and the moment it touched my thigh, I arched, thrusting my chest forward on an agonized moan, as pulses of radiant heat shot beneath my skin. The flames snaked and rippled through my veins to my core, sending tiny vibrations of heat to my womb.

Still grinding on the mattress, I bit my lip, mindlessly intoxicated and aching all over again.

"Zevander, please," I whispered. *"Da'haj mihirit dimitszia."* I frowned at the words that'd spilled from my mouth. Even more disturbing was that I knew their meaning. *Give me your release.*

He let out a long, tormented moan through clenched teeth, his head tipped back to show the veins in his neck protruding, just as before. Hot fluids sprang forth from the tip of his cock, spilling in white jets across my belly. Pulse after pulse shot out of him, coating my skin in his release. Wild fascination claimed his eyes as he stared down at me and ran his palm over my skin, spreading the fluids across my stomach. Marking me. "You are mine, moon witch. For all eternity and whatever lies beyond it. No soul has ever been more intricately woven into mine than yours."

My heart lurched with his words, the cynical creature inside of me loosening its grip. I ran my fingertips over his cheek and the wretched black scar there. "And you are mine," I whispered.

* * *

The room darkened as night fell. I lay beside Zevander, coiled tightly against his body, watching shadows move outside. The pale creatures with black eyes. In the hours that we'd lay exploring each other, their numbers had increased, the growls and snarling heightening with the rising of the moon. Though none had yet attempted to breach the ward, just knowing so many prowled outside of the small hovel stirred fears of being consumed alive by them.

Only the steady beat of Zevander's heart at my ear kept me calm.

"We'll return in the morning," he said. "Hopefully there will be fewer of them then."

Nodding, I clutched him tighter. While the thought of abandoning my sister's search left a heavy ache in my chest, I couldn't risk the possibility of something happening to either one of us.

My thoughts drifted back to the creatures I'd seen in the woods after I'd fought Elowen. What they would have done to me, had they caught me. Tearing into me with teeth and claws, or worse, attempting what Uncle Felix had tried back at the house. I flinched beside Zevander and nuzzled my face into his chest.

A gentle hand stroked my hair. "What troubles you?"

"You once asked me what I fear. I've since learned of another." A shaky breath sputtered out of me, as if in that moment of calm, the trauma had finally found its home inside my chest. "Despair. I fear being so helpless that all hope is lost."

"You're not helpless. You're strong, Maevyth. You fought, and you lived."

A visual of lying beneath Uncle Felix, desperate and grasping as he tore away at my clothes, stabbed at my thoughts. "I was afraid. I reacted out of fear."

"Fear inspires strength."

"I didn't feel strong. Not with Uncle Felix, or Agatha. Not

with Elowen, or the creatures that chased me back to the cabin. I felt lucky, and luck eventually runs out. If those things come for us in the night—" A suffocating sludge of panic gripped my lungs, choking my words.

"I will not let anything hurt you." Finger hooking my chin, he tipped my head back, his eyes glowing pools of molten lava. "I have killed in a variety of ways, Maevyth, but anything that dares attempt to harm you tonight will suffer the most violent of them all," he said in a voice that was somehow fierce and chillingly calm at the same time. "Believe me when I tell you this." His lips pressed to mine, and I clutched him tighter, letting him wind me in his web of safety. "They'd be fools to tempt such fate. Not a single creature would be spared when I burned it all to the ground."

"I never should have come back to this place. Never should have left Aethyria. I just want to go back to Eidolon."

"I'm going to take you to Calyxar."

"Will you stay with me?" I asked.

"Yes. The king will be searching for me. He'll likely put me to death, or arrest me, for having abandoned my guard."

I buried my face in his chest again, the remorse chewing at me. "I'm sorry. I shouldn't have—"

"Don't be sorry. I've no desire to spend the rest of my life serving as a glorified nursemaid."

The comment tugged a smile from my lips. "And so, you'd choose to be a glorified nursemaid to me? Watching over me all hours of the day?"

His lips curved to a smirk. "I'd quite enjoy watching over you all hours of the day." He wrapped me tighter and kissed my forehead. "Particularly when your shirt is hiked up and your hands are bound. I'd never take my eyes off you."

I thought back to that moment and the words that'd spilled out of me. "I don't know what language that was. What I said to you."

"You spoke Primyrian. The ancient language."

I remembered Dolion had once said it was the language of the gods. It made no sense, though, particularly when I knew nothing of the Aethyrian gods. "How would I know it, let alone speak it?"

He exhaled a sigh and stroked his thumb over my cheek. "The mystery of you never ceases to intrigue me."

The growls from outside had me lifting my head, and I peered through the dark window that showed nothing but the faint rays of moonlight. They were out there, though. Waiting. Pacing. "Do you think the ward will hold?" I asked, nuzzling closer to him.

He lifted his head toward the window, then lay back down, tucking his arm beneath it. "Hard to say. I suspect it's the only way the old woman survived this whole time."

"Those things ... they're terrifying. What is it that this Cadavros wants?"

Gentle strokes of his calloused hand across my arm sent a calm through me. "If it's true that he embodies Pestilios, then he yearns for chaos and the power to control life and death."

"Is it true that my blood could have prevented this? That the bloodstones are powerful enough to stop him?"

"It doesn't matter, Maevyth," he said, with a bitter amusement in his voice. "If preventing this plague means sacrificing your life, then I've no interest in saving everyone else. The whole world could perish of disease and famine, for all I care."

"Some would call that selfish." I traced my finger over the deep ridge in his chest.

"Then, I am selfish."

"And Rykaia? You could watch her perish, as well?"

He snorted. "Rykaia would be first in line for my head, if I sacrificed you."

The thought of that made me chuckle. "I look forward to seeing her again."

"As do I."

A horrific sound gurgled in my stomach, and I pressed my hand to my belly. "Speaking of being famished."

"I suspect there's stew." He raised a brow. "If you dare."

I'd have liked to imagine that pot only carried the remnants of one night, but given the lack of meat, I wondered how long she'd been scraping leftovers into it. "I think I saw some jars in the cupboard. I'll see if I can scrounge a meal out of it." I pushed up to climb off the bed, and he grabbed my arm, lifting his head off the pillow for a kiss. My stomach growled again, and I smiled against his lips. "I'll be right back."

"Good. I'm starving, as well."

I left him lying there and padded toward the kitchen. Halfway to the cupboard, though, one of the floorboards seemed to shift beneath my feet. Frowning, I backed up a step, noting the quiet creak of the wooden planks, and when I stepped forward again, it shifted a second time, as if loose. I pushed up to the ball of my foot, noting a slight give. A carpet covered the board, which I peeled back. Beneath, a section of the floor seemed to have been carved out from the rest. Like a door.

From the table across from me, I swiped up the firelamp and turned it up, illuminating the irregular planks, one of which held a metal loop handle. A shadow of movement stirred in my periphery, and I glanced up to see Zevander at the threshold of the bedroom doorway. Arms over his head, he leaned into the frame, his brawny form a momentary distraction.

He nodded toward me. "What'd you find?"

"A door of some sort."

Brow kicked up, he tipped his head. "Have we not learned to stay away from doors in the floor?"

Smiling, I looped my finger into the hole. "I'm curious. But, just in case, don't go anywhere."

He huffed and strode closer, looming over me as I pulled the door open on a groan of tired wood. Darkness below made it difficult to see, but as I swept the firelamp over the opening, I could just make out the presence of something there.

A body.

With a gasped breath, I jumped backward.

Zevander caught me before I tumbled onto the floor, and swiped up the firelamp from my grip, holding it over the opening. "Gods be damned ..."

I scrambled forward and fell to my knees, peering down into the crawl space. My heart caught in my throat, as a needling shock crawled over me.

There, curled into herself, lay my sister.

Aleysia!

Thank you so much for following Zevander and Maevyth's journey through The Eating Woods. Your connection to this world and these characters means so much to me and their story is far from over.

I'm thrilled to inform you that Eldritch, the second book will be available in 2025 and will pick up where book one left off.

If you'd like to keep up with release announcements and all the fun extras, I'm most active on Instagram and in my reading group on Facebook.

Instagram: /kerilake
Reading Group: The Gothiphiles

You can also sign up for my newsletter, The Raven's Scroll. Visit my website www.kerilake.com for more details and links.

OTHER BOOKS BY KERI LAKE

ABOUT THE AUTHOR

Keri Lake is a gothic romance writer who specializes in demon wrangling, vengeance dealing and wicked twists. Her stories are gritty, with antiheroes that walk the line of good and bad, and feisty heroines who bring them to their knees. When not penning books, she enjoys spending time with her husband, daughters, their rebellious Labrador (who doesn't retrieve a damn thing) and rescue pup. She runs on strong coffee and alternative music, loves a good red wine, and has a slight addiction to dark chocolate.

Keep up with Keri Lake's new releases, exclusive extras and more by signing up to her newsletter, The Raven's Scroll

Join her reading group for giveaways and fun chats:
THE GOTHIPHILES

She loves hearing from readers ...
www.KeriLake.com